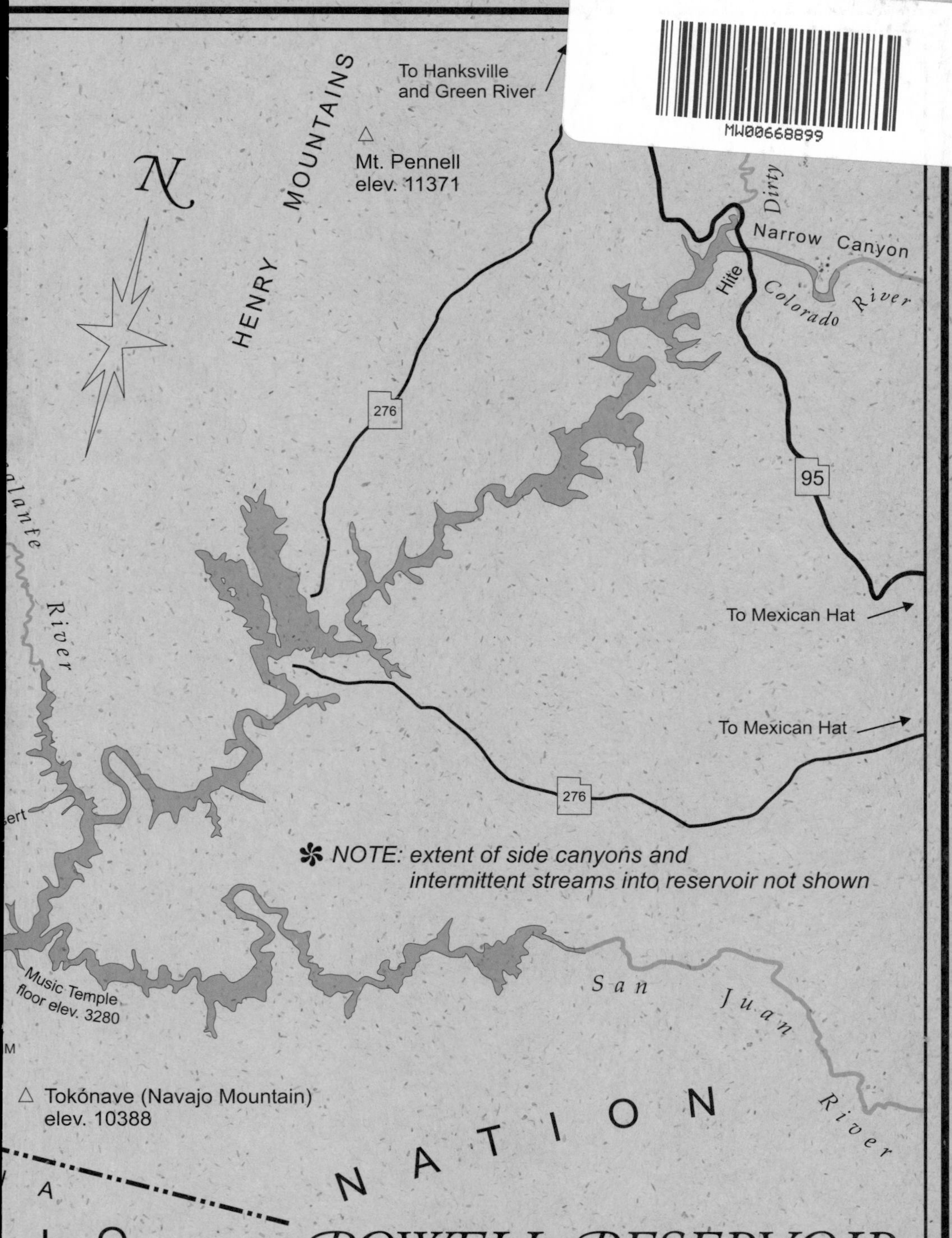
HENRY MOUNTAINS
To Hanksville and Green River
Mt. Pennell elev. 11371
N
Dirty
Narrow Canyon
Hite
Colorado River
276
95
To Mexican Hat
To Mexican Hat
276
River
Music Temple floor elev. 3280
NOTE: extent of side canyons and intermittent streams into reservoir not shown
San Juan River
Tokónave (Navajo Mountain) elev. 10388
NATION
J O
POWELL RESERVOIR
0 10 MILES 20 30

GLEN CANYON

Glen Canyon

A Novel

Steven Hannon

Kokopelli Books ✳ Denver

Published in the United States by Kokopelli Books,
an imprint of Blackacre, Inc.
66 Ash Street, Denver, CO 80220

Library of Congress Catalog Card Number 96-78757

ISBN 0-9655125-0-9

Book Design by Kokopelli
Cartography by Steven Hannon
Illustration by Pamela Reitan

Printed on Fraser Papers HALOPAQUE ®

100% Total Recycled Fiber
20% Post Consumer Fiber
Acid ∞ Free
Elemental Chlorine Free

First Edition

Manufactured in the United States of America

98 00 02 03 01 99 97
2 4 6 7 5 3 1

for Susan.

and for J. F. S.
—thanks for your prayers.

Contents

Photographs and Illustrations

Photographs

ILLUSTRATIONS

PROLOGUE

ZAGORSK RESERVE MATERIEL DEPOT, NORTHEAST OF MOSCOW
JANUARY 18, 1989

Three officers stood in the bitter cold, the winter-slanting afternoon sun shining brightly on the braided gold and powder blue bands on their caps and epaulets. The distinctive insignia were reserved for the Komitet Gosudarstvennoy Bezopasnosti, the Committee for State Security—in particular, the intensively screened members of the Moscow Guards Directorate.

They watched the forklift driver move the last of the diesel fuel drums into the marine container. Eighty-three of the light green 200-liter barrels rested in the shipping container—indistinguishable from the thousands of similar storage and transport units in the sprawling military depot. The fuel drums had been removed from another container on a flatbed truck.

The senior officer nodded at the junior of his two companions. Major Beznemov walked over to the forklift driver. "Sergeant, come with me. I want to inspect the other one." He pointed to the container on the flatbed.

"Remove that empty pallet." The sergeant went to the front of the empty container and stooped to pick up the wooden platform. Major Beznemov stepped behind him, drawing a 9mm Steyr from beneath his greatcoat.

The officers outside heard a single gunshot, the metallic report muffled by the insulated container and the icy wind. Major Beznemov walked back onto the loading dock. He closed the container doors, locking them.

"Is that the last of them, Nicolai?"

"Yes, Comrade General. No one remains."

"And the empty box?"

"It will go east, to the disposal yard at Druzhina. We have full control there. It will never be touched."

They stood silently, staring through the open doors at the neat rows of pallets, each wooden platform supporting a single fuel drum.

"And the rest, Sergey? All are in place?"

Colonel Drozdov turned to light another cigarette, cupping his hands against the wind. "Yes, Comrade General. At Symferopil and Odessa. Same arrangement as here."

"Damned Ukrainians . . . I don't like the situation."

"I agree, sir. But, logistically, it is necessary. With the fleet headquarters at Sevastopil, we will maintain control. Ukraine or not."

"I still don't like it," the general said heavily, accepting one of Colonel Drozdov's cigarettes, a Marlboro. "If things go completely to shit, will General Nastenko be loyal to us or to Ukraine? That is the big question."

"We could never have done this without him."

"We could never have done it without people like Sergeant Varensev back there, Comrade Colonel," the general snapped.

"And many like him," the colonel said quietly.

"A great many more good people died at Stalingrad and countless other places in the Great Patriotic War, comrades," Major Beznemov added without emotion.

"For my part, I'm glad the wet affairs are now over," the senior officer said. "Lock it up." Major Beznemov swung the doors shut and spun the combination lock on container K17756MB.

The general looked down the long row of similar storage units, extending in both directions as far as could be seen. "So now we are only seven, gentlemen," he said softly, his voice barely audible over the sharp wind.

"Yes, sir. It is only the seven of us now," Colonel Drozdov replied.

The general's scowl deepened. "He's going to give it all away. Our glorious General Secretary is going to give away the entire Union. His glasnost and his perestroika. Openness. *Horseshit!*"

"The new treaty is before the Politburo now, Comrade General. We acted just in time," Major Beznemov said, crushing out his cigarette and lighting another. He and Colonel Drozdov joined their commanding officer as he started toward the sedan. The usual driver was absent; Major Beznemov would drive the Zil.

The black sedan disappeared down the long row of storage and shipping containers, and except for the relentless wind no sound broke the silence of the vast depot. Container K17756MB, like its thousands of companions, would not be disturbed without specific instructions from a senior Moscow Guards officer at the headquarters on Dzerzhinsky Square in the heart of Moscow. And except for seven officers, no one within the elite unit, or the rest of the KGB, or the entirety of the military and political apparatus of the Soviet Union, had any knowledge of the contents of K17756MB. Secured within the eighty-three 200-liter drums were a like number of variously configured tactical nuclear weapons, with yields ranging from thirty to eighty kilotons. Except in the minds of the seven men, no memory remained of the existence of the weapons or of the others stored at Odessa and Symferopil. Over a period of three years, all physical evidence and paper and electronic records had been expunged, along with the people who possessed the memories. The weapons did not exist. They would not be accounted for in the Tactical Arms Reduction Treaty.

GENTLE CANYON

1

The Great River, midsummer of the year 1294 by the Julian calendar

Tuvi looked over the edge of the smooth orange rock. Far below, his father stood on a ledge, squinting up in the brilliant light. It was time for Tuvi to begin the climb down the evenly spaced notches in the sandstone. He adjusted the cotton strap that held his pottery canteen until it rested on his back, next to the quiver of arrows and the bow. His hands had to be free, and adjustments would be difficult once he started down.

The half-hemispherical steps in the sandstone wall had been carefully carved, just large enough to admit the toes of the twilled yucca-leaf sandals securely laced to his feet. The steps also provided firm handholds. Twelve winters before, as soon as he had begun to walk with strength and balance, he had learned to climb the canyon wall in their village. He had been instructed to wait until the person below finished climbing before he started down so that a fall would not carry away the climber beneath him. People did fall. He did not think about it as he stretched a foot down to the next indentation in the warm rock while reaching for a corresponding handhold. He felt the reassuring friction of the rough yucca fiber against the course stone. Tuvi seldom thought about falling anymore. His life ending in a fall from the cliff would be no different than the many other events that rested in the hands of the Creator.

He stepped onto the ledge where his father waited. Long ago the Ancient Ones had carved the steps in the cliff Tuvi and his father used, placing them on the inside of a turn in the river where the stone was somewhat sloped—not vertical, as it was on the outside turns and along straight reaches of the canyon. His father started down the last portion of the cliff to the gentler slope of rounded and domed rock descending to the sandbar. The long reach of sand and its lush willow thicket filled the inside curve of the wide turn of the canyon below, and across the sand, barely visible against the sheer black-and-orange-striped wall on the opposite side, Tuvi could see the river's thread of clear water as it slid slowly beneath the cliff. For as much as he could remember of his seventeen winters, this was the familiar view of Pisisvayu, the Great River.

His father said the river had another mood, but Tuvi could not imagine it. Many years before, in place of the thin stream of clear water, each year after the planting time Pisisvayu had filled the bottom of the canyon.

The old people said it ran fast and brown with the soils it carried, but the last time had been three winters before the year of his birth; each year thereafter the water in the canyon diminished. Now, up on the plateau there was almost none. Long discussions were held in the kivas about whether the North Village clans should move into the canyon as the People had done before, but more than once the Great River had come in an angry flood and swept away the fields, villages, and many of the People. Mother Earth had told them that they must not live in the canyon. Nothing here was permanent except the great expanses of the orange rock Tuvi now descended, and all that remained of the ancestors' work were the steps and the long-abandoned granaries high on the cliffs. The clans now came to the canyon to fish, hunt, and gather wild plants—but they could not live here. The great canyon belonged to Pisisvayu.

"Tuvi, my third son, take my canteen and fill it. I will meet you in the Place of the Flute."

He gazed a long moment into his father's wrinkled face, framed by white-streaked hair that hung in bangs nearly to his eyebrows, almost to his shoulders on the sides, and tied in a knot in the back—all encircled with a woven headband. It was difficult now for the old man even to eat, but he no longer complained about the pain in his remaining teeth, ground to blackened stumps. The People knew that the life-sustaining corn of Mother Earth, even the sacred white kernels, also served to shorten their lives. Tuvi's father's mother and then his wife had fed him the corn that the women ground with the *mano* and the *metate*, and mixed with the ground meal was the fine sand from the grinding stones. Tuvi knew this would likely be his father's last year; he had lived forty-one winters—beyond the time the Creator had given him. The People were thankful for their lives, which were longer than nearly all of the animals'.

Tuvi watched his father walk across the fine amber sand, through the willows, and into a grove of trees clustered around the opening of a narrow side canyon. He knew his father wanted time alone. The old man would think of many things while he sat in the quiet mystical place he had first visited as a small boy, and among the myriad wonders of the canyon of the Great River Tuvi knew the Place of the Flute was his father's favorite.

The river canyon was hot, much hotter than the rim, and like his father Tuvi wore only a woven cotton breechclout, comfortable in the canyon's heat. This was Tala'ti, the hottest time of summer. Normally they would come to the Great River in the winter, but now there was no time. By winter the rest of the people in their clans would be gone.

His feet sank into the scorching sand as he walked toward the river. The air hung heavy, hot, and still in the canyon; the occasional buzz of an insect and the soft crunch of his sandals accented the breathless silence. One of the great blue wading birds suddenly rose, without a sound, from a clump of willows and rushes at the water's edge. The slow movement of the bird's wings carried him silently down the canyon, his long legs trailing behind as the rising thermal current lifted him toward the rim. Then Tuvi began to hear a sound, quickly increasing in intensity—like the wind blowing through a thin crevice in the rock. He looked up at the arch of blue above the cliffs, seeing nothing at first. Then he saw them: two dots plummeting toward the heron as it glided down the canyon. The falcon and her smaller mate swooped past the large, lumbering bird, sharply pitching upward as the momentum of their stoops carried them nearly back to the rim. Tuvi knew the falcons were not seriously attacking the heron; he'd seen them do the same thing many times—celebrating their mastery of everything that occupied the skies above Mother Earth.

At the water's edge, he could see where the heron had been wading, looking for small fish and frogs; the deep imprints of his feet were still visible in the soft mud. A large, humpbacked fish wriggled through the reed-choked shallows, trying to reach the safer holes in the main channel. Tuvi and his father would come to the river in the evening to shoot their arrows at the squaw fish, now such easy targets.

He filled the canteens and then knelt to sip the clear, warm water from a still pool at the river's edge. Strider bugs darted across the surface and cast sharp shadows on the rippled sand. *I should take water to my father . . . No, I must not disturb him yet.*

His thirst satisfied, Tuvi sat down, cross-legged in the hot sand. Across the narrow strip of water, the sheer cliff rose sharply above the outside turn of the canyon. High overhead the guttural croak of a raven broke the silence. The bird's wedge-shaped tail and broad wings fanned out, balanced on the imperceptible upwelling of hot air from the depths of the canyon. The young man leaned back on his elbows, digging them into the sand so they would not be burned, and stared up at the expanse of rock arching high above him in the brilliant light. Panels of long, wide stripes—dark brown to nearly black—ran down the face of the stone. The unstained rock appeared dull orange, but the coloring was subtle: it changed with the hour of the day and the angle at which light fell upon its varied cleavages, textures, and surfaces. The colors ranged from light tan, buff, and taupe to a deep iridescent chocolate; from a gentle pink to salmon, orange, and dull red; even from a pale green to nearly black.

Tuvi knew that the wide black lines were only on the surface, just like the overall colorings of the sandstone. He had watched his father patiently chip the clan stories and passage records into the dark color, the figures standing out brilliantly in the exposed rock. The stories of the Ancient Ones were still sharply visible where they had long ago been pecked into the stone, each dot-formed figure created slowly and with great deliberation—not random, casual recordings, and not mere art. Neither did they say too much, as the spoken word does—subtly but inevitably diluting and corrupting fact and knowledge with each telling. And they were done by the slow, patient thinkers in the clans, not the glib and voluble leaders and politicians who were seldom the wisest. Tuvi was proud that his father was one of the few men permitted to write the new *tutuventingwu.*

He looked down at the two pottery canteens resting in the sand. His was colored a deep orange, overlain with dark red and black geometric patterns, suggesting the visage of the cliff across the river. The other was old, made by his father's mother when she was a young bride, and was nearly black; only thin lines of the gray-white pottery slip appeared between the broad black patterns. He smiled as he remembered his father saying that he did not like the new style of pottery: "we should not alter the old ways," his father had said many times to the other village elders.

Most of the people of their clans were gone now from the three canyon villages of Kawestima. In their village in a high cliff cave, only four families remained. Soon they, too, would travel to the south, across the black mesa, to follow the others in the final portion of the ancient migration that had carried them in the four directions since the Emergence. Spider Grandmother told them to go south to where the Bear, Parrot, Eagle, and Badger Clans were living near the three mesas. Many years ago the four principal clans, having finished their migrations in the four directions, had settled at Sichtilkwi, the Flower Mound. It was the place that had been prophesied so long ago at the Place of Emergence. Tuvi's Snake Clan, joined by his father's Horn/Flute Clan, had finally received the permission of the Bear Clan who lived at Shongopavi on the second mesa. Their families would be allowed to settle at Koechaptevela at the end of the first mesa.

Mother Earth had given them many signs. The corn, beans, and squash no longer grew well in the canyons of Kawestima, and even the cotton grew miserably in the deeply arroyoed floors of the gorges. Tuvi's people had moved farther and farther up the canyons seeking good ground to plant, but the crops were still poor or failed entirely. The enemy people, the Kononpaiochi from across the Great River, attacked the North Village clans more frequently as the time of thirst grew longer: they robbed the granaries, stole their turkeys and dogs, and even took the crops in the fields. The anger and killing forced the People to live in the villages up in the cliff caves, just as the other clans far to the northeast at the green mesas had done. The animals were nearly gone, and the wild plants now offered little food. Even the durable piñon and the juniper, needed for construction and fuel wood, were disappearing from the canyons and plateaus. Many of the people were sick, and most of the babies died. Mother Earth was clearly speaking to them. The time had come to move south.

As Tuvi thought of these things, he abruptly realized that he should not be sitting out in the open. *The Kononpaiochi could see me here!* He cringed at the thought of the barbarians from the north, "the people who do not comb their hair." *They are so disgusting. So filthy. They live in dirty huts and they want only to rob and kill.* During the last raid by the enemy people, his best friend had died. Unconsciously, he felt for the reassuring bow and quiver of arrows.

Tuvi set the canteens in the cool rushes and started across the river. The sand was firm under his sandals, the warm water rising only slightly above his ankles as he strode easily through the quiet flow to the steep slope of sand and willows. He smiled, thinking of the first time his father had shown him the hidden place that lay just ahead of him up the rock slope. He vividly remembered the wonder and reverence he had felt when he was led into the mysterious side canyon ten winters ago. The entrance was completely invisible from the river, guarded by the shoulder of the giant sentinel of rock soaring above him. He stepped out of the shallow water, scrambled up the slope, then pushed his way into the thick growth of willows and chokecherry bushes.

He found the opening in the cliff and struggled to enter the passage, hidden from view by a sharp left turn the side canyon made just beyond its entrance. His father had told him that many times in the past, long before Tuvi was born, water would race through the hidden place, gouging out everything down to the bare rock and sweeping most of the accumulated sand and vegetation out into the river. Many years had passed since the last flood, and the growth at the entrance made it difficult to enter the passage.

The air and the sand beneath his feet suddenly cooled. The cliff walls rose far above him. He stretched out his arms, nearly able to touch both sides of the deep, narrow cleft in the side wall of the Great River's canyon. The passageway twisted and turned as Tuvi walked farther in, the walls sculpted and fluted as if carved with a giant chisel; the layers of stone eroded differently as they were dense or more friable. Only a sliver of sky gleamed high above him, and in a few more steps he could not see the sky at all; the light in the narrow cavern was suddenly transformed into a phantasmagoria of greens and dull orange. It was not only the color of the rock, the very air seemed to be tinted with the strange, somber, ever-changing hues. He felt as though he were being swallowed by the earth.

The towering hallway through the stone opened and closed as it penetrated deeper into the canyon wall: now widening to reveal a maze of cliffs and domes and the reassuring arch of blue; then closing again in a confusion of smooth, dark, purple-green and orange-ochre rock. Where the floor curved up into the vertical walls of the passage, thin layers of the sandstone were chipped and flaked off. The exposed rock interrupted the random patterns of lichen—splashes of red, orange, green, and gray scattered across the weathered surfaces. He passed by a column of stone, shaped like a slender beehive, two dozen times his height.

For much of its length, the floor of the twisting slot canyon was bare and rounded, littered with smooth stones and pebbles, witnesses to the scouring floods that had formed the slender channel over countless centuries. In other places it was paved with tracts of fine sand, frozen into ripples as though water were still flowing over them. The stretches of bare rock and sand were interspersed with potholes, holding captive the stones that had carved them.

Water partially filled some of the potholes in still, crystalline pools. Like coins of cold, molten silver the tiny ponds alternately reflected bright orange walls and cobalt sky or dark, sunless reaches of black-streaked and patinated stone. Wetted pebbles were of enameled bronze in muted sympathy to the high burnt-red glare. Tuvi could see that the water came from long horizontal cracks in the rock above him. Clustered along and beneath the thin cracks were profusions of ferns and mosses, glowing in brilliant greens where the sun touched them, then sinking into deep purple-greens and near-blacks in the shadows of the high walls. Below these islands of life, water sheeted thinly down the vertical stone, a glistening texture trickling over dagger-like stains. Where the seeps were dry, or nearly so, the dyed rock became a kaleidoscope of blues: a deep, iridescent blue-black to metallic cobalt to chalk-white. Where the sun shone on the stains, the blacks changed to chocolate browns, and the pale blues and whites were dazzling in their brilliance.

The colors of the sandstone echoed in the adornments and woven cotton fibers Tuvi wore: about his neck a double-looped choker of earthen-toned stone, shell, and bone beads suspended a black lignite pendant, carved in the shape of a frog with eyes of inset turquoise; lignite and turquoise repeated in the pendants that hung from each ear; a red stone ring decorated a finger. The same theme of color, dominantly black, light blue, and tan, appeared in his woven cotton quiver and the band that encircled his head. All the People of the high plateau honored Mother Earth by wearing her sacred colors.

Tuvi walked around the last of the twists in the passageway. The narrow cleft widened into a vaulted grotto, and above the overhanging lip of the cavern he could see the passageway continuing at a higher level until it was out of sight. The high, burnished walls of the receding canyon were splashed with bright midday sunlight and surmounted by an arc of sky. Over the lip of the grotto, through a turquoise- and black-stained notch in the rock, a thin thread of water plunged into a dark pool that filled the bottom of the cul-de-sac. The tiny cascade made the reflection of the grotto walls seem dreamily out of focus in the surface of the pool. The air was damp. The clusters of dagger-shaped fronds of tiny fern leaves and mounds of dark moss rioted in their perfect environment. He stood still, listening to the steady, hollow plash as the filament of water spread into a stream of drops near the bottom of its plunge.

Tuvi reluctantly turned to retrace his steps through the magical hidden passage. Soon he was probing his way through the thicket at the entrance. Nearly blinded by the incandescence of the river canyon, he stopped to let his eyes adjust and heard, faintly but clearly from across the gorge, the sound that always made his whole body smile. His father's flute. Tuvi scrambled down the slope, splashed across the river, scooped up the canteen straps, and ran up the beach toward the grove. He entered the wooded side canyon, wider than the hidden place across the river. The music was louder now; each note rang sharp and resonant, but the tones seemed to have multiplied as if several flutes were being played.

Only my father can play the flute in such a way, Tuvi smiled as he marched up the sandy bottom of the side canyon. At a small cluster of trees the canyon made an abrupt right-hand turn and exploded into a massive cavern. Not like the dim, intimate grotto at the end of the hidden passageway, this was a huge theater, partly sunlit, the remainder a recession to twilight. But like the grotto at the end of the hidden passage, the overhead rock was stained blue, black, and white over which water had flowed from a slot high in the dome. Through the twisting spillway, extending hundreds of feet to the canyon rim, a narrow piece of blue appeared. Seeps emerged from the back wall, and a faint sheen of water appeared below the clumps of mosses and the masses of dagger-shaped fern fronds. Clusters of yellow blossoms engorged the seeps where the sun struck the cavern wall, and where a pool had lain in years past, a large basin of fine sand awaited the end of the long drought.

Tuvi strode into the cavern, toward a large boulder centered under the half-domed vault. The old man reclined against the rock with the flute pressed to his lips, his left ankle crossed over his right knee. Tuvi stopped and stood quietly, listening to the rising and falling tones echoing in the vast chamber. Many times he had heard his father play in the plaza above the kiva, and the sounds were always delightful; but here, in this magic place, the effect was astonishing, the delicate tones filling the entire amphitheater, closing in on him from all directions.

How can such sound come from such a simple thing? Tuvi thought as he watched his father play the tiny instrument. The flute was made from the forearm bone of the black eagle. One end of the ulna bone was plugged with cotton and piñon pitch, and near this end was a small oval hole into which his father somehow blew a stream of air from his stretched lips. At the center of the bone was another hole, followed by two others, their spacing uneven but carefully calculated, over which his father placed his fingers.

Tuvi had tried many times to play the flute, invariably succeeding only in making a harsh, rushing sound. His father would patiently show him, again and again, but Tuvi's efforts would finally send his father into spasms of laughter, usually ending with the admonition that he should be content with his work with the irrigation dams and ditches. Others in the village could make notes with the flute, even connecting them in pleasant arrangements, but only Tuvi's father could make the flute sing and sparkle with crisp, clear notes—rising and falling in cascades of long, short, and staccato tones linked together in patterns and rhythms so pleasing that Tuvi's whole being was filled with joy.

As his father played a long, descending scale, Tuvi thought of the song of the tiny wren of the river canyon. He loved the call of the little bird: the plaintive, descending, measured tones cascaded down the canyon like the wind and the water. And the imitative sound of the flute was so appropriate in this magical place at the edge of the Great River. But in the same moment Tuvi realized the wonderful sounds would probably never be heard again in this place.

"Tuvi, my third son," his father exclaimed as he turned toward his favorite child. "The flute has taken my breath. I am very thirsty." The old man reached for his canteen, glancing askance at his son's polychrome vessel.

"The sounds of the flute are so beautiful, my father," Tuvi said, kneeling in the soft sand.

"Ah, not so good any more. Without strong teeth, my mouth puckers up like an old dried yucca fruit." His father smiled, revealing the few ragged stumps remaining in his mouth.

"You are the only one in your clan who says this, my father," Tuvi replied, shaking his head. "Even the other Horn/Flute elders say you are the best." The young man's smile broke into a laugh, the sounds of his voice making the great chamber vibrate with echoes. "My father, when I came in here you looked like Kokopelli, hunched up against the rock with your legs crossed and playing the flute."

"But, my third son, I do not carry a sack of seeds on my back. And your mother tells me there is little seed left here," he roared in a contortion of laughter, while grasping his breechclouted loins.

"My father, it *is* you I see in the clan stories and travel records carved on the rock. With your gift with the flute you *must* be Kokopelli."

The old man smiled and leaned back, resting his head against the boulder and staring at the cross-bedded and tapestried ceiling high above them. Then he quietly broke the silence that had fallen over the great room. "Long ago when I was a young man," his near-whisper softly echoed, "before the time of thirst, I would see water fall through the opening up there." He pointed to the cleft in the roof, stained with the minerals of countless years of intermittently flowing water. "It would pool in that basin of sand. There were many red and yellow blossoms in the spring and early summer and over there . . ." he turned and pointed toward the area in the sunlight. "Over there, that small tree, it bloomed with the most brilliant red flowers and bright, heart-shaped leaves you have ever seen. There were many such trees in the canyon, but most are dead now. Mother Earth has taken their water."

The old man and his son rested in the sand, the whir of a grasshopper's wings occasionally breaking the silence. A hummingbird darted among the flowers clustered along the sun-splashed seeps. The tiny bird's iridescent body flashed in a shaft of light that penetrated the dim recess of the back of the grotto and pooled in a sharp yellow spot on its dark floor. Fine particles of dust moved slowly in the light's column.

"Shall we eat, my father?" Tuvi reached for the cotton pouch his father carried. The finely woven bag was similar in appearance to the young man's quiver, the cotton strapping suspending their canteens, and the headbands both men wore. Each had been carefully woven by his father on the loom in their kiva. The black, light blue, and tan cotton yarn was woven in a slit tapestry manner into diagonal patterns of hooked triangles, parallel lines, and squares with center dots. Besides the functional headband, the old man's only adornment was a bracelet of woven dog hair and fine yucca fiber, studded with dried juniper berries and turquoise and lignite beads. A few small pieces of opalescent seashell accented the finely crafted band. The shell had been traded through many hands, beginning its passage with the people who lived far to the west at Patowakacheh, the Great Water. The pieces of shell were very important to all the People, but particularly to his wife's Snake Clan. Tuvi and his brothers and sisters were among the latest members of the ancient clan

"Yes, my third son, Tuvi, I am hungry. Perhaps the *piki* and your mother's chewed bread."

"We also have some of the dried prairie dog, baked with the *tuitsma* leaves you like, and yucca fruit, my father," Tuvi said, digging through the contents of the pouch and withdrawing the rolls of thin blue corn cakes and the chewed bread.

"No, just the *piki* and the chewed bread. The meat is too tough for me."

Tuvi and his father both greatly enjoyed the *someviki*, the sweet bread the women made by chewing the cornmeal dough until much of the starch was turned to sugar by their saliva. The dough was mixed with juniper ashes, wrapped in corn husks, then baked on a hot stone.

"Are there any of the soft nuts your mother shells for me?" the old man asked. He continued to gaze up at the ceiling, studying the coloring and sculpting of the ages.

"I am sorry, my father, there are not." They both immediately thought of the disappearance of most of the wild seeds, nuts, and fruit—one of the many reasons the clans were moving south to join the rest of the People.

The old man turned to look soberly at his son. "As the Creator gave me the skill to make pleasing sounds with the flute and so to give pleasure to my people, so you, my strong third son—you were given the skills to capture and distribute the precious water to our corn, beans, squash, and cotton. When we settle again in the south, the People will look to your Snake Clan to bring us the water our crops will need.

"We knew, back when I was a boy, that we would make our home in the bottom lands and in the cliffs at Kawestima for only a short time. That is why we built the North Village crudely. It is only twenty-seven winters past that I helped in the construction of the dwellings. I chipped and carried so many stones up to the cliff site, I . . ." The old man paused a long moment. "Now we have to live up there all the time because of the raids from the Kononpaiochi." Tuvi's father continued to gaze at the layers of 100-million-year-old petrified dunes. "Just a few winters after we finished, the time of little water began, and then the sickness and the raids . . ." The old man's voice trailed off. They continued to eat in silence, both thinking deeply about this last day they would be together in the magical place by the river.

"My father," Tuvi said, interrupting the overwhelming calm of the great cavern, "tell me about your travels in the canyon of the Great River."

"A large and wondrous place, my third son. While I can honor this cavern with my flute, the canyon of the Great River has many—so very many—other places with their own wonders: strange, twisting, dark and narrow passages—like the hidden place across the river. Did you visit there today?"

Tuvi nodded. "Yes, my father, during your meditation."

"That was thoughtful of you—to give me the time alone," the old man continued, patting his son's knee. "Many other side canyons are wide and sunny, filled with groves of the water-loving trees, the hard-wooded, sharp-leafed trees, and the lovely spreading ones whose berries the squirrels like so much . . . Most are dying now." Tuvi stroked the smooth surface of his canteen while his father paused. The old man was thinking about the many changes he had seen during his long life.

"Large terraces of land are found along the river, where our ancestors used to plant; but Mother Earth has told us, reminded us many times, that we must not live down here."

"How great were the floods?" Tuvi asked, sparked by his lifelong interest in irrigation and what made the waters flow.

"Many accounts of great floods have been handed down in our stories. It is important that we remember such things. The great floods have not occurred in my life, nor in that of my father or his father, but they have come many times, and they will surely come again. Do you know the point high on the cliff, above the entrance to the hidden place, where the rock becomes more narrow?"

"Yes, I saw that today."

"Many years ago the water came halfway up to that point."

"That cannot be true, my father! Such an amount of water would have partly filled this great cavern where we sit."

"It is true, my third son," the old man nodded gravely. "In my travels up and down the river I have seen places where logs are wedged into the rocks high on the canyon wall. Only a great flood could have put them there. Remember, my third son, this wondrous place is for us to visit, and to hunt and fish in. It is a favorite creation of Mother Earth, but once in a while she decides she does not like her trees, plants, and animals she has put down here. And she wants to move her rocks and boulders around a little bit. So she sends down a great flood, then allows everything to grow back again, as lovely as before."

"How far have you traveled in Pisisvayu's home, my father?"

"Many years ago, and then again just in the past few winters, I have traveled far up and down the river's great canyon. You remember the past two winters, when I asked if you wanted to go, but you preferred to be with your young friends and to watch the girls? I have seen you looking at them as they grind the corn."

Tuvi felt his face grow hot. "Yes, my father. Yes, I know. I was very stupid."

"I was the same when I was your age, my third son. Your mother knows. Anyway, during the long dry time we have had, I have been able to travel far up and down the river. I have been four long, running days up the river's path from here, past where a large stream, filled with muddy water, used to come in from the north. Two years ago it went completely dry. Past that place the canyon gets very narrow and dark, and it winds and twists beneath high cliffs of a much darker color. The water flows more quickly, often over boulders and falls, and I could go no farther. Few trees grow, and none of the beautiful side canyons are found—no grottos with ferns and flowers like we have in this great canyon. But all the way up to the dark place, the canyon is like it is here. The river runs slowly and gently with so many beautiful side canyons that one man could not search them in a lifetime. You know the other river that joins the Great River on the south, just a short way upstream from here?"

"Yes, it comes from far to the northeast, from the lands of the clans at the green mesas."

"They are no longer so green. My clan stories tell us that they were once covered with the soft nut trees and the blue berry trees, but most are gone now, replaced only with grass." The old man sat in contemplative silence again. "Too many people . . . and now the long time of thirst."

"Are their people dying like ours, my father?"

"Yes. Mother Earth did not intend for there to be so many of us. Now her land has grown weak. Your mother and I should have stopped with you, my third son," the old man smiled, winking at his favorite.

Tuvi thought of his four younger brothers and sisters and the several more who had died as infants. He felt uncomfortable. Guilty. "You were going to tell me about the river that comes from the green mesa people."

"I have been far up that river, to where it twists and winds like the neck of a goose. More painted grottos, waterfalls, pools, and side canyons—all filled with ferns, mosses, flowers, and seeping water."

"What about down the canyon from here? I have been only as far as the wide place with the many hard-wooded trees."

"The Great River and its canyon widen in many places. Deep side canyons go farther than a man can run and return in a day, and in many of them the walls curve back against each other—like the hidden place across the river, but much larger. It all finally ends in a long, narrow run of the river with very high, steep walls. There the canyon just ends. It spreads out where many years ago, before the time of thirst, another muddy stream entered from the north—where the People gathered to trade. Below that point the river again enters a dark, winding canyon of different rock. It starts to run faster, and there are many waterfalls. I have never tried to go past that place.

"Beyond the place of the many hard-wooded trees, which you have seen, I have found more terraces and fertile areas where our people used to make their farms. The canyon walls contain many records of the travels and important events in our history. In fact, most of the story of our people is told in this canyon, to be seen and read by all who come by for as long as this great canyon remains."

"Is it not wrong, then, for us to leave it, my father?" Tuvi asked hopefully. "Where else will we find the hard stones Pisisvayu gives us to make our tools and arrowheads?"

"Such choices are not for us to make, my third son," his father said sternly. "We must follow our destiny. And now we have seen the blue star—the signal that was foretold at the Emergence. Mother Earth has also been reminding us that it is time to leave. She will continue to provide for us wherever we go."

"I wish I had come here more times," Tuvi said with a hint of tears in his eyes. "How stupid of me to ignore this place and waste my time with my friends back in our village."

"My third son, it is often the case in life that we do not appreciate something until we are about to lose it, or worst of all, until after it is gone. Mother Earth puts these places here for us. It is up to us to find them and to cherish them."

The sun was high on the eastern wall of the canyon. In the cavern it was nearly dark when Tuvi and his father finished their meal of the fish they had shot in the pools along the river and the tubers they collected in the marsh at the end of the sandbar. The light from their fire flickered on the high walls of the cavern, reflected in the thin seeps of water that tried to reach the grotto's floor. Tuvi leaned back against the block of sandstone. He watched his father closely while the old man once again produced his magic from the tiny flute. As small as it was, the instrument was limited to high pitched notes, but somehow his father played it so softly that the tones perfectly matched the acoustics of the grotto. After some time the lilting notes stopped, replaced by the old man's steady breathing as he settled into sleep in the warmth of the fire and the sand.

Tuvi awakened in the dim, gray morning light. He heard his father moving about, collecting their possessions and wrapping up the remainder of the fish that had dried over the fire during the night.

"When you grow old, my third son, you will also go to sleep early so that you can cherish each day," his father said as Tuvi got up, grumbling and shaking the sand from his hair. His father walked over to a large pile of sandstone boulders in the far recess of the cavern. When he returned he was carrying a very old kiva jar. It was the most beautiful piece Tuvi had ever seen, perfectly shaped and polished and with a fine, intricate pattern of concentric black triangles. It had been made by his father's mother, still remembered for having created the finest pottery in the Horn/Flute Clan, and his father had caused much trouble when he had removed it from the kiva to bring it here to the river many years ago, before Tuvi was born. The village *kikmongwi* and a few of the elders were still angry that it had been taken, nonetheless Tuvi's father resolutely insisted that it was his by right and, furthermore, that it belonged in the Place of the Flute.

His father sat down, with some ceremony, then placed the tiny flute and a prayer feather *paho* into the nearly spherical vessel. He sprinkled both with the sacred white cornmeal that he always carried, reciting a prayer as he did so. From the cotton pouch he then withdrew a wad of piñon pitch, wrapped in a corn husk, the amber sap still soft and sticky from the heat in the sand. Many of the men in the village liked to chew the pitch while they worked, but Tuvi did not like its strong odor and pungent taste.

"What are you doing, my father? Are you not going to take the flute?"

"It will remain here where it belongs, in the Place of the Flute, my third son," his father answered while he mixed the piñon's resin with sand and fibers from a cotton boll. He spread the tacky mixture around the recessed lip of the jar and then pressed the small lid into place.

"But do you not want to take it with you now, this last time we will be here? It is your favorite flute. And . . . and the kiva jar."

"You are right, it is my best flute. That is why it must remain here where it plays the best music. And it deserves to rest forever in this fine jar. I would never enjoy it as much in another place—I want to remember only how it sounded in this gentle canyon. Now help me hide the jar so the murdering Kononpaiochi will never find it."

His father set the old pottery urn in an obscure recess in the back of the cavern. "There. It will rest in peace," he said, satisfied. He placed the last of a pile of rocks over the recess and walked back into the dim, early morning light. "Come, my third son. It is time to leave."

The sun was just rising over the vast expanse of bald sandstone domes, cliffs, pinnacles, and buttes to the east when Tuvi joined his father on the rim. To the west, the bright dawn was creeping, copper and gold, down the peaks toward the darkened canyon and its river far below. To the south, rising sharply above them in the brilliant light, was the peak of great Tokónave, on whose flanks the Snake Clan had once lived.

"When I was a boy, patches of snow would remain up there throughout most of the year," Tuvi's father said while observing his son looking up at the broad, wooded mountain, rising above timberline near its summit. "It was from Wuhkokiekeu that your clan moved to Kawestima many years ago, my third son. We have all moved enough. Now we have earned the right to settle for all time at Flower Mound," the old man added wearily.

"My father, do you think that our long-lost white brothers, the *pahanas*, who departed from us when we emerged at the Sipapuni, will finally join us all at Flower Mound?"

Tuvi's father squinted into the brilliant light of the east and shook his head slowly. "Remember, my third son, our white brothers took the witch woman, Powaku, with them when they went east after our emergence from the Third World. So, they will know both good and evil. We must be very vigilant if they return to rejoin us."

"But, are we not awaiting the one *pahana* who it is told will bring us great benevolence, my father?"

"Yes . . . But we must be certain when the *pahana* arrives that he is the awaited one."

With a last long gaze down into the canyon and the intimate places they had both loved through their lives, the two generations of their mothers' ancient clans turned southeast from the rising sun and began the long walk home.

2

The Colorado River, August 1, 1869

"Andy, Missouri, bring the sextant and tripod up from the *Kitty*. This will be a good place to fix our position."

"On the way, sir," came the reply from one of the two men dragging the oak dory onto the gently sloping beach. Two other boats, one identical to the first and the other smaller and made of pine, rested on the sand, their bows pulled halfway out of the turbulent brown water running past the beach. The river made a long, wide turn beneath a sandstone monolith that rose above the outside curve of the canyon.

Ten weeks earlier the three boats and a fourth one had been painted a gleaming white. Loaded heavily with equipment and provisions, they had cast off from a sand spit at Green River City, Wyoming. The departure point was just below the new Union Pacific Railroad bridge, which marked the railroad's progress toward the historic meeting earlier that month with the rival Central Pacific Railroad at Promontory, Utah. Now only patches of white remained on the boats, their hulls scraped and gouged, the planking smeared with pine pitch to seal the seams.

"Look at that, Andy," Billy Hawkins said as he pointed to another of the heavy double oak frames that had detached from the planking of the *Maid of the Cañon.* Slivers of light shone through some of the seams in the boat's hull.

"Aye, I saw it when we left Cataract Canyon," Andy Hall replied grimly, the young Scotsman's face appearing much older than its nineteen years. "Has'na been a prooblem through this quiet water, but we canna' leave it be. I dinna ken when the river will be ugly again, but it sairly weel."

Billy Hawkins dug through the forward locker in the other heavy oak boat and hauled out the sextant box and the tripod. "*Kitty*'s lookin' pretty sorry, too," he concluded after carefully examining several of the sprung and cracked frames in *Kitty Clyde's Sister.*

"Sairly wish we still had some'a those tools we lost. Make it a la' easier to make the boats right."

"Well, if we still had all that luggage we wouldn't have made it this far. I think the Major wants to stay here a couple'a days, so we'll have time to make some more patches and saw some oars. Seen a lot of driftwood at the head of the bar when we pulled in."

They both looked up as two other men came down the sloping beach to the boats. While all of the nine men in the party had blended into a common physical appearance wrought by ten weeks at the mercy of first the Green and now the Colorado River: shaggy, matted, and sand-filled hair and beards; sun- and windburned faces and arms; ragged and torn cotton shirts; wool or buckskin trousers; bare feet, sodden shoes, or hand sewn moccasins; the two men walking down to the boats differed from the younger men—not in appearance but in demeanor. They were sober and detached, with a bearing possessed only by men who have not only experienced combat but who have been forced to order others to their deaths. They had survived the long, terrible war in the East, and along with the other Union veterans in the river expedition they had fled into the new, open, free, and anonymous expanses of the far West. Nonetheless they would carry with them for the rest of their lives the profound emotional trauma the war had inflicted. Both George Bradley and Walter Powell were coolly competent, possessed little humor, seldom spoke, and often stayed to themselves when circumstances permitted.

"An' where would Dunn and the Howlands be off to?" Andy Hall asked while Bradley and Captain Powell reached into the *Emma Dean* to remove another armload of gear. The smaller pine boat had fared better than her more heavily laden companions.

"Went back into the trees up there to find a camp. Probably get windy out here tonight," Bradley answered. "And we better get to work on the boats. No telling when this quiet water is going to end and down we'll go again."

Whether jovial or somber, carefree or meticulous, every member of the party was constantly aware that they still had over 2,000 feet to drop in the canyons ahead before they reached the known elevation at the mouth of the Virgin River. The longer they floated through the nearly flat, gentle reaches of this red sandstone canyon, the faster they would eventually have to fall. And at any time they might come to a place in the canyons where the river fell too steeply for the boats to run, where there was no place to portage or line the boats through—or even to climb out. They grumbled increasingly about the continual stops their leader required to make his sextant and barometer observations of position and elevation. Now stops were being made to inspect the Indian ruins they saw along the walls and rims of this quiet canyon. Besides the general urge to get on with the trip, there was the shortage of food. Their ten months' supply was now reduced to about 200 pounds of mildewed flour, less than fifteen pounds of sour bacon—already boiled several times—two bags of dried apples, and a sack of coffee. Each stop on the river, seeming unnecessary to most of the crew who had no interest in scientific observation, meant they were that much closer to running out of food.

"Anything left of those sheep we got up in Cataract Canyon, Billy?" Captain Powell asked. Billy Hawkins preferred to be called "Missouri," a reference to his service in his home state's militia, but the name had not stuck with most of the men.

"Nope. The last of it turned yesterday, what with this heat. Maybe we can jump somethin' in the willows along this bar. Good job for Oramel and Dunn when they get back." Billy Hawkins was the expedition cook, carefully monitoring and husbanding the dwindling food store. The heavily-built young man was always ready with a laugh or a joke when things went badly, but no one, not even the expedition leader, argued with him about his food rationing decisions.

The two men who stood farther up the beach were also Union army veterans. Jack Sumner was a lightly built, cat-quick man, uniformly acknowledged to be the best boatman in the group. Together with Bill Dunn, it was his job to respond quickly when the *Emma Deàn* was scouting the river ahead of the other boats, probing for the best route through a runable rapid or scuttling ashore above a dangerous one. A wave of their leader's red handkerchief as he stood on the mid deck of the *Emma Dean* would send the heavy oak freight boats toward shore upstream. After scouting the rapid, he alone would decide whether to run, to line the boats through the rocks near the bank, or to carry them around the fall in the river. His decision meant the difference between a twenty- or thirty-second—but perhaps expedition-ending—run, a difficult lining among the boulders, or several hours of back-breaking portaging of gear and heavy boats. Most of the men thought their leader was too cautious, since it was not his back being broken by the endless portaging. But the same men did not share his deep concern for the precious sextants and barometers and even for the boats themselves—the concern that made the difference between a successful scientific expedition to chart the course of the Colorado River or a mere adventuresome frolic.

The man standing with Jack Sumner gazed up at the huge sentinel of rock towering above the rim of the canyon across the river. John Wesley Powell resembled the rest of the ragged crew in general physical appearance. His stylish, mid-Victorian mustaches and heavy sideburns had degenerated into a tangled black and graying mass. A stranger happening upon the scene on the beach would quickly surmise, however, that he was in command. The stranger would also notice that the abrupt, busy man was missing his right arm below the elbow, the victim of a Confederate Minié ball it had received in the fierce battle at Pittsburgh Landing, Tennessee. But the loss of his forearm to the 53-caliber rifled slug caused Major (Brevet Lieutenant Colonel) Powell little inconvenience. Although he did not routinely bend to the tasks of lining and portaging the boats, he regularly and persistently climbed the steep side canyons, cliffs, and talus slopes in order to make observations of the surrounding country and to measure the heights of the canyon walls by means of the glass barometer he would carry. His climbs were often hurried, and consequently even more dangerous, because of the need to make the barometric readings at prearranged times to match corresponding readings on companion equipment at the canyon floor. This double procedure guaranteed an accurate measurement of the relative change in atmospheric pressure and helped account for the vagaries of local conditions. Long before the camp awoke and long after it retired, Major Powell would be recording his observations and keeping his journal.

"You're welcome to take the latitude observations at noon, Jack," he said to the intense man standing next to him. "You're getting mighty good with the instrument."

"Thank you, Major. I do like the precision and order of the celestial work." He followed his leader's gaze up the high rock across the river. Jack Sumner had been a co-planner of the expedition and among all the men he possessed by far the most wilderness experience.

"That is, unless it will interfere with your name carving. How many trees and rock walls have you left your mark on now, Mr. Sumner?"

"I just want people to know I've been by here, sir. That's all."

"There will be no question of that," Major Powell said with a slight smile. "Now, I'm going on up the bar to see if I can find a way out. Where's Oramel? Not back yet? He'll probably want to go along. Here comes Bill."

Bill Dunn emerged from the willows that extended down the long bar of sand. His jet-black hair hung to his shoulders, and unlike the others, he wore a full suit of buckskin, dark and shiny from untold months of dirt, grease, and sweat. When not out on the river, Bill Dunn was happiest on a quiet hunt for whatever game animal happened to be near.

"Nothin' in there, Major," the wiry former soldier announced as he walked up, placing the butt of his rifle in the sand.

"Where are Oramel and Seneca?" Major Powell asked. "They find us a camp yet?"

"They went snoopin' around back there." Bill Dunn waved toward a copse of trees at the mouth of a narrow side canyon.

"Don't you ever get tired'a messin' with that mop'a hair?" Billy Hawkins grinned at Bill Dunn while he unshouldered the heavy oak tripod and spread its legs in the sand.

"Now, Missouri, you just tend to your cookin' and let me be about my hair. If the good Lord meant for us to be all the while a'croppin' our hair, we'd'a been born with shears."

Major Powell helped their young cook set the sextant on the tripod. "Mr. Sumner here is getting pretty good with the instrument," he smiled at the fair-haired Jack Sumner, the man the usually gruff, former officer most respected and relied upon among all the men. Despite the rigors and strains of the long, dangerous trip down the unknown river, neither of them displayed a hint of the mutual animosity that would grip them years later. "We're about two miles down from the confluence with the San Juan, and I want to get a good fix here. The government maps are all wrong about where the rivers join."

"Major Powell! Come on up here, you've got to see this!" The seven men on the beach all looked up at Seneca Howland, shouting from the grove of trees near the cliff.

They ran up the beach and pushed through a thicket of cottonwood, box elder, and hackberry trees, following Seneca up the vegetation-choked passage. Soon they were walking between high, curving, tapestried walls of darkened sandstone. Less than fifty yards into the passage, at a small stand of redbud trees, the younger Howland brother led them through a sharp right-hand turn. The cluster of men stopped abruptly.

George Bradley exhaled a long, breathy whistle. The group continued to stand in silence while the last faint reverberation of the sound faded in the stillness of the soaring cavern.

Blue-eyed Andy Hall spoke for them all: "Aye, 'tis the very hand'a God Himself ha' done this," he said quietly.

"Captain Powell," the expedition leader said to his brother, "we'll bring our camp in here tonight. Right next to that big rock over there. And Missouri, try not to disturb the sand in that pool. I think we'll all enjoy just looking at it lying still."

They had been a party of ten in four of the small boats when the expedition departed from Green River City, Wyoming, on May 24. The venture down the unknown canyons of the Green and Colorado Rivers was not a lark. It was a serious, well-planned expedition to explore the last uncharted region in the United States, to document carefully the course of the rivers through their mysterious canyons, and to record what was found along the route. Major John Wesley Powell had assembled a competent and enthusiastic group of men for his venture. All were motivated and strong, most of them disciplined from the ordeal of the Civil War, and together they brought to the expedition a fine combination of wilderness survival skills.

Their leader had also gathered the best information available for the design and construction of the wooden boats that would carry the men and their stores and equipment through the unknown region. He'd had a glimpse of what he would face during two previous years in the mountains of western Colorado, but he had no way to know of the terrible demands the river and its canyons would make on the boats and their crews. Despite the careful preparations, the heavily loaded and only marginally stable wooden dories, manned by men who were strong and willing but inexperienced with the power of a great river, were often swamped and overturned. In the upper reach of the Green River, in a place they had named the Canyon of Lodore, the expedition suffered its first great misfortune. One of the boats, the *No-Name,* together with nearly all of its cargo, was lost. The boat, some of the instruments, and the one-third of the expedition's food stores it carried, were crushed in a rapid the men later named Disaster Falls. One week later more of the gear, including much of their bedding and clothes that had not been lost with the *No-Name*, and nearly all of their mess kit, was left when the men were forced to retreat into the river from a wildfire the cook fire had started. The remaining three boats were crowded, causing one of the crew members, himself particularly chastened by the river's unexpected violence, to abandon the venture shortly thereafter when they passed near the Indian agency on the Uinta River.

On down through the canyons—named by them Desolation, Gray, Labyrinth, and Stillwater—to the junction of the Grand and Green Rivers, which combined to form the Colorado, the three boats and their crews descended. They glided smoothly through many sections, but crashed, spun, and rolled through others when decisions were made to run the rapids rather than to line the boats through or carry the vessels around the obstacles.

Past the junction of the two rivers, they were faced with a canyon that was a nearly continuous series of rapids. When they were finally spit out of this maelstrom, named Cataract Canyon by unanimous agreement, they entered a section of serene water. It would continue for nearly 160 miles through the red walls and domes of the Kayenta and Navajo sandstones. The expedition's landing on the bar just below the confluence of the Colorado and San Juan Rivers came after they had floated peacefully for a little more than three days, and the idyllic canyon and the gentle river had done much to mitigate the traumas of the previous two months, the worries over the diminished and spoiled food supply, and the knowledge that they still had a long way to drop before they reached the mouth of the Virgin River. As anxious as they were to move on, the hidden cavern and its setting held the men strangely captive. Repairs and other work were needed. Observations had to be taken. Excuses were found to ignore their growling stomachs and stay in the magical place.

Bill Dunn watched while the Howland brothers finished carving their initials and last names next to his. The bright sandstone shone through the centuries of desert varnish where the steel knife blades had gouged it away. At other places throughout the great canyon, other men had long ago carved figures and symbols into the rock. The old inscriptions had been made unhurriedly, with great planning and ritual; done without the advantage of sharp steel. And they told far more than a name. No living eyes remained that could read in precise detail the stories told in the rock.

"Ye're all gettin' as bad as Jack, a-carrvin' yeer Johnny Hancocks all over the place," Andy Hall said, watching Oramel Howland finish the last letter. "Now, if ye're not too busy, give Missouri and me a hand siftin' the flour. Ye do want to eat, don't ye?"

"That rotty old mosquito net is more hole than net," Seneca answered.

"Jus' shut up an' help us push the lumps through," Billy Hawkins shot back.

The sun was high on the eastern wall above the river. Back in the water-hewn grotto, a fire blazed and snapped against the large boulder where the camp had been gathered. The several conversations filled the great room with a confusion of echoes, overlapping and blending into a single background murmur.

"I sure do hope Captain Powell don't sing 'Ol' Shady' again," Seneca Howland whispered to his brother. "You'd'a thought he would'a got the message when we started callin' him Old Shady."

"Somehow," the elder Howland replied, "it won't bother me so much tonight—here, in this place." The two men and their regular companion, Bill Dunn, were leaning against the opposite wall of the cavern, staring up at the vault of carved rock, water stain tapestry, and seeps.

"The Major couldn't get up them *moqui* steps he found, so I guess we'll be stayin' tomorrow while he tries across the river," Bill Dunn said quietly. "Give us plenty'a time to caulk the oak boats and finish sawin' them oars. Tomorrow, Oramel, you get to be in the pit pullin' on that whip saw with the dust fallin' in your face."

"My old back just isn't as good as you young bucks'," the older Howland brother groaned. At 36 he was the oldest man in the expedition, a fact reinforced by his long, graying beard. He was most similar to their leader in education and interests; accordingly, he functioned as a much-needed buffer between the intense, often pompous, overly cautious John Wesley Powell with his preoccupation with matters of science, and the former soldiers who unavoidably harbored some animosity toward a former officer. Oramel Howland's close camaraderie with the other men and the fact of his not having been an officer did much to control criticism of their leader by the men whose labors made the expedition go forward. "We're gonna need those oars, though, soon's this river decides to get nasty again. Oughta be glad we found the cottonwood logs, I guess."

"Now, Oramel," Bill Dunn said after a moment. "Don't be complainin' so much about the sawin'. You spend most of your time workin' on them damn river charts the Major wants done so bad. You're lucky you're an artist and not just a strong back like me'n Seneca here."

"Yeah," Seneca chimed in, "and Sumner and Bradley are all the time sneakin' off to write in their own diaries or climbin' with the Major or messin' with the barometers. And Captain Powell's about worthless. That leaves Missouri and Andy, and me and Billy, to do all the shit work around camp. And we're all starvin'. We just can't keep up all this heavy work on what food we get. And the Major—he don't seem to notice. Just goes off climbin' up and down every other cliff he sees."

"Seneca, I've explained to all of you, over and over, how important the scientific observations are." Oramel Howland avoided telling the men that an eclipse of the moon would occur in a few days and that would necessitate another day-long stop for a climb to the rim to make observations. With the time of the eclipse exactly known, they could confirm their time and, accordingly, their exact longitude. "And don't be talkin' that way about the Major," the older Howland warned his brother. "I mean, everybody likes you an' all, but if old Bradley heard you he'd skin your ass."

"Better not be Cap'n Powell calls you out. I'd take care of him," Bill Dunn growled. Early on in the expedition the former soldier and mountain man had clashed with their leader's moody brother.

"We ought'a just be thinkin' about gettin' on outta here, that's all," Seneca snapped. Like his companions, the younger Howland was torn between the welcome respite in the peaceful place and the overarching reality of their situation. "I mean, I don't think the Major has any real idea where we are, much less what we're gonna find ahead of us."

"Seneca's right, Oramel," Bill Dunn nodded grimly. "When we see the chance, we ought'a just leave. I'm not gonna starve to death in this canyon while I wait for that damn river to kill me."

Major Powell sat by the cook fire, watching Missouri pile coals on the lid of the big camp kettle, a fortunate survivor of the wildfire debacle in the Canyon of Lodore. Its precious load of pan bread, scraps of bacon, some stewed apples, and coffee would be their meal—tonight and for the next month, unless some game were found. He fully appreciated the food situation and he was not unaware of the griping among the men, but his steadfast belief, born of years of military service, was that such grumbling was normal, even desirable. So long as joking and laughter mixed with the complaints, he was not concerned; and so far that had been the case. But he was growing aware that the Howlands and Dunn were drawing apart from the others in camp. They continued to interact with the rest of the men, and there had not yet been open dissension, but Major Powell knew he had to keep the men busy. Idleness—idleness and deadly silence—were the things to be avoided at all cost.

The spirits of the men, even the Howlands and Dunn, had started to lighten during the past four days in this peaceful sandstone canyon. Everyone, despite the limited food and the uncertainty of what lay ahead, had marveled over the canyon's abundant vegetation, its great royal arches carved in the high cliffs, its mysterious side canyons and twilit alcove gulches, its streaked and colorful walls, and its many glens of ferns, mosses, and flowers. Now, in this inspiring and dramatic cavern surrounding their camp, the men seemed very nearly at peace. John Wesley Powell reflected on the discovery of the great cavern. Mere fortuity could not have led them to stop at this particular place.

"You ready for supper, Major?" Missouri's inquiry broke his reverie.

"I certainly am," he answered, stooping to examine the contents of the dutch oven. "You're doing a fine job stretching the bacon."

"I cut some up and mixed it in with the bread. Gives a little flavor and goes a long way. It's not so noticeable it's been boiled a couple'a times already."

"We're fortunate to still have the apples. Did they get a good drying today?"

"All afternoon. They keep us from scurvy, I guess."

"Just don't let Andy collect us another mess of greens like he did at the mouth of the White," the Major barked. A chorus of laughter and groans erupted from the rest of the men, now gathering around the glowing fire.

"Ye willna' le' me forrgit that, will ye?" Andy Hall shot back to an explosive increase in laughter, now accompanied by catcalls. The great room thundered with the happy sounds of the clutch of men crouched far beneath its arching ceiling, the laughter in response to the still vivid memory of the food poisoning they had endured. The passage of a month had not erased vivid recall of the wretched aftermath of eating the potato tops Andy had gathered from an Indian garden on an island in the river.

As for Missouri's cooking, however, all joking had long since been abandoned. The canyons, rapids, and falls that lay ahead were uncertain, but the quantity of food remaining was clearly defined—something less than one month, with the fare soon to be reduced to bread, stewed apples, and coffee.

"'Tis a sartin we need to find a couple'a wee sheep," Andy said after the laughter died away. In an instant everyone remembered the feast back in Cataract Canyon when Dunn and Bradley had managed to shoot two young bighorns.

"Yeah, but next time we're gonna jerk all the meat so's it'll last," Missouri said conclusively. "Just broke my heart dumpin' the last of it two days ago. Almost as bad as when the beans sprouted and spoiled."

Jack Sumner carefully took his piece of the pan bread. "Remember the sugar?" he sighed.

"All right, everyone, that's enough," Major Powell commanded. "In all these fine, wooded side canyons we're bound to jump some game. As far as we managed to climb up the Indian steps we found today, Bradley and I got a good view of the big, dark mountain just to the south of here. There will be plenty of game in that area, and we can augment our supply of piñon pitch." A glance at his sleeveless good arm would remind every man that it had been their leader who only a few days before had climbed out of the canyon to find the desperately needed caulking resin. He had used his shirt sleeve to carry down the quantity he had collected. After more than two months in the deep canyons, not a man in the group failed to marvel at his leader's ability to climb with only one arm. Major Powell was often able to go where no one else would, or even could, follow.

"How about a tune, Captain?" George Bradley asked. As highly as he thought of his like-minded companion, he also hoped there would not be a repeat of "Ol' Shady."

Everyone had settled back, most resting against the convenient slope of the large boulder. The moving light of the fire reflected in the seeps running down the back recess of the cavern and in the still surface of the plunge pool. The crackling fire echoed softly. Every man retreated into his own private world while Walter Powell's deep bass voice began to ring through the air. He had a fine voice, compensating for his otherwise dour disposition—a depressed condition from his time in the Confederate prison camp at Fort Sorghum. Everyone always enjoyed Captain Powell's occasional serenades at camp in the evening, but this night, in the grand cavern, what the men heard was far more than pleasant singing. All had gotten used to the murmuring echoes of their talking, but now the ever-present background growl underwent a profound change. A single human singing voice became a choir. Nearly six centuries had passed since the great hall had responded to the ordered succession of tones and cadences that the human ear finds so pleasing, and buoyed by the amplification and chorus of his voice, Old Shady brought forth his finest effort. The sculpted and domed expanse of ancient rock responded in kind: the result lovely, inspiring, and grand beyond description. With the end of each rendition came demands for more until the amateur voice finally began to falter.

> " . . . Let the Hero, born of woman,
> crush the serpent with his heel,
> "Since God is marching on."

"That's all, boys," Walter Powell announced. "There's no more music left in me. And it's a good note to end our Sabbath."

"Amen," George Bradley said. The former sergeant was very serious about keeping the Sabbath, necessary repairs to their boats and scientific explorations excepted.

"This is truly a place that was meant for music," Major Powell said thoughtfully, reflecting the happiness that had settled over the group.

"Na' just a place, Major," Andy Hall said. "'Tis a grrand temple'a music."

"That's it, then," George Bradley added with uncharacteristic enthusiasm. "We should call this place Music Temple."

"And so it will be recorded in my journal this evening," Major Powell exulted with a slap to his thigh. Unanimous nods and silence endorsed the most appropriate choice of the name.

The nine men would spend another day of work and exploration and another evening of song at the enchanted place on the wide curve of the river. As the human mind tries to expunge the horrors it witnesses, so it also seeks to amplify and preserve what is pleasant. Of the six men who survived the remainder of that journey in the summer of 1869, all would remember for the rest of their lives the two days and nights at the very special place—the Music Temple in the lovely, gentle and quiet reach of the river they would name Glen Canyon.

Cathedral in the Desert, 1959 (*Tad Nichols*).

3

Music Temple, April 19, 1963

Throughout the uncounted millennia during which the great layers of sandstone in the Colorado Plateau were uplifted and eroded, the dominant mechanism of change had been moving water. Like the many side canyons, arches, alcoves, glens, and grottos along the length of Glen Canyon, the particular cavern located in the east wall of the Colorado River canyon, seventy-one miles above Lee's Ferry, Arizona, was also formed by the movement of water: the slow seeps from cracks and fissures in the ancient rock; the regular, storm-born freshets cascading from the canyon rim; the infrequent cataclysmic floods that roared down the main stem of the river and inundated the chamber with churning rock- and sand-filled whirlpools, forever demonstrating Nature's disdain for finished product. For a million years before a creature even remotely resembling a man had stood upon the earth, such had been the forces that formed and sculpted the Music Temple.

On this arbitrary day in the spring of an arbitrary year denoted 1963, the timeless cavern at the wide sweep of the river was experiencing something entirely new. It had begun a few days previously at the great turn below the monolith of sandstone when the ancient flow of the river ended as it entered a quietly swirling pool of frothy, flotsam-choked slack water. As each day passed, the point where the free-flowing river entered the dank rising water moved farther and farther up the canyon. And with each day, the trash-laden still water advanced up the amber sandbar and through the bank of willows and chokecherry bushes above the bar to the base of the high sandstone cliff. On this particular day, a long finger of the quiet water intruded up the narrow side canyon and probed into the temple in the stone. In the shallow, rising pool on this bright morning, the brilliant pink blossoms of a hedgehog cactus shone up through the silty water, patiently reaching for, celebrating, the life-giving light and heat from the sun. As the days passed, the petals and sepals of the little cactus plant blossoms gathered less and less light, finally closing permanently in the strangling, unending night.

What the river and the Music Temple were experiencing had begun three months before at a place fifty-six miles down the river's course. An enormous dam had been erected across the ancient bed of the river. On a January day, with the man-made monolith nearly complete, the entrance to the west diversion tunnel around the dam was slammed shut. The water suddenly stopped and, with nowhere to go, began to back up behind a cofferdam, just upstream from the 4.9-million-cubic-yard block of concrete wedged between the red sandstone walls. When it had risen thirty-three feet, extending a 119,000-acre-foot pool of water nearly fifteen miles upstream, the river was again liberated through the east canyon wall diversion tunnel.

On March 13 the east tunnel was closed, with only 1,000 cubic feet per second allowed through to keep the river alive below the dam: the filling of Powell Reservoir had begun. Farther and farther, back and up the gentle slope of the river, the dank pool of water crept, flooding the tranquil meadows and cane-filled marshes, drowning the sun-dappled groves of Gambel oak and cottonwood and the thickets of willow, chokecherry, acacia, and mesquite. The myriad side canyons, each a microcosm of the mother canyon, also fell victim to the rising flood. The huge amphitheaters with their cool, shady springs and seeps, engorged with profusions of ferns, primroses, and soft emerald mosses—all disappeared, strangled, and died. The towering arches cut into the sandstone, the intimate cloisters, and the tapestried desert-varnished walls—all slid beneath the still, black water.

At the wide curve of the river fifty-six miles above the obstruction, in the grotto of the Music Temple, the water crept above the clumps of grasses, sedges, rushes, and reeds that grew in the soft, fine sand, then started to climb the trunks of the box elders, the Fremont cottonwood trees, and the hackberry trees whose fruit the squirrels loved to eat. The debris-laden water spilled into and contaminated the crystal pool at the base of the back wall of the cavern and began to inch up the stained and varnished rock toward the profusions of life that hung along the seeps. The worn and weathered boulder resting in the sand floor of the Music Temple became an island and then, too, slipped beneath the rising surface.

In the farthest reach of the cavern, the insistent water tried to lift an old, finely glazed pottery jar, but the buoyant force was stopped by a pile of sandstone rocks and slabs. Within the watertight spherical vessel rested an ulna bone and a clutch of downy breast feathers from a golden eagle. Both the segment of bone and the feathers had been changed and formed by the hand of a human into things of use and reverence to him.

In the sunlit portion of the ancient temple the water reached for the brilliant magenta-red blossoms of the redbud trees and climbed toward the explosions of monkey flowers and fleabane, the delicate golden columbines, and the orchids and cardinal flowers growing with the ferns and mosses along the seams in the rock. In the innermost reaches of the temple, the arrowhead-shaped fronds of maidenhair fern and the cushion tufts of mosses succumbed to the dark, lifeless water. The daggered tapestry stains of the ages now ended abruptly at the fetid, advancing surface; in time, even the top of the intermittent waterfall vanished, no longer able to plunge into its crystal pool. Inexorably, the whole of the Music Temple disappeared beneath the stagnant water. The only evidence of its existence was a narrow, winding arm of the reservoir extending back into the stone—what had once been the crescent-thin skylight, soaring hundreds of feet above the floor of the great cavern.

Seventeen years would pass before the contained waters finally lapped at the tops of the spillway gates of Glen Canyon Dam, at an elevation exactly 3,700 feet above sea level and 420 feet above the floor of the Music Temple. Behind the structure stood 27 million acre feet of water: enough to cover 2.7 million football fields ten feet deep. The expanse of slack water extended upriver 186 miles, swallowing the entirety of Glen Canyon, Narrow Canyon, and the lower reaches of Cataract Canyon. Over the ensuing years, the level of the reservoir would alternately drop and rise according to the demands for irrigation and for the electricity produced by releasing the impounded water through generating turbines at the base of the dam. Dry years with diminished runoff would cause the lake level to drop farther. A huge, lifeless ring formed around the perimeter of the reservoir as the stagnant water leached the color from the surface of the sandstone. Except for the summers of the years 1980 through 1984, when the reservoir has filled, anyone floating on its surface is surrounded by the bleached and sterile border. Although it is named Lake Powell, the huge impoundment is not a lake. A lake is a living, natural thing, slowly built by the patient forces of Nature in a controlled scheme, in total symbiosis with its surroundings. What stands behind the Glen Canyon dam is a reservoir—a tank with a leached and lifeless rim, relentlessly filling with the entrapped sand and silt so needed to sustain the natural life of the river below the dam: throughout the course of Marble Canyon and the length of Grand Canyon National Park.

Far beneath the surface of the reservoir, down through the narrow, twisting crevice in the ancient rock, the Music Temple rests in cold, dead, slime-laden, ink-blackness. No evidence of life remains save for the occasional intrusion of fishes able to withstand the crushing pressure of the water. And so the Music Temple waits.

But waiting is a component, a feature, of the passage of time, and Mother Earth and her river have no recognition of time. Time is a concept needed only by the recent man creature, who is granted so little of it. When the now-cemented sands of the Music Temple were first being laid down in wind-driven drifts, the South Atlantic Ocean had not yet formed. The eastern bulge of South America rested against the curve of the West African coast, the nascent ocean a mere rift in the land mass. Between that time in the history of the earth and the present, the now-recognized continents drifted apart, the Atlantic Ocean was created, then in a relative instant of recent geologic time, the whole of the sandstone-laden Colorado Plateau uplifted and the river cut through it, forming the great canyonlands. Such is the nature of the thing man calls *time*. And so the Music Temple waits.

Glen Canyon Dam (*Bureau of Reclamation*).

The river at Hidden Passage, 1960 (*Tad Nichols*).

1968 (*Tad Nichols*).

1993, with bathtub ring (*S. Hannon*).

4

GLEN CANYON DAM, JUNE 6, 1983

Six men stood on the top of the dam near the left elevator tower. Each looked intently down at the foaming white plume of water arcing out over the river from the deflector bucket at the end of the left spillway tunnel, 550 feet below them and 1,300 feet down the left wall of the deep gorge. Through the soles of their shoes the men could feel the vibration that accompanied the intermittent rumbling coming from deep in the sandstone canyon wall. Two of the men studied the emerging water through binoculars.

"Yeah, there's definitely material in the jet."

"Yes, I see it too," the operations and maintenance chief agreed. "When're the people from Denver getting here?"

"They should be landing any time, Randy," the O&M chief's assistant replied.

"Okay, Salt Lake authorized us to cut her back from 20,000," Randy MacConnell said while the group walked back along the crest of the dam toward the left spillway inlet. "We're to try 10,000, with the right side opened to 10,000. And tell the guys to bring the cart topside."

After twenty-five years with the Bureau of Reclamation, it grated on Randy MacConnell a little bit that he had to clear all water releases with the Upper Basin headquarters in Salt Lake. As the number two man at the Glen Canyon unit, this was *almost* his dam, after all. But he also realized that only the headquarters was in a position to coordinate and manage all the dams and structures throughout the 108,000 square miles of the Upper Basin of the Colorado River.

The tunnel spillways were cut into the Navajo sandstone just upstream from either end of the dam. Water may first enter the spillways when the surface of the reservoir rises to 3,648 feet above sea level, seventy-one feet beneath the 3,719-foot elevation at the tops of the parapet walls on the crest of the dam. Curved steel radial gates hold back the reservoir up to a level of 3,700 feet. When the gates open, rotating upward, water enters each spillway at the 3,648-foot level, under the lower edges of the gates. From the inlet, the released water descends 600 feet at a 55° angle through the wall of the canyon. At the bottom of the incline, the water turns in a smooth curve into a horizontal section of tunnel, discharging at the bottom of the canyon 1,300 feet beyond the toe of the dam. Then as it exits the tunnel, the water hits a curved flip bucket, directing the jet of water away from the canyon wall and arcing it upward to dissipate its kinetic energy.

Any impoundment of water must have a spillway: a controlled means to bypass excess water accumulating behind the dam structure. Spillways are sized, after a careful investigation of the highest flood flows that may occur in the watershed intercepted by the dam, in a trade-off between the probability of water flow and cost of construction. At Glen Canyon Dam, each spillway tunnel was designed to transport up to 138,000 cubic feet of water per second, but even at this rate of flow the tunnels would not be completely full. A portion of each tunnel's cross section must be exposed to atmospheric air pressure as though the tunnels were simply inclined, open flumes. The tunnels must never be completely filled, for then they would become pressure conduits, a regime they were not designed to withstand.

Today, a cautious United States Bureau of Reclamation engineer would likely say that he does not like tunnel spillways. His counterpart in the early 1950s when the dam was designed would probably have said the same thing. But the engineers were told to build a dam at this particular place in the canyon, and the location mandated tunnel spillways according to the technology and the budget available at the time.

Early on, long before the era of great dam building by the Bureau of Reclamation, engineers, dreamers, politicians, and bureaucrats recognized that gently sloping Glen Canyon would be a marvelous place to build a dam. With an average incline of only two feet per mile, the canyon would impound far more water with a given-sized structure than would, for example, the Grand Canyon with its average slope of eight feet per mile. By the time the federal government and its water- and electricity-using clients became serious about building a dam in the lower end of Glen Canyon, investigations had revealed only two feasible sites. The candidate eleven miles downstream from the one selected, located on a sharp gooseneck turn in the canyon, could have avoided tunnel spillways. An over-the-crest spillway could have been used, with the power plant located around the bend in the river; the powerhouse penstocks would then have been tunneled through the inside turn of the canyon. However, that site had serious foundation rock problems, notably a thick seam of Chinle shale that would have dissolved under the weight and water pressure of a large concrete dam. The selected location had acceptable foundation rock, the geologists and engineers decided, but in the narrow, straight section of canyon where the dam would be built, the hydroelectric plant could only be located at the foot of the dam. Accordingly, a simple over-the-crest spillway was not possible. The spillways would have to be tunneled through the foundation rock and around the dam.

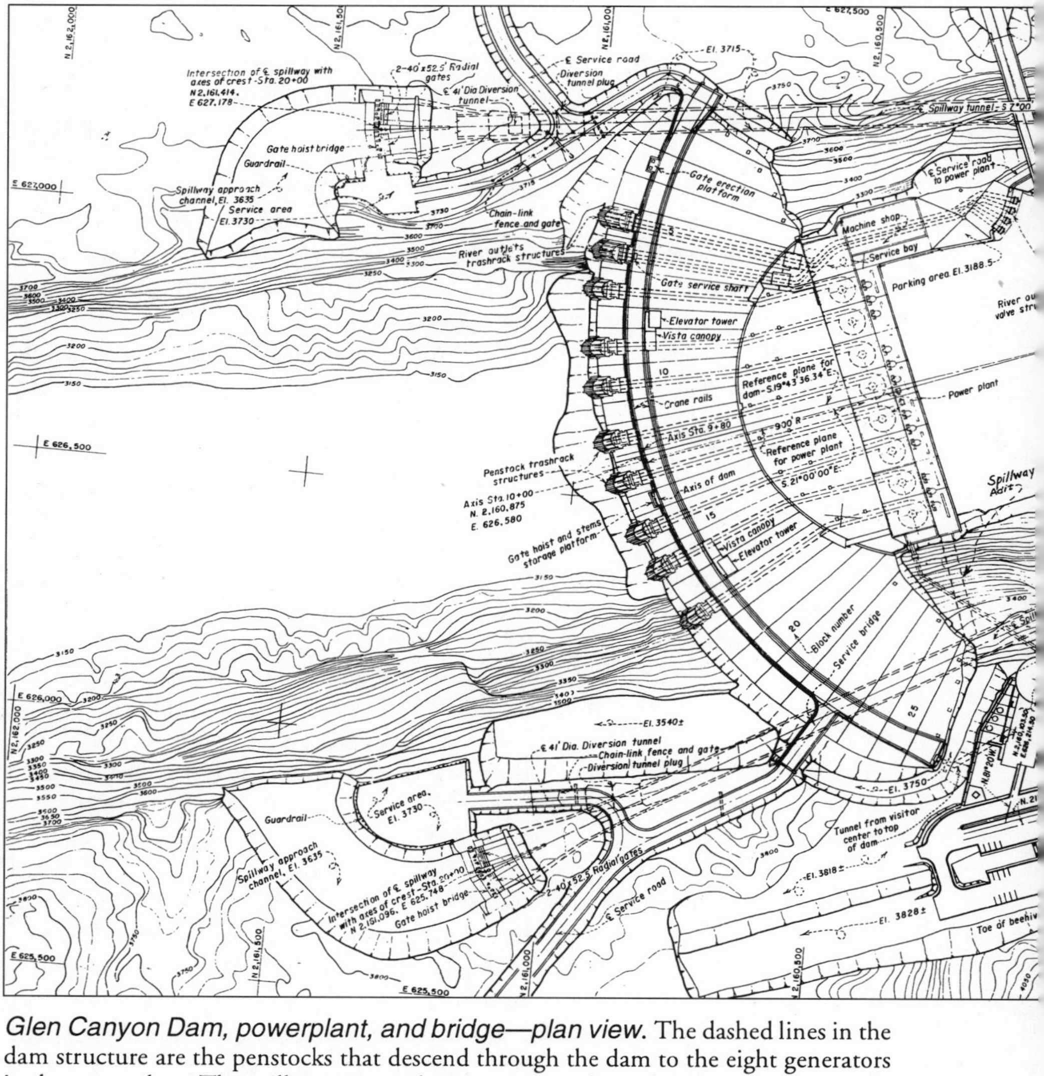

Glen Canyon Dam, powerplant, and bridge—plan view. The dashed lines in the dam structure are the penstocks that descend through the dam to the eight generators in the powerplant. The spillway approaches are cut into the east and west canyon walls at the reservoir surface level, and the exits are seen below the dam at river level. Not shown are the inlets for the river diversion tunnels, farther upstream to the north.

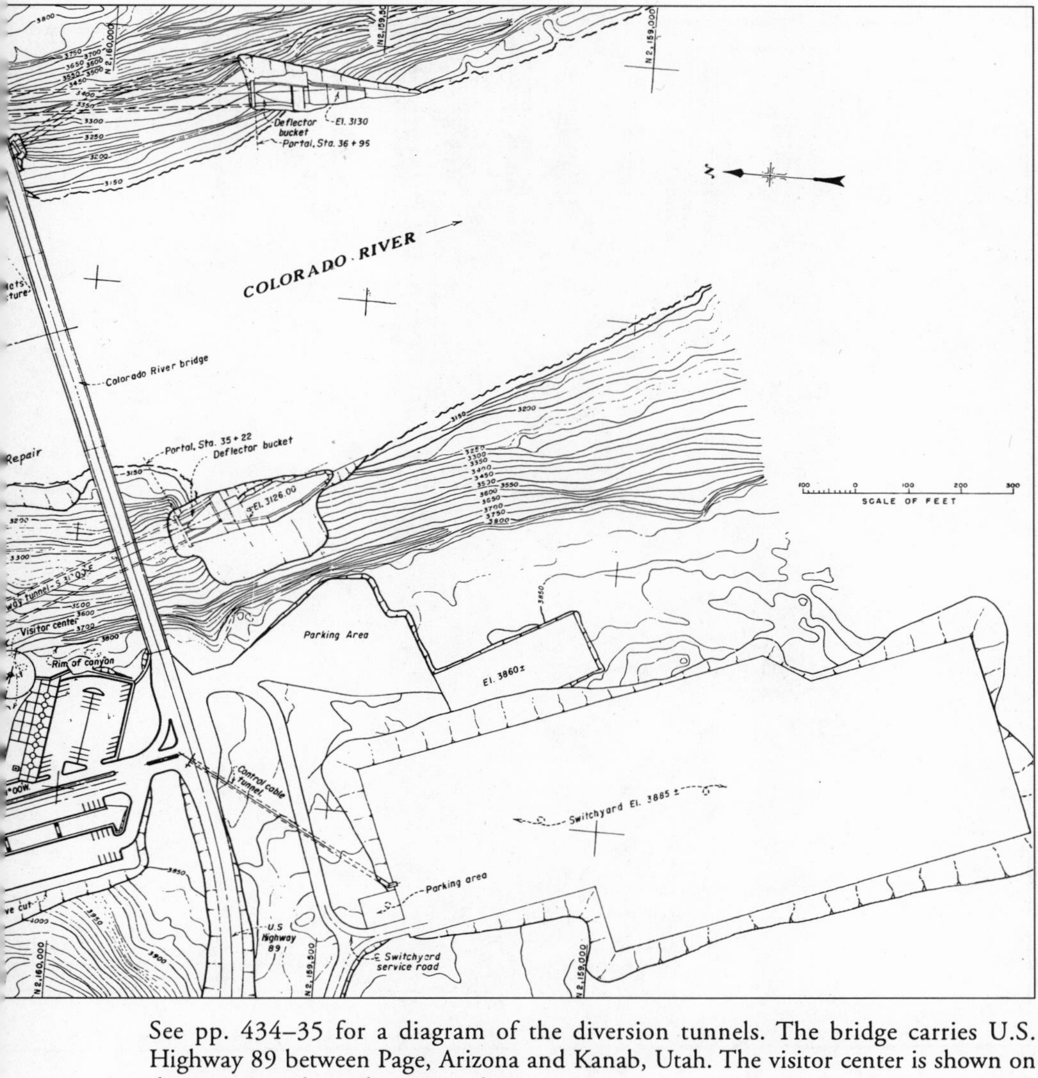

See pp. 434–35 for a diagram of the diversion tunnels. The bridge carries U.S. Highway 89 between Page, Arizona and Kanab, Utah. The visitor center is shown on the west rim, above the power plant.

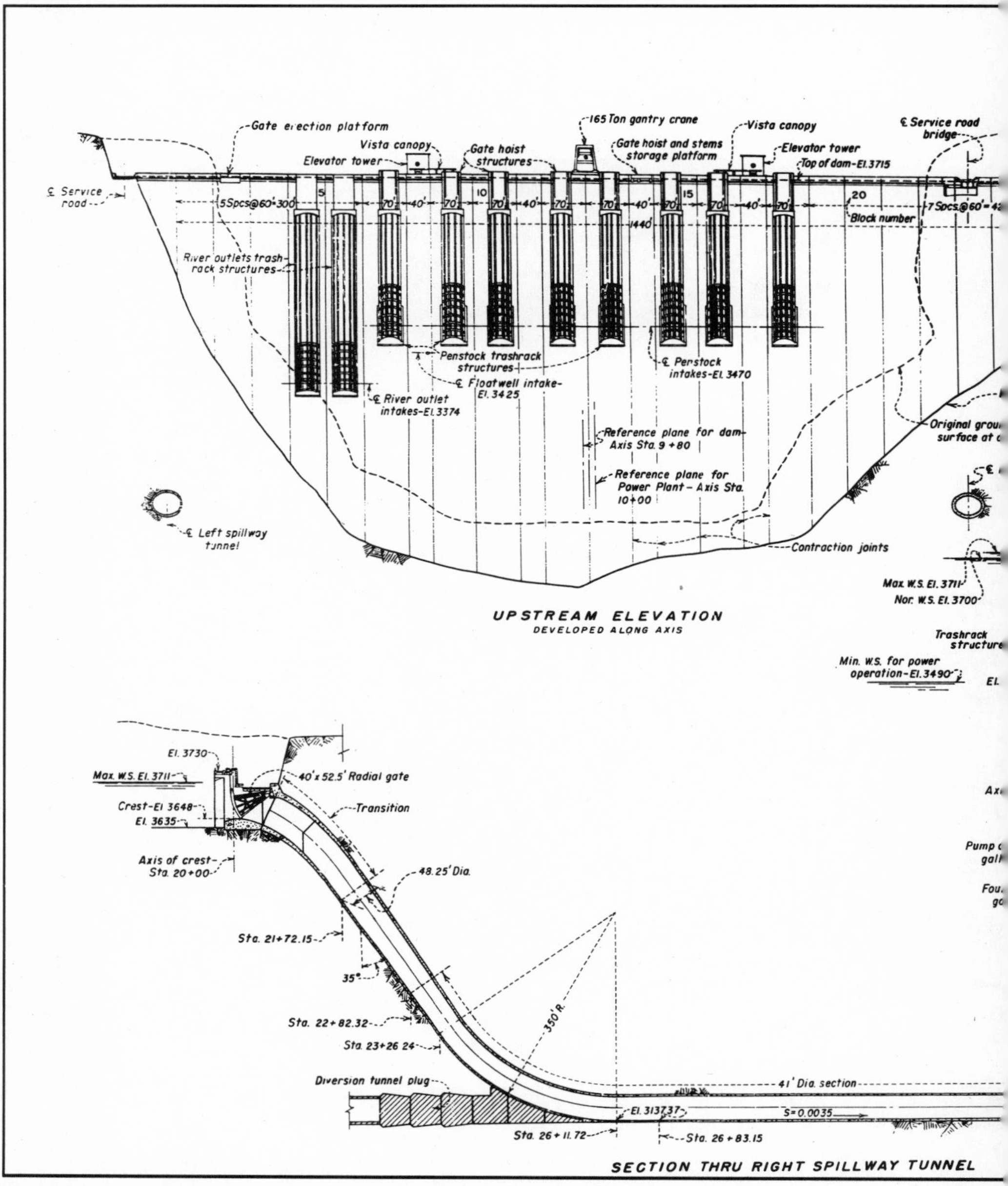

Glen Canyon Dam; spillway—elevation view. The upstream elevation shows the penstock inlets and the inlets for the river outlet works. Note that the reservoir may not be drained below elevation 3374. The dashed line in this view shows the original profile of the canyon at the dam site. The sections show views through a penstock and

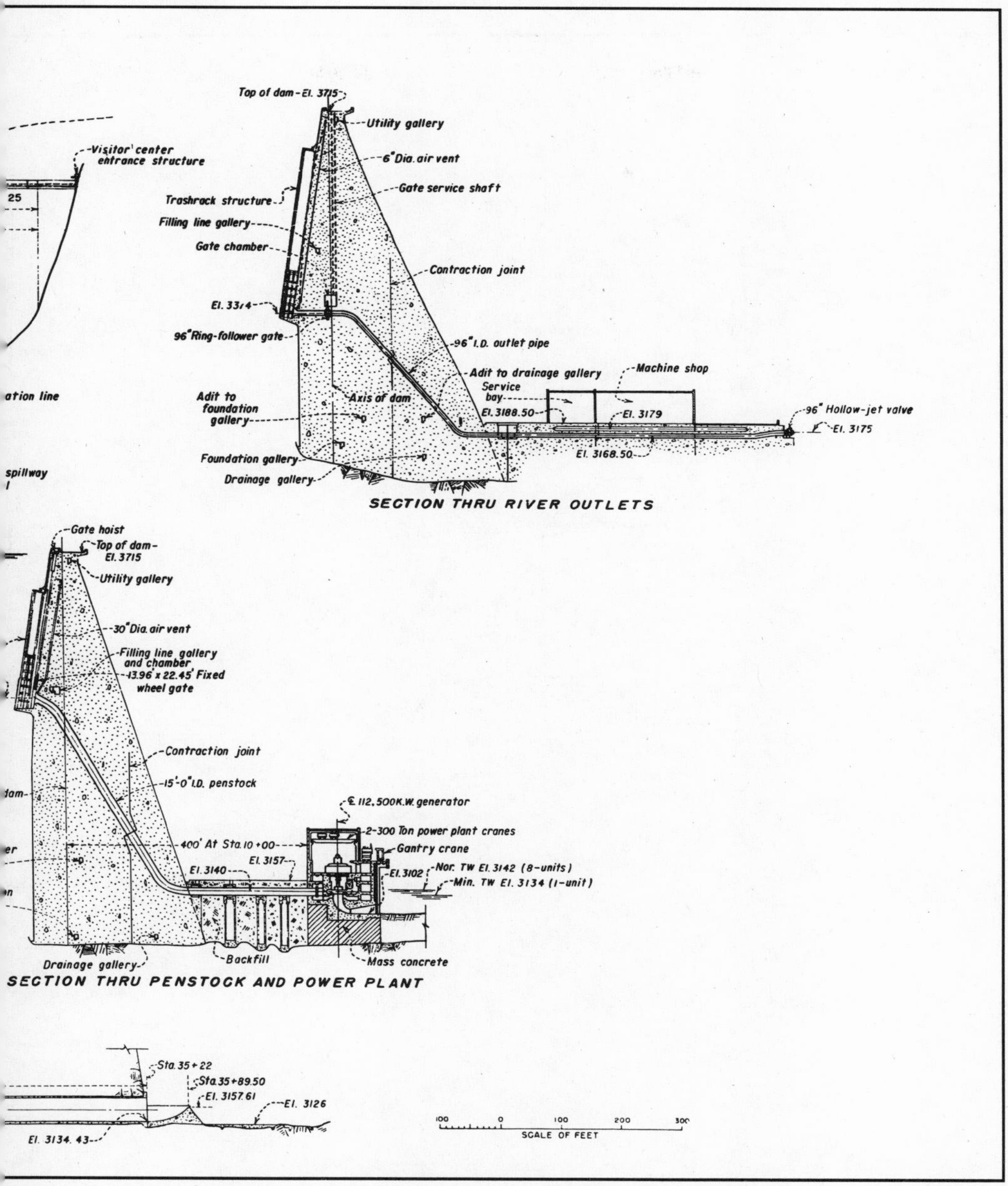

the power plant, and through the river outlet works. Note the position of the two spillways through the east and west abutments. The spillways are circular in cross section, appearing elliptical in the drawing only because of the angle of the sectional view.

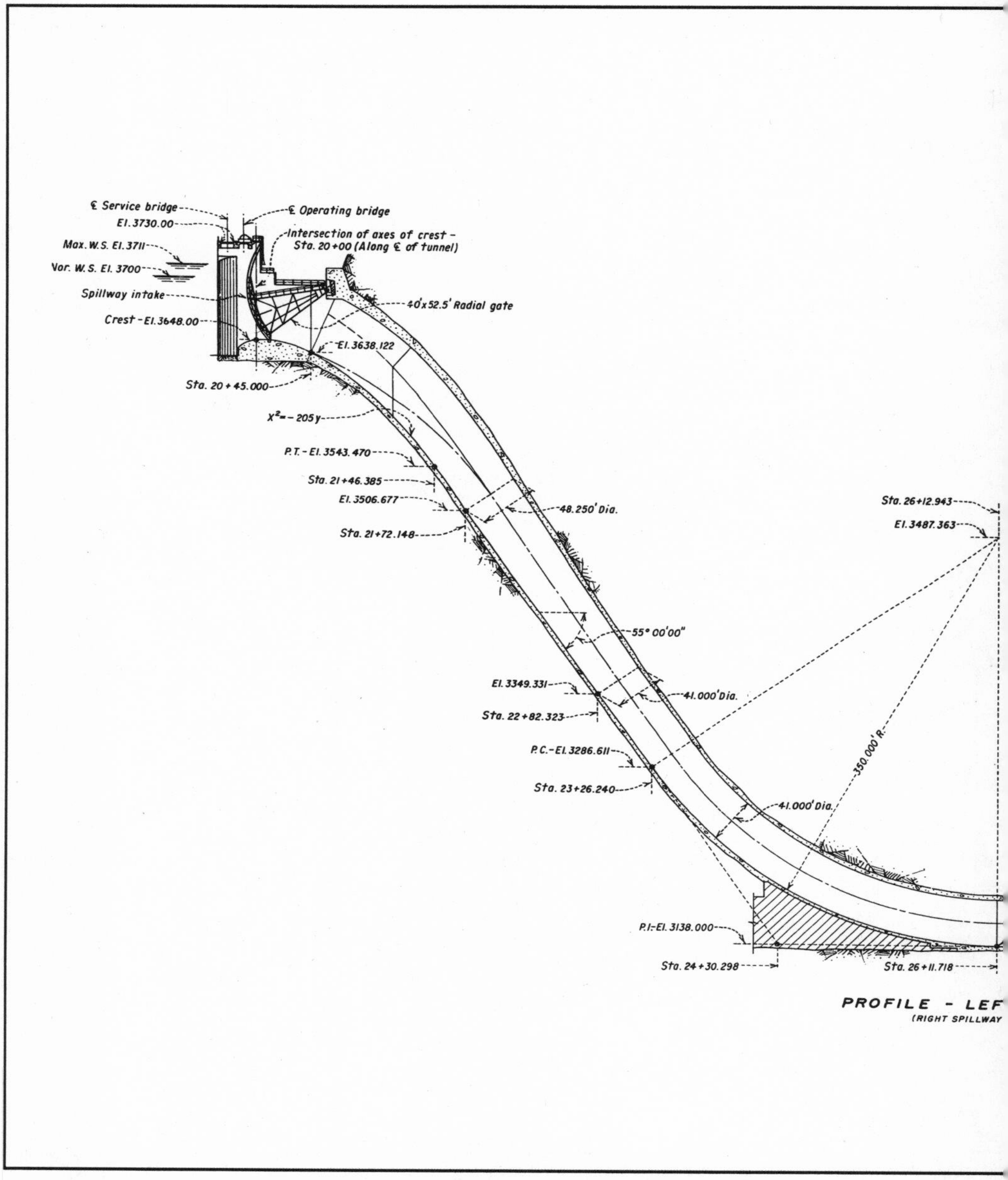

Spillway—profile view. The radial gate at the reservoir level rotates upward, releasing water under its lower edge if the elevation of the reservoir is above elevation 3648. The cross-hatched area adjacent to the curve in the spillway represents a portion of the diversion tunnel plug. The horizontal portion of the spillway uses the

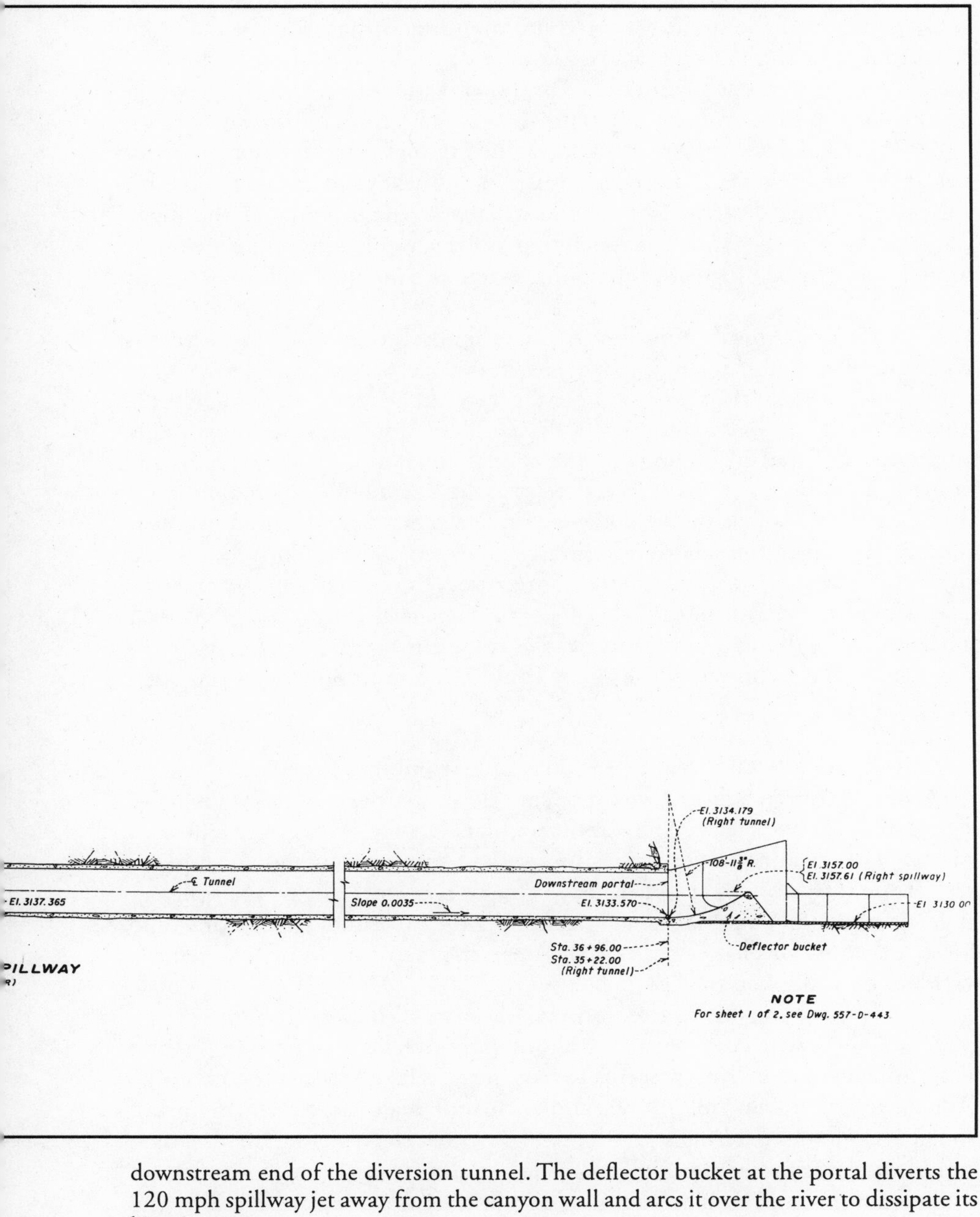

downstream end of the diversion tunnel. The deflector bucket at the portal diverts the 120 mph spillway jet away from the canyon wall and arcs it over the river to dissipate its kinetic energy.

However, an economic advantage encouraged this arrangement. The lower portions of the spillways could use the tunnels that would have to be cut through the canyon walls at river level to divert the river around the dam site during the years of construction. The upper sections of the spillways would be tunneled upward from a point approximately one-third of the way up each 3,000-foot river diversion tunnel. The inclined tunnels were designed to break out of the canyon rims at a predetermined point near each wing of the dam, with the spillway diversion works constructed at these points at the high-water level of the reservoir. The remaining, upstream portions of the diversion tunnels were to be plugged at the point where the inclined spillways started up.

Cutting a nearly fifty-foot-diameter hole through solid sandstone is big, expensive, time-consuming work. With the selected spillway design, one-third of the original river diversion conduits would be retained, doing double duty. The scheme was economically efficient; nevertheless, careful hydraulic engineers still had misgivings about tunnel spillways. Hoover Dam, the original learn-as-you-go giant dam project of the Bureau of Reclamation, built in the early 1930s, has tunnel spillways. When they were first used in 1941, the linings of the tunnels were seriously damaged by the relatively modest flows they had carried. The damage was repaired, the cavitation phenomenon that caused the damage studied, and corrective measures investigated. But what bothered the naturally conservative engineers was that the capacity of the tunnels was definitely finite. They could not accommodate an unanticipated flood.

At 10,000 cubic feet per second, some rumbling persisted. Salt Lake decided that the left spillway would be shut down for inspection. Two massive steel gates, each 40 feet wide by 52.5 feet high, slowly lowered and squeezed off the water rushing under them, the reservoir lapping to within a couple of feet of the top of each gate when they came to rest on the lip of the spillway. A group of maintenance men were assembling the cable and winch that would lower the four-wheeled cart down the steep incline of the tunnel. The little cart had been dubbed the "I Challenge U 2."

"What's the rate of rise, Johnny?" Randy MacConnell asked.

"She's still coming up at about point eight feet per day," John Patterson answered. "Inflow seems to have just peaked; starting to taper off." With a reservoir 186 miles long, and with four major rivers and scores of smaller tributaries entering it, both men knew that the water level at the dam would continue to rise after the inflows leveled off far upstream. Even though water is an incompressible fluid, it still took time for things to stabilize in a tank the size of Powell Reservoir.

July 7, 1983. The *I Challenge U 2* at the top of the left spillway behind one of the radial gates. The level of the reservoir behind the gate is 60 feet above where the men are standing and only 0.5 feet below the tops of the steel flashboards. Note the water leaking under the gate. The men are tied in with safety lines as they prepare to descend in the cart down the spillway bore to inspect the damage (*Bureau of Reclamation, Tom Fridmann*).

The *I Challenge U 2* being lowered down the left spillway. Just ahead of the cart the slope of the spillway increases to 55°. Note the streams of water falling from the drain holes (the reason for the umbrella), and the water leaking under the lower edge of the spillway gate. The men had their wills prepared before they volunteered for this job (*Bureau of Reclamation, Tom Fridmann*).

The O&M chief looked down into the yawning maw of the spillway. Randy MacConnell shuddered at the prospect of being lowered down by a thin cable into the dark, gaping void—the top fifty feet of a 168,000-acre, 186-mile-long reservoir held back by gates. A long-experienced Bureau man should not even think about the prospect of the gates rupturing and flushing whoever was in the spillway like a bug in a toilet bowl. That could never happen, after all. *Not my job, thank God,* Randy MacConnell thought. The hotshots from the Engineering and Research Center were on their way down from Denver in a Bureau plane. *They're the experts. It's their job to go down there. They know what to look for.*

The team from E&R arrived. After a short briefing on what had transpired over the weekend, they got into the little cart to begin the winch-controlled roll down the steep tunnel. One of the men carried a waterproofed Nikon. They both wore heavy rain gear.

Throughout the length of the tunnel, hundreds of holes were drilled through the concrete lining into the sandstone. Under the enormous pressure from the reservoir, water was slowly forced through the porous rock, with the drain holes needed to relieve the water pressure. Hundreds of similar holes were driven into the dam abutment keyways and into the foundation rock below the 9.25-million-ton dam.

In the whole length of the left tunnel, over 6,000 gallons per minute leaked out in streams through the drain holes. As the men disappeared down into the dark, the water poured out of the holes ringing the tunnel—increasing in pressure the farther the cart descended. More water sheeted around the wheels of the cart from leakage under the spillway gates.

Definitely earning their pay now, Randy MacConnell thought while he watched the spewing streams of water dance in the flashlight beams.

"There's a lot of damage right along the line of the invert, starting at the curve and getting worse through the curve and down into the tangent. There's a series of six holes, from elevation 3,140 and on up the invert about sixty feet. At its worst, the full three feet of concrete lining's been removed, with deep erosion into the rock. How long'd the tunnel run at 20,000?"

"Less than twenty-four hours," Randy MacConnell answered. "We cut back to ten this morning and then shut it just before you arrived."

"We've got to get flashboards on top of the gates. It's clear that we'll go into surcharge as the reservoir tops out," the lead engineer concluded. "Run the left at 2,000, drop the right to four, and open the river outlet works' hollow jets to a maximum of 15,000. Let's bring the power plant to 28,000, but don't push the ROW beyond the 15,000. We've got to keep the velocity in the conduits below seventy-five feet per second—may have a problem with leakage in the expansion joints at higher velocities. That'll all give us forty-nine kay. Salt Lake thinks it should be enough. How soon can you get the flashboards in place?"

"With four-by-eight, one-inch ply we can have them up in less than twenty-four hours. Gonna have to rig safety nets before I send any of my guys out over those spillways, though."

"Sure, of course," the engineer nodded.

The difference between theory and practice, Randy MacConnell thought when he headed back up to his office to make out the day's log.

***

June 9

National Weather Service forecasts increased rain showers and higher temperatures in the Upper Basin. At current discharge of 49,000 cfs, reservoir forecast to crest at 3,702.5, 1.5 feet below flashboard rims. Vibration sensing equipment being prepared. ROW discharge to be increased while monitoring for cavitation damage. Left spillway to be shut down.

June 13

Reservoir rising fast. New NWS forecast predicts 500,000-acre-feet inflow increase through July 31 to 3,000,000. Noise and surging in ROW conduits; throttled back to 13,000. Left spillway reopened. Total reservoir discharge increased to 53,000, with projected maximum reservoir elevation of 3703.7.

June 16

Reservoir still rising at six inches per day, even with 53,000 outflows. Discharges increased to 12,000 in left spillway; 4,000 in right. Decision made to reserve the right spillway as long as possible in the event NWS forecasts inaccurate. Further decision to increase discharges from Hoover to make space for higher Glen Canyon releases.

***

Randy MacConnell watched from his usual vantage point on top of the dam. The condition of the flow at the outlet of the left spillway tunnel had changed. The discharge was supposed to be a smooth sweep of water, but the sweep had been getting weaker in the last two days and now it was entirely gone. Instead of hitting the flip bucket where the 120-mph flow was turned up to arc high into the air, the water emerged in a churning boil, filling the tunnel outlet.

"Those tunnels are not designed to handle that kind of flow," he said.

The Denver E&R man was grim faced. "We've got a hydraulic jump.

It has to be somewhere just past the elbow. Randy, we're gonna have to increase the flow to restore the sweep."

"And by increasing the flow, we'll be aggravating the cavitation problem—setting it up for an even bigger pressure differential," Randy MacConnell responded quietly.

"Right. But we've got no choice. Salt Lake says bump the release to 17,000. That'll put us at 61,000, total. The inflows seem to have topped out at about 75,000. We should be okay."

***

June 20

NWS forecasts increased rain showers in the Upper Basin. Unseasonably warm temperatures on the western slope of the Southern Rocky Mountain high country.

June 23

Flow rate in left tunnel increased over past three days to maintain sweep. At 21,000 cfs, jet again lost its sweep. Noise levels increased. Discharge lowered to 10,000 and right tunnel opened to 15,000. Total outflow now 69,000, with all eight turbines running at maximum discharge and the ROW at 75 percent. Denver Operations orders discharges through Hoover increased to 14,000 per spillway. NWS predicts rains will increase throughout Upper Basin. Reservoir at 3,704. Now impossible to completely shut flows in our spillways; closing gates will cause flashboards to overtop and fail. Decision to replace four-foot wooden boards with eight-foot steel flashboards. Spillways could then be shut so long as reservoir stays below 3,708.

June 27

Inflows now at 104,000 cfs and still climbing. Apparent that reservoir will exceed 3,708 feet. Salt Lake orders our discharge to 80,000 cfs in the evening with further increase to 92,000 cfs tomorrow. Known damage in left tunnel; right tunnel held in reserve in event of increased rain. Sweep in left tunnel reestablished at 25,000 cfs; rock and debris in jet.

June 28

Rumbling noise from spillways increased dramatically. Left discharge increased to 32,000 cfs to move hydraulic jump away from damaged area and out toward spillway exit. Intensity of noise and vibration worse, with loud thumping sound audible on dam crest. Sweep at left flip bucket lost. Material from tunnel causes river to turn amber color. Large chunks of concrete lining, sandstone, and sections of rebar clearly visible in jet. Left reduced to 20,000; right increased to 27,000 cfs. Noise in left quieted, but debris now seen in jet from right tunnel; sweep faltering.

Workers' view into spillway (*Bureau of Reclamation*).

* * *

Deep in the foundation walls of the canyon, tunnels are driven into the dam keyway abutments from galleries within the dam structure. The lowest tunnels—referred to as adits by the engineers—are over 450 feet below the dam crest and extend more than 400 feet back into the canyon walls on either side of the dam. Their purpose is to intercept and monitor the water slowly pushed through the porous rock by the hydrostatic pressure of the reservoir. The lowest foundation adits cross over the spillway tunnels sixty-nine feet above the crowns of the spillways, and drain holes extending down from the adit floors reach to within twenty feet of the spillway ceilings. Intercepted water is carried away through the dam by a network of galleries and drains, joining the water from hundreds of additional drain holes bored from the dam into the surrounding foundation rock.

Randy MacConnell lead one of the engineers from the concrete dams division back into the lowest adit on the right side of the dam. Water poured from the drain holes and ran down the walls and across the floor of the tunnel. It was like being in a rain forest monsoon.

"It's just up here," he shouted to the engineer. The noise from the spillway, running less than seventy feet through the sandstone below them, was deafening.

Another seventy-five feet into the adit the two men saw that a number of the drain holes in the floor surged violently with water and air. High-pressure spurts shot up through the holes and impinged on the ceiling of the abutment tunnel.

"I don't like this at all, Randy. We're going to have to cut the flow through this spillway. Can't say what the hydraulic connection is, but there's no doubt that it's there. This adit is off limits."

The surging abated when the discharge through the right overflow was lowered: obviously, a connection existed through the rock jointing between the drain holes and the high-velocity water in the spillway. No surging was found in the adit above the left spillway.

With the runoff appearing to have crested, the total outflow was reduced to 85,000 cfs, both spillways running at 20,000. Salt Lake estimated that the reservoir would later crest just above elevation 3,707, one foot below the tops of the flashboards.

* * *

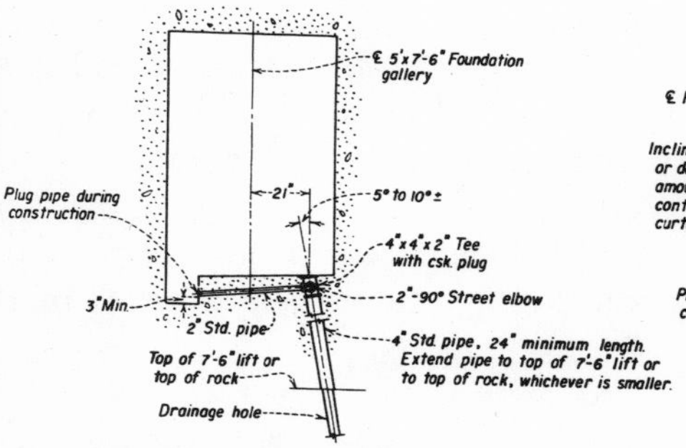

TYPICAL SECTION THRU
HORIZONTAL FOUNDATION GALLERY

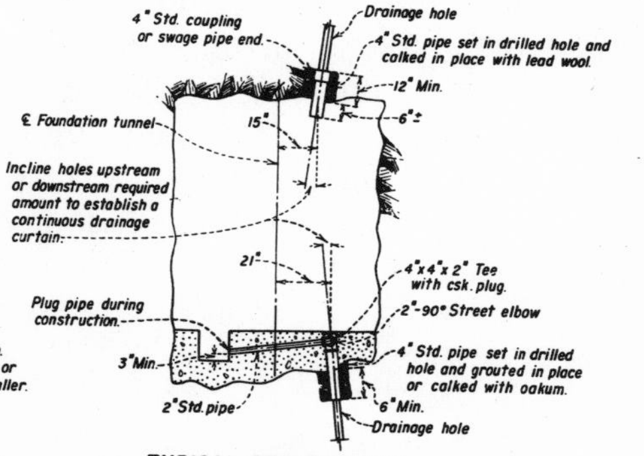

TYPICAL SECTION THRU
HORIZONTAL FOUNDATION GALLERY

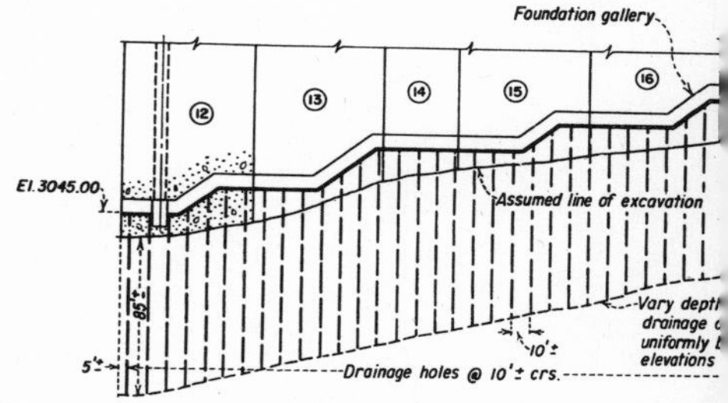

Foundation galleries, drainage, and spillway. Hundreds of drain holes are drilled into the dam abutments and foundation to relieve pressure from the impounded water.

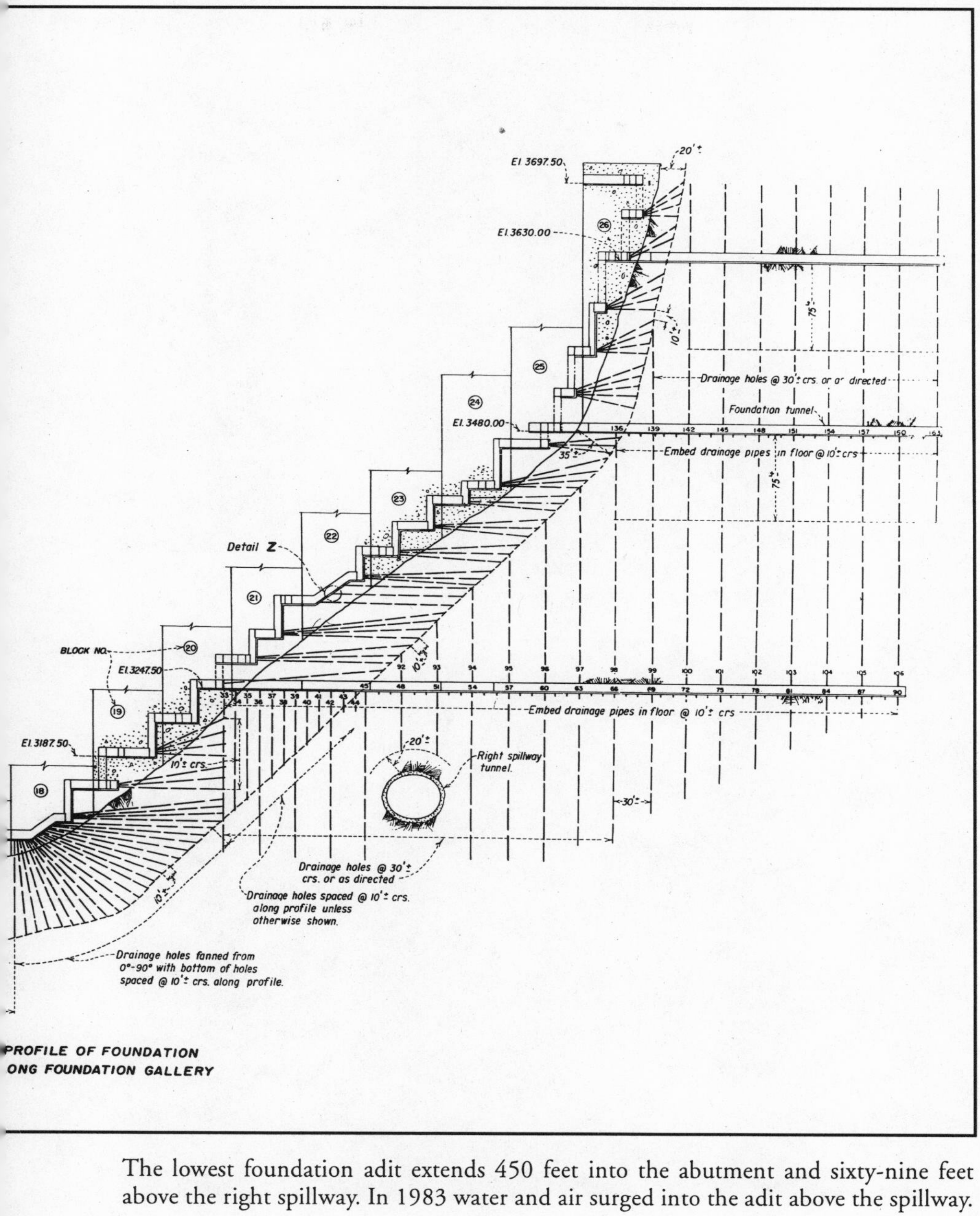

The lowest foundation adit extends 450 feet into the abutment and sixty-nine feet above the right spillway. In 1983 water and air surged into the adit above the spillway.

Installing one of the 8-foot steel flashboards. The gate is raised about two feet so the water does not spill over its top (*Bureau of Reclamation, Tom Fridmann*).

Steel flashboard and braces installed. The other gate in the right spillway, which is not raised, retains a four-foot plywood flashboard (*Bureau of Reclamation, Tom Fridmann*).

Close-up of a four-foot wooden flashboard. The reservoir is standing about one foot below its top, but the water is backed up 190 miles behind it. Note the water leaking under the flashboard (*Bureau of Reclamation, Tom Fridmann*).

July 5

More surging in bottom right abutment adit. Flow reduction not possible due to left spillway flashboard installation. Worker safety nets over spillway inlets. Reservoir at 3,706 and still rising.

July 7

Left flashboards completed, gates closed for inspection of spillway. Less than one-half foot freeboard on flashboards with gates closed, allowing only brief inspection. Wave action in river from ROW, turbine, and right spillway outflows precluded entering left tunnel from river. Inspection cart access revealed major damage. Holes in tunnel lining and protruding rebar prevented cart from proceeding into curved section.

July 8

Right spillway flashboards completed, cart lowered for inspection. Damage similar to left tunnel; rebar protruding from damaged lining described as appearing like "spaghetti." Able to descend into curved section; large hole observed in bottom lining and rockfall on right-hand side of tunnel. For safety reasons, unable to get dive team into pool to examine hole. Damage far more extensive than anticipated. Flow in right tunnel kept at 5,000 cfs after inspection.

July 15

Reservoir peaked at 3,708.34 feet, 10.66 feet below parapets. Total discharge to remain at 60,000 cfs, gradually reduced as reservoir starts down.

July 23

All spillway gates closed at 8:00 A.M.; reservoir at 3,707.8. Catwalk to be built to left tunnel portal to permit access by boat. Violent wave action in tailrace totally eroded old access road.

* * *

Randy MacConnell waited impatiently while the boat was lowered into the tunnel behind the upsweeping ramp of concrete at the portal. A five-foot-deep layer of rubble lay in the flip bucket: chunks of concrete and sandstone, twisted and broken lengths of rebar.

Before the pumps had been brought in, the water had stood twenty feet deep in the tunnel, dammed up by the flip bucket at its portal. As the boat was pulled into the spillway, the water was six feet above the invert, with the five-foot-deep layer of rubble extending 200 feet back, barely beneath the water level.

The maintenance foreman pointed his flashlight up the tunnel. "My

God, Randy, look at that!" Resting in the spillway was a sandstone boulder, eight feet high by ten feet wide. When they pulled the boat up to the block they saw that it was fifteen feet long, with another layer of rubble, again five feet deep, extending 600 feet behind the boulder toward the spillway exit.

"I don't think I want to see where this thing came from," Randy MacConnell said while they maneuvered the boat around the huge sandstone slab.

One hundred and fifty feet farther, just below the point where the tunnel started to curve up toward the spillway inlet, they saw the source of the boulder. The beams from their flashlights could not plumb the bottom of a giant hole in the invert of the spillway.

"It's got to be fifty feet deep, Randy." John Patterson pointed his light at the upper wall. "Shit, look up there." Mats of rebar had been pulled out of the concrete like bones from a piece of cooked fish. Only the crown of the tunnel retained its lining: hundreds of tons of the three-foot-thick concrete hung precariously above the men in the boat, while all around them water poured out of the exposed sandstone. The hydrostatic pressure from the reservoir was at its greatest at this point beneath the dam abutments.

"Damn, the cratering even goes back into the plug." Behind the ragged concrete, water stood in the remainder of the river diversion tunnel, connected to the bottom of the reservoir. The pressure behind the plug was nearly 50,000 pounds per square foot.

Divers entered the "big hole" just downstream of the plug in the left tunnel, discovering a cavity in the sandstone forty-three feet deep, fifty feet wide, and extending135 feet downstream. Approximately 2,300 cubic yards of sandstone had been excavated below the concrete lining. Inspection of the right spillway revealed similar but less extensive cavitation, including another large hole carved into the sandstone at the foot of the inclined section.

As soon as the level of the reservoir fell far enough to provide adequate freeboard on the spillway gate extensions, work began in earnest to repair the damage. At least one of the spillways had to be operational by January, in anticipation of possible winter storms, and all work had to be completed before the next season's snow runoff.

By May 1, 1984, the reservoir had been drawn down to elevation 3,674, twenty-six feet below the tops of the gates. On May 30, about one month earlier than the highest flows the previous year, inflow to the reservoir peaked at 115,260 cfs—even higher than the year before. The reservoir rose to 3,700 feet, the elevation of the tops of the spillway gates, on June 26, and remained above that level until mid-September. The spillways had not been needed only because the eight-foot flashboards were still in place.

The river had again tested the obstruction in its canyon.

Left spillway inspection (*Bureau of Reclamation*).

"House rock," the boulder found in the left spillway after the water had been pumped out. The block of sandstone had been excavated from the "big hole" and deposited farther down the tunnel (*Bureau of Reclamation, Tom Fridmann*).

Catwalk to the left spillway portal, before the water was pumped out. Note the wave action from the river outlet works discharge (*Bureau of Reclamation*).

Left spillway debris, after water had been pumped out, August 9, 1983 (*Bureau of Reclamation, Tom Fridmann*).

Close-up view of damage in the "little hole" in the right spillway, looking toward the portal. Note the broken and twisted reinforcing bars (*Bureau of Reclamation*).

Close-up of damage to the left spillway at the elbow. Water is spilling from the drain holes drilled through the concrete tunnel lining to relieve the water pressure from the reservoir (*Bureau of Reclamation*).

The left spillway at the elbow when first inspected. The water has been partially pumped out, revealing erosion clear through the three-foot-thick reinforced concrete lining. Note the stair-stepped cavitation erosion through the concrete in the elbow. Behind the elbow is the river diversion tunnel plug with 50,000 pounds per square foot of water pressure at the bottom of the reservoir (*Bureau of Reclamation, Tom Fridmann*).

Same view in the left spillway as in the previous photo, but with the water pumped out. The "big hole" was nearly 50 feet deep and extended 135 feet down the spillway from the elbow. Some of the new reinforcing bars have been placed before filling the hole with concrete (*Bureau of Reclamation, Tom Fridmann*).

View across the "big hole," down the left spillway tunnel. Dewatering the tunnel in order to place concrete in the excavated area was a major construction problem (*Bureau of Reclamation, Joe Dahilig*).

CACTUS CLUB

Lower Escalante River, 1960 (*Tad Nichols*).

1

San Francisco, November 10

Best time of the year, Stan Bellamy thought as he nudged his old Jaguar out into the relatively spare midday traffic on the Bay Bridge. *Days are still warm, no fog, lots of wind so no smog, the hordes of tourists are gone, and there's no rain yet.* He craned his neck to look over the bridge railing. Past the dense cluster of high-rises in the financial district he could see the lovely outline of Coit Tower on top of Telegraph Hill and the streets and buildings slanting up Nob and Russian Hills. Stan still didn't like one of the newer San Francisco landmarks—the Transamerica Tower. The building was okay, he just didn't like insurance companies. He'd practiced law too long. The downtown district slipped behind as he settled into the 65-mph stream hurtling across the bay.

Lots of boats out, for a weekday. Wish I was, he thought while he loosened the knot under his stiff white collar. With occasional glances in the mirror at the woman half a car length behind him, he managed a scan of the bay. The sailboats heeled sharply when they emerged from the lee of the city and got the full brunt of the westerly wind coming through the Golden Gate. Stan thought of his Olson 30 sitting quietly in her slip at the St. Francis Yacht Club as he watched the pattern of whitecaps between the city and Alcatraz. *Nice breeze. About 25 knots.* Atop the city's hotels and skyscrapers, flags and proprietary banners all pointed stiffly east; Angel Island, Mt. Tamalpais, and the hills of Marin County beyond were sharply etched against the cloudless blue sky.

Emerging from the tunnel through Goat Island, Stan confronted the specter of the East Bay. The best part of the drive was over. From the city to the island, the bay was spanned by a handsome, four-tower, double suspension bridge, one of mankind's most artistic and inspiring inventions to link points of land. On the other side of the tunnel, the bridge transformed grotesquely into a series of cantilever and deck trusses, these devices being among the bridge-building fraternity's least endearing creations. *Point A to point B connection is all this thing has going for it* he thought as he passed under the section of the upper deck that had collapsed on that World Series day in 1989. The apparently more delicate sister bridge to the west and her cousin spanning the Golden Gate had come through unscathed. *Got to be flexible to survive, I guess.*

When the bridge spit him out, Stan scanned his planned route on the East Bay freeway. *Must be a wreck. Complete parking lot. Have to go cross-country. Another fifteen minutes.* He glanced down at his watch.

As much as Stan Bellamy loved his lifelong home of San Francisco, he despised the East Bay. He looked down at the freeway he'd planned to be on. Its normal, round-the-clock speed approximated the flow of slightly inclined warm mud; but the ooze was now completely stopped. Stan tried to imagine what the dense conurbation had been like when first seen by the Spanish padres: a gentle slope of grassy meadows and meandering streams with occasional arboreal intrusions and tidal marshes, abundant with birds and aquatic life. *The Miwoks and Costanoans must have had a really good life here—until the Spaniards showed up.* He descended into Oakland and headed for Telegraph Avenue, the celebrated entranceway to the Berkeley soviet.

Telegraph Avenue near the campus hadn't changed much over the years, excepting the intense proliferation of every conceivable variety of ethnic restaurant. The entirety of the Middle East, Asia, and much of Africa and South America were represented. Not America north of Mexico, or even Central Europe. Not sufficiently correct. *Berkeley. I'm supposed to love this place. I graduated from here, after all.* But the seediness, particularly on the south side of the campus, annoyed him most. *Maybe it's always been like this; I just didn't notice when I was a student. No. No way. It's much worse now.* For a fine university of international stature, the University of California at Berkeley was unique in its immediate proximity to a Western version of a Moroccan suq.

Stan glanced up the slope of the Berkeley Hills, rising above the main part of the campus. Academic credential and tenure increased with corresponding increases in elevation and proximity to lovely Tilden Park, high in the Hills. There lived the academic elite, many spending their days exhorting students to challenge everything establishment and then retreating, wholly removed from what they preached. Contrary to its image worldwide, Berkeley was not a vast, swarming collection of students and dissidents. Much of the upper Berkeley Hills would rival Shaker Heights, Grosse Pointe, or Greenwich.

Above the main campus, he glimpsed the familiar rounded dome of the cyclotron building. What went on in there was a world away from the teeming undergraduate masses surging in and out of Sather Gate at the end of Telegraph Avenue. The atomic particle accelerator dominated the center of the venerable Lawrence Berkeley Laboratory. *Had to change the name a while back. Being called the Lawrence RADIATION Laboratory made the university elite a little too uncomfortable, I guess. Didn't change what goes on in there, though.* The laboratory was a world center for atomic research, providing marvelous advances in nuclear medicine and a growing understanding of the fundamental nature of matter. But, together with its sprawling cousin over the hills in the Livermore Valley, the "Rad Lab" had long been the home to, and persistent perfecter of, the hydrogen fusion thermonuclear bomb. The laboratory's existence in Berkeley, and squarely in the middle of the campus, must truly be the very definition of irony, Stan had always thought. *That place exists solely by the largess of the United States government, and much of the hundreds of millions in funding for the laboratory's research and operations finds its way into the general coffers of the university.*

As he curved around the campus to the North Side, the environment starkly changed. The mêlée of undergraduates, tourists, shoppers, merchants, and mendicants on Telegraph Avenue moderated in clamor, appearance, and odor to a scene of orderly collegiate life. The immediate North Side, by reputation, was the realm of austere ecclesiastic institutions, graduate students, and lesser faculty members. In fact, Stan knew full well, it was a rabbit warren of cramped student housing. Legions of graduate students occupied every building from basement cranny to attic loft, ignored by those responsible for the enforcement of the local health and fire codes. The secreted population was subtly revealed, however, by the complete absence of any vacant street parking space. Nearly all the parked cars were permanent fixtures, ensconced in the fall and not moved until the end of finals in June, by which point each was a gummy cocoon of tree drippings, leaves, and fossilized bird shit.

But Stan did not have to hunt for a place to park. He pulled into the Cactus Club parking lot. Until the lot had been built, club members could never find a place to park anywhere within reasonable walking distance, and they invariably got tickets. The bird-shat cars never got tickets while club members seldom escaped the sanction of an overtime stay. That the parking lot existed at all was the culmination of a protracted squabble, instigated and prosecuted in the grand and archetypal Berkeley tradition.

The site had been a vacant lot adjacent to the clubhouse, the property having belonged to the club since its founding just before World War I. Nevertheless, according to paleo-Berkeley municipal thinking, one who purchased a parcel of real estate, paid taxes and insurance premiums on it, and was responsible for its maintenance, was not necessarily the one who determined its use—zoning compliance notwithstanding. Over the years, as residences filled the immediate area, the lot began to serve, by prescription, as a de facto city park, vegetable garden, trash dump, long-term camping area, short-term love-making area, dog-relieving area, neighborhood playground, and, in later years, a north campus drug dealing venue. Some number of years ago, the club announced its intention to build the much-needed parking lot on the property. The outcry—verbal, physical, and editorial—was immediate, universal and stentorian, and largely generated and enflamed by a number of the princes of academe who looked down, literally and figuratively, upon the club from their comfortable perches in the Berkeley Hills. Pickets, demonstrations, marches, sit-ins, candlelight vigils, campus orations inciting riot, riots-in-fact, collective and in-personam threats, street blockades, arson, and three lawsuits resulted. Four and one-half years elapsed before the first earth mover arrived, and only then after massive expenditures of time, money, and energy for lawyers, landscape architects, mitigation specialists, and laboriously negotiated mitigation-in-fact. Today, in the minds of the defeated crusaders, the parking lot stood as a continual reminder of the evil that was the Cactus Club, with no effort spared to keep the legend of the travesty alive. And for members of the club, the simple act of parking an automobile served as a happy, warmly anticipated preamble to each visit.

The comfortable fragrance of old wood, fabric and carpet, well-worn leather, dust, and a hint of mildew welcomed Stan. This base was overlain with the aromas of the day's luncheon specialty and a touch of tobacco smoke. Here, and only here in Berkeley public, could Daphna Flanigan, adjunct professor of African studies, enjoy her intensely pungent Jamaican cigarillos. Beyond the foyer and coat room, Stan entered the gathering hall, filled with the day's assembly of members and guests. Through the windows a striking view to the west revealed the city, her bay, and her bridges. On the opposite side of the building was the dining hall, from which the members could gather the equally satisfying view of their parking lot.

Big crowd today. The friendly theater of effervescent discussions, barks of laughter, and the clink of cubes in iced tea glasses filled the room. He felt his whole body relax in the familiar setting. To a man or woman, the members assembled largely to escape from what it was they did for the rest of the day, and in a fashion few of them enjoyed either at work or at home, to talk freely about what they really thought. A visit to the club was a form of group therapy.

Stan scanned the medley of tweed, cardigans, bow ties, and business suits.

"Stanley! Over here," boomed across the room. The source of the voice was not hard to distinguish. Malcolm Renslaer stood six and one-half feet tall and weighed well over 300 pounds. The large man stood with Waddy Temeseh and Saul Kalinik. Malcolm and Saul were Stan's oldest and closest friends. Waddy, a former client, had become Stan's newest friend.

"I'm glad you could break away from teaching your young lawyers how to protect the guilty," Malcolm said as he clapped Stan on the shoulder. He glanced down at their guest. "Uh . . . sorry, Waddy." The year before, Stan had managed to rescue Waddy from a difficult legal entanglement in Colorado.

Waddy met Malcolm's glance from nearly a foot below it. "It's all right, Malcolm, I *was* guilty—at least in the eyes of your *pahana* law."

Stan seized the opportunity to avoid another of Malcolm's lawyer-bashing exchanges. "One hit at the legal community is all you get today, Malcolm. Why don't we find out what Waddy's been up to since we last saw him? *Lawful* activity, I hope," Stan smiled at Waddy.

Saul nodded. "Yes, picking on lawyers is just too easy."

"Saul, don't *you* start. Nuclear weapons scientists are hardly in a position to attack lawyers."

"Okay, okay," Malcolm interrupted, holding up his ham-sized hands. As much as he loved his argument-filled visits to the club, he also wanted to hear from Waddy. They didn't get to see him often enough.

"Nothin' new, really. Promised Stan I'd be good, so I have been. Just here on my normal sellin' trip. Same old, same old. But actually, Saul, I wanted to talk to you about this latest nuclear test crap."

"Wait a minute," Malcolm broke in, "We can get to that in a minute. Today—right now—I want a clear explanation from our desert merchant here just what he really, actually, is selling to the natives."

Waddy snaked his way over to the sideboard, intent upon one of the last canapés of salmon gravlox. "Malcolm, I know what you're thinkin'. What you're all prob'ly thinkin'. I would very likely suspect the same thing if I were you; and, frankly, I'm surprised you haven't already cross-examined me about this. No, absolutely no, I'm *not* sellin' artifacts of the Ancient Ones. In fact, I'm one of the most determined ferrets in the Hopi Tribe when it comes to findin' the people stealin' those precious links to our past."

"Yeah, you're related to the Anasazi, aren't you?" Malcolm said.

"Malcolm, this is not the right environment to give you even a brief summation of my people's ties to the Ancient Ones."

"Anasazi is a Navajo word, isn't it?" Saul interrupted. "What was the real name for the people?"

"We call them Hisatsinom, 'our ancestors.' The head pounders call them Anasazi, 'ancestors of the enemy.'"

"Head pounders?" Malcolm asked with a quizzical smile.

"The Tasávu. The Navajo. When they first crawled into the western parts of Tusqua, our land, in what you call the fifteenth century, they made a practice of crushing the heads of their captives. They still call us 'corn eaters.' They breed like rabbits, and now they own practically all our land. They have a lot of lawyers." Waddy glanced at Stan.

"I'm sorry I interrupted you," Saul said. "You were going to tell us what the ancient people actually called themselves."

"You asked, Saul, but I was not about to tell you," Waddy smiled coyly. "We prefer to keep such things to ourselves. We're rather like the followers of Siddhartha Gautama, the Buddha, in that regard. Before we'll tell you anything of the Hopi Way, we have to be asked, sincerely, several times. Even then, most Hopi have no interest in satisfying *pahana* curiosity. Since I've come to know and trust all of you, I would be pleased to tell you some details of our history and what it means in today's world. But we'd need far more time, and this isn't the right place."

The chef's assistant hit the gong, sending everyone flooding into the dining room to select seats at random. A fixed seating order would not have been tolerated—the president's chair at the head of the center table being the only exception. Platters of grilled red snapper with jicama melon relish and asiago polenta were passed down the long tables, followed by tureens of cream of artichoke soup and bowls of tomato and buffalo mozzarella salad. Fresh berry cobbler waited on the sideboard. Because the chef concentrated on a single entrée and accompaniments, staff was reduced to a minimum. At the end of the meal, members bussed their own dishes. As the groups took their seats and settled into continuing discussions, they were silenced by the ring of flatware struck against an empty glass. The president rose to announce a special event. Boisterous table thumping and applause greeted the news that the following Wednesday there would be a reading of one of Wallace Stegner's unpublished short stories.

"So, Waddy, what's your complaint about the next nuclear test in Nevada?" Saul asked.

"Okay, just tell me," Waddy immediately grabbed the invitation, "if we've signed this START agreement, at least with the important parties, why do we have to keep blowin' up the desert? And don't we have a new tactical arms treaty to begin tearin' down all the thousands of smaller nukes? Besides, I thought there was a moratorium on more tests."

"Congress passed new legislation even though, under the 1992 moratorium, we were actually permitted a few tests. Waddy, I'd rather not waste our day getting into all the politics about why the new law passed, but from a strictly scientific standpoint, we really need the information. Further testing may get shut down again—permanently if we enter into the last phase of START. The tests have been planned for a long time as part of our overall development program, a lot of money has already been spent, and besides, we're conducting them in conjunction with the Brits."

"Hasn't the U. S. conducted over 900 nuclear weapons tests since 1945? And you still don't have it right? I mean, a bomb is a bomb, isn't it? Are there any parts of Yucca and Frenchman Flats you guys haven't already blown up?"

"Well, technology improves. We're constantly upgrading the efficiency and safety of the devices and their triggering systems, while decreasing the physical size and weight of the weapons. It's no different than any other high tech industry."

"But we no longer have to keep up with the Joneses, do we? Isn't what we already have plenty good enough? Pretty soon we'll just be havin' to disassemble under START and—what do they call the tactical weapons treaty—*TART*?" Waddy was unable to contain a smile. "Just tearin' apart what we're now buildin' and testin' at great expense of resources and our environment. Can any of you think of any other human endeavor in which such a massive amount of time, energy, and resource has been expended only to throw it all away? Surely there must be *some* way to use those damned things."

Saul shifted in his chair, then stared out the window at the bay.

"Let me butt in here a minute," Stan said, hoping to soften Waddy's bluntness. "Saul is not at liberty to discuss the details of his or others' work at Livermore; and without that information there's no way we can get anywhere with this subject. We'll just have the usual speculation on our part and the usual silence from Saul. Waddy, the three of us have been through this a lot of times before." Malcolm nodded in agreement. Saul concentrated on his plate.

"Okay, I'm sorry, guys. It's just that it all seems like such bullshit."

"Much, if not most of it, is, I will tell you," Saul said, looking up. Stan and Malcolm stared at him for a long moment. It was the first time they had ever heard Saul say anything negative about his work as a physicist at the Lawrence Livermore National Laboratory.

Stan examined his old friend's familiar face. He'd long ago decided that Saul looked like a melanistic Vincent Van Gogh. In place of the red hair, ruddy complexion, and green eyes, Saul had thick, gray-flecked black hair, an almost olive complexion, and very dark eyes. But Saul's face mimicked the beetle brows, small round ears, high cheekbones, pointed chin, and full, pursed lips of the tortured artist: the vision captured in the self-portraits done by Vincent while he lived in his beloved yellow house at Arles.

"Want to elaborate on that comment?" Malcolm asked.

"Forget it. I shouldn't have said anything. But to sort of answer Waddy's question about other possible uses of the weapons, twenty-five years ago the Atomic Energy Commission planned to detonate a number of large devices underground in western Colorado to release natural gas from oil shale formations. Trouble was, the gas companies weren't too excited about having to sell radioactive unnatural gas. Of course, contamination of the ground water from so many of them concentrated in one area would have been worse than a meltdown of a nuclear power plant."

Stan nodded. "And remember the plan to build another canal across Panama, using a line of medium yield weapons to excavate the trench?"

Saul looked out at the bay again. "Yes, that's right. I forgot about that," he said distractedly.

"Well," Malcolm added, "we probably should keep a few of the really big ones around, loaded aboard Titan rockets, so we could deflect an asteroid . . . But if we do go the way of the dinosaurs there won't be anything left except coyotes, cockroaches, and lawyers." His big grin accompanied a clap on Stan's back.

Stan knew that Waddy, and probably Saul, were dying to correct Malcolm's prediction, to point out that actually there would be only two distinct species of survivors. He responded to the circle of suppressed smiles. "Keep it up, Malcolm. One of these days you're going to get yourself into something where you'll really need a good trial lawyer—and I don't mean one of those stuffed suits you've got holding down chairs in your offices."

Everybody concentrated on the chef's creation for a while, until Waddy spoke up. "Uh, somethin' I've been wantin' to ask. Could one of you explain why this club is so despised here in Berkeley?"

"Oh, hell, that's a long story," Malcolm grinned. "Everybody in this place is a member *because* of those academic shitheads and their P.C. thought control."

"But some of the members are university professors."

"Mavericks all," Malcolm answered. "They're tenured. Can't be fired, and they don't give a damn what the rest of the university nitwits say."

"Waddy," Saul said, "the club's position of ignominy within the sacred Berkeley precinct is largely because free speech is truly practiced here. Not merely a politically correct form of free speech—I mean the freedom to speak, completely uninhibited, on *any* subject."

"Without labels," Stan added. "Bigot, racist, fascist, queer, sexist, homophobe, pro-lifer, and so on—you'll never hear them used here. If someone does resort to a label, he'd better be prepared to explain, in detail, what he means by it. It's a particular issue in the club, because in Berkeley labels are commonly used to end discussion—to brand someone to the smug satisfaction of the label user." He thrust his chin toward Malcolm. "Except the big guy here. Everyone's about given up trying to sort out his particular hangup."

"Don't encourage him, Stanley," Saul frowned.

"Like your calling us *pahanas,"* Malcolm said. "I know it's simply your Hopi word for a white person, but it seems to smack of something derogatory. Saul, remember? When Daphna got pissed at something you said and called you a honky?"

"Yes, what a day that was," Saul smiled. Malcolm was positively radiant. Discussions about race were his favorite. The subject was endless, unresolvable. Much better than religion.

"Well, it took over the whole afternoon's discussion," Malcolm continued. "Everybody jumped in. I sure learned a whole lot about the origin of that word. Then when Saul took the position that Jews aren't white people—that *really* pissed her off."

"Well, we're not. We're Semitic."

"That explains it," Waddy said. "I didn't think you were a *pahana*, Saul."

Oh God, it's starting again, Saul thought. *We'll be here all afternoon.*

Malcolm was building up steam. "But Semitism's not a racial categorization. It's just a subfamily of Afro-Asian language grouping: Aramaic, Arabic, Ethiopic, as well as Hebraic."

"Malcolm, you're being too simplistic," Saul sighed. "So long as the summary term *white* remains in the lexicon, I'm afraid we'll have to insist upon not being included."

"I defy anyone here to even define what a white person is," Stan jumped in. "What? A Caucasian? And what's that? Someone from the Caucasus: maybe an Abkha, a Circassian, a Kartvelian, a Georgian, a Chechen, an Ossetian? But those people are nearly all Muslim, and most are thought to be descended from ancient inhabitants of Persia. Therefore, they are *white*? What nonsense. We're all descended from the original people, who were African."

Saul saw that Waddy was going to raise a big objection to the last statement. "Oh, please! Not today. Let's not get into all this again."

"Okay, back to Waddy's question about the club. Let's not forget our membership policy," Stan said to a gale of laughter from Saul and Malcolm.

"There *is* no membership policy, Waddy," Malcolm thundered, gathering a scatter of glances from around the room. "Even the ACLU, the NAACP, and the Asian American League, among others, would have to admit that we're about as diverse as is possible given we're limited to an array of eighty-five: the size of this dining hall plus room for guests."

"I'll bet the Daughters of the American Revolution wouldn't want to join," Waddy said.

"Well, I beg to differ. If I were female I'd qualify for membership in the DAR. Anyway, money, social standing—whether high, middle, or low—academic achievement, character, personality, number of friends in the club, political, sexual or religious persuasion, power—none are determinative here. This place is perfect disorder, Waddy. Outrageous, fecund, wholesale disorder. The academics hate it. Hell, *you'll* be a member one of these days." Malcolm surveyed the room. "Isaack over there hit the beach at the Bay of Pigs, and that guy he's huddled with spent a couple of years down at Soledad for something having to do with an Episcopal Church treasury. And there's Manuela. She was a Sandinista, trained in Cuba." Malcolm turned back to Waddy. "We're very proud of our position as the most noxious thread in the Berkeley fabric. There's just nothing better than being hated by knee-jerk, P.C. yo-yos."

Waddy took his turn studying the collection in the room. From the little he knew about the people assembled, he suddenly realized the extent of the eclectic mix. Bland people with remarkable views and acid wits mingled with electric people of conventional views and little wit. "I guess I understand. Anyway, tell me—how *are* members selected?"

"First of all, somebody has to move far away or die. Nobody quits. Then at the annual meeting there's a vote. Actually, there's seldom much dispute; it's amazing how general consensus just builds over the year . . . Waddy, you'll never be a member until everyone understands all that business with you and the Navajos, and the *pahana* thing."

Waddy continued his examination of the rest of the people in the dining room.

"We still haven't heard much about what's going on in your life," Stan said. "When do you start back to work in Grand Canyon?"

"Oh, next month. We haul a lot of tourists down to Phantom Ranch during the holidays. Pretty nice down there then. Also, this fall I started helpin' run the scientists and bureaucrats down the river—the ones doin' the environmental impact statement on the Glen Canyon Dam releases."

"Yeah, that's right. The EIS should be finished pretty soon," Stan said distractedly. He and his two old friends looked intently at each other.

Long moments passed. "So, what's the matter?" Waddy scanned the trio of solemn expressions. "What did I say?"

"I guess we were all thinking the same thing," Saul said. Stan and Malcolm nodded blankly.

Malcolm said quietly, "In 1958 the three of us—it was after our first year in college—we floated Glen Canyon."

"You . . . you saw Glen Canyon before it was flooded?" Three nods answered the question.

"Oh, man!" He searched the faces of the three older men sitting beside him and across the table. A great deal of intense, silent communication occurred amid the murmurs of conversation and the clinks and clatters surrounding them.

"I was only six years old in 1963 when the reservoir started to fill. Others in my clan only told me about the canyon when I was old enough to understand."

"What is your clan?" Saul asked.

"I am Snake Clan. My father is Horn/Flute. Both have very strong ties to the canyon of the Great River."

"So your clan affiliation derives from your mother," Saul nodded. "I didn't know Hopi society was matrilineal."

"Sort of like you Jews, Saul. Anyway, the Snake Clan were the last to leave from their homes in Kawestima. You probably know the place as Betátakin—what the Tasávu call it."

"That's in the Navajo National Monument, isn't it?" Malcolm asked.

"Damn Tasávu! They have no claim to the ancestral home of my people. We lived in the region for thousands of years before the first head pounders started wandering around in Tusqua."

"So you are directly related to the Kayenta Anasazi," Saul said.

"*Kayenta* is another Tasávu word—the Anglicized version, that is. Should be pronounced *tkeyh-in-deh*. Means somethin' like 'quicksand whirlpool. If you fall in you don't come out.'"

"Why don't the Hopi insist upon the use of the correct names?" Malcolm asked bluntly. "If you just stand by silently, the world will only know the Navajo names for the places so important to your people."

Waddy glared at him. "You're right. The problem is that my people are not self-glorifiers like the Navajo. It is not the Hopi Way."

"Perhaps it should become your way," Malcolm persisted, "before your culture is just swallowed up by the Navajo like they have swallowed up your land."

Waddy paused a long, pain filled moment. "You certainly know how to cut deep."

"You're way off base, Malcolm," Stan said. "Why don't we change the subject."

"It's all right. He's correct, actually. In fact, I have argued exactly what he said. But tradition and a people's ways change slowly, if at all." Waddy looked at Malcolm intently. "The head pounders and their legions of lawyers may have taken our lands but they will never destroy our culture."

"Why don't we just talk about Glen Canyon?" Saul said, exercising his skill at maneuvering things out of an uncomfortable impasse.

"One day," Waddy said pensively, nodding at Saul, "it is our belief that the great canyon of the River of my People will be both physically and spiritually restored to us. The natural land is our heritage. No matter what changes are made by the puny efforts of the *pahanas*, one day all will be returned. The natural land lives forever: in that sense, past, present, and future become one."

"I'm truly sorry that you and everyone else only shortly past our generation has been denied that treasure," Saul said softly.

"Yes," Malcolm sighed. "Remember Cathedral in the Desert, up Clear Creek on the Escalante?"

"How could we forget?" Saul whispered. "That grand cavern at the end of the long, winding side canyon, with its plunge pool and the tapestried walls, and . . . well, you remember."

"The next day we stopped at Music Temple," Stan quickly added. "We camped there just like John Wesley Powell did on his two expeditions. Wasn't that place something?"

"You . . . you were at Music Temple?" Waddy said as he clutched Stan's arm. His dark eyes betrayed a hint of excess moisture.

"Yes, we stayed there two days and we explored Hidden Passage just across the river. Wonderful broad sandbar and lots of wildlife in the willow bog at the end of the bar. We camped right in the great cavern, next to the pool." Saul and Malcolm smiled silently.

"Any particular reason for your interest in Music Temple?" Stan asked their guest. Waddy still had a grip on his arm.

"It's just . . . it's a very special place to my clan, that's all." Waddy released his unconscious grasp and stared out at the parking lot. He was not familiar with the parking lot saga.

"Waddy," Saul said, "it should be a satisfaction to you that our memories of our experience for those few days in 1958 stands as living proof of the special place it was."

"*Is*," Waddy corrected.

Saul nodded. "The special place it *is*. For me, it's like it happened last week. In this sense I feel I can understand what your people believe about the spirituality of nature and the timeless joinder of earth and man."

"Okay, can we move on to something else?" Malcolm said soberly. "This is all just too depressing."

"Well," Stan said, "moving from one depressing point to another. Waddy brought up nuclear testing. What about all those bombs in the former Soviet Union? Aren't we now in an even more dangerous situation with the fragments of the Soviet Union each controlling their own supplies of bombs and missiles? Kazakhstan, Turkmenistan, and Uzbekistan are almost wholly Muslim. How long will it be before some bunch of crazies in neighboring Iran get their hands on a nuke and take out a big chunk of Israel? What about it, Saul? Do you think the new independent states will be able keep the tight control the Soviet Union maintained?"

"That's what START is all about. The new tactical weapons treaty, too. Very tight inventories and controls are scheduled. The problem is that Ukraine, in particular, is dragging her feet. But it's not the big strategic weapons that are of concern to me. It's the thousands of small tactical rockets and bombs. They have the greatest risk of being obtained by extremists in the Middle East. Like Stan said, Turkmen borders Iran on the north, and the Turkmeni are closely linked to the Uzbeks and Kazakhs, who had a lot of the smaller weapons. The Russians *claim* that all the small tactical weapons are under their control, but I don't know. That whole region is solidly Muslim, and there has historically been a lot of resentment against Russia. The strongest emphasis must be placed on rounding up all those little guys—and I mean right now."

"Fat chance," Malcolm said.

Saul shrugged. "Frankly, I'm afraid that it's going to take an incident—probably an actual explosion somewhere—to really wake everybody up. The consensus seems to be that the crisis will, indeed, occur in the Middle East. Remember how much trouble we had controlling the Israelis when Saddam was lobbing Scuds into their country? All bets are off if Muslim extremists use even a small nuke in Israel. Damascus, Baghdad, and Teheran would be leveled in less than an hour. Maybe Riyadh, Khartoum, and Tripoli, too. And remember, START, democratization, and all the rest do not disarm all the weapons that're probably remaining in the independent countries. It's at least a possibility that Israel's eye-for-an-eye reaction to nuclear attack would suck us into a nuclear exchange with some part of the former Soviet Union."

"Is this official thinking we're hearing, Saul?" Waddy asked. "I mean, you people at Livermore have your hands right on those bombs."

"No, nothing official. Of course, since we're all so close to it at work, there is a lot of talk. The people at the lab can speculate, like anyone else." Saul stared out at the parking lot for several long moments. "A few of us feel that a controllable incident, well away from Israel, is what it will take to really shake everybody up and get some effective safeguards in place. The CIA has certainly arranged accidents before to accomplish strategic objectives. I know this sounds crazy, but is it not more crazy to just sit back and wait for the inevitable to happen in Israel?"

Waddy shook his head. "Saul, do you have any instinct at all that this has been considered by our great leaders, and, even if considered, does anyone at that level have even the *REMOTEST cojones* needed to actually do what you suggest?"

"Yes, I'm sure the accident scenario has been well analyzed; as for the more important question—no, not a chance."

The universally acknowledged problem with lunch at the Cactus Club was that the time was always too short. It was quarter to two when Stan glanced at his watch. While he had no afternoon classes, he still had to finish his law review recommendations. Then as if suddenly waking from a pleasant but overlong nap, Malcolm got up and fled in a mild panic, responding to the duties attendant to being grand master of vast assemblies of people, commerce, and industry. Even Waddy exhibited some urgency to be off to meet with one of his Hillsborough customers; but Saul was bound by the most relaxed schedule and luxuriated over his coffee, as though government weapons scientists were blessed with the mellow environment of the most obscure university researcher. Saul and Stan were among the last to leave, repairing to the beloved parking lot.

"Good to have Waddy back for a while," Stan said. He started focusing again on what remained to be done with the day.

"He always does get us thinking about things, doesn't he?"

Saul's detached look did not communicate with Stan. "Something particularly profound in today's ramblings?" he asked, joining Saul's gaze across the bay.

"Think about it, Stan. Just think about it."

Stan watched his old friend get into his car. *I missed something today*, he shrugged. *Think about what?*

2

EIGHT HUNDRED THIRTY MILES ABOVE THE INTERTROPICAL CONVERGENCE ZONE EASTERN PACIFIC OCEAN, NOVEMBER 10

Topex/Poseidon silently completed its ground-trace sequence after 127 revolutions. It was back at the precise point above the Pacific Ocean where it had been ten days previously. The oceanographic data accumulated in its onboard recorders were played back to earth through the NASA Tracking and Data Relay Satellite System, and soon the billions of bits of information would be passed on to thirty-eight participating atmospheric and oceanographic research institutions around the world.

The $600 million, 5,800-pound bundle of some of the latest space technology was jointly sponsored by the United States and France. Since its launch aboard an Ariane rocket in August 1992 from the space center in Kourou, French Guiana, the altimeters and orbit location instruments had completed their assessment and verification phases. The satellite was now in the process of completing its mission: precisely mapping the topography of the world's oceans, 66° north and south of the equator.

The satellite's sophisticated instruments focused on the Eastern Pacific Ocean's surface that lay immediately beneath its current pass. The bulges and depressions it detected were caused by three phenomena, but Topex/Poseidon concentrated on separating and precisely measuring the smallest component. The gravitational attraction of the uneven and non-homogeneous land mass lying beneath the seas caused much of the sea's variation in elevation, and superimposed upon this topography were the hemispherically-wide bulges and depressions from the pull of the moon and the sun. Finally, there were subtle variations resulting from the weather and climate, producing interactions between the ocean of water and the atmospheric ocean riding on its surface.

It was this third component—the dynamic ocean topography—that Topex/Poseidon had been sent into orbit to investigate. Although the gravitational attractions produced a global altitude variation of nearly 500 feet relative to the center of the earth, the dynamic component was normally less than seven feet. In order to accurately map this tiny fraction of the overall ocean contour, the position of the satellite and its altimeter readings were measured precisely to within a few centimeters. The NASA Topex altimeter and its French counterpart each measured the height above the waves with a similar accuracy, and from these data the dynamic ocean surface could be mapped. Assisted by hundreds of thousands of observations of the physical characteristics of the oceans and atmosphere around the world, the movements of the gigantic masses of heated and cooled waters could also be calculated and mapped.

One of the movements of ocean water of particular interest to oceanographers was that which caused the phenomenon known as "El Niño." Long before meteorologists and oceanographers were aware of it, much less able to attempt to explain it, the fishermen of Chili, Peru, and Ecuador had known of the strange event. Every ten years or so, at the time of year of the birth of the Christ Child, unusually warm water would appear along the equatorial Pacific coast of South America. Through the preceding summer and fall, heavy and continuous rainfall would occur along the normally arid coastal region. Fishing was completely disrupted as the usually cold water and the upwelling of marine flora and fauna were cut off. The huge schools of anchovy and sardines retreated southward to deeper and cooler waters, out of reach of the purse seiners, and the local fishermen also lost their traditional prey, the *pejerrey, lenguado,* and *cojinoba*. These were replaced by enormous quantities of swimming crabs and rays, damaging the fishermen's nets and filling them with a catch that could not be sold.

The most recent El Niño, that of 1982–84, was by far the most intense among these anomalies that had been recorded since measurements began in 1935. Rainfall was 1,000 percent above average along the South American coast, and unusual weather patterns had also been seen in North America, particularly in the basin of the Colorado River. The sea surface temperature, the principal indicator of an El Niño event, reached 84°F off the coast of Ecuador in 1983, nearly 8 degrees above normal, and the elevated sea temperatures covered a wide area of the eastern equatorial Pacific during the mature phase of the El Niño. Across the expanse of the Pacific the normally uniform trade winds diminished, and the equatorial westerlies extended eastward beyond the International Dateline. The low pressures in the Gulf of Alaska sank to near-records, the high pressure area in the Eastern Pacific increased dramatically, and the mid-latitude westerly winds north of the Pacific High also increased substantially. The southern branch of the jet stream intensified and migrated south as far as Baja California, from December until well into spring. With the removal of the usual high-pressure ridge that blocks the flows of polar fronts from the Gulf of Alaska, large quantities of late-season snow fell in the mountains ringing the Upper Basin of the Colorado River: from the San Juans in Southern Colorado to the Wind River Range in Wyoming to the Uinta and the Wasatch Ranges in Utah. The United States Bureau of Reclamation had been caught with too much runoff and too little space in its system of reservoirs on the tributaries and main stem of the Colorado River. The Bureau announced one year later that it had modified the spillways so that the damage caused by the 1983 event could never be repeated.

If human eyes were looking down from Topex/Poseidon on this day they would have seen the envelope of bright blue atmosphere etched in an arc against the black void of space. The human brain connected to the eyes, regardless of the brain's store of scientific knowledge or training, would have been struck by the profound fragility of the skin of life-sustaining atmosphere, marked by the whorls of clouds over the expanses of brown and blue. Back on earth, hundreds of atmospheric scientists struggled to find links, correlations, and clues between the chemical changes in the thin shell of air, the movements of the world's ocean currents, and the weather and long-term climate. Topex/Poseidon was not in existence in 1983–84, the years unusual floods occurred in several areas of the northern hemisphere. The satellite was not there to see the subtle changes in sea surface elevation that correlated with the increased and broadly expanded range of surface temperatures in the eastern equatorial Pacific. But had it been there, it would have observed changes in the ocean surface elevations that were greatly exceeded by the ones it was witnessing on this day.

Getting started, 1956 (*Bureau of Reclamation*).

Now, the dam, 1959 (*Bureau of Reclamation*).

UKRAINE

Tapestries in Twilight Canyon, 1960 (*Tad Nichols*).

1

Sevastopil, Crimea, November 15

Kateryna Kovalevska walked along the sea wall, gazing out at the armada of naval ships in the roadstead. Down the long expanse of water to the west, the near-winter sun settled, brassy orange, into the gray horizon of the Black Sea. Scattered across this arm of the inland sea, extending up to the Crimean port of Sevastopil, most of the ships of the Black Sea Fleet rode at their anchors. All were pointed into the setting sun as the tide water flooded into the Sevastopil'skaya Bukhta.

The sun was surprisingly warm in the late afternoon. The "velvet season" still lingered in Crimea. She smiled at the thought that far to the north, in the sleet and cold of the beginning Russian winter, many of the Moscow elite yearned for their private dachas on the lovely mountainous coast of this peninsula jutting south into the Black Sea.

A fisherman hurried along the seawall, glancing nervously away while he passed the tall, slim woman in the uniform of a field grade security officer. She was oblivious to the man's passing. She pulled off her mink shapka, loosened the clip that held her fine, obsidian black hair in a tight bun, then let it fall in a thick mass over the collar of her greatcoat. She closed her eyes, absorbing the last of the faint heat from the departing sun and listening to the wavelets that sporadically struck the rocks of the seawall.

Lieutenant Colonel Kovalevska was ethnic Ukrainian, a blend of the ferocious Cossacks who had peopled the steppe since the fifteenth century and the equally fierce Tatars who had long ago come from the far east. Few of her Tatar people remained in Crimea. Nearly all of the descendents of the ancient people had been slaughtered by the Nazis; then most of the survivors were killed or deported by Stalin for supposed collaboration with the enemy. But those who remained in Crimea and across the breadth of Ukraine were fiercely independent, only grudgingly tolerating the long, overpowering occupations by foreign rulers, most recently the Russians.

The historic Ukraine spread from the Slavic-peopled Carpathian Mountains in the west across the undulating, fertile land of the steppe to the gentle Don River in the east; from the Black Sea on the south to the ill-defined transition to Russia in the north. For as far back as history was recorded, the people of the Ukrainian steppe had worked the rich black *chernozem*, producing an abundance of wheat and other grains, but for a millennium the industrious people of Ukraine had been forced to give up their bounty to feed the voracious Russia, then the Turks, then again the Russians. Potentially, Colonel Kovalevska's Ukraine was the most productive of all the republics in the new Commonwealth of Independent States. It should have the best chance for survival in the post-Soviet crash into a free market system, but the thirty-eight-year-old woman knew that a prosperous Ukraine was unlikely—as unlikely as her own prosperity. The Ukrainians were largely a peasant people, and corruption among their leaders was endemic, fueled and encouraged by the omnipresent Russians upon whom Ukraine was dependent for nearly all of her oil and natural gas. And the trade of foodstuffs for energy had by no means been even. Huge sums were owed to Russia, with Ukraine's giant neighbor driving a hard bargain: Russia wanted the fleet and all the nuclear weapons; then, many feared, their beautiful peninsula—ultimately, the whole of Ukraine.

She had devoted her life and career to the service of the Soviet Union, and like the majority of her fellow officers, soldiers, sailors, and airmen, she still could not fully accept that her beloved, vast and powerful, Union of Soviet Socialist Republics was no more. She had been taught to believe in the right, the superiority, of the great socialist system. And she did believe it. Less vigorously now, but she still believed it.

A graphic reminder of the recent upheaval were the small changes in insignia and decoration of her proud uniform. In place of the Soviet star and the hammer and sickle, her uniform now displayed the trident of Saint Volodymyr, the martyred saint who in 988 had brought Christianity to Ukraine from Constantinople. The uniform that only a few short years earlier had represented the armed forces of one of the two greatest powers in the world, now represented only an obscure country on the shores of an isolated sea.

Along with the changes in the uniform she had worn for the past thirteen years, another change was conspicuous to Kateryna. The banner of azure blue over golden yellow, representing the expanse of sky over fields of grain, had been gone beyond the memory of all but the oldest of her people. The Ukrainian national flag again flew over the principal buildings of Sevastopil, the capital city of the Krymska Oblast, and all across Ukraine, but none were flying from the yardarms and transoms of the ships in the roadstead. She stared at the scores of Soviet naval ensigns, their familiar red shapes sharply accentuating the gray scene. Kateryna was certain that, in the end, the entire 600-ship fleet would fly only the white, royal blue, and red flag of Russia.

She had been a career officer in the Soviet State Committee for Science and Technology. With her doctorate in nuclear physics and her initial employment at the prestigious Kurchatov Institute, Kateryna had looked forward to a career in nuclear power development. But her talents had been directed elsewhere, first to weapons design, and then to the ultra-secret studies of special missions and sabotage deployments. Then, because custody and transport of all nuclear devices were under the control of the Committee for State Security, the young physicist had been drawn into the massive organization. She had even been required to endure the intensive and often brutal training at the Committee's Moscow center—the "Manger," as it was called, for the unrelenting mass of KGB fodder it produced. Now even the mighty KGB was no more, replaced by hastily created intelligence commands in the newly independent republics, each formed around the fragments of the former security agency. In fact, the core of the KGB still existed, though now exclusively Russian, with its principal offspring being the Russian Federation Foreign Intelligence Service and the Ministry of Security. And the Russian military was still hugely dominant, just as it always had been for as long as organized countries had existed in this part of the world.

Kateryna stood at the end of the seawall. She watched the clouds of sea gulls following the returning fishing boats, the birds' cries reinforcing the pungent odor of the sea. But again her eyes were drawn to the huge fleet, ships that had been the counterbalancing force against America's Sixth Fleet in the Mediterranean. *At least those naval officers have a navy,* she thought, also understanding that practically all of the officers were Russian. *What is to be the rest of MY career?* She was painfully aware that Ukraine could not maintain its own nuclear research program and arsenal, and she was also aware of a more fundamental aspect of life in Ukraine: women were always removed from employment before the men. *And what have I to do other than be merely a watchdog over steadily decaying and unneeded weapons? No one is going to threaten us with nuclear war because of our wheat, sugar beets, and coal.*

Kateryna had far darker thoughts—the fear always with her, though not always in her consciousness. She knew of things she was not supposed to know. She was confident that no one yet suspected her secret knowledge, but her fear was that it would be discovered by one of seven former Moscow Guards Directorate officers: six were now in the transformed Russian Ministry of Security, the seventh in Ukraine. Major General Pavlo Nastenko was Kateryna's commanding officer.

The anxious dread that regularly spiked into her awareness faded again; her thoughts extended beyond it and beyond her career, her Ukraine, and the loss of her once mighty Soviet Union. She stared down the sound, toward the Black Sea and the cold sun settling into a hazy gray horizon. Her entire consciousness involuntarily flooded back to a day in early April 1986. She was with Anatoliy and little Sofiia, then just starting to walk. They were in the garden of a small whitewashed and tiled cottage in the rolling foothills of the Carpathian Mountains. It was Anatoliy's family home. Springtime engorged the orchard-dotted countryside, and the sun was warm on a late Sunday afternoon.

"Tolik, when are Mama and Papa coming home?"

"Soon. They probably stopped to buy fruit," Anatoliy said as the screen door to the garden slammed behind him. He scooped up his little daughter then plopped into the wicker swing beside his wife. Sofiia giggled and squirmed as she played with her father's beard.

Kateryna looked closely at her husband. Fifteen years her senior, he was a tall, broad-shouldered man with a thick thatch of hair, more blond than his closely trimmed beard; his wide, open face was grooved with deep smile lines. He looked at Kateryna, and Sofiia also looked up at her mother. Father and daughter both had the piercing azure eyes so common among the Slavic people of western Ukraine, but the little girl had gotten her slightly olive skin tone from her mother. It accentuated the straw-blond hair and the startling eyes. She would also likely develop Kateryna's thin, willowy figure. *Sofiia is going to be a beautiful woman*, her mother thought.

Sharing Kateryna's gaze, Anatoliy absorbed his wife's countenance: "How fortunate I am to have you, Katrusia," he said, leaning over to kiss her cheek. She turned in the swing, her hands cupping Anatoliy's face—a ruddy, freckled face that contrasted sharply with the smooth, olive-toned hands holding it. She kissed the face she loved. As his eyes opened, Anatoliy saw his wife's: they were slightly almond-shaped, set below dark brows, and separated by a thin, delicately pointed nose. Her eyes were the very opposite of Anatoliy's—dark and multicolored like the matrix of an opal. They always seemed so wise and all-knowing to him. He kissed the nape of her neck, burying his big face in her thick, silken hair.

"As am I to have you, my love," Kateryna said softly. Sofiia wriggled off her father's lap and stooped, rockily, to gather a handful of plum blossoms, now falling from the garden trees. In little clenched fists she offered them to her father and mother.

"We must leave soon, Katrusia," Anatoliy murmured. Out through the birch grove at the rear of the one-third hectare plot, they heard the unremitting chorus of frog ribbets, broken occasionally by woodpecker taps and songbird calls. Black currant bushes blossomed around the perimeter of the garden and filled the dappled sunlight spaces between the underground root cellar, the barn, the outhouse, and the little outdoor kitchen used during the hot summer months. Mama Kovalevska's flowers were erupting everywhere in carefully tended plots.

"Oh, Tolik, the time has gone so quickly. We must go back tomorrow. My flight to Chelyabinsk is Tuesday morning."

"You have much more responsibility with your promotion. My pretty wife is now a major," Anatoliy said proudly while they watched their daughter playing in the grass at their feet.

Kateryna thought of the many things that awaited her return to the sprawling nuclear weapons complex, beyond the Ural Mountains in faraway

Russia.

"And you, my handsome doctor, you have much to do back home."

"I am being sent up to Prypiat for perhaps three weeks. We are finally permitted to conduct the testing we have urged for so long, to see if there is anything to the complaints we have had about the cancer rate among the Chornobyl workers."

"Tolik, must you go to that place?" Kateryna asked with undisguised anguish. She knew the Chornobyl reactors were a mistake, hurriedly and poorly designed. Even more were planned at the huge complex 120 kilometers north of Kyyiv.

"Just as you must go to Chelyabinsk, Alatov, Nizhnyaya Tura, and wherever else your duties demand."

Outside the close confines of her work, Kateryna was forbidden to talk to anyone about anything relating to her duties. Nearly everything she did was classified Most Secret. The huge, Russian-dominated security agency had its tentacles everywhere, and the thousands of operatives in the Second Chief Directorate were particularly determined to know of the activities and, if possible, the very thoughts of the people who had intimate knowledge of the Soviet Union's nuclear arsenal and its deployment. Major Kovalevska was involved in far more than mere custody and transport of the weapons—and she was conspicuous in the huge agency, a fact that added to her need to follow the rules precisely. Being both ethnic Ukrainian and a woman were highly unusual for a KGB officer involved with nuclear weapons.

Kateryna hated the separations from Anatoliy, now made even more painful since Sofiia had come into their lives. How she longed for a normal, stable home life. With her husband's essentially permanent assignment to the Center for Radiation Medicine in Kyyiv, Kateryna dreamed about resigning her position. But she knew she would not be permitted to leave. Her superiors had made that clear when she had casually inquired about reassignment to the Ukrainian department of the State Committee for Science and Technology in Kyyiv. The state had invested too much in her very specialized training, in particular, the matter of certain deployments of tactical nuclear weapons. Additionally, and most ominously, Kateryna knew too much about the KGB. That fact alone would assure that she and would never be permitted to leave its service. Her personal concerns and wishes were irrelevant.

"Tolik, I hear them." The sounds of the old carriage and the clip-clop of the horse came from the lane in front of the house. Anatoliy picked up Sofiia and followed his wife into the little cottage.

Kateryna and Anatoliy knew that Mama Kovalevska had gone to the Orthodox cathedral while her husband shopped in the Sunday market. She always wore her best head scarf and dress when she planned to go to the cathedral in Lviv. The old woman would stand in the huge, crowded church throughout the five-hour service, singing and listening carefully to the liturgy, sung in Old Church Slavonic. She would wait in the long line to kiss the icons and to be blessed.

Were his time with Kateryna not so precious, Anatoliy would also have gone to the church with his mother. But his father would not. As Kateryna's father had been, Leonid Kovalevska was devoted only to the all-powerful state, and also like Kateryna's father, even though they were of wholly different ethnicities, the old man considered the church to be a sign of weakness, of fatuous dreaming—something only for women to be concerned with. Women were meant to do most of the heavy and menial work; if they needed the church to assist them in their lives, that could be tolerated.

"Did you have a good trip to Lviv?" Kateryna asked as the old couple entered the house, first pausing to change their shoes for slippers. Aneliia Kovalevska looked up at Kateryna. The small, stooped woman was nearly half as wide as she was tall: a product of her ethnicity, the Ukrainian diet, and the circumstance of sixty-seven of her seventy-eight years having been spent in heavy toil on the state and collective farms. Her nearly-circular face, wrapped in an embroidered babushka, was deeply creased and leathered by her lifetime in the fields, and the old woman's reaction to Kateryna's greeting sent the creases and lines into an effusion of happy, sparkling smile. As Kateryna stooped to kiss her, Aneliia reached up to hold her daughter-in-law's face. The tiny gold wedding band, deeply embedded in the finger of her right hand, had not been removed for sixty years.

"My pretty Katrusia, our Sunday is perfect! Even Papa found little to complain about," she said, turning her smile to her lifetime partner. Leonid nodded with a glance at his old wife, then headed for his chair in the garden. "Come, Katrusia, help with things Papa got at market. Then we must start supper. Tolik, go sit with your Papa and have cigarette. He will tell you many new anecdotes he heard at market."

Kateryna shared her final Sunday supper with Anatoliy's family in the tiny house in the verdant foothills of the Carpathian Mountains. The evening had been spent in quiet conversation about the waves of change everyone saw on the political horizon. Gorbachev now even permitted the bells to ring in the churches across Ukraine, and there was talk that people would be permitted to own more than the one-third hectare to which they had long been limited. The turmoil in the Baltics was thought to be a portent of change in many of the other republics. Many even spoke of significant disarmament, but the people of western Ukraine, like most of the people along the frontier with the West, were fearful of giving up their defenses. The old people vividly remembered that the last great assault on their lands had come from the west, as it had at the beginning of the nineteenth century.

The family also spoke of Anatoliy's and Kateryna's plans for a little sister or brother for Sofiia. Mama Kovalevska had been very happy to hear that her stubborn and career-oriented daughter-in-law was beginning to understand that family was all that really mattered. And while Kateryna was with Sofiia, Anatoliy, and his parents—the only family she had—her duties and her career seemed so far away and irrelevant. The evening had ended with everyone listening intently to the words of Taras Shevchenko, the poetry recited reverently by Anatoliy's father in the soft language of Ukraine.

A wind started to build, coming up the sound from the west, pushing gray waves before it. Kateryna turned up the collar of her greatcoat, quickly reknotted her hair and snugged down her fur hat; but she was oblivious to the sudden drop in temperature replacing the departed sun. Her thoughts concentrated on what had happened three weeks after that last Sunday in the little cottage near Lviv. What had happened in the early morning hours of that day at the end of April when Reactor Number Four at Chornobyl exploded. What had happened to change her life.

Those Russian fools and their carelessness! WHY, my Tolik? WHY did you go to that place! she asked for the uncounted time. She knew the answer, of course: the same answer to why she obeyed the commands of her own superiors who forbade her to go to Chornobyl after the terrible accident.

Because of his oncology specialty and training in the treatment of radiation sickness, Anatoliy had been needed to work right in the midst of the worst area of contamination. After he became ill from the radiation, he had died before Kateryna was released from her duties. The last time she had seen him was the Tuesday morning she had left for Chelyabinsk after their visit to Lviv. Anatoliy's death had shattered the frail old people and less than a year later they too were gone—first Aneliia, then a few weeks later her patient husband.

Kateryna longed to remember as many of the details of that last time as she could: the precious memories of that long-ago two weeks with Anatoliy, now slowly fading with her anguish. Over seven years had now passed, yet Kateryna remained haunted by the memory of her strong, handsome Anatoliy. He had personified the Ukrainian national character of simplicity, frankness, and openhearted warmth, and he had loved Kateryna and their little girl with such fervor. The unbearable despair that had lasted for the first two years had slowly subsided into a detached yet constant ache. Only little Sofiia had kept Kateryna going—that and her pride in being an officer in the service of her country and directly involved in its first line of defense. Now it was only Sofiia: "Sofiyka," as Anatoliy had called her when she was born.

Kateryna looked at her watch. She quickly started back along the sea wall. Sofiia would be coming home from school soon.

The little girl broke away from her companions, all alike in their brown dresses and black aprons, their brown trousers and white shirts. She ran across the street and up the stairs of the row house on the narrow street.

"Mama! Mama!" the slight and willowy nine-year-old called out as Kateryna watched her through the window. She burst through the door, clutching a sheet of paper. "Oh, Mama, look at my marks!"

Kateryna swung her daughter around while holding her in a tight hug. "Sofiia, you make your mama so very proud!" Immediately she thought of how equally proud Anatoliy would have been. She tried to force the thoughts from her mind.

"Here, let me read this." She needed a few moments to hold back the welling tears and to avoid the little girl's wide, searching blue eyes. While she started to read the school form, Kateryna was overwhelmed with another thought, pushing out any comprehension of the yellow sheet of paper. *She is just like Anatoliy, this little one. Nothing escapes those big blue eyes. I can hide nothing from her*. Her mind once again focused on the piece of paper, and, reading it slowly, she was finally able to concentrate only on Sofiia and her world.

"This is wonderful, little one. Perhaps it is time for you to be in the Plast."

"Oh, Mama, yes!" She hugged her mother again. "I want that so much!"

For Ukrainian little girls like Sofiia, only the Plast, a sort of Girl Scout organization, remained in the suddenly changed system. Kateryna recalled her own progression from the Oktobrists at age seven, to the Pioneers at age ten, finally to the Komsomol, the Young Communist League, when she was fourteen. She had joined the Party at eighteen, a highly unusual accomplishment for someone outside the Russian elite and doubly so for a young woman. Her father's status as a loyal Party member and not an "exploiter" had helped greatly. In Ukraine, only Party members had any chance of going on to university.

Still needing to avoid Sofiia's inquiring little face, Kateryna took her hand and led her down the hallway to the kitchen. "Come, we will make the *bigos* we were going to save for tomorrow night. We must celebrate the good work of my smart little girl."

She is becoming more and more a young woman every day, Kateryna thought, while watching her daughter carefully assemble the savory sauerkraut and pork sausage. As she looked at Sofiia's slim little body, not yet starting to show the promise of womanhood, Kateryna was reminded of herself at Sofiia's age. How she had wanted to be a dancer!—a career she had begun when she was five and been dedicated to until she was nearly twelve. But she had done too well on her school examinations, and it had been decided that Kateryna would best serve the state by having a technical career. She was forbidden to spend any more time with her dance, commanded to concentrate solely on her technical studies. Personal desire was irrelevant. Kateryna had been placed in a severe academic curriculum that eventually led to her obtaining a degree in physics. Ultimately, she had earned her doctorate in high-energy physics, with assignment to the KGB soon following—an amazing accomplishment given that Kateryna was a Ukrainian woman in a system dominated by Russian men.

She well realized that her daughter was still in the same system. Even after the recent dramatic events that had so altered her country, change would likely come too late so far as Sofiia was concerned. At the level of the working people, things were still moving very slowly in Ukraine. Kateryna remembered what Anatoliy had said, shortly before he died, about change in Ukraine: "The wind blows the tops of the trees, but down in the forest it remains quiet."

Sofiia had taken off her coat and gloves when she came in, but she was still wearing her head scarf. She never took it off except to bathe and when she was alone in her bed. She was ashamed of her dull and patchy short hair. Although the radiation and chemotherapy treatments had been over for three months, she was still self-conscious about her hair. Kateryna often heard her cry when she looked at herself in the mirror.

Four years after the horror at Chornobyl, Sofiia had been admitted to Hospital No. 6 in Moscow, where she received the best care available despite the fact that she was ethnic Ukrainian. The daughter of a KGB officer got the best care, ethnicity notwithstanding. Sofiia had apparently recovered—until the discovery six months ago: she had developed a cancer, a form of lymphoblastic leukemia that was particularly resistant to treatment. With the dissolution of the KGB, Kateryna could no longer claim any priority for Sofiia's access to the drastically declining specialized care; it was all she could do to get her daughter some initial chemotherapy when the cancer was detected. Since then, all priority at the Moscow hospitals had gone to Russians, and the two radiation treatment hospitals in Kyyiv were overwhelmed with the steadily increasing numbers of new patients.

After the breakup of the Union, Kateryna's status as a Ukrainian had quickly begun to work against her. The ancient ethnic hatreds between the Russians and Ukrainians surfaced almost immediately as old KGB contacts quickly turned against her. Sofiia had not had any treatment for three months because the waiting lists at the hospitals in Kyyiv were hopelessly long: Chornobyl had become Ukraine's problem; Ukraine was left to deal with it. Although her daughter was now in apparent remission, the cancer would grow and probably metastasize if left untreated.

Day by day, Kateryna was seeing the last of her world being snuffed out, while the basic structure of a person's life in Ukraine—country, work, family—was slowly being denied to her. Having grown up in a nation dominated by communism, Kateryna had not acquired the fourth component of the basic life structure that is so taken for granted in the West: a faith in God. Her father, a dedicated communist, had taught Kateryna that the only god was the all-powerful state, and Kateryna's mother had not dared to speak against her husband. Anatoliy had enjoyed a strong though suppressed faith—he regularly, patiently, often subtly, urged his wife to see the truth, nonetheless Kateryna had repulsed his attempts to share it with her. Now she was denied the opportunity to draw from the great well of hope that a strong belief in God would have given her in her crisis. The god she had been taught to believe in and to give her all to, her great and powerful Soviet Union, the one she loved and for whom she wore the uniform, was now gone. Her husband was gone, her own and Anatoliy's parents were gone; now the last little part of her family was slipping away.

Kateryna was certain that her position in the Ukrainian security agency, such as it now was, would soon be eliminated—her fear based upon more than her increasingly irrelevant nuclear weapons specialty. She had made a serious career mistake several years ago, having written reports to her immediate commander critical of the means being employed to dispose of chemical and radioactive waste materials. Large areas near the weapons laboratories and depots at Ust' Kamenogorsk, Chelyabinsk, Tomsk, and Krazniarsk were catastrophically polluted, with some areas in danger of becoming wholly sterile, unable to support any kind of life. A huge cutback in the officer corps was now inevitable. Kateryna was increasingly convinced that this blot on her record would put her on the retirement list.

But it was Sofiia who dominated Kateryna's thoughts. Although she could do nothing about the recurring, withal diminishing, pain from the loss of her husband, any more than she could do anything about the loss of her proud Union and the destruction of her career, Kateryna would not—could not—accept the fact that her daughter would be consumed by the same horror that had taken Anatoliy.

2

Headquarters, Crimean Security Command, November 16

"Good morning, Comrade Colonel."

"Good morning to you, Comrade General Nastenko," Kateryna crisply responded in the old way to humor the senior officer. *The old man still has not accepted it.* She knew the changes were hardest on the few officers who still had personal memories of some of the founders of the Revolution. Perestroika and all the other Gorbachev policy changes had been anathema to the old guard, many of whom still believed that the new regime would be overthrown and that proper order and the Revolution would be restored. "I am looking forward to meeting the delegation from the West this morning. Do you think we are really any closer to some agreement on this START treaty?"

"Ah, remember, Comrade Colonel, Ukraine must be very careful not to be duped by the West; nor by the Russians—especially the Russians. The fools in Belarus and Kazakhstan may agree to give up their weapons, but we in Ukraine must not be so stupid. The Russians know that we are very near to breaking the targeting codes for the SS-19s and -24s; of course, the Americans know that we will then be able to retarget anywhere we wish."

We will never move forward, Kateryna thought as she looked at the old Ukrainian warrior, almost the perfect stereotype of a nineteenth century Cossack, even to the huge bushy mustaches he wore. *Until these old Chekists either retire or die, there is no real hope of moving toward the Western policies that have proven to work so well in many areas.*

The heavy, broad-shouldered old man slowly got up to pace about the room, hands clasped behind his back. "Comrade Colonel, it has been decided that you may best serve our Ukraine with an exciting new assignment."

Here it comes. The beginning of the end.

"You have served with great distinction, Comrade Colonel," the forty-five-year veteran went on, in preamble, "and your particular skills in representing Ukraine's position in the START talks have been most valuable . . ."

Kateryna continued to analyze what General Nastenko was saying, trying to keep a step ahead of him. She had honed that particular skill in her career with the deadly KGB, where mere survival, much less advancement, was like walking through a minefield. Kateryna recognized that she had a good chance to prolong her career if she could be included among the elite cadre of professionals needed in the disarmament negotiations. For the talks, Ukraine needed people with strong technical training in nuclear weaponry, unquestioned loyalty to the state, the cunning and street savvy that came from working in the KGB, and of particular importance, facility with the English language. All Soviet physicists had to learn English as part of their technical training: every serious nuclear physicist in the world had to be fluent in both Russian and English, the languages in which nearly all professional publications on atomic research, historic and current, were written.

". . . but we are concerned that, perhaps, you might have the tendency to be too . . . how shall I say . . . too aligned with the Western position on certain matters," the old officer continued.

There it is. The environmental report problem. The command believes I will be too lenient with the Western demands about our cleanup of nuclear manufacturing and disposal areas, which, somehow, has gotten included in these negotiations.

The old Cossack continued his circuit about the room, alternately clasping his hands in front of himself and then behind, "The Russians are taking a very hard approach in certain areas, and it is felt that we should present a united front in such matters even though we, in Ukraine, have legitimate individual concerns in many other areas . . ."

Kateryna tried to concentrate on the old man's droning. *This discussion—this instruction—is so typically old Slavic. Even in a one-on-one conversation between two officers, who have known each other for years and who even hold the same ethnic loyalties, there is this impossibly circuitous manner of speaking. Why doesn't he just come right out and say exactly what the problem is?* Kateryna knew the answer, of course. It was embedded in centuries of customs and practices among the Slavic peoples: communism and the constant looking over one's shoulder had nothing to do with it; it was just the way things had always been done in this part of the world. But for someone trained in the hard intellectual discipline of nuclear physics, overlain with the equally hard discipline of the KGB, the old practice was particularly frustrating. Kateryna also knew that this characteristic of her people was particularly aggravating to the Western negotiators, who were so used to "telling it like it is," as they said in the West.

General Nastenko abruptly sat down in the chair opposite hers at the conference table. He stared across at her for a moment before continuing. "At the talks we have people who know in intimate detail every aspect of the construction and strategic operation of our weapons and, of course, practically all of what the West has deployed. We have others who are trained in analysis—psychological analysis—to keep us protected from their bluffs and to tell us when the other side is not telling us the truth. We have others who are keenly aware of the more practical day-to-day military operational aspects of our weapons deployment. And we have still other people who are perfectly at ease in the use and understanding of their English language so that we will catch every nuance of their conversation with us, and so on, and so on," he said, sweeping his hand between the two of them.

"In you, Comrade Colonel, we have an officer who knows a great deal about all of these important areas . . . all wrapped up in one body." General Nastenko glanced at Kateryna's tailored uniform jacket that could not fully hide the fact that she had retained the figure of a dancer.

"But in your new duties you will be operating without all of the comfortable backup our START negotiators enjoy. There are not many like you, Comrade Colonel, so we have to use all of you in the most efficient way."

Oh, I wish he would get on with this. Kateryna's concentration drifted momentarily to Sofiia, who would be playing with her friends in the care center while the school was closed.

"Lieutenant Colonel Kateryna Kovalevska, I congratulate you! You are to be assigned to command one of the special teams going to America to inspect the destruction of Western nuclear warheads under the tactical weapons treaty." General Nastenko beamed as he got up.

Kateryna automatically jumped to her feet to accept the general's outstretched hand. The old man's words sunk in only after she was halfway out of her chair. In that instant, several questions rushed to her mind, but they were all eclipsed by the aboriginal thoughts of a mother about to be separated from her sick child. Her second dominant thought was that Anatoliy had died while she was assigned away and the same horror could now be repeated.

"Sir," she said abruptly, "what of Sofiia? I cannot leave her, she needs me, she– –"

The old man cut her off with his raised hand. "Everything is already taken care of, Comrade Colonel," the old officer tried to assure the frightened woman standing before him in the uniform of the former KGB. "We have arranged for Sofiia's treatment—everything she will require—at the Radiological Institute in Kyyiv. She will get as good care there as she would in Moscow."

Exactly! The same care as any Ukrainian in Moscow. NONE of our hospitals are as good as their counterparts in Moscow. "But I must be here, to ensure that– –"

"Everything is taken care of. Sofiia will receive the best care. I know you have suffered greatly since the loss of Anatoliy—you are an inspiration to every Ukrainian in the way you have heroically performed your duties while being solely responsible for your daughter's care. We have done everything to keep you and Sofiia together since your husband died; however, we are now at this point where . . . where your duty to Ukraine must come first."

The old man showed his age despite his effort to maintain the correct military bearing as he walked around the end of the table. He took her right hand in both of his. "Kateryna Romanivna," he said with a familiar use of her patronymic that startled her, "believe me. I will personally take responsibility for Sofiia. She will be in school in Kyyiv, and her treatment will be given first priority. It is a fine hospital there in Kyyiv. You know that; Anatoliy was assigned there."

Kateryna had only superficially heard what General Nastenko had said, her thoughts racing through the questions that filled her mind: the many things that could happen while she was gone. "When am I to leave, and how long will I be assigned?" she asked, almost as a demand.

The old officer quickly dropped her hand and stepped back. "You are to leave immediately. Tomorrow. And your assignment is indefinite. The initial duty in America will be for two, perhaps three months."

Her thoughts coalesced. *Those bastards! They could have told me months ago. They knew that Sofiia's school term would be just ending. It will be a convenient time to start her at Kyyiv. They could have easily arranged for her to have treatment during the past months. Now there is no time for me to be with her and no time to explain why I must go away. She knows that I was away when*

Tolik died, and now she is sick with the same thing. Those bastards!

Kateryna also knew that there was a particular reason why she had been selected to head one of the inspection teams. It was the old method of guaranteeing that citizens traveling or assigned to the West would come back to the Soviet Union: even in these times of change and openness, the state still wanted to ensure that its best citizens would come home where they belonged. Her little, sick Sofiia was just a convenient state tool. With a change in demeanor her just-realized thoughts commanded, she asked, "Where am I to be assigned?"

Unaware of the reason for her sudden composure, General Nastenko wrongly assumed that the KGB officer had replaced the mother. "You are to be sent to what is called the Pueblo Army Depot. It is located in America's state of Colorado."

Kateryna was not familiar with the facility at Pueblo. She was intimately familiar, of course, with the United States' nuclear weapons final assembly depot located near Amarillo, Texas, southeast of Pueblo. She had examined hundreds of satellite photographs of the big Pantex facility on the flat plains of the American heartland, located in an area that a First Chief Directorate officer had once told her was "a place that only a Texan could love." She could only imagine what the Pueblo depot at the foot of the Rocky Mountains would be like.

"Will there be time for me to go to Kyyiv with Sofiia, to enroll her in the school and also to speak with the doctors at hospital?"

"Of course, of course. You do not leave for Moscow until tomorrow evening. The rest of your team is already assembling; they should be ready when you arrive at Sheremetyevo tomorrow night. You have the rest of today and all day tomorrow—plenty of time to travel to Kyyiv and then go on to Moscow. In fact, I have already made the arrangements for your transportation and the appointments at the school and the hospital. I told you that I would take care of everything."

The old man returned to his desk. Kateryna walked to the front of the desk; the two officers exchanged salutes. Major General Pavlo Yaroslavich Nastenko watched the tall, slim, raven-haired woman cross the office to the door. He could not help but notice, as he had so many times in the past, that she walked with the level, fluid movement and perfect posture of a dancer. He sighed quietly and wished sincerely that he were twenty-five years younger.

3

National Center for Atmospheric Research
Roberts Mesa, southwest of Boulder, Colorado, November 17

"Boy, look at that, Dr. Heartwood, the temperature anomaly spreads clear up the coast of Central America into Mexico." Paul Heartwood and his assistant looked at a printout from the Cray 3 computer.

"It's going to be a big one, Willie. The sea surface temperatures are already seven degrees above normal."

"Lot bigger than last year and the year before."

"This is starting to look like the biggest El Niño event yet. Clearly it's going to surpass the one in '82 to '84."

"Sure wish we had sea surface elevation data from 1983. That Topex info really fills in a lot of gaps—proves our model is working."

"Topex/Poseidon was just a dream in 1983, Willie. But you're right. I'd certainly like to have surface current information from 1983 so we could have more verification. Lot of water fell out west that year." The senior atmospheric physicist looked directly at the young graduate student. "Always keep in mind what this is all about, son: prediction. People, governments, who want precipitation predictions are the ones paying for all this—the ones who will support your career. No one much cares what all that water is doing up there until it starts to come down."

"Right, Dr. Heartwood. I guess the flooding was bad in the Upper Basin of the Colorado in 1983." Like most budding scientists, the young doctoral candidate was interested only in pure science—in his case, what moved the masses of atmospheric moisture around the earth; more particularly, what happened in a narrow band of the troposphere above 100,000 feet. Once his high-altitude water descended to join the lower-elevation moisture, eventually to land on the earth, it was no longer his concern. That was for the low-level atmospheric physicists and hydrologists to worry about.

"You bet it was. Actually, it was worse in 1984, and now here we are, into another cycle." Paul Heartwood watched the data scrolling out of the printer. "It's pretty clear that we're into a much bigger event than we had in the '80s. Do you know what this may mean, Willie?"

"You mean in the intermountain region—in the Colorado River Basin?"

"Right."

"Well, same story as last year and the year before, only more pronounced. Probable dipping of the Pacific High, therefore more intrusion into the Rockies of mid-latitude storms, bigger snow load, more runoff."

"Willie, have you seen the study done by Appleton-Thompson Engineers for the Bureau of Reclamation? What they call the 'upper limit design rainstorm' for the Colorado River Basin above Glen Canyon Dam?"

"No, sir."

"I suggest you read it. It attempts to look at the worst-case scenarios in the Upper Basin to produce the probable maximum flood."

"Late-season snow and then suddenly warm temperatures and rain, like happened in 1983?"

"Well, that of course, but it's the storm phenomena in their report I find intriguing. The patterns we're starting to see with this El Niño may tie in with the storm patterns the A-TE report analyzed: an extratropical 500-millibar low in the Upper Basin with tropical cyclone involvement. Are you familiar with the incidence of tropical storm activity in the eastern Pacific? I mean, the area of the Pacific right off the coast of Mexico?"

"I've touched on it in my course work, Dr. Heartwood, but it's not in my discipline."

The old scientist sighed heavily. That was the story now. With the explosive expansion of atmospheric science, the young people had no opportunity for more than a brief exposure to anything but their narrow fields of expertise. Everything now had to be done by committee—ever expanding and more complex committees of ever more isolated subcategories of specialty, with computers taking over the integration of thought, analysis, and prediction. In his near-retirement years, Paul Heartwood was very glad that he had had his career when he did.

"Willie, have you ever been to the Grand Canyon?"

"Sure. Even hiked down to Phantom Ranch once. Climbing back up to the Bright Angel Lodge nearly killed me," he laughed.

"What we're discovering with these El Niño/Southern Oscillation patterns ties right in with the current thinking on how that big canyon formed. It wasn't just a grain of sand at a time. 'Uniformitarianism' they call it. Of course, steady erosion occurs, but it's now believed that much of what exists today happened in thousands of cataclysmic events—huge floods, with seismic and volcanic events thrown in now and again. Look at what happened when Crystal Creek flooded in 1966. The pile of giant boulders the flood swept down that side canyon instantly created the worst rapid on the Colorado. And that was just a narrowly confined flood on one of the hundreds of tributaries to the river's main stem. The evidence is growing that there have been unimaginable floods over large areas of the Upper Basin. It all winds up in the narrow trench of the Colorado River."

"Well, we've got good flood control now on the Colorado," the graduate student replied.

"Wrong, Willie. Even the Bureau of Reclamation is starting to wake up. Why do you suppose the A-TE study was commissioned? Even the Bureau may be starting to get a little concerned about what may be *probable* in terms of a PMF."

"Well, sir, since that flood back in 1983, surely the Bureau leaves enough storage space in Lake Powell to contain a big flood."

Paul Heartwood frowned. "Wrong again. The Bureau is not permitted to maintain flood storage space in Lake Powell. That giant reservoir does not have a flood control mandate. It may be completely filled because Glen Canyon Dam was built to generate electric power: the higher the reservoir is permitted to rise, the more water is available to generate electricity. It was also built to enable the Upper Basin to reliably meet its water delivery obligations to the Lower Basin under the 1922 Colorado River Compact and to satisfy the Upper Basin's share of the 1944 treaty with Mexico. Every year 8.23 million acre feet must be released through Glen Canyon Dam to the Lower Basin, no matter what the Upper Basin actually produces. Beyond that, if the river provides the water, it is the mission and intent of the Bureau of Reclamation to top off the reservoir each spring. Every winter, if the reservoir is nearly full, the Bureau juggles releases with estimates of the anticipated spring runoff so that the reservoir will just top off. That's what they were doing in 1983 when they got caught with a lot more late-season runoff than was expected."

"Well, Lake Mead is never allowed to fill; why doesn't the Bureau do the same thing in Lake Powell?"

"It's written right into the congressional authorization. Back in the 1920s, when Hoover Dam was being planned, flooding was a big concern on the lower Colorado, so Congress specified that five million acre feet of flood-control space was to be maintained in Lake Mead. By the time Glen Canyon Dam was being considered, everybody had forgotten about floods—they were concentrating on how much money could be generated by the dam's power plant and the value of all that good irrigation water. It was only the flood-control space in Lake Mead that prevented a really big disaster in 1983. The Bureau was able to hold releases from Hoover Dam to 40,000 cfs, as the much higher outflow from Glen Canyon Dam ran down the Grand Canyon and into the reservoir."

"But Dr. Heartwood, surely since the experience in 1983– –"

"You're not listening, Willie. The Bureau's hands are tied. Congress has *mandated* that Lake Powell be filled if Mother Nature provides the water. Now here we are. The reservoir is nearly full from the last two years of heavy snows and reduced calls for water by the Imperial Valley, Los Angeles, and Phoenix, and we are right in the midst of what is starting to look like the biggest El Niño event yet recorded. Even with that, we don't have the foggiest damn idea about just what kind of precipitation can occur in the Upper Basin. Have you ever seen the rainout from a hurricane down in the southeast?"

"I grew up in Louisiana, Dr. Heartwood."

"Okay, what if that occurred in the Upper Basin?"

"Sir, tropical cyclone activity contains most of its moisture close to the earth. How could such a storm penetrate beyond the Mogollon Rim above Phoenix? It blocks the route into the Upper Basin."

"The Mogollon Rim is only 6,000 feet. Will all tropical cyclone moisture be sheared off below that elevation? Can it rise as it progresses across the Sonoran Desert from Baja and the Gulf of California? What percentage will go over the rim if there is, say, a 500 millibar low settled over the Upper Basin—like is postulated in the A-TE report? And that does happen, quite often, actually."

"I don't know."

"Right. None of us knows, for sure. Since 1900 over seventy significant tropical cyclones in the eastern Pacific have recurved toward North America, with more than a dozen deeply penetrating and raining out in Mexico and Arizona. Look at the data we're getting right now. These sea surface temperatures are a setup for a lot of tropical storm activity in the eastern Pacific."

"I guess the dam was built without a flood-control mandate based on statistical information available at the time."

"That's right. When it was designed, the Bureau had maybe seventy-five years of river gauge records. The whole flood capture and spillway bypass system for the two big dams was based upon an analysis of reliable Colorado River flow records back to about 1870. Engineers want demonstrable, accurate data on river flows before they design a dam and then spend money to build it. Giant concrete arch dams are very costly things to construct, Willie. But I think the engineers overlooked the biggest piece of information they had before them—right under their noses."

"What's that, Dr. Heartwood?"

"A 5,000-foot-deep, 300-mile-long, ten-to-twenty-mile-wide canyon that was created in less than five million years."

Humble beginnings, 1956 (*Bureau of Reclamation, Fred S. Finch*).

PUEBLO

Lower Escalante River, 1960 (*Tad Nichols*).

1

Lawrence Livermore National Laboratory, November 16

"Saul! Hey, Saul! Get over to the director's office. Superman wants to see you right away," the division manager yelled down at the group of people at the bottom of the NOVA laser target chamber room.

The men and women looked at each other in unison, then up at their boss. "I guess he can get away with calling the old man that. Shit would really hit the fan if he heard us say it," Saul thought out loud while the others nodded, again in unison.

"On the way," Saul called back to his boss, leaning over the railing three floors up.

"Remember, grab your ankles and shuffle backwards into the old man's office," one of the men called out as Saul went up the ladder. Their laughter reverberated off the maze of catwalks and beam-line cylinders directed at the 100-trillion-watt laser target chamber. The NOVA research was now concentrated on finding a means to create controlled nuclear fusion, as occurs in the core of the sun, but until recently the primary mission had been to develop an effective way to destroy incoming Soviet ballistic missiles: the prototype Buck Rogers ray gun. Although the current state of world affairs had put the primary mission on hold, it had not been abandoned.

Saul and several of the other people in the target chamber gallery were among the hundreds of Ph.D.s employed at LLNL. Including the additional collection at the companion laboratories at Los Alamos, Kirtland Air Force Base, and Berkeley, they comprised the largest concentration of doctoral-level scientists in the world. The laughter echoing in the huge room was not entirely directed at Saul. It was also a spontaneous release of contained anxiety. Every one of the scientists and weaponeers was concerned about what the end of the Cold War would mean to his or her job security.

Unlike their counterparts on the Berkeley campus and at the Sandia lab, Lawrence Livermore and Los Alamos were principally concerned with putting into practice the deep research done at all four laboratories. Designing ever more sophisticated nuclear weapons, and methods to destroy them, had been the big job at LLNL; now with the end of the Cold War the R&D facilities were particularly vulnerable to severe cutbacks.

Saul was no exception. As he drove through the campus-like laboratory complex it was all he could do to stay within the 20-mph speed limit. He experienced every possible anxiety about being summoned to the director's office—a summons that did not first involve a chain-of-command meeting with his supervisor. Among the staff at Livermore, physics Ph.D.s were as common as bachelors of literature in a newspaper editorial room; accordingly, little formality existed among the staff of almost-equals. But the director was still the director and in ultimate charge of Saul's destiny.

"Good morning, sir," Saul said in as nonchalant a voice as he could manage.

"G'mornin', Saul, have a seat," Tim McManus shot back in his usual rapid-fire manner. "How's things at NOVA?"

"Same story, Dr. McManus. Big difference, it seems, between theory and practice."

"Your team'll get it right, Saul. That's why we hire all you smart guys," the Nobel laureate said. "Listen, the Secretary called this morning about a little problem that's just come up. You've been tagged for the job."

Saul was relieved but puzzled about the "job" reference and the fact that it had come directly from the Secretary of Energy.

"We need you for a little temporary duty over in Colorado. Couple months is all. You'll be in charge of the disassembly team at Pueblo. The regular guy, Jonathan Babcock, had to have some kind of emergency surgery and will probably be out for weeks. Couldn't be at a worst time. The Ruskies are just about on their way over to monitor the teardowns. Energy had to come up with somebody fast—someone who'll make the best fit."

"Best fit?" Saul said weakly.

"Look, there's thick politics on this one, with us eggheads way outta the loop, as usual. Hell, I don't think we'd understand all the protocol if we spent a month being spoon fed. Point is, the Department had a formula for exactly the right person. You're it."

From much past experience, Saul had learned that he just had to interrupt the director if there was to be any hope of turning a meeting with the man into a conversation. Tim McManus was most at ease if everybody else talked as fast as he did—an old habit acquired during his early research days when the best brainstorming among razor-sharp minds occurred with rapid-fire exchanges of ideas and arguments. Corporate boardrooms and military staff meetings didn't use this technique, but then, Saul thought, they weren't trying to figure out what's going on inside an atom. Saul's personality made it hard for him to communicate in the director's preferred mode.

"Dr. McManus, I understand that in our work we sometimes have to make some quick adjustments, but I'm only peripherally aware of what's going on with the TART implementation. What is it that makes me so particularly attractive for this job? I really think I have to know that exactly." Saul felt out of breath.

"I'm not in on all the political details, so I can only pass on the little I was told." Saul watched in disgusted fascination as Tim McManus reached into a mahogany box on the desktop and withdrew one of his notorious, custom-rolled cigars: slug green and the better part of a foot long. Oblivious to Saul's thinly veiled revulsion, the director ceremoniously clipped an end of the cigar, poked a hole in the other end using a little tool specially designed for the two functions, and then rolled the punctured end between his lips in the time-honored fashion. Saul was now fully focused on the flaring wooden match tip while the clipped end glowed incrementally redder in perfect counterpoint to the increasingly larger puffs of smoke. The legend was that the director smoked the cigars to advertise his continual presence around the lab. The cat was never away.

Shaking the match out, Tim McManus got up from behind the cloud of carcinogens hanging over the desk and turned to look out at the green hills of the Livermore Valley. With the view of the low, round hills, verdant from the recent rain, Saul was reminded that where he was going the country would be brown, barren, and windswept—and perhaps 10 below zero on some days.

"The Ruskies are big on pecking order and protocol niceties, Saul. Colonel Babcock getting sick was real convenient, it turned out, since the senior officer coming over is only a lieutenant colonel. The bright idea our brass came up with is that we're going to totally de-emphasize the military crap. The important point is that both sides should be represented by academically equivalent types. She has a doctorate in plasma physics."

"She?" Saul jabbed in. In his entire career, Saul had never heard of the Russians placing a woman in command of a sensitive political assignment.

"Yeah. One real smart one too, I understand. Have to be. Not many women where she's been working. All we know about her, at least all I've been told, is that before the revolution she was a specialist in tactical weapons hardware and, the brass suspects, 'unique tasks deployment,' whatever that means. You two will match pretty well on the hardware score—similar backgrounds on the kinds of machinery you'll be taking apart. Anyway, that's another reason you were chosen. This is supposed to be strictly scientific; our guys want to keep military posturing to a minimum. Hell, you know that anyone over there who winds up with that kind of an education in nuclear physics is almost certainly involved with a technical services directorate in the KGB, or whatever it's called now. I'm sure they operate the same old way when it comes to nukes." The director absently propelled a particularly dense puff of smoke across the room. Saul nonchalantly held his breath.

"Where was I? Oh, yeah, de-emphasize the military aspect and keep things plainclothes and as informal as possible. One physicist cooperating with another one. Another thing—and this is very important to keep things cordial—the Secretary likes your temperament. Hell, the damn wall could fall off the building, and you'd just move your chair out of the draft." The director paused between puffs. "An odd thing, though—she's ethnic Ukrainian."

Saul had to breathe, so he grabbed the opportunity to interrupt. "Sir, am I– –"

"Hear me out on this. Yeah, seems real odd that the Commonwealth team, comprised exclusively of Russians, would be commanded by a Ukrainian, and a woman at that. The Russians and Ukrainians aren't exactly getting along. 'Course they never have. Next—and I'm just guessing because the Secretary didn't say much—it looks like you'll be a good experiment to find out if Boris really is cranking down his espionage system. Apparently we don't know how much they know about that Israeli agent thing you were caught up in, so the snoop brass wants to play some kind of little game. Still doin' it even though the war's supposed to be over. Well, anyway, you're supposed to be a big surprise, so our guys want to see how long it takes them to come up to speed about you. This will help us to understand something about their supposedly relaxed espionage system. Isn't this all a bunch of crap? I thought all that business was over. Taking these damned things apart is harder than building them."

Another puff gave Saul an opportunity to break in, gag reflex notwithstanding. "Sir, am I to be involved in some kind of espionage? Because I speak Ukrainian? Is it because of the accusations about the Israeli?"

"No, Saul, no snooping. It's just part of the friendly environment we're trying to create here. Your Ukrainian *is* perfect. Can't teach that in school. How old were you when you arrived over here? Never mind. Anyway, Lieutenant Colonel Kovalevska is from a tiny village somewhere in Crimea. Apparently our spooks want the Ruskies to figure out who you are and then fall all over themselves saying what nice SOBs we are for going to such an extreme to make this affair so cordial, and—this is very important—it *should* be cordial. Total bullshit, but I'm just following orders. They put all the stuff into the hopper they thought was important about your counterpart and the mission and you popped out." The director was not the least bit out of breath.

Tim McManus sat back down and stretched his arms across the desk toward Saul, suspending the cigar midway between them. Saul got an unavoidably close look at the now-slimy mouth end of the roll of tobacco leaf. "Saul, you and I could not possibly figure out all this political maneuvering. That was the official part, believe it or not. There's probably something else. Nothing was said, but I know the Secretary pretty well. They all feel pretty bad about the way you got beat up over the Israeli agent thing. I think they want to make things right—the assignment could lead to a big job in the whole disarmament process. I guess it's their way of saying that they expect you to be around for a long time. This business we're in can be very strange, Saul, but we don't build Chevrolets, you know."

"Dr. McManus, I'm just a scientist. I've been confined to applied physics my whole career. Tell me. Right up front. Do you think I can survive in this political stuff?"

"Well, we're about to find out now, aren't we?" The director came out from behind his desk and started toward the door. The meeting was over. "Right now, all you have to think about is that you're the handpicked man to head this team. Secretary says you're it, so that's it. Don Haldemann will cover for you at NOVA while you're in Colorado. Did I say? Should be about two months, maybe three. Your cute little cars will just have to get along without you for a while." The director stuck out his hand after opening the door. "Thanks, Saul. Get the details from Teddy over in personnel. Your travel orders should already be cut. And Saul," Tim McManus said as Saul was just leaving the room, "a lot of people are going to be looking at you. Watch your step."

***

Saul rolled out from under the 1935 Packard dual-cowl phaeton, wiping his hands on a nearly spotless mechanic's rag. He lay on the creeper, staring up into the front wheel well of the old touring car. The inside of the fender was painted as carefully as the outside.

I AM being phased out. The Israeli agent episode will NEVER be forgotten. His transfer to the NOVA team had boosted his anxiety. Now this.

He got up and sat on the stool by his workbench. His shop was as organized and nearly as clean as a neurosurgery operating room: everything about Saul's life was order, discipline, and routine—and perfectly made machinery. The perfect machinery at the lab was seldom his to work with personally; at the lab he was a scientist, not a technician. The antique cars served that need in his life.

The weapons teardown is a dead end. The whole treaty thing could stop at any time. I'd never get back into the lab. Too many good people there who don't have a red-tagged personnel jacket.

2

DULLES INTERNATIONAL AIRPORT, NOVEMBER 20

Everything around her in the airplane was familiar: the snatches of conversation in Russian; the lingering odor of *borshchok* and the lamb *shashlik* the flight crew had served while they were over Newfoundland; the civilian clothing she and the rest of the passengers wore—Western at first glance, but still not quite duplicating what photographs in American magazines had taught her. Kateryna stared out the window of the Ilyushin II-96 as the wide-bodied jet touched down and swept past the terminal building. *How beautiful*, she thought, admiring Eero Saarinen's striking creation, with its soaring reach of glass and concrete. The plane taxied to a stop, ending the long, nonstop trip at a line of black automobiles parked at the end of the runway.

"Good morning, Colonel Kovalevska. Welcome to the United States." Kateryna confronted a tall, smiling man extending his hand to her as she stepped off the boarding stairs at the head of the group marching down behind her. From her briefing in Moscow, she knew he was Richard Witherspoon, a career State Department man and an expert on Soviet and Russian affairs. In a glance, she saw no evidence of military presence. Although there were many military officers on both sides of the meeting groups, everyone was in civilian clothing.

"Good morning, Mr. Witherspoon," she said, before the man could introduce himself. "Thank you for welcoming us so generously." The smiling man did not display the least hint of surprise that she knew who he was, even though the Americans had not told her superiors specifically who would be greeting them in Washington. *First rate*, Kateryna thought, appreciating the professionalism the State Department man had just displayed. She recognized one thing about Mr. Witherspoon immediately: although he smiled broadly, with facial lines in all the right places, his eyes showed not the least emotion. *He smiles just like a Russian First Directorate officer. What else do you do, Mr. Witherspoon?*

Kateryna and Mr. Witherspoon got into the lead limousine as her team and the Americans loaded into the rest of the vehicles, their departure smoothly orchestrated by protocol people from the State Department. The line of cars moved across the expanse of concrete and then wound through the airport roads and onto a multilaned highway. Her host remained silent. *This man understands what it means to me to see, at last, what my whole life has been dedicated to defending against.* The alien world swept past in the soft movement and silence of the airtight Cadillac; unavoidably she compared the large, compartmented American automobile with its Russian Zil counterpart. *Militarily, we and America are in essential parity. But this automobile . . .*

While the car sped along the wide, landscaped highway, Kateryna traced a mental map of their route, testing the reality against the map planted in her brain. She knew they were not taking the most direct route into the city; perhaps, she thought, to give her the glimpse she was anticipating—what had been a focus of her life in the KGB. She had known it only as a two-dimensional picture: a collage of overhead imagery, carefully drawn diagrams, and interpretive sketches aided by a few ground-level photographs. She could not resist turning her head to look past the State/likely-CIA officer.

"We no longer need such a large facility, Colonel Kovalevska. I am sure that a CIA officer's reaction to his first look at the building on Dzerzhinsky Square would be the same as yours."

Well done again, Mr. Witherspoon. Kateryna smiled to herself at his reference to the old Soviet address for the KGB headquarters. The Bolshevik secret police leader's name had been removed from the big square, along with other communists' names on streets and squares throughout Moscow. She decided to give the smooth professional another opportunity to think on his feet. "I am surprised that we were not welcomed at your Andrews Air Force Base since it is much closer to Washington than the civilian airport."

"We felt that it was the appropriate gesture to recognize the proper civilian circumstance we have now come to, Colonel Kovalevska," the official responded immediately and without any hesitation. The words flowed out as if they'd been scripted.

Perhaps. But you also did not want us to see the miserable conditions in your capital city that would be unavoidable on a trip in from Andrews.

The highway paralleled a river Kateryna knew to be the Potomac, then soon crossed over to the east bank and abruptly ended in the heart of Washington. Unlike the CIA headquarters, Kateryna had seen many television films taken in and around the buildings of America's capital. She felt she knew exactly what to expect, but she was shocked to see the beauty of the city in real life.

It is so much bigger than my impression. And look at all the cherry trees to blossom this spring. Her thoughts flooded back to the foothills of the Carpathian Mountains, reminding her that she would miss the springtime there, also bursting with fruit trees. A sudden recollection of a long-ago April walk with Anatoliy crushed in on her thoughts. She saw two-year-old Sofiia and plum tree blossoms.

"We will leave you here at your hotel, Colonel Kovalevska." The sound of the State Department officer's voice jarred Kateryna back to the moment. They had pulled under the portico of a large hotel; a brightly uniformed man was reaching for the handle of the car door. Mr. Witherspoon walked around the back of the limousine to join her at the foot of the steps to the lobby.

"You must be tired from your long flight," the graceful official smiled, misunderstanding the cause of her detachment. "Everything you will need can be arranged with Mr. Jacoby," Mr. Witherspoon added as he nodded toward the pink-faced young man standing next to him. "I am sorry that you will not have more time here in Washington, but, to be sure, we will arrange a proper introduction to our city when you return from Colorado. You will be picked up tomorrow morning at nine o'clock. Let me say again, welcome to America, Colonel Kovalevska."

3

Pueblo Army Depot, February 1

Damn, I'll be glad to get out of here. Longest ten weeks of my life, Saul thought as he hurried across the icy concrete toward the mess hall. The wind whipped dust devils of powdery snow across the courtyard, piling it in little windrows on the downwind sides of the leafless trees. *In another two or three months it'll be hotter than the hinges of hell here. No spring in this place. Just winter to instant summer.*

By any civilian standards, the Pueblo Army Depot, now officially known at the Pueblo Depot Activity, would not be included among the garden spots of the Western world. The military services generally do not locate their installations in areas in great demand by settlers, whether the settlers were pioneers in the nineteenth century or Native Americans over millennia. But given the U.S. Army's particular penchant for locating its posts and depots in mosquito-infested swamps, frozen wastelands, or blazing desert hellholes, the Pueblo Depot could have been far worse than it was. The Army Materiel Command depot was spread over the top of a broad barren hill fifteen miles east of the city of Pueblo in southern Colorado. The depot had been chosen for the warhead disassemblies because it was on the Independent Base Closure Commission's hit list and nearly deserted; it was less than 300 miles by remote highway from the Pantex facility near Amarillo where the warhead pits would be sent; and it was isolated enough to not create a big problem if a radiation leak occurred. DOE was fully convinced there was no danger of a nuclear detonation.

Saul looked to the south, where stands of winter-barren cottonwoods along the thread of the Arkansas River promised an eventual eruption of greenery. To the southwest, beyond the dreary industrial city revealed only by the tall smoke stacks of the old Colorado Fuel and Iron steel mill, the solid white of the twin Spanish Peaks abruptly ended the expanse of the Great Plains that began over 800 miles to the east.

But Saul's thoughts were not focused on the crisp, harsh scene around him. He was thinking about his dinner companion. Following a very stiff and formal introduction upon her arrival with the Russian team in November, Saul had gradually developed a friendly relationship with the seemingly indurate Lieutenant Colonel Kateryna Romanivna Kovalevska. The absence of uniforms and the trappings of military custom, as envisioned by the

Departments of State and Energy, had indeed been a good idea. An amicable working relationship had developed between the teams of former Cold War enemies. Honest, if restrained, discourse began to replace rigid posturing and simplistic aphorisms.

Saul also had the Department of Energy to thank for the opportunity to further thaw the relationship. Surrounded daily by harsh Russian, cacophonous English, and the awkward attempts by each group to speak a new language, Saul and Kateryna enjoyed their soft Ukrainian. And little time had passed before Saul came to understand why the Ukrainian woman was able to command the team of Russian men. Though both Russia and Ukraine remained little advanced beyond Saudi Arabia or Iran in their treatment of women, it became clear that all of the members of the Commonwealth team were, very simply, afraid of their leader. The least misstep on the part of any of her team would produce a withering rebuke. Compounding the strength of her position was the fact that her ethnicity derived from the formidable Cossacks of the steppe and the Tatars of the Crimean region. More fundamentally, the Soviet Union had not been gone long enough for decades of fear of the secret police to have been forgotten. Saul well understood that the KGB was gone in name only.

He hunched into the stinging wind, hands thrust into his trousers pockets, jacket collar tight about his neck. He was preoccupied with what had been interrupting his sleep for weeks. The unvarying routine of the warhead teardowns and the quiet boredom of his off-work time blended the days together, but what had been a background, albeit growing, anxiety had now ascended to a nagging urgency. Saul thought nearly continuously about that day at the Cactus Club in November: the conversation about Glen Canyon and the overlapping discussion about control of nuclear weapons. At the same time, he struggled with an unavoidable, fundamental aspect of his character.

Throughout his career, Saul had never even remotely considered that he was anything other than one of the "good guys," using his considerable skills and energy to aid the fight against the "bad guys." The determination of what was "good" and what was "bad" in the greater world picture had always come easily to him: truth, justice, and freedom versus lies, inequity, and slavery, and the Soviet Union had fit the opposing role perfectly. He had had no doubts whatsoever about the correctness of his chosen occupation. Then at some point, and he could no longer remember when, he had begun to examine more closely what was good and bad in his own country. Here the sharp, easy distinctions that ordered his life's work blurred, because despite his rigidity about the Soviet enemy, Saul had always been burdened with his need to try to see both sides of a dispute: to try to reconcile conflicting interests, values, and judgments about a common circumstance. Saul had a very hard time simply accepting and swallowing dogma. With his slavishly disciplined analytic mind, tempered by a capacity for deep compassion that is so often found in persons of his ethnicity, Saul would have been a very effective professional mediator had his other skills and interests not drawn him to the world of applied nuclear physics. And for the most part his need to understand, if not fully reconcile, the conflicts he saw had been satisfied: a woman's right to decide what was done with her own body versus the sanctity of human life; society's interest in controlling what children heard or saw versus an individual's freedom of speech; the needs of the less fortunate in the society versus the need for the capitalist system to operate with unregulated freedom; among many other fundamental and long-standing debates.

However, there was one area where he had been unable to come to a self understanding, unable to accept compromise. He could not countenance the relentless sacrifice of the very special places on the earth: the stands of ancient forest that held the secrets of the ages; the living, free-flowing rivers with their runs of spawning salmon or their abyssal canyons; the margins of the land and sea, with their reefs, beaches, bays, and marshes that nurtured so much of the earth's life forms. It saddened and angered him that the legacy of his grandchildren and beyond was being squandered so recklessly for the immediate profit of a relative few. Now—here, today—he sensed the chance to be able to strike back: to recover some small part of what had been lost. But what he had been so obsessed with he knew to be wrong: "wrong" by the social mores and laws that governed the society in which he lived, though not wrong by the higher standard that to Saul eclipsed the connivings of the groups of powerful men and institutions who set the written standards and who preached the social rules—all to protect their entrenched positions.

The warhead teardowns were nearly complete, well ahead of schedule. Soon he would return to the familiar green hills of California, his beloved cars, his friends—and, he anxiously hoped, his old job at the NOVA Laboratory. Nevertheless, the anxiety remained. It had begun in earnest one evening during a dinner conversation with the Commonwealth team leader. They'd been talking about the unending drama in the Middle East. Saul unwound the yarn ball of that evening's conversation.

* * *

"You know, Colonel, we in the West are quite concerned about the Commonwealth being able to keep track of all the weapons deployed by the Soviet Union, particularly with such a powder keg region so close by in the Middle East."

"Now why would you be, except as an academic exercise? It is no more likely now than it ever has been that North America will be exposed to an attack with nuclear weapons."

"Well, that may be true, but the United States has a strategic concern about nuclear weapons activity anywhere in the world."

"You Americans talk about war like virgins talk about sex. You have never been invaded. You speak from imagined passion, not from experience. You do not know what it is to have your families, your children, wives, husbands, raped and killed; your homes burned by an invading army. You cannot know the terror. And that terror, when it is ended, becomes a component of the national character of a country: a strong, binding force that you do not have here."

Saul was surprised that Kateryna did not know about his background. He assumed she had been fully briefed. "My parents were murdered by the Nazis at Babi Yar."

For the first time in the weeks they had been together, the confident woman's demeanor completely collapsed. "Oh, Dr. Kalinik . . . Saul! I did not know . . . I was not told. We'll not talk further about these things."

"No, no, it's okay. I was very young—only three years old—when they were taken from Kyyiv in 1943. My adoptive parents, from a small *shtetl* outside of Odessa, they were the only parents I knew. It was a long time ago. Please, I enjoy learning of your part of the world."

"I was so presumptuous and arrogant."

"Colonel Kovalevska, I– –"

"Kateryna . . . please."

Saul hesitated. "Actually, I'm encouraged that you were not fully informed about my background. It shows, perhaps, that your country, I should say Russia, has more trust than in the past."

Kateryna smiled. "Saul, you are very good at defusing a difficult situation. Perhaps you should have been a statesman."

"Colonel . . . Kateryna, I was very wrong to even mention what must be a very sensitive subject for you."

"Perhaps we *should* talk about it. After all, there is no reason objectively *or* politically that we should not."

"Are you sure?" He could not believe the sea change in the woman's demeanor. It was as if they were suddenly friends. More than acquaintances, anyway, and certainly not antagonists.

"Saul, believe me, we too are concerned about all the weapons. At least some of us."

"Some of you?"

"Well, many Ukrainians at least, because of our geographical position. It is a very tense situation. Some of us are concerned about the weapons in Kazakhstan, for example, being diverted to other Muslim countries. We Ukrainians have no love for Russia, that is well known, but the feelings toward Russia in some of the Muslim areas of the Union—Commonwealth I mean—are very, very bad. The Russians have treated these people like dirt for hundreds of years."

"Are you saying that the *some of you* you mentioned are being ignored?"

"In a word, yes. Particularly about keeping track of the field weapons, like the missile warheads we are disassembling here. Those are the ones most vulnerable to theft. The eastern people could start some kind of *jihad*, and we in Ukraine would surely be caught up in it. There is the situation with the Chechens, and the Ingush right next door. Those people are solidly Muslim; they *so* hate the Russians, as do the Ossets to the west of them and the Dagestanis to the east. Azeri and Afghan mercenaries are well entrenched in that area, fanning the flames. Then, of course, there is the long-standing war in Georgia and the fierce hatred between the Armenians and the Azerbaijanis. The whole of the Caucasus could erupt in a *jihad*, just across the Black Sea from Ukraine."

"But under the treaty we have been told that all of the tactical weapons—small missiles, artillery rounds, and so on—are under exclusive Russian control. The Russians have represented that all the tactical weapons have been under their exclusive control since July 1992. Only the big strategic weapons remain outside of Russia—in Byelorus, Ukraine, and Kazakhstan."

"Saul, believe me, tactical weapons remain outside of Russian control—many of them, despite the treaty. I find it hard to believe that your government does not know of them. It *must* know. But you Americans only know what your government wants you to know. In that sense, you are no different than we are. Worse, actually, because you in the West are so naïve."

"Perhaps so," Saul shrugged. "And we are not informed about the day-to-day details of the ethnic clashes in the former Soviet Union." Saul immediately regretted using the word *former.*

"You had no concern with our internal problems!"

"Uh . . . perhaps not, but– –"

"And you certainly have enough of your own ethnic difficulties."

"Yes . . . That . . . that is very true."

Kateryna's flare of temper subsided as quickly as it had come. "It is almost always ethnicity and racial conflict that start wars—not governments and not even economic pressures, as you like to believe in the West. Consider the Second World War. Of much more importance than the economic issues involved, the Germans and the Japanese both considered themselves superior to the peoples who surrounded them. Both felt it was their destiny to rule their neighbors."

"The Russians, as well," Saul added.

"Yes, but at least they did not start the war."

"They certainly took advantage when it was over."

"Saul, the dangerous situation with these small weapons we are talking about is not now with the Russians. The real threat occurs when ethnic hatreds are combined with religious intolerance. Look how long the Cross and the Crescent have been battling each other in my part of the world.

Now of course we have the Star and the Crescent in Israel. They all believe in one God. Why must the rest of the world be at risk because Christians, Jews, and Muslims cannot agree on which particular prophet is involved?"

"We . . ." *I'm not going to get into a long discussion with a communist about religion.* "We are fortunate that our ethnic differences here in America are not likely to lead to war."

"I wouldn't be so sure, Saul. Even your great capitalist country could fragment—it did once over the issue of race—and you still have huge groups of people who voluntarily cluster together in mono-ethnic communities: Cantonese in San Francisco, Koreans in Los Angeles, Greeks in Chicago, Russians in Brighton Beach, Cubans in Miami, and so on. They do not aggregate merely for survival or because of discrimination; they mainly come together by choice: for the feeling of community their common ethnicity, culture, values, and language provides—just as in my part of the world. And yet, you in the West refuse to openly discuss the existence of ethnic or cultural differences. What do you say? It is not politically correct?"

Saul frowned. *This is not going anywhere.* "The political correctness thing is—was—just a fad, Kateryna. Most people now dismiss it, recognizing its great potential for damage—like the ultraconservatives in this country who want to categorize and polarize everyone as either liberal or conservative, with no middle ground."

Kateryna wagged her finger across the table. "I don't think so. In any real discussion of ethnicity, most people here scream *racist* and then everyone else runs for cover. You Americans and racial discussions are like the Victorians and sex: they refused to even mention it in public, but they certainly discussed and practiced it with gusto in private. Saul, it wasn't just economics that destroyed our Union, it was hopelessly entrenched and xenophobic ethnic balkanization. To learn from our experience, you must guard against such things here by openly discussing subjects that are now dismissed as racism."

"Easy to say, but hard to do, Kateryna. Remember, you are talking to a Jew. In our history we have often been widely dispersed, seldom by choice, but it finally became clear that survival depended upon our coming together in a place of our own. And, speaking of Jews and getting back to Western concerns about nuclear weapons, many here are concerned about their getting into the hands of the enemies of Israel. We see the situation there as the most likely breeding ground for a scenario leading to a nuclear incident."

Kateryna nodded. "As bad as it now is in the Caucasus, the situation in Israel does remain the most likely cause of a nuclear incident. But it would also likely escalate into more than an incident. If a radical Muslim group detonated a nuclear weapon in Israel, the Israelis would immediately retaliate—massively, and including targets in Kazakhstan, southern Russia, and my country. And I am not confident that the strategic weapons in Kazakhstan would not then also be used against America because of this country's fanatical support of Israel. Under the present agreement, the weapons are no longer supposed to be targeted at the West, but I would not be so certain. Saul, your country's general support of Israel is one thing, but *why* did your government permit the proliferation of nuclear weapons by them? It could be your own undoing."

"That subject is very complex, going clear back to Chaim Weizmann and Ernst Bergmann setting up a nuclear research laboratory in 1948, only months after the birth of the state of Israel. The Zionist lobby has always been very, very strong in this country."

"Your government's position on this issue for the past forty years is absurd. Despite America's refusal to even acknowledge the existence of Israeli nuclear capability, it is widely known that they not only have first-generation fission weapons but thermonuclear devices and the capability to missile-deliver them into Russia as well as throughout the Middle East. Saul, you in the West have long criticized us for not being honest and candid, and yet you have consistently refused to acknowledge what has been known since the early 1960s, when the true purpose of Israel's facility at Dimona was first understood."

"If our government had formally acknowledged Israel as a nuclear proliferating nation, our law would not permit the delivery of any conventional arms to the Israelis. Then, with the massive aid and weaponry the Soviet Union provided to many of the Arab nations, Israel would have been quickly overwhelmed. She would have used her weapons of last resort. To prevent this, we looked the other way concerning Israel's nuclear program, and we provided conventional weaponry as well as general assistance to maintain a balance. Both the U.S. and the Soviet Union were at fault, over a long period of time."

Kateryna stared at Saul for a long moment. "Yes, I must admit you are correct. We both used the Middle Eastern countries as surrogates. But the surrogates remain after the principals have retreated, and so do the weapons in neighboring countries."

"Kateryna, just how possible do you suppose it is that any of those Soviet weapons could actually be diverted into the Middle East?"

"It is more than merely possible. Particularly in the Muslim republics. They are drawing closer and closer to the fundamentalists in Iran and Afghanistan, and without a central security agency, the risk escalates. From our standpoint in Ukraine, the threat is more than palpable. We do not want a nuclear incident near our own country. Don't you have some kind of an American saying that expresses that feeling?"

"Yes, yes, we certainly do. It's called 'not in my back yard.' Just *how* possible is it that such a thing could happen? I mean, time-wise?"

"Oh, no one can say, of course; it is because everything is in such confusion. And money—hard Western currency—is so desperately needed."

"You mean needed by your governments?"

"Well, yes . . . and by desperate people. Surely you know about our weapons scientists, now very nearly out of work. For example, look at the members of my team. They are now functioning merely as technicians. Formerly these very talented scientists were well paid and held prestigious positions in our state. Now many are being courted by Middle Eastern extremists. True capitalism, is it not?"

"Capitalism is not a perfect system either, Kateryna. But are steps being taken to particularly safeguard the most, shall I say, *desirable* of the weapons in the republics? And are the new republics acting together or just individually?"

"I cannot speak of that, of course; however, I will say that if it were up to me, I would do more." Kateryna paused and looked closely at her dinner companion. "You tell me. What do you think should be done to decrease the risk?"

Saul matched the intense look he was getting from across the table. "It seems to me that the world has got to be awakened—very rudely awakened—to the threat."

"And how would you do that?"

"Well, I had a discussion just a while back with some friends. We tossed around the idea of setting up a controlled incident. That our government, or Russia's, or yours, would somehow arrange a nuclear incident, perhaps with the blame laid on a terrorist group. The difficulty, of course, is how such a thing could be effective without people being killed."

"You are very clever, Saul," Kateryna smiled. "You have taken my comment about virgins and applied it to the whole world: the way our governments have talked about nuclear war."

"Nearly two generations have passed since Hiroshima and Nagasaki: the baby boomers too young to remember and their children seeing it only as ancient history. Worse than that, for those who do think about it, the bombs are now largely seen as having been a necessary conclusion to the Pacific war. Except for a few revisionists, most people rationalize what happened because America was at war. After all, the Japanese started it at Pearl Harbor; for nearly fifteen years they had engaged in countless and widespread atrocities throughout the Far East; by 1945 there was hardly an American family that had not already been touched in some fashion by the war; there would have been heavy American casualties and suicidal resistance with an invasion of Japan's home islands—that sort of thinking."

"Therefore you think it is time for another demonstration of just what these weapons are capable of doing?"

"Yes. To get the current generation of politicians off dead center. A carefully contrived incident could instantly galvanize academic talk into profound action. We are now at a crucial point of very relaxed tensions between East and West. With an incident to rally around, we could see a giant leap toward complete nuclear disarmament, not just this token nonsense we're doing here in Pueblo, down at Amarillo, and in Nizhnyaya Tura. Otherwise, who knows where we will be in a few years? Perhaps right back with thousands of missiles pointed at each other."

"Saul, I find it impossible to even imagine that any of the principal governments would have the courage to take such action unilaterally. Of course, it is even less likely they would act in concert. Perhaps the idea would be studied by the security agencies, but that is all. Whether communist or capitalist, East or West, you know politicians are not capable of being that courageous. That is why they are politicians."

"Perhaps a dedicated group of individuals—a group of informed, technically capable people—could do it."

* * *

As he walked into the mess hall, Saul remembered that the conversation had ended abruptly at that point. Kateryna had given him a long, penetrating look and then excused herself. Since then not a word had been said about his abrupt suggestion.

While on duty, business was business and Kateryna did not miss a single particular. The U.S. team could not have hidden the least detail. But since that evening the two of them had been far more relaxed together. His revelation of what had happened to his parents had changed Saul entirely in her eyes: he was no longer merely an American of Ukrainian ethnicity. He was Ukrainian.

Following the rapprochement of that evening, with their arm's-length friendship growing, slowly at first and assisted by their relaxing ability to converse in her native language, Saul began to sense that the strong willed woman suffered from something deeply personal. It was more than the collapse of her Soviet Union and the troubles that weighed so heavily upon her beloved Ukraine. Finally, on a recent Saturday afternoon walk along the nearby Arkansas River, Kateryna revealed that her daughter was ill with cancer. Once she began to talk about Sofiia her anguish flooded out, exposing an entirely different person beneath the flinty exterior of the state security officer.

When Saul walked into the mess hall he knew he was not going to be rid of his anxiety until he found some way to follow up on that evening's conversation.

"Good evening, Kateryna," he said easily as he set his dinner tray down. "May I join you?"

"Of course, Saul, do you think I want to sit in this place alone? I did not believe it possible for your military installations to be drearier than those of ours." At seven o'clock the World War II-vintage mess hall was nearly empty, populated only by a few non-team, Department of the Army civilians.

"Ready to go home?" Saul grinned.

She rolled her eyes, followed by a half smile. "I have a calendar above my bed with big Xs marked over each completed day. And you? Are you anxious to go back to California?"

"Less than three weeks left now; you can't be more ready than I am." Saul immediately regretted his remark, reinforced by the look he got from across the table. "Kateryna, I'm sorry . . . Uh, how is Sofiia's treatment coming?" he asked tentatively, still feeling as though he were walking on eggs when he broached any personal matter with her.

She looked away, down at her plate, then finally met his eyes, the sharp look now replaced by pain. "I really do not know. In her letters she says that everything is well and the school in Kyyiv is good and she has friends. But she is a nine-year-old girl. What can she know about her treatment? My letters to her doctor have been answered with typical, how do you say, 'bureaucratese.' I got the last one from his assistant yesterday, and now I am very worried. He says that he is sorry that they are so limited in what they can do! Saul, there are so many people in Ukraine sick from the Chornobyl disaster. Eighty-five kilometers north of Kyyiv, two-thirds of the way to Chornobyl, it is a dead zone. The few hospitals in Kyyiv and Odessa are overwhelmed. It is even worse in Minsk because they were directly downwind from the radionuclide plume during the first two days. Of course, the Russians offer nothing. They have their own problems."

"It's easy for me to tell you not to worry. I have my own children. They are grown now, but I can understand your fears. It's only a little while longer before you will be back home."

"Yes . . . soon." She tried to smile, with signal failure. She laid her hand on his arm, then looked past him at nothing.

Encouraged by her display of closeness, Saul decided to make his move. "Kateryna," he said tentatively, "There is nothing you can do about when you leave. That day is fixed. Why don't you let me show you something of America besides this dreadful army depot and dreary, wintertime Pueblo?"

"That is very kind of you, but we are scheduled to go on the tour after we finish our work."

"Kateryna, you do not *have* to go with the rest of your team on the tour of Colorado week after next. Why don't you let me show you some really exciting parts of the local country? I don't want you to spend your last days here being dragged around on a bus listening to a tour guide."

"As the team leader I have an obligation to go."

"You are well beyond meeting your official protocol duties. Besides—and excuse me for saying so—I'm sure your people will not question the right of the Commonwealth team senior officer to do as she pleases."

"What about your government? Will they agree to a former KGB officer being turned loose?"

"I cannot imagine there would be a problem," Saul demurred with a backhand wave of his hand. He almost blurted out that possible Ukrainian espionage would not be of great concern to the CIA—instantly very thankful he'd caught himself in time. "And haven't your team members been able to go freely into Pueblo, even up to Colorado Springs, without a chaperone? I think the only thing you have to worry about is what your own people might think. Why don't you contact your embassy and just ask them? Part of enjoying the trip will be having a free conscience."

"I don't know. You know the condition I am in right now." She shook her head, then reacquired her vacant gaze, once more seeing only the institutional green wall of the mess hall. "I don't think I would be very good company. I don't want to be entertained; I just want to get through the remaining time. But I really appreciate the offer." She looked back at him. Saul heard the tone of voice he had learned meant *stop*.

It was now or never. Time was running out. He felt a whole lifetime of social awkwardness closing in on him. *How can I, Saul Kalinik, nerd scientist, possibly play mental footsie with a goddamned KGB officer?*

"Kateryna, we should talk about more than what we will see on a pretty drive through the countryside."

The eyes across the table transformed in an instant—dreamily detached to penetrating, examining. Behind the eyes were not thoughts of how to gently repulse a romantic overture. They were the rapier-quick thoughts of a mind trained in espionage.

"What are you trying to say? I won't bite you," she smiled as she brushed back her hair and leaned forward with both elbows on the table, her fingers laced under her chin.

Thank God she leaned forward and not back with her arms crossed. "Remember the conversation we had a couple of weeks ago about what might be done about focusing public awareness on all the nuclear weapons?"

"Of course," she answered quickly, easing herself back in her chair. The penetrating look intensified: the one Saul had gotten that evening two weeks ago was back.

"We've hardly scratched the surface with the disassemblies here and over in Russia. It's just politics that's driving this limited treaty, not firm resolve of the people, in your country and mine."

"Very true." Kateryna looked around at the people remaining in the mess hall. She took her time, concentrating on each person for a long moment.

Saul pressed on, "Have you ever wished you could undo something—I mean undo a big mistake—something done by your government that is now recognized as having been a big mistake?"

"Of course," she said, again rigidly focused on Saul.

"Such as?"

"Such as the gross radionuclide contamination of some areas in Kazakhstan, for example. That is one of the several reasons the Kazakhs hate the Russians and why it is so dangerous for weapons to remain there. Iran would be more than happy to pay for the cleanup in exchange for a few of the products that caused the contamination." Kateryna's gaze bored even deeper into Saul. "Why are you bringing this subject up again?"

Okay, this is it. Now or never. "I have in mind combining the incident we talked about and ridding *our* country of one of *its* mistakes." He struggled on. "Perhaps you could assist with the incident. Perhaps you could get Sofiia to the U.S., where she can get proper care. You have an opportunity now that you may never have again."

Saul endured the longest, most painful silence his sheltered life had yet exposed him to. Completely foreign. Intimidating. Excruciating.

"I will see you here after work tomorrow evening," Kateryna finally announced, her tone more command than invitation. With that, the sudden stranger got up, walked swiftly to the door, and was gone.

Saul remained riveted to his chair, feeling as though he'd just been kicked in the stomach. He had a cold feeling in his throat and a strange floating sensation, almost like dizziness. He was experiencing shock, a clammy fear, and a profound elation—all at the same time.

The inventory of warheads being torn down to their beryllium, enriched uranium, and plutonium "pits" was almost exhausted. The fat-softball-sized, tungsten-sheathed spheres were being shipped to the Pantex plant in the Texas panhandle where facilities existed for secure storage of the fissile cores. Neither Russia nor the United States had yet figured out what to do with the mounting accumulations of the nuclear material, short of simply vitrifying it for storage or taking the absurd proliferation risk of consigning it to civilian nuclear reactors for consumption. Both governments, as well as the rest of the conscious world, were very aware that a growing number of people were more than interested in acquiring some of the salvaged materials. Accordingly, Pueblo's material, like the estimated 1,300 nuclear bombs that traveled across the country each year, was trucked to Amarillo by DOE's Albuquerque-based Transportation Safeguards Division. Intense security was provided for the unmarked specially-built "Safe Secure Trailers" which made the secret night shipments, and none of the local inhabitants knew that some of the most dangerous substances on earth were traveling through their towns and villages and passing their farms and ranches.

The sleepless night made the following long, frigid day, side by side with the woman in crisp khaki, nearly unendurable. Kateryna occasionally said some necessary thing to him about the work, but she was even more rigid and formal than she usually was on the job. She was absent for the second half of the afternoon's work, a fact that did not attenuate Saul's anxiety.

My God, what have I done! What is she thinking? Where is she? His mind writhed with the possible meanings of Kateryna's summary command and sudden departure the previous evening. *She has reported to her embassy or formally complained to the State Department. No. Why would she direct me to meet her tonight? Perhaps to gloat over me when I'm placed under arrest? That's where she is right now; meeting with her people or ours. What have I done?*

Saul had been in the mess hall since five, having dinner, waiting, having dessert and coffee, waiting, and then having several more cups of coffee, each isolated by long periods of waiting. Kateryna walked in at quarter to eight, fifteen minutes after the steward shut down the hot line. Three army privates sat over in the far corner playing odd-man-out with quarters, flipping the coins into the air, catching them, then slapping them onto the backs of their hands. An ancient Willie Nelson tune whispered scratchily through the speaker in the other corner. A soldier in a white T-shirt and fatigues was starting to stack chairs on the Formica tables.

"Hello, Saul," she said as she walked up and sat down abruptly.

"Hi," was all he could muster. *Thank God there's no one with her—yet.* Every conclusion he'd reached, rejected, and reacquired came to him almost simultaneously as he looked across the table at Kateryna. She returned his gaze without the slightest expression on her face. He noticed that she wore no makeup of any kind, then he suddenly realized that she never had in the past two and a half months. He just saw the unblinking, multicolored-brown eyes lasering into him as though not an instant had elapsed since the previous evening. His mind flashed a vision of himself sitting in a bare, cold room in Lefortovo Prison: the woman staring at him across the table was wearing the brown uniform of a KGB officer.

"Saul, we are going to take the trip you suggested, but modified. Between now and when we finish here, you are going to arrange for me to meet, personally, each of the principals in your enterprise. You will arrange a suitably private place for us to meet, as a group, where there can be no surveillance. When our tasks here are finished and my team leaves on the tour, I shall remain, for a reason they will find acceptable. You will leave a day ahead of me, ostensibly to go home. You will leave your car at the Stapleton Airport in Denver, in the northeast area of outlying shuttle lot number two. The day after you leave, I shall make my way to Denver and pick up your car to drive to our meeting place. How I get to Denver is not your concern. Outside of work, we shall not be together for the rest of our time here except for you to tell me that you have made the arrangements." Kateryna's face then softened very slightly. Saul remained rigid.

"Please do not question my precautions. They are necessary. We shall come through this as we each envision." With that, she stood up and again walked out of the mess hall—but not as briskly this time, and she sent a brief glance and a smile back at him just as she went through the doorway.

There IS no enterprise. Why in God's name did I even suggest such a thing to her? This is insane! Saul sat with his cold cup of coffee until the sergeant walked over and told him the mess hall was closed. He walked back to his quarters, oblivious to the horizontally traveling snow carried by a blast of thirty-miles-per-hour, 15° wind.

Sitting on the edge of his bed, still fully wrapped in his thawing parka, Saul realized he had to talk to Stan and Malcolm. And he was beginning to get an idea about where they could all meet with Kateryna.

4

San Francisco, November 3

"Good morning, Mayacamas International. How may I direct your call?"

"Mr. Renslaer's office, please. Saul Kalinik calling." *Good old Malcolm. Still no voice mail.* A few big companies still realized that a caller's time was worth as much as the company's.

"Thank you. Please hold." His call was switched from what Saul imagined to be a large telephone bank with several operators to the third outer office of what he knew to be a huge suite occupying the top floor of one of San Francisco's financial district skyscrapers. He listened to a segment of "Spring" from *The Four Seasons.*

"Mr. Renslaer's office," a perfect female voice interrupted Vivaldi's classic.

"Yes, Saul Kalinik for Mr. Renslaer."

"What is the nature of your business, Mr. Kalinik?"

"It's personal."

"Just a moment, please." No music this time.

"Hello, this is Toni Wheeler, may I help you?"

Neither of them managed to pass along my name. Still better than voice mail, though. "This is Saul, Toni. Is Malcolm available?"

"Oh, hello Saul. I'm sorry, Mr. Renslaer is out of the office right now. May I give him a message?"

"Toni, ask Malcolm to call me at 719–445–3597. I can't be reached during the day, but I'll be at this number after five-thirty, your time. It's important."

"Mr. Renslaer is out of the country and is not expected back for a few days, but I should be speaking to him in a day or two."

Saul knew better than to even ask where Malcolm was or how he could reach him directly. "Toni, when will Malcolm be back—for sure?"

"Late Saturday evening is the last thing I heard."

"Has he got anything planned for Sunday?"

"Well, you know Mr. Renslaer. He did say he'd be going straight into Napa, so I assume he's planning to spend Sunday at Stony Ridge."

"Please tell him I want to see him Sunday morning at Stony Ridge. It's very important. And Toni, could you try to reach Stan and ask him to go up there, too? Maybe you'll have better luck than I have."

"Hello, this is Stan Bellamy. If you'll leave a message after the beep I'll call you back when I return. Thanks."

"Shit!" Saul grumbled as he heard the recording for the sixth time that night. *It's midnight. You're too old for that kind of running around, Stanley.*

* * *

Stan had a familiar thought when he struggled into his apartment dragging the sundry equipage and refuse common to a week's tour in the backcountry. *Why is it I always feel guilty when I come back from a camping trip? Like now I have to do penance or something. Now the phone calls. Shit. Look at 'em all. Sure am glad I got this caller ID. Hey! Saul called. He called again. Lots of short ones—hang-ups. Uh-oh, he called at midnight.*

"It's Stan. I just walked in and got your message."

Saul groggily tried to focus on the voice from the telephone. The nightstand clock said 2:30 A.M. He'd been asleep for less than an hour.

"Stan . . . Hey, Stan! Where the hell've you been? I've been calling you since yesterday evening." Saul was now fully awake.

"I was down in Baja. Gimme a break. I get vacations, too, you know. So what's going on?"

"Can you go up to Stony Ridge Sunday morning?"

"Yeah, I guess so. What's up? Thought you had another two weeks out there in the frozen wastes."

"Well, yes, that's right. But I have some things I need to do at Livermore," Saul lied. "And . . . I need to see you and Malcolm."

* * *

"Good morning, Canyon Park Company, may I help you?"

"May I speak to Sandy, please?"

"One moment, sir." The operator was immediately replaced by a yelping Garth Brooks. *Why is it that the instant you get five minutes out of any city in America, this is all the music there is?*

"Um hello, this is Sandy, can I help you?"

"Yes, this is Saul Kalinik again. I talked to you earlier about one of your employees, Wadsworth Temeseh?"

"Oh yes, Mr. . . . um . . . Kallick. Well, we're in luck. The wrangler who came up from Phantom Ranch said Waddy's working down there right now."

"Great. Please connect me to the ranch headquarters."

"I'm um sorry, sir. We don't have phone service down there right now."

"What?"

"Yes, I'm sorry, the phone's out. But I'd be glad to send a message down this afternoon."

"Send a message?" Saul thought he knew what was coming.

"Oh, yes. I'll just write down what you want and put it in with the rest of the mail stuff."

"You mean on the mule train?"

"You bet. How'd that be?"

"I guess that would be just fine, Sandy," Saul sighed flatly.

"Um what do you want me to say, Mr. Kullick?"

"Just say 'Call Saul, collect. Immediately. Very important. 719–445–3597, after seven P.M.'" Saul suddenly felt very foolish about the brevity. *This isn't going down into the Grand Canyon tied to a pigeon's leg. Probably might as well be.*

"I've got that, sir."

"Can you please read back what you wrote down, just to be sure?" Sandy read it back.

"Sandy . . . Let's start over." Saul recited the message again.

"Okay, I got it."

"Please . . . Just read it back again," Saul said, as evenly as he could manage. Sandy complied.

"That's three-five-NINE-seven, and I said *PEE*-em!"

"Sorry about that. I'll just fix it right now . . . There. It'll go down today, Mr. . . um . . . Colon. I'm gonna put it in an envelope right now." Saul was thankful he'd fashioned a pigeon leg-length message.

This is great. Just great. We have a lady who might be in a position to sell us an atom bomb, and I have to send messages by mule team.

* * *

"Hello?"

"Hey, egghead, thiz ol' Waddy."

"Waddy! Thank God. Why'd you wait so long to call?"

"Wait, shit! I just got your note late this afternoon. The wranglers brought it down with the ranch stuff. I dropped everything—prob'ly get me fired—and then spent the last three hours almost killin' a good mule gettin' up here. What the hell you want?"

"I'm sorry, Waddy. Damn, I left the message yesterday morning."

"Well, I just got it. What's up?"

"Listen . . . Are you where you can talk comfortably?"

"Sittin' in a nice chair in the El Tovar lobby."

"Oh, never mind." *Can't talk about this over the telephone.* "I need to ask a big favor."

"Shoot."

"Is there any way you could put together a river trip? From Lee's Ferry to Phantom Ranch?"

"When?"

"Uh, well, starting a week from Sunday."

"No way. 'Sides, we'd freeze our nuts off. You crazy?"

"Waddy, we can just dress for the trip. Can't you try? It's for the Commonwealth team leader. A raft trip on the Colorado would be the best vacation experience she could have while she's here."

"She? What's the deal? You want me to boat-grunt a trip in the middle of the winter so's you can get laid? You *pahanas* sure do have to work hard to get fucked."

Saul sighed audibly. "Waddy, that's not it. Let's just leave it at that, okay? And there'll be two other guests."

"Even if I could find a boat there's no way to get me, four passengers, and all the winter shit we'll need into one raft, even an eighteen footer. It's four or five days down from Lee's Ferry, and what am I supposed to do with the raft when we take out at Phantom? No road back, you know. Who're the other two?"

"I hope it'll be Stan and Malcolm. I'm going to be seeing them this weekend out in California."

"*Absolutely* no way. We'd need a whole boat just for Malcolm."

"Waddy, please try. Let me just say that you will really enjoy the trip yourself—I mean more than usual."

"Whadda ya' mean?"

"You'll see."

"Well, I'll tell ya' what. It just happens that I'm also headed out to the Bay Area for my last sellin' trip. Leavin' tomorrow. My last chance before I have to start mule-haulin' tourists first of the month. We can talk about this when I get out there."

"Can you meet with us at Stony Ridge on Sunday?"

"You know, I've not been up there yet. I'd really like to see Malcolm's palace."

"We'll see you Sunday, then. And Waddy . . ."

"Yeah?"

"Try to start putting the trip together before you leave."

"Saul, the big problem, besides the boat and gear, is that I don't think I could get a permit on such short notice."

"It's off season. You must know every river rat on the Colorado. Put the word out about needing a permit. Swap with somebody. Something. Can't you do that?"

"A couple'a guys do owe me some favors. Saved Buck's ass last year. Prob'ly could find a couple'a boats. Who's gonna drive the other one?"

"I guess it'll have to be Stan or me."

"Oh, that'll be interesting."

"Both Stan and I have run the Colorado clear to Diamond Creek."

"Yeah, in your youth."

"It was before the dam."

"I'm still not impressed."

"Try, Waddy."

"Maybe I could find another group to put in at Phantom. Sure would like to see ol' Malcolm go through Hance Rapid."

"I hope we all get the chance to see that." Saul set down the telephone. *What in hell am I doing?*

* * *

Kateryna had also been doing a great deal of thinking and agonizing, her thoughts severely constrained by thirteen years of immersion in the deadly Soviet security agency and the more fundamental indoctrination she had received since she was a little girl. Her adult life had been based upon an assumption of distrust of any human being or institution other than her Soviet state. Even her family was to be watched closely, she had been taught, but Kateryna had always had a difficult time with that command.

The proposal made by the American physicist had been a shock. Of course, her first reaction was that it was merely a crude attempt to compromise her, but she found it very difficult to believe that Saul Kalinik would have been selected to carry out such a deception. He was too transparent. She soon decided that Saul's inept suggestion was genuine. After some weeks, she had come to feel almost comfortable with her counterpart; at length she was convinced he was legitimate: that he was simply what he appeared to be. She had decided to make the necessary arrangements to meet with Saul and whoever else was involved. She knew she was not being entirely rational, realizing painfully that she was reacting to a mother's desperation, not to the cold discipline she had been taught.

But the passage of time with no follow-up by Saul had resurrected her conditioned suspicions; further, she was brought back to the reality of what awaited her when the assignment in America was finished. Sofiia's last two letters made it clear that she was getting worse, and there had been no word from the doctor in Kyyiv for over a month—just the short note from his assistant. Even General Nastenko had been unable to do anything. The void left by Anatoliy was now occasionally replaced by a spate of anger. *Can't you understand, Tolik? I cannot do all of this alone!*

Unexpectedly, Kateryna had managed to find a measure of relief from the relentless, excruciating anxiety over Sofiia. Midway through the tour of duty, during a Saturday afternoon trip into Pueblo when she had been on her own, she happened upon her remedy—a strange, confounding one from a source she never, ever, would have anticipated. She had been wandering around in the downtown area of the city when she saw the building: a little structure on the corner of a side street in a run-down section near the civic center. The neighborhood had small, one- or two-story commercial buildings, storefront shops with apartments upstairs, old houses on tiny, narrow lots with old people who sat on their porches in the midwinter sun and stared vacantly at her as she walked past.

Little distinguished the building she noticed from the commercial and industrial buildings in the neighborhood—little except the object that caught her eye, halting her in mid step. Atop the one-story structure was a small, gold-painted, hemispherical dome: protruding from the top of the dome was the distinctive three-armed cross of the Eastern Orthodox Church. Kateryna had stood transfixed, alone on the strange street in the strange American city. She was flooded with thoughts of home, of Anatoliy, immediately of the little church in the center of the village where she had been born.

Anatoliy had been so devout—secretly but passionately devout in his Orthodox faith—and throughout their courtship and their marriage he had patiently sought to bring Kateryna into the fold of the Church with its secret gatherings of the faithful. But the long years of Soviet schooling in her adolescence and early adult life, her scientific training in the rigid Russian universities, then later the rigors and crushing omnipresence of the KGB had done their job. Now, so many years later, on a late Saturday afternoon in the strange foreign city so far from home, Kateryna experienced a sudden, powerful feeling. It was as though something unseen and indescribable had flowed into her very being. More than anything else at that moment, she wanted to go into the little church. And she did.

The nave had been empty and dark, with just a few candles burning. Three small icons hung on the screen enclosing the priests' sanctuary—like the ones she'd seen in her village church. Practically all of the churches in Ukraine had been destroyed, or converted to museums or warehouses, but the one in her little village had survived. Kateryna did not remember how long she had remained in the church; she was only aware that other people had come and gone. It was dark when she finally stepped outside.

Every Saturday thereafter she had returned to the plain little building. She would stand silently in the small, dark and peaceful place for an hour or more, always wearing a head scarf as the old women in her village had done. The little sanctuary had no pews. Kateryna had been told by her mother that it was disrespectful to sit in the presence of God. She would often look closely at the little gold-paneled paintings on the iconostasis, and after a while she no longer tried to understand them but gratefully accepted the feeling of peace they gave to her—the sensation of relief and warmth the whole of the little church offered with nothing asked in return. She never spoke to anyone, never dared to light a votive candle as the others did, and she made it a point to go to the church only when there was no service or other activity. Kateryna was embarrassed that she knew nothing of the liturgy. She was ever aware that she was not a part of the Church, but she came to accept, then welcomed, then rejoiced that is was so strongly a part of her.

Stony Ridge

Hidden Passage, with admirers, 1960 (*Tad Nichols*).

1

San Francisco, February 6

Stan was still trying to wade through the stack of law review articles. He'd planned his return from Baja so that he'd have all weekend to work, now Saul's telephone call had cut his time in half. *Quarter past ten. Better get going soon.* He looked down at the manuscript on top of the pile: "The Homophobic and Sexist Implications Inherent in the Rules of Civil Procedure." Stan grabbed his jacket and headed for the door.

He'd done his best to locate Malcolm, alas the usual pleading with Toni Wheeler had been fruitless. Stan was often confronted with the regular disappearance of his two closest friends: Saul's travels masked in governmental secrecy—junkets to wherever for arcane discussions of theoretical physics—Malcolm's disappearances driven solely by the paranoid demands of the business world. Now, it seemed, Malcolm had been gone even more than usual, out of the country for a week or more at a time over the past few months. Toni had been particularly protective of her boss's secrecy and Malcolm had not volunteered any explanations.

The morning spread over the city and her bay, brilliantly sunlit. Stan glanced across the Golden Gate from his route along the elevated highway running through the Presidio. In two or three hours, boats of all sizes would be scattered across the water, here clustered at the starting mark of a race and there scudding before the brisk wind under spinnaker and full suit of sail. The great majority of people living around the bay, and who had not ventured onto it, gave little attention to the dense gatherings of sailboats that appeared at select locations around midday on Saturdays and Sundays. The assemblies marked the starts of races. From the shore, silenced and obscured by distance, there was no hint of the high drama being played out in the apparently random but in fact formalized dance of the sailboats as they jockeyed for position just before the counted-down start of the race. From the shore, the event had the excitement of watching paint dry.

No boats yet. Still too early. Crews having brunch, getting ready for battle. Stan loved to race. If he hadn't told Saul he'd go up to Stony Ridge, he'd be out there himself in *Penny Pincher. Looks like a light air day, though. Yeah, I'd rather go up to Malcolm's.*

Once beyond the distraction of the always-spectacular view, Stan got back to serious thinking. He did his best thinking while driving, and a trip up to Malcolm's estate in Napa was at the top of his list of favorite thinking-drives. Stan spent little time anymore in pondering his work. Since giving up his trial practice to settle into the simplicity of academia, he'd had scads of personal time, and things were much easier in his cloistered life at the San Francisco College of Law. No more dealing with the withering stress of daily doing battle in court; now he could just sit back and tell the eager young people how to do it. But the expanded personal time resulted in more and more thinking about himself. As easy as his work was now, for the first time in his life Stan was without direction. He'd spent a long career worrying constantly about clients' problems and their solutions; now he found himself caught up in an ongoing evaluation of what it had all been about. To keep his hand in a little bit he'd taken on a few *pro bono publico* defenses of environmental activists who the timber and cattle industries had demanded be prosecuted to the full extent of the law. And they had been so prosecuted—unsuccessfully, on several occasions, thanks to Stan's efforts and the teams of eager young lawyers he supervised.

We're all getting old, he thought grimly as he turned off 101 and headed for the Napa Valley. *More hair grows in my ears now than on top of my head.* He instinctively leaned over to look in the rear view mirror. *What do any of us really have to show for all the years we've spent fighting the system? Malcolm's been able to do a lot, with all the power and money he has, but he's constantly complaining about how little he thinks it really is. He's probably right. We haven't accomplished squat. And now we're slowing down. Our effective years are now counted in digits, not decades.*

Stan thought about the man he was going to visit. Malcolm's father had been one of the richest men in California, and his only child, from infancy, had had his life rigorously planned: every step carefully calculated to prepare the young Malcolm for his eventual role as the captain of Mayacamas Industries—later to become Mayacamas International under Malcolm's leadership. But the only heir to the dynasty, which had begun in New York when it was still called New Amsterdam, had been denied the excitement and anticipation of making the choices that would fix his destiny. *At least Saul and I experienced that. We really can't understand what it must be like for people like Malcolm. He was resigned to his fate, although he worked very hard to be like the rest of us.* From the beginning, when they'd met as freshmen at Berkeley, Stan sensed that the three of them would probably remain close for the rest of their lives, intrusions of work, marriage, and family notwithstanding. Malcolm had always been the leader, which, Stan supposed, began with the simple fact of his paying for nearly everything—both Stan and Saul being pecuniarily challenged to near desperation throughout their college years. Resentment or discomfort about this largess had never been an issue, and both Saul and Stan felt they were helping Malcolm live vicariously the free life he would never enjoy.

We've had such different lives since college. I guess it's mainly been the environmental stuff that's kept us together, Stan thought while his route curved through the rolling hills of the Carneros region, southwest of the Valley. Outdoor interests had bonded them during their brief, collegiate time of license: their precious summers spent on river trips and on high-country excursions in the then-vacant Sierras. Malcolm had eagerly chosen to spend the summers with his new friends on the squalid-but-forever-memorable treks and floats, eschewing the palmier retreats available to neighborhood young men whose families had inhabited Pacific Heights since San Francisco had been wrested from the elements. They had hiked the John Muir Trail, following the original edition of Walter Starr's guide book, run the Salmon River in Idaho, the Yampa and the Green in Colorado and Utah, and the Colorado through Glen, Marble, and Grand Canyons. During the intervening years, they'd all been involved in the growing activism that came to be known as environmentalism. *We didn't get caught up in all the antiwar frenzy, even being from Berkeley. I guess that was a few years after we left.*

Driving farther up the Valley, the relative newness of the Carneros region transformed into the expanse of long-established vineyards. Whether traveling in the Valley at bud break; in the midst of the hot green summer; after the crush when the leaves turned their many varieties of red; or during the dead of winter when the vines were reduced to pruned stumps, Stan always found the Valley visually intoxicating. *Saul really loves it up here. Forever dragging me to a new winery.*

Things were not so easy for Saul. All that time at the lab—probably for nothing, because of the environmental stuff—then the Israeli spy thing. Carol couldn't take it any more. He really misses her. And the kids. Clear over in Israel now. Stan knew his friend had not advanced as far as he might have in government service because of his crusading for his environmental beliefs. When Saul had accepted a position on the Sierra Club board of directors, there had been quiet censure among his peers and superiors in the old Atomic Energy Commission. He had been particularly criticized within the bomb community for his opposition to the expansion of the nuclear power industry in California. In the early years, being an environmentalist and a Berkeley graduate was equivalent to being a McCarthy-era communist, or nearly so. At least that was the way most government people felt. And then there had been the accusation—later dropped—that he had given information to a Mossad agent. Clearly, Saul had been passed over in his career advancement.

In the heart of the flat, fertile reaches of California's premier wine-making region, Stan slowed for the turnoff to Stony Ridge. The estate was located in the Mayacamas Mountains, between Oakville in the Napa Valley and Glen Ellen in the Sonoma Valley to the west. Malcolm's family had owned the acreage long before anyone even considered planting grapevines in the Valley, much less up in the hills. In the early 1850s, Malcolm's great-grandfather had purchased thousands of acres in what had been Mexican land grants, using the property as a private hunting preserve. The holdings stretched from the bottomlands of the Napa Valley, over the intervening range, to the flats of the Sonoma Valley. The vineyards and winery at Stony Ridge were the first established in the mountain area in the 1920s, and since that time the old stone winery had been expanded with modern equipment, with much more of the estate now planted in vineyards. Malcolm's Stony Ridge label had become a highly prized component of the cellars of serious wine connoisseurs throughout the world.

In the past few years, Malcolm had come to spend more and more time at his Napa estate—his San Simeon sans the gaudy castle and the gaudier people. His most favorite refuge from his hectic life had always been to invite a few friends up for a weekend of riding, good conversation, and the fine dinners prepared by his renowned kitchen staff. In addition, there were the big parties, usually to showcase his wines, but also to meet his obligations to the San Francisco cum Napa establishment. *All that's been slowing down, lately . . . There've been only a couple of parties in the past year,* Stan realized as he geared down his aging XK150 sedan, following the winding road up out of the Valley.

After clearing the guard at the main gate, Stan was greeted with a regular Stony Ridge event. As he began the long, crushed-rock-drive ascent to the main house, he was immediately accompanied by half a dozen of Malcolm's beautiful Arabians in the adjoining pasture. The animals flowed along in their breed's uniquely free, joyful movement, their tails held high, keeping pace with the car just outside the split-rail fence. The regularly spaced red cedars along the drive revealed flashes of the manor house through their picket as the narrow, steadily climbing lane crossed stone-bridged streams, passed a lake with its fleet of plump geese, and wound through a growing latticework of rock-fence-enclosed vineyards and cedar groves. Prolonged views of the old house high on the ridge appeared and the dancing Arabians fell away as the pastures and vineyards became gardens and lawns. Up a slight rise, the drive ended in a huge loop around an ornate stone and iron fountain guarding the front of the massive house. Malcolm was there, still dressed in the morning's riding habit and accompanied by his old Irish wolf hound, limping along at his heel.

"Stanley! Just in time. Anthony's putting the finishing touches on the very best beef bourguignon you've ever had. Hope you haven't had lunch."

"Fortunately I have not, Malcolm. And how are you? Sorry I'm late. When's Saul due?" Only Malcolm's spotless old Rolls was parked in the drive.

"Don't know. Toni just said he'd be here this morning."

"Any idea what this is all about?"

"Haven't talked to him. Got back late last night. He was lucky to catch me; I've got to leave again in the morning."

"And Malcolm, what are *you* up to? You've been gone nearly constantly over the past few weeks—months, I should say."

Malcolm tried to put his hands into pockets that were not a part of his jodhpurs. He looked down and then slowly met Stan's gaze. "Just some personal stuff. I guess it is time I told you two about it. But let's wait; I don't want to go through it twice. Now, how about a sample of the latest and best *meritage* Stony Ridge has ever vinted."

Stan looked down at Hercule, lying patiently at his master's feet, and realized again that time was, indeed, fleeing by. He remembered the old hound in the flower of his lanky youth, when he had been able to keep up with a lean Arabian at full gait. Deep in his dark eyes, even now, lay the reflection of some long-atrophied instinct to chase and kill the Irish wolves, now extinct; to once again put to their patiently bred function those powerful jaws, now useless. Perhaps the instinct would finally die with his generation of the now-irrelevant hunters. Somehow the finality of the old hound's place in the world seemed strangely applicable to Stan—aging, irrelevant.

Malcolm led the way across the drive to the broad stone stairway leading up to the house. Stan loved the old estate, with its collage of wine country smells: of cedar wood, moist stables, and the pungent, musty sweetness of wine-soaked oak barrels. The manor house and stables had been built in 1898 by Malcolm's grandfather, whose passion was breeding and training Arabian horses. True to the name, the buildings on the estate were constructed largely of local stone: a mélange of green and gray serpentine, dark graywacke, and greenstone basalt, now coated with a patina of multi-hued green lichens and dark moss that only the passage of time could effect. Built as it was at the Victorian/Edwardian cusp of American architecture, the Queen Anne manor house was an extravagance of broad porches, turrets, cupolas, and widow's walks; of somber-toned wooden trim, steep slate roofs, dormers, and wrought-iron finials. Encased in their deep earth shades, and betrayed only by the precise, man-made realignments of nature, the house and its accompanying buildings seemed part of the surrounding native assembly of yellow pine, cedar, fir, redwood, oak, and bay laurel.

Crossing the pillared verandah and entering the foyer, the effect was a leap back over a century of time: French-polished Circassian walnut; etched and beveled window panes; parquet marble floors; massive European furnishings; a Ninth Dynasty urn of delicate blues and ivories; ferns perched upon their slender stands; the grand carved staircase ascending and then dividing to disappear to either side; and the whole surmounted by a splendid Italian Renaissance gas fixture suspended from an elaborately frescoed ceiling above faux stone walls, draped with tapestries and hung with portraits of ancient Renslaers, gazing down upon their current incarnation.

"I've always wondered. Do you ever feel uncomfortable being stared at by all those relatives?"

Malcolm laughed. "Fortunately, I don't spend a lot of time in the front hall. I know what you mean, though. I always feel like they're demanding to know what I've done each day to expand their holdings."

Stan followed his host through the parlor and into the adjacent conservatory. The view overlooked the gardens and lawns, the patchwork of descending vineyards, pastures and stone walls among the trees, and the grazing and gamboling Arabians—all painted upon a grand expanse of the Napa Valley with a hazy blue Caymus Range rising distantly beyond. Stan drank in the familiar scene along with the mossy scents of humid soil and greenery.

Malcolm settled his Falstaffian frame into one of the many outsized chairs he'd located strategically throughout the house. A white-jacketed young man appeared without discernible summons and as quickly vanished with Malcolm's cellar order. It had been Malcolm who put Stony Ridge on the enology map of the world. The estate still displayed some evidence of the old stump-like trunks of zinfandel planted by his father in the 1920s, but Malcolm had started the plantings of cabernet sauvignon, merlot, cabernet franc, and malbec—the constituents of the special Bordeaux-style *meritage* blend that had enshrined Stony Ridge.

Stan studied his old friend. Malcolm had, alas, inherited the Renslaer predisposition to poundage: about 325 seemed to be the Fates' historical demand. Somehow, Stan thought, Malcolm managed his bulk marvelously. Perhaps it was because he had accumulated it only gradually, if inevitably, since their early youth at Berkeley that Stan had not really noticed his old friend's relentless accumulation of flesh. Malcolm's large head, crowned with a tousled thatch of gray-streaked black hair, matched the large-boned, six-foot-six-inch body. His head displayed a broad face with chiseled features and intense hazel eyes, surrounded by deep smile lines and surmounting a patrician nose. Stan could not remember whether Malcolm's head had always been so large or if it had grown with the rest of him. He found it impossible now to imagine a svelte Malcolm: the man's dominant mass complemented perfectly his place in the world of industrial giants, and with his girth exceeded only by his gusto, Malcolm was a formidable player in the inner power circle that made everything run.

"So, what *have* you been up to, Malcolm?" Stan tried again.

The large man got up and walked to the twenty-foot-high bay of windows. He stood in baronial silhouette, pondering the panorama of everything that was good about California and his life. As Malcolm absorbed the eastern expanse of his domain, Stan was reminded of the glorious sunrises he had viewed from this room and the languid, shady afternoons he had enjoyed in the garden below the conservatory windows. The silence was broken by Benjamin's entry.

"Mr. Kalinik has just passed the gate, sir."

Malcolm whirled about. "Great! Let's go out and meet him." They went back out through the hovering ancestors and down the marvelously hewn and fitted green and gray steps. Stan caught glimpses of the approaching car, its bright color flickering through the row of cedar trees, with the escorting stream of Arabians winding their way up the ridge toward the house.

A spectacular antique roadster pulled up the last rise and came to a dusty stop next to the fountain. Saul's broad smile radiated through the windshield.

"To what do I owe the grand honor of having the very master of the manor and his minion greet my arrival in person?"

"Oh, stuff it," Malcolm roared as he sprang forward, encircling Saul's slender shoulders with a meaty forearm. "If it weren't for good citizens like me how would you eggheads get the wherewithal to enjoy your sheltered lives?"

Both Malcolm and Stan had always been in quiet awe of Saul's phenomenal intellect, and Malcolm, in particular, felt that Saul's mind was wasted on his chosen field of work. A number of times he had offered both of them very attractive positions in his industrial machine, but somehow things had just stayed as they were. They had also remained good friends.

"Nice car, Saul. How long've you been working on this one?" Stan asked as he admired the raucously yellow Auburn cabriolet, its color clashing painfully with the courtyard's rioting thicket of salmon-pink fuchsias. "About a 1934 model?"

"Thirty-five, and she's been taking my time for over a year," he responded proudly. Saul's only, but regular, diversions from his work were his fastidious restorations of antique automobiles. He had what amounted to a complete machine shop at his home, where he kept, at any given time, perhaps a half-dozen of his treasures in various stages of restoration. From the time they had all met in college, Saul had been fiddling with machines. He had intended to be an engineer, but the sheer force of his intellect took him beyond such pedestrian pursuits, thrusting him into the loftier reaches of applied physics. He still needed to get his hands, physically, into things: if he couldn't do it at work, then his old cars provided the release.

"How much of this one's original and how much has been Saul-custom-made?" Stan asked.

"Lot of work in this guy. I had to build some of the engine and the guts of the transmission by hand. Fortunately, I had a set of original specifications and drawings."

"Come on, let's have some lunch." Malcolm had never had any particular interest in cars other than to get him wherever he was going in the appropriate style for the occasion. Stan glanced at the collection of vehicles clustered around the fountain. It occurred to him—even with the marginal contribution of his old Jag—that the scene would make a nice cover for *Gentleman's Quarterly.*

"Okay, Anthony, everybody's here," Malcolm broadcast from the sitting room as they entered the huge dining hall. "Sorry about the delay."

The three men sat down at one end of the long mahogany table, intended to accommodate forty. The young man in white instantly reappeared, armed with a basket of fresh baguettes, sundry cheeses, and two bottles of Malcolm's *meritage.*

"Tell me what you think of the new blend, Saul," Malcolm beamed. Stan was very glad he hadn't been put on the spot.

Before he pronounced his verdict, Saul went through the standard sniffing, glass-twirling, and mouth-swirling ritual. Long before it had become fashionable for the Bay Area elite to believe they understood fine wine, Saul had been a connoisseur. "Very fruity, especially black currant and some violet nose; frankly, more than I would have expected with a raw wine. I can pick up tobacco nuances already from the cabernet franc, and it seems like you've blended more than the usual amount of merlot from the amount of spice I find. It should be a good one, in time: very soft and complex after the sharp tannins relax a bit."

"Right you are, my boy!" Malcolm gushed as he clapped his hands. "You're spot on. Just about what we've all concluded."

Not me, Stan thought. In all such great wine conversations, he felt left out. He always felt out of place at the wine snob gatherings that were hard to avoid in San Francisco polite society. *It all seems such bullshit. Be damned if I have EVER been able to taste or smell tobacco in a glass of wine.*

"Right, now let's have our meal with some of the '85 so you can appreciate where the new one's going," Malcolm resumed. "Should be spectacular with the beef." Malcolm gave Saul and then Stan a long look, his expression suddenly serious. They had often seen him in these mood swings: like a storm cloud passing over a sunny lawn party. "I'm glad Saul suggested we meet. I have something I need to talk to you both about. But first, Saul, tell us what's on your mind."

Saul's demeanor instantly mirrored that of his host. He squirmed in his chair and glanced toward the butler's pantry. "Uh . . . we should have some privacy."

"Well, actually, I gave the staff the day off. We'll have the place to ourselves after lunch."

"Would you mind going for another ride?" Saul asked. Stan thought Saul was more than serious; he seemed almost anxious. Saul was never anxious.

"Okay. Sure." Malcolm gave Saul another long glance. "In fact, I think that's a real good idea."

"Not Blackjack for me, if you don't mind," Stan said, anticipating Malcolm's delight in forcing upon him the most fractious of the fine horses at Stony Ridge. As seldom as they were now ridden, most could be a handful.

"Relax, guys, we'll just have a nice quiet ride," Malcolm assured him.

Even Saul, a fine horseman, was visibly relieved by Malcolm's pledge.

Stan finished dressing in his room on the second floor. He wound the stock tie about his neck and then threaded a stirrup leather into the belt loops in his whipcord breeches. A long-ago experience with a broken stirrup and a bad fall had started the now automatic practice, originally suggested by Malcolm's father. *That was one of the last days of the Mayacamas Hunt. Malcolm's father awarded me my buttons that day . . . Damn, that was a long time ago.* Stan took his black jacket from the coat tree and paused to examine the bright silver buttons embossed with the Stony Ridge crest. He picked up his cap and the old hunting whip, also given to him when he'd been "buttoned." He stared out the window at the Napa Valley, far below. *So many years.* A rush of memories returned.

When Malcolm's grandfather, and then his father, had maintained the Mayacamas Hunt, the members had assembled and the hounds had been cast from the east garden, right below Stan's window. He remembered mornings with a gathering of seventy or more hunters in their red and white, and black and tan, as eager as the fifty couples of English foxhounds to descend the ridge and begin the hunt. The huntsman's horn and the hounds' excited baying on those bright and crisp, winter Sunday mornings could be heard for miles up and down the Valley. The assembly area had long since been encroached by more gardens and vineyards, but Stan still had strong memories of the lively gatherings when they had all been in college, when Malcolm's father had been master of foxhounds and Malcolm served as one of the whips. In those last days of the Hunt at Stony Ridge, he and Saul rarely missed the colorful events. *We even made a lot of the Wednesday afternoon cub hunts,* he remembered wistfully—*Skipped a few classes.*

Modern-style vineyards, with their trellised vines and irrigation systems, had not yet been developed, and the hunt did little damage to the old head-pruned, dry-farmed, and relatively widely spaced vines. Much of the Valley was then just hay meadow, prune orchards, and open pasture, and the Mayacamas Hunt was part of the Valley color, including in its member roster nearly all of the old landowners. But by the early '60s, the non-hunting vineyard owners in the Valley were starting to complain about the hounds and riders who came roaring down the ridges and ravines and out into the bottomlands. With the explosion of the California wine industry in the mid '60s and the coming of new, serious vintners who were paying the then-unheard-of price of $4,000 per acre, the old tradition soon came to a halt. For a few years the Hunt tried to confine itself to the precincts of Stony Ridge, but the foxes soon learned that safe haven was to be found in the now off-limits Valley-bottom vineyards. Even though the red fox was foreign to California, having first been imported for fur farming and hunting, the crafty little creature had adapted quite well to his new environment, to the great disadvantage of much of the local small animal population. Mr. Reynard still occasionally let himself be seen at Stony Ridge, a reminder that he had won.

Saul and Stan rejoined their host in the east garden below the conservatory, all identically clad save for Malcolm's indulgence of his fetish for jodhpurs. They both relived their relief at the sight of the two aging geldings the grooms had brought up from the stables along with Malcolm's Broadside, a particularly large stallion of handsome conformation but of confounding piebald coloring. Like most of the Stony Ridge horses, Broadside was derived from the old stock left over from the long Spanish and Mexican occupation of California, and like most carefully bred stallions he was always very aware of his immediate equine company.

"Malcolm, Broadside doesn't look very happy," Saul said.

"Fuck him, he needs a little discipline. Let's go."

Deferring to Malcolm's preferred position as master of the manor, Saul and Stan followed their host onto the groomed trail leading up the ridge behind the house, pool, and tennis courts. After about ten minutes at a quiet walk through the soft, sun-dappled duff of the bridle path, Malcolm reined in Broadside. The three riders stood facing one another in a triangle, their mounts' breaths intermingling, while Malcolm quietly surveyed his two old friends. The stallion's nostrils were flaring, and his small, neat ears were just beginning to swivel back. Stan thought he saw a hint of white around the animal's huge dark pupils.

"Okay, Saul," Malcolm said. "You're first. What is it?"

Saul twisted about in his saddle, fumbling with his reins and crop. Stan thought he had never seen his old friend look so uncomfortable. Saul finally answered, "Malcolm, why don't you tell us what you've been up to first? It seems to me that you've been gone, out of the country, more than usual over the past few months. And the last time I went to your offices in the city, it seemed that things were, well, scaled back. What have you been doing?"

"Very perceptive for someone with too much education," Malcolm said disjointedly as Broadside bunched up and finally objected with a rear to breathing the same air as the two old eunuchs facing him. After the big stallion had wheeled about, snorted, bucked a bit, and managed a short hind-leg jab at each of the docile geldings, Malcolm continued. "I'm finally getting out of here—out of California. I'm moving the whole shittin' works. This damned state is just regulating and taxing businesses out of existence. Especially the labor laws. The goddamned labor laws. I don't run my companies anymore, the goddamned Department of Labor runs them. The slightest complaint and we're automatically presumed guilty. What we do is never good enough—never will be good enough. My consultants tell me we're in the top 2 percent of all corporations nationwide when it comes to every kind of compliance in every area subject to regulation. Hell, we've now achieved fifty-fifty gender parity, from bottom to top, in every division. *No* one else can claim that—not even close. *Still* we get get hassled. Well, I've had enough. The State of California can just do without all my taxes. And I want to do something worthwhile for a change. I want the both of you to come along." He brought Broadside to a short, dancing halt from the trot they had started, this time backing the excitable horse away from the others.

"What do you mean, come along?" Stan asked. "Where are you going?"

"Well, once I started the move I began thinking that maybe I should just get the hell out of the whole damned country. In the business world it's getting so that national borders are irrelevant anyway. And I want to be free to do what I want, without countless bureaucrats questioning everything."

"What do you mean, you want to do something worthwhile?" Saul asked, heartened by Malcolm's choice of words.

Broadside decided to dance about on his hind legs again, performing a sort of equestrian arabesque, and culminating in a double hind-leg kick in the direction of Saul's horse, which barely lurched out of range. Malcolm abruptly dismounted and snubbed the nervous animal to the bridle path rail. "Come on, this damned horse is driving me nuts. Let's walk down the hill to the old lodge." He paused. "Oh, hell, we can't leave them here." After three attempts, Malcolm remounted and led the way down the steep hill toward a stand of old-growth redwoods.

The ancient trees were clustered in their preferred locale: the bottom of a steep ravine where the giants could spread their feet into the moist soil and where their large flat sprays of tiny needles could capture and condense the morning fogs that lingered in the sheltered depressions. Above them, on the drier hillsides and ridgetops, complementary stands of arrow-straight Douglas firs were dominant. Though not possessing the bulk of their huge cousins, the tall companion trees were equally coveted by loggers for their dense, straight-grained wood, almost immune to warping.

Entering the grove, Stan became aware of a pleasant déjà vu: the massive dark columns, like the organ pipes of the cathedral at Winchester, became the 400-foot-high tapestry stains of Cathedral in the Desert; the sword ferns carpeting the feet of the great trees became the profusions of maidenhair in Redbud Canyon; the slow trickle of the ravine's cold, clear water was the little creek that slid through the dark serpentines of Aztec Canyon. And more than anything physical was the overwhelming sense of peace, a peace that could only come from the silence of the ages. The remnant grove, a rare island of what had been the primordial California, held the essence of what had been Glen Canyon. It was more than simile. Stan vividly relived the Glen Canyon of his youth as he rode through the dim light, following the old companions who had shared that brief, treasured time.

When Malcolm's great-grandfather purchased the Stony Ridge property, San Francisco was well into the frenzy of building that began shortly after the famous discovery in a sawmill tailrace on the American River. With the immediate environs of the future city nearly devoid of plant life, much less the needed forests of lumber wood, the rapidly expanding hordes of Forty-niners, and those bent upon serving them, spread out in all directions to seek their building materials. The primeval stands of redwood, pine, and fir in the surrounding mountains were attacked without regulation or second thought. As the horizon of leveled hillsides expanded outward from San Francisco, coastal schooners sailed up and down the edge of the Pacific in search of further supplies to quench the relentless thirst for timber.

But the original Malcolm Renslaer's property in an obscure valley north of the mud flats in the upper San Francisco Bay was wholly spared from the loggers' attack. Its stands of fir, while spectacular, were sufficiently scattered to discourage the building of the roads needed to reach the trees. The occasional pockets of redwoods, growing at the extreme eastern fringe of their range, were also isolated. Other areas were more easily reached and logged, a circumstance that spared the Stony Ridge groves. With the exception of the tiny national monument of Muir Woods, and a state park far down the San Francisco peninsula, the Stony Ridge estate was today the only place in the whole length and breadth of the greater San Francisco area where glorious old-growth stands of coast redwood and Douglas fir remained. The insatiable demands of the constantly expanding San Francisco, the construction of the railroads, and the needs of the miners eliminated nearly all the old forests until the devastation was finally halted, to a limited extent, near the Oregon border. Excepting the two parks, all of the other fir and redwood forests seen today in the Bay Area and up and down the immediate coast are second growth, lacking the community of plant life found in forests that have grown, diversified, and been left untouched over thousands of years. The ancient forests were mined, not "harvested," as the logging companies today like to claim. They are gone forever, as "forever" must be viewed within the human concept of time.

As Saul, Stan, and Malcolm picked their way among the huge trunks and the living trees' long-departed brethren moldering into the forest floor, they reacted as though they were intruding into a great stone cathedral during vespers. Despite the urgency of their thoughts, they responded spontaneously to the ageless time capsule they had entered. The only sound was the rhythmic thud of the horses' hooves, the animals' exhalations, and the squeak of leather against leather.

Some of the moss-, twig mold-, and humus-covered decaying trees lying broken at their feet, long preserved after death as they had been protected in life by their heavy concentration of tannins, and after centuries in such repose more earth now than wood, had just begun to sprout in the ravine when the distant ancestors of their horses were being bred to pull the pharaohs' chariots. The giants towering over 250 feet above them, now in the winter of their lives, were saplings when the Romans were in the midst of their occupation of what was to become England. Fragments of the ancient companions of these few remaining trees, which had occupied similar enclaves along the California coast, remained now only in forgotten mine shafts and mills, and as abandoned and broken railroad trestles, snow sheds, and ties. Much of the rest of the cut and dismembered mammoths disappeared in the City of San Francisco on that April morning in 1906.

Shafts of yellow radiance descended through the canopy of feathery fronds high above the horses and their riders. Suspended in the dreamy beams were sparkling particles of dust, lazily propelled by an imperceptible movement of air in a kind of Brownian Motion. Remnants of the morning fog clustered in tiny droplets on the filaments of a spider web, shining like the reflection from a phonograph record. The invading light settled in pools among the massive boles imbedded in the spongy floor, providing brief bursts of energy to the companion flora that had lived with the giants through the ages: tan oak, orange-barked madrone, red alder, and California bay laurel reached and twisted among the red/brown/gray fluted columns to capture the occasional penetration of light and warmth. The understory of the ravine was not a place of brilliant flowers, but of mosses and ferns: things able to thrive in the dim, diffused light. Stan was overwhelmed with his memories of the intimate places in that long-ago river canyon.

Still without speaking, they unsaddled the horses and turned them into the broken-down paddock next to the old hunting lodge built by Malcolm's great-grandfather. Broadside immediately trotted to the far end of the corral, as far as he could escape from the other two, who would be content to stand side by side and nose to tail, one hind leg lifted and the hoof tipped down, as old horses so often do.

"Let's go in and build a fire," Malcolm said. "Should be some dry wood inside."

Saul and Stan followed him into the old lodge, built to serve Malcolm's great grandfather, his family and his friends, just as the house on the ridge had served succeeding generations. The old retreat was crudely but massively built of logs from the firs on the hillside above. The redwood grove had not been touched. The huge fireplace was constructed from the same rock used to create the intricate mosaic of foundations, walls, and walkways that underpinned and defined the newer buildings on the ridge crest.

The hand pump at the sink produced some water, soon heating in an iron pot swung into the fireplace. Malcolm busied himself with the fire, then with a grunt, hoisted his bulk up and immediately back down into one of the old leather chairs, long ago constructed for another oversized Renslaer. "Have you been satisfied with your life?" he asked abruptly, speaking to no one in particular.

"Odd that you should mention that," Stan said, startled that Malcolm seemed to have read his thoughts. "I *have* been thinking about that quite a bit lately—while I drove up here, in fact."

"So what have you concluded?"

"That time is running out. Productive time, I mean."

"What about you, Saul?" Malcolm asked. "You don't get to be quiet, as usual. And what are you so nervous about? I've never seen you fidget so much."

"Malcolm . . . uh . . . in a way, what you're talking about is what I wanted to talk about." Saul squirmed in his chair and then sprang up and walked over to a window. He stared out at the Valley through the streaked, wavy glass. "I guess you both know that what I've tried to do, with my environmental activities, has hurt my career. Now with the downsizing and all at Livermore, well, I'm not real confident about my future." He spun around and faced Malcolm. "Where are you going and what are you going to do? Tell us what you have in mind first. Mine is . . . complicated."

"All right," Malcolm shrugged. He propped his feet onto a footstool, made from an old saddle, and stared at the smoky fire for a few moments. "For the last three years, I've been slowly liquidating and encumbering virtually all my holdings. Now, with just a few quick moves, I'll be entirely offshore. For the time being, a massive layer of paper hides all the financial stuff, but I can't juggle everything much longer. My remaining holdings in California, throughout the rest of the country, and anywhere else in the world where they would be subject to the reach of U.S. authorities or creditors: real estate, shipping, manufacturing interests—everything—has either been mortgaged to raise cash, sold outright, or with a lease back. The goddamned banks who have made so many millions over the years with my business were only too willing to lend me whatever I asked.

"My plan all along has been to move just outside the reach of our government and then use my money to fund worthy projects—things I would not dare do here under the scrutiny of the law, the business community, even the social community. I'm now in a position to take direct action to get things done—not just kiss politicians' asses, fund their campaigns, or contribute to other people trying to work within the system. As of now, I have too much money and not enough years left for any more of that crap."

"What about Stony Ridge?" Stan asked anxiously. "How can you just walk away from this place? Have you sold her too?" He could not imagine never again being able to visit the old estate.

"I've given that a lot of thought. No, Stony Ridge is not sold. Not exactly. I'd like to be able to slip back here once in a while. Relax, Stanley, you'll be able to visit that old grove even if I'm not around. I've set up a way for the place to be used by a consortium of environmental groups and the viticulture and enology department at UC Davis. Stony Ridge would be a perfect classroom for the study of wine making. It would also make a fine conference and research center. The irreplaceable parts of this estate, like the fir and redwood groves, must be preserved. Stony Ridge is like a California time capsule hidden away in 1853. I will not leave her fate to a bunch of accountants, bankers, and lawyers. There has already been enough development. Great-grandfather's goose hunting fields down in the Valley, which became Grandfather's hay meadows and prune orchards and then father's vineyards, are now worth $100,000 per acre to grow grapes for pricey wines. The university could never hope to acquire that kind of vineyard land or even the specialty vineyards I've developed up here in the highlands. I've proven that much of this mountain area is spectacularly suited to growing if sufficient attention is given to grape variety, soil, and aspect of the field. But, I want the enologists and the environmentalists to fight out just what the proper use of the highlands should be—not a collection of three-piece suits. My only concern is that after I start doing my new work, financially aggrieved people may seek to attach or seize Stony Ridge. What do you think, Stanley?"

"About all you can do is hide her under the biggest pile of paper you can create. Even the federal government has to be able to prove that you own the property before it can be seized."

"That's what I've done. I took personal care of most of the details myself. Only I know the whole setup. Actually, it's so complex that I'm kind of afraid I'll forget the route of the paper trail."

"What about your children?" Saul asked.

Malcolm scowled. His children, hopelessly spoiled before his wife died and wholly disinterested in the operation of the Renslaer empire, were not his favorite subject. "I gave them life, an excellent upbringing, education to the extent they felt like accepting it, and they both have a great deal of money—thanks to their grandfather's very generous trusts as well as my own. They're grown. They're on their own now."

Stan knew that the conversation could quickly degenerate into a long Malcolm diatribe about the current generation of young adults poised to take over the operation of the world. "I'm sure you're not able to talk over with your lawyers the planning of all the paper shuffling you described, Malcolm. It must be frustrating to have all those high-priced suits on salary or retainer and not be able to talk to them about this most important thing in your life."

"It certainly is. Everything about the grand plan has, until this moment, been kept entirely within my head. My people do the work, but, like you said, I can't talk to anyone about the overall scheme. No one to help me with strategy, but I've been as careful as I possibly can be to scatter the conveyancing, mortgaging, leasing, and money-moving all over my business enterprises. Even a suspicious, knowledgeable, determined, well-funded pack of ferrets would have a hard time finding their way through all the paper."

"And what do you mean, specifically, by worthwhile projects?" Stan persisted with the question Saul had asked while they were up on the bridle trail.

Malcolm frowned again at the break in his thoughts. "There are so many things that have been and are still being done to our world that the civilized societies simply cannot control, much less hope to correct. Take the Japs, for example."

Oh, God. Japan-bashing time again. Stan was surprised to see a smile on Saul's face. "You're not agreeing with him, are you?"

"No . . . No, of course not. It's just that every time I hear him say 'Jap,' I think of Jewish-American princess."

"Can we get back to this?" Malcolm grouched. "Maybe you two still don't get what I'm talking about here."

"Sorry, Malcolm," Saul said.

"Well, what the Japs are doing is a good example. Our government just continues to kiss their asses. We hear a lot of talk about reducing the trade deficit, but nothing ever gets done. They haul their automobiles over here, but those big ships go back to Japan empty, except for maybe a pile of money. Why can't they take back loads of cattle? America is just a colony, so far as they're concerned. A damned colony, aren't we? They take our raw resources at low prices, then send us finished products at inflated prices. Doesn't that define a colonial arrangement? And we provide a complete, free, defense umbrella to protect their supply of oil."

"Can we *not* get into all this again?" Stan sighed.

Saul: "Wait a minute, Malcolm. Explain one little detail for me. Your senior vice president in the San Francisco office is Kanji Tachibana."

"Kanji's American."

"Naturalized. Both his parents live in Japan—refuse to move here."

"Saul, you just don't get it—never have. It's their fucked up *culture*—how they *do* things—their values—not their ethnicity. And it's not the people, as a whole, but their ruling class. That whole country is still run by a handful of shoguns, like always. And let me tell you this: there's no way Kanji will ever eat some concoction made from bear gall bladders, mountain gorilla hands, or goddamn *tiger* pricks! You getting the picture?"

"Those are principally Chinese customs, Malcolm."

"Oh, *bull*shit!"

"Okay, hold it, you two." Everyone listened to the fire for a while.

"Stanley, the gross environmental degradation those people are involved with, worldwide, is a perfect example of what I intend to target after I get out of here."

Both Stan and Saul admired their old friend for the rigid stand he had long taken among his fellow captains of industry. Although widely respected among his peers, Malcolm was a maverick in the world of industrial giants: in fiscal, anti-governmental, and general business matters he was squarely within the bismarckian standard, but when it came to the environment he was conspicuously liberal. His fellow industrial barons and their political dogs uniformly insisted upon the conservative mantra being recited in unison and in toto, but Malcolm had consistently demurred when that agenda automatically excluded anything the organized environmental community proposed. And Malcolm had always been more than sensitive to environmental criticisms leveled at his companies. Saul and Stan knew that he had spent a great deal of money over the years to make his businesses as environmentally friendly as was reasonably possible, but his most effective contribution had been his role as a standard-setter for his peers. Because he had "done the right thing," his competitors had often been forced to follow his rigorous example.

"Stanley, Saul . . . it is very important for you both to understand exactly what I am asking you to do. I only mention the Japs because what they're involved with is so conspicuous. It's okay for them to strip whole mountainsides up in British Columbia, but they don't cut a single tree on Mount Fujiyama. And where do you think practically all of the hardwood lumber from Indonesian and South American clear cutting is going? Japan has permitted, indeed encouraged, its population to expand to the point that it has hopelessly outstripped its own resources. They are still slaughtering whales, despite worldwide condemnation—calling it research—and they continue to drift net huge areas of the seas, turning them into marine deserts. Nothing changes. Well, once I'm set up outside the reach of U.S. laws, I'll be able to compete more than equally with them. Maybe then I can force a few changes to be made." Malcolm was now at full steam. "As a couple of examples, I have to abide by our antitrust laws here, but the Japanese don't have such restrictions. In many areas I'm not permitted to deal directly with foreign governments, but again, the Japanese business/government *zaibatsu* combine has a free hand. They can sue me under our laws, but I can't touch them in their country, under their laws—just like I could never be a citizen there because I'm not Japanese. Ha! Can you imagine? But, of course, they're free to immigrate here within their very generous quota. Well, once I'm able to play by their rules, without prohibitions by our government and courts, I'll be able to start interfering in their activities in other countries. And—here's the best part—I'm certain that our government will just look the other way, and, to the extent it can, even encourage me." Malcolm lurched up and started to pace. "Let me put it very clearly. I want to . . . no, I intend to declare war on the people and elements in this world that environmental consensus, if not our governments, demands be controlled. Over the years I've tried to get you both to join me, but this time I'm not talking about just a job. I'm talking about major projects where we would all work together . . . So. What about it?"

Stan was stunned. He was unhappy with some of the situation he found himself in at his age—but unhappy enough to give it all up? "I don't know about permanently leaving the country," was all he could say.

"Look, it would take days to go over all the details. I'm just asking you both to give the idea some thought. In any case, I'm outta here. And pretty damned soon." Malcolm turned to Saul. "Now, with that said, *damnit* Saul, what in hell is eating you?"

Saul swallowed hard. *Can't put it off any longer.* "Remember the discussion we had a couple of months back at the club, when Waddy was here? When we were talking about Glen Canyon?"

Malcolm nodded. "You bet. Just the mention of the canyon sure got Waddy's attention." He settled back down in his chair.

"Yeah," Stan said as he recalled the day.

Saul looked intently at Stan. "Stanley, remember the end of our river trip in '58 when we were ordered off the river? Warned to go no farther because we were approaching the dam construction area? Run off like criminals? Remember the shock when we realized that water really was going to back up behind a big dam? When it first really sank in that the paradise we'd just seen was actually going to be flooded?"

"Of course, Saul. I remember like it was yesterday. And then we had to hump everything up Antelope Creek and around to Lee's Ferry."

"Remember the screaming rage and frustration we all felt? Just us three college kids. Nothing we could do about it."

"I don't know about you two," Malcolm said soberly, "but I never got over that day. It was the starting point of all my thinking about what we supposedly civilized people are doing to our world. Stanley, didn't you get the feeling that one day you'd want to finally be in a position to do something about such things?"

"Well, yes, but I think I have to some extent." Stan was suddenly defensive about what he'd been agonizing over. "The law has helped me to– –"

"Oh, horseshit!" Malcolm thundered, his whole body shaking in the overstuffed chair. You've won skirmishes, not battles, and certainly not wars—just like me, and I *know* you want to do more. Remember, it was you who insisted on stopping when we saw that fleet of earth movers. You used a pair of vice grips to twist off the valve stems on one of them. All *twelve* tires. Remember that?"

"The impetuousness of youth," Stan said, smiling at the sudden recollection of a long-forgotten event.

"Yeah, well, I'm still impetuous—and now I have a lot more money and smarts than when I was nineteen years old." Malcolm stared at the fire. "Sorry, Saul. I interrupted."

"I . . . uh . . . Malcolm, what you've just told us about your plans, well . . . it might fit in with something that's recently come up. We're about wound down with the tactical nuke disassemblies at Pueblo, and I'll be going back to work at Livermore, probably back at the NOVA lab, and– –"

"Shit, Saul, just spit it out," Malcolm snapped.

Stan was starting to feel uncomfortable. He pulled at the sweaty stock wrapped around his neck.

Saul swallowed hard again. "There might be a way to obtain a nuclear device—to get rid of Glen Canyon Dam."

Stan was instantly more than uncomfortable. He felt clammy all over.

In Malcolm's highly disciplined and organized life he was very seldom caught off guard—surprised. All he could do was stare at Saul for several long moments. "Judas Priest! One of the ones you're tearing down at Pueblo?"

"No, that would be impossible. A Soviet device."

Stan remembered the rest of the Cactus Club discussion about the weapons in the former Soviet Union. "What are you talking about? How could you *possibly* do that?"

"From my counterpart at Pueblo. She has a big problem in her life, and I think she might be willing to trade the device for what she needs." Saul felt the countless, silent questions raining on him from Stan and Malcolm.

"Okay, let me just start at the beginning." Saul outlined the conversations he had had with Kateryna and what he had come to know about her background. He went through a laborious recitation, trying to include every detail as it occurred, though he was regularly interrupted by Malcolm, who insisted on quick summaries and conclusions. There could have been no clearer demonstration of how differently the two men were disciplined to think. Saul struggled with, finely ground, and then expanded the minutiæ of a situation in the tedious manner of someone who has too long been a scientist. Malcolm quickly gathered details, summarized, gathered more details, added to the summary, and then formed a conclusion. Malcolm just wanted to know what time it was. Saul got caught up in explaining how the watch worked.

After the initial shock, Stan found his thoughts focusing on the absolute unacceptableness of what Saul was suggesting.

". . . and so she wants to meet with everyone involved. Should that be the two of you? Would this be the sort of project you have in mind, Malcolm?"

"Well . . . shit . . . not exactly." He glared at the rough-hewn flooring. "Glen Canyon. Damn you, Saul. Damnit! Of all the ideas you could come up with, why that one?" A long silence ensued. "Summarize this woman for me. Just your overall impression."

"I can give you no generality about her. She's very complex, highly trained—disciplined in ways none of us could understand. She rarely betrays anything personal. She's, well, alien. I'm sure that even among all your industrialist friends you've never been confronted with anyone like her."

"Her daughter is clearly the woman's main concern, correct?"

"That's right, but I think I really got her attention with the notion of setting up a controlled nuclear incident. She spent a lot of time talking to me about the political situation in her part of the world. She's convinced that if a nuclear weapon does get away it will occur somewhere in the southern block of the former Soviet republics and Ukraine is right on the edge of that area. There's no longer just the Muslim-Israeli clash in the Middle East; we now have the situation in the Balkans. And it looks like the whole of the Caucasus is going to erupt: the clash in Chechnya; Kateryna mentioned that the same problems exist in other ethnic enclaves surrounding Chechnya; the ongoing situation in Georgia; to the south the Christian Armenians and the Turkic Muslim Azerbaijanis are hacking away at each other—all those people have despised the Russians since the czars started grabbing their countries a couple hundred years ago. And not so far away are all the Kurds: they'd love to do a number on the Turks, the Syrians, and, naturally, Saddam. Then there's Iran. All right in Ukraine's back yard."

"Saul . . ." Malcolm paused, uncomfortably. "You know I agree 100 percent with what that woman is saying, but a little more focused. If we're going to have a war involving nuclear weapons, it is most likely going to be because of the Arabs and Jews. Damnit, I am *sick* of the whole world being held hostage because of their endless and hopelessly uncompromising dispute over Jerusalem and a tiny piece of desert along the Jordan River! Every other night on the evening news, for the past nearly fifty years, we've had this unremitting squabble."

"Malcolm, we now have the added fact of a big chunk of the former Soviet arsenal close by and under the control of people who are, at least religiously, closely allied with Israel's enemies. But please . . . let's not get into all that again."

"We *are* in it. You're suggesting that I give up what I have carefully planned for several years in order to help prevent a nuclear incident in the Middle East and, by the by, get rid of a piece of objectionable concrete. Just what is your real motivation, Saul? Is it Glen Canyon Dam or protecting Israel? If it's the latter, count me out—at least so far as risking my whole enterprise goes."

"Whether you choose to believe me or not, it *is* the dam, not the consequential benefit of drawing attention to all those weapons that could be used in Israel. As you are American first, and Dutch/English second, that is also my order of loyalty with respect to my own ethnicity."

Malcolm looked closely at his old friend, a smile creeping onto his huge face. "Saul, did you ever hear about that exchange between Henry Kissinger and Golda Meir—during Kissinger's shuttle diplomacy after the Yom Kippur War?"

"I'm sure there were a great many exchanges between them," Saul frowned.

"Kissinger told the prime minister—I'll try to paraphrase it: 'I am an American first, the Secretary of State of the United States of America second, and a Jew third.' Mrs. Meir immediately responded: 'That's okay, sonny, we read from right to left.'"

Saul just stared back at the big man, now grinning widely. "Malcolm, that's very cute, but I stand by what I said."

"Okay, Saul, I . . . I understand that, believe me. And I couldn't agree more with what you've had to say in the past about the Middle East: whenever religion gets combined with ethnicity we have a particularly volatile situation."

Stan had recovered during Saul's detailed recitation of his conversations with the Soviet woman and the current installment of the ongoing Saul/Malcolm exchange over the role of ethnicity in the functioning of the world. He was now far more interested in a more fundamental aspect of Saul's idea.

"What you're proposing is insane." He took his turn to get up and pace about. "That reservoir is nearly full. There are twenty-five or -six million acre feet of water impounded behind Glen Canyon Dam. It is absolutely unthinkable that such a mass of water would suddenly be released. Nothing would be left, all the way to the Gulf. Hell, the flood would probably take out Hoover Dam, releasing another twenty million or so acre feet. It's just unthinkable. Sure, I agree that the decision to flood Glen Canyon was tragic, but that big reservoir is now a reality."

"Of course you're correct," Saul said quickly. "But I've given this quite a bit of thought. There's no need to massively breach the dam. All that's necessary is to wound it beyond repair."

"Oh, how in hell could you possibly finesse such a thing? That's an arch dam. Any significant break in its structural integrity and the whole pile goes."

"I don't agree. It's largely a gravity dam, massively overbuilt because in the '50s the Bureau still was not fully secure in the engineering of big arch dams. I mean, it's not overbuilt to the extent Hoover was, but it's certainly not a thin arch like it would be built with today's engineering. The mass of the dam is over nine million tons."

"Saul, what are you talking about—*wounding* the dam?" Malcolm asked.

"Not the dam itself, actually; I'm thinking about the abutments. Remember, that was the major problem with the Glen Canyon dam site: the Navajo sandstone. The stuff is highly porous, it's poorly cemented, and, if I remember correctly, it has a low modulus of elasticity: it's soft—not soft in the common sense, but not what geologists would call hard."

"Saul," Stan objected, "the canyon walls are massive, surprisingly homogeneous sandstone—porous, poorly cemented, and what you call soft or not. The explosive force needed to even *wound* the site, as you say, would be incredible." He plopped back down in his chair.

"For purposes of general discussion," Saul resumed, "you can broadly figure that it takes about two pounds of sophisticated high explosive to shatter one cubic yard of rock like the Navajo sandstone. Now, under the approach I was thinking about, the objective would be to so fracture an abutment that it would leak like a sieve. The structural integrity of the rock would be damaged to an extent that no amount of grouting and bolting could repair it. The reservoir would have to be drained and abandoned. How much explosive force to do that? Well, I haven't gotten down to those details yet, but it's at least clear that it would require hundreds of tons of conventional high explosive."

Malcolm concentrated on the fire. "So it would indeed take a small nuke."

Stan: "Well, I'm sure the Bureau of Reclamation people are not going to stand around watching someone deposit several semi loads of Tovex into a spillway tunnel."

Malcolm rotated out of his chair to poke the logs. "Let's back up a little here. This Glen Canyon thing is way out of what I've had in mind to occupy myself with when I finally get out of here. My plan all along has been to get involved in projects that our government would secretly like to do but can't—or won't. The Japs are only one example. There are all kinds of things going on around the world that I can happily busy myself with. But destroying a big dam—right here in the States—I don't know, Saul." The fire was going well, but Malcolm kept poking the logs. "On the other hand, I can't think of anything I'd like more than getting rid of that frigging dam. In the final analysis, that one effort might be worth more than everything else I could do . . . But doing it would end forever our days here at Stony Ridge," he added with a glance over at Stan.

"Look, I rushed out here because this is a one-time shot. Colonel Kovalevska will be leaving in two weeks, and that will be it. We really don't have two weeks to think about this and then set up some way for all of us to meet with her."

"*Damnit,* Saul, you know I hate to pass up an opportunity, especially a very unique opportunity. But frankly, I don't know that I want to have anything to do with some Soviet KGB type. What do you really know about this woman? What could you ever know? And, what the hell, if we really did decide to get rid of that dam, why couldn't we just build a bomb? With all the nuclear reactors around the world, and with everything that's been published on the subject, it seems that it could probably be done."

Saul shook his head determinedly. "There has, indeed, been much speculation lately about people getting their hands on fissionable material and building a nuclear device. Well, my friends, it's just not that easy. Outside of the major powers in the world, only China, India, and Israel, for sure, and probably Pakistan, and maybe North Korea and South Africa, have constructed nuclear bombs."

"Those Israelis having the bomb in such a volatile part of the world. How'd we ever permit that?" Malcolm sighed.

"Israel has had nuclear weapons since 1969 and they haven't used them, despite being surrounded by millions of people who only want them all dead," Saul answered, slightly defensively. "Then, now, and always, Israel will not permit the Third Temple to be destroyed. In fact, their nuclear arsenal is code-named the 'Temple Weapons.'"

"My point, exactly, about the danger of ethnicity combined with religion," Malcolm smirked.

"Well, perhaps ethnic/religious intensity is a good thing. Israel peremptorily and unilaterally took out the reactor at Osirak in 1981, and the inspections after the Gulf War proved they were correct about Iraq's intentions."

"What if Saddam had used those nerve-gas warheads we discovered after the Gulf war," Stan said.

"It would have only taken one, Stanley. The U.S. could never have controlled them. Israel was down to what in our military is called Defense Condition One: armed for immediate launch of their nuclear Jericho missiles and aircraft. The use of poison gas in Israel is, of course, a particularly sensitive issue."

"How much of a nuclear arsenal do they have?" Malcolm asked.

"Oh, no one can say for sure. The best published information about the reactor and the underground chemical reprocessing facility in the Negev Desert, based mostly on what Mordechai Vanunu told the *London Sunday Times* in 1986, is that they have probably produced, to date, about 1,000 kilograms of plutonium, and they have acquired an unknown amount of highly enriched uranium: some from their own resources in the Negev, some purchased, and some stolen."

"This Mordechai, whoever, you mentioned. He must have been a Jew. Why did he expose them?"

"A Moroccan Jew. He felt discriminated against while he was working at the Dimona weapons plant." Saul paused. "Discrimination is everywhere, Malcolm."

Malcolm shook his head. "How could they have done it—right under our noses? I've read that as early as the late '50s the U-2s gave us enough information to know that with the help of the French they were building a chemical reprocessing facility right under the big reactor out there in the Negev."

"Privately, Eisenhower thought it was a great idea," Saul answered. "But Kennedy still had the last good opportunity to stop the Israelis' bomb program, that's for sure. The astonishing thing is that nonproliferation was his highest priority."

"Kennedy got 80 percent of the jewish vote." Stan said.

"That's a little too cynical, even for you, Stan. Lyndon also had a chance to stop them, but he was all caught up with his Great Society, and then the war took over. After Johnson it was too late. Israel had the bomb and was in production. Every president since Kennedy has just carried on what has apparently been our enduring policy of using Israel's arsenal to, as it is said, 'still the atmosphere' in the Middle East."

"And Kennedy also had the last opportunity to stop the dam," Stan added. "Construction on the dam itself was barely started by the end of 1960."

"Kennedy was the quintessential Easterner," Malcolm said with a grunt. "He had no concept of, much less interest in Western values. In 1960 there was very little to the environmental movement—Eastern or Western."

They all stared into the fire, finally boiling the coffee in the pot swung over the flames. Malcolm: "Well, with my resources and your talent, you haven't convinced me that we couldn't just build a small bomb to take care of that dam—if we decide to do such a thing. Doesn't have to be highly sophisticated. We're not going to deliver it with an ICBM. What's all the damned hurry with this Ukrainian woman?"

"Technology and materials aside, it still takes a lot of equipment, facilities, and talented people to actually construct all of the components of a nuclear device. Look at all the stuff Saddam accumulated in his quest for the bomb, yet he really wasn't that close. Besides, you don't just build one of these things in a garage—even if you have all the materials, access to all the published information on the subject, the ability to read it, and the people to do the job. As for obtaining a U.S. weapon, forget it. Exactly zero prospect. It would be easier to drive off with a load of bullion from Fort Knox."

"Saul," Stan interrupted, "the Congress's Office of Technology Assessment recently published a report saying that it would *not* be that difficult for an informed group of people to construct a crude weapon, assuming they could get their hands on enough plutonium or enriched uranium 235 to create a critical mass."

Again Saul shook his head. "Setting aside the very unlikely possibility of acquiring enough reprocessed, weapons-grade plutonium or enriched uranium, Malcolm mentioned the availability of reactor-grade plutonium, given all the nuclear power plants scattered around the world. Well, that unreprocessed stuff is very highly radioactive, far more hazardous, ironically, than is weapons-grade plutonium. Just handling that material without all the protective equipment would be a death sentence; furthermore, it is very likely to detonate accidentally. It would take at least fifteen kilograms of civilian reactor-produced plutonium to construct a fractional kiloton device, probably less than a tenth of a kiloton, and the whole thing, with all the conventional high explosives required to try to create critical mass with the contaminated plutonium, would weigh more than the Hiroshima bomb did—a ton, at least. Actually, the biggest risk of someone building such a device is that it would scatter about 99 percent of that screaming-hot, reactor-grade plutonium over a wide area."

"That van parked in the World Trade Center carried about a ton," Stan answered. "The primitive bomb you described would have a yield a hundred times the ton of explosives that van carried."

"Hold it," Malcolm commanded. "I'm not going to sit here listening to Stan-the-lawyer cross-examine Saul about the details of nuclear physics. Stan, you and I should accept Saul's word on this."

"Yeah, you're right."

"Okay," Malcolm went on, "I will concede that the opportunity you think you have with this woman is unique. But I don't feel I want to risk everything with someone I could never know. Hell, it's taken me thirty years to get to know the both of you. And, Saul," Malcolm smiled, "the fact that you're even bringing this up at all is proof that I probably don't know you."

"Malcolm, why don't you at least talk to her?"

"Yes, why not?" Stan agreed, intrigued by Saul's wound-the-dam-only concept. He thought for a moment about the place they were in. The lodge had been built when practically all of the American West was still virgin, essentially unknown to the invading white man. He was certain the earliest discussions in the very chairs they were occupying had concerned schemes for the grossest exploitation of the new land and much of its natural life. The budding captains of industry in the new West had likely sat in this very spot planning the building of empire. *Now, here we are talking about taking some of it apart.*

"I guess I don't know you, either, Stanley," Malcolm replied. He turned back to Saul. "Damnit, why did you have to bring up Glen Canyon? If I think about it much I might just weaken." He paused a long moment. "What have you got in mind about meeting with this woman? No commitments; just tell me what you have in mind."

"A float trip in Grand Canyon: good security, we'd have her alone for several days so we all can have a close look at her, and she'd be able to see what we propose to do. If she even cares, at least she'll see that the detonation will occur in an unpopulated area confined in a deep canyon. The trip would look like a natural thing for a foreign visitor to do—not like hiding out in a hotel room with three guys."

"You have thought about this a little bit," Malcolm grinned.

"I have."

"There's something else I'm sure you've thought about," Stan said as he got up to ladle out the coffee. "The matter of a huge flood aside, what about radiation?"

"Of course I have thought about it; and it has largely influenced my thinking about the placement of the device. All that's needed to severely fracture the sandstone, to cause uncontrollable leakage around the dam, would be one or two kilotons, with the device set well back from the dam itself. Furthermore, my initial thought is to place the weapon under several hundred feet of water, near the bottom of the canyon. The uncontained component of the blast would be vectored straight up, so the fallout area would be minimal. The bulk of the radioactive material would be absorbed in the deep canyon or carried in solution by the water. It would flush down to Lake Mead: the insoluble material settling into the mud, and the soluble radionuclides dispersed to far below any danger level."

"What about Page and the Navajo Power Plant?" Stan probed with the next obvious question.

"Stanley, Page would just go away. With no reservoir, no marinas, and no hordes of power boaters, the town could not survive. And that big coal-fired power plant right next door would also have to close. It needs the reservoir to supply the huge amount of water it uses in its steam turbines and cooling towers."

Malcolm interrupted: "A marvelous side benefit. That goddamned power plant is destroying the air quality in the whole Grand Canyon area. Millions of people come from all over the world to see that national park and for much of the year it is obscured by smog. God only knows how much that monstrous plant is contributing to the greenhouse problem, even with the scrubbers they're putting in to cut the sulphur dioxide. As for Page, it was only built out there in the middle of nowhere as a government town to house and service all the workers who built the dam. For their town site the government stole Manson Mesa from the Navajos."

"Stanley, I'm sure Malcolm with his business view will correct me if I'm wrong, but it seems to me that the radiation issue just gets down to a cost/benefit thing. With the size weapon I'm talking about and with the blast contained as it is, no more than a couple of square miles would have long term contamination. Two miles out of about eighty thousand square miles in the reservoir area: freeing nearly 200 miles of river, countless side canyons, and hundreds of miles of shoreline versus perhaps a quarter mile of river where people would not be able to camp. The contaminated water and the soils it would carry with it would be dispersed down 240 miles of river, with nearly all of it ending up in the Lake Mead delta or diluted in the reservoir. The water would eventually be further dispersed clear on down to the Gulf. More than a couple of miles downstream you would not even be able to measure the radiation above the natural background level."

"Every benefit has a cost," Malcolm said as if to himself. "The only issue is whether the benefit sufficiently exceeds the cost, with the argument finally just getting down to differing views over what is sufficient. Look at all the atmospheric nuclear tests in the Nevada desert, less than a hundred miles from Las Vegas. Weren't there dozens of them, Saul, back in the late '40s and early '50s?"

"There were quite a number, all of them employing weapons many times the yield I'm talking about and detonated entirely within the atmosphere. Even with all that, the earth has managed to cleanse itself fairly well everywhere but at the immediate points of detonation." Saul looked intently at his two friends. "You know, that stuff is still classified."

"Yeah," Stan said with a touch of bitterness. "The government is still using the national security laws to cover up its mistakes—in some cases intentional conduct. I'm sure that with just the information you personally have, many of the people who suffered direct radiation injury at the time of the tests would be able to prove their claims against the government." Stan-the-lawyer had momentarily replaced Stan-the-friend.

"That's damned unfair. We all have constraints under which we work, and discussing that information just happens to be one of mine."

"*Life's* unfair, people," Malcolm interrupted. "Let's move on. Getting back to the meeting with this woman, when do you have in mind?"

"As soon as we can put it together. She has to go back to Washington with her team two weeks from today. We'll have to go next Sunday, at the latest."

"Impossible for me. I'll be halfway around the world to close on some property—the key element in my relocation. I've been working on the details for nearly two years. And besides, how could you set up a Colorado River trip on short notice? The rafting companies don't even schedule trips in the winter, do they?"

"Waddy," Saul answered. "I've asked him to look into it. In fact, he's supposed to be here today. He's out here on a selling trip before he has to go back to work at Grand Canyon."

"Oh, shit, Waddy," Malcolm groaned. "I mean, I like the fellow but we really haven't known him all that long."

"I'd be comfortable with him," Stan said. "During the preparation and then his trial out in Colorado I came to know him very well."

"That sure was good work on that case," Malcolm nodded.

"Lawyers *are* needed once in a while, Malcolm. That land and cattle baron made sure the local prosecutor pushed everything to the limit."

"But what bothers me is that Waddy also pushed those people out in Colorado to the limit. Would he be controllable with this Glen Canyon thing?"

Stan's slight pause said a lot. "Malcolm, you like Waddy. Besides, you saw his reaction when we started talking about Glen Canyon. I thought he was going to cry. I think he'd be a good addition—essential, actually, with his knowledge of the canyon area."

"Sure didn't take Saul long to convince you," Malcolm winked at his old friend.

"Saul's idea is at least worth a look. And remember, I was the one who twisted off those valve stems."

"You're right, I do like that little Indian. But liking him and trusting him with my very existence are two different things." They all stared into the fireplace, each needing the long silence.

"Damnit, Saul," Malcolm said painfully, "Why'd you have to bring up Glen Canyon? Up until this afternoon I thought I had my future plans firmly in mind. Damn you."

Saul leaped from his chair, resuming his place at the window. "There is another element we should factor into this. I've been the direct target of Israeli agents. I've been extensively investigated by our government because of my profile of being a Jew with a presumed pro-Israeli inclination: my parents' fate and because my children live in Israel."

"That Israeli agent thing has to be all forgotten," Stan objected.

"That was just one," Saul said without turning around. "There were a couple of other attempts."

"Haven't you still got whatever security clearance is required to work in nuclear weapons research?"

"Sure, but you don't understand. You can still be carefully watched," Saul answered wearily. He stared across the Valley at the distant Caymus Mountains.

"Saul, how can our government possibly question your loyalty?" Malcolm fulminated.

"Just like your questioning my motivation for this whole plan."

"I was wrong about that. After thirty-five years, I know you better than to question your loyalty."

"That's my point. Governments don't know people."

Malcolm persisted, "I mean, look at the years of dedicated service you've given; the brilliant contributions you've made—with probably a lot more that haven't been publicly recognized. And for the love of God, you received the Silver Star in 'Nam. I know you were wounded at least twice."

Saul waited patiently until Malcolm quit sputtering. "Malcolm, those things are forgotten quickly. Each new bunch of politicians taking over Washington only sees what's right in front of them: a Jew with an apparently strong reason to be very pro-Israel. It's simply an unavoidable situation I live with. If we do go ahead with this, I'll be the first place they'll look."

Another long silence. "Want to go back up to the house?" Stan suggested. "Maybe Waddy's here."

Malcolm got up. "Yeah, let's see if that horse will let me back aboard. Should have the place to ourselves by now."

Broadside was still occupying his place at the end of the corral and it had started to rain. After several attempts, the big stallion finally accepted the sodden equipage on his back; then with Malcolm and a marginally content Broadside well ahead, they rode back up the ridge. Entering the drive area, they were greeted by the sight of Waddy's unmistakable truck and an excited Benjamin running down the front steps. Hercule hobbled along closely beside the man whose age he matched in dog years.

"Sir, excuse me, but there is a person by the name of . . . *Waddy*, I believe he said. Just arrived. *That* is his . . . vehicle. I am very sorry, sir, but he did sound as if he were invited, and– –"

"That's okay," Malcolm responded, to Benjamin's obvious relief, "we were expecting him. Where is he?"

"I believe he is at the stables, sir."

"I told you to take the rest of the day off."

"Yes, sir. But this Waddy person arrived and I– –"

"Yes, of course. Very good of you to stay. I'm sorry. Now, go ahead for the rest of the day. See you tomorrow morning."

"Thank you, sir. Good day, gentlemen."

Stan marveled while he watched the old man walk slowly back toward the house. *Impossible to find such loyalty today.* As a young boy, Benjamin had been a stable groom for Malcolm's grandfather, he had remained through the tenure of Malcolm's father, and now, at the age of eighty-one, he ran the whole estate. Malcolm's family had been very good to Benjamin and his family, even putting all the children through private schools. The attention had been returned many times over.

They rode across the drive and toward the curving, tree-lined and rock-walled promenade to the stables, passing Waddy's truck. The fact of its being made nearly exclusively of steel was its only element of commonality with the other vehicles in the drive. An ancient Ford four-wheel-drive, rusted out in the usual places above the wheel wells and in the lower corners of the quarter panels, not a single part of its body remained unaffected by the countless miles it had lived in the backcountry of the desert Southwest. The truck and attached camper shell were painted in a collage of dappled tans, browns, and black, much like the new army vehicle paint jobs seen during Desert Storm but having been painted by Waddy's hand long before the army paid an obscene sum to a consultant to design a similar color scheme. Affixed to the truck was the usual collection of off-road hardware: spotlights, CB antenna, power take-off winch, lengths of heavy chain, and a sheepherder wagon jack. The rear bumper displayed a stylized Hopi Tribe logo, a no-longer-readable, hand-lettered phrase in English-transliterated Hopi, and a decal informing: "Insured by Smith and Wesson." Even Malcolm noticed how perilously close the truck was parked to his Silver Shadow.

So much for the GQ scene, Stan thought.

The stables, like all the buildings constructed under the direction and careful planning of Malcolm's grandfather, mirrored the great house in architectural style. Built around a large courtyard, the stalls and the second-story accommodations for the grooms and other staff formed a square enclosure. Over the entrance gate an intricate iron herald, delicately composed of a scene of horses, hunters, hounds, and foxes, proclaimed: *Mayacamas Mews.*

Waddy was closely examining one of the Stony Ridge broodmares.

"Hey! What are you doing with my horse?" Malcolm called out across the courtyard.

Waddy turned and loped across the cobbled square, his brilliant grin ablaze. "Holy shit, should I bow or somethin'? A trio of soggy squires returned from takin' the air. What you been doin' to that stallion, Malcolm? Looks real unhappy. What's the matter, big guy, tubby here too heavy? He ought to leave you alone and use a Clydesdale." Waddy laughed out loud as he stroked the big stallion's muzzle and dish-shaped face. The horse relaxed for the first time in the day.

"Go to hell, you little savage . . . Nice to see you, too, Waddy . . . Where've you been?" Malcolm, Stan, and Saul responded, respectively.

"Glad I was late. You didn't expect me to get on a horse dressed in that shit, did you? And those pissy little saddles. All they're good for is to make a woman's thighs nice and strong." Broadside was clearly enjoying Waddy's attention.

"You are particularly crude today," Malcolm rejoined immediately. "No wonder you and this horse get along so well, considering your commonality in testosterone level and, more than likely, genital equipment. And what do you mean *women?* I should think you would be confined to Belgian or Percheron mares—perhaps a rhinoceress. I can't imagine that any young woman could possibly accommodate– –"

"Oh, God, Malcolm. Enough, already," Saul pleaded.

Waddy's grin widened. "It's all right," he chirped. "Old Malcolm just misses his youth. Now he has to settle for ridin' around on one of those silly saddles, dressed up like a nineteenth-century fop."

"Young man," Malcolm fired back, "I rather prefer to ride without the distraction of having my center piece constantly caressed by—what do you call that thing—a pummel? Very appropriate. Of course, it gets mighty lonely out where you western types live, I imagine."

"Touché, old bulgy sire. Okay, truce. How are you guys? Tell ya' what, let's take care of these horses and then you can get outta that crap you're wearing. I'll just keep laughin' as long as you're in those rigs."

With the grooms gone, as directed, they led the horses to their stalls. Waddy insisted upon a complete wipe down and fresh hay and straw before they went up to the house.

Everything was familiar in Stan's old room overlooking the east garden. So comfortable. Since he'd started college at Berkeley, Stony Ridge had become his second home. In fact, he thought, it was his only real home now. He had no more family. Malcolm and Saul and their children—they were Stan's family.

He sat on the edge of the bed and looked out over the vineyards and groves that dropped away to the Napa Valley. How many mornings had he awakened to the sun streaming through the old stained glass-bordered windows? *I'll never be able to come back here.* He got up to look at his reflection in the oval cheval glass standing by the bureau. Malcolm's father had given him the tan and black riding boots; even the little bootjack resting on the floor. He wedged the heel of a boot between the outstretched legs of the little bronze fox and then stepped with his other foot on the animal's crouching rump to pull off the paw-clamped boot. *How many times have I done this?* He tilted the mirror in its frame. *Still pretty trim.* He got undressed, hung the riding clothes on the carved rack, and shoved the wooden trees into the tall boots. On his next visit everything would be cleaned, pressed, polished, and saddle soaped—just as it had always been done throughout the entirety of his adult life. He laid out a change of clothing on the bed and went into the shower.

Stan found Waddy in the kitchen, busily at work at the huge, maple-topped prep table which occupied the center of the room.

"Man, look at this place. Whoever set up this kitchen really knew what he was doin'. All the best equipment, in the right place, completely organized. I feel like I know exactly what's gonna be in every drawer, bin, and cupboard."

The big kitchen they were standing in was laid out to prepare a banquet for a sit-down party of forty. Now, other than the occasional dinner for a few of his fellow growers in the Valley and the annual bash hosted for the wine writers, there were only a couple of the big parties each year. Malcolm had become increasingly withdrawn in the past few years, despite the pleasure he drew from using the big house as it was intended. Stan now understood that his reclusiveness had coincided with what he'd been doing with his business empire.

"Well, go grab a jacket and apron and give me a hand, huh? You can start by breakin' down that hotel rack." Waddy pointed to the center section of a lamb carcass lying on the prep table.

By fortuitous coincidence, Stan knew about lamb racks, an exception to his generally feeble grasp of things culinary. They had been his long-term, almost-wife's favorite specialty; accordingly, he'd been pressed into learning the details of their preparation. He hacked out the chine bone with a cleaver, then went to work "frenching" each of the rib bones. He wondered how many apprentice chefs had suffered through the incredibly labor-intensive procedure as he finished one bone in five minutes. Seventeen remained.

"Hey, not bad. I thought a lawyer couldn't even line up the sides of a sandwich," Waddy clucked. "Better speed it up, though, we're not havin' that for breakfast." He grabbed the other rack and finished it while Stan completed his third bone.

"How'd you learn all this?" Stan watched Waddy meticulously clean and sharpen the boning knife before he put it away. Throughout their time together in Colorado, Waddy had never even mentioned this piece of his history.

"BIA-sponsored school and apprenticeship when I got out of high school. Spent my last year at the Four Graces in New York. All paid for by you *pahanas*—your guilt over the way you've treated the poor Indians."

"Ever been employed as a chef?"

"Couple'a years in New York, is all. Had to get out of that city. But there's not too much demand for French cookin' in the Arizona outback and I don't like workin' seventy-hour weeks, year 'round."

"Then why'd you go through all the school, apprenticeship, and work in fine restaurants? You must have known you couldn't stay away from Arizona."

"Now, Stan. What did I explain to you guys the last time we were at the club? Think about who I sell to. Last night I put on a spread for three of my best customers and their families down in Pebble Beach. By the time they finished the *zabaglione* I'd sold them about $10,000 worth of stuff."

"You *can't* have had that in mind when you went through all the chef training," Stan protested. Waddy just smiled and finished carving another perfect, seven-sided tournéed potato.

"So, what else are we having?" Stan said when he realized Waddy wasn't going to answer any more questions about that particular detail of his life.

"From his *mise en place* in the walk-in, I'd say Malcolm's chef planned to serve the lamb racks, some kind of couscous, sautéed baby veggies, and baked, candied squash. I found an apple cobbler. Good solid winter meal, but I can't stand couscous, so we're havin' *pommes cocottes.*

"That's what you call those little football-shaped potatoes you're whittling?"

"Boy, you're ignorant for an educated person. Here, try his glaze for the lamb. Tastes like Bordeaux mustard, balsamic vinegar, ancho peppers, roasted pecans and honey. Some spices I can't identify: might be tamarind and galangal."

Malcolm came into the kitchen, resplendent in a moss-green cashmere jacket emblazoned with a gold Stony Ridge pocket crest, white shirt, club tie, fawn slacks, and tasseled cordovan loafers. "Well, well, well. It seems that Anthony may only be 90 percent missed this evening. But do either of you clowns really know what you're doing?"

"Ah, the master of the manor," Waddy parried. "I suppose you're one of those highly critical gourmands. Poor Anthony."

"Where's Saul?" Stan interrupted, hoping to cut short another Malcolm/Waddy machismo exchange.

"Where he always is. Ensconced in the library with one of grandfather's old books."

"Wait 'til he smells these lamb racks. He'll come out," Waddy smiled.

They grouped for dinner at one end of the long table. High overhead, beneath the vaulted and timbered ceiling, rows of herald banners hung over the hall. Most of the west wall, from floor to ceiling, was an expanse of leaded, clear glass panes with numerous coats of arms displayed in stained glass panels. Stan remembered the grand summer dinners, with the great room awash in sunset light.

"You know, on many occasions John Muir sat at this very table," Malcolm said as he followed Stan's gaze up to the flags. "He was a great favorite of Grandfather's."

Stan stopped in mid bite. "Malcolm! You never mentioned that before. Here? Here at Stony Ridge? All these years and I didn't know?" Stan was more than a little hurt in addition to being surprised.

"Grandfather said he could identify and explain in detail the coats of arms on every one of the flags up there and in the window panels. Of course, he knew all the Scottish clan tartan setts mounted above the fireplace too. He hated the city but loved to come up here. He, Will Colby, Frederick Badè, Little Joe LeConte, and the rest of the early Sierra Club leaders would come here to discuss their environmental battle plans—particularly when they were fighting to save the Hetch Hetchy.

"When I was a little boy, I remember grandfather talking about those old days. He told us about one time—it was just after the earthquake and fire—Muir and Professor Badè were exhorting grandfather not to permit any of the old groves to be cut. The San Franciscans were desperate for lumber, you know, but practically everything had long since been reduced to stumpage. The small park near Santa Cruz and the grove below Mount Tam that the Kent family donated and then named for Muir—that's all that remained in 1906, besides what's here."

"John Muir walked through the grove above the old lodge?" Stan asked, his fork still hanging limply in his hand.

"I was told it was his favorite spot here. He always refused to stay in this house, preferring the old lodge. Louie Wanda and their girls would stay in the house, but Grandfather said Muir often slept back in the grove. He must have been nearly seventy then."

"Wouldn't you love to hear again what these old walls heard, Malcolm? I mean, to hear the discussions, the planning, the political maneuvering as those men tried to save the grand canyon of the Tuolumne River—the companion to the Merced River Valley?" Stan pushed his plate aside and stared out through the expanse of glass.

"Stanley, I didn't know you had such an interest in that particular piece of history," Saul said.

"Damn, Saul, that was the very first great environmental fight. It launched the battle that rages to this day: conservation-for-use versus conservation-for-preservation. And those two sides of the same coin fighting the rape, pillage, and burn."

"Isn't that what killed him?" Waddy asked. "Didn't he die shortly after final Senate approval for San Francisco's reservoir in Yosemite Park?"

"He lived just another year," Stan answered. "John Muir died on Christmas Eve, 1914—alone in a hospital in Los Angeles." They all gave Waddy a long look, surprised that an Arizona Hopi Indian would know details about a long-ago battle for the heart of the Yosemite.

"Hey, look people, don't be so surprised. What John Muir knew instinctively about the Creator being in every single piece of fur, feather, flesh, foliage and rock: that's what's at the heart of the Hopi Way."

The conversation stopped. Only the snaps and pops from the burning cedar logs broke the silence.

"Come to think of it," Waddy continued slowly, thinking out loud, "the last passenger pigeon died in 1914 too. September. She was named Martha. Toppled off her perch at the Cincinnati zoo. Twenty-seven years old. I remember John Muir wrote about that shortly before he died. When the *pahanas* came here, there were a couple billion of 'em. Killed 'em all. Pigeons. Just harmless pigeons. Sort of like all the Indians." Malcolm and his guests continued to eat in silence.

"So, why am I here?" Waddy asked. "And Saul didn't come all the way out here to go for a ride."

Saul and Stan looked over at Malcolm. He held their gaze for a moment, then nodded.

"Waddy," Saul said hesitantly, "do you remember the discussion we had at the club back last November?"

"My second trip out here? Let's see . . . Yeah, we talked about Glen Canyon."

"And you know about the work I've been doing with the new Tactical Arms Reduction Treaty—the warhead teardowns at the Pueblo Army Depot."

"Yeah?" Waddy abandoned his lamb chop and sat up straight. "We talked about nuclear weapons that day at the club too."

"Well, I may have stumbled upon an opportunity to address both of the subjects we discussed."

Waddy looked closely at Malcolm and Stan, then back at Saul. "The dam?" he said very quietly.

"Yes."

"Son of a *bitch*." Waddy again made the circuit of intense looks. "You're serious, aren't you?"

"We're just talking about it," Malcolm said. "Before Saul got here today, Stan and I had no idea about this opportunity he may have. We're just talking about it and we want your input."

"One of the weapons you're dismantling at Pueblo? How could you possibly get away with one, Saul?"

"No, it would be a Soviet device; arranged through my counterpart on the Commonwealth team."

"So *that's* why the river trip. You want to show her what you have in mind."

"That's part of it. The trip would provide a secure, intimate environment so that we could all talk it through."

"Why would some Russian want to give you a nuclear bomb?"

Saul outlined what had transpired during his tour at Pueblo, with Malcolm again restless during the painfully detailed recitation.

"A KGB officer—a woman at that. How could we possibly believe anything she said?"

Stan smiled to himself. Within a day of meeting him, he had come to know that Waddy distrusted anything governmental, the police in particular, and he was not closely allied with the feminist movement.

"Well, that's another reason for the river trip," Saul answered. "You know better than any of us what the river does to people—how everything just seems to get down to simple, honest basics. Somehow that river and the canyon strip away human bullshit."

"Very, very perceptive for a *pahana*, Saul. You sure you're all Jew and not part Indian?"

"Now wait a minute," Malcolm interrupted, seizing the opportunity to digress into a nice discussion of bloodlines. "Don't give me that *pahana* crap. You didn't get that wave in your hair from pure Hopi ethnicity. You're partially Anglo, aren't you?"

"*Very* partially. My grandfather was an Irish priest—sent out to convert the heathen. My grandmother managed to convert him, though. Sure am glad he was black Irish; I was spared the devil-blue eyes you poor bastards have. Not you, Saul, you should be thankful. Damn wavy hair, though." Waddy held up his hand when Saul passed the bottle of pinot noir. "Can't do it. Indian *and* Irish is a bad combo."

"And tell me," Malcolm persisted, "how in hell did you get a name like 'Wadsworth?' I've wanted to ask you that for a long time."

"Simple. My mother loved to read; especially the early American poets. She read probably every book in the bookmobile that came around the reservation."

"I'll bet you had some trouble over your name, growing up on the reservation." Malcolm couldn't have smiled any more broadly.

"You got that right, Malcolm. But most Hopi in my generation have Anglo names, in addition to our clan names."

Saul realized that Malcolm didn't seem too enthusiastic about the whole Glen Canyon idea. The conversation had headed off into Malcolm's favorite topic, doubtless to further degenerate into an uncontrollable, Japan-bashing episode. Saul lunged at the momentary lull to get the conversation back on track. "Waddy, were you able to get anything together for the river trip?"

"Yeah, I spent the whole afternoon the day I talked to you and most of the next morning. Got us two Avon sixteen-footers and most of the gear. I'll have it all together at Lee's Ferry a week from tomorrow. Also found an outfitter with a commercial trip who'll take the boats on down to Diamond Creek. Trouble is, who'll drive the other boat? Guess it'll have to be you, Malcolm. You'll need the whole boat for you and your stuff anyway."

"Waddy, I won't be there. We'll all get together after the trip."

"What the hell? I jumped through my ass to set this up on one day's notice. Got everything set for five people—even a wet suit that'll fit you. That was *really* a bitch."

"Waddy," Malcolm continued patiently, "I think it would be most effective for me to meet the woman here. I really think Stony Ridge would make a better impression than me standing on a river bank in a wet suit."

Waddy's grin reappeared. "Prob'ly right about that."

"Besides, I have a conflict for the next week or so."

"Conflict? Big guy, what could possibly be more important than this? Haven't you got *enough* money already?"

"It's not money. The culmination of about two years' work is going down, starting this coming Friday and into the next week, halfway around the world—the crucial part of my relocation I've been working on. It would take all day to explain it."

"Try."

"I just can't do it."

"*Can't* usually means *don't want*, Malcolm."

Stan could think of less than half a dozen people on the face of the earth who could get away with talking to Malcolm Renslaer as Waddy was able to. There was no question in his mind that Malcolm was fond of Waddy. "Let's just take one raft," he said. "That'll be adequate for four of us, won't it? Besides, that solves the driver problem for a second boat."

"And we can't have any strangers along," Saul appended.

"Yeah, I guess. But it'll be really tight what with all the extra crap we'll have to drag along to keep that woman happy."

"Here's what we'll do," Malcolm said quickly. "Of course I must talk to the woman, but it's probably best that you all soften her up some before I take my shot. When you finish the trip, go on up to the South Rim from Phantom Ranch on—what? Will Friday morning give you enough time to float from Lee's Ferry to Phantom?"

"Well, it'll be just enough time if we make four long days and have no problems with any of the rapids. I'd planned on five days."

"Okay. I'll arrange for you to be picked up in front of Bright Angel Lodge at—will three in the afternoon, Friday, work?"

"Just barely, Malcolm. If—and I say if—there're no problems on the trip, and if there're no problems with the mules, we can be on the South Rim by three. What's the rush, anyway? Saul said she doesn't have to be back to Pueblo until Sunday."

Saul shook his head. "We'll be coming out to California after the trip, and we don't know whether we'll have gotten anywhere with her. It may be entirely up to Malcolm. It could take some time."

"That's right," Malcolm went on. "You can fly out of Flagstaff and go right into Napa. We can meet here Friday night and whatever it takes Saturday. I'll have the lady back to Pueblo on Saturday or Sunday—whenever we're through. No commercial airlines or paper trails."

Stan was once again reminded that he was in the company of a man who could basically do whatever he wanted, anywhere in the world, at any time.

Waddy: "Malcolm, I was really lookin' forward to seein' you have a little white-knuckle experience through some white water. Do you some good, for a change, to be in a situation where you had no control."

"Look, you little heathen, I'm confident you'll manage to arrange another shot at me. Better luck next time."

"Oh, hell, your raft would be damn near awash. You'd never make it through Hance and Sockdolager." Waddy thought for a moment. "You know, I forgot about somethin' else. There'd be no way to get you out of the canyon—'cept maybe a Sikorsky. You sure as hell couldn't walk out. Riders on Canyon Company mules can't weigh over 200 pounds. Two hundred and one pounds and you don't climb into a saddle. Buck Johnson's allowed some people, up to maybe 225 pounds, on a couple of his big guys, but that's it. How'd I forget about that?" Waddy shook his head. "Prob'ly could rig a travois, though."

"See? The gods never intended for me to go down there," Malcolm grinned.

"So, we're all set then," Saul said.

"Well, not quite. I don't have a permit."

"Oh, shit," Malcolm groused, "it's the middle of the goddamned winter. What difference does it make? Just go."

"Park Service is real touchy about that, Malcolm. We'd get arrested. They'd send a chopper down to pick us up. The Russian lady would get discovered. We don't wanna do that."

"Just another example, folks, of why I'm getting the hell out of this country. Frigging bureaucrats. Every time you turn around you trip over one. Costs me millions every year." Malcolm had always tried to focus on *effective* environmentalism. He had little patience with the government's efforts that very often only served to harass the individual citizens—the big polluters and exploiters got away with murder.

"Waddy, what's the chance of getting a permit?" steady Saul asked.

"I can be back there by Tuesday, midday, if I get an early start in the mornin'. I got some chips I can call in. Shouldn't be a problem—I hope."

"And if you don't get a permit, I guess we can just bring the lady out here," Malcolm concluded. "But I really think the river trip is a good idea. Do your best to make it work, Waddy."

Throughout the conversation, Stan had again been distracted by more fundamental matters and the discussion about John Muir. "Look, I'm having a real problem with the whole idea. I mean, in the abstract it's a wonderful dream, to restore that river canyon, but damnit that huge reservoir is a reality we have to face. Releasing all that water is just unthinkable. Why don't we consider a more manageable enterprise? And hear me out," Stan said as Waddy shifted in his chair, mirrored by Saul.

"What about O'Shaughnessy Dam? The Hetch Hetchy Reservoir only holds about 375,000 acre feet, and it would probably all be contained in the Don Pedro Reservoir farther down the Tuolumne Canyon. No one here can deny that in significance, if not in size, that dam in the heart of the Yosemite is at least as monstrous as the one plugging up Glen Canyon. Furthermore—this is perhaps the most important point—the necessary damage could be done with high explosives. Even just wounding Glen Canyon would, indeed, require a small nuclear device. I mean, it's fun to talk about, but, well, I just have a real problem with the whole notion." Stan turned to Malcolm, who nodded.

Stan looked up again at the old herald banners. "Saul, I know you believe you could finesse an explosion to just damage an abutment, but you'll have to admit that there is a clear risk of breaching the structure. And there's another point. Powell Reservoir is used by millions of people every year. Right or wrong, it's there, and lots of people enjoy it, ignorant of what it once was. But the Hetch Hetchy Reservoir—the city of San Francisco won't let anyone in their water supply. It's an off-limits enclave right in the middle of America's finest national park. And remember, there has even been talk about tearing it down."

"Hey, I forgot about that," Malcolm said. "Wasn't it an Interior secretary, no less, who suggested that it be removed?"

"Yeah, wasn't it Jim Watt?" Waddy asked.

"No way it was Jim Watt," Stan laughed.

"Let me tell you this, folks," Saul said. "The Bureau of Reclamation actually has a section, at its headquarters in Denver, that is figuring out ways to take dams *apart.*"

"You're kidding," Waddy said. "I don't believe it."

"No, it's true."

"Typical bureaucracy," Malcolm grumped. "First and foremost is self-preservation. Those guys are smart enough to read the writing on the wall about all those dams, so they're cranking up for another generation of activity."

"So, should we wait for them to get around to Glen Canyon Dam? Is that what you're saying?" Waddy asked with little enthusiasm.

"I'm sure that none of their flagship dams are under consideration," Saul replied. "The study group was probably only set up when their boss at Interior made his comment about O'Shaughnessy Dam. Look, people, the issue right now is whether we are going to take advantage of a very unique opportunity. There's just no time for a long debate. I have to be back in Pueblo in the morning. The Commonwealth team is going on a tour after we finish up this Friday, and as soon as I get back I'll have to convince her that she should go on our trip. As the team leader she'll be expected to go with the others. Anyway, right here—today—we have to decide if we're going to at least make an effort to talk to her. We can argue about all the details later." Saul paused. "We don't have to actually use the weapon. We'll have plenty of time to think everything through."

"Set it up, Saul," Malcolm decided. "Stan and I can talk some more before I leave. I can put my trip off for a day."

"Yeah, you people wrestle with your consciences," Waddy said. "In the meanwhile I'll get the river trip put together. Saul's right; might as well have a nice run through the canyon. Hell, we don't even know if she'll actually be able to get us one of those bombs. How do we know this isn't just a whole bunch of bullshit?"

"Indeed, there are a lot of issues," Saul admitted. "Even if Colonel Kovalevska could obtain a weapon, there is the matter of it being the proper yield; and we would have to be provided with the arming code. Those systems are guarded at least as carefully as the weapons themselves. Secondly, we—I—would have to design and build a whole new arming and triggering mechanism, or at least the circuitry. It is very complex."

Waddy got up to stretch. "You guys've been through all this twice today. The moon'll be out full soon, so I'd like to go for the ride I missed."

"Go ahead. There're a couple of western saddles and the rest in the back of the tack room. Help yourself, but don't try Broadside. He may tolerate a western saddle, but not the bridle. He'd pitch your ass clear down to Napa."

"I won't need a bridle; just a halter will do. Has he ever been ridden bareback?"

"Yeah, about ten years ago. But watch it. He's a handful."

"There isn't a horse alive I can't ride, Malcolm," Waddy said with finality. Everyone believed what he said.

2

Pueblo Army Depot, February 10

"Damnit, Waddy, this is Thursday. Tonight's my last chance to talk to her. Tomorrow's the ceremony and the party and all the rest of the hoopla, and then she'll be off on the tour. It's probably already too late."

"What the fuck you want me to do? You don't understand what a hassle the river permit system is. Look, I've got one more chance. I'll let you know by four this afternoon. Besides, can't you just go on out to Malcolm's with her, like he said?"

"I think she'd balk for sure at going clear out to California. Once we've done the canyon trip, I can tell her about California."

"I'll call you at four, one way or the other."

Kateryna was sitting with her team members when Saul walked into the dreary mess hall, its baleful odor of rancid grease now familiar. They were all there, including the Russian embassy man who had come out to Colorado when the teams had first arrived.

Oh, shit, that's right. The damned PARTY *she told me about. I'm screwed. She'll never get away from them for the rest of the evening.*

"We all hope you can join us at the reception after the ceremony tomorrow, Dr. Kalinik," Kateryna said, speaking in Ukrainian, as Saul walked past. Her comment made it clear that he was not invited to the private party the Russians were having. It was also clear that the party was well under way.

"Of course, I wouldn't miss it." With that, he got his food and sat down across the room. *Well, tomorrow's the last chance. We've got to use that river permit Waddy finally found.*

As if to punctuate affirmatively the end of the tour at the Pueblo Army Depot, southern Colorado displayed a bright blue winter day. Friday morning found a pellucid, cloudless sky, a slight chinook breeze, and a relatively balmy temperature of 50 degrees rapidly melting the previous evening's thin blanket of glistening new snow. The dramatic prominence of the Spanish Peaks to the southwest, Pike's Peak to the northwest, and the intervening Sangre de Cristo Range were etched in white against the sea of cobalt. A faint smell of spring teased the air.

All the work had been finished two days before; now everyone was dressed up in anticipation of the celebration scheduled at noon. Military, Energy and State Department officials, and the Colorado governor would attend. Big semis from the television networks were setting up, satellite dishes sprouted like mushrooms, and a few of the celebrity news people appeared, strutting and posing among their network logo-emblazoned RVs and trailed around by their handlers, and makeup and wardrobe people.

Saul finally found Kateryna sitting alone in one of the director's chairs the TV people had planted on the winter-dormant lawn in front of the depot headquarters building, next to the static displays of retired Pershing and Honest John missiles. *Last chance,* he thought as he waved to her. Soon they would be rounded up to be briefed for the afternoon's formalities. Both of them, as leaders of the respective teams, were scheduled to make abbreviated comments, to be followed, of course, by the non-abbreviated speeches and posturings of the politicians and elevated bureaucrats. The Russian ambassador and a deputy Secretary of State would be the most long-winded. Of all the people scheduled to speak, only Saul and Kateryna knew any of the details of what had been going on at the depot for the past three months. But that was not important. What played right for international television was important.

"Do you have your lines memorized?" Saul grinned as he sat down.

"Of course. And you?"

"Well, the little I have to say doesn't take much organization . . . Kateryna, it's all set. Everything's arranged."

She hesitated, looking down. "Saul, it is not possible now; you have taken too long . . . I must go on the tour—it is expected. The Russian ambassador made that very clear last evening."

Saul reacted as he had never reacted to anything in his life. He jumped to his feet. "Goddamnit to hell! This isn't some little game, woman! Do you want to save your daughter's life or not?"

Kateryna glanced quickly around, then looked up at him. "Sit down."

He remained standing, glaring at her.

"I said . . . please . . . sit down."

Saul sat down, but he was not through. "You have avoided meeting with me since we talked a week and a half ago. In the meanwhile, I have done everything I could. I even went out to California to put together the meeting you demanded. *Demanded!* Well, it's done. This is your last chance."

"And it was yours, as well," she snapped.

"Okay, forget it!" He bolted from his chair and started to walk away. In a moment he felt a firm hand on his arm and Kateryna was standing beside him.

"Saul . . . Saul, please. Meet me back here in one hour. This must not end in angry outbursts."

He turned to face her—glared at her—for several moments. "All right.

One hour."

Kateryna was sitting in the same chair when Saul walked back across the parade ground. He slumped down in the chair beside her.

"I'm sorry. I had no right to say such a thing about Sofiia."

"No, you were absolutely right. We both must stay focused on what is important. And I *do* understand that you must have had some difficulties putting this together. Now, tell me about your arrangements."

"You can avoid the tour?"

"I am going to do what I must do. Now, please, explain what you have organized. We do not have a great deal of time."

He hurriedly outlined the planned trip, surprising himself by just launching into the details as though there would be no objection at all. Kateryna did not interrupt while Saul ran through the itinerary. Perhaps his outburst and the cooling-off time had been fortuitous. He did not mention the detour to California. He could deal with that after the river trip was agreed to, or begun, or sometime later—anytime—but later.

"The Grand Canyon? For anyone from my country, a visit to your Grand Canyon would probably be the first choice; we know there is nothing else like it in the world. But for our present needs, is it necessary? We have so little time for a trip of that sort, and what of unexpected contingencies? I cannot be late in returning to Pueblo. And one other thing . . ."

"Yes?" Saul said, failing entirely to conceal his anxiety.

"I cannot possibly leave here until Sunday morning. I simply must spend tomorrow with the Russian officials; of course, I will need ample opportunity to explain why I must have some time to myself and so on. Will we then have enough time?"

"The time remaining will be adequate. Don't you agree that the river trip will give us the privacy we need?"

"You are right. We would be completely secure. And such a trip would be perfectly understandable if I am ever confronted with having to explain."

She has to be taking some risk in going with us. That means she must really believe she can deliver.

"Saul, is there some other, more particular reason why you chose the Grand Canyon? Does it have something to do with what you are asking me to provide to you?"

"I would prefer not to get into that." *Damn! It's like she can read my mind.* "At least, not right now. I think both of us need to keep things undefined until an agreement is reached, don't you?"

"Very well. Now, what do you suggest about travel arrangements? Will I still need to go to Denver?"

"Why can't we just take my car? After all, we've certainly been seen together a lot here already—if not in the past week and a half." Saul couldn't resist his last comment.

"No, it is very necessary that we take the precautions I have mentioned. I know you are not so naïve as to believe that we are not being watched—by both our governments."

"I suppose you're right . . . Uh . . . there's something I have to ask you." *Maybe I should just let it go.* "Where have you been going on your Saturday afternoons the past few weeks? Is it something we should all know about?"

She smiled softly. "It is nothing, Saul. I have been going to a church in Pueblo—to help me cope. Do you understand? Did you think I had a lover?"

A Soviet secret police officer—in church? "Oh, yes, of course. I . . . I'm sorry." *That was well done, you idiot.*

"Saul, there is one thing that is very important. Please hear me clearly. I must meet with the people who will be in a position to make the whole arrangement work. Is that understood?"

"That has been one of the problems: why everything has taken until this last minute. I can tell you now that it's all arranged." *I can't tell her about California. Plenty of time once we get on the river. But she'll know as soon as she meets only Stan and Waddy. How will she react? Maybe I should level with her now . . . No, better wait.* "Now, about the travel details. Instead of going to Denver, it will be far more convenient for you to go to Albuquerque. That's south, in New Mexico, but it's over twice as far as Denver. Can you make your arrangements to go there?"

"Yes, go on."

"I'll leave my car in the airport parking garage: on the east side of the lowest level in the short term parking area. There's always space there. The long term parking lot is small and it might be filled. The Albuquerque airport is much smaller than Stapleton, but I'm assuming that no one is going to be paying any attention to me after we're through here. You know—security people." Kateryna was smiling slightly.

"So, you pick up my car and then drive west on highway 40 almost to Flagstaff—that's in the next state, Arizona. Major interstate highway all the way. Just east of Flagstaff turn onto U.S. Highway 89, going north. Stay on 89 to Page—it's the only town out there. We'll meet at the West Court Inn. It's right on the main road through Page, on the west end, just as you come into town. There's a reservation for Catherine Jensen. Albuquerque to Page is about 450 miles . . . uh, 700 kilometers, little more. Should make the drive in about nine hours, with stops. Watch your speed, especially on the reservation. I'll have to get a flight from Albuquerque to Flagstaff and then rent a car or just get one in Albuquerque. I don't know yet; I haven't thought it all through. Remember, it's over twice as far from here to Albuquerque as it is to Denver. Take that into consideration when you change your arrangements. And you'll need some personal items for the river trip. Here's a list."

By the time Saul finished, Kateryna had lost the struggle to contain her laughter. "Saul, I think you missed your true calling. You should have had a career in the discreet service to your country."

Saul joined in Kateryna's fit of laughter. It was such a relief.

"Saul, we'll have to talk later." They were being approached by a group of people from both of their teams, and it was evident that someone had already broken out the refreshments.

The political/media circus started right on schedule, followed by the party in the post officers club. Saul had managed to stumble through his prepared speech, but Kateryna had been magnificent, immediately delighting the New York and Washington press and TV people and fortified by the fact that, for the first time in the past three months, she had dressed to the nines for the occasion—a natural for the talk-show circuit, she had politely declined each invitation to the beaming pleasure of the Russian ambassador. Surrounded by the politicians and the polished and poised television interviewers, Kateryna had been as smooth as old ivory.

Good God, Saul thought, *that woman could make me believe anything she wanted to. What have I gotten all of us into? What if she's just setting us up?* Saul worried over that for a while and then started worrying about something else. *What if she's forced to spend the rest of her time here doing the media thing? It could easily happen. Those State Department people had to have seen what a public relations gold mine she is. Might even wind up with the President on the south lawn of the White House.*

Later on in the evening, Kateryna caught Saul's eye and gave him a nod and a smile. Somehow she'd managed to break away from the surrounding admirers to change her travel arrangements. Even through the glow of the fine vodka he'd been forced to drink, it suddenly hit Saul that what had started out as casual, wishful thinking was now on the way to becoming reality. He was terrified.

3

National Center for Atmospheric Research, February 11

Paul Heartwood stared at the latest printout for the eastern North Pacific model. Data from thousands of space, atmospheric, marine, and ground observation points all around the world had been fed into the new Cray 4 computer recently installed in the basement of the Mesa Laboratory. The latest collection of $10 million wizardry from Cray Computer Company was needed to fit the millions of pieces of information into the thousands of highly-paid-nerd-generated equations that comprised the atmospheric simulation program. The whole effort was intended to model the weather pattern for a large area of the Pacific Ocean.

"No doubt about it now. She's a big one, Willie."

"Definitely a lot bigger than the '82–83 ENSO."

"Look at that spread of anomalies. They extend clear up the coast of Mexico to Baja." The chart showed that the sea surface temperatures as far north as Cabo San Lucas were already more than 8° Fahrenheit above normal.

"And look at the wind data, Dr. Heartwood; there is a clear trend of diminished trade winds, and the equatorial westerlies now go almost across the Pacific belt, well east of the dateline. The midlatitude westerlies, above the Pacific High, have also shot up."

Paul Heartwood examined the higher elevation graphics. "The southern branch of the jet stream has migrated almost down to the tip of Baja."

"What are we getting from the correlative programs?"

"Not integrated into the Pacific model yet. Even with the new Cray, we can't grid the whole El Niño/Southern Oscillation area—not clear across the Indian and Pacific Oceans. Impossible amount of data and computer time would be needed. As it is, our grid intersections are too widely spaced to really crunch what's happening with the data we've got. The upper Mississippi flood numbers and the stuff from the winter storms in western Europe are still being incorporated. Lots to crank in. When it's done, we'll see if the forecast model comes close to duplicating what actually happened last year."

"The record precipitation in North America and later in Europe should give us a good extreme-case scenario," the young man said.

"Yes, that and the equally anomalous lows we got in the eastern U.S. in January and February and the highs down in Australia. Lots of good data to check out the model extremes. Here, look at this."

The next printout showed the isobaric pattern of the Pacific High atmospheric pressure zone, generally centered between Hawaii and the West Coast of North America.

"It's moving south, Dr. Heartwood. How far do you think it will dip?"

"The forecast model should tell us as soon as we get all the data in. But just from what we can see here, the Sierras and the Rockies are going to get a lot of late snow with the high pressure ridge moving out of the way. The storms'll just keep boiling across from Asia, through the Gulf of Alaska. You going skiing, Willie?"

"Spring break, Dr. Heartwood. I can't wait."

GRAND CANYON

Fern Glen Canyon, 1960 (*Tad Nichols*).

1

NORTHERN ARIZONA, FEBRUARY 14

From the point where the Colorado River enters the canyon lands near the Colorado-Utah border, and for the length of its course through the rugged and remote region of southern Utah and northern Arizona, few places are found where the virgin river permitted a crossing by man, beast, or machine. A few miles downstream from Glen Canyon Dam on the Colorado River, and situated at about the midpoint of the river's travels through the canyon country, is the historic crossing known from the earliest visits by white men in the last century as Lee's Ferry. Major John Doyle Lee, adopted spiritual son of Brigham Young, husband to nineteen women (many at the same time), a principal organizer of the Mormon slaughter of 120 of the 137 men, women, and children of the non-Mormon, Fancher Party near Cedar City, Utah in 1857 (children under seven, deemed too young to remember, were spared), and a common ancestor of a great many people now living in Utah and Arizona, including the Department of Interior Secretary who gave the final approval for the filling of Powell Reservoir, in 1871 opened a toll ferry at the remote river crossing—penance along with Mormon excommunication for his role in the massacre that was not properly avenged until his death before a firing squad in 1877.

For tens of hundreds of years before 1871, the native inhabitants of the region made use of this break in the river's continual sequence of canyons, coming to hunt, fish, and trade at the broad, gentle reach of water where a tributary of the river entered from the north. Approaches from each canyon rim, although not easy, were well traveled. The Pais—the Havasupai and the Hualapai—who lived west and south of the river gorge knew the place, and even their enemies, the Yavapai, occasionally visited. The Paiutes from north of the river, the Utes from the northeast, and the Navajos and Hopis to the southeast came here. The Hisatsinom, the Cohonina, and the Sinagua were here centuries before, and before them the people of the Desert Archaic culture made use of the place. The most recently arrived people are slowly beginning to unravel the long history of this remote area of the Southwest, but they have much to learn. The members of the native cultures who still live in the region know a great deal, but they choose to say little.

This point on the river also marks a sharp transition in its character. Before the construction of the great dam, to the north and east was gentle

Glen Canyon, where the river flowed for over 150 nearly rapids-free miles. The canyon floor was often wide, spotted with meadows, marshes, and lush riparian growth and abundant with wildlife. To the south and west of Lee's Ferry, the river and its canyon change character dramatically: the tranquil gradient of two feet in each mile of river through Glen Canyon abruptly increases to eight feet per mile as the river enters Marble Canyon, to drop in a stair-step fashion with stretches of gentle water interlarded with boulder-strewn rapids. The peacefulness of Glen Canyon as it existed before the erection of the huge concrete structure at its lower end is gone with the river's descent through progressively older rock formations. And as the river cuts more deeply into the ancient rock, the surrounding land rises higher and the upper canyon walls spread farther apart, striking downward in slopes of crumbling shales and in cliffs of the harder sandstones and limestones. The canyon rims rise ever higher above the narrow, sheer inner gorge; the plunging rapids increase in frequency and ferocity. This is the entryway to John Wesley Powell's Marble Canyon and the introduction to the vast area that has come to be known as the Grand Canyon.

Saul found Kateryna in the lobby, engrossed in the local newspaper. "Happy Valentine's Day." As he said it, he realized he didn't know if Ukrainians paid any attention to St. Valentine.

"Good morning, Saul. And the same to you," she smiled.

"Did you have a nice trip from Albuquerque?"

"You should know. Your following me was so clumsy." She was still smiling. "You had better stick to your physics."

"Yes, well . . . driving from New Mexico was more convenient than flying and then renting a car at this end, so– –"

"We have to start trusting each other at some point, Saul. Can we start now?"

"When I left my car in the airport lot, I did wait to see if you picked it up okay . . . I guess I did follow you . . . Kateryna, I'm sorry."

"Come on. Let's go meet your friends."

Stan noticed the woman as soon as she entered the dining room. What he saw was the antithesis of what he'd expected. He'd been looking for someone on the order of a shaved bear or an NFL lineman: anthropoidal—no neck, minimal forehead, eyebrows grown together. *Typical Saul. Not a word about what she looked like.* Stan spilled his coffee as he set the cup down half off the saucer.

She was about five ten and had a slightly olive complexion. Coal-black hair was pulled tightly back from a thin face with a prominent, delicate nose; but despite her sharp features, Stan thought she looked somewhat Asian: slightly elevated cheekbones, full lips, and almond-shaped eyes. It was the woman's eyes Stan concentrated on as she came closer. They were large, luminous, and darkly multicolored. She was very slim, like a model, he easily observed in the slacks and thin sweater she wore; and as she followed Saul through the crowded dining room she seemed not to walk but to float.

"Stan, may I introduce Kateryna Kovalevska."

Stan had to struggle to glance back at Saul. *This woman has the most beautiful eyes I've ever seen.*

"I guess the first order of business is a nice tourist visit to the local attraction, Glen Canyon Dam," Saul hesitantly volunteered as they sat down.

Stan smiled his agreement then continued his observation of the obviously foreign woman sitting across from him. Somehow, she seemed familiar. He could not understand how someone so unfamiliar could feel so familiar.

"Yes, I would like to see it," Kateryna replied, her British accented English reinforcing Stan's alien image of her. She refocused on Stan. "But I am also looking forward to meeting Mr. Renslaer and your Waddy who Saul has told me so much about. He is a North American native, true?"

"Yes, but Waddy is truly unique," Stan said. He now found it hard, for some reason, to meet her steady gaze.

Saul squirmed noticeably at the mention of Malcolm. *Can't put this off any longer.* "Kateryna, I'm afraid there has had to be one small change in plans." He immediately received the penetrating look she could muster in an instant. "Malcolm cannot make the river trip, but we've arranged for all of us to meet with him right after we leave the river on Friday. Besides," Saul continued quickly, "Waddy decided there simply would not be room for five of us in the raft with all of the equipment and supplies we'll need." He glanced anxiously at Stan. "Another raft would have required a hired boatman, a complication we don't need; lastly, there would be a problem getting all of us out of the canyon. You'll understand when you meet Malcolm. You knew I was having trouble arranging all of this, so . . . well, he just couldn't make it."

Throughout his explanation, Kateryna's face remained stiff. It then relaxed into her familiar smile.

Thank God.

"Is Malcolm an important part of your enterprise?"

"Uh . . . well, yes, he's the most important part."

"You are assuring me that before I must return to Pueblo I will have the opportunity to meet with him?"

"Oh, yes," Saul and Stan responded in unison.

"I didn't know how to bring this up when I found out that Malcolm couldn't be with us here. I didn't want to mislead you, I– –"

"It's all right, Saul. I understand. Now, don't we have a tight schedule ahead of us?"

A mile north of Page the broad expanse of Manson Mesa was cleaved by the Colorado River gorge as though cut with a giant knife. Two man-made structures, one of delicate, arching, steel lattice and the other of massive, alabaster concrete, emerged abruptly, spanning the 1,100-foot-wide, 650-foot-deep cleft in the Navajo sandstone. They drove slowly across the bridge, staring silently at the curving gray-white expanse of man-made stone that filled the width and most of the height of the canyon.

Saul pulled into the parking lot for the Carl Hayden Visitor Center, perched on the west rim precipice of what remained of Glen Canyon. "Okay, let's be tourists. There's a great view down into the canyon from inside."

Before entering the building, Kateryna paused to examine a large piece of sandstone displayed just outside the entrance. Embedded cleanly in the rock were several footprints of a three-toed, bipedal dinosaur, *dilophosaurus.* The evidence of the one-ton carnivore's few seconds of travel across the ancient mud that became the Kayenta sandstone had been frozen in time for 170 million years. What Kateryna did not see or understand was that the fragment of rock before her was but a tiny fraction of the ancient clues to that Mesozoic world now lost beneath the waters of Powell Reservoir, along with thousands of the more recent treasures left by the Fremont Culture and by the Hisatsinom and their predecessors. Below Glen Canyon, in Marble and Grand Canyons, the remains of the Triassic, Jurassic, and Cretaceous periods had been erased—to the top of the lower canyons' 240-million-year-old rims, the beginning of the age of the dinosaurs.

"It is startling," Kateryna said while she stared down through the outwardly sloping windows at the massive intrusion between the walls of orange sandstone. Far below, the river swirled emerald green from the power plant at the toe of the dam. The dam's engineers had made no effort to blend their creation by color, shape, or texture into the natural scene. The dam was purely utilitarian. Functional. Stark.

"Saul, what is the reservoir capacity?"

"Twenty-seven million acre feet when it's filled to the spillway gates."

"I don't see spillways."

"Tunnels," Saul answered with a point into the canyon. "You can see the outlet of the one in the east wall down there. Tunnels had to be bored through both walls to divert the river around the dam construction area. The spillways are now incorporated into the lower ends of the diversion tunnels. You can see the approach to the spillway inlet cut into the east wall, up there at the surface of the reservoir."

"Tunnel spillways? This looks like sandstone."

"It is."

Kateryna slowly shook her head. She continued to stare at the more than nine million tons of concrete wedged between the opposing walls of the river canyon.

View southwest toward the City of Page, May, 1983. With the reservoir nearly full, water has entered the inlet channels to the spillways. The visitor center is on the west rim, across the highway from the switching yard. The protrusions on the upstream face of the dam are the guides for the gates used to close the penstock inlets and the river outlet works (*Bureau of Reclamation*).

"Come on, let's go down to the crest of the dam," Saul said. "They have an elevator that goes clear down through the dam to the power plant."

"Was that man a military hero?" Kateryna asked as she paused before a bronze bust of Carl Hayden.

"No, but he was certainly a political hero to the people who wanted to build a huge city a couple of hundred miles south of here." Saul could not hope to explain the complicated political intrigue, over decades, that had resulted in the building of the great dam they had just seen.

Carl Trumbull Hayden had been a senior senator from Arizona and chairman of the powerful Senate Appropriations Committee during the crucial dam-decision period in the early 1950s. He had represented the citizens of Arizona for fifty-seven consecutive years in Congress, from 1912 until 1969, but unlike the great majority of his weathercock brethren in the Congress, Senator Hayden was driven by a mission both singular and focused: the delivery of Arizona's share of water allocated in the 1922 Colorado River

Compact. To achieve this goal, he masterminded and bulldogged through Congress the authorization to construct a 9.25-million-ton concrete arch dam in the lower end of Glen Canyon, designed to impound 10,000,000 million gallons of water. Then, to transport the water to the confluence of the Salt and Gila Rivers and beyond, he obtained for Arizona the construction of a $3 billion, 336-mile-long conduit across the Sonoran Desert to Phoenix and Tucson and the construction of power transmission lines from the new dam to provide the electrical power to keep the desert metropolis, where temperatures reach 120°F, cool as well as green. Senator Hayden's career-crowning achievement stands as the acme of monumental pork barrel projects, never before, since, or ever, to be surpassed.

In the House of Representatives at the time, Wayne Norviel Aspinall represented the western district of Colorado. Congressman Aspinall had also been a politician his entire adult life, starting out on the town council of Palisade, Colorado in 1926. As chairman of the House Interior and Insular Affairs Committee, he was in a position to roadblock virtually any major construction legislation before it could go to the House floor for debate. Congressman Aspinall used his position with consummate skill in horse trading for his beloved western water projects. He sponsored the Colorado River Storage Project Act, legislation anticipating the building of nearly forty reclamation structures, including seven large dams: Flaming Gorge near the Utah-Wyoming border on the Green River; Echo Park at the confluence of the Green and the Yampa Rivers in northwest Colorado; Split Mountain on the Green River downstream of Echo Park; Navajo in northwest New Mexico at the confluence of the Piedra, Los Pinos, and San Juan Rivers; and the Curecante Unit, consisting of three impoundments on the Gunnison River in western Colorado. Largely through the efforts of Congressman Aspinall, all of the dams were built—with two exceptions: the Echo Park and Split Mountain dams would have been located in Dinosaur National Park. A coalition of environmental groups, led by the Sierra Club—which still painfully remembered its failed effort, led by John Muir forty years before, to halt the construction of a dam in Yosemite's Hetch Hetchy Valley—successfully stopped the construction in Dinosaur National Park. But the success was at a terrible cost. The coalition agreed not to oppose the erection of Senator Hayden's substitute dam on an obscure reach of the Colorado River above Lee's Ferry. No one among the environmental groups' decision makers had ever been there. Glen Canyon was traded away because it was a place no one knew.

The third member of the powerful trio responsible for the building of the six dams and reservoirs was Floyd Elgin Dominy. Mr. Dominy's rise through the ranks of the Bureau of Reclamation had been nothing less than astonishing. He had joined the Bureau in 1946 as a land settlement specialist. By 1953 he was chief of the irrigation division, Assistant Commissioner in 1957, Associate Commissioner in 1958, and Commissioner of Reclamation in 1959, a post he held for ten more years: all accomplished by a non-engineer in an organization composed dominantly of engineers. But, far better than being an engineer when it came to getting things done in Washington, Floyd Dominy was a skilled politician. And above everything else he loved to build dams. He'd started out in 1934 authorizing and helping to build stock ponds for ranchers when he was agricultural agent for Campbell County, Wyoming. As the actual or the effective Commissioner of Reclamation during the Bureau's great dam-building era, Floyd Dominy, with his powerful friends in the House and Senate, made sure the Bureau got to build dams.

A fourth element was involved, closely allied with Senator Hayden: a relative handful of Tucson and Phoenix landowners and existing or would-be corporate farming giants who would benefit hugely from the construction of the dams. The profligate mining of the precious groundwater from beneath the Salt River Valley surrounding Phoenix had created a problem for the people who wanted unlimited growth for the man-made, fountain- and golf course-filled, ephemeral oasis that is Phoenix. Nobody considered that perhaps this phoenix would best serve the people who would be asked to pay for the transport of water across several hundred miles of desert by simply settling back down into the ashes from which it rose. The Hohokam Indians had abandoned the valley near the confluence of the Salt and Gila Rivers centuries before, realizing that there was not enough water to support even their small, stable population.

To solve the self-generated problem, the latter-day inhabitants of the parched desert valley decided that Colorado River water would have to be impounded—again, because the millions of acre feet behind Hoover Dam were not enough. But Phoenix was over 150 miles by the shortest, crow-flying route from the river, well down its course to the Gulf of California, and Tucson was another hundred crow miles deeper into the Sonoran desert. These distances were not a problem, determined the powerful old men in Phoenix, Tucson, and Washington. It would only require the further expenditure of billions more of the taxpayers' dollars to pump, tunnel, channel, and invert-siphon the water through fierce desert mountains and across furnace-like valleys from the river to Phoenix and on to Tucson: the Central Arizona Project. A succinct description of the area this water diversion system would have to traverse was set forth by the Bureau of Reclamation:

> "Below the canyons, the Colorado flows through wide, sloping desert plains bordered by low mountain ranges—the hottest, driest region in the United States. Temperatures run as high as 125 degrees Fahrenheit. The sun shines almost every day of the year and, except for the devastating thunderstorms now and then, there is very little rain. Bone-dry and shimmering in the heat, this is an American Sahara." *Hoover Dam*, U. S. Department of the Interior Bureau of Reclamation, U.S.G.P.O. 1985-585-725, at p. 9.

By the time the system is completely finished and fully operational, water at an initial rate of 3,000 cubic feet per second (1.5 million acre feet annually) will be lifted nearly 2,900 feet in elevation by fourteen pumping plants, powered principally by electricity from Glen Canyon and the giant coal-fired power plant that stands next to Powell Reservoir on the Navajo Reservation. The water will flow through three tunnels, eight inverted siphons, thirty-nine check stations, on-stream reservoirs, open canals and pipelines for a total distance of 336 miles. And hugely more water than is needed to slake the thirst and cotton-growing demands of the expanding Phoenix and Tucson will have to be impounded and transported.

It happens that water vaporizes only reluctantly before an assault of heat energy. A single British thermal unit is required to elevate one pound of water 1°F, but 1,000 BTUs are needed to evaporate that pound of water. Desert animals and plants have learned, through millions of years of evolution, to protect their precious body fluids from the merciless heat of the desert, but the desert of southwest North America possesses a limitless quantity of BTUs. Standing or placidly flowing water has no chance. It disappears into

Inspection trip to Powell Reservoir, November 8, 1964. From left to right: Edwin Davis, Sen. Hayden's assistant, standing in front of Secretary of Interior, Stewart Udall; Commissioner Dominy; Senator Hayden; Congressman Hosmer, California; Congressman Johnson, California; Congressman Aspinall (*Bureau of Reclamation*).

Senator Hayden and other dignitaries enjoying more of the November 8, 1984 inspection junket (*Bureau of Reclamation*).

Congressman Aspinall is present for the topping out of one of his six Colorado Basin reservoirs, June 23, 1980 (*Bureau of Reclamation, Vern Jetley*).

the boundless, harsh blue sky without the formation of the tiniest cloud. That was not a problem, it was decided by the few men. Just build more dams, impound more water, flood more canyon, and divert more water through the conduits. And the entire system has very nearly been completed, operated by an entity named the Central Arizona Water Conservation District.

Stan noticed Kateryna carefully observing the security guard sitting at a desk at the entrance to the elevator that descended to the top of the dam. The unarmed rent-a-cop was engrossed in a *Guns and Ammo* magazine and did not pay the least attention to anyone entering the elevator. Kateryna was shaking her head slightly as the doors closed.

Wouldn't dare arm that guy, Stan thought. *Probably dreams about being able to blow somebody away.*

They walked down a long tunnel, emerging on the crest of the dam to be further herded along in a tour group taking the next elevator that would descend into the dam's bowels. Looking over the parapet wall, down the 75°, curving face of concrete, the visitors paused to take in the view 578 feet above the river where water was being released from the power turbines. In the other direction, the reservoir spread out of sight around domes, buttes, and cliffs protruding above its surface. According to the gauge on the upstream face, the water level was fifteen feet below the 3,700-foot elevation of the reservoir's designed high-water line—the "conservation pool"—and the tour guide proudly predicted that with this year's expected runoff the reservoir would fill, "really improving the recreation experience on Lake Powell." Kateryna gave Saul and Stan a prolonged, searching look as they followed the group into the elevator building. Before they entered the lobby, Stan saw Kateryna take another long look at the empty guard kiosk on the dam crest roadway.

Over a minute was required to descend the hundreds of feet through the mass of concrete. They exited into a narrow corridor extending transversely within the dam, then turned at a right angle into another corridor running 200 feet out to the downstream face. At the tunnel corner the tour guide explained that the group was separated by 100 feet of concrete from the water near the bottom of the reservoir, where, he further explained, the pressure was 40,000 pounds on each square foot. He also pointed out a locked gate leading to a labyrinth of tunnels and vertical stairwell shafts throughout the dam, all diagrammed in a display mounted on the gate. The tunnels gave access for inspection of the structure and provided a means of releasing water leaking through the sandstone into and around the edges of the dam itself. The sound of the water rushing through the maze of galleries echoed in the tile-lined hallway. It was not a place for someone who suffered from claustrophobia.

At the end of the tunnel, the group was suddenly confronted with the incredible mass of concrete soaring above them and curving out to meet both canyon walls; then after crossing a short causeway, they entered a cavernous, three-story room that extended nearly 600 feet across the bottom of the canyon. Stan was struck by the fact that the great room with its row of eight huge whirring machines was vacant. Not a worker could be seen to attend to the needs of the power turbines, all purring in muted unison like so many contented felines. Responding to Stan's inquiry, the guide explained that the system was almost fully automated: astoundingly, at any given time only a handful of operators were on duty throughout the dam and generator complex. He quickly added that in the case of an emergency, although highly unlikely, a force of technicians could come from Page in a matter of minutes.

Before leaving the visitor gallery, Stan watched a digital counter that was continuously presenting the cumulative sum of money collected for the electrical energy generated since the dam had been built. *There's the cash register.* He thought of the electricity required to pump millions of acre feet of water over hundreds of miles to Phoenix, Palm Springs, and Los Angeles, so that cotton and blue grass could be grown in the desert and tens of thousands of swimming pools could be filled. He thought of the water fountain at a big development east of Phoenix, where the highest man-made geyser in the world, requiring pumps rated at 5,400 horsepower, sent water to a 630-foot apex in the desert air. The fountain was created by the same company that had brought London Bridge to Lake Havasu.

Everyone trooped out of the generator gallery to the transformer deck. They stood at the railing, staring down into the clear green waters flooding into the tailrace pool beneath them. Having released its gravity driven potential energy to the electrical generators, the suddenly freed water seemed to mill about in the revolving pool before slowly relenting to the gentle pull of the earth in what remained of Glen Canyon.

Kateryna was concentrating on a tourist exhibit that displayed a long steel rod, two inches in diameter and threaded on one end. Saul pointed up at the wall of the canyon. Embedded in the sandstone by the hundreds, from near river level and extending in a random pattern to the precipice, were square steel plates held in place by rock bolts drilled into the cliff face. The seventy-five-foot-long bolts were giant versions of a device known to generations of rock climbers, but in this case they were intended to hold the rock itself rather than the weight of a suspended climber.

While staring up at the mechanically stabilized sandstone wall rising 700 feet above them, Saul thought of the geology report he had read about the construction of the dam.

> "The Glen Canyon dam site is in the Jurassic Navajo sandstone . . . There are no faults in the immediate vicinity of the dam site. The area is characterized by relatively few joints, of two distinct types: (1) Steeply dipping subparallel joints restricted principally to a single set trending NE-

Originally built as 125,000 kilowatt units, each of the generators has been upgraded to 168,000 kw at 150 rpm, giving the power plant a total output of 1.344 gigawatts. The full output is seldom utilized because to do so would release water well above the targeted maximum flow down the Colorado of 20,000 cfs (*Bureau of Reclamation, V. Jetley*).

SW diagonally across the axis of the dam, and (2) stress-relief joints roughly paralleling the canyon walls . . . .

* * *

"Thin shale seams were encountered at elevations 3115 and 3065 at the base of the right abutment keyway. The seam at elevation 3115 varied from one-eighth of an inch thick to about 4 inches thick and had a water flow of 2 to 3 gallons per minute . . . The seam at elevation 3065 varied from a thin shale parting in the sandstone to a shale layer 1 to 2 inches thick and had a waterflow of 75 gallons per minute . . . .

* * *

"Although the Navajo sandstone is remarkably uniform and yields remarkably smooth excavation surfaces, it had two principal characteristics which contributed to design problems. The stress-relief jointing parallel to the canyon walls showed a tendency to open slightly with time and slab or peel off onionskin fashion. The second defect is that the rock had a fairly large percentage of 'set' or unrecovered strain occurring during the first loading of the sandstone. . . .

* * *

"Stress-relief jointing, along with undercutting by water discharging from the right diversion tunnel, caused a large rock slab, estimated at 18,000 cubic yards, to fall into the outlet portal of the tunnel . . . .

* * *

"Excavations in the power plant area near the right canyon wall and in the machine shop area near the left canyon wall were troubled with slabbing along stress-relief joints. . . .

* * *

"Zones of less well-cemented sandstone encountered in the keyway excavations, although surrounded by normally-cemented sandstone, required considerable local resloping to meet existing design concepts. A program of extensive rock bolting and drainage immediately downstream of the dam was accomplished to securely anchor large slabs of rock which were the result of jointing. . . .

* * *

"Porosity of the Navajo sandstone ranges between 20 and 25 percent, so the bank storage or waterholding potential is considerable. The reservoir started filling in 1963; and since that time a program has been underway to determine the volume of water in bank storage . . . A slight movement along an existing joint was observed on the right side of the reservoir several miles upstream of the dam. It is assumed that such slight readjustments are occurring elsewhere in the reservoir area as the reservoir level reaches successively higher levels. This movement is a normal reaction and represents readjustment along existing joints resulting from the increased waterload of Lake Powell. Future movements will be recognized, as in the case of the other large reservoirs, only as slight shocks on seismographic instruments.

* * *

"Because of vertical and near-vertical joints encountered in the upper parts of the abutments, adits paralleling the abutments were constructed in the dam between elevations 3157.5 and 3630 . . . One near-vertical joint, called the A-joint, was observed in the right abutment above elevation 3120 and required special grouting . . . .

* * *

"A joint opened up between the rock-contact line at the right abutment, block 26. This break in contact between the concrete and the rock extended about 30 feet down the upstream and downstream faces of the dam. Since the upper grout lift in the dam is ungrouted, no arch action was transmitted to the abutment. It was necessary to grout this joint to prevent water from leaking around the abutment.

* * *

"In view of the stress-relief joints that have developed, or may develop, in the abutment rock downstream of the dam, particularly in the right abutment, and the increase in the rock stresses that will result from the arch thrust, the Board is of the opinion that extensive anchorage and drainage should be provided to ensure the stability of these rock masses. The more critical areas of the abutment appear to be those below about elevation 3450 in the right abutment [the area of the location of the right spillway] . . . Of special importance is the rock mass lying riverward of relief joint "A" where, in the right abutment in the lower part of the keyway, the intrados is riverward of this joint." Technical Record of Design and Construction, *Glen Canyon Dam and Powerplant*, U.S. Bureau of Reclamation, Denver, Colorado, 1970, at pp. 13-34.

Kateryna was looking at Saul for an explanation. "Stress relief jointing in the canyon walls. Like in all sandstone canyons, the rock near the river-eroded wall becomes unloaded and wants to exfoliate: what created all the beautiful arches you see—used to be able to see—in this formation through Glen Canyon."

"How far back into the walls does the jointing occur?"

"I don't know. I do know that when the diversion tunnels were bored they found them quite a ways back. This was an ideal site from the point of view of getting the greatest amount of storage for the size of the impoundment structure, but the rock is certainly not ideal. Of the several sites considered in the lower end of Glen Canyon, this one appeared to have the fewest problems, so the Bureau dutifully did its job despite the geological difficulties that arose during construction. What you see is the dental work needed to stabilize this surface rock. Still leaks, though."

Kateryna pointed out the small torrents of water running down channels near the juncture of the dam and the sandstone wall, matching seeps and runs down the face of the wall itself. On the other side of the chasm they took in a similar scene of hundreds of plates and bolts and the seeping and flowing water.

"I have seen a number of similar structures in Russia, China, and in

South America, but I've never seen an arch dam abutment leak this badly; you could hear the water rushing through the dam when we stopped back in there at the dam gallery display. It makes me a little nervous, standing down here, even though I know this amount of leakage cannot threaten the dam structure."

"I know what you mean," Saul said. "We're told there is no problem. All dams leak to some extent, like you said, but this sure is a dramatic demonstration of the enormous pressure from all that water above us pushing through the sandstone."

"But the spillways are another matter. Our engineers would never design tunnel spillways through such low-modulus sandstone."

"There was no choice here. The primary function of this dam is power generation, and at this site the power plant could only be located at the toe of the dam. If it were being built today, and if cost were no object, I suppose it would be built with a ramp spillway over the power plant, like they're doing in China now. How do you happen to know about dam spillways?"

"Oh, just one of the many things we are required to know," she answered with a quick glance. "Where are the spillway tunnels in relation to where we are now?"

"I'm not sure, but I believe they're about at the same level we are here, maybe a little lower."

"How far back in the canyon wall?"

"Over 200 feet, I think."

"Have they ever been used?"

"Yes. The Bureau had a problem with the spillways back in 1983. Unexpected rain and snow runoff hit the reservoir when it was nearly full. Other than a short run in 1980 when the reservoir filled, that was the first time the tunnels had to be used, and they suffered extensive cavitation damage. We're told the problem has been fixed, though. Too bad. See that big steel door?" Saul was pointing at the closed entrance of a truck-sized portal into the wall of the canyon, directly opposite the row of twelve single-phase, 13,800-volt to 345,000-volt transformers that extended nearly the width of the canyon in front of the powerhouse. "There's an adit behind that door that leads clear back to the spillway; another one like it is on the other side. They were used to haul in the equipment and materials to repair the damage."

"Are you saying that the construction adits were left in place? They were not plugged after the spillways were repaired?" Kateryna stopped to stare at Saul even though the docent was trying to herd the mob of tourists back toward the dam and the waiting elevator.

"They have little concrete plugs with man-doors right at the spillway tunnels. Otherwise there's an open, fifteen- or twenty-foot-diameter passage back to the spillway behind that door."

On the drive from the visitor center, back across the bridge and along the edge of the canyon to the road down to Lee's Ferry, the three were silent.

Saul and Stan wanted Kateryna to concentrate on what she had just seen.

"In Ukraine we have two great rivers. The Dnieper flows through the center of my country and south to the Black Sea; and the Don, lying near our eastern border, also runs into the Black Sea. Our Dnieper has many dams from Kyyiv downstream; in fact, it is now just a series of reservoirs throughout most of its course.Other than at the river estuary across from Odessa, the only free-running reach is that entering the reservoir near Chornobyl, but now we cannot . . ." Kateryna stared down into Marble Canyon as they drove over the old Navajo Bridge, adjacent to a nearly completed spandrel arch structure that was a near-duplicate of the one built in 1929. Stan and Saul waited and then glanced over at her. She continued, distracted. "None of the dams on the Dnieper is as great as the one we visited. They are all necessary to generate the power for our industry. Is not this one needed for such things?"

Saul looked over at Stan, who spoke first. "*Need* is one of the things we should talk about in the next few days, Kateryna. Let me just say that I imagine your country's requirements for electric power are different than ours

The right spillway construction access adit, August 31, 1983. The tunnel was bored into the west wall of the canyon to the spillway from the end of the deck in front of the power plant. Note the size of the tunnel in comparison to the front-end loader. Rock bolts anchor the highly stressed sandstone abutment. The temporary walkway was needed for access to the spillway portal (*Bureau of Reclamation, Tom Fridmann*).

because we waste so much here."

They pulled into the nearly deserted parking area adjacent to a wide launching ramp that sloped down to the river's edge. "Such extensive facilities in so remote a place," Kateryna said as she looked around at the U. S. Park Service's effort to provide all the conveniences that most Americans now take for granted, no matter where in the outback they go.

Saul followed her gaze around the area. "If this were a day in June the ramp and parking lot would be jammed with busses, big trucks for all the gear, and lots of rafts, including big motor-powered pontoon boats. There'd be outfitters and boatmen running around everywhere and scores of tourists. Mountains of gear and provisions."

"Must all the river trips start here?"

"Yes. Since the dam was built it's the only place with road access. Lee's Ferry is a madhouse from spring through the fall, for both private and commercial rafting."

"What do you mean *commercial*?"

Oh, no. Not this time. I do not want to get into another big discussion with a communist about capitalism. "Well, rafting companies taking paying customers down the river."

"But is this not one of your national parks? Is not commercialism

A slow day at Lee's Ferry, 1984. The commercial boat men and women are waiting for their customers to arrive by bus from Flagstaff (*Bureau of Reclamation*).

forbidden in your parks?"

Here we go again. "Commercialism *is* permitted in our national parks, however, it's rigidly controlled. Our government decided long ago that private companies could do a better job than the bureaucracies in operating the necessary tourist services." *This is going to get complicated.*

"So the citizens must pay to use their parks. What, for example, would someone have to pay to take the trip we are going on?"

"Uh, well, let's see. I think eight hundred to a thousand dollars, not counting the mule ride out of the canyon. That would be another couple hundred."

"Could people just take their own boat on the river?"

"Sure, but private parties have to wait six or seven years to get a permit."

"So, as a practical matter if someone wants to take a river trip he must pay a commercial service."

"No, that's not right. There are many private trips on the river; it's just that there is a long lead time for them during high season. The United States Park Service allows only a rigidly controlled number of boat parties on the river in a given season, primarily because of the limited camping sites and to try to ensure that everyone will have a reasonably uncrowded experience on the river. The camping situation is getting worse because of the steady erosion of the river's beaches."

"Over two hundred dollars per day seems like it would be out of the reach of most of your citizens."

"Yes . . . Yes, it is. But to take a private trip, there is the matter of having a very expensive boat and all the necessary gear. And as you are about to find out, it takes a great deal of skill to pilot a boat down this river. You can get killed if you don't know what you're doing. Without the commercial companies, even with the matter of cost aside, much fewer people would be able to make the trip. And organizing these trips is also a big production, as you will soon see. Actually, the commercial trips are no more expensive than practically all the other specialized guide services for different outdoor activities: sailing, pack trips in the mountains, photo safaris, and so on. If you want expensive, take a look at what outfitters charge for a big game hunt, or what it costs to go on a peak climb in Asia or South America."

Kateryna considered what Saul had said for a moment. "And by permitting mostly commercial companies, with presumably qualified operators, your authorities have fewer problems with people getting in trouble on the river."

"Now you're getting the picture," Saul frowned.

"Saul, I'm sorry. I know it upsets you for me to question such things, but I am only trying to understand details of how your system functions. We in the East are now being encouraged to follow your example, are we not?"

Three gear-loaded inflated boats sat on the ramp next to the river's edge: two a bright blue and one navy gray. Stan examined the modern hypalon creations with their custom-fitted aluminum and plastic storage boxes and efficient rowing frames. He remembered their own provisioning for the trip thirty-six years before: a trip that had started over 150 miles upstream at the foot of Narrow Canyon and had run the length of Glen, Marble, and Grand Canyons to the Hualapai Indian Reservation at Diamond Creek. Their boat had been a World War II surplus U.S. Army assault raft, with all of the gear and provisions completely disorganized in six army duffel bags. Stan smiled when he recalled Saul's failed effort to waterproof the bags with layers of rubber cement. Everything had been wet for a month.

"Ready to go, tourists?" They turned around to find Waddy standing behind them.

Kateryna was confronted with an individual unlike anyone she had ever seen. Standing closely in front of her and looking directly up into her eyes was a stocky, powerfully built man about thirty-five years old, with a torso the shape of a beer keg. On his head was a large-brimmed hat of the American West variety: old, torn, heavily stained, and displaying a band made of some type of reptile skin with a white-tipped, barred feather thrust between the beaded skin and the hat felt. Around his neck was a chain of small, bright blue stones set in ornately shaped pieces of silver. Also around his neck, a pair of sun glasses hung from a woven and beaded thong. The rest of his clothing consisted of a pair of short nylon pants, more a loin cloth than pants, and a pair of Japanese-style rubber sandals. Bangs of blue-black hair protruded beneath the hat to the man's eyebrows; on the sides, the hair hung in waves nearly to his shoulders. In back, from what Kateryna could see, it appeared to be tied in a sort of bun. His eyes, remotely Oriental in shape, were nearly the color of his hair and contrasted starkly with the most brilliant grin of large, even, white teeth Kateryna had ever seen. The black and white were set in a large flat face with high cheekbones and decorated with a prominent nose, the protrusion of which was surpassed, perhaps, only by ones she had seen in the bazaars of Istanbul. Dominating all beyond the scant clothing was a skin the color of old mahogany and seemingly as smooth as polished stone. Kateryna was suddenly aware of a large, callused hand thrust toward her.

"Hi, I'm Waddy. I'll be your boat coolie for the next four days." Saul and Stan winced in unison.

"I'm very glad to meet you, Waddy. Saul has told me a great deal about you."

"Well, old Saul here, and Stan too, haven't ever seen me in my natural element. This is my country, pretty lady, and I'll be very happy to show it off for you." Saul and Stan again cringed, less obviously, at the sudden familiarity, but Kateryna displayed nothing but apparently sincere pleasure.

"Our turn'll be comin' up pretty soon. Boat's loaded; the ranger's checked us out and cleared us for launch. Better smear on that crap you white folks need to keep from gettin' your hides burned off. It may be February, but that sun'll still burn. Did you bring all the stuff and clothes on the list?"

"Yes, Waddy, I have brought everything, as instructed."

He turned to Saul and Stan. "I know you guys've done a lot of boating, but hear me out since you haven't been down the canyon in February. We really won't get a whole lot more sun once we get on the river 'cause we'll be goin' into Marble Canyon. Everybody put on the wet suit pants now. When we get outta the sun you'll want to put on the tops. It'll get real cold, real fast when that water hits you with no sun. And make sure you tie some kind of chin strap onto your hats. See mine here?" Waddy grabbed at the finely braided and bead-decorated loop hanging loosely from his hat. "We can get sudden gusts of wind in this canyon, and you'll need both hands to hang onto the boat goin' through the rapids. You're really gonna need those hats. Everybody got tennis shoes? Good. Easy on the boat, don't matter if they get wet—which they will be all the time—and good for walkin' on the rocks. Won't stop a snake, though." Waddy grinned at Kateryna.

The people in the other party were getting ready to shove off, making a last-minute check of their gear. They were going all the way to Diamond Creek, 226 miles down the river, so unless it happened to be available at Phantom Ranch, they would have no chance to replace a forgotten article for the next two and one-half weeks. With a strong push off the ramp, the two boats drifted out of the eddy and were soon caught in the current. Everyone waved as they slowly retreated down the wide channel of clear green, gently waving water.

The last boat remaining on the ramp was a sleek gray sixteen-footer with a yellow stripe girdling the perimeter of the outer inflated tube. Set atop the outside and thwart tubes was an aluminum-tube frame holding a seat with a strong back support, heavy oar locks with two long sweeps, with a big aluminum box hung under the front. A plastic chest occupied the space under the seat, with two smaller boxes hung under the sides of the frame, completing the square. Spare oars were lashed to the raft's sides. A large pile of neoprene bags and miscellaneous items occupied the rear of the boat, all covered and lashed down with a heavy rubber net. Small metal boxes were tied to the top of the frame, two empty five-gallon plastic buckets hung down into the boat, and a large mesh bag with aluminum beverage cans was suspended in the water to complete the equipage.

"Where do you want us to sit?" Kateryna asked.

"Just pick a spot on the outside tube or the forward thwart, like you saw the other people do. Hang on to the strapping around the outside of the boat or grab the bow line. The wettest ride is in the front, the wildest in back. I want to watch you for a while before I let you sit in the hot seat in back, though." Waddy then went through all the safety instructions, including what to do if anyone went overboard.

". . . so remember, if you go into the water, keep your feet in front of you. You'll move right along, goin' a little faster than the raft, like you were sittin' in a lawn chair, with your life vest keepin' your head above water. Use your arms to slow down. Remember, keep those vests tight. If they're loose, the vest will float just fine but your head'll be wedged down inside—not floatin'. No problem gettin' back aboard. You'll be amazed at the motivation you'll have. Even if the boat flips, we'll all just float along together 'til we hit some quiet water where we can swim ashore and turn it back over. Don't get caught under the boat, though. Remember, the people in front sit mostly on the thwart tube goin' through a rapid. Move fast if I yell 'high side.' Keep the bilges bailed with those buckets. Okay, everybody got it? No problem. Now let's get your stuff stowed in these bags."

"When will we leave?" Kateryna asked.

"We'll give the other party enough time so's we won't be pushin' 'em. There's a big commercial charter ahead of us too. Left this mornin'. Unusual that the big commercial trips go in the winter. Here comes the Smoky to check us out."

The ranger walked over with her clipboard, gave the raft and its contents one last check, then nodded with a smile. "You're in good hands, folks, Waddy is one of the best on the river. Have fun."

"Hey! Let's go boating," Waddy shouted. With that, the three passengers jumped aboard as Waddy waded out, pushing the raft ahead of him. The river current quickly began to carry them down the canyon.

"Waddy, what is all the water in the reservoir used for?" Kateryna asked while everyone got settled.

"I really don't know all the politics about the water. I do know that a whole bunch of it evaporates while it just sits up there."

"I can explain a little bit about that, Kateryna," Stan said, seizing the opportunity to talk to the strange, attractive woman. "The place we left from, Lee's Ferry, is the water accounting division point for the whole river, separating the Upper Colorado River Basin from the Lower Basin, with all mileage measured up and down river from that point. The states in the Lower Basin are supposed to share the river equally with the headwater states, with some of the water passed down to Mexico under a treaty. Glen Canyon Dam is up there largely because of a water accounting error made back around World War I."

"But the dam wasn't built—completed—until, what did the man say, 1963?"

"Kateryna, I'm sure you are very familiar with bureaucratic decision making."

"Of course, it has been my life, Stanley," she smiled.

"After years of negotiation, the seven Basin states entered into a compact in 1922, spelling out how the river would be divided up. Then it took many more years for the legislatures of the seven states to ratify the agreement. One state, Arizona, where we are right now, held out until 1944 because it believed California would get nearly all of the Lower Basin water until Arizona developed the means to use its share. Arizona was afraid California would not give back the allocation once it started to use it because California had a lot more people in the Congress. There was a big court fight and Arizona finally prevailed in the U.S. Supreme Court. Anyway, when the engineers, hydrologists, and negotiators were originally trying to figure out how to divide up the water in this river, it happened that they took flow records from a twenty-four-year period of time that was wetter—a lot wetter—than the true average. Then, many years later, when it became clear that the agreed upon flow was actually more, on a ten-year running average, than the river could deliver, the river in the Upper Basin was considered to have a *deficit* flow."

"How could such a fundamental error be made in such a very simple calculation?"

"The usual: carelessness/ignorance/stupidity/arrogance."

"So just change the flow numbers to reflect reality."

"Most of the country in the Southwest looks much like what you saw driving out here. Anything having to do with water involves big-time politics. That water accounting error, incorporated as it is in a document like an interstate compact, is engraved in bureaucratic stone as unyielding as the Vishnu shist and Zoroaster granite underlying the whole of this canyon country."

"Are you saying that big reservoir was created so the Upper Basin could store water in order to augment supposed deficit flows downstream that don't really exist? I mean, don't exist because of how the deficit is defined?"

"That was one of the reasons. The biggest reason." Stan was at a loss to try to explain to a lifelong communist the details of Western political wrangling and deceit: at once the worst, and in a perverted sense the best, example of what made the American system function. "The responsible agency, the Bureau of Reclamation, knew long before Glen Canyon Dam was authorized by Congress that the Upper Basin could not produce, on average, the basic 7.5 million acre feet it was obliged to deliver to the Lower Basin under the compact. Actually, it has to deliver 8.25 million acre feet because of the treaty with Mexico, but it gets credit for the small inflow from the Paria River you saw when we left Lee's Ferry." Stan paused again. *I'll never make her understand. I barely understand.* "You see, Glen Canyon Dam, and the other big dams farther up the river and its tributaries, could never be justified on the basis of return on investment from sale of agricultural water. Only by generating electricity for sale all over the west could the cost/benefit analyses come even close. In fact, about 90 percent of the cost of the dams must be repaid from electrical power sales. A big part of the water goes to a relative handful of large landowners whose land would have been worthless without the water."

"Your citizens must pay all that money to keep a handful of capitalists rich?"

"Yes . . . that's it." *She picked up on that in a hurry.* "But the consumers *are* getting a commodity for their money."

"Nevertheless the citizens are having to pay for theirs, while the capitalists are getting theirs essentially free."

"The traditionalist elders of my tribe would like you, Kateryna," Waddy said.

Waddy and this lady are going to get along just fine, Stan thought. "So, it is critical that the reservoir fills in order to guarantee the year-to-year power head for generating electricity. If the Bureau had admitted that the water actually was not there year after year to fill the reservoir, it could never have justified building the dam. The Bureau simply had to be able to promote the dam as a surefire, electricity-producing cash register."

"You're telling me then, that a handful of unelected powerful people make decisions for the whole rest of the country but largely for the exclusive benefit of the elite; just like the Soviet Politburo made decisions for all of us. I don't see any fundamental difference between your system and ours."

What do I say to that? "I guess you can sort of look at it that way."

"The water accounting error you spoke of. In my country, even in the Soviet Union, an absurd error such as you describe would have been simply corrected, bureaucracy or not."

"The Lower Basin states, particularly California, would never have agreed."

"But it was a *mistake*. They should not be permitted to withhold agreement."

"California never would give up such a windfall."

"Perhaps our Soviet system wasn't so bad after all." Kateryna shook her head, watching the sandstones and limestones of the 250-million-year-old Toroweap formation slide by.

Waddy had been pulling harder and harder on his oars, more than was necessary to overcome the head wind coming up the canyon. "Just because some stupid *pahanas* had their heads up their butts and then another bunch of them insisted on takin' advantage of the mistake and then a small bunch of bureaucrats and their land baron friends lied to the people, we lost that beautiful canyon. I can't get it out of my head. That tranquil Eden—isolated, silent, and alone without an advocate—was doomed forty years before the dam was even built because of *pahana* stupidity, greed, and arrogance."

Kateryna looked at the intense young man straining against the wind waves slapping the raft's bow. She instantly realized there was far more to him than the apparent backwoods ruffian. "But what of flood control, Stanley? I imagine huge floods have flowed down through these canyon lands. There is no soil to absorb water."

"Certainly. I must agree that a palpably proper reason for damming Glen Canyon would have been to create another flood control structure for the Lower Basin. During the seventeen years, 1963 to 1980, when it was initially filling, the Glen Canyon reservoir functioned as a flood control structure. It took that long to fill because, indeed, the river produced much less water than it was supposed to and most of the water had to be passed through to meet downstream needs. Anyway, the river was under complete control, with any flood flows swallowed wholly in the huge container behind Glen Canyon Dam. An entire generation of people growing up on or moving in along the lower Colorado were unaware of any possibility of flooding."

"But isn't it a flood control structure?"

"No. The Bureau of Reclamation is required to fill it if the river will provide the water. The more water, the more turbine head, the more electrical power capability. Remember, first and foremost, Glen Canyon Dam is a power production cash register."

"That is equally as insane as the matter of the error in the river accounting." Kateryna wiped the perspiration from her forehead. The direct sunshine was hot in the rapidly deepening gorge; the bulky life vests and wet suit pants were uncomfortable, compounding the heat. "Waddy, must we wear these heavy things? The river is so placid."

"Sorry, those are the rules; and this time the bureaucrats' rules are actually based on reality. Just jump overboard if you get too hot; it'll give you good practice gettin' back aboard when you get ejected against your will." Kateryna looked back at Waddy's grinning face. "The temperature will seem to drop immediately when we go into the shade of the canyon wall. Then you'll want to put on the tops."

The river flowed gently over the first few miles, carrying the raft and its passengers down the almost imperceptible gradient. The smooth current was interrupted by only a couple of mild riffles as the narrow cleft of Marble Canyon descended into the surrounding plateau. The initial surge of conversation and excitement abated into quiet reverie as the vastness and awesome spectacle of the deepening canyon had its effect. It was impossible to take it all in. Concentration on a detail of the canyon wall or the shoreline gliding past would suddenly be interrupted by a surge of awareness of the whole immense scene. Waddy tried to point out and explain the geology of the rock formations, their creation, and their relationships to each other, but Kateryna, in particular, found it impossible to absorb and understand scientific details in the face of the dramatic demonstration of the insignificance of human life and its time frame that surrounded them. Upon departing Lee's Ferry and entering Marble Canyon, they were in the Kaibab and Toroweap formations of limestone and sandstone. When they reached Phantom Ranch four days later, these same formations would be barely visible at the top of the outer canyon, nearly 5,000 feet above them and ten miles away up the Bright Angel Trail to the south rim.

The rafters' first adrenaline rush came up suddenly at Mile 8, two hours after their launch. Since passing under the span of Navajo Bridge and its new companion, the river had descended through the Kaibab formation, the Toroweap formation, and the Coconino sandstone and was well into the softer, sloping Hermit shale. The still-gentle river was about 700 feet below the rim when Kateryna heard an initially faint, then increasing roar coming from down the canyon.

"Waddy, is that a—what do you say—a rapid we hear?" she turned to ask.

"Yeah, Badger Creek. I don't usually stop for this one but we'll go ahead and pull over to take a look."

"It is so deceiving. The river seems so placid."

"Always is, upstream from a drop. The river sort of dams up. Look over there; that's Badger Canyon comin' in. And that's Jackass Creek on the other side. These rapids are practically always at places where a side canyon enters. Flash floods and debris flows down the side canyons deposit boulders in the river channel, so a rapid forms."

"But doesn't the river spread out the side canyon debris?"

Waddy ferried the raft into the backwater above the fall, raising his voice to be heard over the roar of water. "That is exactly as Mother Earth designed it. Trouble is, with that big-assed dam up there, no more floods come down to smooth things out. Eventually, some of these rapids are gonna get too steep to run."

"Is this a big one, Waddy?" Kateryna asked as they all looked down the short but steep drop of frothing white water.

"All the rapids on the Colorado are rated on a 10 point scale. This one is about a 5 with the flow we've got. It does get sort of technical at real low water."

"Will we go through a 10?" Kateryna shouted above the roar.

"Almost. About eleven miles above Phantom Ranch we'll go through Hance. At the flow we should have it'll be a 9. Another ten miles below Phantom is Crystal Creek Rapid. It's a 10. It's the worst—*best*, I mean. Sorry we have to miss it," Waddy grinned.

Kateryna stared at the boiling water erupting below the smooth stream of green at the head of the rapid. "Do you just go straight down or is there some special technique, I mean– –"

"Yeah, this one's pretty standard. I'll just follow the tongue, where the flow concentrates. The only possible problem is that hole on the right just as we go in."

"Hole?"

"That smooth dome you see just above all that churning water below it is caused by a submerged boulder. As the flow crashes down below the boulder a back wave forms. That's a little hole. With a big one the boat can get caught. Okay, let's go. Remember your chin straps."

Waddy guided the raft into the tongue, the glassy smooth, narrowing spillway that poured the ponded river into the head of the rapid. He immediately pointed the boat straight downstream, passing just to the left of a bulge of clear water sheeting over a submerged ten-foot-diameter boulder. Past the hole they bounced and crashed through a series of closely-spaced waves, accompanied by whoops and yells from Kateryna and Stan. Saul was his usual composed self. It was over quickly, and they were bobbing along in gentle waves.

"Good work, Waddy," Stan said. "When's the next one? I don't remember."

"Three miles down. Longer but probably a little more gentle." A chorus of boos and feigned complaints echoed in the canyon.

"Is this the best you can offer?" Stan grinned back.

"Okay, people, we're gonna finish the day with a run through House Rock. It's rated higher than the last one. It's steep and nasty. Four years ago, at only a little bigger water, I flipped the boat in the big vee wave hole on the left side. Satisfied?" Half smiles and no more commentary.

Without stopping for a scout, Waddy executed a headlong run through the combers and rolling waves of Soap Creek Rapid. This time he let Kateryna sit on the pile of gear behind him. Without a hint of apprehension, she had quickly accepted his invitation to sit in the hot seat. *She doesn't say much. Real cool lady, but strange. Nice wet suit, though.*

This is perfect, Saul thought as they glided down the ever-deepening canyon, the river now cutting through the Supai Group of sandstones, limestones and conglomerates, 290 million years old. *Kateryna seems to be positively entranced. I can literally watch her relax.*

And Kateryna was relaxing as she took in the awesome spectacle of the ever-widening and descending canyon. She felt surprisingly at ease in the company of the three men, only one of whom she knew at all. Her instinctive caution and even her ever-present thoughts of Sofiia were overwhelmed by what she was seeing around her. Everywhere she looked in the deepening gorge she was made aware of the immense power of Nature and the insignificance of man in this place where time had no meaning. She was beginning to understand what it was that was driving the three men to do the thing they had in mind.

Stan found himself paying increasing attention to the quiet, detached woman sitting next to him. He was oddly excited by the prospect of being in such close company with her for the next few days. But these thoughts were eclipsed by larger thoughts. *This is serious business. No, this is insane business,* he realized while he tried to analyze his feelings. *Sitting next to me is a former Soviet security officer. My God, what has she experienced in her life? What in hell am I doing admiring the back of her neck?* His contemplation was interrupted by her voice.

"Saul, you were going to tell me about how the spillways were damaged at one time," she said, turning around. He was taking his turn on the pile at the back of the raft.

"Do you really want to hear about it as we float along with twenty-some million acre feet of water poised behind us?"

"Yes, please," she said without hesitation.

"Well, like Stan said, it really gets down to the usual old story of human greed and reaction to powerful pressure. Lake Mead, the big reservoir about two hundred miles down the canyon, must maintain at least five million acre feet of flood control capacity each year. Its principal mission, ahead of water storage and power generation, is flood control. Unbelievably, as Stan told you, Lake Powell has no flood-control component. When Glen Canyon was approved by our congress, it was authorized to be filled to maximize power generation potential—to pay for it. Then– –" Waddy started to laugh, interrupting Saul's explanation. "Waddy, what's so funny?"

"Oh, it's nothing. I thought of it when Stan first mentioned the Congress. You know what a congress is? It's a collection of salamanders—like a bevy of girls, or a covey of quail, or a herd of elk. That's what it's called—a congress of salamanders. Slimy little lizards, workin' in the dark. Very appropriate." They each smiled, understanding a little more of how Waddy's head worked.

"A newt is a type of salamander, isn't it?" Stan said. "Sorry, Saul, we interrupted you."

"Anyway, they didn't want any wasted space in the reservoir. Most Bureau people now have second thoughts about the original insistence on filling the reservoir, but that's the law and now they're stuck with it."

"But what if a big flood occurs when the reservoir is full?" Kateryna asked.

"That is exactly what happened in 1983. In 1980 the reservoir filled for the first time, and through the next two seasons the Bureau was able to keep refilling it from the spring runoff. Then in the spring of '83 there was a heavy snowpack in the mountain ranges ringing the Upper Basin. Temperatures stayed cool, with snow remaining late in the season. Suddenly it got real warm—I mean, it went from cold to the '80s in a matter of a couple of days—then on top of that, heavy rainstorms occurred all over the Basin. The spillways are designed to carry a total of about 275,000 cfs, so there should not have been a problem. Well, there was a problem. When the flows in the spillways were each only at about 10,000 cfs, the tunnels started to cavitate."

"From shock waves?" Kateryna asked. "How were they formed?"

"Right. As the water flowed over little mineral deposit bumps in the spillway linings, tiny vacuum bubbles formed just downstream of the bumps. When the bubbles imploded from the force of the water, minute shock waves started to erode the concrete lining of the tunnels. As the eroded cavities got bigger, the shock waves got bigger, then the damage increased rapidly. Once the holes got big enough, just plain mechanical erosion took over."

"Did they try to control the flow?"

"Yes. They built flashboards on top of the spillway gates to increase the elevation of the reservoir. At first they used plywood sheets. Plywood. Can you imagine?"

"They're beavers. Whadda'ya expect?" Waddy groused.

"Well, the reservoir kept rising, so big steel flashboards were fabricated in a hurry and bolted to the tops of the gates. Even with that, the Bureau still had to release water under the gates and the cavitation kept getting worse. At the peak runoff, the spillways were passing a total of about 50,000 cfs, with the penstocks and river outlet works dumping another 45,000. They were maximizing the flow through the turbines and the outlet in order to keep the spillway flows as low as possible."

"What finally happened?"

"The Bureau got lucky. I say the *Bureau* got lucky because it got the blame for the flood. But it wasn't entirely the Bureau's fault. The people managing the dam were just doing the best job they could, given the ridiculous and dangerous job they'd been given—to try to keep the reservoir topped off. The current generation of dam managers has to deal with the situation the Bureau created when it was struggling to justify building the dam in the first place. The people down river want it both ways: maximizing water and power production while at the same time expecting security against flood. Ridiculous. Anyway, the snow runoff peaked and it quit raining. The reservoir topped out at about 3,708 feet—that's its elevation above sea level—only seven feet below the crest of the dam. When they were able to get into the spillways, they found severe erosion at the elbows, 40 or 50 feet into the sandstone. I've talked to a guy who worked there at the time. He said the noise down inside the dam from the shock-wave erosion and the chunks being torn loose was like a steady barrage of artillery."

"You said the spillways have elbows?" Kateryna asked incredulously.

"Yep. The inclined sections of the spillways intercept the river diversion tunnels I mentioned back at the dam. The upstream ends of the tunnels are plugged at the elbow sections—that's where the erosion in the tunnels was the worst. The Bureau was really worried while the damage was occurring that the plugs or the sandstone around them might be eroded enough to connect to the water at the bottom of the reservoir."

"If a hydraulic connection did occur, no matter how small, there would be no way to stop the flow under the full pressure of the reservoir," Kateryna quickly concluded.

"How do you know so much about dams and reservoirs?

"Saul, don't your American universities require a broad education of physicists?"

"Not really. I happen to know about the 1983 event because I was just curious. I read the Bureau reports about the incident and how they fixed it."

"So tell me about the repair job," Kateryna asked, dodging Saul's curiosity about her training.

"Air slots were cut in the tunnels about halfway down the inclined sections. As water rushes over the slot, which runs around most of the circumference of the tube, air is drawn in and entrained in the water flow. Any bubbles that form at bumps in the lining will then be cushioned by the air when the bubbles collapse. Cavitation does not start, so there's no erosion."

"Was the repair tested?"

"The next season. The runoff in 1984 was actually bigger than '83, but the water and power demand over the winter had drawn down the reservoir enough so it didn't spill—barely—when the snowpack runoff came. The reservoir again rose above the tops of the spillway gates and only because of the steel flashboards did they avoid another bypass. After the snowmelt season, the tunnels were run for several days at 20,000 cfs and through the left tunnel alone, for about an hour, at 50,000. No cavitation damage."

The aeration slot—four feet wide by four feet deep—extends around three-fourths of the spillway bore, halfway down the 55° slope. The men are secured by a rappelling cable (*Bureau of Reclamation*).

View from above the switching yard on the west rim, August 12, 1984. The left spillway was tested for one hour at 50,000 cfs after completion of the tunnel repairs and construction of the aeration slots. At the portal the water is jetting properly at a speed of 120 mph before it hits the deflection ramp. The river turbulence upstream is being caused by simultaneous discharge from the river outlet works (*Bureau of Reclamation*).

"Are you saying the air only gets into the water through the exposed ends of the slots?

"That's right. They remain open to atmospheric pressure above the level of the water flowing in the spillways."

"But what if the tunnel runs so full that the slot is fully closed off by the water? No air could enter the flow, and the cavitation would begin again."

"They're never supposed to run that full."

"But if an unexpected flood occurred, and they did run full enough to close off the air, the spillways could be massively damaged, right?"

"I would imagine that is correct."

"And what if the flood was sufficient to completely fill the spillways? Are they designed to operate as pressure conduits?"

"No, they're not."

"Saul, looking at this great canyon it is not hard to imagine that there have been many floods in excess of the—what did you say—the 275,000 cfs the spillways are designed for. I just cannot get over the folly of relying on limited-capacity tunnel spillways through sandstone—with curved sections, no less."

"You know very well that engineers have to design everything based upon probabilities and costs: in this case, probability of a given flood balanced against cost in preparing for the flood."

"Why wasn't a ramp spillway used? With the power plant beneath it. That arrangement will handle any flow."

"Cost, once again. That and because the Bureau had never built a dam with that configuration. The river diversion tunnels were already there, so it was just a lot cheaper to use part of them for the spillways, just like the Bureau had done down at Hoover Dam."

"How long has the river flowed through this canyon, Saul?" Kateryna asked with a mischievous smile.

"In its current configuration, nearly five million years, so far as we know."

"And there is no way to really know just what quantities of water have flowed through here during that five million years, is there?"

"Probabilities, Kateryna. All we have to work with are probabilities based upon extrapolations of known data."

"We were told today that the reservoir would likely fill with this season's runoff. How accurately can the predictions of runoff be made?"

"There are hundreds of telemetry-monitored snowpack gauging stations throughout the basin above the reservoir. A computer model continually updates the quantity of water in storage in the snowpack and in the tundra above timberline. If it looks like the reservoirs are going to fill, the Bureau juggles releases so that there will be enough storage space to avoid a big spill."

"How large is the basin above the reservoir?" Kateryna persisted, her curiosity undiminished.

"More than a hundred thousand square miles: from Teton Park in the north, to the southern San Juans on the east, then to the Uinta and Wasatch Mountains in Utah on the west. A huge, mountain-ringed basin."

"I think I understand what Stanley said about the justification for building the dam, but why is not *some* storage space left in the reservoir? Twenty-seven million acre feet cannot possibly be needed."

"Money. Money and politics. The engine of our capitalist system."

"We in the East are being encouraged to follow your example, are we not?"

"You must learn from our mistakes, Kateryna."

"And you all want to undo what you perceive to be a particular mistake—the one we saw this morning."

Saul paused before answering. "In a nutshell, yes."

Waddy quit rowing in the quiet water, letting the raft drift slowly. *So there it is. Saul finally got to the point. Now what?*

Kateryna broke the silence. "You feel that what would be regained by restoring the flooded canyon would offset the damage from the release of all that water?"

"Kateryna, there's no need to destroy the dam. We just want to damage it sufficiently so that it cannot be repaired—so that it will have to be abandoned and eventually torn down." Saul noticed that Waddy started to say something but did not interrupt. He clenched his jaw and resumed his rowing.

"I think that would be impossible to accomplish, Saul. You obviously don't know a great deal about concrete arch dams. Any significant damage would cause the whole structure to fail." Stan nodded in agreement.

Saul: "All we have to do is fracture the sandstone in one of the abutments enough that the leakage could not be stopped."

"To do that, you would necessarily have to interrupt the canyon wall support for the dam. The dam itself would collapse without its needed abutment support, unless, of course, only a spillway was affected. From what you have told me it seems that the spillways are the weak points in that structure, especially considering that they are cut through very porous and probably fractured sandstone."

"Augmenting the fractures in the sandstone around a spillway tunnel is what I have in mind."

Waddy pulled through the foamy division between the river flow and the shoreline eddy to land the boat. A broad delta of boulders spread out from the base of Rider Canyon, pinching off the river's channel as it curved beneath the sheer east wall. A series of large chunks of Esplanade sandstone had tumbled from the wall, further restricting the channel. "Okay, folks, come along and take a look at this little puppy." Everyone followed Waddy across the boulder field to the edge of the boiling flow through the narrow channel. The rapid was short but its ten-foot drop warranted its 7 rating at the present river flow.

"This is one where we don't want to just follow the tongue into the rapid. It leads right into two big holes on the opposite side as the river curves around the delta. See the first one? It's where that big wave angles out from the left wall and a second wave in mid channel intercepts it, forming a vee. Just past that is a bigger hole from the usual pourover of a boulder. Finally, we have to avoid the big rock sticking out from the east side at the end. That first hole below the vee is where I flipped."

"What's your plan?" Saul asked. "I vaguely remember we just pulled hard to stay right."

"That's it. I'll set up close on the right goin' in, stern first, and then ferry right as we curve around. This sucker gets real technical at lower water 'cause there's not enough room on the right to avoid the holes that get even worse at low water. Just be glad we got this much water. Must'a been a little warm down in Phoenix."

"What happens if the boat goes into a hole?" Kateryna asked.

"If we get turned sideways, the water coming over the boulder above the hole can bury the upstream tube and flip the boat. With a really big hole, the boat may get stuck. That back wave action at the end counterbalances the flow, so you're caught—gettin' the crap pounded out of you, maybe bein' sucked under. Those two aren't big enough to be keepers; but since they're so close to the left side you could get shredded on the rocks.

"And another problem with a hole is all that frothy water in the bottom. Air doesn't support a loaded raft very good, so you sink in farther."

Kateryna: "Archimedes' Principle."

Waddy bobbed his head. "Uh huh, that's right." Saul was also smiling his agreement and even Stan the history/law major understood. Stan had made himself understand whatever was necessary to operate a boat—in his case, a sailboat.

"How would you get out?" Kateryna asked the next obvious question.

"Unless the current around the edges grabs you and flicks you out like a dead fly, you don't get out. You just drown. So we try to stay out of holes. Anybody wanna walk around? I can pull back in that eddy below the rapid to pick you up." Silence. "Let's go." Continuing silence as they trooped back to the boat.

"Okay, everybody's grommet tight? Good. 'Least water won't leak in there. Let's hit it." Waddy set the boat diagonally stern first into the right side of the flow, then as soon as he'd passed a small rock sticking up through the swiftly flowing water, he pulled strongly back with three hard strokes. On the last stroke, his left oar hit a barely submerged rock and came out of the water. The full pull with the right oar then spun the front of the boat toward the center of the river just as the raft approached the vee-wave hole. The boat was poised to slide into the right edge. It dipped into the lip of the churning white water, nosing downward and revolving counterclockwise into the back wave.

Kateryna stared down into the foaming, spray-filled cauldron that bottomed out five feet below her perch on the edge of the raft. She was showered with icy water, some finding its way down the back of her neck. She felt the raft tip, but the fringe of the back-curling wave kicked the boat and the current slid it past the hole. It was now pointed, stern first, at the dome of water pouring into the big hole.

"Hang on!" Waddy yelled. A strong pull on his right oar swung the boat, followed by three deep, two-oar strokes that pulled the raft's center of gravity to the right of the next boiling depression in the 8,000 cubic-foot-per-second flow. They slid past the second hole, past a point of rock protruding from the east wall, then continued through the waves backward, each pounding collision with a curler showering the raft. Cheers from everyone, including Saul, filled the narrow canyon when they abruptly found themselves bobbing along in the tailwater.

"Well, that's a good demonstration of how not to do it," Waddy proclaimed while Stan and Kateryna manned the five-gallon plastic buckets to scoop out the water that nearly filled the boat.

"Kind'a thought we might get wet in that one, so we're gonna camp on the left side about a mile down—where the river turns more toward the west. Should get some late afternoon sun from down the canyon to dry us out."

Waddy's camp selection at 18 Mile Wash managed to optimize the conflicting conditions of a nearly 2,000-foot-deep canyon and the low arc of the winter sun. The sun stayed above the rim just long enough for everyone to get out of their clammy wet suits and into warm, dry clothing.

"Sorry about pushing things, guys. I don't like to camp late, but I wanted to buy us some time tomorrow so we can explore a side canyon. We really should have a couple more days on the river to do this trip right."

"Everything is perfect, Waddy," Kateryna said while she and Stan finished setting up the second of the two tents. She helped Waddy unload the remainder of their gear from the back of the raft. "Is this our toilet?" she asked as she removed an army surplus rocket box and attachments.

"Yeah, that's the latest contraption the Park Service makes us use. It's called a *groover*, don't ask me why. We gotta use that thing for all number two duty. The Park Service has developed specific guidelines for the number of turds per person per day. We gotta account for every one," Waddy said with perfect deadpan seriousness. "With the four of us, and the length of the trip, and considerin' what we'll be eatin' an' all, the guidelines say we gotta have thirty-eight individual droppings in that little box when we take out at Phantom Ranch. A Park Service guy'll be there to count 'em and I'm in big trouble if we're short." Kateryna continued to stare at Waddy as he went on. "I do always try to sneak a couple into the river, though, just to add my little contribution to the pile in the bottom of Mead Reservoir." At this point Stan lost his composure, followed immediately by Saul and Waddy.

"Oh, you people," Kateryna said, her face flushing as she joined in. "I'm not going to believe anything more you tell me, Waddy."

"Seriously, Kateryna, go ahead and pee in the sand right near the river so's it'll get flushed. The solution to pollution is dilution. But ya' gotta use the groover for the rest."

Stan shook his head. There was simply no way to control Waddy's crudity. He was what he was. "This is going great," Stan said when the laughter died down. "We'll have plenty of time. What is it, only about seventy miles down to Phantom, and we've got three more days? We made nearly twenty today. I'd say you planned this perfectly."

"How *did* you manage to get this together on such sort notice?" Saul asked.

"Called in a few chips, is all. Isn't that little Avon boat a beauty? She's the private yacht of one of the commercial company big guys. Never expected for us to have a rig like that. Just lucky, I guess."

"Oh, sure, just luck," Stan said. "It's pretty clear a lot of people around here like you."

"You've also saved some people's butts," Saul added. "I heard about you fishing that tourist out of a grotto down at Havasu."

"Yeah, well . . ." Waddy's mahogany color brightened.

"Oh, leave him alone, you thugs," Kateryna interrupted with a laugh. "Can't you see you're making him uncomfortable? Now, Waddy, let's prepare supper." She linked her arm in his and walked over to the roll-up, slat-top table that had emerged from the pile in the back of the boat.

A hearty dinner on the beach, a sunset radiating from behind the canyon rim, a nice view down the darkening river canyon, the gulps and gurgles of the river sliding by, and the occasional delight of the descending call of a tiny canyon wren ended the first day on the river.

"Can we build a fire?" Kateryna asked.

"No firewood," Waddy shrugged. "And fires right in the sand aren't permitted, even if there was some wood. So many people camp on these beaches that if everybody built a fire there'd be a big mess. Because of the dam, the beaches aren't scoured and replenished with new sand by the floods. All the driftwood just floats around up in Powell Reservoir. Big log occasionally sinks one of those speedboat assholes runnin' around up there, though," Waddy smiled. "You ought'a see all those little side canyons up on the reservoir. At the upper ends of nearly all of them, there's just a mass of scum and driftwood and shit floatin' around. They look like cesspools. You sure don't see pictures of that in the promotion brochures for the *Jewel of the Colorado*."

"How much soil did the river carry before the dam?"

"Believe it or not, over a hundred million tons annually. That's why the river was named the Colorado—also what built the huge delta where the river flows into the Gulf of California."

"Then all the suspended soils collect in the reservoir."

"That's right. In fact, that's the third reason the dam was built. First there's the water accounting bullshit Stan told you about; then there's the need to generate power to pump water across 200 miles of desert to fulfill Senator Hayden's scheme for a new Los Angeles at the confluence of the sucked-dry Gila, Verde, and Salt Rivers, and to keep all those *pahanas* cool in the summer. Next, the fuckers had to have a place to store mud. About 350 miles down river from here is another big dam, about the size of the one you saw. It wasn't long after that dam was built, back in the 1930s, that the beavers realized it was gonna fill with dirt a whole lot faster'n they'd planned on.

Instead of the thousand or so years they'd figured, in less than 300 they'd have a giant rice paddy with a 600-foot waterfall at the end. Dumb shits. So they decided they needed a sacrificial reservoir and created Powell to silt in during the 300 years. Hell, at the rate things are goin', people won't be around in much more than a hundred—'least not all the *pahanas* anyway. A thousand years those arrogant fuckers suppose to plan ahead. Hitler planned for a thousand and he lasted twelve."

"Waddy, the level of the river has dropped since we landed. Is the power production outflow on a regular cycle?" Kateryna asked.

"Yeah, it is now. It used to fluctuate really wild, but there's been so much complaint from the Park Service and the rafters that the Bureau and the Western Area Power Administration keep the river to a pretty regular daily cycle between about five and twenty thousand cfs. It used to be that if it happened to get really hot in Phoenix the river would surge way up and then drop sharply when the sun went down. WAPA gets to really stick it to the power companies at peak demand, you know. Like Stan said, that big sucker's primarily an electrical power cash register. A long study of the river was just completed—what's called an environmental impact statement—that's supposed to decide on a permanent flow regime for the river. But I'll tell ya' what. There's nothin' they can do to run warm, silty water down this river like it used to. And all these beaches are shrinkin'. 'Bout the only thing that might work is a slurry pipeline to bring mud from the deltas formin' at the upper ends of the reservoir. That'd take a hundred-fifty miles of pipe and the water would still be cold from the turbine releases. That water is about 47 degrees The native species in the river have been wiped out."

Stan: "But don't they plan to release a surge of water through the outlet works to try to scour out some of the sand that's on the bottom of the channel? To deposit it on the eroded sandbars and beaches?"

"Right, that'll work a couple'a times, until all the sand is scraped off the bottom; but eventually it's all gonna wind up in Mead Reservoir. The free river, in predambrian time, kept the stream environs in perfect balance with the river. Perennial vegetation existed only above the regular high-water line, occasionally being scoured out by floods. In the zone between the normal annual levels of the river, broad and constantly replenished sandbars and riverbanks were populated each season with a little new growth and nice clean sand. Now, with the daily fluctuatin' flows, nothin' grows in the surge zone, and above the 20,000 cfs level we've got all this foreign vegetation movin' in: all that damn Egyptian tamarisk some stupid *pahanas* imported and all the camelthorn, cheat grass, and ravenna grass. Cheat grass sprouted up all over the West 'cause'a overgrazin', nobody knows how to stop it, so now its down here in the canyon. And that ravenna grass can grow twelve feet high. Some dumbshit Park Service ranger planted it around the dam visitor center. Naturally, seeds blew into the canyon. Now they're runnin' around down here tryin' to dig it out, but they'll never do it. That grass will eventually snuff out everything else—'cept the tamarisk . . . Used to be river otters in here, too. All gone now." Waddy stared across the river at the Manakacha Formation, just emerging from its 280-million-year burial. "Even with the effort to keep the river on a regular cycle, electrical demand in Phoenix largely determines how the river will flow. I'm not holdin' my breath waitin' for that EIS to really change anything."

Waddy walked down to the raft. "I brought along a charcoal pan and briquettes. Maybe a few pieces of wood that got flushed down with a side canyon flood will accidently fall into the fire pan."

After dinner, as the first stars appeared in the purple eastern sky over the rim of the Kaibab formation, now 1,900 feet above them, Saul decided that it was time. The ice had been broken; now it was time to really get into it.

"Kateryna," he began, finally trying to speak the words he had repeated over and over in his mind but forgetting everything he'd planned to say as soon as he began. "I feel that . . . I hope . . . We have much to discuss—things of mutual concern, and . . . I'm sorry that Malcolm isn't here, but nevertheless we should get started." *That was just great.* He decided to try again.

Kateryna rescued him. "Saul—all of you—I appreciate the effort you have made. We have uncomfortable things to talk about, but this place you have chosen could not have been more appropriate. I now have some understanding of your motives. Of course, Saul has told you of mine—my daughter and the very dangerous situation existing in and near my homeland. Let us talk, first of all, about the concern which is shared: the growing possibility of a nuclear weapon being sold or stolen and detonated in a crowded city." Saul looked intently at Kateryna, nodding his agreement.

"From my view," she went on, "it is most likely that such a thing would happen in my part of the world. Then again, there is the recent conventional bombing at the New York World Trade Center. Wherever in the world it occurs, it will probably be somehow related to the Christian/Muslim war, and now the Jewish/Muslim war, we have had off and on in the Middle East since the time of the Crusades. I am quite uncomfortable talking about this subject since I am privy to far more of such information than any of you; nevertheless, for the overall, shall I say, *good*, I will speak as freely as I can. You must understand that my even sitting here with you goes against everything I have learned and done for my entire adult life. And none of us—the three of you and I alone—can have any real assurance that this is not just a clever—how do you say—*setup*."

Waddy spoke up. "I'll answer that by askin'—just sayin', actually—what possible gain would there be? What would you gain by turnin' us in, and what would we gain by doin' the same? I mean, we—the three of us and

Malcolm—really want to blow up that piece'a shit dam; 'course you really want to get your daughter to where she can get the best possible care, and we all—not me, really—are concerned about somebody startin' a nuclear war in the Middle East.

"You have to understand somethin' very clearly about me. I think this is all gonna get down to individual, not group, motivations. All I really care about in this world is this canyon land: the land of my ancestors. I can appreciate other problems in the world, but all I really *care* about is this place. There's more than enough to fix right here without lookin' around all over the world. I just want all of you to know that my role in this, whatever it turns out to be, has a very simple, straightforward motive. Nothing complex. No galactic moral involvement with me."

Saul smiled at his friend. "Galactic moral involvement?" Waddy's abrupt, honest comments had put him nearly at ease. He turned to Kateryna. "At some point we just have to trust each other, like you said back at the hotel. Hell, I have to trust these guys. And Malcolm. If we're going to get anywhere to accomplish our own objectives we're just going to have to take a chance. The time has come—right now—for us to get on with it or forget the whole idea."

"I'm here," Kateryna responded with no hint of emotion. "As beautiful as this canyon is, I'm not here for a vacation. I only mentioned the matter of deception because it had to be said—out loud. Now, I agree, we should get started."

Stan jumped to his feet. "Waddy was candid. So I will be too. That dam . . . the outrageous injustice that it was built—to satisfy the egos of a handful of bureaucrats and politicians and to enrich another handful of people—it was tragic. But to risk breaching it . . . The flood . . . I can't even think about that happening." Stan struggled with the impossible conflict he had felt since the initial discussion at Stony Ridge. "The indescribably beautiful canyon that was behind that dam– –"

Waddy: "*Is* behind the dam."

"*Is* behind the dam. It's not at all like this place. As this canyon is grand, Glen Canyon is intimate. As this canyon is powerful and often violent, Glen Canyon is gentle and peaceful. As this canyon is stark and naked, Glen Canyon is filled with verdant life. In order to fully appreciate both of them, they must be seen together, experienced together. Their being created and existing side by side was not an accident."

"You're startin' to think and talk like a Hopi," Waddy smiled.

"So now, the companion to this grand canyon is under five hundred feet of water, so people can live in Phoenix as though they were in New England; so a tiny few other people can get rich planting cotton and growing grass in the desert to feed cattle!" Stan slumped into the sand.

Saul: "Besides giving you the opportunity to see, up close, what we are obsessed about, it was important for you to see and evaluate for yourself that with proper precautions we can have both the needed nuclear incident and accomplish our objective here without loss of life."

Kateryna responded quickly. "Of course, isn't the issue of loss of life at the heart of any concern over nuclear weapons? I do not know population details, but there must be a number of communities along this river before it reaches the sea. And from what I saw of that dam and reservoir, Stanley is very correct that there is a great risk that a detonation powerful enough to damage it sufficiently will likely cause the whole structure to fail. You all might as well understand that I happen to have considerable background in the subject of hard damage with nuclear detonations. I see a real problem with your scheme to just mortally injure the dam."

"With the proper explosive force and placement, I am convinced that we can just wound the dam. I– –"

"Wound, shit!" Waddy leaped up and kicked a stone into the river, revealing his summer-lightning temper. "We should blow the whole fucker to dust! Are we just gonna dance around? I mean, that thing is killin' Mother Earth—since 1963 and for the who knows how many thousands of years it'll take the natural forces to fill it with mud and then grind down through all that concrete. Wound . . . shit . . ." Waddy sat down, scowling.

"Waddy," Saul slowly continued, "hear me out on this. You'll see what I'm getting at. The idea is not to attack the dam itself, just one of the abutments. If we can damage the rock sufficiently—deeply and completely enough—there is no way the dam site could be repaired. Not with today's construction and safety requirements. Safety and geological concerns brushed aside in the 1950s would not be ignored today. Furthermore, even if it could be repaired, I'm certain there would be a broad outcry against doing so. It was only built because our government—really just a handful of powerful men, as Stan said—kept the people uninformed. With major damage done to the dam, and with the public attention it would receive, all the fallacious reasons for building it in the first place would be exposed. I'm confident that a deep wound is all that is needed. The only issue is how best to accomplish the task."

Kateryna kindled to Saul's spark. "I will agree that if you can avoid serious injury to the structure itself, your plan may work. From what I saw this morning, it would be child's play to gain entry using that elevator into the dam. Security there is ludicrous. There was only a tumbler-lock gate securing access into the galleries and those galleries have to connect to inspection and drainage tunnels back into the abutments. But detonating in an abutment tunnel would be too risky—a direct connection to the dam itself. With a full reservoir the whole thing could fail."

"Great!" Waddy enthused to a unanimity of shaking heads and smiles.

Kateryna thought for a moment. "No, the weak points with that dam are the river diversion tunnel plugs you mentioned. Just enough explosive force to start leakage around a plug. Leave the dam alone. What about access to the spillways? We could not actually see the inlets this morning."

"Both sides are fenced. The only ways to get to them are over the service roads at each end of the dam or by floating in from the reservoir. The roads are gated, of course, and the areas around the spillway inlets are monitored with TV and motion sensors, both microwave and infrared. Probably seismic units, too. Coming in from the lake we'd have to get the device up and over the spillway gates—that could be as much as fifty feet—and then we'd have to rappel down the tunnel. Kateryna, I agree that guard security at the dam is light, but even if we could figure out how to deactivate all the sensors, we would still be screwing around in the area for quite a while. Then the time to get out."

"Yes, time would be a problem." She paused. "And the noise."

"Exactly. Any sound in that tunnel would be transmitted through the rock to the dam like you were using a megaphone. Dam security is pretty sleepytime, but it's not *that* bad."

"What about coming in from the outlet end?"

"Different problems. We'd have to come up the river fifteen miles from Lee's Ferry. Couldn't row it with the outflow from the dam; we'd have to use a motor. Even if we got up there undetected, there'd be a big problem getting into a spillway portal. There are deflection buckets at the ends and no ladders up from river level. Finally, even if we got up to the lip of a tunnel, water stands about twenty feet deep the whole length of the tunnel back to the elbow—over a thousand feet."

"Why the water?" Stan asked.

"The spillways leak like sieves—about six or seven thousand gallons per minute from hundreds of drain holes relieving the pressure in the sandstone. The water doesn't just run out the end of a tunnel because of the flip bucket at the end; it spills over the lip of the bucket and down a 45° ramp to the river. So the water fills up the tunnel until it stands as high as the top of the bucket, twenty feet deep. In addition to rock climbing up to the lip of the outlet and then hauling up the device, we'd also have to take a raft. Same time problem and the tunnel outlet areas are very visible from both rims, the dam, and the bridge.

"Actually," Saul nodded to Kateryna, "you were on to something with the abutment tunnels. There are several at different levels on both sides and they are indeed accessible from the gate we saw this morning near the bottom elevator lobby. Now here's the point. The lowest ones go back several hundred feet, passing right over the spillway tunnels. A relatively small detonation would so compromise the integrity of the rock abutment and interfere with the spillway that it could never be repaired. Exactly what we're trying to do here."

"Not what *I* want to do!" Waddy jumped to his feet. "I want to see big chunks of that fucker launched into orbit. Just a big hole in the canyon where that mother once stood. Where the river would fill the hole, we could call that Lake Powell. Maybe even put up a nice brass plaque dedicating it to Senator Hayden. They sure as hell wouldn't need the Hayden Visitor Center anymore. Better yet, maybe the explosion would blow that piece of shit off the rim too. Maybe it would just launch off down the canyon like a giant Frisbee, scattering those fancy Bureau offices all over the mesa. Maybe– –"

"Waddy, calm down," Stan said. "We're here to talk seriously about this."

"I *am* serious. "I don't know what you all are so worried about. It's over 350 miles down the canyon to Hoover Dam, and beyond that it's what? Another seventy miles or so to the first town. And what town is that? Fuckin' Laughlin, Nevada, that's what. Have you ever *seen* that circus? Nothin' but giant plastic gamblin' palaces, snowbird RVs, hotels, and parkin' lots. They built everything right on the edge of the river, just *askin'* for a flood. They'd

September 14, 1983. Spillway drainage water is being pumped out of the tunnel while it is being repaired. Water seeps from joints and seams in the abutment (*Bureau of Reclamation, Joe Dahilig*).

have hours of warnin' to just walk up the hill, find a nice seat, and watch the show. Hell, there'd be time for people to drive out from L.A. Prob'ly sell tickets, souvenir programs, TV station helicopters, the whole deal. Wonderful, just wonderful."

"Waddy . . . Waddy," Saul said patiently. "The flood would probably take out Hoover Dam too. That would add another twenty-plus million acre feet. There would be nothing left. Absolutely nothing, all the way to the Gulf."

"We could have riverboats again, just like back in the 1800s. Paddle wheelers comin' up from the Gulf, clear up to Black Canyon. Take tourists up to show them where Hoover Dam once stood. We could run the river all the way from Brown's Park on the Green clear to the Gulf. Mother Earth would have her river back. She's gonna get it back one day anyway."

By this time, Stan and Kateryna were laughing uncontrollably.

"Oh, Waddy," she said, catching her breath, "if this weren't so serious, I could listen to you go on all day."

"But I *am* serious." Everyone else just smiled and shook their heads. "Okay, fuck it!" He got up and stomped down to the boat.

"He is so intense," Kateryna observed quietly. "Can you trust him not to—how do you say—go off half cocked?"

Stan and Saul did not answer immediately. "I certainly hope so," Stan said, as Waddy tossed a fist-sized stone clear across the river. "Come on back, Waddy," he yelled. "You have to be in on all of this."

Waddy trudged back up the beach and sullenly sat down.

Kateryna asked, "What about triggering?"

"Yes, that *is* the next problem. Every time I've thought through a scheme for remote triggering I've also thought of several ways it could be compromised."

"What about just standin' there and pullin' the pin? . . . I'd do that," Waddy whispered darkly.

Stan: "Now, Waddy, we don't want– –"

"If that's the only way, I guess I can do as much as those guys over in the Middle East. I would liberate the river of my people for all time."

Stan thought for a moment about what Malcolm had said about the joint effect of ethnicity and religion. "I didn't know Hopis practiced kamikaze warfare," he said, trying to lighten things up.

"Oh, come on, Stan, you're starting to sound like Malcolm," Saul snapped, suppressing a sigh. "Let's get on with this." Saul glanced again at Kateryna, who had remained expressionless during the last exchange. "Heroics aside, you have to understand the forces that will be brought to bear to interrupt our little plan once the authorities understand what's going on."

Kateryna nodded, almost imperceptibly.

"Well, why do they have to know?" Waddy demanded. "I mean, just put the fucker in the dam or a spillway, set a timer, and run like hell. Job completed."

"Okay, that's enough, Waddy," Saul said. "That is just out of the question. If you persist in that nonsense, I don't see how we can have you involved with this." An uncomfortable silence settled over the group.

"Yes, there must be adequate warning," Stan said firmly. "There's no way I'm going to have any part in sabotaging that dam without warning. Even if we can manage to finesse the explosion to accomplish just the necessary damage, there's still likely to be one hell of a flood down the canyon if one of the old river diversion tunnels gets seriously opened up. And no matter how carefully we try to calculate just the right explosive power and placement of the bomb, there will always be the risk of a catastrophic failure of the dam or an abutment. If the reservoir's full, that's twenty-seven million acre feet of water. Waddy, I can assure you that Malcolm feels the same way."

A sterile silence again settled over them. Throughout the conversation, Kateryna had closely observed her companions. Since they had met at the hotel in Page, she had searched for any break, any hint, that would reveal deception. If what she had just witnessed was choreographed, it would, she thought, be worthy of praise from the master of the Kirov. "Saul, have you come up with any ideas to solve the placement and triggering problems?"

"Yes. I think so, that is. Lot of technical problems to solve, but conceptually I believe it will work. But first of all, let me say, I do not agree that it would be as simple as you suggest to take the bomb in through the dam to an abutment tunnel. Even if there's only a small chance of getting caught, why take the chance if there's another way to set the device without detection? I think the solution I have come up with will avoid the placement risk, and I also believe it will have a more secure triggering system."

Everyone was listening closely, even Waddy.

"I think we should set the device in the lake behind the dam, submerged next to a canyon wall near the inlet to one of the diversion tunnels. Wherever it's set, we can simply float it into place at night without any of the difficulties involved in trying to breach the dam security. The main problem is where to place it so that the blast is directed principally at the sandstone and not the dam."

"And initiating the fusing?" Kateryna asked. "Sonar?"

"Exactly. Arming can be done when we place the device. For fusing, a coded digital signal would be sent from any one of a number of transmitters set in the lake. No need to risk a land line to the device and no need to somehow string the long antenna required if it were placed in a foundation tunnel. Just come in by boat and set it anywhere we like, anchored and buoyed at a precise depth."

"How would you prevent a diver from just going down and deactivating the device? You would not know it was being done." Kateryna answered her own question as quickly as she spoke. "A proximity fuse?"

"Right again."

"But your government has sonar countermeasures, correct?"

"Yes, and there are counter-countermeasures."

"Oh, bullshit, Saul," Waddy said irritably. "Just float it in, get the hell out of the way, then set it off with a simple radio transmitter. Job done." He got up to get a soda out of the drag bag.

"Waddy seems to have a different moral ethic than you do," Kateryna said quietly to Saul and Stan.

"What you're seeing is the end result of the centuries of bad treatment his people have had at the hands of white people in this country," Stan said, shaking his head.

Saul: "I don't agree entirely. The Hopi people, as a group, have a stronger moral sense than do the members of the so-called mainstream cultures and religions, including my own Jews. The Hopi have been treated badly but their beliefs are so strong that they simply rise above it. They believe that after the *pahanas* burn themselves out, they will survive. They are very peaceful, adhering closely to their ancient virtues. But Waddy . . . he's sort of a maverick among his people."

"You're right," Stan nodded. "It seems he can't always follow his peoples' teachings. Malcolm would probably say it's his Irish streak."

"We have the same situation in several parts of the Commonwealth, the result of heavy-handed treatment of minorities by the Russians. That is the precise reason I am so fearful that a nuclear weapon will be used in one of our cities—why I am sitting here with you right now."

Waddy came back and sat down. "Look, people, please understand. I'm not devoid of conscience. Hell, a lot of my friends work here on the river and at Phantom Ranch. But dammit, this is war so far as I'm concerned. In any war, casualties are taken. If we screw around with a lot of warnin' time and talkin' and so on, we'll just wind up havin' the bomb defused. I don't know any of the details like you, Saul—I just believe that they could undo anything you could come up with. Remember the KISS principal."

"What?" Kateryna frowned/smiled.

"It means 'keep it simple, stupid.' An old army saying," Saul laughed. "I will admit there's definite validity to the axiom."

"Same thing in the Marine Corps," Stan said.

"About the warnin'," Waddy went on, "other than Hoover Dam, it's over four hundred miles down to the first inhabited place on the river—Laughlin. Wouldn't it take, I dunno, maybe half a day for the water to reach there even if the dam failed suddenly? If someone dragged his feet and tried to empty his slot machines, well, that's his choice. What about just a short warnin'? Just enough time to sweep the river for rafters, boaters on Lake Mead, and warn the 'Pai's and the people at Phantom Ranch."

"Waddy," Saul responded with his usual patience, "you know that all the rafters would first have to be located and then most of them removed with helicopters. Even right now, in the off season, there are quite a few hikers on or near the river. Locating everyone would take a lot of time—three or four days, at least—plenty of time for the authorities to disable our bomb if it's just simply placed. No, with even the kind of reasonable warning time to clear just the river corridor and Lake Mead, we're going to have to have a sophisticated triggering system."

"He's right, Waddy," Kateryna said, taking sides for the first time.

"There's something else, people," Stan said. "The FBI and ATF will quickly understand that we're not threatening the destruction of the dam in order to accomplish some other purpose. They'll know it's the dam itself that's the issue, not just a tool we're using. They'll have nothing to lose by being aggressive in their efforts to stop us. No negotiating, either. What? That they'll promise to tear down the dam if we defuse the bomb?"

"That is also correct," Kateryna said. "I know very well how my people would handle the situation."

"Yeah," Saul said wryly. "It's no accident that terrorists don't hijack Aeroflot planes."

"But would your authorities act so decisively, as Stanley suggests?"

"Why don't we get back to more basic things," Waddy said abruptly, "like whether or not you're actually gonna be able to get us a bomb?" A painful silence fell over the group. Saul and Stan both tried to think of something quickly to soften the effects of the typical-Waddy direct confrontation.

"Yes," Kateryna smiled, seeing their discomfort. "We need to talk about that."

"Kateryna," Saul said awkwardly, "it's just that with the recent changes in your part of world, we thought– –"

"Why do you presume that our security in Ukraine is any less rigid than yours? Do you suppose that the reciprocal teams working at this moment at Nizhnyaya Tura would have any more opportunity than we had at Pueblo or at your Pantex facility?" The gradual relaxation she'd displayed since the river trip began was gone in an instant.

Saul almost groaned out loud. *Oh, shit. That made it worse.*

"You must think so," Waddy said trenchantly, "or you wouldn't be here right now."

Oh, no! You damned fool, Waddy, Stan winced. He glanced at Saul, now seeming to be in physical pain.

Kateryna's carefully poised demeanor slipped another fraction. "So, Waddy, you can certainly cut right to the issue," she said after a moment's pause. "Yes, it is true that under certain circumstances there may be an opportunity at this particular time. Before I came here with all of you, I had no idea if what I perhaps could offer was what you had in mind. With my visit here, and after hearing some detail of your plan, I can say that yes, I might be able to fill your need."

"So what makes it any easier in your country?" Waddy persisted.

"That I cannot say. I am not here to compromise the details of our security systems—only to help prevent the eventual escape of a weapon that would, very likely, be used in my part of the world—and to make this exchange of hardware for something I personally need."

Stan spoke up. "Look, Waddy was way off base there. We have no need whatsoever to know any details. We take it on faith that because you came on this trip you'll make the effort and that there is some chance of success. Frankly, discussion of details, if any, is properly between you and Malcolm. After all, he's the one who will be meeting our part of the arrangement."

"I agree," Saul added.

"I'm sorry," Waddy said sincerely. "I'm not into all this politics. It's just the way I am."

Kateryna softened, her smile reappearing. "Yes, I know. This is hardly a casual matter for any of us, each for our own reasons, as Waddy so correctly observed." She got up. "I'm tired. What are to be the sleeping arrangements?"

"Yours is the little gray tent," Waddy answered. "These two city pansies can have the big one. I like to sleep on the back of the boat to stay away from the snakes."

"Snakes? Your rattlesnakes I have heard about?"

"I was just kidding," Waddy grinned. "Our little pink Grand Canyon rattlesnakes are gentle pussycats."

"Yeah, for you they are," Stan said. "Kateryna, Waddy is a member of what his people call the Snake Clan. Of course he gets along with rattlesnakes. Zip up your tent."

"Seriously, we do have scorpions," Waddy added. "Lots of 'em. It's the tiny little ones that are the problem. Night is their time. Just be sure to zip up the screen fly—and keep your shoes in the tent."

* * *

After a winter-dawn wake-up, thirteen miles of river, an ever-deepening canyon, and an exhilarating morning running the many rapids of the Roaring Twenties slipped by before eleven o'clock. Just past Mile 31, and upstream of a large side canyon, Waddy ferried the raft over to the west bank.

"You've got to see this area up close. There's a big cave and a nice hike up South Canyon. Later, we'll go down to see what my people call the Two Springs waterfalls." Waddy led the group up to Stanton's Cave, named after a nineteenth century surveyor whose employer wanted to construct a railroad down the Grand Canyon. On the way, on a bench above the river, sat the remains of the dwellings of the last people who had occupied the area over

1,100 years before.

"What are these ruins?" Kateryna asked.

"Seasonal homes. They had some terraced fields, irrigated with water from South Canyon up there. Good drinking water from Two Springs. Also some granaries up the side canyon. Reasonable access to the rim. Three families lived here." Waddy was not particularly effusive in his explanation and Stan realized that Kateryna had a lot more questions. He caught her eye, ending further inquiry with a slight frown and a furtive shake of his head.

"Do you all feel like a good hike up South Canyon or a decadent sprawl in the warm sand by the river?" Waddy asked.

"Let's be decadent," Kateryna answered. "I'd like to go for a swim."

"It'll be more like a quick dunk. That water is still less than 50 degrees. Come on, you guys, walk off some of that fat."

"I think I'd rather lay in the sand too," Stan said.

Saul and Waddy left for their hike while Kateryna disappeared into the rocks above the beach to change. What Stan saw when she reappeared more than confirmed what he'd imagined. She wore a European-style bathing suit of the type common on the beaches of the Côte d'Azur, and from what Stan knew of the price of women's bathing suits, he guessed that Kateryna's must have cost about $10 per square inch of material. He failed entirely in his effort not to gawk. "Aren't you afraid of getting burned?"

"Oh, I'll be okay for a little while." She kneeled down in the sand next to him, negating most of what the tiny patches of fabric tried to accomplish. Kateryna's hair, heretofore kept tightly wound in a knot under her hat, had been released and now fell in cascades of glistening, inky waves. It covered her shoulders and arms as she lay propped up on her elbows looking out at the river.

"Can you please put some sun cream on my back, Stanley?"

"Of . . . of course. Sure." He leapt to comply as she rolled over. He felt hard, well-toned muscles under soft skin. "How about the backs of your legs?"

"All right," came languorous agreement from beneath the extravagant pile of warm hair. Stan found even tighter muscles and even softer skin. When he finished he got up, ran to the river, and dove in. The shock propelled him immediately back out of the water like a recoiling spring. Waddy was right.

"My, that was impulsive," Kateryna smiled when he rejoined her on the narrow blanket. She laid a warm hand on his wet thigh. "Ooo, that water must have felt good." She got up and walked slowly down the beach and into the river as though she were on a south Florida beach. Stan stared in amazement while she eased herself into a pool near a large boulder, completely submerging herself several times before she got out. Her hair hung in thick ropes halfway to her waist as she stood above him, drying herself off and rubbing heavy rolls of hair between her hands with the towel. Stan noticed with increased agony that the cold water had produced firm bumps under the tiny patches of cloth partially covering her breasts.

She sat down, her cold thigh brushing against his, now warm and dry. "You should have waited to put on the sun screen," he said.

"Then you'll have to put some more on, won't you?" Stan again complied, with the familiar emotion. He stroked the oil into her cool, damp skin while she combed the knots out of her hair.

"Are you enjoying yourself?" he asked. "I mean, are you glad you came here with us?"

"Oh, this is just marvelous. Everything is perfect." She turned around and took the tube of sun screen to continue the anointing herself. "We have so much to see . . . and to talk about. I am so sorry that there are only a few more days until I must leave." She frowned slightly. Her statement was about 10 percent true. Ninety percent of her was anxious to return home, to be with Sofiia. The canyon trip was just speeding up, however slightly, the torturous wait until she could go home.

"Stanley, why did you stop my asking Waddy about the aboriginal ruins?"

Smiling at her odd reference to the Anasazi site, Stan quickly realized again that she was, indeed, foreign. The bikini-exposed body and delightful face seemed familiar, but the life experiences and the mind of the woman sitting next to him might as well have been extraterrestrial.

"Those ruins and hundreds, perhaps thousands, of others like them, were left by what we call the Anasazi, the direct ancestors of Waddy's people. He probably knows more about those ancient people than do all of the Anglo anthropological experts combined. He's also very protective—secretive is more like it—about his Hopi origins. In his mind, who the Anasazi were, how they lived, why they suddenly abandoned these canyon lands, even what they called themselves, is not the business of inquisitive Anglos. Those foundations we saw are as much a part of Waddy's life as if the people who built them were still there. To the Hopi, the people, the land, and everything that grows and lives upon it are woven together in what Waddy refers to as the Hopi Way. Western religions exist apart from the land, focusing on a detached God and the central importance of the human species. To Waddy, God *is* the land and every living thing on it, with humans no more important than any of the Earth's other inhabitants." *She's a lifelong communist. I'm probably wasting my time.* "Shortly after I met him, I made the mistake of inquiring why he didn't assist in the excavation of Anasazi sites. He pointed out that Anglos don't dig up their own cemeteries."

Kateryna nodded slowly while she gazed with unfocused eyes toward the river. Her hair nearly dry, Stan couldn't help staring at the now curly mass of thick, warm, blue-black locks.

"Hey, you two look pretty cozy," Waddy said as he and Saul emerged from the rocks above the beach.

"You guys look like you could use a dip in the river," Stan replied, flushing slightly, suddenly self-conscious of his sitting closely next to the nearly naked woman on the skimpy blanket. Saul and Waddy took the suggestion and were soon back on the beach, dripping and reaching for towels.

"Boy, Kateryna, you sure don't look like you have a nine-year-old daughter," Waddy blurted as he plopped down in the sand. Saul looked away with an audible sigh; Stan looked down, shaking his head. Waddy had struck again.

Kateryna smiled back, "I have to work at it very hard. Do you?"

Touché, Stan thought.

"Ooooh kaayyy," Waddy responded with a roll of his eyes. "Let's head on down so we'll have time for more exploration tomorrow." After a quick stop to top off the water cans at Vasey's Paradise, known for over 2,000 years as Two Springs to the Hopi and their ancestors, and a near-disaster when Kateryna started to climb to the falls through a mass of poison ivy, they were back on the river.

"Another fifteen miles to camp," Waddy said, his voice echoing softly between the immense walls of red-stained limestone. "We'll have some company. I know that big commercial outfit planned to stop there, but there're a couple'a nice big beaches with plenty of room. No more rapids today, just some glorified riffles, really. We'll stay nice and dry."

They were soon floating past a huge, sand-floored cavern extending along much of the outside of a big turn. "That's Redwall Cavern," Waddy announced. "John Wesley Powell stopped there on his first trip through the canyon. All those scientists we got comin' down here to study the effects of the dam on the river environment proved what I was sayin' about the beaches wearin' away. A fellow who lives down in Tucson was brought along. He had taken a bunch of pictures of the canyon back in the '40s and '50s so he set up another photograph at the exact spot where he took a picture of Redwall Cavern. Comparing the new picture with the old one proved that the level of the sand has dropped twelve feet since then. Eventually the cavern floor will be gone and it'll just be an undercut of the river."

"Just a quick stop here," Waddy announced when they floated through quiet water at Mile 39. The canyon walls were nearly sheer from river to rim; conspicuously, tailing piles from tunnels on either side spilled into the river. "This is where the Bureau of Reclamation planned another dam, Kateryna. Everything you've seen, clear back to Lee's Ferry, would have been gone. Thought you'd like to consider this when you think about Glen Canyon."

"There's not enough water, on average, to fill the two big reservoirs they've got," Stan said. "They even planned another one, below the park at Bridge Canyon."

"Why weren't they built?"

"After the Glen Canyon disaster, a whole lot of people raised hell, mainly organized by what, at the time, was a small conservation organization called the Sierra Club."

"Yes, I've seen their beautiful books. The books have inspired such groups to form in Ukraine and some of the other republics."

The vertical Redwall limestone, its blond and black layered core stained red by iron oxides leached from the Supai Group above it, shortly gave way to lighter-colored, softer, slope-forming limestones, all of which had been formed by the gradual accumulation of the shells of countless decillions of marine animals in long-ago seas. When the party approached their camp at Mile 46.5, the Kaibab formation, entered at river level at Lee's Ferry, was now over 3,000 feet above them at the canyon rim. They had descended in a little over one day through formations created over a period of more than 300 million years. At evening's camp, the river had cut through the dense limestones and was just entering the much softer Bright Angel shale, its purple and green hues occasionally breaking through the talus of Muav limestone.

"Saul, why don't you and I take a little walk?" Kateryna suggested as she helped haul the last bag up the beach. "I think it's time you and I talked about a few technical details. We don't want to bore Stan and Waddy, do we?"

"Well, okay," Saul stammered, glancing at Stan, who appeared more than a little disappointed. "I guess we should get down to specifics."

She looked at Stan and Waddy. "I hope you understand. Last night got a little intense, and I have only just met you both. I need to retreat a little bit, okay?"

"Hell, yes. Have at it," Waddy said. "There's a real nice trail up the side canyon; starts up the slope behind where you should find that commercial party. Most of them will probably be on a big beach that was scoured out of the river bottom during the 1983 flood—just over that little hill with all the mesquite. They get the nice big beach but we get the last of the sun down Saddle Canyon. Have fun." Stan still looked disappointed.

Saul and Kateryna walked down the beach, then scrambled over limestone rocks and occasional exposures of the vividly-colored Bright Angel shale. Sure enough, when they threaded through a dense grove of mesquite, they found a large group of people spread out in a big camp in the grove and across a lagoon of the river. Dome tents sprouted like mushrooms in little sandy patches among the mesquite and tamarisk thickets. What looked like an army field kitchen was arranged at the foot of the sloping beach where most of the party had gathered around as people always do in any kitchen, even a temporary one in the bottom of Marble Canyon. A drifting cloud of smoke and the fragrance of burning charcoal, kerosene starter, and grilling steaks filled the air. Most of the men had a hand wrapped around a can of beer.

"Kateryna, what you see here goes on in back yards and city parks all over America. Look, they've even got a volleyball net set up. And a horseshoe pitch."

"Is volleyball so popular here?"

"Are you kidding? Remember the last Olympics? This is typical American summer activity and they're getting a nice early start this year. Outdoors, casual, sports, barbecue, beer, just hanging out with friends in a big group."

They said hello to several of the clusters of people before starting up the steep, talus-littered trail to the mouth of the canyon, groved with hackberry trees and box elders which would proliferate farther up the box canyon. They dodged the mesquite thorns but their shorts were occasionally snatched by acacia catclaws: the "wait-a-minute" bush and their mesquite companions grew in dense profusion along the trail together with redbud trees, soon to blossom in magenta-crimson extravagance.

"Saul, think of how much anxiety and trauma we could have saved if groups of my people, from all over the Soviet Union, could have met and talked and, as you say, *hung out* with people like those."

Saul glanced over at the determined woman puffing up the steep trail beside him. "Very true, Kateryna, very true. But, you know, our system isn't perfect either. I think that where the world is ultimately headed is toward some amalgam of your old system and ours. Like you said, so many people in this country would never in a lifetime have the resources to go on a trip like this."

"But they still have their barbecues in the back yard, do they not?"

They stopped at a promontory overlooking the river to absorb the spectacular view of Marble Canyon with its deep alcoves eroded into the limestone walls.

"Saul, the sun is very hot. Let's go farther into the canyon. It looks delightful." Beyond the steep climb up the talus they entered a narrow, intimate canyon. A clear stream trickled along its shrubbery-dotted bottom.

"This place would be incredible in the spring," Kateryna said. Dense groves of winter-barren hackberry, box elder, and redbud trees now filled the canyon. Following a scramble up to the lip of a pothole shelved into the streambed, their exploration ended at the base of a thin waterfall.

"So . . . let's talk," Saul said after they'd nearly drained the canteen Kateryna carried.

"Saul, I have thought about it a great deal. I still feel that a foundation tunnel detonation would be most efficient—but, of course, it could breach the structure. Also, I will admit there could be difficulties with dam security. Looking at your proposal for an underwater detonation directed at a canyon wall, there are weapons I believe I could provide that would do the job."

"Is a one- or two-kiloton device available?"

"Yes, two, what you call kilotons.

"You can obtain a two-KT, freestanding device?"

"Yes, I believe so," Kateryna responded flatly and without hesitation.

"What configuration?"

"A demolition munition."

"We *thought* you had those, but we had no certain intelligence."

"We patterned ours after your W-45."

"That's an old design. We retired that particular ADM in 1984. Did you follow our design exactly?"

"No. By the time we obtained the information on your weapon, our state of the art had expanded considerably. Among other upgrades, ours is boosted."

"How will you know the exact yield? I mean, have the tritium reservoirs been serviced? You know, with the short half life . . ."

"These weapons do not have tritium injection. The pit core is a first-generation urchin constructed as a lattice of polonium and beryllium, with the lattice filled with lithium 6 deuteride. We use a deuterium gun for initial neutron flux. The inclusion of the urchin is simply a backup."

"Initial neutrons come from sort of a supercharged model T . . ." *DAMMIT, control your smart mouth!*

Kateryna did manage to control her instinctive response. "I guess you could look at it that way. These particular weapons had a mission that demanded both reliability and a long shelf life—what I believe you refer to as *wooden* bombs."

"The yield is not variable, like our W-45," Saul said, not as a question.

"No. Incremental yields are fixed with different levels of deuterium injection, mass of fissile material, configurations and detonation matrices of the HE lenses, and also the reflector, tamper and levitation configuration—the usual."

"What about the event counter? I mean, is it up to the sophistication of the ones at Pueblo? I understand you've had some problems."

"I cannot tell you the details; however, you can be confident that it's well beyond the early defaults you refer to."

Saul understood that *cannot* meant *would* not. "Consistency of yield and reliability with this boosted device?"

Kateryna paused a moment. Her reaction did not escape Saul's notice. "I have personally witnessed the repeated testing of this family of weapons. The results were acceptable."

"Is there a problem?"

"I am sure you can understand that I am not able to simply walk into one of our arsenals and select a weapon off the shelf. Only certain weapons may be available. And yes, they have what could be considered to be a problem, as you said."

"What?"

Kateryna hesitated again, her mind filled with the many conflicting considerations in telling the American physicist about a certain design flaw in a certain component of a certain generation of weapons. *It doesn't matter. They don't use this system. Theirs work better.* "It is a switch in the detonator circuit."

"The krytrons?"

"No. Before entering the krytron-switched leads to the detonators, there is a main switch, somewhat like a krytron, that releases the impulse from the capacitor bank. There have been some failures with these switches. Testing has shown that they fail to open 8 percent of the time."

"Is that why you can get access to these weapons? They are being retired or reconfigured?"

"I am not going to get into that."

"You do understand that I have to have reasonably detailed specifics. We'll only have one chance at that dam."

"And I will have only one chance to obtain a weapon."

"Of course . . . I'm sorry."

"This is difficult for me, as well, Saul."

"Yes . . . Perhaps before we get into more detail about this ADM you should explain why you're not considering artillery rounds, a naval torpedo, a missile warhead, and so on."

"Only the ADMs and missile warheads are available. Besides, the only other weapons in the yield range you require would be tube-fired projectiles, which would be difficult to modify for your purposes. Unlike the U.S., we did not get into sophisticated development of artillery. Both the arming and fusing systems would present difficulties in modification for your proposed use."

"So what about the missile warheads?"

"The available warheads have the same switch fault as the ADMs, but . . . there is a more fundamental reason why those would not be . . . would not be available to you. Those weapons are our—how should I say?—our *pièce d'résistance.* Except for the detonator switch problem, they are some of our best creations. Besides, unless you have very technical facilities and particular expertise in the area, you would find great difficulty in penetrating and overriding the PAL, as you call it—the permissive action link. You may find it strange, given that I am here, but I am not willing to reveal the details of such weapons. If their particulars are disclosed under the treaty, that is fine. Saul, I am driven by personal concerns, and I also fear greatly what you and your friends discuss academically: the acquisition by terrorists of nuclear weapons in or near my country. I am not a traitor."

"I know this is very difficult for you; I can only imagine the conflict you must feel—I have two children of my own and I also served in my country's military. Also, despite what I—we—propose doing, we are not traitors, either

. . . But I guess most people would probably say we are." Saul paused to collect his thoughts. "We have no choice but to accept what you can provide. I'm not going to examine the teeth of a horse being given to me."

"Saul, this is not a gift. And until I meet your Malcolm and see that he will truly be able to assist my daughter, there can be no commitment."

"Believe me, Malcolm will arrange anything Sofiia needs. Now, please, you mentioned permissive action links. What access protection exists on the ADMs?"

"That is a main point in their favor for your purpose. The demolition weapon I have in mind does not even meet your category B system, much less your multiple-code, limited-try, two-person, category F."

"Are you saying that it's simply a single digital code?

"Yes."

"Kateryna, I can't believe your people would make access so simple. It's so risky."

"Precisely. And by spiriting one over here to blow up some sandstone in a remote desert, my people—and your people—will definitely be awakened. Perhaps then we can *really* get serious about destruction of all these weapons."

"Will I be able to bypass the PAL?"

"Not unless you are particularly skilled in electronics. The link goes through the event counter; consequently, if the counter does not like what has been done to the circuit it will not function."

"Then I'll have to have the code."

"I . . . I don't know yet. If I can get the weapon I should be able to obtain its code."

"Tell me more about the demolition piece."

"It is not a stone age relic. The switch problem aside, the guts of the ADM—the warhead, including the nuclear system, the nuclear safing system, the implosion system, the firing system, and the mechanical details to assemble them—is a modern, as you say, off-the-shelf item. This device, while not up to the level of the very latest missile hardware, is a basic component of a number of our weapons. It is employed in torpedoes, aerial bombs, and standoff weapons; but the main purpose for this particular design is demolition: for placement where the weapons would have to remain for long periods unserviced. Most importantly to your placement scheme, it has been configured in naval depth charges and marine ADMs."

"Deep water placement?" Saul's eyes glowed.

"Yes, but let me continue. As I said earlier, we used your W-45 as a starting point. Your weapon was first deployed in 1960; by the time we received intelligence on it we had moved far ahead. Our weapon's fissile core and the tamper and reflector assembly is quite modern, with a 41 percent fissile core efficiency. For the tamper we use very highly enriched U 238 and the purity of the beryllium in the reflector is, frankly, better than we have seen in your weapons. The whole tamper/reflector arrangement is far superior to the tuballoy used in your W-45. The fissile core is constructed of super-grade, 98 percent plutonium 239, concentrically matrixed with shells of highly enriched U 235. Furthermore, the weapon employs nearly the latest advancements in the chemical explosive lens component. We have solved much of the neutron flux absorption problem while retaining near optimum push properties. We also solved the difficulties you had with voids. Our HE has very reduced shock sensitivity and high heat resistance. All of these improvements led to our resolving your W-45's principal problem. What was it, 200 kilos? And about sixty centimeters in diameter by 120 centimeters? What we have is a very good field weapon: approximately forty centimeters in diameter by seventy centimeters in length, with a weight of forty-five kilos. Two men can deploy it."

"What was their primary mission? It's not just curiosity; I really need to know everything you can tell me about the device."

"All right. They were for a particular task in the European theater. I'm sure your military command know the details. They were deployed along the entire length of the Russian, Byelorussian, Moldavian, and Ukrainian frontiers—to stop armored advances by creating physical barriers. Hundreds were in place."

I'm sure they remain in place. Saul remembered the Russians' fanaticism about invasion of their borders. *They will never forget Genghis Khan, the Teutonic Knights, Napoleon, and Hitler, among many others.* "You've convinced me. Now tell me about the underwater version."

"The same weapon but slightly heavier and larger. With the pressure case requirements, size and weight were increased to about fifty centimeters by eighty centimeters and, for the two-kiloton device, a weight of about fifty-five kilos. Increased bulk and weight were not so critical since the weapons would normally be deployed from shipboard."

"Used as depth charges, they must be much lower yield."

"Well, certainly. As depth charges we have fractional kiloton weapons. Our destroyer crews were not intended to be kamikazes, Saul. But the counterparts to the land mines are the same yields."

"And they were to be used for . . . ?"

"Underwater deployment at critical naval choke points, such as the Bosporus Strait, the Dardanelles, Suez, Gibraltar—for protection against your Sixth Fleet."

"And Panama, too, I'll bet."

"Among other places," Kateryna replied abruptly. "Saul, we are not concerned here with details of military tactics"

"These naval weapons still retain the simple PAL?"

"Yes, because they also had a mission for covert or battle deployment by special underwater teams. The command staff prevailed in the requirement that they could be reliably armed, even by a single person, under intense combat conditions. The decision was made to compromise safety and security for reliability in a combat stress environment—the same reasoning that demanded a simple boosting arrangement not relying on a tritium reservoir, insertion mechanics, and so on."

"Within the pressure case I assume you have retained the usual sealed nuclear unit?"

"Yes, of course. We used argon in these weapons."

"I'll have to get into the physics package to access the arming and fusing circuits. What am I going to do with the gas?" Saul thought out loud. "I'm glad to hear that the plutonium is nearly pure 239 isotope. At least once the gas is disposed of, I won't have a very hot environment to work in."

"That's right. Once the argon is removed you could safely work around the core, but get a suit anyway. You'll have to devise something to pump the gas to another sealed container. The nuclear unit has a connector for such purposes. The service-necessary components—the power source and the neutron generator—are accessible from outside the hot unit, but you will have to get into the case to get at the arming and fusing mechanisms."

"Right. In order to adapt the weapon for our arming and fusing requirements, I'll have to dig into the guts of it. Does that bother you?"

"You'll not see anything much different from what our other teams are taking apart in Nizhnyaya Tura. And without particular expertise in electronics you'll discover nothing about the event counter. Basically, this device is well within the scope of what you are doing over here. The scientists at your Sandia, Lawrence Livermore, Berkeley, and Los Alamos laboratories are highly respected by our people. Further, we realize that your espionage has been nearly the equal of ours."

Saul was thankful that Malcolm wasn't present to hear this. He would have doubtless pointed out that the "our" Kateryna referred to was no more. Waddy could make insensitive comments that didn't faze her, Saul thought, but Malcolm could shove a big political foot into his mouth and blow the whole deal. *I've got to remember to woodshed Malcolm before he has a chance to talk to her.* "What do you think about my idea to employ sonar-activated fusing?"

"That depends entirely upon the level of sophistication of the sonar signaling system, whether it can be compromised, and, of course, whether you can get your hands on such devices."

"Can you help at all? The underwater versions you've described would have to have sonar-activated triggering like I propose to use." Saul knew he was on thin ice with his undisguised overreaching.

"We have such devices, of course, for both triggering and detection systems, similar to the ones your latest nuclear attack submarines employ. Even the sonar buoys used by your antisubmarine aircraft are functionally similar. But to answer your question, I really doubt that I could help. Saul, all of you have to understand that I will not be informing you of the details of how I will gain access to the weapon or even where it will come from. I will tell you that the weapons and the sonars are probably not in the same locale, therefore to attempt to acquire both could cause the whole scheme to fail. That is as far as I am prepared to go in explaining the problems I would face."

"I had no business trying to push you that far, Kateryna. It's just that the matter of safeguarding the triggering of the bomb is as important as the weapon itself. It will be my biggest problem to solve—both technically and logistically. Let me ask you this. Does the marine version of the ADM have a variable proximity fuse system?"

"They have provisions for including such systems, but they are not actually installed in the particular weapons I'm talking about." She shook her head. "Saul, with the placement scheme you have in mind, I see a significant problem."

"The mass detection component."

"Yes. Naval proximity fuses do not have to be highly sensitive since they need only detect large ferrous or titanium masses. Even so, the matter of electronic and even mechanical countermeasures and corresponding counter-countermeasures for these systems is an area of great sophistication in naval subsurface warfare. I am afraid that is well out of my knowledge."

"Yeah, me too," Saul admitted. "I'm open to any suggestion you have."

"Perhaps you should rethink the whole concept of an underwater detonation. You may be too focused on that approach and fail to see solutions to the problems you foresaw with the other placement locations. The underwater weapon would be applicable to whatever plan you employed—just a little bulkier than necessary for dry land placement."

"So the punch line here is that you may be able to obtain a weapon with a yield and configuration that are ideal but there is an 8 percent chance that it could malfunction."

"That's it."

"Why don't we head on back?" They scrambled down the slick chute from the pothole and were soon back in the harsh winter sunlight, overlooking the canyon.

"I'm definitely ready for another dunk in the river. In the summer, this canyon would be worse than Kazakhstan."

They walked back through the crowd of happy campers on the beach, waving to people they'd talked to earlier. "Saul, will you tell me about your Stanley Bellamy?"

Saul glanced at her as she looked away. *Just part of her evaluation of us, or is there more? That would certainly add another wrinkle to the whole thing.* "What you see is pretty much what there is. I've known Stanley for, what? Thirty-six years. He's my closest friend. I think I could ask him for anything and he'd break his neck to accommodate. I feel the same way about him. So does Malcolm, and probably Waddy too. Stanley is trained in the law: started out with the State Department, then private practice, now he's teaching at the San Francisco College of Law. He's comfortable now preparing new lawyers for their lives of relentless ridicule."

"What do you mean?"

"Our legal system works, in the true democratic sense." *Uh-oh. Shouldn't have said that.* "What I mean is– –"

"I know, Saul, we have a great deal to learn in that regard. Go on."

Boy, she really is interested if she'll just let that one slide by. "To make our system work we have to put up with a lot of bullshit. Most lawyers, I think, feel that way too. The basic premise is that our system should free a thousand morally guilty persons rather than convict one innocent one. Does that make sense to you?"

"No. It doesn't."

"In the process of bending over backward to protect that one innocent person, the other thousand get away with murder—in some cases, literally. As a consequence, lawyers are subject to a constant barrage of public opprobrium because they use what people think of as technicalities to set guilty people free. Stanley finally had enough of the lawyer bashing. Even at the State Department, he found that being a lawyer was often a liability."

"Does he have children?"

"Stanley has never been married—and I don't think he has any children," Saul laughed. *Shit, that sounded like something Waddy would say.*

"What has he said about the prospect of being a fugitive after you all go ahead with this?"

Saul stopped and turned to her. "We're all struggling with that one. Aren't you and Sofiia going to have to leave your country permanently if you deliver the weapon to us?"

"I suppose that is part of what Waddy meant last night when he referred to this thing getting down to individual, personal resolutions of issues."

"I'm confident Malcolm will do his best to soften the blow, you and Sofiia included."

They were almost back to the camp when she asked: "Does Stanley have a serious personal relationship he would have to give up? I mean, do you think that is going to be an issue for him?"

"No. No, I don't think so." *Is she just trying to figure out our depth of commitment, or is there something else?* Back at the beach, Saul watched the tall, graceful woman walk straight to Stan.

"Okay, people, we're gonna have a little change of program today," Waddy announced after they crashed through the short but violent Kwagunt Rapid at Mile 56. "The Little Colorado will join the river just up ahead, and

I'll be leaving you for a while. You guys take the boat down past the river junction and pick me up right where you'll first see the Great Unconformity. The Tapeats sandstone sits right on top of it. Can't miss it. Okay? Got to visit some old friends."

Saul and Stan nodded. Kateryna gave Saul a puzzled glance.

"I'll explain later," he whispered.

The canyon was becoming grander and grander as the high ramparts of the limestones and sandstones extended farther out from the river above the sloping shales. The vertical walls of the harder rock broke off in slabs as the soft shales eroded from beneath them. By this recession of cliffs the canyon widened, generally retaining an established profile, while the river cut deeper into the progressively older formations. By the time the Little Colorado joined the parent river, sixty-one miles below Lee's Ferry, the canyon rims rose 4,000 feet above the river and were separated by several miles.

The Little Colorado River had carved its own canyon, draining much of northeastern Arizona and some of western New Mexico, including the entirety of the Painted Desert and Petrified Forest regions. Except during the regular summer rainy season, or when occasional storms pass through its basin, the Little Colorado is a hot, dry gash in the desert landscape for all but the last few miles of its course. When the tributary river does run in flood, unchecked by any dam, it injects thousands of tons of sediment into the main stem of the Colorado in an effort to restore its eroding beaches, banks, and bars. But the frugal infusions of life-giving sediment are not up to the task of restoring the river, running cold and clear from the turbines of Glen Canyon Dam. The continual, daily-fluctuating outpourings from the still, sediment-free pool behind the dam more than undoes what the adolescent stream and other tributaries try to build.

At the extreme lower end of the Little Colorado, just a few miles above its confluence with the mother river, a series of wellsprings arise from the lower Tapeats sandstone and continue up into the Bright Angel shale and the overlying limestones. The springs are remarkable for their production of vivid, turquoise-blue water. Some of the color of the "Little Caribbean" is caused by dissolved calcium carbonate, but most derives from the interaction of algae and bacteria teeming in the warm, petri-dish environment. A particular spring forms a deep pool within a huge formation of travertine mineral deposits the bubbling water has built up over the unknown time it has flowed. This place and one other occasioned Waddy's announced detour.

Just above the confluence at river left, he pulled the boat into a little beach overhung with ledges of Tapeats sandstone, tamarisk, and mesquite. The anticipated aquamarine stream was a roiling tumult of mud and debris.

"Shit. Had a storm upstream. Wish you could'a seen the natural water from the springs. This looks like what we get during the summer monsoon."

When the brown current debouched into the clear green water of the Colorado, the intrusion formed a dense, contrasting finger thrusting into the river, then slowly diffused. From this point on, the river would continue to have an opaque tan tint until the sediments settled into the still, upper reach of Mead Reservoir, nearly two hundred miles downstream.

"So you only have to take the boat about two miles down. Can you guys handle that?" Waddy grinned as he hefted a rucksack to his shoulder.

"If we can't, I guess you'll have a long walk, won't you? Take your time; we're way ahead of schedule."

"How're you going to get across that running mud pie?" Saul asked.

"Guess I'll get wet." He started up the broad stepping-stone ledges of Tapeats forming the north bank of the Little Colorado. "See ya later. Maybe five hours."

Kateryna could contain herself no longer. "Are you going to tell me what this is all about?"

Saul found a comfortable seat on a warm ledge of Tapeats and peeled off his wet suit jacket. The canyon had been cold, out of the direct sunlight, but the exposed river junction was bathed in warmth.

"Why don't we have some lunch and we'll tell you what we know," Saul said as Kateryna watched the roiling brown water flow around a large, boulder strewn island where the rivers joined: the official end of Marble Canyon and the beginning of the Grand Canyon.

"Hard to believe now, but for most of the year the Little Colorado flows as a beautiful stream of bright blue water, sort of the color of the turquoise in Waddy's necklace. Archaeologists figured out that this area has been occupied by people for at least 2,000 years—some ruins remain, across the river a ways upstream. It's generally accepted now that Waddy's Hopi are the direct descendants of those ancient people. Of course, the Hopi know for sure; it's only us non-Indians who are just now beginning to figure things out. The blue water flows from a series of springs up the canyon. Waddy is going to one of the springs, very sacred to them: they call it Sipapuni. To the Hopi it is the place of emergence from their previous third world, and it is there that they can communicate with departed souls. So that's why we're not tagging along."

"Yes, I see," Kateryna said slowly. She gazed up the wide canyon where Waddy had vanished, her examination of the scene finally being drawn to the summit of Cape Solitude which dominated the south rim.

Saul pointed to the other side. "That's Chuar Butte, with Temple Butte right next to it. They still hold the wreckage of a TWA Constellation and a United DC-7 that collided in 1956. Have you ever heard of our Federal Aviation Administration?"

"Of course. It was the prototype for our own . . . the Russian agency."

"That crash is what started the FAA. It was only a couple of years before we had our trip down from the head of Glen Canyon. It seems almost like yesterday. Right Stan?"

"Yeah . . . That's what this canyon does," Stan said without looking over.

Kateryna looked to Saul for an explanation of Stan's cryptic response. He shrugged. "Remember the Redwall we entered back in the Roaring Twenties and the big cavern below Vasey's Paradise? That's the Redwall clear up there now." Kateryna followed the direction of his hand to the sheer cliff high above the terraced formations between it and the river. "And that's where we started," he continued, indicating the Kaibab formation at the rim of the canyon, now its natural blond without the vanished Moencopi to stain it red.

"How far up is it now?"

"Nearly 4,000 feet. The river will sink more than another thousand."

Kateryna's attention was again focused on the tributary canyon. "Do all of Waddy's people make pilgrimages to their shrine?"

"I don't think so. What about it, Stan; you've spent a lot of time with Waddy."

"I don't know."

Saul: "I believe only certain people are permitted to visit because it is so sacred. The Navajo stay away too. From the little I know, it seems that that area should be completely off limits to anyone other than the Hopi. Trouble is, it's very accessible to all the river traffic."

"Then Waddy has some special stature among his people if he is going there."

"He's a member of his tribe's One-Horn Society and I believe they are among the few permitted to visit the Sipapuni. At least he used to be a member, but I think something happened. He's mentioned that in the past year he has spent less time at Hopi. The only hint I got was one time he commented that he had failed to follow the Hopi virtues. Maybe that has something to do with what he's doing today. What do you think, Stan?"

Stan shrugged and shook his head.

"Where else is he going?" She concentrated on Stan as Saul spoke.

"A couple miles down the river the Hopi have another sacred site. A salt mine. The salt is still used in their ceremonies."

"Salt has been revered in many cultures," she said distractedly as she got up and sat down next to Stan. "You're being pretty quiet today, Stanley. I'll give you a valuable Russian ruble for your thoughts."

"Oh . . . It's nothing. I was just thinking about how shallow our modern Anglo cultures are. There's Waddy, going up to commune with 2,000-or-more-year-old ancestors, and I couldn't tell you who my great-grandparents were, much less what they did and thought and believed. Saul's people keep track of where they came from, but I'll bet he doesn't know details about his great-grandparents, either. Right, Saul?" Saul smiled and shook his head. "What about your people, Kateryna? "Stan asked.

"In Ukraine we are very much aware of our origins. Having been overrun so many times in the past, we are an amalgam of many ancient cultures. We in the south have much eastern influence—from the Tatars. Can't you see it in the shape of my eyes?"

Stan leaped at the opportunity. Within the almond contours, set under strong, black brows, he could at last try to plumb the colors in the huge, dark pupils, partially eclipsed by lash-heavy lids. He found flecks and flashes of purple, green, and gold, blended in a deep chocolate matrix of melted opal.

Saul couldn't help but notice that Stan's close examination, with his index finger gently tipping up Kateryna's chin, was concerned with more than a mild interest in ethnicity.

* * *

"Okay, people, we have *got* to take a close look at this one," Waddy said after he pulled the raft through the foamy eddy line. They had spent the previous night on a beach that afforded the maximum late afternoon exposure before the sun disappeared, too early, behind the rim of the Kaibab Plateau. Their camp, in the area of the river known as "Furnace Flats," was at the bottom of the famous Tanner Trail, one of the few paths from the rim that descended all the way to the river. They had enjoyed an evening of lively conversation with a group of young backpackers on a month-long adventure exploring the trails of the south rim.

From down the canyon the deep rumble was felt as much as it was heard. They were just across from a large side canyon with a boulder-strewn dune at its mouth as Waddy led the way up a steep slope above the right side of the river. Across the river canyon, splotches of bright red shale glowed brilliantly, illuminated by the harsh winter light. They stared in silence down the canyon. Below them, boiling and churning through a chaos of white water, the river descended through the notorious Hance Rapid.

At thirty feet, the "Rock Garden" is the greatest descent in the entirety of Marble and Grand Canyons: a continuum of waves and deep holes interspersed with exposed rocks or barely-covered "sleepers." Only the fact of its relatively long course keeps it from being the worst stretch of white water in the whole course of the Colorado River. But like all the major rapids in the canyon, Hance exists at a point where an entering side canyon occasionally deposits its load of debris in the river channel. The situation at this place is magnified by the coincidental fact that at some point in the ancient past the layers of sedimentary rock had been intruded by a basalt, an igneous rock much harder than the surrounding material. The river has had a difficult time carving through the obstruction, so it just pours over the boulders that rest on top of the basalt. Waddy was trying to figure out the least dangerous route through the obstacle course marching down the river below them.

"At low water it's easiest to pick out the route from this vantage rather than from the dune across the river," he said. "It's gonna be a bitch with this low water. Can't be over 6,000."

"Those look like big holes along the right side, and the left side is very rocky at the top," Kateryna said.

"You've got that right. Those holes are boat swallowers. Land of the Giants, it's called."

Stan: "So maybe go in just to the right of the rocks in the center, then across that flat stretch."

"Looks like a big hole right at the end of the flat water," Saul cautioned.

"Yeah, that area is called the Duck Pond," Waddy nodded, "and there sure as hell is a big hole at the end. At higher water the hole wouldn't be so bad, but it'll be deep today."

"It looks like a right-to-left ferry past the hole at the end of the Duck Pond, but I can't tell what happens after that," Stan said.

"Past the pond we just have to stay away from the Rubber Magnet that tries to draw you over toward that big domer and into the Land of the Giants at river right. Past the Rubber Magnet we just crash through a series of closely spaced waves. Very little choice today." Waddy continued to examine his planned course. "This thing just keeps gettin' worse with the rocks that keep comin' down Red Canyon. Damn that damn dam!" Once again, albeit not as enthusiastically, everyone declined Waddy's suggestion that they walk around.

"This water was released a little after this time yesterday," he said. "Runs about ninety miles per day. Must've been zero peaking demand at midday down in Phoenix for the water to be this low. The Navajo Generating Station provides the steady power to Phoenix."

Waddy pointed out that Hance was rated 9 at the present flow and less than two miles below it was Sockdolager Rapid, almost a 9. Then at two and a half mile intervals would be Grapevine (8) and Zoroaster (7), the latter named for the bright rose-colored granite that would soon be seen striking into the equally hard, black Vishnu shist, the oldest rocks in the canyon at about 1.7 billion years.

Starting just below Hance Rapid, the whole character of the river-level Grand Canyon changes. The fairly benign, slow descent through the colorful, sun-drenched limestone and sedimentary formations narrows abruptly to a dark channel through the twisted, grotesquely deformed Precambrian shist and granitic intrusions. The fossil-bearing Cambrian Period ends with the Tapeats formation. Below that is the Great Unconformity, where the formations deposited over hundreds of millions of years were eroded away before the sandy-brown Tapeats sandstone was laid down. Hundreds of pages of the geologic record are missing. The river cuts quickly through the few surviving formations below the Great Unconformity and then comes to the ancient metamorphic shist, itself lying under another "Great Angular" unconformity. Between the two relatively closely spaced unconformities, 1.2 billion years have disappeared. The river then tries to continue its downward erosion, with little success. Through the reluctantly yielding shist and granite, far into the lower Grand Canyon, the river's erosion has been nearly stopped at the floor of this vault of earth's history.

Waddy drifted the raft sideways down the smooth approach to the cataract, standing up on the seat to get what view he could over its rim. The tops of the first group of waves protruded sporadically above the glossy smooth, undulating sag at the lip of the fall. The bright sunny slopes of Hakatai shale suddenly dimmed. A heavy bank of clouds blotted the sun, seeming to magnify the roar that filled the canyon. Drifting toward the fall, Waddy lined up to pass the protruding rocks. He thought of the low flow and the sharp rocks just beneath the surface, so to avoid the rocks he set up farther to the right than he'd planned.

He glanced back at Saul, perched on the gear pile, and realized another mistake he'd made. Through Furnace Flats everyone had shed their wet suit tops. Preoccupied with the run through Hance, Waddy failed to notice that Saul had not put his back on.

"Saul! Get that wet suit top on!" But Saul had no time. With both hands he clutched the heavy netting over the gear pile as the whole descent of the rapid came into view.

Waddy crashed the boat directly into the first series of waves as he passed the mid-channel rocks, heading toward the flat of the Duck Pond. He'd planned to row forward across the pond, but he found himself well to the right-hand side and his forward rowing position did not give him the power to ferry across the pond as he could with strong backstrokes. *Damnit, I should have gone in stern first.* The glossy dome of the pourover into the hole at the end of the pond was coming up fast. *Too late to go left.* Waddy cranked back hard on the oars, to pull the raft around the right side. He almost made it, but the bow went over the dome and crashed into the edge of the hole, spinning the raft violently counterclockwise when it swung down into, then past the six-foot-deep boil of white water.

Being well into the series of steep waves and holes past the Duck Pond, a major course change was not an option; then any change of course or attitude vanished when Waddy lost his grip on the left oar. Hance Rapid had the unfortunate property of getting more violent as it progressed into its middle section and beyond, and to make matters worse he was now sliding toward the Land of the Giants. The raft rode sideways in the current when it rose to the crest of a large wave and crashed down the back side into the trough beneath an even larger, back-curling comber. This time the boat slowed in the trough, but the tons of water coming from behind did not.

"High side!" Waddy yelled as the crashing water submerged the upstream tube. But it was too late. In a perfect demonstration of moment arm mechanics and angular momentum, the raft rolled over, counterclockwise. Waddy heard a muffled cry above the toneless, pounding roar. He thought first of Kateryna, but it had come from behind him. Stan and Kateryna had disappeared in the wall of water coming over the side of the boat. Waddy felt himself falling, endlessly falling, down and down, surrounded by churning, frigid water.

It seemed forever before his head burst through to the air. The frothy water sloped above him in every direction; the raft was beside him, upside down. Before he was thrust under again, he saw two heads and the tops of orange life vests a few feet ahead at the rim of the crater of water surrounding him. *Stuck in a hole. This is bad. Real bad.* He was again sucked under; once again he felt himself being drawn down, turning end over end, collisions with boulders knocking the air from his lungs. Another endless time passed before he was pitched into the cloudy light. The raft was now on the other side of him and it seemed that he was out of the hole. Bobbing in the waves just ahead of the boat were two heads and life vests. *Kateryna and Stan. Where's Saul?* "Saul!" He looked around. Nothing. *Shit, he's under the boat!*

Stan and Kateryna had slowed themselves and were even with the front of the boat, now revolving slowly in the rapid's tail water. "Stan! Uncoil the bow line and toss it over the back of the boat." Waddy struggled to pull himself under the raft, fighting the Extrasport foam vest that was specifically designed to keep him from doing what he was trying to do. He groped around under the load of equipment and rowing frame, now functioning as a perfect keel, until he found a leg. With one hand gripping the leg and the other reaching around the perimeter tube, he struggled to pull Saul out from under the raft, but Saul's vest was doing its best to stay under the boat. Just as the raft was heading into Son of Hance, the combined struggles of Waddy, Stan, and Kateryna extricated Saul from beneath the raft. "Hang on to him while we're goin' through this one!" Waddy shouted.

Using the bow line now stretched over the length of the boat, Waddy was able to scramble out of the water. Then, with an amazing vault, Kateryna seized the bow line and pitched herself up so that she was sprawled over the tube. Waddy grabbed a fistful of beautifully-filled wet suit and pulled her the rest of the way onto the bottom of the boat. Stan quickly followed, and the three tried to drag Saul's dead weight up over the side. There was nothing to brace against until Waddy tied a hitch around Saul with the bow line and then cantilevered himself over the bow at the end of the line. After several attempts, Saul was finally atop the overturned raft.

"Do you know CPR?" Waddy asked Kateryna.

She nodded.

"Get to work. Stan and I have to swim this thing into an eddy somewhere." Waddy scanned the long, dark channel ahead of them; the vertically foliated black shist and dikes of rose granite erupted in a ragged wall from either side of the swirling water. They were more than midway between Hance and Sockdolager Rapid. He thought of the series of fierce waves, holes, and pourovers coming up, a near repeat of the now-forgotten Hance. *Be more like Rockdolager at this flow.* As far as he could see down the gorge, the dark walls of shist and granite thrust vertically from the river. No sloping shales; no beaches: a ragged tunnel leading directly to one of the major rapids. He couldn't remember. He just couldn't remember where the next landing should be. He thought there was a small beach at Asbestos Canyon riffle. *Are we past it? Ought to be able to spot Asbestos Canyon.* Everything looked the same in the dim canyon. No landmarks. The outer rim was now out of view from the narrow inner gorge. He tied the end of the bow line around his waist and started toward the right side.

Kateryna loosened Saul's vest and cleared his airway. She and Stan were just starting the breathing and chest compression routine when Waddy suddenly saw Asbestos Canyon coming up on the right. "Stan! Into the water! We gotta try to eddy-out up there." Once they were in the water, Waddy realized they'd never make it, and he was almost certain there was no other possible place to land on the right side before they got to Sockdolager. He thought he remembered a tiny beach on the other side, at the head of the rapid. *Yeah. Hance Creek.* "Other side, Stan, we gotta swim it to the left side. Come on! We'll never make that one on the right." Waddy swam diagonally left down the river, dragging the heavy raft.

He could hear Sockdolager just around the bend in the dark canyon. "Swim, Stan! Push! Frog kick!" The river was moving more swiftly now as the canyon narrowed; when they rounded the bend the sounds of the rapid filled the ragged gorge. Cold rain began to pelt the water. Waddy caught a glimpse of the little beach: a tiny, steeply slopped patch of sand right at the head of the rapid. *There's got to be an eddy there. Has to be an eddy. Otherwise there'd be no beach.* Waddy realized he wasn't thinking entirely coherently. *Hypothermia. Deadly. Damn that cold reservoir water. Fuck that dam!* He glanced to the right, downstream. He could see the leaping tops of what he knew was a long run of closely-spaced waves, interspersed with holes and pourovers. *We can't go into that fucker. We'd never make it.* "Swim Stan, swim!" Waddy thought he could feel the current start to accelerate. Suddenly he felt it slow, then reverse. *The eddy!* "Keep pushin', Stan!" Waddy's feet touched rocks and soft mud and then he was on the bank struggling up the beach and tying the line around a boulder.

They dragged Saul up the little beach to the flattest place they could find. He was nearly the color of the hypalon raft and Kateryna had not been able to get him to breathe. Everyone went to work. Kateryna had the breathing detail when Saul came back to life with a convulsion of retching, coughing, and shivering. She spat out a mouthful of what had surged from his stomach.

The rain stopped, but a strong wind blew up the dark inner gorge. The sunless, 50° wind-chilled air was like ice. With the accompanying lack of strength, coordination, and judgment caused by their exposure, Waddy knew the first order of business, starting with Saul, was to get warm. "We gotta get the stuff outta the boat." He crawled into the water under the raft and went to work on the webbing holding the frame to the D-rings. *Just take your time.* His long-ago river mentor had driven home the wisdom of the need for extreme care when razor sharp knives were used underwater in the vicinity of tender flesh and thin hypalon.

"Okay, it's cut loose. Help me lift the raft off." The bottom of the Avon was soon resting on the beach; Waddy then went to work cutting the webbing and tie-downs on the bundle of gear. They quickly separated the "Bill's bags"—the ingenious synthetic rubber duffels, with their clever roll-up closing mechanism designed long ago by some resourceful river rat, produced warm, dry clothing and sleeping bags.

"Looks like you learned how to roll up a river bag right. They're nice and dry. Let's get Saul out of those wet bottoms and into his bag. Kateryna, strip down and get in with him," Waddy commanded.

Despite his anxiety over his old friend, Stan felt a sudden wave of envy as Kateryna crawled into the polypro bag clad only in a pair of bikini panties and a turtleneck. He went back to cranking up the Coleman stove to start a pot of water for soup.

"Well, that certainly enhanced our day, didn't it," Waddy said with a little laugh.

Stan immediately rejoined: "Yes, we had a good hance-on experience." He looked down to see if Kateryna had appreciated their absurd little repartee and was met with a smile and a shake of her head. The three of them started to enjoy the buoyancy of relief which seems always to follow a close call with disaster—just one of the defense mechanisms of the human mind.

After about thirty minutes with a pair of long, warm, dry legs wrapped around him in the packed sleeping bag, Saul started to recover.

"My, Colonel, is this a Ukrainian tradition?" he said groggily to a chorus of relieved laughter. "Throw me back in the river so we can do this again."

"Stay in there until he starts to get a hard-on, then you can get out." Even in his diminished state, Saul managed a cringe. Kateryna blushed even more deeply than she had when she'd reacted to Waddy's explanation of the toilet.

"Waddy, no wonder there are only 9,000 of you Hopis left," Stan said.

"I'll bet there is only one like him," Kateryna smiled.

"Stan, why don't you and I climb up Hance Creek to see if the spirits left any combustible flood debris for us." They disappeared up the steep gully and soon returned with two big armloads of wood, some still dry. Kateryna was out of the sleeping bag and spooning some of the hot soup into a slowly recovering Saul.

"Well, this is not exactly an ideal camp," Waddy said, "but it sure beats the shit outta dyin' in that river."

"Amen to that, my friend," Stan said. Everyone stared out at the violent boil of water stretching down the canyon below their perch on the beach. Little was said as they sat huddled around the smoky fire, thinking about what had almost happened. This was their last night on the river.

Maybe that happened on purpose, Waddy thought. *Nothin' like a close call like that to bring people real close together.* He glanced over at Kateryna, sitting very close to Stan. *Yeah, I think what happened was just what we needed.* "Tomorrow mornin' we have nine miles down to Phantom Ranch—and I'll be more careful through this one." He nodded toward the river. "Past Sockdolager we only have Grapevine, probably not as bad, and then Zoroaster and 85 Mile."

After a fitful night on the rocky, slanted shore, everyone was up and packed with the first dim light seeping into the inner gorge. High above them and out of view, the sun blazed yellow on the Kaibab formation at the canyon rim.

"With this start, we'll have plenty of time to make our appointment topside," Waddy predicted when they pushed off into the cool morning air, hanging motionless over the river. "Ready to get nice and wet again so early in the morning?" Waddy laughed as he quickly pointed the boat headlong into the fury of Sockdolager.

Just after nine o'clock they floated under the black steel Kaibab footbridge, where Waddy pulled the raft over to a long, willow-bordered beach. Below the landing, Bright Angel Creek came bubbling into the river from the right-hand side of the canyon.

"Let's just leave our crap in the boat. I can bring the mules down here to load up."

"What a delightful place this is," Kateryna exclaimed. They walked up the well-worn trail through the shady, sun-dappled groves of cottonwoods and oaks covering the floor of Bright Angel Canyon. They were suddenly back in civilization, with groomed campsites and the ubiquitous dome tents scattered regularly through the stands of trees. The Bright Angel campground was always popular because it was the only place in the whole length of Marble and Grand Canyons where a traverse between the canyon's rims was possible.

A short walk up from the river found them among the buildings of Phantom Ranch, long a resort run by the Canyon Park Company, operator of all of the concessions within Grand Canyon National Park. A main cantina and dining room and a number of guest cabins clustered along the thicketed bank of the creek. Everything was artfully laid out, with stone-bordered trails winding among the buildings and groves. Most of the people they encountered around the resort buildings had neither walked in under a heavy load nor floated in but had ridden down on Canyon Park Company mules from the sprawling resort on the south rim.

"Go on and look around while I see about our transportation up the hill," Waddy said with a wave as he headed toward the corrals. "If you run into a worn-out, cowboy-lookin' guy named Buck, tell him where I am."

A likely-Buck was spotted immediately in the little canteen, busily holding forth to a group of people, many of whom wore "I love Philadelphia" T-shirts. The Easterners were among the few lucky visitors at Phantom Ranch who had reservations for the resort's handful of cabins.

Unlike most of the dude ranch wranglers who spent a few months each year escorting tourists up and down the Kaibab and Bright Angel Trails between the south rim and Phantom Ranch, Buck was a legitimate cowboy. He looked like the squeaky-clean Marlboro Man should have looked: a cadaver-white, almost-bald pate and a dark brown, leathery complexion, extending from the eyes down, gained from forty years of living outdoors under a broad-brimmed hat. His feet had never been shoved into perfect, $500 lizard skin boots intended solely for the wilds of a dance floor; rather, his old Tony Lamas were mostly worn at the ball of the foot where they were nearly rubbed through after nearly 5,000 miles in a pair of stirrups. Buck was as thin as a coach whip except for the paunch starting to protrude over his old rodeo buckle (awarded, not purchased) as a lifetime of beer drinking was beginning to overtake his fading metabolism. The buckle and its stained and scarred belt, with "Buck" carved in the back, held up a pair of old tight Levis whose pockets contained not a thing and which ended in tatters and folds over the insteps of the rowel-spurred Tony Lamas. Tucked into the top of the old Levis was a faded plaid cotton shirt, displaying no hint of excess capacity and with its little mother-of-pearl snap buttons strained to their own capacities above the rodeo buckle. The single pocket in the shirt front contained a little bag of Bull Durham loose tobacco and a packet of cigarette papers. Buck was not aware that the papers now outsold the tobacco bags by a large margin. The sleeves of his shirt were snapped shut at the wrists with a trio of the same fake pearl buttons. All Buck needed to do to dress up was to remove the oversized bandana knotted around his neck, close the top fastener of his shirt, and hang a turquoise and silver bolo tie under the collar.

"Are you Buck?" Stan inquired when they walked into the little dining room with its blue Formica tables and wicker chairs.

"You got'im, mister," came the reply from behind an intermittent row of Beechnut- and Bull Durham-stained teeth. A hand rolled cigarette bobbed on Buck's lower lip. "Who's askin'?"

"We're friends of Waddy. He's looking for you at the mule barn, and we've got a boat down on the river waiting for your people."

"Right on time. S'cuse me, folks; gotta go see my favorite little Injun." Buck extracted himself from the crowd of Philadelphians and led the three strangers down to the corrals.

"So, which of these roach-backed, cow-hocked nasties you gonna permit us to use today?" Waddy called out while he walked over to greet his old friend. "We're gonna need four for ridin' and two for packin'. Make that three packers."

"Nothin' but the best for you, my friend," Buck said as they shook hands. "Take your pick. Here, I'll help ya'." Buck and Waddy waded into the crowd of mules and soon had seven of the animals tied to the corral rail in front of the tack shed.

"Will they all work together? I don't know any of these critters."

"Yeah, these are all mine. You ride Buster there, the others'll follow okay. Better put sorry ol' Biscuit in the middle, though; he don't like suckin' hind titty. The lady can ride Huckleberry and for you, big fella, we got Tuffy here," Buck nodded at Stan as he slapped a thick young sorrel on the rump. "Saul, is it? You ride little Notch. They're all real gentle. Won't be a problem at all."

"Can we help?" Stan asked.

"Naw," Buck drawled, "Waddy'n' me'll handle things jus' fine."

Stan, Saul, and Kateryna watched in quiet fascination as the two men quickly and efficiently outfitted the mules with halters and leads, bridles, and riding and pack saddles, smoothly cinching, buckling, and tying off the latigos, breast collars, breeching, connecting, and myriad other straps used on a modern Decker pack saddle. They rigged cargo slings and hung panniers.

"You plan to load up down at the river, Waddy?"

"Thought that'd be easiest. What about the boat?"

"Three people'll be here to join a group comin' down river tomorrow. It's a big outfit, so's if your boat's short somethin' there won't be a problem. I'll make sure the boat and your gear gets back where it belongs in Flag. No problem there either if you've got everything marked like it's s'posed to be." Buck winked at his friend while he finished rolling another cigarette. He was one of the few who could do it with one hand, a skill derived from growing up in a saddle.

"Of course, Buck, of course. Now let's get movin'. We gotta get topside."

Down at the river, Saul, Stan, and Kateryna continued to watch in admiration as the belongings and equipment going up the trail were loaded and balanced in the panniers and tied on with cargo slings. Two pairs of leathery, gnarled hands worked in a blur, throwing and tying clove and tandem hitches, cinches, buckles, and bowlines, and finishing off with a marvelous diamond hitch that secured the top-loaded gear on one of the mules. Each animal carried no more than 180 pounds, pack equipment and contents included, evenly distributed on each side and placed at just the proper spot behind the animal's withers. The whole was accomplished without a kick, bite, or apparent objection from any of the three pack mules or their four companions who were to carry the human cargo up to the south rim.

"I'd planned to get here last night an' get a real early start this mornin'," Waddy apologized. "That little debacle yesterday sort of screwed things up."

"What happened?" Buck quickly asked, hoping for a chance to rag his friend.

"Oh, I flipped the boat comin' through Hance."

"Well, now, everyone'll be pleased to learn that you're human after all."

"Guys, by the time we get up to Bright Angel Lodge, everyone on the river from Lee's to Diamond Creek will know about our little experience," Waddy grumped as his friend clapped him soundly on the back.

Buck ground the quarter-inch-long butt into the sand. The cigarette had not left his face since it had been lighted and burned down. "Have fun, people." They mounted the patient mules and started down the trail to the Kaibab Bridge. "He really is a better wrangler than a boatman," Buck shouted after them.

"How long will it take to get to the top?" Saul asked when they started over the suspension bridge. Across the river the span ended at a tunnel cut into the canyon wall.

"Well, we're supposed to go up the Kaibab Trail." Waddy pointed up at the switchbacks carved into the steep slope of the canyon. The Kaibab formation they'd left at Lee's Ferry was now nearly 5,000 feet above them and ten miles away by trail.

"Stock comes down the Bright Angel Trail and then up the Kaibab, so's they don't have to pass. Not enough room to pass in a lot of places. But if we go up the Kaibab we'll wind up miles from Bright Angel Lodge and we'll be late. So we're goin' up the Bright Angel. Buck said there's only one late party comin' down and we should meet them on the Tonto Plateau; plenty of room to pass up there. How long to the top? 'Bout four hours, I guess. Gonna have to take it slow and stop a lot for these animals. Malcolm's pilot's just gonna have to wait."

"Pilot?" Kateryna twisted in her saddle to look back at Saul.

Oh, shit. "Kateryna . . . Malcolm will not be able to meet us here, so we're going to have to go to his home."

"Another change in plans you neglected to tell me about? And just where *is* his home?"

"California."

Kateryna reined in Huckleberry abruptly enough to cause Notch and Tuffy to dance and jump about behind her on the narrow bridge.

"Whoa! Watch it, people, these guys don't much like this bridge as it is," Waddy shouted back.

"I'm sorry, Waddy," Kateryna called over the three pack animals. She turned around to deliver a marginally sublethal glare in Saul's direction. "You tell me right now what you have planned. I have to be back in Pueblo early Sunday morning, at the latest. That's less than two days—and we are going to California?"

"Kateryna, there was just no way we would have had room for Malcolm on that raft. You'll understand when you meet him," Saul said.

"Boy, that's for sure, and there ain't a mule alive could carry him up this trail," Waddy called back, hearing Saul's comment. "Sure wish he'd been aboard for our little experience at Hance. Chance of a lifetime," Waddy laughed, with Stan joining in.

"With the short time we had to organize this trip," Saul blundered on anxiously, "there was just no way Malcolm could get away for several days. And rather than his coming out here, it will be about as fast and a whole lot more private for us to meet at his home. It's very secluded and comfortable there. We can fly to California in a couple of hours and then back to Pueblo about as quickly."

"Why didn't you tell me earlier?" Kateryna bored in with the crucial question.

Saul hesitated, unsure of what to say. "You . . . you would have thought the whole was trip too complicated for the time we had. Please, trust me, it's all going to work out just fine."

"That is not the issue."

"I can only apologize, Kateryna." The group fell silent as the mules approached the tunnel at the end of the bridge.

Kateryna turned around in her saddle to look at Saul. "I never trust anyone who says 'trust me.'" A few moments later she turned around again, this time with a smile and a wink.

"Came through here with a big string at night once," Waddy said when he started into the tunnel. "It was rainin' pretty good, and a bunch'a backpackers'd decided to camp in the tunnel to get outta the rain. Whole gang of 'em were hunkered down in here. Couldn't see shit, and pretty soon I had mules stompin' over sleepin' bags, and people screamin', and people'n mules tryin' to go in every direction. What a mess. White goose down was floatin' outta here for two days after that." Their laughter still echoed in the tunnel as they emerged into the bright light.

After climbing several switchbacks they left the Kaibab Trail and traversed the canyon wall above the river until they intercepted the Bright Angel Trail, where it joined the route over its own bridge from Phantom Ranch. After paralleling the river downstream for a mile, the trail turned away from the gorge and followed a narrow, hot, side canyon: Pipe Creek flowed thinly through its cleft in the shist and granite from a source high on the Tonto Plateau. The little creek's deep canyon ended at a steep talus slope with the trail switchbacking up toward the plateau.

Waddy stopped to give the mules a short drink before heading up the trail cut into a steep slide. The broad, gently sloping area of the Tonto Plateau, formed from a bench of Bright Angel shale and Tapeats sandstone, separated the sheer inner gorge and the river from the wide expanse of the upper canyon, now stretching more than twelve miles between its opposing rims.

The trail switched back and forth up the wide slope between promontories of black, folded and twisted, nearly-two-billion-year-old Vishnu shist and dikes of pink and gray Zoroaster granite that had intruded into the ancient rock. Near the head of the talus the trail notched into a wall of shist and granite to carve its way around the right-hand promontory. Stan marveled when he thought of the work it had taken to hack the trail by hand through the dense, dark rock, laid down as a layer of ocean sediment and shells when only primitive life occupied the world's original sea. The limestone and shale had then metamorphosed under the heat and weight of long-eroded mountains for nearly a third of the life of the earth.

Waddy stopped to rest the mules in a bit of shade as the trail turned away from the sun to enter a narrow ledge around the sheer cliff. "This is the worst of it, guys. Up on the Tonto there's an oasis called Indian Gardens where we'll stop for lunch. Plenty of water and shade. From there on up it'll keep gettin' cooler. It's over 8,000 feet at the top."

Stan and Kateryna gazed down the several hundred feet of precipitous drop into the canyon. A glimpse of the river appeared at the far end where the thread of Pipe Creek debouched from the narrow gorge.

Saul tried not to look over the edge. His mind would only let him focus on the fact that he was sitting helplessly on the back of an animal one short step away from oblivion. When he'd planned the trip, his acrophobia had been overlooked. "Waddy, can we please move this operation along?" Waddy nodded and nudged Buster up the trail, now curving sharply in and out of clefts in the vertical rock face.

Through this segment, the trail had a low wall of rock on the outside edge, forming a guard rail. Over the many years since it had been built, sections of the barrier had fallen away and were not repaired by the Park Service. Neither had they been repaired by the commercial company whose regular use of the trail earned it a corresponding regular profit. In the absence of the human attention needed to maintain the trail properly, Nature steadily worked at reclaiming the artificial cut in Her canyon wall.

Waddy slowly walked his mule around a sharp turn. Without warning, a group of three teenaged backpackers appeared in front of him, running wildly around the blind corner and leaping from rock to rock with their heavy loads. The leader let out a whoop as he dashed around the tight bend, causing Buster to back up with a jump. The mules behind repeated the lead animal's maneuver, coming together like a pack of cars suddenly braking in freeway traffic. The chain reaction moved rearward, each mule having to jump farther back to avoid the one in front. At the end of the train, Notch bumped sharply into Tuffy, forcing Stan's mount back suddenly and blindly where a section of the safety wall had long ago fallen away. Tuffy's right rear hoof slipped off the unprotected edge of rock. As it did, Stan glanced back, pulled his right foot free of the stirrup, then lunged toward the cliff on the inside of the trail. But as he started to push off from the saddle, his left foot wedged into the stirrup—at the same instant the scrambling animal lost the struggle to keep its center of gravity over the trail. With a frightened bray, the young mule plunged from the precipice. Stan's foot broke free of the stirrup just as the animal fell.

Tuffy dropped to a narrow, steeply sloping ledge about twenty feet below the trail, but his frantic scrambling was unable to hold him there. Slowly, he slid from the ledge and fell into a steeper chute down the rock face, finally coming to a stop nearly a hundred feet down the narrowing crevice in the rock. The still canyon filled with the agonized sounds from the stricken animal. As the mule hit the first ledge, Waddy was off Buster and running the few steps up the trail toward the trio of shocked teenagers.

"You little cocksuckers! You're goin' over, too!" he screamed in rage. Even before he had begun to swing his leg over the saddle, Kateryna was out of hers and running between the pack animals and the inside cliff face. She arrived at the group of boys, frozen in their steps, just as Waddy was drawing his arm back to deliver a blow calculated, and now adrenaline-fired enough, to crush the first young man's face.

Years of discipline and training had overtaken the woman who now intervened. In an instant Waddy was on his back in the trail, gasping for the air he'd quickly exhaled following a hard knee kick just below his sternum. By this time Stan and Saul had joined the scramble of activity taking place on the narrow ledge 700 feet above the bottom of the canyon.

"Jeez, mister, we didn't mean to . . ."

"Shut up, you little bastard!" Stan snarled as Kateryna grabbed his arm. Stan looked down at Waddy and then glared at the ashen-faced boys. "Sit down and shut up. Not a fucking word."

Waddy was getting up, now restored to reality between gasps for air.

"I'm sorry, Waddy," Kateryna said, "I had no choice. You could have killed him."

"You're right, babe, I would have killed him. *Still* might." Waddy stared at the terrified boys with the eyes of a rattlesnake. In the hot silence, everyone was aware of the muffled sounds from the mule. Waddy went back and looked over the edge.

"Can't move his hind legs. Back's busted."

He resignedly walked back up to the first pack mule and removed a large stuff sack. He upended it in the trail, dumping out a coil of 10.5mm kernmantle climbing rope, a harness, and a rack of miscellaneous aid climbing and protection gear. Having managed to get himself "rimmed" on a number of Grand Canyon excursions in his youth, Waddy no longer went anywhere in the canyon country without his climbing equipment. He stepped into the harness, rigged a figure-eight rappelling device, then looped a pair of webbing runners around a horn of shist that protruded from the cliff above the trail. A carabiner was clipped into the runners and the rope fed through the carabiner to its mid point. Waddy knotted the ends, rewound the rope into four coils, and individually tossed them down to the ledge where Tuffy was lying. The young mule's struggles were inching him closer to the edge of the long plunge to the bottom of Pipe Creek.

Waddy inspected his anchor carefully. "Kind of a sharp place here. Let me know if that rock starts to cut through the runners," he nodded to Stan and Saul. "Long fall if they cut through. That shist can be as sharp as flaked obsidian." Stan and Kateryna exchanged a glance. Saul shuddered.

Below a section of the steep chute in the shist and granite face, Waddy had to free rappel past an overhang, then traverse over a section of rock before descending down the chute to the ledge. As the rope was pulled sideways across the lip of the overhang, it slid across a section of shist that, three winters previously, had freeze-spalled off a small flake. When Waddy's weight stretched the rope over the lip, the sharp edge cut through the outer sheath of one of the strands of kernmantle and into all six braided sections that comprised the rope's core. The neat slice was nearly invisible, masked by the mottled appearance of the sheath, but the rope's strength was instantly reduced to a fraction of its mandated rating of 2,700 pounds. Within the sheath the strands in the core of the rope started to elongate, some of their tiny filaments stretched beyond their tensile strength, as half of Waddy's 165 pounds bore down on them.

He reached the ledge, paused a long moment, then ran his hands over the thrashing animal's withers. He sat down on the ledge and held the struggling mule's head in his lap. Tuffy relaxed under Waddy's touch. On the trail high above, five of the six people watched in fascinated horror as Waddy withdrew his knife from its sheath and cut the helpless animal's throat. The sixth person watched as well, but also observed her two companions. In less than a minute the rattling of air in and out of Tuffy's lungs stopped, and the crimson spurts of blood from his severed carotid artery no longer cascaded into the void. Waddy sat motionless for a minute or two, Tuffy's head now still, the young mule's final agony ended. Slowly, Waddy edged out from under the dead animal. He unbuckled the blood-soaked bridle, cut the saddle cinch webbing, and tied both to the climbing rope.

"Haul 'em up—and *don't* lose the rope through the carabiner when you untie the end or I'm stuck down here."

It took him thirty minutes to climb and prusik the eighty feet. He'd been busy with a sticky section of free climb, with a tough, 5.8 move, when he came to the damaged place in the rope. He didn't notice it as he moved safely past the spot. By the time he got to the lip of the trail his shirt was soaked with sweat and partially congealed globs of mule blood, mixed with dust and sand. Waddy pointed at the saddle and bridle. "Pick'em up."

"You can't make us . . ." This time Waddy got to the largest of the three before Kateryna could intervene. In a split second the boy, a head taller than Waddy, was doubled up on the trail with both arms clutched to his midsection. He was fortunate that Waddy had just climbed up eighty feet of rock.

"Now, you two want to pick it up, please?" The other boys jumped for the saddle, struggling to figure out how to carry it along with their heavy backpacks.

"One more little squeak and you follow that mule you killed. Got it? Now, we're all goin' up to the Gardens to turn you over to the ranger."

Waddy realized that if he let them go, by the time they reached Phantom Ranch their teenaged testosterone, enflamed by the confidence of brash youth, would have blossomed the event into an entirely different story. The story would be sent up to the rim, where it would undergo further metamorphoses, and a battery of rangers would be waiting for them with questions. Lots of questions. A similar scenario had occurred to Kateryna, entitling Waddy to a look from her that amounted to professional admiration. Stan and Saul, without the latent instinct or professional training to anticipate such trouble, wondered why the forced march of the boys was necessary. *After all,* Stan-the-lawyer thought, *they hadn't really done anything except be typically felony-stupid, totally irresponsible, wild teenagers.*

Waddy marched the sullen teens to the ranger station above Indian Gardens. *Good thing it's Liz Rafferty on duty here; she's got a level head and she knows me. Glad I didn't beat the crap out of that big prick. Be hard to explain.* Waddy was counting on the ranger to just accept his story and not require statements from Saul, Stan, and Kateryna. The last thing they needed was a paper trail. As trail wrangler, his story alone should be accepted.

"These three young lads owe Buck Johnson for the price of a good strong mule, and they almost caused the deaths of four people," Waddy began. He concisely related the whole event, interspersed with observations about the irresponsibility of the teens on the narrow trail used by a lot of pack stock. The boys were contrite in the face of authority.

"I think they ought to be denied the privilege of enjoying this national park," Waddy said when the ranger told him he could go back to his customers. "Your choice, though, ma'am. Also, I'd appreciate it if you'd radio down to the ranch to tell Buck so's he doesn't find out on his own. He's gonna be really pissed."

The caravan continued up the Bright Angel Trail. "I think those three will be very glad to just let the thing go," Waddy mused out loud. He thought some more. "But, you know, they could change their story later."

"I think you handled it perfectly," Stan said. He and Saul had finally realized Waddy's damage control.

"I'll call Buck as soon as we get to the top, if he hasn't already headed up to the Gardens to get his tack . . . and I'll leave him a note and a check; those little *pahana* fuckers'll never pay him."

When they got to the rim, Waddy was in a big hurry to sort out the mules, make his call to Buck, and then leave as quickly as possible. They found Malcolm's driver standing near the entrance to the Bright Angel Lodge, holding a sign that said "Stony Ridge." They were on their way south to Flagstaff minutes after Waddy turned the mules over to Buck's wranglers.

"You never know how these feddies will react," Waddy said. "Some desk ranger could decide that to cover his ass he had to have statements from each of you. Best to just clear out."

Three miles south of Flagstaff the driver turned off the freeway onto J.W. Powell Boulevard. When they pulled into the parking lot of the general aviation section at Pulliam Airport, Kateryna immediately noticed the Cessna Citation III. "Mayacamas" was lettered in contrasting silver and black above the turbofan engine mounted on the rear of the fuselage. They had just entered the Arizona Air Service pilots' lounge and she was being introduced to a gray-haired man wearing four bars on the epaulets of his starched white shirt.

"I'm very glad to meet you, Captain Rogers," Kateryna smiled at the man, the archetype of a commercial pilot. "How long a flight will we have?"

"About an hour, is all, Miss Jensen," came the smooth reply. Captain Rogers glanced askance at Waddy, still wearing his mule-blood-encrusted clothing. Dan Rogers' world of gleaming, multimillion-dollar, precision aircraft, strict routines, and impeccable dress was a world apart from the little Hopi standing before him, a man who shortly before had climbed down a precipice in the Grand Canyon to cut the throat of a helpless, suffering animal.

"Dan, can I interrupt here for a moment?" Stan asked. "Is there any chance you could modify your flight plan so we can get a good view of the Colorado River, from Laughlin down to Yuma?"

"This plane has a pretty tight schedule. I'll need to check with the home office." Captain Rogers went over to the telephone in the lounge.

Kateryna grabbed Stan's arm. "Now what? More delay?" Saul reacted as if he were about to be hit.

Stan: "This has to do with the *personal* decisions Waddy mentioned the other night down on the river. Do you remember?"

She nodded.

"This is a perfect opportunity for all of us to get a good look at what's down there. Highways don't follow even half of the river, and besides, the aerial view is just what we need to see—at least I do." Stan looked around at the few other people sitting in the lounge. He nodded toward the door and they went out into the open hangar.

"Kateryna, we have to look at the worst case of there being more of a flood than we intend. It won't delay the flight even an hour."

Captain Rogers stuck his head out the door. "Mr. Renslaer says that its up to you, but we can't go into the Mexico. That would take a whole lot of time to arrange. And, sir, he'd like to speak to you."

"Well what did the great man have to say?" Waddy asked after they'd settled into four of the six first-class-sized leather seats in the passenger cabin. A desk and two swivel armchairs occupied the rear of the airplane. Everyone except Waddy was instantly aware of grimy river clothes and smelly bodies.

"Nothing, really," Stan answered. "Just asked about our trip. I told him about Saul's adventure in the sleeping bag." Saul and Kateryna both pinched their lips together in tight smiles and shook their heads.

Captain Rogers accelerated the swept-wing jet down the runway and into a steep, curving climb out over the ponderosa-timbered plateau that surrounded the city of Flagstaff. The little plane climbed at about four times the rate of a 727 but something well less than an F-16, and they were soon flying above the San Francisco Peaks, rising snow-capped just to the north of the city. Waddy gazed down at the home of the katsinas on the flanks of Neuvatikao. He studied the slopes until he could almost pick out the site of one of the most important shrines; then his eyes were drawn farther down the mountain to a ski lift. He turned away from the window.

Kateryna also stared out at the mountain and the expanse of desert country surrounding the forested plateau. She had no way to know of the importance the dead volcano had to the young man she had only met four days before but who already seemed like an old friend. In a few more minutes, Kateryna was able to peer down into the vast canyon in which they had been swallowed up only a few hours before. *Two more days and I'll be on my way home to Ukraine.*

"Folks, coming up right below will be a good view of the Supai Indian village and Havasu Creek." Captain Rogers steeply banked the Cessna, changing its course toward the west. Everyone looked down past the dipped left wing at the huge gash of the Grand Canyon and the thread of river at its bottom, glinting in flashes in the sunlight. "We'll follow the river on down to Lake Mead, then turn over the dam to the south."

"How low are you permitted to fly, Dan?" Stan asked the intercom next to his seat.

"I have to stay well under the traffic in and out of L.A. and above the local corridors, so we'll cruise between seven and ten thousand. Will that give you a close enough view?"

"Perfect, captain," Stan answered. He turned to Kateryna. "That's a whole lot of canyon for water to travel down before it even gets to Mead Reservoir."

Kateryna pointed to the intercom by her seat and then forward. "Why don't we just enjoy the view?" Saul and Stan looked toward the closed hatchway to the flight deck and nodded agreement.

Captain Rogers banked the Cessna in a slow turn over the Colorado River's first big reservoir. "That's Hoover Dam," Stan said, leaning across Kateryna to point out the strikingly contrasting, alabaster arch wedged into the andecite breccia of Black Canyon. In relation to the size of the reservoir extending far behind it, the dam appeared tiny.

"It contains over four million cubic yards of concrete and stands 725 feet above its foundation rock, about the size of the Glen Canyon Dam." To the north and above the reservoir, they could see Boulder City, originally sprouted from the desert in the 1930s to house and serve the dam construction workers, just as Page had been born in the 1950s. Beyond the Bureau of Reclamation town, Las Vegas sprawled in the distance, glittering dully through its ball of smog.

"Can we drop a little lower while we go down the canyon, Dan? And please, slow down as much as you can when we pass over Davis Dam."

"I can go on down to 6,500, but that'll be it," the voice came back.

Below Hoover Dam the Colorado River lay still. Sixty-seven-mile-long "Lake" Mojave backed the river up behind its own dam, all the way to the outflow from Hoover. In this regard it fulfilled nicely the Bureau of Reclamation ideal: a river converted to a stairway of reservoirs, with no wasted (flowing) water.

The narrow canyon reservoir quickly passed under the aircraft, and Captain Rogers slowed their speed as the communities below the earth-fill Davis Dam came into view.

"That's Bullhead City, Arizona, on the left; across the river is Laughlin, Nevada," Stan announced as they felt the airplane slow and nose-up in its effort to keep flying.

"Look at that Laughlin pile of shit," Waddy griped. They all looked down on the strip city of fluorescent-hued high-rise hotel/casinos, giant neon and electronic signs, imported palm trees, grass-green-painted concrete, and acres of RV-filled parking lots, all strung along a single boulevard on the west bank of the river. Even at 6,500 feet, Stan imagined that he could read the mammoth sign next to one of the gleaming casinos. It would hawk $3.95 steak and lobster dinners, $19.95 water bed rooms (free HBO), a generous slot machine come-on, and the name of some country-western singer. Just downstream of a steamboat-shaped casino, a four-story-high cowboy waved from a rooftop, welcoming visitors to the oasis.

"One of the buildings is shaped like a boat," Kateryna pointed out her window. The River Queen Hotel and Casino covered most of a city block and rose twelve stories above the adjacent river. It was equipped with 100-foot-diameter paddle wheels, two huge, river boat-style smokestacks, and about twenty-five miles of lights and neon tubing—all visually dominating yet blending perfectly into the carny atmosphere of the new city.

"Why is that commercial area built down there, so far from anything?" Kateryna looked out to an endless desert, filling the horizon.

"Legalized theft," Saul answered. "Those are all gambling casinos, exploiting one of mankind's oldest and most tragic addictions."

"Dan, can you slow down a little more and maybe take a turn around the area right below us?" Stan said, keying the intercom.

"Folks, this is no Piper Cub," came the quick reply. "She's real unhappy and about stalled out as it is. Any slower, this little gal will fly about like an anvil."

Saul winced involuntarily as he looked down at the wing, its flaps extended to their fullest. Ever the physicist, he imagined the turbulent-flow boundary layer advancing forward on the upper surface of the airfoil, destroying lift as it progressed. With no propellers, the airplane required speed to maintain the necessary Bernoulli-effect pressure differential over its airfoil surfaces. The slight—and growing—vibration Saul felt through his seat was not his imagination.

"Stanley, how far down the river are we from the Glen Canyon Dam?" Kateryna asked, still examining the florid development spreading below them.

"About, oh, 400, maybe 425 miles, I would guess."

Kateryna pictured a several-hundred-foot head of water being released into Marble and Grand Canyons and she imagined it engulfing the demonstration of capitalism run wild she viewed below. *At least twelve hours.* Even in the rugged, twisting canyon, and with the huge backwashes that would surge up the side canyons, the massive wall of water suddenly released from its captivity would not run at the usual four miles per hour. *Little accumulated debris to slow it down. Thirty to forty miles per hour, average.*

Stan looked down at the frenzy of building activity promising Laughlin's continued expansion. Founded in 1967, by 1984 the town had only ninety-five permanent residents and one small casino, but by 1992 the population was 7,500, over eight thousand hotel rooms were available, nine high-rise hotel/casinos lined the riverbank, and over four million people visited Laughlin that year. Nearly all of the thousands of casino workers lived across the river in Bullhead City where they could afford the rent.

"I don't suppose there's any chance that Laughlin's a ground zero on your Strategic Rocket Forces' SS-18 hit parade, is there?" Waddy asked with a grin that enveloped his whole face.

Kateryna looked over, her head cocked to one side. She returned an impish smile. "Only on the odd chance that one missed your Hoover Dam. I doubt that the little dam we just saw and this tourist city were strategic targets, Waddy."

"Just imagine what twenty-seven million acre feet of water—maybe fifty million—going by on its way to the Gulf would do to that pile of shit down there."

She frowned and pointed forward again. "We've had this discussion." She turned back to the view out the window.

Bullhead City ("Butthead City," to many of the younger lounge lizards in Las Vegas), named for a distinctive rock formation now mostly submerged beneath the waters of Mojave Reservoir, stretched for miles down the river on the Arizona side: an agglomeration of motels, neon-colored real estate offices, gas stations, fast food restaurants, mini-malls, bowling alleys, drive-through liquor stores, video rental shops, RV parks and sales offices, swap meet lots, and more imported palm trees and electronic signs. But unlike its glitzy neighbor on the opposite shore, Bullhead City had some grass, non-palm trees, and landscaped areas.

They could feel the little jet nose down, accelerate, stop vibrating, and contentedly begin flying again as Captain Rogers finished his turn and pointed her south. They passed over a big loop in the river with its interior entirely filled with several thousand mobile homes and double-wides. The huge, river-level area was the newest extension of Bullhead City, and besides providing seasonal homes for northern snowbirds, it was needed to house the workers who kept the gambling Mecca across the river making money for its handful of mostly-non-resident owners.

Riverbend, Holiday Shores, and Riviera will sure be goners, Stan thought. *Why in hell do the local planning commissions and the Bureau of Land Management let people build right in the flood plain? That area should be for wildlife, or a greenbelt, or even a park or golf course—not houses. Just plain stupid.* He looked out at the tens of thousands of available acres only a short distance away and safely above even the wildest level of the river.

A few miles below Bullhead City, highway 95 ran beeline straight for twenty miles down the Arizona side. The adjacent Colorado wound among the sand dunes, farm lands, and wild areas of the 38,000-acre Fort Mojave Indian Reservation which occupied most of both sides of the river and extended to the next town, Needles, California. The Mojave Indians had largely avoided building permanently along the river bottom, preferring instead to use their fertile enclave for crops. Their memories of river floods went back about 2,000 years.

"Stanley, why do your authorities permit residential construction in the flood plain right next to the river?"

"Because the smug city fathers of Laughlin and Bullhead City are content in their ten-year, boomtown time frame and have not the least idea of the history of the river nor the remotest inclination to educate themselves. Back in the '70s, when Powell was still filling, all the floods that came down from the Upper Basin were wholly contained behind Glen Canyon Dam. New city council people, county commissioners, and federal bureaucrats have forgotten or never have known that really is a river down there."

"*Pahanas* have always clustered in flood plains," Waddy smirked. "—where the water, game, fertile land, and timber are—so they don't have to work so hard."

"Historically, of course," Kateryna nodded. "But it should not be tolerated once people know better. How long have the floods on that river been accurately recorded?"

"A little over one hundred years," Stan answered. "Prior to the construction of Hoover and Glen Canyon Dams, June flows of 70,000 cfs were a regular event, and flows of over 100,000 cfs came along every few years. Floods peaking at over 200,000 cfs were known, and those of 400,000 or more were suspected. A few people—very few—paid attention to what the local Indians had to say. Look at that big vacant area. The Mojave Tribe knows better than to build right in the bottom. The non-natives just go ahead and build and then look to insurance companies and the state and federal governments to bail them out when the inevitable occurs. In a few other parts of the country, people have the same attitude. Whether in the Mississippi Midwest; along the barrier islands of the Southeast and Gulf coasts; or along fault-latticed, fire- and flood-prone regions of California, people demand to build their homes where the occurrence of a natural disaster is not a question of whether, just when. And the whole country gets to pay for their insistence on living where Nature has amply demonstrated that they should not live. Every ten or fifteen years or so, our taxes pay for the low-interest loans to rebuild all those zillion-dollar homes in Malibu and Benedict Canyons."

"A miracle of your capitalism, Stanley."

The old Santa Fe Railroad town of Needles, California, passed quickly below the Cessna as Captain Rogers turned southeast toward the Havasu National Wildlife Refuge. The core of the old town was built above the river's high-water line, in accordance with sound railroad practice and simple common sense. But relenting to withering political and financial pressure, the town had in recent years acquiesced to developers' pleas to construct, for their unknowing customers, luxury homes, condo villages, RV parks, and marinas right on the riverbank. During the 1983 Glen Canyon spill, the area had been badly flooded, but that event had soon been forgotten. New customers arrived regularly to purchase the expensive riverfront homes.

Beyond Needles, they soon passed over the bridges at Topock, Arizona. They could see the massive Santa Fe Railroad bridge and the recent span for Interstate Highway 40. Just to the south of the freeway bridge was the lovely old steel arch bridge, built in 1916 and immortalized by John Steinbeck and the later 1960s television program *Route 66*. The bridge now carried only a gas pipeline, en route from west Texas to deliver its continuous high pressure stream to Los Angeles for conversion into smog.

As the bridges fell away behind them, they passed over a group of volcanic minarets, the inspiration for the naming of Needles. At the base of these jagged mountains and standing within the crevice of Mojave Canyon was the beginning of yet another reservoir: "Lake" Havasu spread down the Colorado's last canyon. The Havasu National Wildlife Refuge continued to occupy both slopes, sharing much of the western shore with the Chemehuevi Indian Reservation, with the refuge and Indian lands remaining almost entirely wild or desert bucolic. Not so the 4,000-odd acres of private land about halfway down the reservoir's Arizona side. Sprouting like a gaudy *Amanita muscaria* mushroom, Lake Havasu City filled the shoreline and the nearby island. Connecting the island with the shoreline city was a structure that served to define the word *incongruous*.

In 1831 a simple and harmonious bridge was constructed across the Thames River near the heart of London. The five lovely keystone arches of the span, constructed of fitted and bordered hand-hewn granite blocks, witnessed the passing of countless Thames River barges and 137 years of London history—until 1968, when Mr. Robert McCulloch, Sr., of America and of outboard motor fame, purchased the 1005-foot-long bridge: before, then, and now the largest antique ever sold. He then moved it, every stone cataloged and numbered, down the Thames River, through the English Channel, across the Atlantic Ocean and the Caribbean Sea, through the Panama Canal, and up the Pacific coast to Long Beach, California, where the 10,276 granite blocks, most weighing a ton or more, were reloaded onto a caravan of trucks and rolled across the Mojave Desert. At his new development on the shore of Lake Havasu, Mr. McCulloch had the peninsula into the lake severed, creating his island, whereafter the old bridge was reassembled across the new channel. The entire enterprise provided a limitless font of ruthlessly witty commentary on BBC-4 and in pubs, clubs, and homes across Great Britain. In mitigation, however, the lord mayor of London graciously accepted an invitation in 1971 for the rededication of the bridge at its new desert home.

Below the splash of snowbird habitat at Lake Havasu City, the shores of the reservoir were reclaimed as an Arizona state park, dotted with numerous boat ramps and campgrounds, clear to the lower end of the impoundment at Parker Dam. At this end of the reservoir were structures marking two of the reasons for the construction of the massive dam far upstream at Glen Canyon. On the west side, the California Aqueduct commenced in a massive pumping plant. Three pipelines, like giant straws, sucked a continuous flow of water into the pump house for transmission across the Mojave Desert and several desert mountain ranges (more pumping) to be evaporated from lawns and swimming pools, with the remainder converted into sewage in the Los Angeles Basin. On the other side of the reservoir, another pumping structure started a competing flow into Senator Hayden's Granite Reef Aqueduct for delivery to Phoenix and Tucson. What remained propelled the turbines of Parker Dam, marginally helping to supply the diversion systems' electric pumps. The bypassed water then traveled on down the river to be diverted and largely consumed in the fields surrounding Yuma, Arizona, and in the Imperial, Coachella, and Mexicali Valleys of California and Mexico.

"Look at that, Stanley." Kateryna pointed below Parker Dam. The "Parker Strip" extended nearly fifteen miles down the narrow canyon, ending at the next structure interrupting the river. The stilled river behind Headgate Rock Dam was nearly lined with houses built wall to wall on the shoreline. In some places canals paralleled the river/lake, enabling more homes with water frontage to be built.

"You should see that place in the summer," Stan said while the urban strip passed beneath the Cessna. "It's a madhouse. The retired people who come out here in the winter go back home to Canada and the Midwest, replaced with hordes of young people. It starts in June, as soon as school's out. Maybe 150,000 people are down there on a weekend, mostly from L.A. and Phoenix. It's B.U.I. City."

"B.U.I.?"

"Boating under the influence—of alcohol. I've heard that a million cans of beer are consumed down there on a weekend. Most of the cans are probably on the river bottom."

"It would be impossible to evacuate," Kateryna said as she looked intently at Stan. They both looked down at the two-lane road paralleling the river. It provided the only way out of the narrow, development-ravened canyon.

Once again the existence of an Indian reservation arrested the stream-side development, and the last of the Parker Strip vanished under the wings of the Cessna as Captain Rogers took a little more advantage of the jet's potential to travel at 800 kilometers per hour. Past the reservation the river flowed for nearly 100 miles with only occasional human habitation on its shores. They passed over the old town of Parker, Arizona, and 1916's Blythe, California, both built well above the river in respectful recognition of its history.

"That next dam doesn't impound much water, Stanley. What's it for?"

"Imperial Dam. It was built solely to divert the taxpayer-subsidized river water into the All American Canal for delivery to the farm gentry of the

Salton Sink. See the canal snaking away to the southwest? That diversion to the Imperial Valley was the prime political reason for the construction of Hoover Dam. And that's Yuma, Arizona, just ahead, where the Gila River joins the Colorado. Except during a flood, the Gila's always dry because the water is entirely consumed in and around Phoenix."

Kateryna looked down at the largest city on the lower Colorado River. A long levee curved around its north and west sides, between the course of the river and the old town. Another levee protected the lands in California and Mexico.

"We're only about twenty miles north of the Mexican border here. Below that, the trickle left in the river continues to wind through some farm land and then a lot of desert. It ends in a maze of salt marshes before it even gets to the Gulf, with nothing left for the Cucapa Indians. Like the Nile River, the Colorado was vitally important to the whole ecosystem in the huge delta . . . So much was lost that will never even be known."

"I don't see any water at all in the channel."

"What's left is practically always diverted by the Mexicans there at Morelos Dam. See that wing wall extending most of the way across the river channel, beside the levee and just south of the city?"

"Oh, yes, I see it now."

"The water they get is treated to remove salts at that big plant you see just up from their dam. The salts build up in the river because of the archaic irrigation practices the farmers use. Rather than use drip irrigation they just flood their fields, soaking the earth, which causes the salts to wick up to the root zone. Then they use more water to flush the ground through drains, with all the salt-laden water going into the river to have the process repeated at the next diversion. Naturally, the Mexicans complained about the quality of water they were getting; so American taxpayers got to pay $360 million for that big reverse osmosis desalinization plant. And see the canal leading away to the west from the Mexican dam? That's the Alamo Canal. It follows the old course of the Alamo River. It's actually an alternate route for the Colorado River, which eventually turns north and flows into the Salton Sink. Some of the water is even pumped clear across Baja to Tijuana."

"Do you mean the river has flowed into the interior, away from the ocean?"

"Yes. This whole area below us is the Colorado River delta. Over much of it the sand and silts carried down by the river are more than 2,000 feet deep. Practically all the rock converted to sand in the Grand Canyon is spread out down there. The paleo-history of this area shows that on many occasions the river has decided to flow into the Salton Sink rather than down into the Gulf. It has happened at least three times in the past two thousand years: 'Lake Cahuilla' they call it, and it filled the entirety of the below-sea level area out there, called the Salton Sink. The last time it happened was in

1905 when the entire flow of the river went down into the sink—but that time it was caused by human error, and the present-day Salton Sea was created in the process. We'll see it as we turn north."

"That looks like a huge irrigated area to the west and off to the north."

"The Mexicali Valley and the Imperial Valley across the border; they're both part of the Salton Sink—and practically all below sea level. The part north of the border is irrigated by that big canal we saw branching off the river at Imperial Dam."

Early in the Anglo colonization of Southern California, a few of the settlers had recognized that much of the land in the Salton Sink was extraordinarily fertile, excepting an area at the bottom of the northerly end of the valley, 280 feet below sea level and holding the alkaline remnants of an evaporated sea. As the foodstuffs demand of the expanding Los Angeles grew in the late 1800s, attention was directed to the relatively accessible and fertile Salton Sink, later to be grandly renamed the Imperial Valley. But no water was available in the valley and rainfall was minimal. A great deal of water was needed to make the valley bloom, a situation magnified by the fact that during much of the year the temperature in the area exceeded 100 degrees.

Less than seventy-five miles to the southeast from the center of the Salton Sink/Imperial Valley lay a potential solution: the Colorado River flowed by on its way to the Gulf of California. It also happened that for a short distance the river ran only slightly to the east of the southeastern rim of the huge depression. The developers decided to construct a canal—the Imperial (Alamo) Canal—from the river to the fertile lands of the valley. It was done, the valley bloomed, the farmers became very rich, and Los Angeles got its fruit and vegetables. But most of the water, then and now, was used to grow grass to add money-making flesh and fat to livestock.

The course of the Imperial Canal, with its diversion point where the river curved around the northwest corner of the leveed Yuma, was parallel to the river for about four miles, whence it looped to the west within Old Mexico to enter the ancient channel of the Alamo River and descend into the Sink. During the spring of 1904, a flood had badly silted the four miles of canal paralleling the river, making diversions impossible. For the 1904 irrigation season, a quick fix was achieved by cutting a bypass channel directly from the river to the canal that led, in turn, to the old Alamo River. No gate was put into the bypass because everything was to be repaired in the regular canal by the next spring. The stage was set for the occurrence of a wholly unanticipated hydraulic event on the Lower Colorado River.

During the winter of 1904–05, a series of three floods occurred on the Colorado, including one on the Gila River at Yuma. Winter floods were unusual but known, at the time, to the point of reasonable statistical predictability. Then came a larger than normal spring flood. In a panic, efforts were made to plug the temporary bypass, but it was too late. The river entered the bypass and relentlessly began to cut a new route through the soft soils. At this point, the Colorado River was about 100 feet above the level of its outlet in the Gulf of California but 380 feet above the bottom of the Salton Sink, about the same distance away. Naturally, and in accord with good physics, the river chose to follow the path with the steepest gradient. The waters of the Colorado River will always choose to flow downhill, with the exception of two arrangements: the diversions to Los Angeles and to Phoenix and Tucson, where the water surges uphill toward money and political power.

The entire flow of the flooding Colorado inexorably diverted into the ancient Alamo River channel where for a period of sixteen months it continued to course unimpeded into the Salton Sink. No effort by the combined force of farmers, the State of California, and the federal government could stop it. Finally, with the assistance of the competent engineering staff and equipment of the Southern Pacific Railroad, the river was turned back to its former route to the Sea of Cortés. In the meantime, southern California had been blessed with the creation of the Salton Sea which remains in existence to this day: an area of about 370 square miles, possessing a salinity approximating that of the Dead Sea, and an odor and level of industrial, fertilizer, and pesticide pollution far, far worse.

The great flood was not soon forgotten, and the cry for control of the Colorado River became a firm plank in the campaign platform of every politician from the lower Colorado River area. The flood control and guaranteed irrigation water demands of the increasingly powerful Imperial Valley farmers and their politicians finally led to the construction of Boulder (Hoover) Dam in the 1930s. Along with the dam, a new "All American Canal," (entirely within California) was included as part of the project to serve the 600,000-acre potential of the Imperial Valley, the Coachella Valley that encompassed the extreme northerly end of the Salton Sink above the new sea, and the few hundred farmers in the valleys who had grown quite accustomed to being very rich. Starting with the first deliveries of water into the 15,000-cubic-foot-per-second, three-million-acre foot-per-year, All American Canal, and continuing to the present day, the farmers of the Imperial and Coachella Valleys have paid not one cent for water delivered to the headgate of their canal. A $165 million (1928 dollars) project to store water and control flooding and siltation was built, and the valleys' lands were transformed from potentially fruitful but economically worthless because of the lack of reliable water to fabulously productive acreages. Currently, the value of the crops grown in the area is over $1 billion annually—nearly $2,000 per irrigated acre per year—and collected by fewer than 700 farmers in the entire region of the Imperial and Coachella Valleys: agribusiness welfare at its most egregious extreme.

"Stanley, if there were a big flood on the river, those levees and canals would keep it flowing to the sea, would they not?"

"I don't know, Kateryna. I just don't know."

"Have you all seen enough?" came the voice from the flight deck.

"Lets go see Malcolm, Dan."

"We're cleared for a straight run to the city. We'll be there in an hour." Captain Rogers put the silver and black jet into a wide, curving climb as he pointed up to his cruising altitude of 38,000 feet to pass over the air traffic entering and leaving San Diego and Los Angeles. As the little aircraft began performing as the Cessna engineers had intended, Kateryna looked down at the expanse of the Salton Sea shimmering in the northern end of the vast checkerboard of the Imperial and Coachella Valleys.

"There it is. That's where much of the water released from the dams winds up, Kateryna. Billion-dollar-per-year economy down there."

"Those look like orchards in the area north of the sea."

"Much of it is citrus orchard and date palm groves. Even starting to put in some vineyards—good for raisins and jug wine, is all. There at the extreme northern end of the valley is a place called Palm Springs. They irrigate hundreds of acres of golf-course grass and fill thousands of swimming pools in 115° heat with Colorado River water. They even have canals so homes can have waterfront sites, and there's a big hotel with an indoor lake where people are ferried around in boats."

"What about the very large area south of the sea? It is all row crops, is it not?"

"Most of the water in the Imperial Valley is used to grow grass. Grass to feed cattle. They can get eight or ten cuts of alfalfa a year down there."

"Not fruits, vegetables, soybeans?"

"Grass, Kateryna. Grass."

Like so many people throughout the world, Kateryna was fascinated with California. From the perspective of her rigidly controlled Slavic life, this most Western part of America was a distant, perpetually sunny land of prosperous, if decadent, contented people: people who enjoyed every variety of material thing the world could produce. Hollywood and Madison Avenue had reached into most corners of the former Soviet Union despite the determined efforts to stop them; accordingly, Saul and Stan had spent the past hour answering a relentless stream of questions from their guest.

"Our turn's coming up," Captain Rogers announced. They had been orbiting in the fading daylight, awaiting a controller's decision to put their non-priority flight into the procession of commercial jets descending across the south arm of the bay to land on the peninsula a few miles south of San Francisco. Kateryna was oblivious to the delay. She remained glued to her window, taking in the grand view of the bay and its jewel of a principal city.

After a quick descent, they were soon taxiing into a hangar containing three other sleek black and silver aircraft.

"End of the line, folks," the intercom said as they heard the engines' whine start to drop in pitch. Captain Rogers and his young copilot came through the hatchway from the flight deck and opened the exit door. Immediately the travelers were invited into the back of a limousine parked in the hangar.

"Do we have much farther to go, Stanley?" Kateryna asked while they settled into another set of plush seats. "I would very much like to have a bath."

"We'll be there soon. Dan told me earlier that we had to come into San Francisco rather than go straight to Napa. Something about the plane needing to be serviced and then going right out again. I guess our little detour down the river caused the problem. It'll only be another hour," Stan stretched the truth as he thought of the Friday evening traffic through the city and across the Golden Gate Bridge. "We're all tired, and it's been a long day. But we're almost there," he assured Kateryna, trying to pump up his own anemic enthusiasm.

Everywhere she looked, she found reinforcement of her expectations. "Oh!" she breathed softly when they exited the Presidio and headed across the Golden Gateway's span. She looked back at the city, the densely-clustered houses and apartment towers on the hills glowing in the fading sunset. "It is so very beautiful. How fortunate you and Saul are to live here, I . . ." she caught herself too late. The life Stan and Saul had long enjoyed in this so-desirable part of the world was soon to end.

Stan awoke abruptly, his head resting on Kateryna's shoulder, as the automobile slowed and turned into the entrance at Stony Ridge. He saw the guard go back into the gatehouse and the big iron gates slowly swung aside in the headlights of the limo. Saul and Waddy were sound asleep, but Kateryna was fully awake.

Faithful old Benjamin was there to meet them in the courtyard. Only a soft glow from gas lamps shone through the parlor window lace curtains and out the cut glass-paneled doors of the entrance hall.

"Mr. Renslaer suggests that you retire to refresh, and then, if you should desire, we will have a late supper. Miss Jensen, Mr. Temeseh, may I show you to your rooms?"

Stan awoke again with a start, this time with the strange feeling that often accompanies waking up at an odd hour. For a moment he didn't know where he was. It was nearly ten o'clock. He dressed and went down the stairs into the dimly lit entrance hall, following the light and the faint sounds of conversation coming from the direction of the library. He found Saul and

Kateryna engaged in happy conversation with Malcolm, who, as always, commanded the room with his Jovian presence.

"Good evening, Stanley," he boomed, "we thought you were out for the count." Saul and Kateryna joined in Malcolm's hearty smile. "I'm just getting acquainted with this lovely young lady," Malcolm beamed at Kateryna. She looked up at Stan when he entered the room, holding his gaze while he took his seat.

"Good evening, everyone. I feel really spacy after that little nap. How're you all holding up?"

"I'm okay," Saul yawned, still convinced he would never get warm.

Kateryna smiled and nodded as she continued to study Stan. "We were just about to give up on you and go in to eat."

Stan suddenly realized that since breakfast on a cold dawn beach at the head of Sockdolager Rapid, all he'd eaten was a sandwich on the airplane. The planned lunch at Indian Gardens had been forgotten. "Yeah, I'm starved. Where's Waddy?"

"Out in the kitchen interfering with Anthony," Malcolm said. He hoisted himself out of his big leather chair and headed for the dining room.

"Malcolm, we sure needed you when we went through Hance." Waddy and Anthony were carrying in serving platters of vinaigrette baby-leaf salads, fresh baguettes, and a big tureen of ham and bean soup. "For sure, we wouldn't'a flipped."

"Am I to understand that this incompetent little heathen managed, somehow, to overturn your raft in one of the lesser rapids on the river? Now, if it had been Crystal or Lava Falls, I could certainly understand, but– –"

"Lesser, shit! It was running a 9 when we went through."

Malcolm's big face dazzled with his surprise discovery of a particularly hot Waddy-button. "Well, I'm sure that if you had scouted the water more carefully– –"

"Malcolm," Saul interrupted, "it was really bad. I would have drowned if these three hadn't fished me out." He laid his hand on Kateryna's arm. "Please understand that these two derive some testicular satisfaction in trying to best each other." Waddy and Malcolm were now both grinning at her. "They haven't seen each other for a while, so they have to catch up." Saul turned back to Malcolm. "Can we please move on to something which might be less offensive to our guest?"

Kateryna: "It is quite all right, Saul. From the little I have seen it is apparent your two friends care a great deal for each other."

"Well, I don't know about that," Waddy said, leaning over toward Malcolm.

"He's tolerable . . . in brief doses," Malcolm added. "Now, tell me about the trip, Kateryna."

Until she began to relate in warm detail the particulars of the four days they had spent on the river, Stan had not realized just how much Kateryna had enjoyed their journey through the Colorado River canyons. While he listened to her relive the moment-by-moment details of their adventure in Hance Rapid, he realized that it had been the near tragedy that had brought them all together. It was as if the normal months- or years-long process of building a friendship had been condensed into a few minutes. The latent but powerful distrust that had existed between the group of Americans and the visitor from an unknown place had vanished. Somehow, Stan also realized, an unspoken resolve to proceed with the plan had been forged at the same time.

Malcolm listened intently, closely observing the foreign woman while she recounted their experiences. As his three friends added to the story, he always managed to refocus on Kateryna's narrative. He also noticed that throughout the late supper conversation Stan rarely diverted his eyes from the new guest at Stony Ridge.

"So, what do you think, Waddy? Is there going to be anything further about the encounter with those three boys? Looks to me like you smoothed that over."

"Prob'ly have to make a formal statement when I go back to work." Waddy rubbed his tender abdomen. Kateryna gave him another "I'm sorry" look.

"I'm glad you were able to see the rest of the river," Malcolm went on, again directing his attention to Kateryna. "That was a good idea of Stan's—so that you could see the whole picture in context. Whole lot of reservoirs and developments strung along the river, aren't there?"

Saul interrupted, reminded of the conversation they'd had when they drove down to Lee's Ferry. "Didn't you say the Dnieper River is also dammed continuously?"

"Yes, all that is left is the area near the delta into the Black Sea and then above, where it goes into Lake Kyyiv. It used to be so lovely . . ." She stared vacantly. "Will you please excuse me," she mumbled. She got up and left the room.

"What in hell?" Malcolm turned to the others after watching Kateryna's exit.

Saul: "She sometimes gets moody. There're a number of things going on in her life, but mainly it's her daughter. She's very sick." Saul explained the little he knew about Sofiia.

Ten minutes later, Kateryna came back and sat down, nearly as abruptly as she had left. "I am very sorry. You must . . . please . . . forgive me." She paused as if planning carefully what she was about to say. She looked down at her watch. "We have little time left, and we have much to talk about. Mr. Renslaer, are we able to speak freely here?"

"Malcolm, Kateryna, just Malcolm. When a young woman calls me *mister*, I feel twenty years older. And yes. Everyone is gone." Malcolm pictured Anthony and his sous chef in their apartments above the stables, Benjamin long asleep on the fourth floor, and David, Benjamin's young protégé, down in Napa trying to salvage what remained of his Friday night. The rest of the house staff were also gone for the weekend. "Please tell us what's troubling you."

She began slowly, her composure fully recovered. "I understand, I believe, what it is you want to accomplish. Thanks to our wonderful river trip I also now understand, to a large extent, your motivations—group as well as individual." She nodded at Waddy. "Now, in the little time remaining for us, it is important that you know what is important about me. That is, why it is that I am here and what I believe I can do." Kateryna gazed disarmingly at each of the men. Malcolm was startled by the heretofore unrevealed intensity of her steady, luminous eyes.

"The terrible tragedy at Chornobyl on April 26, 1986, is at the heart of why I am here to help you—and to help me. More precisely, to help my daughter." Kateryna continued her stare at the huge man sitting across from her, his bulk framed by the expanse of night-darkened, leaded glass windows rising twenty feet above him.

"When reactor number four at the complex exploded that night, my whole life changed. My husband was a physician, assigned to the Center for Radiological Medicine in Kyyiv. I was stationed at Chelyabinsk-40. Our daughter, Sofiia, was with Tolik at our apartment in Kyyiv. She was two years old. The medical staffs at Chornobyl and at Prypiat—the power plant is between the two villages, about 140 kilometers from Kyyiv—the local medical staffs were overwhelmed. Tolik happened to be in Prypiat at the time, temporarily assigned for some research. He became involved immediately with the treatment of the technicians. Soon he was also treating the fire fighters who were trying to contain the blaze, to keep it from spreading to the other reactors. Try to understand, conditions were so bad that for the ten days after the initial explosion and before the reactor was sealed, anyone working within the reactor building was exposed to a lifetime permissible accumulation of radiation in a matter of minutes. Radionuclide levels were 200 times greater than at Hiroshima immediately after the detonation. Obviously, many people were greatly overexposed. There was nothing to be done. So many people were being terribly injured, and the convective plume of radionuclides was spewing death three kilometers into the atmosphere."

"Weren't personnel being rotated into the area?" Saul asked.

"Oh, Saul! This was the world's first experience with a truly disastrous compromise of a nuclear reactor. The release at the Sellafield reactor in England in 1957, which the West so cleverly covered up, was nothing compared to Chornobyl. Even the most disciplined people failed to appreciate the radiation they could not see, feel, or smell. By the time a person can taste the metallic taste, he is dead. Still walking, but dead. People just reacted heroically to a terrible, fast-moving situation." Kateryna did not tell them that thousands of Estonian military reservists were conscripted for the death-penalty tasks along with the local Ukrainians. Very few White Russians were sent to Chornobyl.

"Tolik was there in Prypiat continuously for three days, treating the technicians, the firemen, and then the miners sent in to shore up the foundation to keep it from collapsing under the core. There were also the helicopter pilots who dropped the tons of dolomite, boron carbide, clay, sand, and lead to try to stem the neutron flux, to cut off oxygen and filter the radionuclides in the plume."

Saul nodded. The others stared at Kateryna, appreciating if not fully understanding the details.

"They were desperately trying to prevent a meltdown of the reactor core. I was told later that Tolik's dosimeter had turned black—completely black—so great was his exposure from the people he treated and from the fallout at Prypiat. After the first three days he was ordered home to Kyyiv. He died two weeks after the explosion from acute prodromal syndrome." She stared past Malcolm at the dark windows. "I did not see him. I was not permitted to leave Chelyabinsk."

"What of your daughter?" Saul finally asked.

"She was in Kyyiv with Mariia, an old woman who cared for her while Tolik was at work. She was a very kind, caring woman. Her husband had been killed during the German siege of Stalingrad, and she had lost her whole family during Stalin's starvation of the Ukrainian and Georgian people in the early '30s. So many died so terribly."

"It was like the Holocaust," Saul said vacantly.

"Saul, you in the West speak of *the* Holocaust. Well, what Stalin did to our people—*nine* million died—that was *our* holocaust, and yet it is never even *mentioned* in the West."

"Kateryna, please. I'm sorry . . . please go on." Saul wanted very much not to get into a discussion about which particular program of genocide was the more terrible. For an absolute certainty, Malcolm would launch into a long recount of the millions who had died at the hands of the Japanese during their many invasions and later in hundreds of prison and labor camps throughout the Pacific war zone.

She paused again. "Such a simple, innocent thing Mariia did. She had no means to know." Kateryna again stared, unseeing, at the expanse of glass across the room.

"Mariia took Sofiia's blanket from the back seat of Tolik's automobile. It had been left there when he went to Prypiat; then he had thrown his overalls on top of it. Mariia wrapped Sofiia in it. The blanket had been on the seat of the automobile for the three days in Prypiat, with the window open, and then had lain under Tolik's clothing. Of course, the heaviest, most deadly radionuclides fall out first: the cesium 137 and iodine 131 are the most concentrated; there would also be much krypton 85, strontium 90, and plutonium 240. The wind had been toward the northwest from the reactor site, with Prypiat directly in the fallout path. For two weeks Sofiia had the blanket with her in her bed. We don't know, but it was estimated that she received two grays."

"Grays?" Malcolm frowned.

"A new unit of radiation measurement—100 rads," Saul said.

"When Tolik came home he was already suffering from acute gastrointestinal illness. Mariia said he was vomiting continuously and he could not control his bowels. He was probably not much aware of what was going on around him. One week before he died, Tolik—somehow in his terrible suffering—realized that the blanket he saw wrapped around Sofiia had been in his automobile. He realized what it meant. His final days were filled not only with his own physical agony but with the despair that he had brought the same suffering to his little daughter. I was told that his last hours were spent screaming his agony for Sofiia."

"Kateryna, you needn't tell us these intimate things," Malcolm said when she paused.

As though she had not heard him, she continued. "When I arrived home, my husband had died and was already buried. Sofiia was still there but was soon to be sent to one of the sanitoria in Crimea, along with thousands of other children from Minsk to Kyyiv. Children are so much more vulnerable, especially from iodine 131 contamination of the milk. Along with all the other children, she had been given potassium iodide tablets to saturate her thyroid so that it would not absorb the radioactive iodine. She was sent away, and I was required to return to my duties. In the next months I visited her in Dzhankoy as often as I could get away. She had never had any symptoms of acute poisoning, also we had no way of knowing how many millisieverts she may have absorbed. The blanket was destroyed, so we had no way to measure the relative biological efficiencies of the radionuclides. Without this information, the doctors had no way to predict any possible effects. Of course, with so many, terribly sick children in Ukraine, Sofiia had no priority for preventive treatment.

"I was able finally to have her with me as I moved to different duty stations. It was in her fourth year that she started to have symptoms from the radiation exposure. My superiors arranged for Sofiia to be sent immediately to Hospital No. 6 in Moscow. That was the hospital where your Dr. Robert Gayle came to perform the bone marrow transplants. It was arranged for him to travel to Russia by Mr. Armand Hammer. Your American folk singer—what is his name—John Denver—he also traveled there to give benefit concerts. Sofiia was diagnosed as suffering from lymphoblastic leukemia. She was immediately started on an intense therapy of vincristine and prednisone and some other collateral components of the chemotherapy. It was apparently successful, and she was in remission, symptom free. I had arranged to be transferred to Moscow. That was possible only because Tolik had been decorated posthumously as Hero of the Soviet Union and because of my position in the chief directorate which worked closely with the physicists at Moscow University. When in remission, Sofiia was placed on a consolidation therapy to try to eliminate any nests of leukemic cells in her body. She continued stable and was doing well in school.

"In December of 1991, with the breakup of the Union, I was included within the state security counterpart in the new Ukrainian state and transferred to Sevastopil. Ukraine had become independent in August, and I no longer had the influence to keep Sofiia under treatment at the fine hospital in Moscow. The old hatreds between the Russians and the Ukrainians surfaced immediately. The fact that Sofiia and I were ethnic Ukrainian suddenly became a liability, and it was also forgotten that Tolik had been given the high decoration. Everything changed so quickly. In Sevastopil no treatment was available for Sofiia; the hospitals in Kyyiv were overwhelmed with all the new patients. Every year there are more and more. Last fall Sofiia began to exhibit symptoms of relapse, and I used every influence I could to get her some new chemotherapy treatment in Kyyiv. She is now in partial remission, but they have found evidence that she has developed meningeal leukemia."

"I've never heard of that," Stan interrupted.

"It is leukemia that invades the central nervous system. Treatment for this illness is largely beyond what is available in Kyyiv, or even in Moscow now. She has had some radiation treatment of her head and spine, but it is not adequate. Her doctors have as much as told me so."

Malcolm jumped up and paced down the length of the dining room. "I've heard enough. We're going to get Sofiia out of there right now. I'll have her in the Alfred Hoskins Center in Seattle just as quickly as one of my airplanes can get over there to get her."

"Mr. Renslaer—Malcolm—the authorities would not let Sofiia leave."

"What do you mean?" Malcolm demanded, his voice matched by his worst corporate-tyrant demeanor. "Everything is supposed to be wide open now, isn't it?"

"Some things do not change," Kateryna said patiently. "Because of me, Sofiia could not leave. If they let her leave, the state's hold on me would be gone. I know too much, and to some extent I am still too valuable to the Ukrainian state. Now, as I am sure you read in your newspapers, Russia and Ukraine are moving farther apart. Old—centuries-old—rivalries and hatreds are reemerging just as they have in other parts of the Soviet Union. My superiors are realizing that people like me who had access to the most intimate Soviet and Russian secrets may be increasingly valuable to Ukraine.

My little Sofiia has become just another pawn to keep me there, even though I may never actually be used by the state."

"It seems to me that it would be in your government's interest to provide Sofiia with the best possible care," Malcolm said, unaware of how cold his statement might sound.

"Yes, of course," Kateryna replied, seeing a clear example of why leaders in her country and in America were much the same. "But she is just one of so many competing for the limited resources. The whole Ukrainian state is in such a condition of flux and uncertainty that subtle political details are not now the highest priority."

"Why not *make* a political issue of Sofiia? A couple of telephone calls from me and she would be instant news. How could your government explain why they would not let a sick little girl go to America to receive lifesaving treatment?"

"Would you risk your whole enterprise with that big dam out in the desert just to save one little girl?"

Malcolm met Kateryna's gaze for a long moment. *How can I answer that?* He was instantly reminded that the attractive woman sitting across from him was a highly trained former KGB officer. "That is an unfair question."

"You at least acknowledge that the situation is not simple."

"Yes. Yes, of course. I should not just think out loud before considering all of the ramifications." Kateryna could not know that that was an unheard-of admission from Malcolm Renslaer.

The other house guests had sat transfixed during Kateryna's quiet, staccato summary and the exchange between her and Malcolm. Saul intervened at the uncomfortable impasse. "How quickly could you arrange for us to get the sort of device we discussed?"

"At this moment, I do not know. I am reasonably certain I can obtain a weapon of the type we talked about, but I will not know until I return. I did not have such things in mind when I came over here."

"Yes, I understand that you do not have the particulars, but can you give us some idea what the *possible* time frame would be?" Saul had lost all inhibition about pressing Kateryna for details.

She sighed. "Whatever I tell you would be inaccurate. And I just cannot—I won't—tell you what the problems are."

Malcolm started to interrupt. Saul was well aware of what their host was about to say, despite the careful coaching he had given him about avoiding sensitive political issues. Saul held up his hand. "Malcolm, we have only two distinct issues here: the bomb and Sofiia. Let's keep it that way, okay?"

Malcolm paused, nodded.

Saul: "All right, let me put it this way. If you could act quickly enough, we could just move you and Sofiia and the weapon at the same time."

"And let *me* put it *this* way," Kateryna responded stiffly. "I will do everything in my power to move things as quickly as possible. Within a couple of weeks of my return, a month at most, I can tell you if I will be successful and give you a specific timetable."

"That sounds good to me," Malcolm declared with a slap of his hand to the table. He handed Saul a look that would have wilted any of the hundreds of Mayacamas executives scattered around the world. It was an unmistakable *shut-up-and-sit-down!* "Now, why don't you two bomb experts tell me what it is we're talking about."

"They haven't told us, either," Waddy said, looking at Stan.

Saul summarized the discussion he and Kateryna had had while huddled in the waterfall pothole in Saddle Canyon.

"Sonofabitch," Waddy gushed. "That thing is perfect! Can you really get your hands on that kind of a nuke?"

"Such a weapon exists in our arsenal. I sincerely believe that I can obtain one." Kateryna focused her intensity on Malcolm again. "Please try to understand that I have a very good reason for not telling you about the specific problems I will face. Some of those problems create the time uncertainty. Sofiia also has a time problem. I don't know what more I can say."

"What about that switch, or whatever it is?" Malcolm asked.

"That situation just exists," Kateryna quickly answered. "Something you have to consider in whether to go ahead with this."

"Ninety-two percent sounds plenty good enough, I'd say," Waddy shrugged. "Nothing in life is certain. That's one of the problems with the whole *pahana* outlook."

"I'll be able to take a look at that detail when I actually see the device," Saul said. "Meanwhile, I'll have time to do some research."

"People," Stan said, getting up to duplicate Malcolm's pacing, "I would like to discuss a practical aspect. Assuming you can acquire the weapon, where would it be made available?"

"Stanley, the only chance I have is in Ukraine. Another source is under Russian control, but is so far in the interior that moving the device without detection would be impossible."

"I've thought about the transport problem a great deal," Malcolm interjected, "ever since we first talked about trying to get a Soviet weapon." Saul glanced over at Kateryna but detected no reaction to Malcolm's admission of the arrogant presumption. He knew she had to be very angry, but she displayed not a clue. Like Malcolm, she was doing her best to avoid a political clash.

Unconscious of his faux pas, Malcolm pressed on. "Ever since that bunch of Syrians tried to smuggle in plutonium and other equipment, shipments from even remotely suspect debarkation points have been scanned for radioactive material. Masking a radioactive source is nearly impossible, given today's sophisticated detection equipment. And, you know, you can't just land a commercial ship or an aircraft anywhere you choose. Furthermore, paper trails are as long as your arm."

"Don't forget NEST," Saul added. Malcolm nodded.

"NEST?" Stan asked.

"Nuclear Energy Search Team, part of the Department of Energy. It's headquartered at Nellis Air Force Base near Las Vegas. The organization has over eight hundred members on standby, with an undisclosed number on active duty. They have extremely sophisticated radiation detection equipment, and nobody at Livermore I've talked to really knows what they're up to. Malcolm's right. It could be very risky bringing the weapon in through any commercial clearance."

"But we have hundreds of commercial ports of entry. Lots of obscure ones," Stan noted hopefully.

Malcolm: "Sure, but then there's the matter of crew. They would be curious about why a ship or plane, so expensive to operate, would go to all the trouble to arrive at some out-of-the-way backwater, even if I had a whole cargo of extraneous stuff to cover up the existence of the one particular item. I could hire a special crew—which might also create an infinity of trouble. I'm not going to set myself up to be blackmailed."

"Malcolm," Saul broke in quietly, "I'm sure you've thought about all this at length, but with your shipping resources certainly there must be *some* way to– –"

"Of course, I could *probably* slip it through. In fact, very probably. There is, nonetheless, unacceptable risk. I know, I know, the drug bosses do it every day. But if they get caught, they just write it off, hire a new bunch of mules, and ship another pile of dope—just raise their prices to cover the loss. We don't have that luxury. We only have one chance."

Saul yawned. "Can we pick this up again tomorrow? I can hardly see, I'm so tired. I need a nice warm bed."

"Good idea," Stan said. "Malcolm, I have a thought. Why don't we continue our discussion tomorrow morning on *Samora*. Take her out on the bay. Perfect seclusion and Kateryna will get a view of the Golden Gate and the city that'll beat the hell out of the Red and White tour boats."

"Also a good idea," Malcolm agreed, "but impossible. *Samora* is gone."

Stan's heart plummeted at Malcolm's statement. The old Renslaer yacht had been the source of some of Stan's greatest pleasure over the past twenty-five years. "Gone? Sold? Not sunk!"

"No, my friend, relax. She is alive and well, and I have her safely hidden away. Part of my relocation plan."

"Can you tell us where?" Stan regarded no man-made thing more highly than the old Sparkman & Stephens-designed schooner: ninety feet of delicately crafted teak, a soaring spread of sail, and lines that would give chills to any lover of traditional wooden sailing yachts.

"Considering what it is we're talking about here, I guess there're no secrets. She's laid up in Malta."

Waddy spoke first: "Planning a cruise through Mr. Gadhafi's Gulf of Sidra, Malcolm?"

"Malta is only about 1,300 kilometers from the Dardanelles," Kateryna thought out loud.

"Judas Priest! That's it! Malcolm's 325 pounds exploded out of his chair. "Stanley, are you ready to skipper *Samora* again?"

Stan had been thinking the same thing even before Malcolm got the words out. Kateryna was already thinking about how and where she could arrange a transfer in the Black Sea, and Waddy realized that he was about to learn how to sail a big yacht across an ocean. Saul was quietly thinking that somehow fate had intervened.

Malcolm quickly produced a bottle of Louis XIII. "A toast! Everything is starting to fall into place."

***

While San Francisco lay shrouded and cold in a February morning fog forty miles to the south, Saturday morning broke bright and clear on the forested ridge above the Napa Valley. Stan had slept little. Since they'd come off the river, the whole insane scheme had started to focus into reality. Kateryna was real: not just the intriguing woman but the Ukrainian intelligence officer. Her motivation—her daughter—was real. *Samora* was real. What had been only conversations among friends was about to become the first step in conspiracy. A felony. Continuing and compounding felonies, to end with a massive destruction of property and, possibly, loss of life. Prison. Or worse.

An abrupt and irremediable change in his life was going to commence on this bright morning. Decisions—commitments—had to be made. Kateryna would leave today to return to Pueblo, then to Washington, then far around the world to a life Stan could only vaguely imagine. Everything was further complicated by the rapidly growing feeling he had for the strange yet delightful woman. She was a woman who would turn his head on a street in San Francisco—familiar, yet alien—intriguing physical beauty. But there was so much more. He was beginning to feel the weight of her coming absence.

"Good morning," he said cheerily, joining her on the east terrace below the conservatory. "Sleep well?"

"Of course not. And you?"

"I'm sure none of us did." He followed her gaze down over the vineyards, groves, pastures, and Arabians, across the Napa Valley and up into the Caymus Mountains, blue and hazy under the bright sun rising above them.

"I was up very early and took a long walk," she said. "This is such a lovely place. Down the ridge over there," she pointed in the direction of the old lodge, "I found a grove of the largest trees I have ever seen. I had no idea such giants existed. What are they? How old?"

"Redwoods. Some of the few ancient ones left. There are several in that grove nearly 2,000 years old."

"Stanley, it was so . . . I cannot describe it . . . It was so peaceful, but it was more—like there was no sense of time at all. I felt so insignificant, and yet . . . and yet filled with some sort of deep understanding. It was astonishing. Even a little bit frightening. Do I make any sense? Do you understand?"

Stan looked into the luminous, multicolored eyes blazing back with such intensity. Part of the alien disappeared in that moment. "I know what you mean exactly. It's the same feeling I experienced exploring the deep grottos in Glen Canyon. In some odd, unexplainable way, that old grove always reminds me of Glen Canyon, yet two places could not be more different. I've given up trying to understand."

"Caught you two again," Waddy chirped as he walked across the mosaic of evenly-fitted gray and green stones. "Remember, this is business." Saul and Malcolm were right behind him.

"So, where do we go from here?" Kateryna asked Malcolm.

He settled himself into another of his Papa-Bear-sized chairs. "First of all, we have the matter of demonstrating good faith." He gestured toward Stan. "What the lawyers would refer to as *consideration.* By the time you arrive in Sevastopil, there will be an account in the downtown Geneva office of Credit Suisse in Sofiia's name, with you as trustee. You will have no problem—at least no financial problem—leaving Ukraine."

"That is not necessary," she said firmly. "Just help me with Sofiia's treatment."

"Of course it's necessary. Also by the time you get home, arrangement will be made for Sofiia's treatment at the Alfred Hoskins Center in Seattle. It's the best. You need to be convinced that you and your daughter will be provided for. We do not know if you will actually succeed in getting us what we need, but I must feel that you will make your best effort."

Stan felt that this was particularly harsh, even by the usual Malcolm Renslaer standards. His glare directed at Malcolm did not communicate.

"Very well," Kateryna nodded, once again reminded that she was dealing with the very personification of the capitalism she had long been taught to despise, "but I am new to your capitalist methods."

"This is, first of all, a business transaction. My experience is that a deal has the best chance of succeeding if all parties are fully informed and clearly understand, from the outset, what each one's duties and benefits are.

Action starts today. I hope everyone here understands that." Malcolm turned to each person in the group. "Once Kateryna begins whatever she has to do to perform her part of the arrangement, it will be very difficult to turn back. Is everyone agreed?"

From the demeanor of the people sitting around the white iron table, Stan realized that each person had thought through some species of the thoughts he had wrestled with so painfully during the sleepless night. Nods came from each of the silent people facing Malcolm. He slammed his palm on the table. "So we are agreed. Now, how can we stay in touch after you go back home?" Malcolm turned his chair so that he was squarely facing Kateryna. "We really can't take any significant action here until you notify us that you can definitely acquire the weapon."

"Saul and I can set up our communication. We've got some time before I leave with the rest of my team. Since we were together so long at Pueblo, I don't think questions would be raised about our staying in touch."

"But how do I contact you after I organize the boat in Malta?" Stan asked.

"I think that arrangement can wait until I contact Saul, don't you think?" Of course, she was right, Stan realized. He hoped his desire to see the lovely woman again was not completely transparent. He knew it was.

"Kateryna," Saul said carefully, "with all the time we spent together, if one of your weapons disappears I will certainly be an immediate object of investigation."

"Yes. I am sure that already there are detailed reports by our security, as well as your FBI, covering our time at Pueblo. Furthermore, our going missing for the past few days has probably created particular curiosity. This is a situation that now exists and simply has to be dealt with." She concentrated on Malcolm. "Let me just say this about my acquisition of the weapon, without getting into unnecessary details. It will probably—and I emphasize *probably*—be some time before the loss of the weapon is discovered. However, as soon as Sofiia and I leave you may be investigated concerning our disappearance and having nothing to do with the weapon. Even when the loss of the weapon is discovered it is unlikely that your authorities would be notified. The source of weapons I have in mind is . . . well . . . very sensitive, politically. I can tell you nothing further. I have already told you far too much."

Saul frowned. "I can understand how your authorities might be reluctant to admit that one of their weapons was headed over here, but I cannot imagine that the loss of the device will not soon be discovered."

Kateryna remembered Saul's comment when they left Phantom Ranch. "Trust me," she said to him with a wink. "But . . . if your authorities *are* notified about the weapon you will have to disappear on very short notice. I'm sure you all understand that."

Malcolm nodded. "Everyone Saul ever said hello to will be contacted.

Our little group will surface immediately—and you'll be in there too," he said to Waddy. "The time we've spent at the club will give you away. A few of the members understand that we might actually *like* you."

"Thank you, Malcolm, I appreciate that," Waddy grinned.

"Kateryna," Malcolm went on, "we have understood from the outset that if we were able to acquire such a device our lives here are over. I have already put nearly everything into place for all of us to simply vanish, and I've arranged a place for Saul to make any modifications to the weapon or assembly of other equipment that might be needed." The last comment earned Malcolm a surprised glance from Saul. "All we need is the word from you."

"And you will get it, rest assured."

"Fine. Now let's have some breakfast and then take a nice, long ride through one of the best little parts of California."

Malcolm didn't use the Napa airport except under very unusual circumstances. Excluding weekends, even if he was at Stony Ridge and needed an airplane, he preferred to drive clear down to San Francisco International. The Napa airport was not a dirt strip with a wind sock. It had intersecting 5,000- and 6,000-foot runways easily able to accommodate the Mayacamas executive jets. It also boasted most of the gadgets necessary to satisfy his and his fellow wine barons' pilots, including VOR and localizer approaches available through the Oakland Air Traffic Center; and uncluttered descents to the field were readily at hand over the north arm of San Francisco Bay. But the irreconcilable problem from Malcolm's point of view was that the Napa County Airport also hosted the Japan Airlines Training Center.

The origins of his initial, unreasoning, generic hatred of the Japanese were with his father during Malcolm's early youth. Malcolm's Uncle Jeb, his father's favorite brother, had been killed at Bataan during the long march to prison camps in which thousands of soldiers had been murdered. It was not so much the fact of his death as its manner and motive. Uncle Jeb had been executed by having a bayonet shoved through his lower intestines. His crime had been an attempt to help a struggling fellow soldier.

When Malcolm was growing up, his nanny was a young Korean woman who had come to the United States just after the war. She had been one of the "comfort women" liberated in the Philippines. As soon as he was old enough to be told, Malcolm learned what had happened to the woman who, in all practical respects, was his mother. The flame of the young Malcolm's smoldering hatred was regularly and resolutely fanned by his father, whom Malcolm was determined to emulate in all things, personal and industrial. As Malcolm gradually ascended to the helm of Mayacamas Industries, the fact of the company's worldwide reach brought him into inevitable contact—and conflict—with the Japanese industrial/government *koreitsu* machine. And as he came to understand how the Japanese establishment conducted its business, his attitudes toward things Japanese descended even lower. But in the process he acquired a more refined focus for his hatred—away from the Japanese people and squarely aimed at their ruling class. Ever since that afternoon at Stony Ridge when Malcolm had revealed how he intended to spend the rest of his life, Stan and Saul were convinced that the principal object of Malcolm's environmental self-help would be the Japanese industrial apparatus. Glen Canyon Dam was but a brief diversion that had happened to intrude upon his grand plan.

Malcolm accompanied his house guests on the leisurely drive through the Napa wine country, ending the tour at the airport. The fact that the JAL facility was closed on Saturday morning had much to do with his decision to come along to say good-bye to Kateryna. Once again, a small black and silver aircraft—this time a gleaming new Lear—was waiting for them at the edge of the transient parking area just outside the small terminal. A nearly exact copy of Captain Rogers, complete with starched white shirt and smart black and gold epaulets, also waited at the open door to the aircraft along with an equally familiar young copilot.

Stan wondered how Napa County could justify covering three square miles of such valuable property with concrete. Then he remembered that the airport had been built by the military during World War II, a time when priorities in California were very different.

"Saul's car is back in Albuquerque, and Stan's and Saul's rentals have been taken care of," Malcolm said as he walked toward the waiting airplane, his arm around Kateryna. It looked to Stan as if Malcolm could wrap his big paw clear around her slender waist. Malcolm stood with his back to the Beechcraft Bonanzas and Queen Airs lined up in perfect rows outside the perfectly manicured, perfectly designed, deco-modern JAL building. Nodding to the smiling pilot, Malcolm continued: "Bob will drop Waddy off at Flagstaff and then Kateryna and Saul at Albuquerque." No one had wasted any effort in asking Kateryna how she had arranged her travel from Pueblo to Albuquerque or how she would return.

Malcolm asked his pilots to step inside the airplane. He held Kateryna at arm's length, his voice barely audible over the whine of the outboard engine. "As soon as you give us the word, we'll have Sofiia on her way to Seattle for whatever she needs. That clinic and its staff are the best."

Kateryna smiled up at the huge man. "I know you will, but please understand that I will have much to do when I get back. You will just have to be patient. You will hear from me as soon as I have solved some problems." She stepped up into the open doorway, hesitated, then quickly came back down. "I guess I'll see you somewhere in the Black Sea, Stanley." She hugged him tightly for a long moment. "Don't worry," she whispered in his ear. With that, she disappeared into the plane, followed by Waddy and Saul.

Stan watched intently as the sleek jet accelerated down runway 36 Left and climbed steeply through the fingers of pewter fog reaching up from the bay.

"Well, I guess I'm just about convinced," Malcolm interrupted Stan's trance. "Saul's right and Kateryna's right."

"Malcolm, even if she is able to deliver, that doesn't mean we have to use it."

Malcolm turned back to the waiting limo. "Sure, we've got time to think about it. But in the meantime, we've got a lot to do."

2

Upper Colorado Region Headquarters, U. S. Bureau of Reclamation
Salt Lake City, February 21

"You seen the pile of stuff we got from NCAR?" the senior hydrologist asked. "Randy MacConnell got it too; now he's calling me daily. He really thinks we should schedule more drawdown in Powell."

The Region Director looked impatiently at the twitchy little engineer. "I'll talk to Randy. We're not going to change the operating plan for the whole basin just because those pointy-headed types back there in Boulder are running around like Chicken Little again. Damnit, I wish they'd butt out. That one jerk, what's his name? Heartwood. He's been bugging the people in Denver, so, of course, the turds start rolling down here." Doug Foreman had one more year to retirement. He had little patience with interference in his region from people outside the Bureau, especially the theoreticians at the atmospheric physics laboratory in Boulder. So far as Doug Foreman was concerned, Boulder was equivalent to Stalinist/Leninist Moscow.

"Sir, if I might. This new El Niño data is very dramatic; we've never seen anything like it before. And it's not just the NCAR people. The Geological Survey's Desert Research Lab at Tucson and even UN Reno are coming up with the same forecast. The Pacific High is already starting to weaken in the north, and the whole thing is shifting south. That matches what happened in 1983 and '84, except this year it's starting much earlier. I--"

"Ortwin, you called this pile of crap a *forecast.* I'm surprised at you. These are not forecasts, they're guesses, nothing more. And guesses based on what? The El Niño/Southern Oscillation theory. Guesses based on abstract theories. Great for overpaid, grant-suckling physicists to masturbate over, but I've got to run a frigging river basin! None of those shitheads has to deal with the people at the Western Area Power Administration. If we bypass water outside of the scheduled operating plan, we will have very unhappy people over at WAPA, as well as the growers down in Phoenix, Yuma, and the Imperial Valley. I just don't want to deal with it. Glen Canyon is not a flood control structure, okay? Sometimes you all lose sight of that very simple fact. Power production, Ortwin. That's what that dam is there for, then ag water, then water for Phoenix, and *then* for those atheists out in L.A."

Doug Foreman was an elder in the Mormon Church. The Saints had been largely responsible for the development of irrigation farming and hydroelectric power production throughout the Southwest and were heavily represented throughout the Bureau, particularly in the Salt Lake regional office. Although the southern Californians purchased much of the Bureau's electric power, Doug Foreman had very little concern for the gentile inhabitants of the latter-day Sodom which now occupied what Brigham Young had dreamed of being the western extremity of his Deseret; and Doug Foreman had never been able to understand how his brethren in religion, including the agents who dominated the FBI's L.A. field office, could stand living on the southleft coast.

"Yes, I do understand, sir; it's just that this time my people think there's a significant chance that late-season precip will be far above normal."

The old man sighed. "Look, I appreciate what you're saying. None of us wants to get caught again like in '83. But, as you also know, we've got yet another factor layered on the situation besides the power people, the irrigators, the municipal water users, and those clowns who run the resort concession at Powell. They really scream if the lake level drops. They complain about the smell and—what do they call it—the *visual degradation*. Have to move all their docks, and then tourists run boats into exposed rocks and all the rest. Now the latest problem is the frigging environmental impact statement for the river between Powell and Mead. The draft EIS is out. Lots more environmental nitwits worrying about counting tweety birds and dandelions. If we mess with the outflow beyond what we've agreed to during this assessment phase, there'll be hell to pay. Denver made that real clear."

"I don't have to remind you, sir, that the Bureau's prime mandate is safety of the structure."

"Oh shit, Ortwin, that'll never happen even if those numbnuts over in Boulder turn out to be more than right."

A flash flood from a sudden rain squall spills over the east rim near the left spillway portal, July 27, 1983, as the river continues to assault the obstruction in its channel (*Bureau of Reclamation, Tom Fridmann*).

Norman Rockwell, 1969 (*Bureau of Reclamation, W.L.Rusho*).

View southwest from the confluence of the San Juan River, joining the Colorado from left, 1973. Hidden Passage is opposite the small island in the channel downstream of the confluence. Music Temple is in the side canyon just beyond the island. Compare photos at pp. 6, 36, 37 (*Bureau of Reclamation, V. Jetley*).

View up the Escalante River arm of the partially-filled reservoir, five miles above the Colorado River confluence, 1973. Davis Gulch enters in left foreground. When full, the reservoir extends beyond Coyote Creek, entering from the left at the top of the photograph (*Bureau of Reclamation, V. Jetley*).

The auto ferry at Hite near the junction of the Dirty Devil River and the Colorado, 1964. Utah highway 95, between Mexican Hat and Hanksville, now bridges the reservoir which flooded the river crossing, 140 river (reservoir) miles above Glen Canyon Dam (*Bureau of Reclamation, W.L. Rusho*).

SAMORA

Aztec Creek, 1960 (*Tad Nichols*).

1

Pillar Point Harbor, Half Moon Bay, California, April 5

"Where'd you find it?" Police officer Tom Dawkins looked down from the end of the pier at the trim racing sailboat bobbing in the water alongside the fuel dock.

"I own the *Lady Gay* over there," the fisherman nodded toward the commercial berths. "We were heading back in late this morning when we saw her. Could tell she was adrift. We went over and saw she was abandoned. Just about three miles offshore and maybe a little bit north of the harbor here."

"Did you look around for anyone overboard, Mr. Souza?"

"Oh, yes, sir. We got on the radio and notified the Coast Guard, too. They had a chopper out in maybe fifteen minutes; then the motor lifeboat from Golden Gate Station showed up. Couldn't believe how fast they got here. They told me to tow her in."

"That's correct, Officer Dawkins," the Coast Guard bosun's mate said. "We were notified yesterday that she was missing, but with the bad weather we had our hands full. We were already on our way to check out this area. Had a radio call earlier this morning about a sailboat adrift."

"So who has jurisdiction?" The police officer started to think about all the paperwork.

"The Coast Guard will take it from here, Officer Dawkins," the skipper of the motor lifeboat responded. "No problem."

"Do you know whose boat this is? I mean, is he one of our residents?"

"No. The guy lives in the city. He and his buddy were out practicing for the Farallons Race. Picked a ratty day to do it, though; dumb shits went right out with a small craft advisory in effect."

"The other fellow wasn't from Half Moon Bay either?"

"No, he lives in Oakland. Relax, you're out of the picture."

"What about the boat? What is it? Looks expensive."

"She's an Olson 30. Hot little item. What's it look like down there, Carl?" he called to another Coast Guardsman emerging from *Penny Pincher*'s little cabin.

The young seaman walked up the gangway from the floating dock. "Lot of water in the bilge. One hatch broken. Life rings, Dan buoy, and strobe are still in place. I'd say she got knocked down, maybe rolled. Safety lines are still below. Bozos were out sailing in a half gale and didn't have their safety lines clipped on. Found four life vests in the cabin, too, so they probably weren't wearing vests, either. These guys were just plain old, dumb-ass stupid. Shark shit by now."

"What happens to the boat?" fisherman Souza asked. He was vaguely familiar with salvage rights on abandoned vessels.

"We'll impound her here with the San Mateo County Harbor District. The harbor master said she'll go over there with those purse seiners and trawlers on the commercial side. You'll need to go on down to Moss Landing to make out a salvage claim. They can answer all your questions."

The crew of Coast Guardsmen reassembled on the trim forty-four-foot motor lifeboat, the bosun's mate taking his place on the coxswain's flat.

"Thanks for your help, Officer Dawkins," the bosun's mate yelled up to the dock. "Your department will be kept informed. We'd appreciate your cooperation in getting the word out around here about the missing men."

"Yeah, you bet." He watched the white-hulled boat with the distinctive blue and red diagonal stripes across her bows head out of the inner harbor toward the breakwater.

2

Malta, April 8

Stan looked down past the dipping wing of the airbus at the oval-shaped island, the larger of the two he'd seen as they started their slow turn and rapid descent to Luqa airport. Past the airport to the northeast he could see the old walled city of Valletta, which occupied the battlement-fortified peninsula intruding into the remarkable harbor, a harbor that had been fought over for centuries.

The island of Malta and its smaller neighbor to the northwest, Gozo, were the principal islands in this small archipelago rising from the Mediterranean Sea about sixty miles south of Sicily. Even on the early spring day, the one hundred square miles of limestone and sandstone island looked bleak: bare, rocky, and uniformly dun-colored, with just a hint of green starting to show. The islands appeared unbroken by any significant forest or watercourse.

As Air Malta flight 101 from London made her approach, Stan began to see the proliferation of small villages spreading inland and up and down the coast. Lush vegetation poked through the anonymous brown. The splotches of dull ivory-colored towns became identifiable clusters of buildings set into the jagged coastal pattern of fawn and azure blue that looked as though it had been cut out with a keyhole saw. The harbor and its peninsular capital city was the focus of the intricate scene.

Stan was still comfortable with foreign travel; his many years with the State Department had taken him to much of the world. Over twenty years had passed since he'd last visited this particular place, but the fruit of long experience told him that he would quickly adjust. He had no anxiety as to place, only as to what he was doing here. Not so the intent young man sitting next to him, Stan thought. Waddy's culture shock, which had begun mildly at Heathrow, would certainly jump several more quanta in the next few minutes.

During the interminable five-week wait for Kateryna's message, Stan and Malcolm, with Saul's more subtle urging, finally convinced Waddy that he would have to shed the trappings of his Southwestern culture. A Hopi Indian, with Waddy's self-accentuation, had little chance of moving about unnoticed, even in the Mediterranean. Besides accouterments, only a simple change was necessary, despite the extended debate that had been required to get it done. Waddy's short, styled hair now had only a suggestion of the wave which had been so conspicuous in his vanished mane. He was dressed in conservative British clothing, and no hint of his beloved turquoise and silver remained. The plan was to present him as a British Columbian of native North American descent. For the same convenience of language, Stan also carried one of the perfectly forged Canadian passports Malcolm had arranged.

The man at the customs and immigration counter gave Waddy a long look as he took the passport. He was quite similar to Waddy in stature, being about five foot seven and carrying a mesomorphic build. He did not have Waddy's distinctive, keg-shaped torso, however, a feature that no attempted deception by clothing, cosmetics, or coiffure could disguise.

Stan watched the Maltese officer give Waddy the visual once-over. Even after all his years with the State Department and his countless contacts with these officials, Stan was invariably amazed at how they were all the same the world over. Whether north, south, east, or west; white, black, yellow, or brown, every government managed with uncanny consistency to find these unique people with their latent, unlearnable ability to detect something that was not "right." They could be fooled, of course, something Stan counted on today.

"Will you be staying in Malta long, Mr. Barrows?" the customs officer asked, glancing at Waddy's hands and then concentrating on his eyes.

"No, not long. Just a vacation," Waddy answered as he had long practiced, even dragging out his O's.

"May I see your return ticket?" the official continued, almost satisfied that the voice sounds he heard were what he'd expected but wanting to hear a little more. Waddy handed over the Air Malta folder containing a ticket to London, scheduled thirty days hence.

"A nice long vacation, Mr. Barrows. Friends or relatives here?"

"No, my doctor told me to take an extended vacation, so my travel agent came up with your lovely island." Another answer according to script.

Stan recalled the long discussion and debate that had gone into this little detail. He had argued that they should be well clear of the Med before some computer matched up a declared departure date with actual airline flight manifests. Fortunately, for stays of less than three months, visas were not required for citizens of EC or Commonwealth countries, even self-governing Commonwealth nations like Canada.

The Maltese was not through with Waddy yet. Stan watched the officer scan the entry stamps in Waddy's passport. Stan felt their passports had too many stamps for their apparent age, despite the declared dates of issuance.

"Have you traveled abroad recently, Mr. Barrows?"

"Let's see." Waddy paused. "I last traveled to London. It was in February." He'd memorized the stamps and visa endorsements.

"I wasn't aware that Great Britain required passports for visiting Canadians," the officer said, handing back the passport. He continued to concentrate on Waddy's eyes for any evidence of confusion from his lie.

"Oh, yes, sir. Since we've been self-governed, passports have been required."

The customs officer made a cursory inspection of Waddy's duffel and then waved him past. "Have a pleasant stay in Malta, Mr. Barrows."

"Thank you. I intend to."

"That guy was like a ferret," Waddy said when they walked out of the terminal toward the taxi rank.

"They're the same the world over," Stan smiled. "But you did just fine. Now you understand why we drilled you so mercilessly."

""He really scrutinized my passport. You think these things are okay?"

"They're fine, Waddy. Perfect, I would say. Malta has gotten a lot of attention since the Pan Am 103 thing in 1988. The two men identified by American and British intelligence as being involved with the Lockerbie crash were traced through here. Probably every terrorist in the Middle East or North Africa travels through Rome or this airport . . . Hell, here *we* are," he said with a weak grin. "The Europeans accused the Maltese of having been too lax in the past, so they're trying to be more cautious. These people are much more laid back than their northern European neighbors. They drove the British nuts. Maybe that's why the Brits finally gave up here."

"I'm looking forward to meeting some of the normal people." Stan knew Waddy was referring to normal *female* Maltese.

"We will, starting at the boatyard, I'm sure."

"Why'd Malcolm pick this place?"

"Because the people *are* so laid back—a product of their convoluted history. Things racial are a lot more complicated throughout the Mediterranean than they are in our Southwest but particularly so on this little island.

Malcolm could occupy himself forever trying to sort through it all. The Maltese consider themselves to be directly derived from the earliest Phoenician traders, but a lot has happened since 1500 B.C. These people are a collage of everything from Africa to the Baltic, from Persia to Spain. Although their language is Semitic, the people are now dominantly Roman Catholic. That started when Saint Paul shipwrecked here in 60 A.D. This was a British colony from about 1800 until 1964, so it's well organized and practically everybody speaks English."

"They do? Uh, we gonna have time to . . . you know, look around a little bit?"

"Sure. You're going to find out that we'll be spending a lot of time waiting for things to get done. The clock ticks a lot slower here than in northern Europe. And this place isn't just Mediterranean in life style, which I'm sure you've read about; it's also African. Very warm and friendly but with a kind of formality that is more than just a leftover British veneer. These people draw the best from a mixture of racial strains—like the whole world should become."

The cab driver skirted the main city and wound around Marsamxett Harbor toward Manoel Island. The narrow, obviously British roads were choked with traffic, including dozens of the unique, colorfully painted Maltese buses. Since Stan's last long-ago visit, the maritime economy of Malta had been converting from dominantly commercial shipping to an emphasis on tourism, including the booming yacht service business. The shipyard on Manoel Island now had facilities to handle the special needs of both motor and sailing yachts up to fifty meters.

Stan remained continually apprehensive after Malcolm had disclosed that *Samora* had not only been refitted but had been altered to disguise her appearance and to modernize her for more efficient sailing by a small crew. His well-entrenched memory of the old yacht was of her distinctive, gracefully sheared black hull with its gleaming, varnished teak trim and gold-leaf striping. Her schooner rig had carried tanbark sails set on varnished spruce spars. Ten strong athletes had been needed to sail her properly, to manage her huge spread of sail. Stan remembered the boisterous runs across the Pacific in the venerable Tahiti Race, broad reaching on a schooner's most efficient point of sail and carrying every square foot of canvas *Samora's* spars and rigging could suspend, including the giant black and gold spinnaker emblazoned with the Mayacamas crest. He could still vividly recall the sensation of standing on the sloping deck, his hands on the six-foot wheel, the huge yacht being overtaken by monstrous following seas in mid-ocean and being sailed by the closely knit crew of friends who pushed her as though she were a dinghy scudding across San Francisco Bay.

Stan had prepared himself as well as possible for what he would soon see. *Samora* would no longer be a gleaming black but ubiquitous white, to blend with the thousands of other large sailing yachts in the Med and around the world. She was no longer a schooner; she'd been re-rigged as a ketch: also a two-masted sail plan but with the taller spar now in the forward position for more efficient windward performance. Her distinctive red-brown, tanbark sails, which had so complemented the dramatic black hull, would also be white to further blend *Samora* into the flocks. The massive wooden masts had been replaced by ultramodern and efficient anodized aluminum extrusions, capable of being bent and shaped by hydraulic "vangs" and stays to stretch a sail to its most efficient aerodynamic shape. The masts would also carry the main and mizzen sails in roller furling mechanisms so that changes in sail size could be accomplished by the press of a button. No longer would a platoon of powerful backs and arms be needed to reef the mainsail, wrestling hundreds of pounds and thousands of square feet of sail stretched and flogging in a stiff wind.

Her deckhouse arrangement had been changed to further alter her changed-rig profile; she would carry Portuguese registration and ensign; and worst of all—most sadly worst of all—to complete her metamorphosis, she was no longer *Samora*. She was now *Aletheia*: "truth" in the Greek language. This last detail troubled Stan greatly. He was well aware of the ages-old and firmly entrenched belief of seamen across the world that it was bad luck to change the name of a sailing vessel.

Stan had questioned Malcolm at length about the details of naval architecture involved in changing *Samora*'s rig. He'd agonized with his fear that the fundamental design of the yacht would be upset. She was intended to carry the big mainsail aft with her strong, full hull sections rearward of the yacht's center of gravity. Wouldn't she be wholly out of balance with the new tall rig forward? Malcolm had confidently assured Stan that a fine, if anonymous and unrecognized, naval architect had redesigned the sail plan and changed some hull configuration, with all of the work having been done under the architect's direct supervision at a small yard on the Caribbean side of Costa Rica. The final detailing of the now unrecognizable *Samora* had been accomplished at the fine yard in Palma de Mallorca. "Olin Stephens would have fully approved," Malcolm had said, referring to the grand old man of yacht design.

The cab drove into the big shipyard. Like a mother looking for a lost child, Stan anxiously scanned the array of sail and motor vessels drawn up on their slipways. As prepared as he was for the new vision, he did not recognize the yacht at first glance.

My God, there she is. That it had taken a double take to see her was proof of the success of her visual transformation. Stan and Waddy got out of the cab in the shadow of the glistening white hull towering above them.

"Shit, Stan, I had no idea just how big this mother would be."

Stan clenched his teeth slightly at the irreverent reference to his favorite lady, even with her as-yet unfamiliar face lift. "Waddy, try to understand that this big *mother*, as you called her, has been a close friend for nearly twenty-five years."

"Hey . . . I'm sorry, Stan," Waddy said sincerely, instantly aware of how he had reacted to coarse references to important things in his own life. "Can we go aboard?" Waddy was looking at the rollaway stairs standing next to the beached yacht.

"Not until we get sorted out with the yard master. I'm sure Malcolm's arranged everything; it's just that the people who run places like this look very unkindly toward strangers who simply climb aboard their charges."

They headed for the aircraft hangar-sized building where the big yachts could be worked on during the rainy months. Walking under *Samora's* gracefully tapering stern, Stan grimaced when he looked up and saw "*Aletheia*" in ornate gold leaf and black enamel script on the transom. Beneath the yacht's name, "Lisboa" appeared in complementary block letters.

"Good afternoon, Captain Thompson, we have been expecting you." A swarthy, rotund, and impeccably dressed man strode forward to greet them. "I am Augúste Blaquiére. *Aletheia* is ready and waiting for your journey to the South Pacific."

Fucker looks sort of like a fat Navajo. Don't trust him.

"Good day, sir," "Philip" answered, followed by his introduction of "John." Malcolm's cover for *Samora* was that she was going into charter service in Fiji. Philip Thompson and John Barrows were her delivery skipper and mate for the trip through the Mediterranean, across the Atlantic, through the Canal, and across the Pacific. Indeed, *Samora* was going to wind up in Fiji, but not in charter service, and she would take a small detour from the declared route.

Stan explained to the yard master that they would need a few more days hauled out, with access to the yard facilities. Some mechanical pieces were required; of course, it would be appreciated if the yard could fabricate the needed items. But thank you, he and his mate could take care of the installation themselves.

Mr. Blaquiére received this information with slightly raised eyebrows. Yachts of the caliber of *Aletheia* were always professionally maintained; however, the yard master was well experienced in dealing with the idiosyncrasies of many of the richest people in the world. His job was to facilitate, gracefully and efficiently, never to question, and certainly never to *ask* questions.

As soon as Kateryna transmitted the go-ahead signal to Saul, soon followed by details of the gross dimensions and weight of the weapon and its container, Stan, Saul, and Malcolm had poured over the yacht's docking plan and schematics, conveniently available because of her recent overhaul. They designed exactly what would be required to create a secure and seaworthy hiding place for the weapon: one of the stainless steel water tanks, located right over the keel in the midsection of the yacht. The device would be lowered into position through the deck hatch over the salon, using the mainsail boom as a crane. Stan had brought along the drawings and specs of what would have to be fabricated as well as a list of tools needed to cut into the water tank and the flooring over the tank. He and Waddy would have to make the necessary incisions, then fit the newly fabricated, removable pieces so that the storage compartment would be wholly secreted. All the pieces the yard was to fabricate were nondescript and consistent with some reasonable modification of the interior of a sailing yacht. The only questionable item was the cradle necessary to secure the weapon within the water tank. It was designed in sections: merely an accumulation of mounts and flanges for the installation of some item of mechanical equipment.

"Captain Thompson, we can have these items fabricated for you in one week. Will that be acceptable?" The yard master's accommodating demeanor, manner of speech, and reserved aloofness were not unlike that of a maître d'hôtel in a fine Paris restaurant.

"That will be more than adequate," Stan responded in the careful fashion common to those responsible for the well-being of multimillion-dollar yachts or aircraft and answerable to the demanding people who own them.

Built in 1936 under the supervision of the twenty-six-year-old naval architecture genius, Olin Stephens, *Samora* epitomized the standard for private vessels intended for the enjoyment of the New York captains of industry and their yacht-conscious friends. Even in those Depression times, Malcolm's father had maintained a "cottage" at Newport, essential in the days when New York was still the center of everything. But when Malcolm had assumed the mantle of Mayacamas Industries, the Renslaer family's home venue, San Francisco, became the focus of corporate power as well. World War II had effectively catapulted California into the lead of the rapidly expanding nation, and by 1970, when he was finally in command, Malcolm had taken full advantage of the continuing boom.

Stan had assisted in the delivery of *Samora* from Newport to her new home at the Saint Francis Yacht Club. Even with the convenience of the Panama Canal, it had been a journey of over 6,000 miles. With her schooner rig, *Samora* had been forced to follow a route north from Panama that had carried her far out into the Pacific, close reaching before the northeast trade winds. Not until they were several hundred miles northeast of Hawaii had they been able to turn eastward with the westerlies to stand in to the California coast. Stan had enjoyed every moment of the trip. He had fallen in love, never to recover.

Waddy was stunned by the opulence of *Samora's* interior. They stood in the middle of the recessed main salon looking up at the ornate, beveled-glass overhead hatch, formed in a gently sloping, hip-roof shape, nine feet above the salon floor and reinforced with thick lexan. The yacht's entire interior was composed of finely fitted dark mahogany, accented and brightened with ivory-enameled panels; forest green settee cushions around the main salon table blended perfectly with the old varnished wood.

Stan looked down at the cabin sole with its long, polished lengths of Burmese teak, spaced with strips of blond holly protruding slightly above the planking to provide secure footing when the boat heeled. Stan and Malcolm had carefully thought through the needed modifications; *but that was theory. Now we've got to do it.* The interior of any proper yacht is designed to be disassembled; especially with a wood vessel, access must be available to every space and crevice, a task made possible by hundreds of carefully fitted pieces and ten times as many bronze screws and bolts. Part of Stan's and Waddy's job was to modify the flooring—to cut it into smaller sections so that it could be taken up quickly under rough conditions at sea.

Stan winced slightly at the prospect of cutting into the beautiful flooring. Both his conscience and their mission demanded a perfect job. "Waddy, there's no way we can do the joinery properly. Be too obvious. We'll have to get the best artisan we can find here to do it. With all these zillion-dollar yachts sitting around, there has to be a good local work force. We'll take care of the tank, though, as planned."

He was once again standing in front of the yard master. "*Aletheia* will be going into charter as soon as possible after arrival in Fiji, and there are a number of items of equipment that must be installed in her bilges: dive air compressor, additional hot water tankage, air conditioning—the usual. The charter business has gotten very competitive."

"Indeed, Captain Thompson, indeed."

"Considering the tight schedule (pronounced "shed-ule") we will have after arrival in Fiji, I would like to get the joinery work done here in addition to the mechanical items I specified. After again inspecting the interior of *Aletheia*, I have decided that we could only butcher what your legendary craftsmen could accomplish with ease and perfection, Mr. Blaquiére."

"I can assure you that we are well equipped to accommodate the needs of any vessel, Captain Thompson," the yard master nodded with an almost imperceptible bow, augmented by his ever-present, supercilious smile. "Now, if you will kindly explain what it is you desire, I will see to its fabrication immediately."

Mr. Blaquiére watched Stan walk back out into the sunny boatyard. *Ah, another smuggler.* The yard master shrugged slightly with the centuries-old ease of his countrymen as he rolled up the drawings. How the owners of these beautiful yachts managed their affairs was none of his concern, he thought. He only cared that he earned a very good living doing his work to perfection and minding his own business—unless he was paid handsomely not to mind his own business.

3

STONY RIDGE, APRIL 9

"We're very sorry to bother you on a Saturday, Mr. Renslaer," the neatly dressed man said when Benjamin escorted him and his companion into the conservatory. The second man was nearly an exact copy of the first, wearing a Brooks Brothers-style, blue business suit.

"Not at all," Malcolm replied. "You're lucky to catch me, what with all the traveling I've had to do lately. How can I help you?" Malcolm had been expecting the visit from the two special agents assigned to the FBI's San Francisco field office.

Special Agent Timothy Simmons glanced around the opulent room with its perfectly pruned collection of exotic flora and dominated by the expanse of leaded glass overlooking several million dollars worth of Napa Valley vineyards. He felt intimidated. He'd much rather have had the interview at the Bureau's office in the city. The special-agent-in-charge had carefully briefed him about who it was he would be interviewing, in strict accordance with the very careful instructions the SAC had received from a deputy assistant in Washington; unfortunately, the agreed-upon interview could only be done at the man's home in Napa. The FBI was always supposed to take charge—be dominant—but Special Agent Simmons did not feel that way at the moment. "Sir, we greatly appreciate your time. We will be as brief as possible."

Malcolm smiled condescendingly, watching the nervous agent try to suppress a swallow.

"As you know, sir, we are investigating the disappearance of a Saul Levi Kalinik and his companion, a Stanley Ward Bellamy. Kalinik's employment with the Department of Energy involves some, uh, sensitive matters."

Why do cops always refer to a person as A *so-and-so? Like there are several hundred Saul Kaliniks and Stan Bellamys, and they're just part of the fungible collection.* "Yes, I've known Saul and Stan for over thirty years. Even so, I don't really have any idea what Saul did out there at Livermore."

"Yes, sir. We don't have to get into that. Can you tell us why he might have been aboard a small sailboat out beyond the Golden Gate on a stormy day—a midweek stormy day?"

"I was out of the country that week, however, I do know that Stan had planned to enter the double-hand Farallons Race this year, like he always does. Perhaps Saul was going to be his crew. Held when it is, the race often involves challenging weather conditions. Perhaps Stan saw the opportunity to practice with his crew under race-typical conditions—and the right conditions just happened to fall on a week day. I don't know. Just a guess."

"Do you know Kalinik to be an active sailor?"

Can't fudge on that one. They know, of course. "No, he wasn't, but I do know that they've sailed together on the bay. Saul and Stan were very close. If Saul were going to crew in the race, it seems logical that he would go along for a race practice. Wouldn't get me out there, though," Malcolm said, not smiling.

"Race practice aside, why do you suppose an experienced sailor like Mr. Bellamy would go out with an apparent novice—with a small craft advisory in effect?"

"Maybe the conditions deteriorated after they went out."

"Don't you own a yacht yourself, Mr. Renslaer?" Special Agent Simmons had now fully reacquired his normally confident (mildly arrogant) demeanor.

"Yes, my family has maintained a cruising vessel since the 1930s. But *Samora* is not a thirty-foot, featherweight racing sloop, Agent Simmons."

"Mr. Bellamy has served as the captain of your yacht, has he not?"

"Yes, on several occasions he has skippered *Samora* in ocean races."

"Then you certainly must consider him to be a very competent sailor to entrust him with such a valuable boat. Isn't that right, sir?"

"Absolutely, Agent Simmons. Stan was a fine sailor."

"Have you given up all hope of their being found? It's only been a few days and they could have made it ashore down the coast. It's happened before."

"Not in a lot of years it hasn't. I don't know how much you know about the area between the Gate and the Farallons. It's not like the Bay out there, and with all the sea lions, elephant seals, and otters that have taken up residence lately, there are a lot of great whites. Yes, I have accepted the fact that they're gone."

"Where is *Samora* now, if I may ask, Mr. Renslaer?"

I don't have to answer that. But if I don't, being a cop, he'll really investigate. "She is in charter in the South Pacific. Actually, at this moment, she is in transit from the Baltic, but I'm afraid I cannot tell you exactly where she is. The delivery skipper has a great deal of latitude in the route he will follow."

"Who is the delivery skipper, Mr. Renslaer?"

"Agent Simmons, can you tell me what all this has to do with Saul and Stan? They were aboard *Penny Pincher* on Monday and *Samora* was several thousand miles away."

"Sir, our job is to investigate everything that might be relevant." Timothy Simmons knew that he had gone far out on a tangent, but he had been taught never to back off a line of questioning. Such a retreat would shift dominance.

"Frankly, I don't know who the delivery skipper is. That would be handled by the brokers who arrange the charter activities for *Samora.* I'm sure you can understand that with all I have to keep track of in my life, I cannot concern myself with these details. I do not function like Jimmy Carter, Agent Simmons."

The special agent and his partner finally broke into smiles at Malcolm's remark. They also knew they'd about run out of gas with this lead. "Thank you, Mr. Renslaer. You may be hearing from us again as the investigation continues."

"Of course, gentlemen. Just arrange a time with Toni Wheeler, my executive assistant. I hope I was of some help."

Malcolm watched through the parlor window while the agents got into their car. *You'll need a battery of people a whole lot smarter than you are to find your way through* Samora*'s pile of paper.*

* * *

Working in the bilges of a boat, even a gracious lady like *Samora*, was an unpleasant job when the work was being done in a humid, semitropical environment. Without the cooling water of the sea to carry away the accumulated heat through the hull, the job was doubly uncomfortable. By the time Stan and Waddy had gotten all the flooring unscrewed from the crossbeams, they'd decided that it was time to take a break and explore the delights of Valletta.

"This is night and morning work," Stan said, now having filled in the blanks in his understanding of the Mediterranean custom of siesta. He also realized that with her new low-latitude assignment, black would not have been a good hull color. Even Waddy had a sheen of perspiration. "Come on. Let's go around to the city and have a look."

Stan organized the rental of a Fiat, followed by a reacquainting with the joys of driving on the wrong side of the road. The trip around the perimeter of Marsamxett Harbor, with its narrow, winding roads and dense traffic, compounded the detail of trying to remember to stay to the left of the approaching traffic. With auto travel now severely limited within the old city, Stan was relieved to park the car and walk through Kingsgate, the peninsular entrance through the high walls, battlements, towers, and ramparts: built to secure the city during its endless wars and sieges.

Waddy felt more culture shock as they walked down Kingsway through the heart of Malta's densely populated capital. Constructed largely of the native limestone, Valletta's texture was quarry-like and remained strangely medieval despite its veneer of modern civilization: a collage of southern Mediterranean, North African, and Middle Eastern cultures with a formality and orderliness which only 160 years of British rule could implant.

Waddy did experience one familiar phenomenon. Stan noticed that more than occasionally he would see a slight smile and the flash of an interested glance directed at his friend. They did not come from Maltese men.

"Stan, as long as we have to be here a couple'a weeks, why don't we move over here to the city? Sure would beat the hell out of that crappy little room we found near the boatyard."

"Okay, but you drive. These people drive worse than Italians, if that's possible."

"No problem," Waddy exclaimed as they turned into one of the stair-stepped side streets, too narrow to admit vehicles even without the stairs. At the top they looked down over the battlements to the moat-like harbor surrounding the old city. The harbor was ringed with forts and ramparts perched on the tips of the several smaller peninsulas jutting out from the mainland toward Valletta. They were like the sheared-off spokes of a giant wheel with the hub of the old city suspended in its center.

Waddy was ecstatic. "Just let me enjoy this for a little while." He watched the young waitress approach with their order of the delicious meat-and-ricotta-filled *pastizzi*. "We'll get out of here on schedule."

There *was* a schedule, and it was tightening, Stan reminded himself. The rendezvous in the Black Sea near Sevastopil was fifteen days away. At least nine, perhaps ten days would be spent refitting and provisioning *Samora*, and Stan was uncertain about the timing in traversing the Turkish-controlled straits between the Aegean and the Black Sea. He and Malcolm had researched the Turkish government's requirements thoroughly; nevertheless, Stan was burdened with his long experience at sea, at the mercy of arbitrary maritime officials. Formal, governmental requirements could be predicted, but the vagaries of the petty bureaucrats could not. If he left too much time to provide a hedge against possible delays in Istanbul, he could wind up having to mill about in the Black Sea. Large Western yachts were still rare in the formerly exclusively-Soviet lake. *Samora* would be conspicuous.

Mr. Blaquiére provided as promised. The next day three Maltese appeared, then in four more days painstakingly accomplished the needed modification of *Samora*'s salon flooring. All Stan and Waddy could do was wait, with excruciating patience, while the methodical craftsmen worked their art. In Holland the same job would have been quietly finished in a day, with no siestas, but when the constantly laughing and joking islanders finally finished their work, Stan was more than pleased. He was convinced that their counterparts in 1930s Newport and Mystic would also have approved

With the joinery completed and the workers departed, Stan and Waddy set to work on the modification of the water tank—then waited two more days for Mr. Blaquiére's workers to deliver the mechanical parts. The water tank would still provide water, albeit reduced by the volume of the canister that would fit into the cradle installed under the new tank cover, but the reduction in sweet water capacity would not be a problem because Malcolm had ordered a new reverse osmosis seawater converter.

Most of the yard workers turned out when *Samora* slid down her slipway into the waters of Valletta's beautiful harbor: to once again enter her proper world. With friendly waves from Mr. Blaquiére's accommodating staff, Stan motored the big yacht around to the Ta Xbiex yacht basin on the adjacent peninsula, where, as in all Mediterranean ports, he was obliged to moor the yacht stern-to: held off the limestone quay by a pair of bow anchors. Anticipating this seemingly easy but actually very tricky maneuver, he had enlisted the hands of knowledgeable locals. A sailboat hull and rudder are designed for forward travel, and single-screw propulsion and tidal currents further complicate the situation. Stan knew full well that if he collided with an adjacent vessel while backing up to the quay, maritime law would demand automatic payment for damage to the other yacht; and *Samora* would be impounded until the damage was repaired to the satisfaction of the other vessel's owner, who could be half a world away. The long-standing law was actually quite reasonable, recognizing as it did the fact that an offending vessel could simply sail out of the jurisdiction and avoid reparation. Stan was very careful.

Two tasks remained. They needed to lay on supplies to carry them for the entire voyage to the Black Sea and then back the length of the Mediterranean and across the North Atlantic to the Gulf of Mexico and Galveston. Stan also had to locate crew to help sail the yacht to the island of Limnos in the northern Aegean. From that point into the Black Sea, Stan and Waddy would be on their own; there could be no extraneous crew to observe what would take place off the Crimean coast. Stan could only hope that between here and Limnos, Waddy would learn enough to be an able hand for the trip into the Black Sea.

Stan carefully studied the faces of the young French couple sitting across from him in *Samora*'s salon. He would not have the luxury of checking their references; he'd have to rely solely on the instinct derived from the many such transactions he'd conducted in the past. As so many like them, these young people were spending their summer bumming around the Mediterranean, helping to crew yachts to wherever the boats were going. When they made port, another ride would be sought, and so on, until they found their way back home at the end of the season. Stan had to be very careful, however. The whole spectrum of humanity could be found milling about the docks of the yacht harbors of the world, and some of the innocent-looking, happy young people were drug couriers. In other, isolated cases, their plan was to make a false claim of assault or rape so that money could be extorted from the owner of the yacht. To avoid seizure of the vessel, the uniform maritime sanction throughout the world, and to further avoid prosecution under laws that presumed guilt until innocence was proven, money was simply paid and the incident forgotten. Stan hated this exposure, but it could not be avoided. He and a complete, withal well-intentioned, novice could not hope to safely control a ninety-foot sailing yacht in the open sea. Malcolm, if not Waddy, had understood the necessary risk in hiring crew.

"What was your last boat?" Stan asked, wanting to talk to their previous skipper. No luck; she had already sailed. "Have you ever been to Limnos?" Their passports said they had not, he saw, when he searched for evidence of regular, repeated passages among the myriad entrance stamps: evidence that they were other than summer holiday adventurers. Now, under the European Economic Community, there were no longer passport requirements among the EC nations. All Stan saw were the old entries. He felt the same helpless, lost feeling that he had when he selected a civil jury panel. With the relatively few questions he was allotted, he had to discover the essence of the persons before him. Skilled psychiatrists spend years on such difficult inquiries.

A quick turn around *Samora*'s decks revealed the couple to be experienced sailors. The least unfamiliarity with what should have been familiar would have exposed them as wannabes, not the seasoned crew he needed.

Stan conducted the next test of his prospective crew. He asked them to deliver funds sufficient to cover their travel back to their original port of embarkation, Marseilles. Under maritime law, well established since the old days of shanghaied sailors, a crewman could demand at any time that he be returned to his original port. The issue was not merely the funds involved; the vessel would also be impounded until everything was arranged, at the convenience of the crewman and the local authorities. Stan was relieved that the young couple were well aware of the requirement and turned over the necessary money without comment—further proof that they were knowledgeable. He was also convinced that they would not object when he searched them and their sea bags as they last stepped aboard to start the journey.

"Okay, we'd like to depart the day after tomorrow. Will that work for you?" Happy nods sealed the contract.

As part of the voyage plan Stan and Malcolm had worked out, Stan reported to the Maltese maritime officials that he and his crew would be taking *Aletheia* on a shakedown cruise to the Greek Islands, returning to Malta before heading out on the delivery of the yacht halfway around the world. Of course, this was reasonable and only displayed good seamanship. Besides, the officials would certainly recognize, the Aegean would be lovely at this time of year: winter was gone, but it was still too early for the hordes of summer tourists. Should not the hardworking minions of a nameless billionaire have a little relaxation before their long voyage? And when *Samora* returned, there should be no formal customs reentry of the yacht. After all, Malta was *almost* a member of the EC and such procedures were now overlooked for travel to a member country like Greece. Malcolm's careful investigation had revealed that, indeed, the comings and goings of the many private yachts from adjacent Mediterranean countries were not subject to the scrutiny accorded commercial airline and ship traffic.

4

Foothills of the Wind River Range
Ten miles northeast of Pinedale, Wyoming, April 18

The Wyoming Game and Fish officer looked around at the scattered, smashed, and ripped remains of what had been a reasonably well-kept collection of trash cans. Lying at his feet was a crumpled piece of hammer-toned galvanized steel that had, until the previous early morning, been the door to a large, outdoor walk-in cooler behind the kitchen of the Mountain High Guest Ranch.

"Sure am glad I wasn't around when that sombitch moseyed in here," the manager of the dude ranch said, shaking his head as he examined the wall of the walk-in where the hinges had been ripped out.

"Yeah, it was old Beethoven, all right," the officer said, struggling to control a smile. He squatted to examine a sixteen-inch-long by nine-inch-wide print in the snow and mud. "Look there. It was him, for sure. See the way his hind right foot toes in?"

"How big *is* that grizzly?" the manager asked.

"In the fall, before hibernation, he'll weigh in at about nine hundred. Probably down to about seven-fifty now. Damned hungry, I'd say."

"What's goin' on? We never get grizzlies down here," the manager whined. "How'm I supposed to get this cooler fixed? We're supposed to be opening in less than two weeks."

"Don't know why he left his den early, but grizzlies don't sleep all that sound anyway. They often wake up in midwinter. But he's up for good now, and he can't get at those glacier lily bulbs the bears gorge on in the spring." The wildlife biology-trained officer kicked his foot at one of the garbage cans, ripped apart like a Styrofoam cup. "You've been dumping grease in here. You're supposed to use that sealed unit over there. That old boar could smell this stuff ten miles away."

"Sir, the unit is full, and it's been frozen. They won't come to dump it until it thaws out. It's this damn winter; just goin' on forever."

"Old Beethoven's usual denning area is way up in the Stone Creek drainage. There's absolutely nothing for him to eat up there; snow must be thirty feet deep near the divide, so he must have had to come clear down this far to find anything at all. We've had a few other calls, but they've all been blackies. Real unusual for grizzlies to have to come down into civilization like this."

"Do you think he's still around? Will he be back?"

"For sure. He got a pretty good meal in that cooler, looks like." The officer glanced at the shredded remains of what had been several cases of smoked sausage and bacon. "I shouldn't have to remind you that grizzlies are protected." The officer wanted to say that the bears were here first and that people who elect to set up business in bear country should be prepared to buy insurance as businesspeople everywhere had to do. He couldn't say anything, of course. In this cattle country it was an undisputed, God-given right to employ any degree of self-help necessary to protect property. Only very reluctantly were the few remaining grizzly bears kept out of the rifle sights of the corporate ranchers who turned their tens of thousands of head of helpless cattle and sheep into the backcountry every year; even so, the officer suspected, more than once the three S's had been employed: shoot, shovel, and shut up.

"Well, what should I do?"

"Clear everything out of the cooler, scrub it down with ammonia, and scatter moth balls all over the area. Haul the refuse to the dump, where it can be dozed under right away."

"What's he gonna eat? I mean, where'll he go?"

"He'll probably go after those elk over in Peterson's pasture. Had'ta been a thousand of them in there when I drove by. Peterson's gonna be hauling in his cattle any day and then he'll be wanting us to clear the elk out. Nowhere for them to go, either. Gonna be calving pretty soon, too."

"Guess that old griz'll have his choice between slow elk and regular ones," the manager smiled.

"That is a common misconception, sir," the wildlife officer snapped. This time he had to speak up. "Even with those tens of thousands of absolutely helpless critters turned loose into his country, the grizzly only *very* rarely takes one. An occasional bear develops a taste for beef, but ninety-nine times out of a hundred it's an already-dead animal he's seen feeding on—usually one that died of some injury, rancher negligence, or natural causes. Big brisket disease kills a lot of calves because of the altitude. Often it's one the wolves got. Grizzlies love carrion. It's their favorite food and they can smell a dead animal from clear across a mountain range. Of course, when a rancher sees a bear feeding on one of his cattle he automatically assumes the bear killed it. They still operate like it was the nineteenth century—they know everything, right?" The game and fish officer was immediately sorry he'd spouted off. He'd probably hear about it at the coffee shop in Pinedale. "I'm sorry I laid into you, sir; it's just that I hate to see the last of these magnificent animals cut down by those slobs who call themselves ranchers. Can't fight money and stupidity."

"Have you seen the weather forecast, officer?" the manager asked, to change the subject. "Supposed to keep on snowin', isn't it?"

"Just saw the stuff on the weather channel last night. Clear across the Gulf of Alaska there were two or three big storm swirls. They're even talkin' about another Alberta Express—this late in the year. All the bears'll be waking up soon, and with all this snow and what's comin', they'll have to come down."

"Guess you fellas'll be pretty busy."

"You could say that."

* * *

Samora glistened with readiness as she lay quietly at her cables, provisioned and cleared for sea. Waddy's all-encompassing delight was replaced in Stan with the more focused anticipation of just how *Samora* would perform. He had to set aside nearly twenty-five years of preconception.

To ensure that a sea breeze had built, Stan waited until midmorning to motor out beneath the towering walls of Valletta. No matter how he tried, he could not get used to seeing the Portuguese ensign streaming two-thirds of the way up the mizzen backstay. Malcolm had seen to the smallest detail, Stan thought, smiling as he looked up at the distinctive red and green flag, nearly eight feet long: exactly the right size for a yacht of *Samora*'s length. *Since 1936 only Old Glory has flown from there. I suppose it's necessary.*

Once out of the lee of the headland, Stan turned the big yacht into the wind and activated, with signal amazement, the new mechanical systems that unfurled *Samora*'s also-new suit of sails. While the huge Ratsey and Lapthorne dacron sails rolled smoothly out, their sheets trimmed through the three-speed stainless steel winches handled by Jacques and Chántal, Stan allowed the yacht to fall off before the north-northeasterly twenty-five-knot breeze. The phalanx of waves marching down from the north were blue-green, breaking whitely in the brilliant sunshine. A powerful close reach awaited *Samora* on her due-easterly course to the Stenon Andikithiron, the strait between Crete and the last small island in the chain stretching south from the Greek mainland. The famous passage had been used by mariners for thousands of years—for exploration, commerce, and war.

Stan set Samora on her course. He watched with approval while his young French sailors trimmed the sails, with no instruction necessary, to draw the wind perfectly for her point of sail; then, with her booms extending out to starboard and vanged down hard, the big yacht leaped into the building seas. From his perch on the bow beneath the giant Genoa headsail, Waddy watched in amazement as *Samora* slowly leaned over and came to life.

With the apparent wind on her port bow, *Samora* heeled less than ten degrees, with only an occasional splash of green water from a wave peak breaking over her windward topside as she accelerated to a smooth twelve knots. The engine was silenced; the only sounds were from the bow wave, some vibration in the tapered-rod standing rigging, and a slight flutter in the trailing edges of the sails: nothing was loose, slapping, or adrift. Jacques competently eased the main sheet until the mainsail back-curved slightly just aft of the mast, while Chántal cinched the boom vang winches tighter and cranked the Genoa sheet lead forward. Soon all leech flutter was gone, and some turbulent flow behind the sails was replaced by the more aerodynamically efficient laminar flow. The digital knotmeter showed an increase of over a knot, and the only remaining sounds were those of the sea and the bass-tone hum of the rod rigging. Standing at *Samora*'s helm on the gently sloping deck, Stan smiled as he watched Waddy. The subtle sail changes were lost on him, but he would learn quickly. He was already questioning Jacques closely about the adjustments that had just been made.

Stan set the autopilot on 87° true, releasing the wheel when he felt the computer-controlled steering take over. He recalled the several occasions when *Samora*'s old simple-but-durable autopilot, affectionately named "Fred," had carried the burden of steering the yacht across the Pacific. *We'll name this new one Fred as well,* he decided as he settled into the helmsman's chair behind the wheel. The new autopilot computer automatically cranked in local magnetic variation, compass deviation, and the leeway the yacht was making. *Super. This may be easier than I thought.* He watched the big spoked wheel turn slightly in response to the demands of the electronic gyrocompass and its computer. With the autopilot steadily correcting *Samora*'s rudder, nothing would have to be done to sail her unless the wind direction shifted. The weatherfax printout below in the navigation station said that it would not.

Stan looked aloft up the triple-spreader mast, 115 feet to the cluster of lights and antennas and the anemometer spinning at the masthead. Fleecy clumps of cumulus clouds moved slowly back and forth in a dome of azure above the apparently-fixed masthead. He was back. Back riding a close reach through building seas on *Samora*. He reached down and selected a cold bottle of Heineken from the cockpit cooler. Once again, after so many years, Stan began to feel the great security of the sea: the sense of removal from the unrest of landbound concerns. For the briefest of moments he forgot why he was back at sea aboard *Samora*, his mind focused only on the fact that he was there once again on a glorious, windy spring day, and that life was very good.

With the speed he anticipated, Stan calculated that they would reach the strait the next day near evening. That was another reason he'd delayed their departure from Malta. He didn't want to traverse the channel, with all of its fishing boats, in the dark; and he also wanted to go through when there would be the least amount of traffic. Fishermen would be asleep by early evening, their days beginning in the very early morning hours, and all of the major ship traffic would be in the next strait to the north, the shortest route between Gibraltar and the entrance to the Black Sea. Even with the concentration of commercial shipping, it would be safer in the northern passage without the small, barely lit, often negligent, cross-trafficking fishing boats that might still be in the Stenon Andikithiron; nevertheless, he wanted to avoid commercial shipping and naval vessels as much as possible. The less he was seen by conscientious, log-keeping watch officers, the better. Neither would a paper trail shadow *Samora*, excepting that derived from the single unavoidable stop she would make. Unlike an aircraft, a noncommercial vessel at sea was not required to file a sailing plan; accordingly, Stan would not be following the shortest distance from point A to point B, but rather the least conspicuous route, as much as possible out of the shipping lanes. He could do nothing about his vessel's more than conspicuous size, however. Somehow he had to juggle safety of the yacht and crew, offbeat routes, crew limitations, and the time restrictions.

Predictably, Waddy bent to his learning in earnest. Stan had rented a sailing dinghy back at Malta and given him lessons tacking and gybing around in the harbor. The theory behind sailing a dinghy was the same for a big yacht, Stan had told him. "You just have to plan ahead more, move more slowly, and rely on mechanical assistance with a large boat." The desert-raised Hopi Indian had learned quickly, almost instinctively. Like professional athletes who always seem to be able to play most sports well, Waddy the river rat and all-around backcountry athlete took easily to sailing.

Once past Crete, the trip would slow as they wound their way up through the Greek islands, having to tack before the anticipated winds. The plan was to arrive at Limnos in the middle of the night, discreetly anchor out in the ample harbor, and behave like an ordinary yacht delivery crew. Stan and Waddy would firmly plant with Jacques and Chántal their intention of waiting around for the owner of *Aletheia* to show up. Big yachts like *Aletheia* commonly spent the summers in the Aegean and then went to the West Indies for the winter season; lots of people like Stan had full-time employment making sure the boats were in the right place at the right time, with the right crew and the right provisions. Stan hoped that Waddy's obvious novice status would not raise conversation in the relatively small world of yacht delivery sailors. It could be an intensely gossipy and nosey world.

Samora plunged effortlessly through the bright water. Stan was amazed at her performance: she sailed like a modern yacht except for her slow tacking caused by the drag of her long, old-fashioned keel. On the other hand, the wine glass-sectioned hull and keel gave *Samora* the tracking ability of a heavy railroad car. She was not the nimble but squirrelly, over sized dinghy like so many of the big new yachts.

The voyage up through the Cyclades Archipelago, extending out from the Athenian Peninsula, had been as lovely as the most glowing travel agent descriptions promised: Milos, Sifnos, Siros, Tinos, Andros—all had drifted past, with the latter three, fortunately, in full daylight. Stan had often heard that the blue of the Aegean Sea was unique. It was not the powdery aqua blue of the South Pacific islands, the blue-green of the Caribbean, the bright blue of the Gulf Stream, or the deep, inky blue of the vast ocean seas. *This is incredible,* Stan thought as he gazed into the dazzling, cobalt-like depths.

To stay out of the shipping lanes, their route took them close by the island of Lesbos, immortalized since antiquity by Ovid's satirical allusions to the poetess Sappho and her companions, not drawn to the company of men. It was just before dawn the following morning when *Samora* quietly slipped her anchor onto the rocky bottom of the harbor just off the village of Moúdhros on Limnos Island. They were fifty-five statute miles from ancient Troy on the Turkish coast and the entrance to the Dardanelles.

Later that morning, when the somnolent Greek paradise began to show signs of awakening, Stan took Jacques and Chántal ashore in the dinghy to report to the Greek customs and immigration office. Another big yacht was of no particular concern to the official when Stan presented the passports and ship's papers; then with proof to the satisfaction of the officer that his departing crew had funds for passage off the island, Jacques and Chántal were released from Stan's responsibility. They left happily, to continue their summer adventure. Stan and Waddy now had to continue alone on the next step in theirs.

By previous arrangement between Kateryna and Saul, the rendezvous place and hour off the Crimean peninsula was set. Stan had no idea how Kateryna would meet them at a point some sixteen miles out into the Black Sea from the southwest tip of Crimea; the details of her arrangements remained an intriguing mystery. All he had to do was get *Samora* to the prescribed point in the sea at the prescribed time: latitude–44 degrees, 28.9 minutes north; longitude–33 degrees, 02.2 minutes east; time–4:00 A.M. This morning he was to receive the date, which was to be as consistent as possible with the work at Malta and the transit to the Black Sea.

"Hello, this is Malcolm Renslaer. I'm sorry I missed your call. I expect to return on April 23. If you leave your number, I'll call you back. I promise. Thanks for calling."

Right on schedule. Stan hung up the receiver and walked slowly back to the dock where he'd left the dinghy. *That's 4:00 A.M. this coming Saturday. This is Wednesday. Perfect. Well, I'll have to drag my feet a little bit. But it does leave me some time if there's a problem. Looks like she timed it to leave Sevastopil late Friday night. Maybe that's party night in Ukraine. People do that on Friday night. Probably even in Ukraine. Probably especially in Ukraine. Maybe she won't be missed until Monday. Smart lady.*

Waddy started to help Stan hoist their little lapstrake dinghy back aboard. "Stan, I've been thinking. What say I just row on in there to that nice big beach and find myself one last little bit of companionship, huh?"

"No way. You took off with that hotel concierge back in Valletta. God, but you are a horny bastard. No, no, it's too risky."

"Stan, I can't help it. I'm not like you and Saul. I'm not a monk."

"Sorry, Waddy, no time. And besides, this is Greece. In a month of Sundays you couldn't score with one of those proper, island Greek girls. You'd get thrown into jail."

Waddy absorbed the achingly beautiful scene. "*Look* at this place," he sighed.

"We have to get moving right away because things are going to slow down. With just the two of us, we're going to have to motor, and there'll be a lot of traffic in the Dardanelles. We can't risk the two of us trying to sail this big yacht in confined waters."

Navigation to the rendezvous point would be easy since Malcolm had equipped *Samora* with the latest global-positioning-satellite navigation system, the civilian version of the location equipment used by the soldiers in Desert Storm. While the civilian version was not permitted the pinpoint accuracy of the military devices, because both systems used the same satellites the reliability was the same. Kateryna, so far as Stan knew, would not have the benefit of the new high-tech navigation tool.

Stan sat down at the chart table in the nav station. He stared at the chart of the southwestern coast of the Crimean peninsula which jutted south into the Black Sea. He hadn't plotted the rendezvous point in the event *Samora* was boarded by inquiring officials, but after examining the chart for a while, he realized that the point had not been arbitrarily selected. A smile slowly crept across his face as he took in the cryptic maritime notations scattered across the British Admiralty chart: a convenient aid to navigation, a lighthouse, was located on the westernmost point of land where the Sevastopil'skaya Bukhta, the fjord-like channel that led into Sevastopil, commenced; and a pair of range lights were also located on the headland. When lined up, one above the other, the range would point on a bearing of 47° true, as seen from ships approaching from seaward. So long as arriving ships kept the lights aligned, they would approach the entrance to the channel exactly, lined up like ducks, until they could pick up the lighted channel buoys. The rendezvous point was fifteen miles out along the reciprocal of the range light bearing—227° true—and then five miles on a right-angle turn to the northwest on a bearing of 317°. Stan checked the location of the point and then noticed another fact that increased the smile on his face.

The charted characteristics of the light on the tip of Mys Khersones said that it just became visible over the curvature of the earth at a range of sixteen miles. The rendezvous point was exactly sixteen miles out to sea along the hypotenuse of the right-triangle legs Kateryna would follow to reach the rendezvous. At that point, the light would just be visible at a bearing of 68°, changing from an over-the-horizon loom to a distinct flash—providing verification that the rendezvous had been reached. Stan saw that the point would also be out of the shipping lanes around the southern end of the Crimean peninsula.

His research had revealed that in late April in the northern Black Sea fog was unheard of and the weather was generally mild. Nevertheless, if the range lights were obscured by weather it would be necessary for Kateryna to dead reckon the sixteen miles directly to the rendezvous point. But even in the worst weather, the flash of the headland light would almost certainly be visible. *Not as accurate, but it should still work. All you have to do is watch the commercial ships. They'll be lined up precisely on course with their radars and GPS equipment.* Stan noticed that the rendezvous point was near an area where the bottom shelved off to 1,500 meters. *I don't know how you figured all this out, Kateryna. I know you aren't a sailor. Standard KGB training?*

Stan shook his head as he got up to go back on deck. His anticipation of once again seeing her had been building steadily since that day at the Napa airport. Throughout the interminable wait he had carried with him the image of the delightful Kateryna, and the promise of seeing her again had accelerated when he and Waddy had boarded the flight to London. The happy anxiety filled every part of him that was not occupied by his task of delivering the big yacht into a strange, unknown sea.

"Stan, tell me about this place Malcolm picked out to move to," Waddy asked while they got *Samora* under way again.

"I've never been to the Seychelles Islands. It's a widely scattered archipelago just a bit south of the equator in the Indian Ocean, centered about 900 miles southeast of Mogadishu, Somalia—due east of Kenya and Tanzania. All I've ever read or heard about, and that's not been much, is that it's a virtually unknown paradise way off any beaten track of the tourist industry. Because it was formerly a British colony, it is very well organized and civilized. Britain left it in very good shape to carry on independently."

"How can he run his whole empire from an isolated place like that?"

"I have no idea how he has everything set up. But in this computerized and electronically networked world we now live in, it doesn't really matter where a business headquarters is."

"Yeah, that's one of the problems with the *pahana* world. Just press a button and fuck up something thousands of miles away. Absolutely no sense of place with your people anymore."

"Are you saying that you *are* going to stick around or you're not going to stick around in the canyon country afterwards?

Waddy hesitated before answering. "I don't know. I'll probably go with the rest of you for a while, but you know I won't be able to stay away from my country." He stared out at the brilliant blue water on *Samora*'s heading, east toward the narrow gap in the Turkish coastline that lead to the Black Sea.

"Other than its isolated setting, is there any other reason Malcolm picked that place out of the whole rest of the world he had to choose from?"

Stan smiled, his thoughts racing back over the decades he had known his friend. "Malcolm loves Africa. He settled for being off the coast because the weight of his money will give him a lot more control in that little island republic. I just can't tell you how much Malcolm loves Africa. His wife was Ethiopian."

"Malcolm was married to an *African*?" Waddy's previous assessment of the overbearing but pleasant man changed in an instant. "But . . . but how, I mean, why . . . I mean . . ."

"Oh, God, Waddy, you should have seen her. She was probably the most beautiful, most charming woman I have ever met." Stan hesitated, thinking of Kateryna. "Malcolm didn't have a chance; he was captured from the moment he met her."

"But Malcolm was married a lot of years ago. I mean, today, no big deal; but shit, back then . . ."

"That's right, it was really a flap. In the late '60s when he got married, a young man in his situation did not just pick a wife at random. Things were arranged—set up from the time he first showed some interest in one of the proper, thoroughly vetted young ladies who ran in the same circle. They weren't marriages, they were mergers. That's how big fortunes stay big fortunes—and get bigger. And, more than money, it's a matter of breeding. People in that stratum are only comfortable—expected to be only comfortable, at least—with others of their own caste. It's just a more subtle, refined form of ethnic isolation, leading to unhealthy inbreeding."

"Yeah, I've seen the result; when I was workin' in New York. You know, those watery-blue-eyed, Marfans-tall people with lank blond hair and oversized teeth. Generally not real bright, either. Good thing they have money."

"That's right," Stan said, once again marveling at Waddy's depth of perception about matters far removed from his desert southwest homeland.

"How did it happen?" Waddy was at a total loss, but very interested.

"When Malcolm was twenty-five, he was posted to Nairobi to oversee the African operation. At the time, he was engaged to a young lady from San Francisco, a member of the Mayacamas Hunt who he had known since he was ten years old. From the time he was eighteen or so, it was just expected that he would marry Binky. Well, only a few months after he was sent to Kenya he met Almaze. Like I said, Malcolm didn't have a chance. I can't explain, Waddy, you'd have to have met her. She was taller than Kateryna—about six feet, I'd guess—and she was the very definition of statuesque. The most dignified, beautiful, charming woman I had ever seen. But more than her physical beauty, Almaze was, well . . . I don't know what to say. She just captivated everyone around her."

"Did she captivate Malcolm's family?"

"Oh, hell, I was there the day Malcolm brought her home. I thought his mother was going to go into apoplectic arrest. Almaze was *very* dark. Fortunately, his father thought it was 'bully,' as he said at the time. Nevertheless, as liberated as San Francisco may be now, among the elite in those days it might as well have been London in the 1890s. And it wasn't just Malcolm's family. I understand her father was even more upset than Malcolm's mother. Almaze's family, from Addis Ababa, was sort of the social and economic equivalent of the Renslaer family in San Francisco. They certainly had other plans for their daughter."

"When did she die?"

"It's been about ten years now. Malcolm's never even looked at another woman since the plane crash. I guess it's just been his business that's kept him going—that and his environmental campaigns."

"Maybe I should take a run over to Ethiopia when we move to Malcolm's place," Waddy said with his impish grin. "What's the country like?"

"Much of it is very mountainous. It's the headwaters of the Blue Nile."

"Lot of pretty women? I mean, was Malcolm's wife unusual?"

"No, Ethiopia is famous for its beautiful people, men as well as women. But they're very tall."

"No shorter ones?"

"I'm confident you'll manage to find them, Waddy."

According to plan, it was past sunset when they could first pick up the light, flashing white every five seconds in the darkening east over *Samora*'s bows. The light marked the north headland of the entrance to the Dardanelles. A little over an hour later the flashes on Ilyasbaba Burnu changed from white to red, indicating they were entering the strait itself. Stan planned to motor up the channel in the darkness and then into the mini-sea, the Marmara Denizi, that lay between the Aegean and the Black Sea. They would find a rest stop at one of the obscure islands.

Being a major shipping lane through a narrow choke point, the strait was well lit with navigation aids. A great deal of complementary and opposing traffic occupied the channel, and *Samora* was regularly passed by large ships, even a Russian naval vessel of the Black Sea Fleet. Stan knew that an alert and careful watch officer will usually shine a powerful search lamp on a small vessel that the ship is passing, particularly in close quarters. He was relieved that the passing ships were operated by persons who were either negligent or who didn't care. *Probably just using their radars.* Samora*'s size will give them a pretty good blip, even without the radar reflector I took off. And* *without a light they can't see her name on the transom.*

"Okay, Pal, here's your first little lesson in coastal piloting," Stan announced as another ship overtook *Samora*, passing closely on her porthand side. "Through the Dardanelles, until we get to the Marmara Sea, the red lights will mark the left side of the channel and the green lights the right. So long as you leave the green ones to starboard and the red ones to port, you'll have a clear channel, even though we can't see the shoreline. The trouble is, these big ships not only have the legal right of way in this waterway where they're constrained by their draught, they follow the more fundamental human nature demand that *biggest* has right of way.

"As a ship comes up from behind, just ease over to the right. But watch the depth sounder. *Samora* draws eleven feet, and it shoals up fast, quite a ways out from the shoreline. Since we can't see the shore, all we have is the depth sounder. The radar's not accurate enough when we're so close in. Just as the ship passes, cross sharply over the bow wave and then slip in right behind." Stan demonstrated, turning *Samora* across the wave veeing out from the passing freighter's hull. "We don't want to get shoved any farther over and she won't roll as badly. Just up ahead is an area called the 'Narrows'; don't have to tell you what that means. We'll wait to go through with no traffic around."

"I'll let you have the wheel goin' through there," Waddy said, taking *Samora*'s helm.

"Well, if you like, but there's nothing to it. The weather's good, so there'll be no problem finding the marks. Every navigation light has a unique characteristic in flashing manner and frequency so that it cannot be confused with nearby lights. Look here." Stan pointed to a small-scale chart of the Dardanelles. It was attached to a chart board illuminated only by a soft red light to protect their night vision in the solid blackness of the sea channel. "The next one coming up is supposed to be green—that means it's on the right side—and it'll flash singly every three seconds. Count 'one-thousand-one, one-thousand-two, one-thousand-three' to verify the frequency."

"This sucks, not bein' able to see where we're goin'."

"Now you know what I meant when I told you about feeling safer when we're well out to sea. *Samora* can handle the ocean seas. It's rocks and big masses of steel that can sink her."

"Yeah, this is crazy havin' to drive through this invisible channel in the dark with big ships blowin' right by us."

"As bad as driving a raft through Hance Rapid?"

"Worse, ol' buddy." Waddy kept his eyes fixed on the darkness ahead. "At least there I can see what's tryin' to kill me—and it's just me versus the river."

"I've plotted the magnetic compass course between each light on the chart. This is just a backup. Glance down at the compass once in a while; it adds a little confidence that the course to the next light is correct. Also, it'll give you something to use if the light gets obscured by fog or a rain squall, or if a ship's in the way or whatever." Stan chose not to tell his novice that in many parts of the world outside of U.S.- or British-controlled waters, aids to navigation were often missing, set in the wrong place, or carrying the wrong light signal. It didn't take much sailing about the world to come to greatly appreciate the U.S. Coast Guard and its counterpart in service to Her Majesty.

"Stan, I can't find the light ahead."

"We're coming up on the Narrows, plus there's a town on the shore: the light is lost in the background city-light clutter. Just concentrate on the general area where you expect it to be and watch your compass course."

Waddy picked out the navigation light before Stan found it. "I got it. Boy, with all those shore lights on both sides, you can't see at all where the channel is. Here, you take her."

Stan took the wheel and throttled down the six-cylinder General Motors diesel. No ships were coming up the channel behind them, and none appeared in the narrow waterway barely evident among the shore lights and their reflections on the water. "Okay, let's run it." Stan cranked down on the throttle; *Samora*'s thirty-six-inch bronze propeller soon had the yacht moving at hull speed into the thin part of the strait.

By daylight they were well out of the passage from the Dardanelles, into the open water of the Marmara Sea. The sun was high when *Samora* settled into the lagoon on the east side of Imrali Adasi, a small, sparsely populated island in the eastern end of the sea.

"Let's grab some sleep, Waddy. I'm definitely not going past Istanbul in the daylight. This, and the trip back, will be the only times when we'll have to pass closely by a big city. *Samora* will stand out like a mosque minaret in downtown Des Moines."

* * *

Once again motoring along in the dark, they approached the entrance to the second, and narrower, of the narrow channels leading to the Black Sea. The old city of Istanbul—Constantinople of antiquity—occupied the western side of the entrance to the Bosporus Strait. In modern times, the city had expanded across the sea lane, spreading over the opposing point of land, and the unfamiliar confusion of lights surrounding the channel entrance, like the Narrows in the Dardanelles, made it appear that they were going to sail right into the city itself. In the early evening a lot of traffic was heading in both directions in the strait and darting back and forth between the shores.

While they passed close by the waterfront, Stan could see the outlines of the slender, pointed minarets rising above their mosques. Many years had gone by since he'd heard the cry of the muezzin calling the faithful to worship. To Stan, the five-times-daily summons was the most foreign sound he had ever experienced: the entrancing, hornlike voice cast across, echoed, and repeated to the limits of the city and beyond, rising and falling with breath-stopping pauses between phrases.

Stan had no obligation to report to the Turkish authorities because they would not be making any port in Turkey. Nevertheless, he anxiously watched for the black and white speedboats used by their maritime police. Even at night, with all the light from the city *Samora* had to be conspicuous. They were also moving slowly against a six-knot current running from the Black Sea. The only way to have avoided the flow would have been to wait for slack tide, but then it would be almost daylight. Stan wanted to be well into the open water of the Black Sea before the sun came up.

"Sonofabitch, Stan, that guy's comin' right at us!" Vessels traveling in the opposite direction were often just drifting in the current to conserve fuel, and one was headed right toward *Samora*. Unless a boat is moving with respect to the water, it has no steerageway. Waddy instinctively jumped to the port side as though he planned to fend off the huge trawler. Stan swung the wheel to head toward the eastern bank of the channel; he watched the depth gauge LCD dropping quickly. The drifting boat went past and Stan again spun the wheel, turning *Samora* back into the channel—with the gauge reading five meters.

"That was close," he breathed. "This old gal doesn't exactly handle like a dinghy." He moved around a fishing boat, redlining the big diesel to gain speed against the current and to fall in behind a small freighter heading up the channel. He squinted to read the Hong Kong vessel's name, barely visible through the rust streaks on the ship's transom. "We'll just let *Gargoyle* here run interference for us."

"New rules now," Stan announced when they began to clear the city. "From here until we reach the Black Sea, the red lights will be on the right."

"What the hell? How're you s'posed to keep track? Get mixed up and you'll drive right into the shore."

"Actually, it's consistent. The Turks put their red marks to starboard for seaward-bound traffic. They have two seas, the Aegean and the Black Sea, so the marks have to be reversed."

"I'd hate to have to reason through that in the middle of a storm."

"I agree completely." Stan thought for a few moments, trying to decide whether to add more confusing information for his novice. "The Turks and a few other countries follow the British rule. Everywhere else in the world, the rule is red marks to port for vessels bound to sea. The Brits are just different, sort of like how they drive on the left side of the road."

Waddy shook his head.

"They think they're perfectly correct. It's the whole rest of the world that's wrong. They're just British, Waddy."

"No wonder your ancestors revolted against them."

5

Upper Colorado Region Headquarters, April 22

Doug Foreman perused the reservoir status printout. He focused on the large ones, the ones he would have to rely on to hold the runoff: Flaming Gorge on the Green River–96 percent; Blue Mesa on the Gunnison River–95 percent; Navajo on the San Juan River–96 percent; Powell on the Colorado River–97 percent. The Upper Colorado Region Director glanced across his desk at the little hydrologist, nervously twirling the hair at the back of his head with his fingers. The Director looked back to the papers spread in front of him, this time concentrating on the summaries from the U.S. Soil Conservation Service. The summaries spelled out the calculated snow load in the Upper Basin.

"Ortwin, I'm not all that convinced this SCS stuff is correct. It's well beyond what our guys predicted last month, and we've had trouble with their SNOTEL data before." The Region Director's attitude, accurately reflecting the attitude of bureau officialdom in general, was that *his* bureau did not make mistakes. Errors were always in another agency, therefore any evidence that might suggest a mistake by his bureau must be faulty. Since its birth in 1902 (when it started out as a mere *service* and not a bureau), the Bureau had made no significant mistakes—known to the public—in either the designs of its dams or the operation of the vast network of impoundments and plumbing it managed, notably excepting the very close call with Glen Canyon Dam in 1983 and the collapse of Teton Dam when it first filled in 1976.

"Sir, we've spot-checked, and we believe it is accurate."

"How many spot checks?"

"We just don't have the resources to do a thorough job. You know, with all the cutbacks it's hard to justify a duplication of what the SCS snow survey teams are doing."

"How *many*, Ortwin?"

"Um, eight, sir: one in each major watershed; and we've asked SCS to send out their own teams again. They say their stuff is accurate, and so far they've refused to cooperate." The United States Soil Conservation Service also had a high regard for its own abilities.

"Arrogant bastards. All they have to worry about is measuring. I have to *deal* with that friggin' snow when it decides to become water." The Director held up the snow load projection he'd received from the SCS telemetry office in Ogden. "Your guys really think this stuff is right? Not just another of their computer glitches?"

"We think so, sir." The veteran hydrologist also wanted to say "I told you so last February," but, naturally, he controlled himself.

"Damn." Doug Foreman glanced back at the reservoir status report. "Where's Mead?"

"A little problem there. The Lower Basin has held back releases because it's been so wet downriver, and there was a pretty big runoff a couple of weeks ago from the Virgin River. Mead's only got 3.6 million acre feet of flood reserve."

"Damnit, they're supposed to hold a full five million. What's the Lower Basin call projection?"

"Not much help there, sir. It's been wet as a spring duck everywhere. The Imperial Irrigation District doesn't want any, Granite Reef Aqueduct is about shut down—we're even getting reduced calls for the California Aqueduct."

"Those assholes out in southern California don't even want any? Greedy fuckers normally suck everything they can get out of Lake Havasu."

Ortwin swallowed hard. He now had to say something he knew the Director did not want to hear. "I guess we'll have to recommend a spill to the Gulf, sir."

The old Bureau man stared at his lead hydrologist. What he was suggesting was anathema to anyone in the Bureau who truly believed in what they did. More fundamentally, engineers hate to throw anything away. "No. No way. Even those nitwits over at NCAR aren't all that sure this weather is going to hold. Haven't you noticed, Ortwin? Their barrage of paper has started to slacken off; haven't heard from that Heartwood jerk in several days now. Besides, the Mexicans still have a mess at Morelos Dam. They'd go apeshit if we released while they're trying to fix their fucked-up dam. What a piece of crap that thing is. They *still* haven't fixed their gates since the flood down the Gila last year. Besides, that's the Lower Basin's problem and so is all the politics with that friggin' treaty." After nearly forty years with the Bureau, and with less than ten months to retirement, the Region Director was comfortable with passing on problems to another link in the bureaucracy.

"Give me the punch line, Ortwin."

"Sir, it's inevitable that Powell will spill. Not too much, we think, what with the remaining capacities in the Upper Basin. At least we'll have a good test of the spillway repairs." The hydrologist's hopeful grin immediately collapsed before the cold stare from across the desk. "And the Powell releases can probably be held in Mead. With the likely return to normal late spring conditions, there shouldn't be a problem."

* * *

A dull gray was forming in the east—a smudgy line beginning to isolate sea from sky when they exited the Bosporus Strait.

The Black Sea.

Throughout Stan's cognizant life, this place in the maritime world had been totally off limits, unknown and unknowable: the Soviet Union's private lake, with the Turkish occupation of its southern shore but grudgingly tolerated. Seven hundred miles east to west, an average of 250 miles north to south, Stan clicked off in his mind the string of wholly foreign, formerly East Bloc countries that ringed the shores: past Turkey to the west was dark, repressive Bulgaria; then came Romania, land of the Transylvanian Alps, followed by the great breadbasket of Ukraine, long suffering under Russia's heavy thumb. A small piece of Russia followed to the east, then Stalin's Georgia, now aflame in civil war, and back to Turkey at the east end of the sea. Stan suddenly felt very alone. World traveler that he was, he might now just as well be on the back side of the moon.

The sea was dead calm. Hugely flat. Her oily ambit of stillness reaching to infinity. Stan had been to Istanbul once, so Turkey was a knowable place; but he felt a complete intruder as *Samora* motored along on the viscous mirror, leaving a wake stretching in a perfect vee to the horizon. He glanced at his watch. Five o'clock: twenty-three hours and 210 nautical miles to where he must be; an average of just over nine knots. He eased the throttle forward until *Samora* was gliding over the surface at ten knots.

Nineteen hundred rpm. She'll guzzle fuel. Stan glanced at the diesel gauges and then, by habit, at the liquid crystal screen of the satellite navigation computer. He felt an instant, cold knot in the pit of his stomach as his eyes found the string of blinking *eights* on the display.

"Feels like a pretty good breeze, Stan. Want to put up the sails?"

"There's no wind. Just the apparent wind from the speed of the boat."

Waddy looked out at the sheet of glass and quickly realized the common error of a new sailor.

"I've got to go below for a minute. Let me know if you see a ship." Fred would keep *Samora* on a precise course of 049° true.

Stan sat down in the comfortable seat at the navigation station and got out the book on the new GPS navigation system. He read the trouble-shooting checklist and then punched in what the book instructed him to. The message on the screen told him there was an "intersect error." The microchip brain in the little box behind the console was confused with the signals it was receiving from several of the twenty-four Navstar satellites that were currently at least 5° above the horizon. Stan read what the book had to say about intersect errors and punched in the next group of letters and numbers, again according to instruction. After a short pause the screen flashed a collection of programming data and then told him to contact a factory-authorized service representative. *Goddamn black boxes. They either work or they don't work. Nothing in between to salvage. Impossible to fix. Why can't the people who build these things understand that when you really need to have them work there will not be an "authorized service representative" anywhere within five thousand miles?* Stan had no backup GPS unit. The civilian version of the military navigation system was still new, and hand-held instruments being available to the public remained a dream.

He glanced around at the array of electronic equipment staring at him from their perfectly-fitted recesses in the mahogany paneling above the chart table. The weatherfax could give him a printout of an isobaric chart to help predict the weather for 500 miles around him. It could not tell him where he was. The radio rack contained an eighty-five-channel VHF unit for short-distance communication and the powerful shortwave radio telephone that could receive from, or call to, anywhere in the world. *I could always ring up Malcolm and ask for help.* Next was the radar screen. *That will give me a rough position—too rough to find a small, probably unlighted vessel in the dark, sixteen miles off shore, unless I'm right on top of it. Can't be running up to every boat out there to ask if they have a bomb aboard.* The LORAN navigation unit would be no help because the LORAN nets, with their land-mounted antenna arrays, had only been established on the shores of friendly areas heavily frequented by U.S. naval vessels, submarines in particular. Naturally, the Black Sea had not been included. Next, the familiar Brookes and Gatehouse radio direction finder, complete with headset and remote compass. *No good. Not until I get close. There's a Racon on Mys Khersones that'll give me a line of position, but not a fix. And I'll be too far offshore to use the RDF beacons along the Romanian and Ukrainian coasts to get an intersect.* Stan skipped over the IBM PC screen built into the console and the collection of wind direction, wind speed, and boat speed gauges. He stopped at the depth sounder. *I can plot soundings and compare it to the charted depths.* He examined the chart. *No good. The bottom's about as uniform as the Colorado River canyon country.* He looked further, taking in the precision chronometer, accurate to within a tenth of a second per month as it ticked out Greenwich Mean Time. His eyes stopped on the log. The mechanical counter clicked off the nautical miles passing under *Samora*, converting the impulses sent from a little paddle wheel and magnet device set into the yacht's hull.

"That's it, then," he said out loud. He got up, walked across the salon, and withdrew a polished rosewood box from the locker above the portside settee. Opening the old brassbound wood box, Stan looked down at the odd-looking instrument which, to the uninitiated, would probably resemble a piece of turn-of-the-century dental equipment. It was Stan's beloved thirty-five-year-old Plath sextant. He glanced back at the gorgeously assembled collection of $150,000 worth of the sailing world's latest and finest electronic equipment. *Completely worthless right now, except for the log and the clock.*

As he climbed the stairs up the companionway, Stan reflected on the fact that the piece of heavy lacquered brass in his hand was not seriously unlike what Cristóbal Colón had used on his journey across the Atlantic 500 years before.

"What in hell is that thing?" Waddy demanded with a quizzical grin.

"A sextant." Stan sat down with his back to the main mast. "The GPS is dead. We're back to stone age navigation."

To get out of the shipping lane, Stan had diverted slightly to the west from the direct course to Sevastopil from the Bosporus. No ships were in sight despite the flat sea. Once they were out of the direct line between the two shipping destinations, he corrected *Samora*'s course to put her on the estimated bearing to the rendezvous point. In the pond-like conditions, he felt that his calculated position was accurate. Nevertheless, the caution derived from thirty-five years of experience at sea, and the tendency toward anal retention after a career in the law, demanded verification of their position.

With his left hand Stan slowly rocked the sextant held to his eye while turning the micrometer wheel with his right hand. Through the lens of the little four-power telescope he saw the reflected image of the sun, dimmed by a dark filter and superimposed on the view of the horizon. He had some trouble with the eye/two-hand coordination necessary to perform accurately the very unnatural combination of activities. Continuous practice was the only means available to master the delicate skill, and it had been years since he had handled the instrument on the moving deck of a sailing vessel. He was thankful that *Samora* was only slightly rolling from side to side and that he didn't have to further coordinate his sight with the lifting of the yacht to the top of a wave crest. *The sea is forever looking for a way to catch you. Fancy black boxes. Let you down when you need them most.*

At the exact instant that he brought the image of the sun's disc just into tangency with the horizon, he counted off two seconds while releasing the micrometer wheel and clicking the stopwatch hanging around his neck. He mentally subtracted the two seconds from the reading on the watch and went below. Stan had started the stopwatch at an exact minute, as shown on the chronometer, and by adding the modified stopwatch time to the chronometer time he had the precise time, within less than one second, of the instant when he had taken his reading of the sun's angular distance above the horizon. He punched the angle and time information into the little navigation computer which immediately spit out the information needed to plot a line of position on the chart. Later in the morning, again at noon, and every two hours throughout the afternoon, he would take additional sights and then project the lines of position back to a common point at noon. If all the readings were accurate, the LOPs would intersect at a common point: *Samora*'s position at noon, Local Mean Time.

Just after four o'clock Stan completed the last of the LOPs, with the five lines nearly intersecting at a common point. He read off the bearing from the plotted position to the rendezvous point and then adjusted Fred to correct *Samora*'s course, taking into account the slightly deviant route they'd been following. He was confident of his position, within a mile; at evening twilight he would get a round of stars to give him a new verified position. From that point, they would have to travel by dead reckoning, relying on the log and compass to reach the rendezvous, assisted by what the large-scale radar screen would tell him. He would also have an added LOP from the radio beacon signal he should be able to pick up from the Crimean headland. He went back on deck and looked out at the still-somnolent sea, appearing as a slightly undulating mirror stretching to infinity. But there was a hint of wind, revealed by an occasional cats-paw: a dark ruffled patch on the smooth surface of the sea that recorded the passage of an imperceptible zephyr.

The first stars began to appear in the darker, eastern half of the perfect hemisphere above *Samora*.

"Okay, Waddy, you're going to have to help me this time," he said as he handed over a notebook, pencil, and the stopwatch. The notebook had four columns with the names *Arcturus, Deneb, Alpheratz*, and *Venus* labeled above them. "I'll tell you the name of the celestial body, and then when I say 'mark' you record the stopwatch reading. When I read off the sextant angle, write that down below the stopwatch time."

Stan stood facing the east where the horizon was quickly becoming obscured. "Alpheratz. Reaaadyyy . . . mark." Waddy clicked the stopwatch, recorded the time under the Alpheratz column, and reset the cumulative-time watch. "Okay, 31 degrees, 18 point 4 minutes." Waddy noted the arc reading, and Stan quickly faced in the remaining three directions, sighting the celestial bodies he had preselected to give him four good intersecting lines of position. He finished with the brilliant planet Venus, descending toward the still-defined western horizon along with the slivered arc of a new moon. Stan gathered up the notebook and stopwatch and went below to make his calculations.

Waddy looked up at the canopy of stars, increasing in profusion as the western horizon faded into night. The scrap of the moon, like a discard thrown up from the vanished sun, rested on the sea; while to the east the horizon was almost lost, only faintly illuminated by the sun's penumbral light. The tiny points of light overhead had a far different meaning to him than to Stan—more than a convenient reference to determine one's position on the surface of the earth. They were a part of the earth and the life on its surface. His belief was reinforced by the glittering pattern overhead, identical to the one he would see on an early spring evening in his desert land. He felt comfortable in the familiar surroundings, despite his knowledge that he was more than two-fifths of the way around the globe from his home and gliding along on an alien sea.

Waddy dozed in the helmsman's seat, nodding off and awakening in jerks. The only light now was the glow from the red bulb in the compass binnacle and the similarly illuminated dials in the instrument panel. Thousands of stars peppered the black above him, and the hint of moon to the west was gone. Fred only occasionally corrected the wheel in the still-calm sea. The only sounds were the muffled rumble of the diesel engine, the burble of the engine exhaust and cooling water, and the hiss of the big yacht's hull slitting the water. The engine caused a slight vibration, and *Samora* rolled and pitched very slowly, responding to the remnant of a long-quieted storm far across the inland sea. Waddy verified the work of the autopilot by seeing no variance in the position of Polaris above *Samora*'s port bow: throughout the night this star would be the only one that would not move. The fact of this relatively obscure star being located nearly directly in line with the polar axis of the earth had long been of crucial importance to northern hemisphere travelers. For Waddy it represented one of the fixed points in the rhythm of life.

"Okay, buddy, we're spot on," Stan announced when he bounded up through the hatchway, splintering Waddy's reverie. "That fix put us right on the dead reckoning plot. If the seas stay flat, we'll be on the rendezvous in six hours and twenty minutes." Stan checked the fuel gauges and quickly envisioned the prospect of having to motor clear back to Malta. *Malcolm's new engine gobbles too much fuel. Unless the wind comes up, we'll have to make a stop before we get back.*

At quarter to four Stan throttled *Samora's* diesel to idle and disengaged the forward drive transmission. The polished hull continued through the water for about a quarter mile while they searched the surrounding line where the profusion of stars abruptly stopped. A breeze had come up in the past hour; small wavelets slapped at *Samora*'s hull while she gradually stopped, rocking slowly in the awakening sea. Overhead, just beneath the starboard lower spreader of the main mast, the small Turkish courtesy flag—white crescent and star on a field of red—fluttered in the growing breeze. High on the mizzen backstay, the broad red and green ensign rolled languidly.

Scanning the black void, they saw nothing except the periodic loom of the light on Mys Khersones. After fifteen minutes Stan engaged the transmission and increased the diesel to 1,200 rpm. *Samora* was soon moving at eight knots in the direction of the looming light. In two miles the light's loom became a distinct flash over the small wave tops. They were exactly sixteen miles off the headland. Stan sighted over the compass at the light, mentally correcting the magnetic reading. The flash bore 68° true: they had arrived. He disengaged the transmission and turned *Samora* in a tight circle to slow her way and maintain her position. Four o'clock.

Stan went below and broke out the radio direction finder. He was soon hearing the Morse Code letters "S-W" through the headphones. When he rotated the RDF compass to get the lowest "null" in the signal, the compass also read 68° when corrected for variation and deviation. Confirmation. In just over an hour, the first eastern light would appear. Nothing to do but wait and scan the circle around them.

"Cut the engine, so we can hear another boat," Stan said. *Samora* lay quietly, pitching and rolling slightly as her bows fell off the growing breeze, the irregular sound of the wavelets breaking the stillness. The spinnaker halyard hit the mast with an occasional ring. The flag on the backstay rippled and popped lazily. The breeze smelled fresh and pungent—anticipatory. "It's going to blow like stink in a little while," he said.

Waddy sat motionless in the darkness and studied his friend. He had come to appreciate Stan's instinct for things having to do with the sea, understanding that it wasn't just the result of the many years he had spent around boats. *Like I belong in the desert, Stan belongs out here.*

"Stan! Straight abeam—to starboard!" Waddy whispered and pointed.

Stan looked quickly to the southeast but saw nothing in the near blackness. A few seconds passed. *There!* He picked out what looked like a small shape on the horizon. No actual horizon was visible, just a sense of where the sky ended and the sea began: where the roof of stars vanished. The shape became larger. Stan began to hear the faint sound of a motor, and he thought he could identify what looked like masts sticking out of the shapeless form. "That must be her!" He strained to see what he wanted to see.

When the apparition appeared to be about a mile away, it started to take on the hard lines of a man-made object. Then it quickly began to look like a boat—a small fishing boat with some sort of booms protruding above it. Stan reached down and snapped on the navigation light toggle switch, waited two seconds, and clicked it off. A few moments later a red port light and a white mast light appeared on the boat-shape for two seconds and then vanished. A cold knot in Stan's gut was suddenly added to the rest of his emotions. *A trap?*

He started the engine and slowly motored in the direction of the little boat. In his hand he held a powerful searchlight, wired directly to the full wattage of the engine generator so that it would produce a brilliant illumination. The light would blind the operator of the other boat, but it would also destroy his own night vision. *Won't matter soon.* A hint of gray was now visible on the horizon behind the little boat bobbing sharply in the rapidly building waves. Further to the southeast, Stan could also see the white fore and aft mast lights of a freighter approaching Sevastopil in the ship channel, about ten miles away, but that separation would be cut in half as it passed them. As he approached the little boat more closely, Stan desperately wanted to turn on the searchlight, but the watch officer on the approaching freighter would surely see it. If he was a responsible officer, he would inquire whether there was a problem. Stan hoped that *Samora* and the little boat would show only as a single blip on the freighter's radar and that the watch officer on the ship had not noticed that two blips had actually converged. *We'd only look like two fishing boats working closely together. Wouldn't we?*

He turned *Samora* alongside the boat, a troller with tall booms that could be extended out to either side. He could make out two figures standing inside the tiny cabin; one person was much shorter than the other. He saw the door to the cabin open, and the taller person stepped out. "Kateryna?" he called, just loudly enough to be heard over the rumble of the two motors.

"Stanley!" came quickly in response. Stan's heart jumped into his throat.

"Kateryna! Thank God! Let's get the hell away from that shipping lane. Stay close. Right behind me." Stan turned *Samora* to the northwest, at right angles from the track of the approaching ship. The two boats ran together for eight miles, consuming well over an hour at the little boat's maximum speed through the building seas.

Stan's thoughts ran deep while they motored along in this most foreign of places. *There she was, right on schedule, with her daughter and that thing, out at sea in a little boat. She could not go back. Would I have had that faith? But I can't go back either. I'm supposed to be dead. But I* CAN *go back—go off with Malcolm to his new home halfway around the world. But Kateryna has cut all ties. What if we hadn't showed up?*

Gray daylight accompanied the wind that could no longer be called a breeze when Stan slowed *Samora*. He looked at the aft deck of the little boat as it pulled abeam. Standing on the deck just behind the hatch to the fish tank was what looked like a fifty-five-gallon oil drum. It looked just like any oil drum he had seen, but it was painted an odd, light green color and had several numbers and words stenciled on the top and sides in the strange lettering of the Russian cyrillic alphabet.

My God, there it is. He stared at what was immediately the most alien thing he had ever seen. His weeks of growing anticipation—and cold apprehension—over this rendezvous on a foreign sea was now replaced by a rain of new emotions—all focused on the green barrel lashed to the deck rolling below him. *This is madness!* The strongest urging in his mind was that he wanted to be away from this place. Back in his comfortable apartment on Russian Hill. Out with *Penny Pincher* on the bay on a brilliant Sunday morning to begin a race. His friends. Familiarity. Safety. But his little race boat was gone. He was far around the world on *Samora*, but even she was now disguised, unfamiliar. He was surrounded by alien.

Waddy ended the trance. "Hey, Cap'n, how 'bout pulling the little boat alongside up near our bow so the main boom will swing over the drum?" Waddy was preparing docking lines to lash the two boats together.

"Yeah . . . Yeah, that's perfect," Stan responded, forcing himself to focus on the reality of what they had to do. "Here, let these down between the boats." Stan handed Waddy three large rubber boat fenders, unconsciously responding to his instinct to protect *Samora*'s topsides. *What the hell am I doing?* he thought after a moment, but Waddy had already dropped the fenders between the boats and was tying them off to the lifelines. "Make the forward lines fast to those bollards," Stan shouted forward in the growing wind. "I'll handle the ones back here."

Kateryna quickly looped the lines Waddy had thrown over the fishing boat's mooring bollards and repeated the maneuver with the lines Stan threw to her. "Okay, now let's rig two spring lines, bow to stern."

The two boats were soon firmly lashed together. Stan looked up at the sky, much darker than it should have been at quarter to six. The waves were building quickly, the wind already at thirty knots. "This is going to get real bad, real fast. We have a lot to do."

Samora did not wallow as badly as she might have without what amounted to an outrigger lashed to her starboard topsides, but it was still very rough. Stan and Waddy got only a brief introduction to Sofiia before she retreated to one of *Samora*'s forward cabins, her little babushka-swaddled face pale and filled with fear.

While Stan and Kateryna worked to detach the flooring in the salon, he saw that she was also affected by the rolling of the yacht. *Could be a long trip for you, lovely lady.* Just as the last of the flooring and the tank cover were pulled up, revealing the open cavity of the stainless steel water tank and the new cradle, Waddy opened the overhead hatch. Water in the partially-filled tank sloshed into the bilges.

"Give me a hand. I'm ready to lower her in."

Stan leapt back up the companionway. Waddy had swung the six-part block and tackle attached to *Samora*'s main boom over the afterdeck of the fishing boat; secured to the other end of the tackle was a rope sling suspending the green drum—an apparent match to the cradle they'd installed in Malta. Stan was again, uncontrollably, focused on the object swinging beneath *Samora*'s main boom.

"You gonna help or just stand there with your thumb up your butt?"

Stan jumped to pull in the boom with the mainsheet while Waddy raised the drum with the block and tackle. It was shortly being lowered through the hatchlight into *Samora*'s salon and down into the cradle in the water tank.

By the time the steel drum was made fast to its cradle, *Samora* was rolling violently "Okay, people, we've got to get under way. We can finish securing the tank lid and flooring later. Right now, we've got to get rid of that fishing boat before she does some real damage." He glanced at the chart on the navigation table. According to his DR plot of their flight away from the shipping lane, they were now in over 1,800 meters of water. "There's a big trench here. Did you plan that too?" Kateryna managed a weak grin. "Get topside. You'll do better up in the air where you can see the horizon." She took his suggestion immediately.

"Okay, buddy, let's get rid of this baggage." Stan jumped onto the deck of the troller. The little fishing boat was now held only by the fore and aft lines as Stan and Waddy went to work below. Stan found three sea cocks while Waddy laid into the bilge of the old wooden boat with a large sledgehammer. *A sledgehammer. She brought along a sledgehammer. She must have thought through every step.* Stan continued to grope through knee-deep water for more of the valves. The sea was quickly filling the troller when they abandoned their effort and scrambled over *Samora*'s lifelines.

"She's going down!" Stan yelled over the sound of the wind, now shrieking through *Samora*'s rigging. "Cast off the lines!" He motored the yacht away as the little boat rolled slightly and then disappeared, stern first beneath the now substantial waves. He headed the yacht into the forty knot wind while partially unwinding her huge mainsail. *Hell of a way to find out if Waddy has really learned anything.*

Stan pondered the fact that he was now headed off on an ocean sailing voyage in a ninety-foot yacht with two non-sailors, a little girl, and an atomic bomb. *This is truly insane.* His mind then flashed back over thirty-five years. For just a few moments he was transported from the madhouse scene, far around the world to a long ago place of overwhelming peace. A campfire flickered against a boulder beneath the arching cavern of Music Temple. It was warm and quiet. He was aware of trickling water and tapestried walls of sandstone. Quiet conversation and warm food. But then it was over when a wave top broke over the bridge deck, lashing him with green water and spume. As *Samora* leaped before the howling wind and mountainous seas, Stan set Fred on a course to the southwest where the big yacht would be reasonably content sailing before the building gale.

6

Sevastopil, Saturday, April 23

Aleksei Davletbaev could not believe it. He stared at the empty space in the water below the quay. His lovely little *Kristya* was gone. Vanished. He had run up and down the quay to his friends and the other fishermen. She had been there yesterday afternoon, he had been told, but last night, or early this morning? Everyone had just shrugged. Few of the men fished on Saturday morning. Saturday morning was spent recovering from Friday night. Besides, with the weather forecast, even the most intrepid would not have ventured out.

Aleksei was frantic. He had gone up to Minsk to visit his mother the week before, for a two-week stay, but had returned early because he needed the money from the fishing. The boat was his only source of income. How would he live? The concept of insurance was unknown to Aleksei—and unavailable even if understood. Since the breakup of the Soviet Union, so many things had changed; the old system was bad, but at least it had been predictable and stable.

One major thing had not changed. Nearly everyone was afraid of the police because they knew that the police had not changed. Together with nearly all of his countrymen, he had spent his life avoiding any encounter with the authorities; now he had no choice. Things would be worse if they discovered the boat missing and then came to him. *They will think that I have illegally sold Kristya on the black market,* Aleksei agonized while he slowly walked up to the state security building at the entrance to the military vessel area. Ukraine was not as free as people in the West now believed. Some things change slowly.

"I am Junior Lieutenant Metlenko. What is the matter?"

He looks like a Russian. He has no neck. Aleksei fixed his eyes on the floor in response to the scowling presence across the high counter. A lifetime of fears rained down upon him.

"Speak up!" boomed across the counter.

"My fishing boat is gone, Lieutenant Metlenko, sir. Someone has taken it."

"What? This is home port of the Black Sea Fleet. This is not criminal-infested Moscow! No one steals a vessel here!" the crisp young officer responded in a rising voice. "Come. Show me."

Aleksei followed the security lieutenant out of the building and down the quayside. As they approached his mooring place, the fishermen quietly strolled away or disappeared into their boats. The quay was deserted by the time Aleksei pointed to the empty space between the trollers.

"When were you last here?"

"Lieutenant Metlenko, sir, I was away to Minsk to visit my mother. I left last week. On Friday. I had fished that morning."

"Give me your travel papers," the officer said, reaching out his hand without looking at the terrified fisherman. Aleksei quickly complied. Junior Lieutenant Metlenko slowly and thoroughly perused the document. "You were not to return until next week," he snapped, fixing his glare on Aleksei.

"I needed to get back to work. My family needs so much."

The officer stared at him for a moment and then abruptly jumped down onto the deck of the adjacent fishing boat. "You down there, come up here." Aleksei's old friend Vasyl was soon standing before the officer, back on the quay.

"When was the last time you saw his vessel?"

"Comrade Junior Lieutenant . . . I mean, sir, *Kristya* was here in her berth yesterday afternoon when I came back in. I was cleaned up and gone by 16 hours, and she was just there." He pointed down at the empty space.

"Did you see anything unusual or strange in the past few days?" The fisherman hesitated and glanced at Aleksei. The event did not escape the young officer. "Well? You know something! Tell me!"

"A drum of diesel fuel was left here on the quay, right in front of *Kristya*'s berth," Vasyl blurted out. Aleksei looked wide-eyed at his friend, his mouth opening slightly.

"When? Who left it? Tell me everything!"

"Yesterday, sir. The army brought it here and just left it."

"The army? What? What are you saying?"

"Three soldiers came with a truck, unloaded the drum, and then drove away. They just set the drum here and left. That is everything I saw. There was nothing else to see. Everything seemed official—normal. It was late afternoon, just as I was finishing."

Aleksei was aware that the two other men standing with him on the quay were likely thinking the same thing he was. Stealing military equipment and supplies and selling them on the black market was now rampant in Ukraine and throughout the former Soviet Union. But this was so blatant and right in the middle of the Black Sea Fleet headquarters.

"Why did you not report this?"

"Sir, nothing was suspicious. Right out in the open. I do not question what the military does—certainly not here at Fleet headquarters. And the navy often uses this quay. We are ordered out until they are through. I have seen military equipment delivered here before, many times."

"Yes, yes, of course. You both must come to the security station and make out full reports."

* * *

Stan looked down at the weatherfax barometric chart while it slowly scrolled out of the printer. *Where in hell did that thing come from?* He frowned at the unmistakable pattern of isobars indicating a severe low over the southeast sector of the Black Sea. The needle on the wind speed dial above the chart table was oscillating unsteadily near the fifty knot mark. *Full gale, and I have no way of knowing where in hell we are.*

Even in the huge seas, Fred was holding *Samora* securely on her course of 250° true. Since leaving the rendezvous point, Stan had decided to get completely out of the ship traffic to and from Sevastopil and had set *Samora*'s course more to the west. The course had also been dictated by the direction of the wind. *Samora* rode most comfortably in the big seas with the wind on her quarter. If she sailed directly downwind, she'd roll like a barrel. Later in the day, Stan planned to turn back to the southeast to stand in to the mouth of the Bosporus, but first he wanted to get closer to the coasts of Romania and Bulgaria so that he could pick up the radio direction finder beacons. He also hoped to verify his position with the radar and with the ship traffic that would be on rhumb lines from Constanta, Romania, and Varna, Bulgaria, bound for the Bosporus.

Now, in the building wind and seas, he was having growing doubts about his plan. *I must be crazy to rely on a damned Bulgarian radio beacon for my principal navigation aid. And I'll have to be too close to shore for the radar to give me a good position. Too dangerous in this weather. God only knows how accurate this chart is.* Stan knew full well that the British had not exactly had free access to the Bulgarian coast when the chart was drawn. A glance at the 1973 revision date on the legend made up his mind. He ran the parallel rules across the chart to plot a course from where he guessed he was back to the ship lane between Sevastopil and the mouth of the Bosporus. *Don't dare gybe over. We'll have to round up, tack, and fall off on the new course.*

Stan felt the old, familiar rush when he opened the companionway hatch and stepped from the warm, wood-paneled cabin into the wind, stinging rain, and cacophonous sounds on the deck of a sailing vessel crashing through the ocean in full gale. He loved it. This was sailing. He'd regained much of his old confidence in *Samora* as he'd adjusted to her performance with the new rig.

"Change of plans, folks," he yelled to Kateryna and Waddy, huddled under the partial protection of the canvas dodger at the forward end of the bridge deck. He quickly explained the reasoning behind his decision to opt for better navigation at the expense of frequent observation by passing ships. "They won't see much in this weather and will probably just laugh at us pansy Westerners for being driven out of their sea by a little storm. Now, we have to turn this big lady, and here's how we'll do it . . . ."

Stan started the diesel engine and clicked off the autopilot. He instantly felt the pull of the six-foot-diameter wheel when he took manual control of *Samora*'s rudder and slowly turned her back into the wind. As instructed, Kateryna hauled in the mainsail sheet while the big yacht rounded up. He had to take things slowly with his novice crew, but *Samora*'s motor would help her to "power tack" across the wind and onto the new point of sail. Waddy cast off the port-side Genoa sheet just as *Samora*'s bows moved across the wind. He quickly took up the other sheet on the starboard-side winch. Kateryna let out the mainsheet, easing out the roller-reefed mainsail as the boat fell off the wind.

"Good work, people." Stan settled *Samora* onto her port-tack course to the southeast. "We'll do the same thing in reverse after we cross over the ship lane.

"So much more wind when we turned around," Kateryna said.

"Same wind. It's just that now the boat speed subtracts from the wind speed to make it seem like there's less wind. When we turned you felt the full force of fifty knots." Stan looked down at the knotmeter, its needle steady at fifteen. "Now it seems like it's only blowing about thirty-five. Nice introduction to sailing for you," he smiled. "How's Sofiia?"

"She is so sick, Stanley. She says it feels very much like when she had the chemotherapy, and I cannot stay with her very long or I also get sick. I should look after her again." Kateryna disconnected her safety line and went below.

Stan had said little to Kateryna as the three of them worked to get *Samora* under way, settled down, and sailing. He had his hands full keeping the ninety-foot yacht under control while carefully explaining to his crew what needed to be done. He thought of the tacking maneuver they'd just accomplished and then thought back to the last Tahiti race. South of Hawaii they had had a similar fifty-knot gale blowing them toward the South Pacific. He recalled his ten old friends, like a pack of nimble gorillas, gybing the huge schooner mainsail and the storm spinnaker for downwind course changes. *That was cutting-edge racing and this is cautious survival.* He dialed in the autopilot course and clicked Fred back on. *Samora*'s helm abruptly turned a few degrees in response to the computer and midship compass correction of the less-than-perfect direction the human operator had been following. "All right Fred, I won't argue with you." He tweaked the sheets to match the computer's slight change in heading.

"Okay, boss, everything's buttoned up down below." Waddy sprang up through the companionway and leaned against the weather lifeline. Stan was much relieved that his first mate had turned out to be one of those fortunate few people who are blessedly immune to motion sickness.

"Clip in," Stan commanded. "No macho aboard this boat. If you went over we'd never find you by the time we got turned around."

Waddy saluted and snapped the stainless steel safety line clip onto the lifeline harness built into his foul weather parka. "Wherethefucarwe, oh captain, my captain?" he laughed, while resituating on the sloping seat in the bridge deck cockpit.

"Damned if I know. Somewhere in the Black Sea," Stan laughed back. He looked out at the confused seas, now with wind-rounded tops streaming a steady parade of spume before the gale. But the Furies had relented with their rain. To windward, occasional shafts of light illuminated the leaden seas in little patches of emerald among the fingers of ragged scud. "Looks like it's breaking up, but that's not what the baro chart said an hour ago—so don't get your hopes up. Stay on deck. I want to check the weatherfax again."

Stan had just opened the hatch when Kateryna, her face nearly the color of the seas, pushed past him, headed for the leeward lifeline. He followed her and kept a firm grip on the back of her belt. *Yeah, this could be a real long trip.*

Samora entered the mouth of the Bosporus at 5:00 Sunday morning, after milling around outside the channel to let two Russian freighters pass through. Shipping routes from all over the Black Sea converged at the only outlet, and Stan knew that *Samora* had probably been noted on more than one watch officer's log. They'd doused the sails and were motoring along the narrow channel to Istanbul and the Marmara Sea, with the yacht now riding as smoothly as a Pullman coach.

"Well, hello, young lady," Stan said when Kateryna led Sofiia on deck. "Are you feeling better?"

"Yes, sir, I am feel much happier now," she responded in her Slavic-accented English, underscoring her mother's perfect British voice. In the growing light of the storm-free morning, Stan noticed the little girl's brilliant blue eyes for the first time. He glanced over at Kateryna, whose Tatar-Cossack eyes were also fixed on him. *Sofiia's father had to have been from western Ukraine.*

"We're about to pass through one of the oldest cities of the world, Istanbul. Have you studied this city's history in school? It was once known as Constantinople."

"Yes, sir. We learn of Istanbul and Constantinople. Is source very much our history. I am very happy to see." Stan was a little relieved when the riveting blue eyes were finally directed away from him and toward the passing suburbs of the ancient Turkish city.

"You call this boat *Samora*, yet I saw the name *Aletheia* on the back," Kateryna said. "'Truth?' Perhaps she should be named *Pravda*."

"*Aletheia* is her new name. I've known her for over twenty-five years as *Samora*, and I love this old boat even more than Malcolm does. With your training, you would really appreciate what he went through to disguise her, both in physical changes and in her legal identity." He waved toward the yacht's towering main and mizzen masts. "Besides her changes in name and hull color, her sail plan is completely different."

"She is lovely. I hope you understand that until just a couple of hours ago, I was not much interested in the details of her attributes. It is so beautiful down in her cabin. I had no idea that boats were built in this way; she is like a vacation palace for a king."

"She was built to be just that—for a capitalist king. I'm glad you and Sofiia are feeling better. That was not a pleasant introduction to offshore sailing."

A frown wrinkled her face. "Stanley, when will we be out of Turkey and into the Aegean?"

"If we don't stop and if there are no delays, we'll pass through the mouth of the Dardanelles around midnight tonight."

"Oh, that is good. We will be well out into Greek waters by tomorrow morning."

"Is that when you'll be missed?"

"Yes. I am scheduled to be at my commander's office tomorrow morning at eight o'clock. We were to have an important meeting out of the city. He will start the search for me then."

"I have to tell you that the way you set up the rendezvous point and the timing was masterful."

"Just using the skills my government spent so much effort to teach me," she smiled coyly.

"Yeah, well, am I to understand that all state security officers are skilled in the particulars of offshore navigation and piloting? The choice of the rendezvous point was brilliant—and even a sledgehammer to sink the fishing boat."

"I will admit that I spent a great deal of time studying the nautical charts and learning what all the little notations mean. I got rather fascinated by the whole subject."

He returned her smile. "You'll have plenty of time in the next month to practice your new skills." *Damn, you're a beautiful woman.* "I suppose it's pointless to ask how you managed to get our cargo from wherever it came from onto that fishing boat."

"Stanley, there are some things you cannot know. We have discussed that. The fishing boat? That was really the only means available. It was just a matter of choosing the right vessel at the right time. The particular boat I selected will probably not be reported missing for another week, and the customary practices of the fishermen also made Friday easiest. I had rather a chore, actually, getting the drum from the quay onto the boat. I had to use the troller booms."

"What will be done to find you?"

"That is uncertain. Everything will depend upon whether there is any suspicion of my using either the fishing boat or this one. Each of the vessels that see this yacht can be a source of exposure when such sighting information is considered with other facts they will have. Such large Western yachts as this are still quite rare in the Black Sea. Once we are in the Aegean, we will blend into the hundreds that are there at this time of year."

"More seafaring lore that you've acquired, I see," Stan said with a shake of his head. "Perhaps you and Sofiia should go below; that looks like a naval vessel coming up ahead. When it passes, Sofiia can stand in the companionway to watch the city."

"I'll make us some breakfast. Sofiia and I are beginning to miss all the food we wasted."

Stan was comfortably settled in the helmsman's seat, admiring the elaborate mansions of Istanbul's exurbanite elite that lined the shores of the Bosporus, when Waddy came up the companionway. Stan saw the surprised look on his face.

"Don't look now, boss, but we have some company right behind us." He nonchalantly sat down, facing the shoreline with his back to the channel.

Stan didn't turn around, but he soon heard the rumble of another diesel engine. Out of the corner of his eye he began to see the black hull of a motor launch, slowly pulling abeam. With as much control as he could manage, he turned and was confronted by a Turkish maritime police vessel closely pacing them. A large red ensign waved from the transom of the black and white boat. Stan glanced up at the little duplicate of the flag fluttering below *Samora*'s starboard lower spreader. *Thank God I remembered to do that. The Turks appreciate maritime courtesy.* He smiled and waved at the two men standing on the bridge of the little boat, both identical with dark-skinned faces, heavy black mustaches, and wearing the trim uniforms and distinctive short-brimmed caps of the Turkish navy. The men did not smile or wave back.

Stan's mind involuntarily shifted to a long-ago conversation he had had with his first sergeant: one of those little pools of long-forgotten memory his brain had kept distilled for recall. The sergeant had served in South Korea after the truce; his unit, part of the UN force, was garrisoned next to the Turkish compound. All of the UN units had been besieged by "slicky boys," the clever young South Korean thieves who raided the compounds; accordingly, the several encampments had been heavily fenced and guarded, to little avail—but not the Turks'. Stan's sergeant said that the neighboring Turkish unit had hung the first captured slicky boy over their front gate, suspended by a rifle cleaning rod thrust in one ear and out the other. Thereafter, the Turks had not been bothered, and their compound continued to need no fences or guards. The UN civilians railed and protested, the South Koreans said not a word—and the body hung there for months. *Even the Soviet Union never dared to do anything about Turkish control of the only access to their Black Sea. Taking on the Turks would have been worse than Afghanistan. Wonder what their reaction would be to someone bringing an atomic bomb into their city?*

The police boat continued to motor next to *Samora*. Stan furtively observed that the men were looking here and there, first at the yacht's hull and rigging and then at him and Waddy. *All they have to do is just wave an arm—motion to me to follow them. Everything would be over.* A minute passed. Another minute. Then the remainder of Stan's stomach came into his throat as he heard the engine of the launch rev. It moved ahead, the men examining *Samora*'s forward section, and then it slowed, once again assuming a position abeam of the cockpit. *Should I call on channel 16? Be assertive? We must look like the textbook drug-smuggling boat: a large Portuguese yacht returning from the Black Sea in April, on a Sunday morning—and if they board they'll find two Canadians and an Englishwoman. Kateryna may fool them, but they'll know that Sofiia is Ukrainian.* More interminable minutes passed as the launch slowed, fell in behind *Samora,* came up on the starboardhand side for a while, and then once again resumed its outboard position. *Kateryna must have seen what's going on. She'd have poked her nose up the companionway by now.* Suddenly, the throaty rumble of the police launch exploded into a roar. The boat sped ahead, its big wake veeing across the channel. In less than a minute it was gone.

Kateryna cautiously came up the companionway to peer after the boat with binoculars. "Did they speak to you? Are they coming back?"

Stan had almost collapsed from relief. "I don't know; they said nothing. We'll just have to sweat it out until we clear the Dardanelles in about fifteen hours."

"Stan," Waddy leaned forward and whispered, "you pissed in your pants."

7

Sevastopil, Monday, April 25

General Nastenko glanced down at his watch and got up from his desk. He walked over to the window to look down at the Black Sea Fleet, scattered up and down the South Bay roadstead.

Kateryna was two hours late. She was to accompany him to Masandra, where negotiations were continuing with the Russians over the details of splitting the fleet. Many other Russian/Ukrainian disputes were on the table, and Kateryna's new involvement in the negotiations since her return from America had been very helpful. In fact, General Nastenko thought, without her the negotiations would not have progressed as far as they had.

He returned to his desk and pulled open the top drawer, withdrawing a framed photograph. *Why must we Slavs always pose so sternly? No wonder the West has been so fearful of us.* He stared at the picture of Kateryna, the while trying to see behind the rigid, expressionless gaze to the warm, sensual woman he knew. *With your knowledge of the West and its capitalism, you can provide much help as Ukraine struggles into their ways, Katrusia.* General Nastenko pondered the upcoming meeting with the Russians. *Even your wonderful sense of humor helps in the negotiations. It is such a breath of fresh air in these dreary meetings with the politicians, the military, and so many state security officers.*

This time Ukraine was determined not to wind up under Russia's heavy thumb, and she was particularly loath to give up too much of the important naval fleet. This afternoon's meeting was to involve the nuclear-capable vessels; therefore, the general realized, the Ukrainian team would rely heavily on Kateryna's expertise.

The old man glanced over the morning précis of security activity within his Crimean command. *Now the citizens are stealing fishing boats.* He half frowned while he read the short account of the disappearance of a troller over the weekend. *So this is the price we pay for capitalism and democracy. The people need the means to become entrepreneurs. If they cannot buy what they need, they steal it from another citizen. We must stop this trend or we will be worse than the West.*

The intercom clicked, followed by Captain Khalavchenko's report that Lieutenant Colonel Kovalevska was not at her residence. The old officer got up, buttoning his uniform blouse. *I will have to do without you today, Katrusia. Where are you?*

* * *

No trace of the storm remained except a scattering of cumulus puffs and the brisk twenty-knot breeze propelling *Samora* through the bright blue water of the Aegean Sea.

Sofiia was standing in the bow pulpit where she'd remained since *Samora* had attracted a school of dolphins. She squealed with delight as the sleek gray mammals crossed back and forth, breaching and sounding just ahead of the yacht's plunging bows and easily matching her thirteen knots.

"Look, Mama. Is so pretty." The little girl pointed at lovely Andros Island with its crystalline-white villages cascading down the steep, rocky slopes to meet the sea. *Samora* would pass closely by the island as she transited the channel between Andros and the Evia Peninsula from the mainland. In the near distance through the strait were the Athenian Peninsula and the Island of Tsia.

"This is all so gorgeous, Stanley. If only we could just anchor in that little harbor and lie on that snow-white beach, then explore the village, find a little cafe for dinner, and . . ." Her voice trailed off while she continued to absorb the spectacular vision of picture-postcard Greece spread before her in the brilliant sunlight.

"Almost as nice as the canyons of the Colorado at sunset," Waddy interrupted with his usual puckish grin. "Such a beautiful place must have equally beautiful girls. Right, Stan?"

"You'll get one night back in Malta, Waddy. Try to hang on. And how are you ever going to choose?"

"Won't be able to. Guess I'll have to have them all."

"Oh is that so, Waddy," Kateryna smiled. "Perhaps you should. We will be at sea for almost a month when we leave Malta."

Waddy's face fell slightly with the renewed realization of the long trip ahead. "Guess I'll have to smuggle a couple aboard."

"He means it." Stan adjusted Fred to change their course. "We'll have to watch him carefully, Kateryna. Now hop to it, hotshot; didn't you notice we've changed course? The sails want trimmin'."

"Aye, aye, Cap'n." Waddy eased out the mainsail, mizzen, staysail, and Genoa sheets as *Samora* ran on a comfortable broad reach before the steady north-northwesterly breeze.

"Kateryna, is there any chance you could rustle up another batch of those . . . what you made yesterday morning? The little fruit-stuffed dumpling things."

"*Vareniki*," Kateryna grinned as she started forward to retrieve Sofiia, still maintaining her dolphin vigil. "You don't have all the really proper ingredients, but I can make do. Sofiia, come and help your mama."

8

Sevastopil, Wednesday, April 27

"Sir, Colonel Kovalevska's Niva was found at the Tatarskaya train station. It was left there Friday evening."

"Thank you, Captain. Continue the search in Yalta." *Why would you take the train for such a short trip?* Kateryna had not mentioned taking the train when she had told him she planned to spend the weekend at Yalta with Sofiia. Her daughter was fond of the resort and all of the tourist activities. *No matter the problem, certainly you would have managed to call by now.* The general assumed his favorite thinking position, standing before the window overlooking the harbor.

As much as he hoped it was not true, Pavlo Nastenko could not resist the thoughts he had: thoughts demanded by nearly forty-five years of service with the GRU, the Soviet military intelligence arm, the KGB's Second Chief Directorate, the Moscow Guards Directorate, and, finally, his position as chief of security for the Krymska Oblast. Kateryna, with her seriously ill only daughter, was a prime candidate for flight. "Defection" was not an appropriate word in these enlightened days, of course; "serious loss to the state" would more accurately describe her leaving the service of Ukraine.

General Nastenko remembered, with a grim shake of his head, the cruel treatment Kateryna had received with the short notification of her posting to America. She could have been informed much earlier so that she could have arranged more time with Sofiia, but the Russians had set up the teams and General Nastenko had had no say in the matter. The general also remembered that she had been denied relief from her duties when Anatoliy was dying in the hospital in Kyyiv. And he remembered, as clearly as if it had happened yesterday, the bitterness she tried to hide when he accompanied her to the cemetery. Then there was Sofiia's deteriorating condition and the declining services available in Kyyiv's overwhelmed hospitals; and he knew that a Ukrainian had little chance of being accepted into the Botkin Hospital in Moscow. Since Kateryna had returned from America, he had tried to use his influence to get Sofiia admitted, with no success. Besides the discrimination, the waiting list was impossibly long. In the old days, he could have simply picked up the telephone and it would have been done.

She has made some arrangement for Sofiia in America. The old general unclasped his hands from behind his back and brought them together in front with a loud clap. *Yes, you are gone, Katrusia. But how?* He would have been informed immediately if she had openly used any public transportation. *And you wouldn't have risked a simple change of identity, would you?* The old security officer decided that the abandonment of her vehicle at the train station eliminated the train as a means of travel. *Unless, my clever one, you expected me to make that conclusion. But a Tatar woman, traveling alone with a child? No, of course not. You always prefer more control, don't you, Katrusia?*

"Captain Khalavchenko, extend your inquiry to Kyyiv and west to the Polish frontier. She may have left us."

* * *

When they'd safely entered the Aegean, Stan used the shortwave radio to reach the high seas radio telephone operator in London, who had connected him to the overseas long-distance operator for a call to an untraceable telephone in San Francisco. He'd left a message for Malcolm—just a number—indicating their arrival date in Malta. A leased airplane would be waiting for Sofiia at Luqa.

The trip through the Aegean and the eastern Mediterranean passed like a dream. They were on schedule, approaching Malta on Wednesday night, when Stan came on deck during Waddy's watch. Since leaving the Dardanelles, Stan, Waddy, and Kateryna had shared deck watches of three hours on, six hours off, and unless they took on more crew, this would be the routine until they arrived at the Texas coast. The schedule was tedious and tiring, but necessary with a crew of only three.

Since passing Crete, Stan had slowed the boat so that they would be sure to reach Valletta late in the evening. The LORAN receiver told him they were twenty-one miles east of the harbor sea buoy, but Stan needed confirmation. He had long-ago accepted the fact that he was a navigation tech weenie; he could never have enough confirmation of his position at sea, and a compulsive, running fix with the sextant that afternoon had confirmed the LORAN position exactly. He now went below to pick up the aero beacon at Luqa with the radio direction finder. The bearing of the "L-U" Morse Code signal plotted right on their course to the harbor entrance.

"We've got the light," Waddy announced as Stan came back on deck. In another few seconds the loom of the Valletta headland light came straight over *Samora*'s bows. Stan replaced the blue-and-white-striped Greek courtesy flag on the starboard spreader with the simple red and white flag of the Republic of Malta.

"Wake me up when we start running out of water."

Stan awoke with a start, as all seasoned sailors do, when he heard/felt/sensed the rhythm of his vessel change. He leaped on deck, dressed only in his shorts, to find Kateryna and Waddy winding in *Samora*'s sails while the yacht headed into the gentle breeze, just off the sea buoy for the channel into Marsamxett Harbor.

"Go back to your bunk, Cap'n, we've got everything under control." Waddy confidently turned *Samora* into the line of flashing lights leading to the harbor entrance.

"Hey, looks like you do. Now let's see if you can follow the correct buoys through the harbor at night, smart guy. I'll get the chart. And remember, the Brits taught the Maltese to do things ass-backwards with their lights."

With only a couple of minor errors, Waddy eased *Samora* up to the courtesy dock at the Manoel Island shipyard. On either side of the dock the quays were lined with scores of *luzzus,* the brightly painted Maltese fishing boats. Decorated as they'd been by the local fishermen for centuries, all of the little boats had eyes painted on their steeply-sheered bows—to spot and ward off danger. Stan felt all the eyes looking at him.

The boatyard was quiet and dark. Only a single light at the end of the long dock and the reflected lights from Valletta across the harbor illuminated the slipways and the channel into the travel lift bay. Despite his recent familiarity with the yard, Stan was apprehensive. Since the rendezvous off the Crimean peninsula and the close call in the Bosporus, this would be the single greatest known risk in the whole operation: everything depended upon *Samora* being simply ignored by the yard crew and the customs people—and the plan Stan and Malcolm had hatched to get Sofiia aboard the airplane had to work.

"Kateryna, familiarize yourself with the passport. The airport customs man gave Waddy's a pretty good scrutiny."

"Are you forgetting who you are talking to?" She shook her head and gave Stan her most disarming smile, then continued her close examination of the document that identified her as Catherine Follows, a British subject. "This is really quite good, actually. Was Malcolm that impressed with my accent?"

"We all are. It's really quite astonishing. You sound just like a County Kent aristocrat. No Slavic accent at all."

"Did you think we have American instructors in Ukraine?" She was instantly serious. "What is the schedule for today?"

"Tonight we'll discreetly get you to the apartment Waddy and I kept in the city, then later on today you will conspicuously come to the boat to be hired on as crew. In the meantime, Waddy and I will see to the repairs and reprovisioning we need. Tonight, just after dark but while the early evening business and traffic is still heavy, we'll rendezvous with the van Malcolm's flight crew has been using to go in and out of the airport. We have only to get Sofiia into the van, then through the gate and aboard the airplane."

"Will we be able to find out first if the van has been able to pass freely in and out of the airport?" The leased airplane, untraceable to Malcolm, was to have had electrical system problems when it arrived at Malta. The carefully selected and obscenely well-paid crew knew only that they were involved in smuggling a very sick child to the United States for medical treatment. The "repair" of the aircraft's electrical problem would require many trips back and forth through the security gate, timed as often as possible when the same gate personnel would be on duty. After enough trips, inspection of the van should degenerate to wave-throughs. Reliance on the universal human trait of laxity born of familiarity, combined with the heavy gate traffic at early evening, was the simple plan. Kateryna was not impressed.

"There is no way for me to get in touch with the flight crew. I only have a description of the van. We have to trust Malcolm on this."

"Stanley, if Sofiia is apprehended, a nightmare of bureaucratic delay could cost her life."

"Yes. Yes, I know." The eyes he was looking into were not those of a trained security officer but of a frightened mother. He reached down and grasped her hand tightly. "Should we keep Sofiia with us for the voyage? We could then fly her from Galveston to Seattle. In the worst case, we would have to drive. The whole trip could take as long as five weeks if we have a weather delay."

"No, of course not," Kateryna replied in frustration.

"Tell you what. I'll drive to the gate area and watch for the van. Maybe I'll see it go through."

"You and Waddy have a lot to do, Stanley; there is no time."

"We'll *make* time. If it looks too risky, we'll call Malcolm and try to figure something else out. Okay?"

They had thoroughly discussed putting Sofiia aboard a commercial flight at Luqa, but a frightened little girl could not be expected to carry through the deceptions required. And since she was unaccompanied and did not have a passport, the Maltese social service authorities would become involved—certainly to proceed at the usual Maltese bureaucratic pace. The same problems would arise if she openly boarded Malcolm's airplane, along with scrutiny of the reasons why an international private flight was shuttling a little Ukrainian girl clear to America. No, Sofiia had to leave unofficially.

Stan watched the Vauxhall minivan drive away from a Gulfstream IV parked at the end of the commercial zone. With her wingtip tanks, he knew that the little jet could easily make the passage with a single stop at Gander, Newfoundland. He imagined the scores of small airfields in the Pacific Northwest where the aircraft could land safely with her powerful Rolls Royce engines. *Nice choice, Malcolm.* He then watched the van drive right through the freight entrance from the Luqa airfield flight line. The uniformed Maltese official only looked up and nodded casually as the van drove past the kiosk. *That's it, then. We're going ahead.*

9

Sevastopil, Thursday, April 28

Pavlo Nastenko impatiently drummed his fingers on his desk while he waited for his scheduled visitor. Captain Khalavchenko had respectfully urged the general to make time to talk with the master of the container ship *Vladimir Rakov*; the merchant officer had an important matter to relate to the commander of security for the Crimean Military District. Meanwhile, the general's operations aide was continuing his investigation. To Captain Khalavchenko, the search for a woman, officer or not, and her daughter, seemed the archetypal military tail-chasing—and the fatuous obsession of a spurned old man. But Sergei Khalavchenko was not a general of state security.

"Why did you not report through the usual channels, Captain Maksamov? This had better be important." General Nastenko glared at the nervous merchant officer.

"Sir, I felt that I must report what I observed immediately to the highest authority. It was most unusual."

"Yes, all right. Go on."

"Sir, we were approaching the range lights on Mys Khersones– –"

"Captain Khalavchenko, get me a chart of the area. Now get to the point, Captain Maksamov."

"Yes . . . yes, sir. My radar showed a small vessel approaching what I had already seen as a larger, stationary vessel off my port bow, about seventeen kilometers as I closed on the range to the headland. The radar reflection showed the smaller vessel to be the size and speed of the seiners and trollers we usually encounter in this area. I noticed the boat because it was the only small vessel of that type out that morning. The weather was building quickly, and it soon developed into a full gale. By the time the two vessels were nearly abeam of me, at about nine kilometers, the radar showed that they had come together and were stationary. Now, this is the very strange part. A CNG ship two hours ahead of me had advised to be on the watch for a vessel that was close to the shipping lane and traveling toward Sevastopil at less than ten knots. The gas ship had not had a visual, but it had observed the vessel on its radar from well beyond the normal fishing area. From the position, course, and speed of this vessel that had been reported, and given that there were no other boats in the area, I believe that it was the same stationary vessel I observed on radar. Now, if two fishing boats were coming together, that is one thing, but a larger vessel coming in from sea and a local fishing boat . . ."

"Show me where you saw the boats as they made contact," General Nastenko said as his operations officer unrolled the nautical chart.

"Just there," Captain Maksamov said, fingering a point southwest of the tip of the Crimean peninsula, about sixteen miles to sea.

"And what else?" the general asked, now much less impatiently.

"I had slowed to mesh into the crossing traffic pattern; then I was forced to heave to, to await a pilot and tug for assistance into the channel in the growing gale. During this waiting time I kept observing the radar blip—the vessels were so close, there was only a single return. It moved slowly to the west-northwest, perhaps fifteen kilometers, and stopped again. Then another strange thing happened. The radar reflection moved at perhaps fourteen or fifteen knots to the southwest."

"So?"

"There was only a single blip on the radar, sir. Those little fishing boats cannot make fourteen knots."

General Nastenko gave the merchant captain a long look, then again concentrated on the chart. "Show me where you saw the change in speed." Where the officer pointed, the sea floor shelved off to more than 1,800 meters. During the brief conversation Pavlo Nastenko's brain had been searching for any connection between the information it was receiving and some bit of stored information. The way in which the old officer's mind worked, it was no accident that he had risen to flag rank in the security services. He remembered the précis he had read on Monday about the stolen troller.

"How certain are you that the moving vessel you first saw was a small fishing boat?"

"Sir, I had no visual on either one. By the time it was sufficiently light, the blip I was seeing and my ship were moving away from each other at a distance of perhaps thirty kilometers. But I can say this. The radar return I saw approaching the stationary vessel was identical to the hundreds I have seen on other voyages in and out of Sevastopil. In every case where I also had visual sightings, the vessels were the small seiners and trollers that are ported in this harbor. Oh, and there is another point. I nearly forgot. At the closest point, when the two vessels were about nine kilometers to my port beam, I saw no running lights on either of them. I should have been able to see a light on the large vessel, at least."

"Any other indication that the stationary boat was the one the CNG ship reported?"

"I never actually saw either vessel. However, from the position, course, and speed reported to me concerning the boat that had been approaching Sevastopil, the position of the stationary vessel on my radar was within the expected area where it should have been. I had only come on the bridge for the approach to the harbor, because of the deteriorating weather. Unfortunately, my first officer had not noticed the stationary blip, so he could not verify when it had arrived, its course, how fast it had traveled, and so on. With the growing seas and all the clutter they produce on the screen, it is easy to miss– –"

"Yes, I understand," General Nastenko said sharply. Such a performance by a junior in the old days would have brought an immediate reassignment to the White Sea. He continued to stare at the chart. "Other than size and speed, is there any further information your radar revealed about the larger boat?"

"There *is* something telling, sir. When the radar return started to move rapidly to the southwest, it was on a course that took it somewhat away from the normal traffic lane to the Bosporus. It was not on a course to any port. While we were waiting for the harbor pilot, I took the trouble to plot its course on a large sailing chart for the western Black Sea."

"So what are you getting at?" General Nastenko demanded. He was not used to receiving circuitous answers to his inquiries.

"General, with the wind direction at the time, nearing gale force, the course was exactly what I would expect for a sailing vessel trying to be on the most comfortable and the fastest point of sail in the given conditions. Sailing a rhumb line for the Bosporus would have put her directly downwind. In such weather conditions, she would have rolled like a log and, in fact, would sail slower than on the very broad reach she was on. With the wind any further abeam, she would sail slightly faster but would take a lot of green water aboard and would be on a wider divergence from the Bosporus. That skipper was holding her on the best possible course, assuming she was bound for the Bosporus. In my opinion, based on over thirty years at sea, what I saw was a sailing vessel, General Nastenko."

"Comparing the size of the two radar returns you saw, and knowing the size of the fishing trollers, can you estimate the size of the other vessel?"

"Sir, there are many variables, most particularly the construction of the vessel, whether steel or wood, her freeboard, her orientation in the water—that is, her profile to my radar, I– –"

"Give me your best estimate, captain."

"Assuming wood construction, nearly three times as large . . . thirty meters."

"So, given that size, and its speed, what *kind* of a sailing vessel?" General Nastenko knew full well that he was asking the merchant officer to base an opinion on a weak assumption about the size of the vessel.

"Sir, I– –"

"Your best assessment, captain."

"It was probably a sailing yacht, sir. Any commercial sailing vessel I have seen anywhere in the Black Sea, or the Mediterranean for that matter, would have to have been considerably larger than thirty meters to achieve that speed, even in the wind conditions."

"Thank you, captain. How long will you be in Sevastopil?"

"We sail in three days, sir."

"Captain Khalavchenko, have my car brought up front."

Junior Lieutenant Yuriy Metlenko sprang to his feet when he heard his desk sergeant in the outer office shout, "Attention!" Five seconds later his office door flew open before a general officer of Ukrainian State Security.

"Stand at ease, lieutenant," General Nastenko said, returning the perfect, military academy salute. The recent graduate assumed an eyes-forward position of parade rest as General Nastenko glanced about the Spartan office. The closest Junior Lieutenant Metlenko had ever been to a general officer was when he had marched by the academy reviewing stand at his graduation. General Nastenko had the young officer's undivided attention.

"Lieutenant, I have come here to inquire further about the missing fishing vessel you reported this past weekend."

Lieutenant Metlenko snapped to attention, his mind racing. "Sir! I have no further information other than confirmation that the vessel was last seen late Friday afternoon this past week, sir!" *Why is a general of state security concerned with a miserable little fishing boat? Why is he here in person?*

"Have you made any investigation of the involvement of army personnel in delivering the drum of fuel you reported?"

"No, sir! I have had no orders to investigate those matters further."

Of course not, General Nastenko thought. *You would not dare, given that much of the theft of military property is by direction of high-ranking military.* He sighed audibly. *We train these fine young officers only to then turn them out into this shit system we have created.*

"Come. Show me where the fishing boat was stolen."

The intense young lieutenant and the old general marched down the quay, accompanied by the general's aide and two guards, their approach sending the population of boatmen, fish vendors, and sundry workers skittering away, this time with no pretense of nonchalance.

"Did the missing fishing boat look like these others?"

"Yes, sir. I have questioned the owner and many of the boat owners up and down the quay; they all report that the vessel *Kristya* was identical to these."

General Nastenko looked closely at the row of small, brightly painted wooden boats. "Did the fishermen tell you anything about the diesel fuel?"

"Sir, the two fishermen who had any information at all said it was a standard army diesel fuel barrel. Almost no one saw the army personnel leave it here because most of the fleet had not returned from fishing. Because there is so much military activity on this quay and since the navy often uses it, no one paid much attention. But, sir, if I may . . ." Lieutenant Metlenko was struggling with his intense military training which forbade a junior officer to be assertive or to volunteer unsolicited conversation with a senior officer.

"Yes, yes, lieutenant. Enough of the protocol nonsense. Just tell me what you know."

"Sir, all of these fishing boats have petrol engines."

* * *

Kateryna and Sofiia said their quiet good-byes in *Samora*'s warm and now familiar salon. Stan and Waddy waited in the cockpit, listening to the soft sounds of the alien language. The tears in the eyes of the woman and child coming up the companionway steps did not require a translation.

"Sofiia is ready to go, Stanley." The little girl was terrified, although she tried her best to conceal it. Stan saw the same fear, nearly controlled, in her mother's eyes.

"We must leave now; it is time," he said. The slipway end of the boatyard appeared deserted, but Stan and Kateryna spent several minutes watching the area to be sure they were alone. Stan picked up Sofiia's travel bag and started down the boarding ladder to the quay. "You will be on your way soon—to America, Sofiia. You must be strong, like your mother." Stan and Kateryna shared a long and uncertain look as they got into the Fiat. In thirty minutes they were to meet the Vauxhall van just outside the gate to the old city.

Stan and Kateryna watched silently from their car, a few hundred feet from the entrance to the security gate into the airport. The little Vauxhall van inched forward in the line of cars. Vehicles ahead of it were visually and sometimes physically searched when they moved through the gate. Many more guards than usual were on duty; several shined their flashlights into the vehicles as they pulled up to the guard kiosk.

"Has to be some unusual security problem tonight," Stan stated the obvious.

"Yes," was all Kateryna responded. It was too late to abort the plan. All they could do was watch and wait.

The vehicle ahead of the Vauxhall was ordered to the side by two of the guards, soon starting to search the car's trunk. The van then pulled up to the gate. Another guard came out of the kiosk. He was talking to the driver. From the Fiat everything was in pantomime; only the sounds of the traffic surrounded them. Seconds passed—hours. *All they have to do is open the rear doors and look under the tarp,* Stan thought for the uncounted time.

Kateryna gasped and clutched his arm when one of the guards walked around to the rear of the van. He pointed his flashlight through the rear windows and hesitated. More hours passed in the parked Fiat. Abruptly, the guard returned to the kiosk and waved the van ahead. Stan closed his eyes, then lowered his forehead onto the backs of his hands, still gripping the steering wheel. Kateryna began to cry softly.

From another vantage point on the perimeter road, they watched the little Gulfstream jet taxi down to the far end of the runway, turn, then point toward them while they stood in the darkness outside the car. The brilliant lights raced toward them, then pointed skyward; the screaming roar of the engines crashed down on them, the airplane flashed overhead, climbing rapidly in a wide arc toward the northwest, its brilliant strobe soon fading with the sound. They watched until the last faint rumble and the winking point of light were gone. Stan had been standing with his arm unconsciously around Kateryna, pressed gently against him in the warm evening air. With the airplane vanished, he was suddenly aware of her closeness, a closeness that enveloped him a moment later when she turned and softly pressed her open mouth against his lips, her hand clutching a fistful of hair at the back of his head. Only the open door of the Fiat kept him from falling over backward.

10

Western Mediterranean Sea, Sunday, May 1

"Okay, Peter, let's do it," Stan shouted up the hatch from *Samora*'s forward sail locker. A pair of powerful bronzed arms reached down and jerked the seventy-five-pound spinnaker and its "turtle" from Stan's grip. When he came back on deck, Peter and Timothy had the chute bag tied to the leeward lifeline under *Samora*'s nearly slack Genoa headsail. They were rigging the spinnaker pole.

What a find they were, Stan thought while he snapped the halyard onto the head of the spinnaker sticking out of the top of the turtle and looked aloft to see that the heavy Dacron line was clear to the sheave at the masthead. The two young athletes ran the spinnaker sheet and afterguy back through the turning blocks and then to the big three-speed winches in *Samora*'s cockpit.

"Now, John," Stan said to Waddy, "when the halyard gets the head of the sail to the masthead, crank back on the afterguy. That will pull the end of the pole aft. I'll handle the sheet. If there's a twist in the spinnaker as it tries to fill, pulling on the guy and the sheet will stretch the foot of the sail and spin out the twist." They always referred to each other and to the yacht by their assumed names, even in private, to help avoid an unconscious slip in front of Peter or Timothy.

"Ready forward?"

"Aye, Skipper," Peter called back the fifty feet to the cockpit.

"Haul away!" Muscles rippled in the arms and bare backs of the two young men while four strong hands hauled down in perfect, paced coordination. Large coils of the spinnaker halyard piled at their feet as the huge nylon sail flared out of the bag and billowed toward the masthead. When the halyard was winched tight and cleated off, Peter helped Waddy with the afterguy and Timothy wound up the headsail that had blanketed the spinnaker after it was set. With the obstruction removed, the 5,000-square-feet of red and white nylon snapped full in the twelve-knot breeze. *Samora*'s speed jumped from five to nine knots. With the light, northeast wind coming off her starboard quarter, the eighty-five-ton yacht heeled slightly on her port bow, responding to the many tons of pressure against the huge sail.

Peter adjusted the foreguy, downhaul, and topping lift holding the end of the spinnaker pole. "All *right*, mates! We're sailing again!"

Stan had been reluctant to set the big sail with his very shorthanded crew, even in the light breeze. In the last Tahiti Race, a coordinated crew of ten had been required to manage the spinnaker and the rest of the boat and sails. But that had been with her old schooner rig, in thirty-five to forty knots of wind and a huge following sea in mid-Pacific. With her new rig and deck gear, *Samora* was now much more labor efficient; but long, occasionally painful experience told Stan that the huge sail could quickly get out of control.

The just-completed set of the spinnaker fully convinced Stan that he'd been correct in taking on additional crew before they'd left Malta. Peter and Timothy had shown up the morning after Sofiia left. The yard master had sent them over, knowing that Stan and Waddy were preparing to take the big yacht halfway around the world. The young English sailors had planned to join the crew of an Italian nobleman's racing yacht, but the long delivery through the Mediterranean and across the Atlantic would pay much more. Even when Stan told them that the trip was only as far as the British Virgin Islands, where another crew was waiting, they still opted for the crossing. Neither of them had been to the Caribbean, and they wanted to get a head start on the lucrative but highly competitive winter season in the West Indies. They could do without the nubile nymphettes of the Mediterranean racing scene. Plenty more awaited them in Road Town.

With a crew of five, watch keeping would be greatly eased, and Stan knew that he would sleep much more soundly with seasoned sailors aboard the big yacht as she confronted whatever the North Atlantic decided to throw at them. Sitting under the gigantic spinnaker towering above him, with *Samora* sailing well in the warm Mediterranean breeze and under the control of a competent crew, Stan came close to relaxation. Three big hurdles had been passed: the weapon pickup, Sofiia's departure, and *Samora* under way to America. They had officially cleared Malta, bound for Tortola in the British Virgin Islands and thence via the Panama Canal to the South Pacific. And before leaving Malta, Stan arranged for a replacement GPS receiver. From the time they transited the Straits of Gibraltar until they approached the coast of North America, they would not have a LORAN net to fix their position. Fortunately, and encouraged by a particularly exorbitant fee, Mr. Blaquiére had been able to locate the needed piece of equipment.

Samora was not unlike the many large charter yachts crossing the Atlantic at this time of year, moving between the West Indian winter playground and the Mediterranean summer playground—except that she was going in the wrong direction. But it was an entirely reasonable time to be heading into the South Pacific if one were interested in avoiding the fierce tropical storms of the world's largest sea. Everything was in order and on schedule, and Stan was as relaxed as he could be knowing that nestled in the bilge of his vessel was enough explosive force to level most of the small city they had left the day before. He also had no way of knowing whether or not some very determined officials in Ukraine were at the moment trying to find *Samora* and their missing nuclear bomb.

* * *

Glen Canyon Dam

I cannot believe I'm doing this. Randy MacConnell could not control a shiver as he watched the mouth of the spillway grow smaller, far up the slope of the tunnel. The Dam superintendent, his O&M chief, and two engineers from the Denver E&R center were riding down the slope of the right spillway, crowded into the *I Challenge U 2.* The little four-wheeled cart was rolling down the 55° incline suspended by a three-eighths-inch steel cable being controlled from a winch on the deck above the spillway gates. Forty-eight point six feet of Powell Reservoir pressed against the back sides of the two gates, now about 250 feet above the four men. Only a tiny half-circle of daylight shined through the aperture of the spillway, over the tops of the gates. The cart was just beginning to roll over a ramp that had also been lowered down from the top to enable the cart to bridge the four-foot-wide by four-foot-deep air injection slot.

At the air slot they were halfway down the slope and being pelted with water draining from holes thirty feet overhead in the crown of the tunnel. Hundreds of other holes were releasing their hydrostatic pressure burdens to run down the curved concrete, with all the flow gathering in the lowest point beneath the cart. Leakage under the spillway gates far above them was adding to the water sheeting under the wheels of the *I Challenge U 2*.

"Look at all of it," John Patterson said, pointing his flashlight at the side of the tunnel. Glistening in the light beam was a surface covered with what could best be described as pimples: a rash on the surface of the concrete with the major eruptions occurring where the most water flowed. Despite the fact that after the 1983 event the bores of the spillways had been ground smooth, in the intervening years the constantly-flowing water had again built up calcite deposits, formed over tiny "seed" bumps and irregularities on the surface of the concrete.

"About like what we had in '83," one of the E&R men said. "Maybe not quite as bad."

"Bad enough," John Patterson said. "Amazing how fast it's built up. I think we should recommend removing it."

"I don't think that's necessary," the lead engineer said. "With the aeration slots we don't have to worry now about cavitation." The lead engineer had been in charge of the design of the slots and was convinced of their adequacy to solve the cavitation problem.

Unless the slots fill with water or the whole tunnel runs too full, the junior engineer from E&R thought. He was one of the newer generation of civil engineers who had a very low regard for tunnel spillways. He had also learned to keep his mouth shut about controversial subjects—particularly in the current era of big cutbacks in the Bureau's engineering staff.

They reached the bottom of the incline where the tunnel started to curve into the horizontal section. It had been here that the erosion through the concrete lining and deep into the sandstone had occurred in 1983. John Patterson radioed up to the winch operators to stop the cart when they reached the level of the water. If they kept rolling they'd descend into the twenty feet of water that stood in the horizontal section of the tunnel. The water from the drain holes filled the whole length of the tunnel to the level of the top of the deflection bucket at the portal, where it spilled over the lip of the bucket to run down into the river. The portal opening was another tiny half-circle, 1,100 feet down the tunnel.

"This is where we think we're getting the increased water intrusion, Frank," Randy MacConnell said to the lead E&R man. "The square weirs we installed at each flip bucket show that the flow through this tunnel is 225 gallons per minute higher than the left side."

(Bureau of Reclamation)

"Randy, I think it's just the fact that there must have always been a little more intrusion through the drains on this side. With both tunnels draining at roughly 6,000, two hundred twenty-five one way or the other is well within the expected variation. We're sure it's been this way since the reservoir filled. I don't see anything significant down here other than the calcite buildup, and like I told you, that doesn't matter any more."

"We noticed what looked like a little more flow through this bore ever since 1983," John Patterson said. "And since this was the side that had the surging through the lower foundation adit just overhead here, well, I thought it might be significant. So, we put in the measuring weirs."

The lead engineer shook his head. "We've looked closely at the 1983 surge event. With all the grout we pumped into the adit drains up there, there's no way we have a leak—just a little more natural hydrostatic pressure flow around this side, that's all. But we needed the spillway drains measured anyway now that we have to account for every drop going down river under the draft environmental impact statement; so the weirs aren't a waste." The E&R man continued to scan the wall of the tunnel with his light.

"If there was a leak associated with the adit surge event, we'd see it right here. Around 200 gpm above the natural hydrostatic pressure flow would certainly show up if it was concentrated in this area. Nope, I'm convinced there is no abnormal leak."

11

Sevastopil, Monday, May 2

Pavlo Nastenko stood in front of the large window overlooking the vessels Russia and Ukraine were still fighting over. It was apparent that Kateryna had stolen the fishing boat to rendezvous with the mysterious vessel. And he had about made up his mind to accept the merchant captain's opinion that the boat she met was a large sailing yacht. But two principal questions weighed on the savvy old officer of state security: why had she chosen such a bizarre, cumbersome, and risky means to escape; and why had she suddenly been receptive to his advances after her return from America?

The matter of the drum of diesel fuel was also bothersome. *A large sailing yacht would most certainly have a diesel engine, and it is logical that it might need additional fuel; they would not want to make a port call in the Black Sea. But only two hundred liters? That most certainly is a factor indicating her range of possible destinations, isn't it? And they would probably prefer to motor, thereby being far less conspicuous than with a spread of sails. Of course, the yacht had to sail in the gale the container ship captain mentioned.*

Once again the old man's thoughts turned to Kateryna, his mind reliving many events. After a respectful time following the death of her husband, Pavlo Nastenko had pursued the lovely and talented woman. He was only thirty years older, after all, and he was not looking for some arrangement; he wanted her for his wife. But Kateryna had always repulsed his overtures—delicately and respectfully, but nonetheless repulsed. Upon her return from America, however, things had been very different. He had not questioned the change in Kateryna's attitude; he was caught up entirely in what could only have been her inevitable realization that he was best for her and Sofiia.

He sighed when he recalled their first intimacy. It was more wonderful than he had remotely imagined, quickly swelling his long infatuation into what, he had been convinced, must be love. With their new relationship, he had done everything he could for her. He had known the weapons disposal assignment was tenuous: the fragile agreement to mutually reduce the stockpiles of tactical weapons could shatter at any time, particularly with the increasing economic and political instability in Russia and Ukraine. Besides, he had reasoned, her talents could be better utilized at home.

He had arranged Kateryna's assignment to the more stable duty of assisting in what would surely be protracted negotiations between Ukraine and Russia over countless issues. He had also placed her in the unofficial position of first deputy, and, he now painfully remembered, it had been Kateryna who had asked to work closely with him. She had said that she did not want to leave Sofiia again. In a way, General Nastenko now realized, what she had said was true: it had all been part of her plan to leave Ukraine with Sofiia—not to have to leave Sofiia again. But *what* plan? He had been forced to investigate discreetly, therefore slowly. He could not have attention drawn to the fact that a general of state security was looking for a missing fishing boat and one of his principal officers.

The intercom buzzer interrupted his concentration. "Sir, I have the information you requested. Three vessels transiting the Bosporus have confirmed a large sailing yacht in the channel on Sunday, last week. The sightings were between 5 hours and 8 hours, and all reported the yacht displayed a Portuguese ensign. One reported the vessel's name: *Aletheia.* I have nothing yet on the vessel's ownership nor anything concerning its recent travels."

"Was more than one large sailing boat, of any kind, observed in the area we are concerned with?"

"Yes, sir, I have reports of at least one other in the southwest sector of the sea. More Western yachts are now cruising in the Black Sea, and there are still the fishing schooners from Bulgaria, I– –"

"Yes, of course. I am aware of that. But were there any others in the Bosporus early Sunday morning?"

"None that have been reported other than the Portuguese vessel."

"Keep tracing her ownership and itinerary, Captain."

"Yes, sir."

The best evidence and General Nastenko's instinct caused him to concentrate his investigation on the mouth of the Bosporus in the early morning hours of the past Sunday. The master of the *Vladimir Rakov* estimated that the boat he had detected sailing in the general direction of the Bosporus would arrive at approximately 0600 on Sunday, assuming that it was a sailing yacht and further assuming that it would maintain its observed speed. It was of course true that the ship could have been going to any port in the southwest sector of the Black Sea, but the old man had decided she was probably going to exit the sea.

"Damn!" General Nastenko slammed his fist on the desk top. In his former Soviet position he would have had satellite surveillance, aircraft, and naval vessels at his instant disposal to find the sailboat. He would have had the entire apparatus of the KGB available with a single telephone call. *Now? Now I am nearly impotent. A general of state security, and I am reduced to overseeing a small portion of a weak, floundering nation. Russia has retained virtually all of the sophisticated materiel and has almost total control over its use. Ukraine is once again just a giant farm and coal mine for the benefit of Russia. Of course, I could call upon some old friendships and get much of the assistance I need. But to find a female officer who was my lover, and her dying child? What was it, Katrusia? Why did you need me so?*

In the late afternoon General Nastenko was about to go home to his empty quarters when Captain Khalavchenko knocked and entered his office.

"Sir, if I might interrupt. I made the routine inquiries about military involvement in the matter of the drum of diesel fuel."

"Yes, Captain," General Nastenko sighed, barely maintaining his patience. He hated to be reminded of the rampant theft that was occurring all over his command.

"Sir, I would not bother you with this, but I thought it odd that the fuel was not taken from the depot here in Sevastopil."

"Where, then?" Something was almost coming together in the old man's gut. Even though he had consciously decided that the drum of fuel must have been needed for the yacht, his unconscious mind still searched—as it had been conditioned throughout a lifetime to do. He sagged in his chair. He had a gnawing feeling—a sense—something. He was nearly afraid to hear what he was about to be told. The old Cold Warrior almost knew it, but it had not yet meshed.

"Sir, the fuel was taken from the reserve materiel depot at Symferopil."

In that instant he knew.

"Sir? Are you all right?"

"Yes. Just leave me, please. And have my car brought around."

When his operations aide left the room, the old officer slowly got up from his chair and went to the bookcase that covered the entire wall opposite his desk. From among the hundreds of books, notebooks, loose-leaf binders, and bound documents, he visually selected a slim notebook located out of reach on the top shelf. Almost casually, he moved the little rolling footstool beneath the shelf and then went to his desk and took from one of the drawers a flashlight and a large magnifying glass. He stepped up on the stool and through the glass he scanned the shelf in front of the selected volume and its companions, shining the flashlight obliquely along the row of books. He examined the length of the top shelf, finding a fine layer of dust along the edge of the shelf in front of the books. Here and there disturbed and smeared dust particles told him that volumes had been removed within the past month—he remembered having removed most of them. He checked the lower shelves. The same. But after fifteen minutes of close examination, he found a tiny section of shelf, at the end of the bookcase on the bottom row, where the dust was heavier—a three month's accumulation since that last time his office was cleaned. The few cleaning workers his command was allocated, desperate to keep their jobs, always did a scrupulous job. He sighed deeply as he withdrew the slim volume from the top shelf.

The ruled pages of the little bound notebook contained entries of meteorological information. Page after page bore columns recording air temperature, dew point temperature, barometric pressure, altitude, and the dates and times recorded. General Nastenko turned to the page where the entries for October 24 began. His eyes momentarily held a flicker of a smile when he recalled choosing the Old Style date of the capture of the Winter Palace to record his special entries in the innocuous little notebook. By reading across the data, combining the numbers in a certain way, instead of meteorological information, the numbers revealed to an instructed reader the designations of eighty-two weapon models, arming lock combinations, and barrel numbers. The last series of coded entries provided the latitude and longitude coordinates of certain warehouses at the Symferopil Reserve Materiel Depot and its counterpart at Odessa, and the numbers and locations of two marine shipping containers within the warehouses.

So this was the reason for your affection, Kateryna Romanivna. This little book and the forged documents from my office you would need to enter Symferopil. How could I have failed to realize this when I learned of the fuel drum? Because my mind, and my heart, could not accept what you have done? I am getting old.

He opened the bottom drawer of his desk and removed a liter of vodka and a 300-milliliter glass that he filled from the bottle. He drained the glass in three swallows, then stared at the little book for several minutes. *You know me so well, don't you, Katrusia? Yes, you knew I would keep this information close by, didn't you? And you knew that I would not have the use of sophisticated cryptographic equipment to record this information—just an old manual code that any high level KGB would recognize. What a treasure you are, Katrusia!* He slipped the notebook into the inside pocket of his uniform blouse, grabbed his cap off the coat tree, then went down to the street to his waiting vehicle.

Although five years had gone by since he'd visited the depot at Symferopil, he had no difficulty directing his driver to the particular warehouse he was looking for. The millions of tons of military supplies contained in the sprawling facility were also the subject of negotiations between Russia and Ukraine. The installation had remained under joint command according to the temporary agreement with the Russians, but it was evident from the recent direction of the Masandra talks that most of the equipment and materiel would go to Russia. That would create a serious problem for the handful of former Moscow Guards officers who had delivered certain important items to Building A-35 in the reserve fuel storage area.

"This will do nicely, Sergeant Astafyev. I will be about thirty minutes." His driver got out and opened the rear door of the aging Voyska sedan. General Nastenko disappeared through the door into the warehouse.

As he walked down the aisle between the stacks of sundry petroleum products and ship containers, General Nastenko thought about the spectrum of sensitive material they contained, including the remains of a considerable number of persons who had been a threat to the Revolution. The problem now was that no one among the coterie of seven patriots had foreseen the breakup of the Soviet Union and the dismembering of the giant security service's apparatus. At three sites in Russia and Ukraine, 165 nuclear weapons were secreted: the forty-one at Symferopil and a like number at Odessa, with the remaining eighty-three weapons stored near Moscow. Seven men were alive who knew of their existence. Pavlo Nastenko was now aware that an eighth officer also knew of the secreted weapons.

He stood in the dim light in front of the shipping container. The marine transport unit looked just like the hundreds of others in the huge warehouse. Only the series of numbers and letters stenciled on the rear doors—K17757MB—identified it as the one he was looking for. Close examination revealed that it had not been moved since he had last visited. He punched in the lock code, recalling his great blunder in putting the combination in the meteorological data book: the idea had been to facilitate passing on all the needed information to another person—quickly, if necessary. *A stupid decision. You must have laughed at that one, Katrusia.*

General Nastenko swung open the doors. The only light came from the dirty clerestory windows high overhead in the World War II frame building. He stared at the rows of two-hundred-liter fuel drums. Even in the dim light, he could clearly see that they had been moved around on the floor of the container; then a quick count confirmed that one was missing. The old security officer withdrew a penlight from his blouse, jumped up on the front row of barrels, and hurriedly began to check off the numbers stenciled on the tops of the drums against the numbers in the notebook. He checked and then checked them all again. It was not enough to know that a weapon was missing; he had to know which one it was. Even with his highly trained and disciplined mind, General Nastenko behaved like a man anxiously looking for his lost pocketbook.

The Chief of State Security for the Krymska Oblast sat down on the top of one of the drums in the front row. He sat there for several minutes, tapping the cover of the notebook with his pencil, oblivious to the heavy layer of dust embedding itself in his perfectly tailored, crisp uniform. He slowly swung his feet, kicking the side of the barrel with his heels as a schoolboy would do. He thought of Kateryna and of how an old, foolish man had been duped; but, strangely, he was not angry. After all, he almost smiled, Lieutenant Colonel Kateryna Romanivna Kovalevska had merely performed precisely as she had been trained to perform. The pliable and receptive clay of youth had been successfully molded and fire-hardened into an efficient agent of espionage. *So, it has finally happened. A weapon of mass destruction is now adrift in the world. And Ukraine has lost one of her brightest flowers. The Soviet Union and now Ukraine, by default, have only themselves to blame.*

As he sat alone in the cavernous, gloomy building, General Nastenko was also thinking about something else—something only he and one of the six Russian officers in the former Moscow Guards Directorate knew. *Sergey would never admit the error. It would be the end of him.* Because of an unavoidable last-minute complication in transporting the secreted weapons in 1989, the ones stored at Symferopil had been switched with the like number in the lot at Odessa. Two identical marine containers had been involved, and the tactical configurations of the two groups of weapons were also identical—except for one difference. General Nastenko looked at the rows of green drums containing the variously configured twenty-kiloton nuclear weapons. *Your clients have gotten more than they bargained for, Katrusia.*

* * *

Waddy gazed forlornly at the distant lights of Gibraltar while *Samora* began her passage through the gateway from the Mediterranean to enter the broad reaches of the North Atlantic Ocean. Peter and Timothy had regaled him mercilessly with tales of the delights to be found in La Linea and across Gibraltar Bay in Algeciras. With a sigh he turned to look into the blackness of the channel leading to three weeks at sea.

The two young Brits had exchanged surprised glances when Stan told them that *Aletheia* would not even be calling at the Canary Islands. A port call at Los Christianos on Tenerife or the neighboring island of Gomera was de rigueur for Med-to-Indies delivery crews. Waddy had argued that a stop in the Canaries would serve to make the voyage look normal, but Stan had decided against it—not because of Waddy's self-serving reasoning, but because of the burden of knowledge that came from many long ocean passages. As much as he liked his two new sailors, Stan was heedful of the ages-old, collective wisdom of the masters of countless ocean-sailing vessels: his competent, conscientious, hardworking seamen could metamorphose, upon release at a foreign port, into total strangers. Stan could not risk even a slight chance that Peter's and Timothy's foray into Los Christianos would end in a rum squall, or worse. Even Waddy, although he did not drink, could easily get into a scrape involving a Canarian young lady. *Samora* would immediately be put at risk, subject to seizure and inspection. Stan had explained to Peter and Timothy that *Aletheia* was behind schedule and the owner was anxious for her delivery to the Leeward Islands.

The route to Tortola in the British Virgin Islands would be along the standard track, not unlike that followed by Columbus a little more than five hundred years earlier when he headed into the great unknown after his last stop at Isla Gomera to take on water and stores and to spend a few days with a mistress. Stan looked at the large chart of the North Atlantic while *Samora* lifted with the passage of a wave beneath her hull. He immediately recalled two memorable downwind "sleigh rides" in the steady, twenty-knot trade winds; the regular, trade-wind-driven wave pattern would be well developed by the time *Samora* passed between Portugal's Madeira and Spain's Canary Islands, four hundred miles off the coast of Morocco. The only trick was to dip far enough south to get well into the trades. The direct great-circle route to the Virgin Islands, while approximately 250 miles shorter, would risk sailing into the Bermuda High, a huge, seasonally wandering region of high pressure and no wind around which the atmosphere and currents of the North Atlantic Ocean revolved in a giant, clockwise pinwheel.

No hurricane threat, either. Peter and Timothy had both asked about the passage being made in May, but the Atlantic hurricane season did not officially begin until June; and early-season hurricanes were nearly always mild. *Samora* was a large, well-found yacht. Stan was reasonably comfortable with the situation.

"But why are the owners giving up the summer season in the Med?" Peter had asked.

"Money," had been Stan's simple response. "The same money that is paying you so well for this delivery." Big yachts were, above everything else, consumers of huge sums of money, and even the wealthy people who owned them generally tried to staunch the hemorrhage. More money was to be made in the growing charter business in the western South Pacific. The unalloyed explanation had summoned the first of Peter's and Timothy's shrugs and grins.

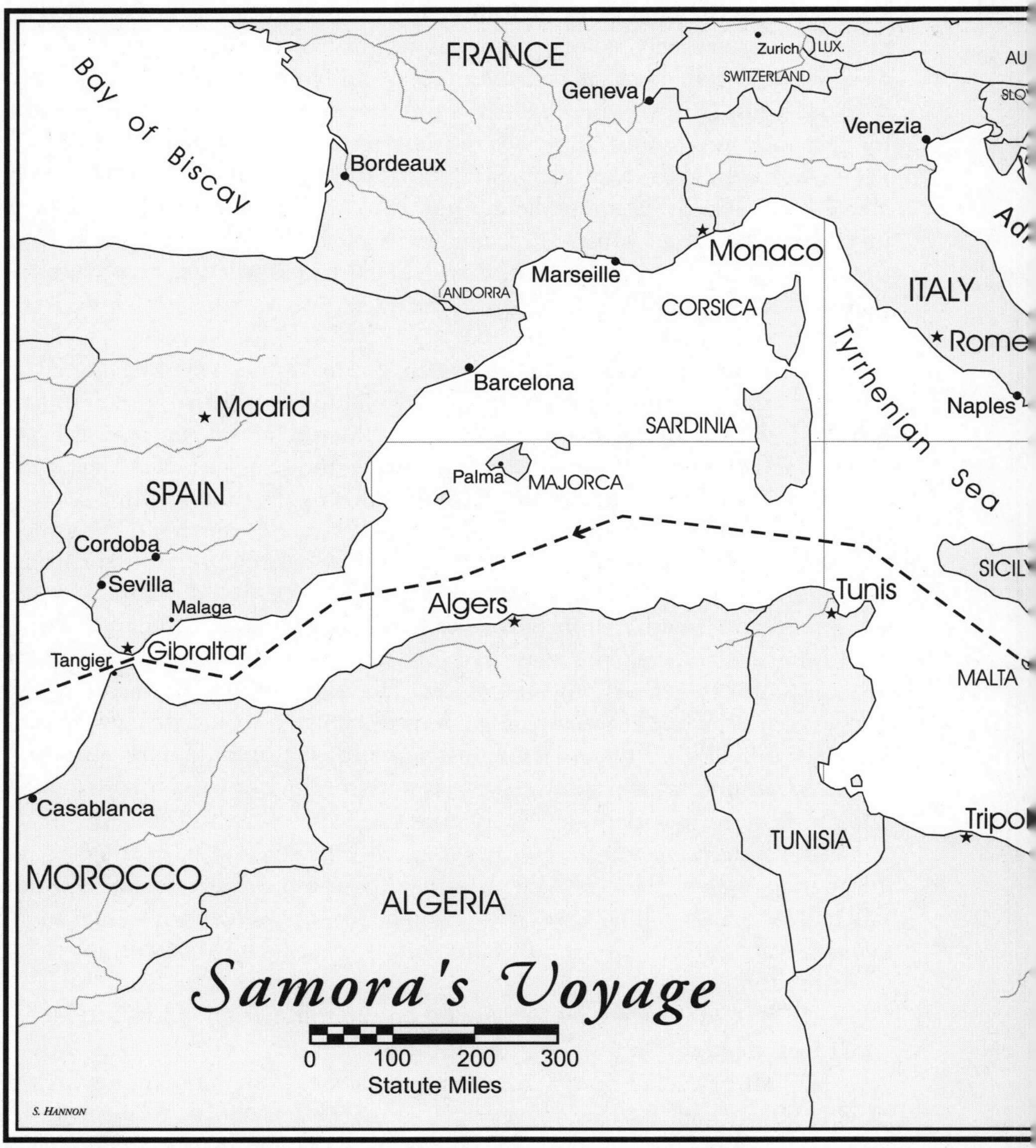
Bay of Biscay
FRANCE
Zurich
LUX.
SWITZERLAND
Geneva
Bordeaux
Venezia
Monaco
Marseille
ANDORRA
CORSICA
ITALY
Rome
Barcelona
Tyrrhenian Sea
Madrid
SARDINIA
Naples
Palma
MAJORCA
SPAIN
Cordoba
Sevilla
Malaga
Algers
Tunis
SICILY
Tangier
Gibraltar
MALTA
Casablanca
TUNISIA
MOROCCO
ALGERIA
Samora's Voyage
0 100 200 300
Statute Miles
S. HANNON

HUNGARY
ROMANIA
MOLDOVA
Odessa
Dneiper R.
UKRAINE
Zagreb
CROATIA
Symferopil
Sevastopil
Yalta
Bucharest
Belgrade
BOSNIA
Sarajevo
Constanta
SERBIA
Sea
Varna
Black
MONTENEGRO
Sofia
BULGARIA
Sea
MACEDONIA
Istanbul
ALBANIA
G R E E C E
Limnos
Ankara
Ionian Sea
Aegean Sea
Lesbos
TURKEY
Athens
Andros
Catania
Milos
Valletta
CRETE
Nicosia
Mediterranean Sea
CYPRUS
Beirut
LEBANON
Tel Aviv
Amman
ISRAEL
Banghazi
Alexandria
JORDAN
Cairo
Suez
LIBYA
EGYPT

Like all of their kind, the young professional sailors rarely questioned the decisions of the often mysterious owners of the grand yachts they crewed—decisions that made it possible for them to pursue their pleasant life-style.

12

Sevastopil, Wednesday, May 4

General Nastenko had spent most of the past two days thinking about, analyzing, and cross-connecting all of the considerations. He had no reason to hurry, after all; by the time he visited Symferopil, Kateryna had been gone for more than a week. The yacht could easily have traveled to any point in the Mediterranean: innumerable places where the weapon could be sent on its way to any part of the world. It was already in the hands of whoever had purchased it, he had nearly concluded.

The yield of the missing weapon was about the same as the one detonated over Nagasaki. If it were exploded in a building in Tel Aviv, General Nastenko had no doubt that the Israelis would instantly respond, massively, with their own nuclear weapons. Five years previously, the best Soviet intelligence had estimated that the Israelis possessed approximately two hundred aircraft- and missile-deliverable weapons, including more than twenty thermonuclear devices. Israel had long realized that her neighbors could not mount an effective assault on her lands without Soviet assistance, and the First Chief Directorate had long known that many of the Israeli missiles at Hirbat Zachariah, including several of the big thermonuclear weapons, were targeted at Soviet cities to discourage another invasion like the one that had initiated the 1973 Yom Kippur War. General Nastenko knew full well that in addition to several large cities, the Fleet headquarters was also ground zero for an Israeli one-megaton weapon.

Mossad agents told us, directly, of the missile targeting, he smiled to himself. As much as he despised the Israelis, for reasons he really did not understand, he greatly admired their militarism and their preparedness—driven by their fanatical determination to survive as a people in a land of their own—just as his own Ukrainians were driven. *But now? Would they strike us now? They would have to know that it was a terrorist weapon, wouldn't they? But Amman, Baghdad, Teheran, Damascus, Beirut, and Riyadh would be flattened. Probably ten million people would be killed. Millions of children would die instantly or later from injuries and radiation poisoning. And all to perhaps save one other child who, ironically, was also injured by nuclear radiation.*

You could not possibly have arranged this before you left for America, Katrusia. There was no time. Although no one had specifically suggested the present problem, the Russians had demanded hurried assignments to the weapons teams to avoid any "unnecessary liaisons." *And you were watched throughout your stay in America—except during the last week. That was when you made your arrangement.*

But in reaction to the instincts that had served him so well throughout his career in the covert service of his beloved Soviet Union, General Nastenko did not believe that Kateryna had made a transaction with Middle Easterners. Sofiia notwithstanding, he felt that she would not deal with them. *No, not at any price—at least not for use of the weapon within the Middle East. That would certainly engulf Ukraine if Israel implemented her Soviet Union-era targeting. Yes, they would correctly assume that it was a Soviet weapon, stolen or not, and strike the former Union out of revenge and frustration alone, if not because it was a continued threat. You know that, don't you Katrusia? Of course you do. I am certain that weapon has another destiny. Perhaps she was contacted by a group such as the one that so bungled the job in New York. Where do they find such incompetent, stupid hooligans? No wonder the Israelis always win.*

A naval demolition device? Was it simply to safeguard the weapon during its voyage in a marine environment? Perhaps. But if the underwater configuration is functionally necessary, that fact greatly reduces the range of intended targets. What will your clients think when it turns out their purchase is of a ten-fold larger yield, Katrusia?

Why that big yacht? The weapon could have been transshipped from the yacht at any number of places in the Mediterranean, but why would they take the risk of another connection? That large yacht was needed for a long ocean voyage. Yes, it has to be going to America. You arrogant, capitalist vermin—now it's your turn. You are the only ones who have unleashed the horror of atomic weaponry upon other people. We have never done it. Our weapons are only for defense of the Motherland. That is precisely why a handful of true patriots secreted a few beyond the reach of the stupid politicians who have been duped by the West. You Western swine certainly deserve to have the little creature you invented afflict your own precious, virgin land.

General Nastenko smiled at his unconcealed hatred for the West, America in particular. A part of him cheered Kateryna on. So, he thought, perhaps nothing should be done. Unless and until it became necessary to remove the rest of the weapons from the depots at Odessa and Symferopil, there would be little chance that anyone else in the group would become aware that the device was missing.

Perhaps, Katrusia, you have given me the opportunity I have waited for—a way, at last, to give something back to the Russians. Throughout his career he had often turned a bad situation to his advantage, yet another reason for the old warrior's flag-rank officer's stars on his epaulets. The general smiled again, recalling his admiration of Britain's World War II prime minister. Sir Winston had often remarked that the Chinese ideogram for "crisis" combined the forms for "danger" and "opportunity." *And so it is. The present situation offers both dangers and opportunities.* He began to sense an opportunity.

"Captain Khalavchenko, I have determined that the yacht *Aletheia* has most probably left the Mediterranean. I need to confirm this. Acquire all information available on a sighting at Gibraltar. The most likely window of transit was Sunday or Monday."

He thought of the real-time satellite surveillance of all the choke points in the Mediterranean. *The pig Russians have a damned picture of that yacht right at this moment!* As sorely as he was tempted, he could not tip the Russians to his interest in the yacht. Until he was entirely sure of his direction, he had to keep tight control. *Yes, I must rely only upon my own resources. I still have a few you Russian swine do not know about.*

* * *

The wind had backed and freshened when the yacht came under the full influence of the northeast trade winds—now driving her southwesterly under full sail at fourteen knots, with the further addition of the Canary current's one-knot drift over the ocean floor as they passed between Madeira and the Canary Islands. They were now well out into the North Atlantic. With the unvarying strength and direction of the twenty-knot winds, *Samora* settled down for the long ocean crossing, her piloting under the continual vigilance and tireless efforts of Fred.

Her crew was also well settled into the routine of the ocean passage. Rather than the rotating watches Stan had offered, they had unanimously opted for a fixed schedule: Kateryna had the midmorning duty when most of the crew would be on deck enjoying the sun and sea during their off watch; Waddy's turn was in the afternoon, followed by Peter and then quiet Timothy, who actually wanted the late-night watch. Stan was on deck with his sextant before dawn, followed by Kateryna to complete the cycle.

Even with the replacement GPS navigation receiver, Stan persisted with his celestial navigation. The episode in the Black Sea had provided a stark reminder of the reality of their isolation on a vast ocean, *Samora*'s sophisticated navigation appointments notwithstanding. Stan was very thankful that the sea conditions had been calm when the GPS failed; typically, such things only happen in the midst of a gale, with the vessel approaching an unfamiliar lee shore at night and probably coincident with the disability of the yacht and/or her rigging or crew. Murphy had been the master of a sailing vessel, Stan was firmly convinced.

He had practiced the ancient form of navigation for over thirty-five years, yet he remained amazed and fascinated by the fact that the points of light wheeling overhead could tell him, within a mile, where he was—anywhere on the surface of the earth. Stan liked being alone on the deck of a grand yacht, surging through the seas at dawn, waiting for the appearance of a horizon sufficiently defined to take his observations before the stars faded from sight. And, unlike the evening twilight, the emerging daylight usually presented a clear horizon.

Kateryna luxuriated in the warm sunshine on *Samora*'s foredeck. Stan had relaxed the safety line requirement during the daylight hours, but only when more than one person was topside. Even Waddy did not have to be told to wear his harness when he was on deck at night. "You look contented," he said, squatting next to her on the large blanket she'd spread across *Samora*'s smooth teak decking. Lying on her stomach, Kateryna was wearing only the bottom of a bikini. Stan's thoughts flashed back to that riverside beach in the bottom of Marble Canyon.

"We've met like this before, haven't we?" he said to the nearly sleeping woman.

Kateryna turned her head, squinting up into the brilliant early afternoon sunlight. "Yes, but the water was colder and there was a nice beach, wasn't there, Philip?" She rolled over, clutching her bikini top to her breasts. Stan could not resist his barely disguised stare. With its slightly Asian skin tone, Kateryna's body had turned golden under the warm sunlight of the Mediterranean and the near-tropical Atlantic. He glanced away as she reassembled.

"Listen." She turned to look toward the cockpit. "I didn't know he played the flute."

"Neither did I." Waddy was sitting in the helmsman's seat, slouched back, one ankle resting on the other knee while he concentrated on his instrument. Stan's thoughts returned to the canyonlands—to a petroglyph he had seen at the mouth of Smith Fork in Glen Canyon. "Come on back. I'm going to give him his first lesson in blue-water helmsmanship." Again he could not divert his stare as Kateryna got up and looped the blanket over her arm, clutching Stan's shoulder for support on the sloping and moving deck. Other than the ample contents of the bright yellow bikini top, nothing jiggled.

Samora was well into the huge waves generated by the steady trade winds. With several hundred miles of "fetch," the wave pattern was well developed and regular, rhythmically overtaking the yacht as the succession of massive undulations caught up with her. Her gracefully tapered stern lifted, then accelerated with the surface of the sea, the wave moving through the water but carrying none of it along; then she settled and slowed behind the broad dome as it continued across the North Atlantic, relentlessly propelled and reinforced by the winds. It was like a gentle roller coaster ride, with the yacht alternately rising and surging and then slowing and settling into the troughs in the steady pattern. Fred had to work to keep the huge yacht on course as each wave tried to slew her stern and throw her beam-on, into the path of those following in their timeless quest for the unattainable horizon.

"He's pretty good, Cap'n," Peter said, motioning to Waddy. Everyone listened appreciatively while Waddy finished the last few bars of *Harlem Nocturne.*

"Is that a native flute, John?" Kateryna asked, looking at the odd instrument in his hands.

He handed it to her "The ulna bone of a golden eagle." She examined it closely and passed it on to Stan.

"How far back in your people's history have flutes like this been made?" Stan also scrutinized the delicate little instrument.

"So far as we know, perhaps 2,000 years. We have even retained some of the melodies the ancient ones knew. They are played in the kiva ceremonies of the Horn/Flute Clan in my native land—what your people named British Columbia." He grinned at Peter and Timothy, with a glance at Stan.

Stan stared out at the endless expanse of sea and thought again about how shallow his own culture was, compared to that of Waddy's people. He shook off the thought. "Well, hotshot, are you ready?" He clapped his friend on the shoulder. "Get a good grip on the wheel."

Waddy straightened around in the helmsman's seat and wrapped his fingers around *Samora*'s leather-covered wheel. The yacht was just slowing and settling into a trough when Stan reached down and clicked off the autopilot. He glanced aft at the foaming crest of the next approaching wave, a half-dozen boat lengths behind.

"Damn!" Waddy exclaimed, feeling the unexpected force on *Samora*'s unassisted rudder.

"Okay, John, as the wave starts to lift the boat, she'll try to round up into the wind. So you have to turn the wheel out of her turn, just like in a car starting to spin out. Also, when she rises out of the trough the full force of the wind will catch her and she'll heel. This will also make her try to round up. Just remember, the boat is always trying to head up into the wind."

The giant mainsail, whose larger, lower portion had been blanketed by the approaching wave, filled and tightened under the full brunt of the fresh twenty-knot breeze. "Son of a bitch!" Waddy turned the wheel to port as the wave lifted *Samora*'s starboard quarter. "Damn! I can feel the whole boat. I can feel the rudder vibrate and the force on the sails!" Even with the great mechanical advantage the six-foot-diameter wheel and the worm-geared rudder linkage provided, Waddy had to brace his foot against the cockpit to control the helm.

"Now, imagine being up here at night, skunk black, in forty knots of wind, squally conditions, with three thousand square feet of storm spinnaker up there, and even bigger waves trying to crawl up your ass."

"No thank you."

"Even an experienced helmsman is good for maybe an hour, max, in such conditions. It's not just physical; it's mentally exhausting. Your constant thought is having the yacht round up and broach, being thrown onto her beam ends, with a giant sea roaring down behind you."

"This is tiring enough. Have to pay attention every second. I just can't believe how alive this big mother feels . . . sorry, Philip."

Peter and Timothy were beaming in unison, watching Waddy struggle with *Samora*'s helm.

"John, the secret is to anticipate," Peter volunteered in his delightful Merseyside accent. Nearly every time Stan heard either of the young Liverpoolians speak, he thought of the Beatles. "Once the wave has got the rudder, you got yourself a la' a work. You have to sense the approaching wave and trim downwind. It's a la' easier then. As she runs down into the trough, turn up the back side of the wave to keep your wind and not lose way. Then turn down into the next cycle as the wind and the next wave take you. It becomes automatic. You'll see. Ready to put up the 'chute?"

"No way, guy," Waddy shot back, concentrating on his work.

Stan knew that Peter and Timothy were itching to set *Samora*'s smaller, heavy spinnaker, but he dismissed the idea as out of the question. A job for at least a half-dozen strong, seasoned, blue water sailors, a spinnaker was still a giant handful in a heavy seaway—even with the new spars and rigging. Regardless, Stan had almost relented, admitting to himself that he longed to feel the big yacht surf down the front sides of the waves, being sailed on the razor edge of her maximum performance. Visions of the last, stormy Tahiti Race filled his thoughts.

The yacht starting to round up brought him back to reality. Peter and Timothy sprang for the wheel, in unison with Stan, to rescue Waddy from a particularly large sleeper that started to turn the huge yacht into the wind, broadside to the wave pattern.

"Once one a those monsters grabs her, it's a toot, huh, John?" Peter laughed after *Samora* once again settled down on her course. "Kind'a lets you know what life would be like for the next couple'a weeks if we lost Fred." Peter's last comment earned him a long glance from Waddy.

"And it's not just the guy driving the boat," Stan said. "Everyone below, lying in his bunk, wonders whether the next one will broach her. Sort of like the rush of fear you get when your raft goes broadside into a hole in Lava Falls, right, John?" Stan added, fielding quizzical looks from Peter and Timothy.

"Yeah, I'd like to see these two on a good ride through Crystal and Lava," Waddy said, reinforcing his self-esteem. He flashed his amazing grin at the two young Brits.

"We're talking about the Colorado River through Grand Canyon, guys," Stan said. "It just happens that our helmsman here is one of the premier boatmen on the river." Instantly, Kateryna gave him a sharp look. *Oh, shit! Shouldn't have said that.*

"Bloody well right I'd go for that," Peter responded, matching Timothy's effusive grin. "I've heard all me life about rafting down the Colorado. It's on me list, mate."

"Well, if you guys ever get up to Vancouver, look me up. I'll give you a ride you won't soon forget," Waddy laughed, glad to have his inning. He was concentrating on the compass when Stan clicked on the autopilot. The wheel turned quickly under the mechanical force, responding to Fred's reaction to the amateur's clumsy effort to sail his boat.

"What about you, Catherine? Want to give it a try?"

"Not dressed like this, I'm not," she said slowly, picturing the spectacle she would provide for the four men sitting around her. "Maybe later on," she smiled, looking intently at Stan while arching her bronzed back. Her thick, loose hair gleamed blue-black in the dazzling sunlight. Stan flushed slightly, wondering if the others had caught Kateryna's subtle double entendre.

The overhead digital clock clicked past eleven when Stan stretched out in the ample double bunk in *Samora*'s aft master cabin. They had all enjoyed a drawn-out supper and quiet conversation in the snug security of *Samora*'s bridge deck cockpit. Following a particularly spectacular conch-pink/indigo satin dusk, everyone had lingered to enjoy the huge yellow moon rising full above the wave tops, relentlessly overtaking *Samora* from the now faraway land masses of Europe and Africa. All was well, Stan thought, recalling the ease with which the old yacht and her crew had settled into the rhythm of an ocean crossing: the continual blending of days and nights; the off-watch leisure time; the dawn routine with the sextant; the exuberant plunging of the sleek yacht through the brilliant days; the happy conversations of her crew.

Samora was large enough for each of her passengers to find a quiet spot to be alone with a book or the deep thoughts that always seem to blossom on a sailing yacht far at sea. The world consisted only of *Samora* and her crew, surrounded by the wave tops disappearing to infinity in all directions and surmounted by the full hemisphere of the sky: cerulean blue and dotted with puffs of clouds by day, an ink-black canopy profused with countless stars by night, awaiting the eerie, ivory glow of the rising moon.

Stan had treated himself to a bath in *Samora*'s opulent marble tub, reserved for the occupant of the master cabin. As he settled clean and fresh into the comfortable bed, he looked up at the soft red glow from the repeater dials built into the teak paneling above the double-wide bunk. A glance at the several gauges summarized the yacht's performance for her master: course, 236° true; wind speed, twenty-two knots; hull speed, fourteen knots, surging to seventeen with the wave crests and falling to eleven in the troughs. The inclinometer showed that the force on the huge spread of sail heeled the yacht 8 degrees.

Stan had assumed his favorite position on the leeward side of the bunk, resting against the hull and listening to the barely audible water rushing past *Samora*'s teakwood topsides. He was almost asleep when he thought he heard the click of the cabin door. His next sensation was the rustle of soft fabric, followed by the gentle touch of hair brushing across his face. The hair was slightly damp and carried a faint odor of balsam and lavender. He was fully awake when his lips felt the same soft, open mouth they experienced that night at the Luqa airport. The delicate sensation on his face was followed by the all-encompassing warmth of a hard, silken body pressing and moving against the whole of him. He started to speak, but two insistent fingers across his lips ended the impulse. Stan felt time and conscious awareness dissolve as he and Kateryna blended into—matching and answering—the rhythmic rising and falling, the surging and settling, of *Samora* and the sea.

"Looks like that nice cabin forward, the one with the shower, will be yours, mate," Peter said to his companion late that evening on *Samora*'s moon-light-washed bridge deck.

"You don't say."

"Aye, I think the lady will be moving into the master cabin."

13

SEVASTOPIL, FRIDAY, MAY 6

"We have a confirmed sighting, sir," General Nastenko's operations officer announced over the intercom. "You were correct. *Aletheia* exited the Mediterranean at Gibraltar last Monday. One of our grain carriers bound for Cuba overtook the yacht at dusk, just inside the traffic lanes through the strait."

"Good work. Anything at all on her ownership, yet?"

"She is Portuguese, at least on paper, but her ownership becomes murky. There seem to be a number of Western-style business groups involved, each one leading to another. As of now, I have her traced to a Swiss company doing business in Singapore, but the Swiss refuse . . . Sir, we do not have the resources to– –"

"Yes, Captain, I understand," the general sighed, reminded again of the now-familiar frustration. *This is absurd. Chasing paper like some Wall Street swine while that capitalist yacht cruises across the Atlantic.* In his Soviet position he could have easily arranged for the yacht to be seized—or simply sunk, once she was clear of the Sixth Fleet's close scrutiny in the Mediterranean. *Now? Now I am nearly helpless . . . but perhaps it is fortunate that it is so. Keeps me from doing something precipitous—losing my chance with the Russians.*

He stared at a large sailing chart of the North Atlantic. *If she did not stop in the Canaries, she should be about there.* He placed his finger at a point one-third of the distance between Gibraltar and the chain of islands ringing the eastern Caribbean Sea. General Nastenko knew that a sailing vessel was constrained by the existence of the Bermuda High, but once the yacht was past the windless area to the north, she could as easily turn up the east coast of North America as she could sail to South America. *Perhaps she is going to Colombia . . . No. No, you would not deal with them.*

Once again the anger welled up under the old officer's starched collar. He glanced at his desk calendar and then got up to assume his thinking position in front of the window. *Those pig-sucking Russians! Over two weeks now.* Immediately after Kateryna's disappearance, he had called the head of the weapons destruction team in Moscow. The man was a former First Chief Directorate officer, now holding a similar position in the Russian Federation Foreign Intelligence Service. He had promised a copy of the surveillance report for the weapons team that had been sent to Pueblo—more specifically, the report detailing the activities of Lieutenant Colonel Kateryna Kovalevska.

Someone or something has intervened here. A simple report. It should not be a problem. It should be no surprise that I have an interest in the activities of one of my officers. He slowly sat back down in his chair. *It is because she has been so effective on the negotiating team. They have something on her and are waiting to spring it. Of course, that's it!* General Nastenko reflected on the irony of the situation. He had put Kateryna on the negotiating team to help Ukraine, and now whatever was in the report that had aroused the Russians' interest would ultimately hurt Ukraine in the negotiations.

All he had learned shortly after her return was that she had disappeared during her last week in America. And that had been gleaned only from an offhand remark by one of the Russians on the team. When he had confronted her about the unaccounted week, she had simply told him that she had needed to get away, had rented a car, and taken a little vacation. The explanation fully satisfied him at the time. His new relationship with her had dispelled any lingering questions. *How very clever you are, Katrusia. I must have that report! But I cannot pursue more contacts in Moscow. They think you are on a special assignment.*

His thoughts were interrupted by his intercom. "Sir, we have further information."

He quickly read the report from the Ukrainian agent in Malta. *Aletheia* had left from there to travel to Greece and had returned a few days later, late in the evening of April 27. The yacht had taken on three crew, one of whom was a woman who matched Kateryna's description. Though she had not been seen, the agent felt that Sofiia had probably left on a private flight from Luqa. *Aletheia* had departed, bound west for Panama and the South Pacific, early on April 29. The report was frustratingly cryptic. The agent had not been alerted to *Aletheia* until after the yacht had departed Malta.

So there was not enough time to travel to the Middle East, yet arrive in Malta late on the twenty-seventh. That settles it—it's not Israel; the weapon has to be going to America. He sprang up to stand in front of his window. He stood there for several minutes, concentrating. *Could the whole strange episode have been arranged by American authorities to embarrass Ukraine and Russia? Does the West need some excuse to back out of the treaty or the continuation of its promised assistance? Another of their CIA schemes . . . ? No, that is too far fetched—and there wasn't time. Kateryna was only selected at the last minute.*

Kateryna's duplicity aside, and despite the welcome prospect of the weapon's use in America, he was fundamentally worried that the loss of the weapon could expose the existence of the others. That, in turn, would have a disastrous impact on Ukraine—and on him. He had almost decided what he must do.

14

North Atlantic Ocean, May 11

Stan was pleased with *Samora*'s performance. She had averaged over 300 nautical miles per day since entering the trade winds, and they were now about 1,200 miles out of Road Town, their landfall on Tortola in the British Virgin Islands. But he was not pleased with what he was seeing on the printout from the weatherfax. For the past thirty-six hours he'd been closely monitoring the tropical weather reports he'd picked up on short wave. It had started out with a report of a "disturbed area" 200 miles south-southwest of the Cape Verde Islands, at the eastern fringe of the reach of the Atlantic Ocean that was the notorious spawning ground for North Atlantic tropical storms. Twelve hours before, the disturbed area had become a tropical depression, moving west-northwest at fourteen knots. *Samora* was more than 300 miles northwest of the center of the depression, but she had slowed and was presently averaging only eleven knots. The collection of isobars on the weatherfax print now showed the classic outline of the leading edge of a developing tropical storm. Stan glanced at the barometer. The glass had fallen fifteen millibars in the past twenty-four hours. The eastern horizon was indistinct: an iron-gray smudge; the sky was filled with thin cirrus clouds that had been shredded into mare's tails by high altitude winds, followed by cirrus streamers advancing over wispy cirrostratus. The weather vanes all radiated from the southeast.

So much for the statistical start of the hurricane season. Looks like Mama Nature decided to move it up a couple of weeks. Strange weather this year: the floods in the Midwest last summer, the winter floods in Europe, record-breaking low temperatures and snow in the eastern U.S. this winter, the rainstorms after the L.A. earthquake, the fire storms in Australia. Now a May tropical storm is catching me out in the open.

The changing weather also disrupted the trade winds. *Samora* was now beam reaching in confused seas, with erratic wind coming from the north-northeast instead of nearly behind her. The steady trades had shifted in response to the atmospheric demand for an air mass to fill the deepening low pressure west-southwest of the Cape Verde Islands. With the changing wind and sea conditions, Stan knew that *Samora* would slow considerably. The winds would continue to back and intensify; as a result, the new wave patterns they generated, each running straight, would begin to intersect the trade wind-driven waves, creating a churning cauldron. Stan adjusted the knob on the shortwave to the frequency used by the National Oceanic and Atmospheric Administration. The detached, female voice he heard reported that since the last broadcast the weather system had been upgraded. With its sustained winds now estimated to be forty mph, the storm had acquired a new distinction: he was now Tropical Storm Alberto.

For centuries seafarers had given feminine designations to two of the most beloved and most respected circumstances of their lives at sea: their vessels and the violent, low-latitude tropical storms—both of which could kill them. Traditionally, the seaman felt that so long as he nurtured and maintained his fragile vessel, it would, in turn, protect and serve him. However, if he should neglect or abuse his ship, it would abandon him without remorse. Accordingly, by their universally adopted, culture- and ethnicity-independent convention, countless mariners carried to sea their perceived experiences on land, and their ships were not "it" but "she." And so it was with the sea itself. So long as the seaman was careful and respectful in his attitude toward the vast oceans of the world, he was safe, indeed happy. But if he were to become careless and trespass upon forbidden areas at forbidden times, he was gravely at risk. Thus, the oceans, in both their peaceful and their angry moods, were also "she."

The long-held conventions had changed in recent times, Stan thought as he plotted NOAA Radio's description of Alberto's position, 320 miles southeast of *Samora*. Men's names were now used alternately with women's to designate tropical storms. The changed convention had satisfied the mood of political correctness that was growing across the land, but it had little impact on those who lived their lives at sea.

The early to mid-season storms tended to plow across the Caribbean rather than recurving up the East Coast, but Stan also knew full well that they could go anywhere in the northwest quadrant. The National Weather Service was still a long way from being able to predict the tracks of the monstrous storms that emerged in the tropical waters of the North Atlantic Ocean. Under normal circumstances, he well understood that the prudent thing to do would be to change course to the north—immediately—to get as much distance as possible between the probable westward track of the storm and his vessel. The situation was the more urgent because *Samora* was in the "dangerous" semicircle of the approaching storm. Neither side was "safe," but in the northern hemisphere of the earth, the semicircle on the right-hand side of the storm, as seen when looking along its path, was more dangerous than the opposing semicircle. In the more dangerous half, the counterclockwise wind added to the forward speed of the whole storm. On the other side of the storm eye—the "navigable" semicircle—the wind speed was effectively reduced by the storm's rate of forward travel. With Alberto's current average rotational wind speed of forty mph, his highest effective wind was now fifty-six mph on the northern side of the storm track.

Stan knew it would be very risky trying to cross the path of the storm to get into the navigable semicircle. The seas would get even worse if he turned south, *Samora*'s speed could be reduced to three or four knots, and the storm path would only require a slight change to pass right over him. *Never, never, NEVER try to cross ahead of or try to outrun a tropical storm,* he recalled the centuries-old wisdom. On the other hand, he did not have the option of heading north. That would put him, at best, hard on the wind in seas that were now approaching the conditions inside a giant washing machine. His only real choice was to change course to the northwest, heading as closely into the wind as the seas and the sails would permit. If Alberto's track stayed generally westward, as such early-season storms almost always did before entering the Caribbean, *Samora* and Alberto would diverge quickly. And when the storm approached more closely, passing to the south, the wind would veer to the east permitting Samora to sail more northerly. But Stan knew it was all speculation, given the capriciousness of tropical storm tracks. One thing was absolutely certain. The last thing he wanted was to be anywhere near the Caribbean islands in the midst of what was likely to be a hurricane. His present course would almost certainly produce that situation.

Peter emerged from his cabin to peer over Stan's shoulder at the chart table. "What's up, Skipper?" he yawned. Following a glance at the chart, he looked up through the companionway at the eastern morning sky, radiating orange to red to murky-gray at the horizon.

The building and backing wind and the churning sea conditions also brought Timothy into the salon. The younger of the two English sailors looked at the plot of Alberto's position and *Samora*'s track. "She might spoil our whole day," he said matter-of-factly.

"Oh, you could say that, fellows," Stan replied as evenly as he could.

"'Bout only one choice, looks like, Skip," Peter observed. Timothy nodded in silence.

"Let's bring her up to 330 magnetic. See if she'll point that high," Stan said, getting up from the chart table and following Peter and Timothy up the companionway ladder. The three sailors turned *Samora* into the wind, reefed her sails, and then kept her as hard on the wind as the old yacht could manage without stalling. Pounding to windward through the churning seas, in gusty, thirty-knot winds under leaden skies, was a significant departure from the experience they had enjoyed for the past nine days in their warm, azure-skied, trade wind roller coaster ride.

"I think she'll hold 330 without pinching, Skip, but she'll be slow," Peter concluded after he'd steered to windward for a few minutes.

"Fall off to 315 and set Fred," Stan shouted back from the foredeck. He checked to be certain there was nothing that could come adrift in the wind-driven spume now sheeting over *Samora*'s bows. Timothy trimmed the sails for the new course and the yacht settled down to a steady eight knots, plunging into the building seas. Both Kateryna and Waddy came on deck to find out why *Samora*'s ride had changed so dramatically.

"To point any higher, we'll have to reef quite a bit more and of course she'll slow down," Stan told his crew, now assembled on the bridge deck. "The old gal just doesn't like to sail heeled past 18 or 20 degrees. Much beyond that and she'll just wallow like a turtle. She's pretty happy right now." Stan glanced at the inclinometer and the knotmeter. "No problem, unless Alberto decides to pay a visit to South Carolina." Stan squinted into the eastern sky which now closely resembled a World War II Japanese naval ensign. Peter and Timothy gave Stan knowing nods. Kateryna and Waddy stared at him blankly, not yet fully comprehending the situation.

"Peter, tell them what's going on. I've got to go below for a minute." Stan had suddenly thought of the forward water tank and the cargo nestled in its cradle. *I've got to transfer water from the aft tank to fill the forward one. No baffles in the forward tank now, just the weapon canister. If the boat gets really thrown around and a two-ton slug of water crashes back and forth in that tank . . . No problem if the tank's full.* Stan started the transfer pumps and went back on deck, thinking about *Samora*'s trim with nearly all the water and the weapon canister now forward of her center of buoyancy. *She'll be jamming her nose into a lot of green water. Can't be helped. She's a stout old lady.*

Following a careful explanation of the situation to Waddy and Kateryna, Stan outlined the watch changes that would have to be made. The comfortable five-watch day would now be reduced to three: Kateryna was likely to get sick, and Waddy would have to have help. He was learning fast, but he had no way of knowing of the greatly increased dangers to *Samora* and her crew.

***

The general watched closely while an overhead crane lowered the shipping container onto the tractor-trailer rig. He took the clipboard with the special authorization form and signed his name across the bottom, handing it back to the nervous senior sergeant.

Why is a general of state security, after duty hours, personally supervising the removal of a container of fuel? the sergeant thought while he checked the tie-downs securing the container to the trailer frame. He handed a copy of the authorization form to the driver of the truck and waved him out of Building A-35. The general got into the staff car and drove off ahead of the truck. *Why is he driving himself?* The sergeant shrugged as he walked out of the building. He had seen so many profound changes in the past three years that nothing really surprised him anymore.

The driver parked the truck in the impound area and walked over to the military bus stop. After the bus came and went, another state security vehicle stopped by the truck; a uniformed soldier got out and climbed up into the cab. General Nastenko would watch four such changes of drivers. After the last change, he drove the truck himself to its final destination.

Late that night, he walked into his office in the nearly deserted security headquarters. He stared out the window at the ships' anchor lights spread up and down the quiet harbor and then sat down at the typewriter behind his desk. The letter he needed to write was the second part of his plan. *At least seven more days,* he thought, glancing at the chart of the North Atlantic Ocean tacked to the wall behind the desk. *Plenty of time.* He stared at the blank sheet of paper in the typewriter. While he carefully considered the content of the letter, he also thought about the following evening's work. He would be arranging for the transport of another container from the reserve military depot outside of Odessa.

He typed in the heading of the letter:

United States Arms Control and Disarmament Agency
320 twenty-first Street, Northwest
Washington, D.C. 20451
<u>Attention</u>: William Grosvenor, Director
<u>Re</u>: Tactical Arms Reduction Treaty
<u>Personal and Confidential</u>

15

THIRTY MILES EAST OF THE BAHAMA ISLANDS, MAY 16

Stan sat at the chart table, his feet splayed out to either side, struggling to hold the parallel rule with one hand and the pair of dividers with the other. He drew a little square on the chart and penciled in *1210, 5/16. Error added to uncertainty added to vagueness.*

Peter looked down at the line of little squares progressing generally westward from the larger triangle, the last good fix noted on the chart. The last satellite fix had been at noon two days before. Peter also looked at the dark gauges and LCDs mounted in the bulkhead above the chart table. Every gauge and liquid crystal display monitoring the instruments located at the masthead was not functioning. A burst of electromagnetic radiation from a lightning strike had fried the masthead equipment. Even the radar on the mizzen mast got zapped. Stan was once again back to Columbus-era navigation techniques.

He placed his hand over the line of little squares he'd drawn on the chart, each of which represented *Samora*'s estimated position based upon his best guess at the course they had sailed and the distance the log showed they had traveled from the previous estimated position. "We're somewhere here," Stan noted quietly as he looked up.

Peter looked down at Stan's hand, resting over a section of the North Atlantic Ocean about thirty miles east of the Bahamas' Turks and Caicos Islands. Peter knew that the area covered by Stan's hand more closely represented the reality of their location than did the latest little square drawn on the chart.

"Maybe we'll get some daylight soon, Skip." Peter looked at the latest plot showing Alberto heading northwest across Cuba's midsection, about 175 miles west of them. The storm had been upgraded to a hurricane when its core winds rose above seventy-four mph three days before, as reported by NOAA Radio: the broadcast told Stan precisely where Alberto was, but it was no help telling him where his boat was. Unless he could take quick advantage of the sun finding a rift to peer through, all he had was his increasingly inaccurate, dead reckoning plot.

"Well, we'd better stay hove-to until I can get some kind of a fix. We're getting too close to all that dirt to the west of us." The last thing Stan wanted was to get *Samora* and her eleven-foot draft anywhere near the Bahama Islands and their banks littered with six-foot-deep water.

"Looks like those poor bastards in Florida are going to get slammed again. They still haven't recovered from Andrew."

"Yeah, looks like it, Peter. But he may yet miss the mainland and go through the Keys; or he may recurve more and head up the east coast." Stan visually extrapolated the now-northwesterly, erratic track of the hurricane.

Samora slowly drifted astern to the northwest, toward the Bahama chain, taking the stiff southeasterly gale broad on her port bow. Balanced with a storm jib and a reefed mizzen, the old Sparkman & Stephens masterpiece rode the still-substantial waves like a well behaved duck.

"So, where to now, Skipper? We can't get down to the Virgins," Peter stated the obvious.

"I'd like to go through the Northeast Providence Channel to Florida. But I'm sure as hell not going in there until things calm down, and I'm also not going in until I'm sure I have the channel. Otherwise, we'll have to go clear up and around Grand Bahama." Stan had another thought that he did not share with his competent English crewmen. It had occurred to him that the Coast Guard would have their hands full with the hurricane and would very likely pay him scant attention. *There's always a silver lining somewhere.*

"Probably be a la' a navigation aids sunk or adrift in the Bahamas, Skipper. I dunno about trying to run through Northeast Providence."

"We'll wait until we have the lights on Eleuthera and Great Abaco. They're land mounted on either side of the channel entrance, and it's then a straight shot to the Great Isaac Light on the other side. They're all far enough north to be okay . . . I think." Stan winked at Peter, who just grinned as he shook his head.

"Okay, Skip. You're more of an optimist than I am. There's bound to be a la' a ship traffic in the channel too."

"I'm counting on that. We can just get in line. But first, we need some sun so I can figure out where in hell we are. And Peter," Stan said with feigned seriousness, "besides everything else, we have another little factor involved here."

"What's that?"

"We are now well within the Bermuda Triangle."

"Should I tell John?" Peter grinned again, with Stan also starting to laugh.

"Peter, you're cruel."

16

U.S.C.G.C. Valiant, Florida Strait, May 19

"No response, Captain," Lieutenant Commander Reuter said after he walked out onto the bridge deck of the medium endurance cutter.

"Did you run through all the working channels, Mr. Reuter?"

"Yes, sir. Nothing." Both officers looked through their binoculars at the large ketch that had just passed the Great Isaac Lighthouse, five miles to the south of them.

"Okay, we'll close and board. This will be a good exercise for our young Mr. Pringle. Stand by at battle stations, Mr. Reuter."

The *Valiant*'s first officer gave the commands that ordered the crew to their battle stations and accelerated the powerful 210-foot Reliance Class cutter toward the yacht. The drug war was handled by the United States Coast Guard as though it were a full-blown shooting war—at least that was the way it was being played in the waters off the southern coast of Florida. The 25mm rapid-fire gun on the foredeck was loaded and manned. Twelve of the cutter's complement, including three determined young women who had managed to fight their way into the formerly all-male bastion, were on deck with automatic weapons and grenade launchers.

"Philip!" Waddy poked Stan in the shoulder and pointed backward.

Stan looked back over *Samora*'s transom at the large bow waves spreading out from a vessel bearing directly down on them. A look through his binoculars revealed a white hull with the distinctive red and blue bow stripes of the United States Coast Guard. *Oh shit!*

When the cutter approached within 300 yards, it bore off to starboard and slowed. Stan didn't need his binoculars to see that the gun on the foredeck was pointed right at him.

"Ahoy, sailing vessel," a loud hailer boomed across the water. "This is the United States Coast Guard. Heave to and prepare to be boarded."

Stan got everyone topside and they all bent to the task of bringing *Samora* into the wind and furling her sails. Stan then went below to gather the ship's papers and all their passports. The cutter was standing off and an inflatable launch was heading for *Samora* when he came back on deck.

The hard-bottomed inflatable came alongside. "All hands are topside, sir," Stan called down as Peter and Timothy lowered the boarding ladder and secured the dock lines the Coast Guardsmen tossed aboard; immediately six seamen scrambled up the ladder, taking positions in the center of the yacht and facing fore and aft. They were followed by a bosun's mate, dragging a large German Shepherd aboard; everyone but the dog wore body armor and carried automatic weapons. An officer then came up the ladder and stepped onto the bridge deck. Stan took another look at the cutter's foredeck gun, still trained on *Samora*; he fully understood that with its firing rate of 200 rounds per minute, the one-inch gun could cut the old wooden yacht in half in a matter of seconds. *Must have changed the rules. Thought they were supposed to safe that gun when the Coasties were in the line of fire.*

"Good afternoon, Captain, I am Ensign Herbert Pringle. You have been boarded pursuant to regulations of the United States Department of Transportation, Coast Guard, governing the operation of vessels in United States waters. I request that you produce your vessel's registration, departure documents, and identification for all persons aboard."

Stan understood that the Fourth Amendment to the United States Constitution did not apply to vessels in U.S. waters. The justices of the Supreme Court, in a rare display of deference to exigency, had specifically said so. He handed over the bundle of ship's papers and passports. *Can't be over twenty-two,* he thought while the obviously newly-minted "nugget"shuffled through the documents.

"Anyone below, Captain Thompson?"

"No, sir." Ensign Pringle motioned Stan toward the companionway. They were accompanied, in advance, by three of the seamen.

Stan and the young officer sat down at *Samora*'s salon table while two of the seamen began to search through the cabins. The third seaman's eyes and his automatic weapon were fixed on Stan.

"Sir, who is the owner of this vessel?"

"Buena Vista Enterprises. It's a Portuguese company, Ensign Pringle."

"Where are you bound, Captain?"

"We were going to BVI for a crew change, en route to Fiji, but Alberto changed our minds, sir."

"Yes, I'm sure he did." The officer glanced around *Samora*'s opulent main cabin. "Get a little breezy a few days ago?" he asked, his demeanor warming up slightly.

"Yes, sir. But we turned north early enough. Wasn't too bad."

"You're lucky he didn't follow you."

"Yes, sir. We all appreciate that. Got a little nervous when Alberto looked like he *was* turning."

"I'll bet. You've made no port calls since departing Malta on 29 April?" He was closely examining the Maltese departure document and checking the stamps in the passports.

"No, sir. Strictly business. My job is just to get her to Fiji as quickly as I can reasonably do so."

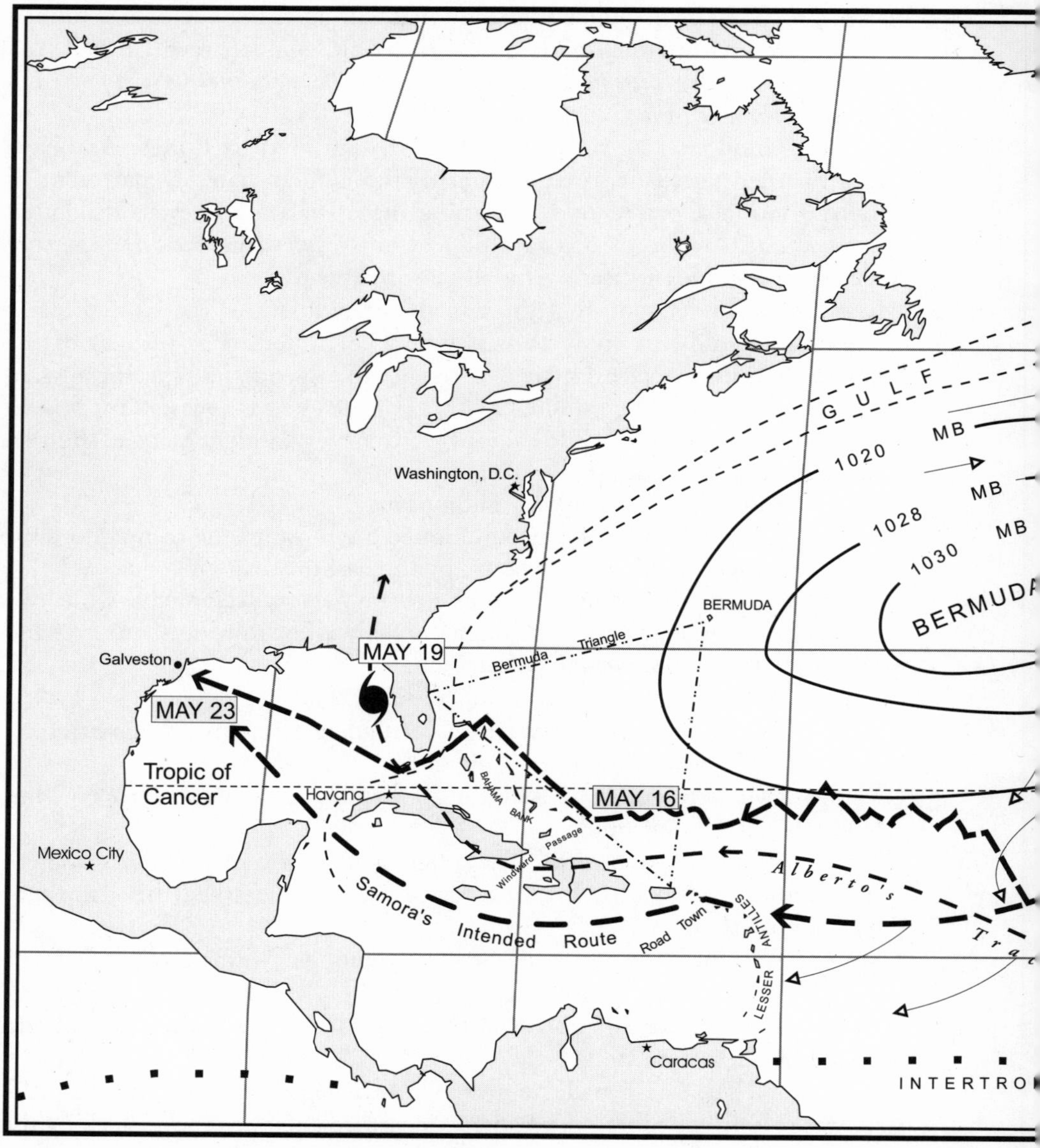

G U L F
1020 MB
1028 MB
1030 MB
BERMUDA
Washington, D.C.
BERMUDA
Bermuda Triangle
MAY 19
Galveston
MAY 23
Tropic of Cancer
Havana
BAHAMA BANK
MAY 16
Mexico City
Windward Passage
Alberto's
Samora's Intended Route
Road Town
LESSER ANTILLES
Tra
Caracas
INTERTRO

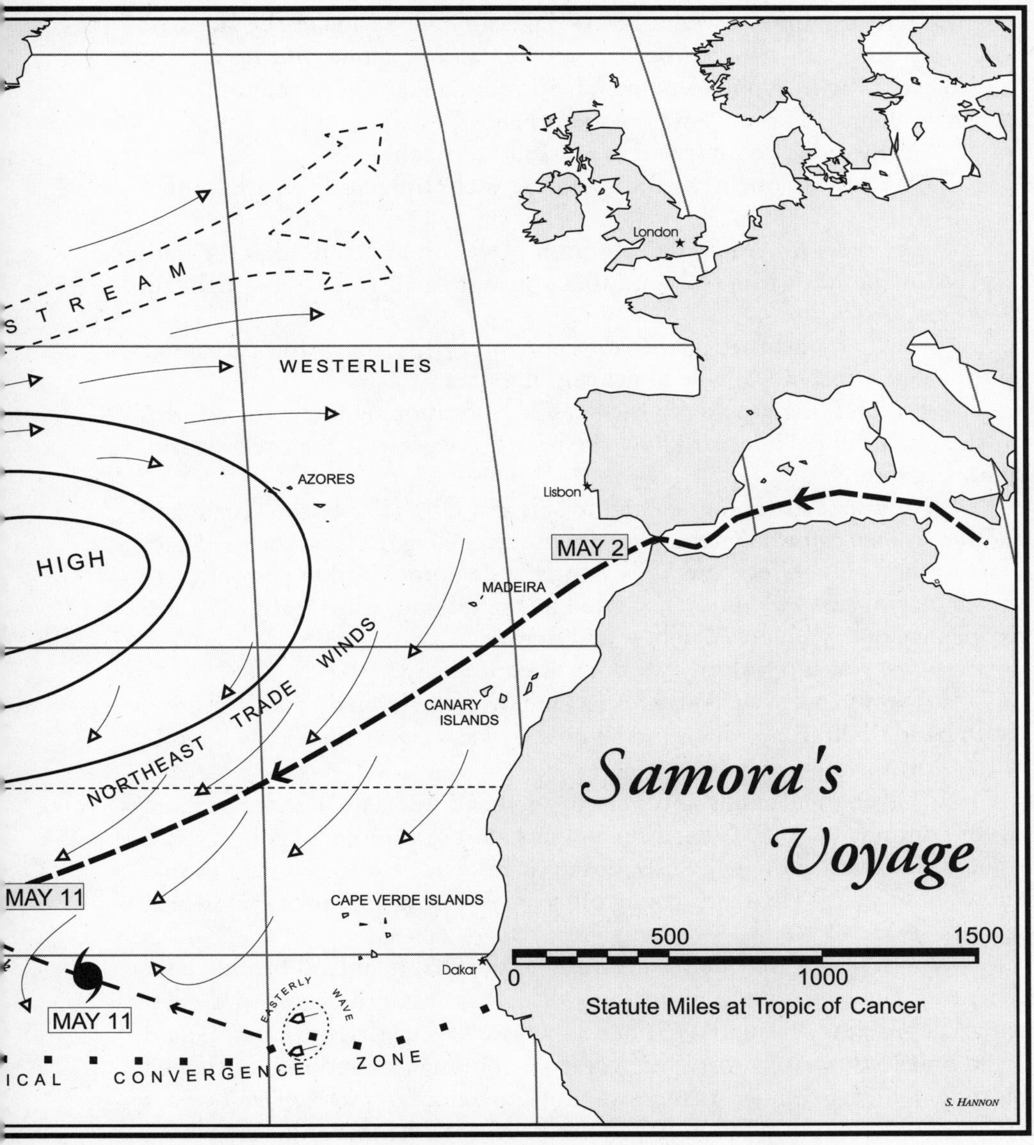
STREAM
WESTERLIES
AZORES
HIGH
London
Lisbon
MAY 2
MADEIRA
NORTHEAST TRADE WINDS
CANARY ISLANDS
Samora's Voyage
MAY 11
CAPE VERDE ISLANDS
Dakar
MAY 11
EASTERLY WAVE
ICAL CONVERGENCE ZONE
0 500 1000 1500
Statute Miles at Tropic of Cancer
S. HANNON

"Just a delivery, then?" The officer stared intently at Stan, the hint of camaraderie shared by storm-tossed mariners now vanished. "Picked a pretty unusual time for a westward crossing, didn't you?"

"The price was right, sir," Stan grinned slightly.

"Isn't it high season in the Med right now, Captain Thompson?"

"I'm just hired to take her to Fiji, sir; I don't make the business decisions. But I can tell you that from a seamanship standpoint it's a good time to avoid Pacific typhoons. Not Atlantic ones, I guess." Stan continued to force a weak grin. The smile was not returned.

"Why didn't you respond to our call on channel 16?"

"We lost all our navigation and radio electronics. Took a lightning hit."

The previous year's graduate from New London glanced at the dark displays in the navigation station. "Bet you were glad to have the light on Eleuthera."

"Yes, sir. Fortunately, the sun came out briefly a few times yesterday and the day before. I was able to get running fixes."

Ensign Pringle looked at the celestial navigation sight reduction forms on the chart table. "Nice to know the basics, even in our high-tech world, right, Captain?"

"You bet, sir. Things can go to shit real fast." The bosun's mate and another seaman came down the companionway, trailing the German Shepherd. Nose to the polished teak and holly floor, the dog proceeded to go over every square inch of *Samora*'s interior, assisted by the seamen, who clearly intended to open every hatch, locker, cubby, and drawer.

"Are you carrying any weapons or contraband?"

"No weapons, sir. And I'm not sure what the United States considers contraband. We did not intend to be in U.S. waters; we're here only because of the storm."

"Given the circumstances of the weather, I understand that, Captain. As for contraband, U.S. Customs maintains a list of prohibited goods. Since you are Canadian and, apparently, in the yacht delivery business, you should know about that." The sharp young officer was once again looking closely at Stan.

"Yes, sir. If I were doing a delivery to the U.S. mainland I would have checked the customs prohibitions carefully." Stan instantly regretted the last remark, bordering on smart-ass, since he was well aware that the Coast Guard could order *Samora* into Port Everglades for a thorough shakedown. He hoped his sudden increase in nervousness was not apparent. *It's clear the Coast Guard assigns their best ones to this duty.* He also knew that the rest of his crew were being grilled, separately, to reveal any discrepancies. It was virtually assured that Kateryna would not slip and refer to the yacht as *Samora*, but Stan did not have the same confidence in Waddy, who was not, after all, highly trained in such matters. *Since Peter and Timothy came aboard, he hasn't missed. Not yet.* Stan had to change the direction of the interrogation.

"Sir, do you have any suggestion about where I could arrange for repairs to my electronics? I cannot properly proceed with *Aletheia* in her current condition. Seamanship aside, the provisions of her insurance contract require me to have the repairs done before proceeding on to the Pacific."

"Well, you can probably forget about South Florida unless you're prepared to wait quite a while. Alberto missed Miami, but he's still raising hell up the west coast and will probably go ashore at Panama City."

"Not even Fort Lauderdale, Ensign Pringle? Everything in the maritime world is available there."

"Negative, Captain. Lots of electronic equipment has been damaged all over the area. I'm sure you'd be way down a long list. Don't you have to go down to Road Town for your crew change?"

"Under the circumstances, sir, I'm sure the owners would agree to air travel for the crew. It would be a bitch getting back to the Virgins from here."

"And just who would you contact to get such permission, Captain Thompson?"

Shit, this little bastard is quick. "My contacts are in Portugal and in Fiji, but actually I don't have to contact anybody. As a delivery captain, I'm generally free to take whatever action is necessary to safeguard the vessel and her crew."

"For the record, I would like to have the telephone numbers and addresses in Portugal and Fiji."

"Sure, I have them right here." Stan went to the chart table and came back with the delivery contract from "Buena Vista Enterprises, Lisboa." Malcolm had arranged a very authentic-appearing Portuguese document, complete with the myriad seals, rubber stamps, ribbons, cheap paper, and misspelled English words a trained examiner would expect. Stan was certain the telephone numbers would be for real answering services.

The officer examined the document closely, noting several details in his contact book. Stan watched the nervous, drooling dog and his handler come back into the salon from the aft cabins. He wondered if the stories he'd heard were true about the drug dogs being addicted to cocaine and heroin to make them really want to find the stuff. The young ensign looked up; Stan caught the slight look from the seaman that communicated "nothing."

"Please stay below, Captain Thompson. I'll be back in a minute."

The officer climbed up the companionway to compare the stories the other members of his highly trained team had heard from the yacht's crew. It seemed forever until Ensign Pringle reentered the salon.

"What are your intentions regarding repair of your vessel? We don't have the resources available right now for an escort into Port Everglades."

"Well, from what you said that would probably just be a waste of time anyway. Although I haven't thought it through entirely, it looks like I have no choice but to put in somewhere along the Gulf coast. Probably faster doing that than to wait around forever in Fort Lauderdale."

"Do you have charts for the Gulf?"

The little fucker is slick. No doubt about it. "Yes, a large sailing chart and a few harbor charts."

"I'd recommend Galveston, Captain. Complete marine facilities in the area around the yacht club. Do you happen to have that one?"

What's the right answer? "I always make it a point to carry charts for all the major ports, even well off my expected route. You never know."

"Right, Captain, you never know, do you?"

Stan went over to the stack of wide drawers built in behind the chart table. He pulled out the master list and then opened a drawer and counted through the numbers on the corners of the charts. He withdrew the British Admiralty chart for the entrance to Galveston Bay. The drawer also contained a U.S. Defense Mapping Agency chart for the same area, which, understandably, was superior to the British version for the same reason that the British charts were superior in areas of the world important to Her Majesty's Royal Navy. *God, I hope the little shit doesn't decide to paw through them.* A duplicate U.S. chart for this one port, far off *Samora*'s intended route, would be hard to explain. "Yes, sir. Here it is."

"Good work, Captain."

"It's my job to be prepared, sir."

"So is it your intention to make port at Galveston?"

I can't believe that I'm actually being invited to take the boat to Galveston. This would really be funny if it weren't for the fact that this little bastard is standing less than ten feet away from a two-kiloton nuclear bomb. Stan decided to try to recover the initiative. "Sir, like I said, I haven't thought it through. Perhaps I should just take the straight shot down through the Windward Passage and get the repairs done in Panama. We've already had a lot of delay with the hurricane."

"Certainly your owners would want you to take the most seamanlike course, Captain. After all, you're delivering a very valuable yacht halfway around the world."

"The time frame is pretty tight, sir. I didn't even take the time to make the customary stop in the Canaries." Stan wasn't sure how the last comment would play. Surely it must have seemed strange that they'd come clear from Malta without a stop. *I should have listened to Waddy. Would have missed the hurricane too.*

"Yes, that *is* a customary watering hole, isn't it, Captain? Why all the rush?"

Stan was once again on the defensive, confronted with the intense blue eyes shining out from under the darker blue baseball cap. "I'm sure you realize, sir, yachts like this are governed strictly by money. There are charter contracts waiting in Fiji, and reputations with the charter brokers can easily be lost. I'm just trying to do my job."

"I don't think you'll like the repair facilities in Colón or Panamá. Not since the Panamanians started taking over the operation of the Canal."

Stan wondered how much propaganda the young officer had received about the United States giving away its Panama Canal property. "You're starting to sound like the U.S. Chamber of Commerce, Ensign Pringle," Stan said, offering his most sincere grin.

The young man finally broke and smiled back. "Not at all, Captain Thompson. Just offering friendly advice. She's your vessel." The officer's VHF radio hissed a command to acknowledge. The ensuing cryptic conversation put Stan's ordeal to an end.

"That'll be it, Captain. Would you please sign here to verify that your ship's documents and passports have been returned and that no personalty has been confiscated?"

"Certainly, sir." Stan complied and the officer started to leave. "I really appreciate your concern for the well-being of *Samor . . . Aletheia* and her crew."

Ensign Pringle turned on his heel. "What did you start to call this vessel?"

"*Samorang*, sir. That was my last delivery. Hard to keep them all straight." *Oh, God.*

Ensign Pringle gave him a long look. "I guess it must be." Stan endured another long pause before the officer turned again to head up the ladder. "Good luck and good sailing, Captain. Consider what I advised you." Stan felt trickles of sweat running down from his armpits.

The Coast Guardsmen were soon back aboard the inflatable. Everyone waved from *Samora*, answered by a trim salute from Ensign Pringle. In less than fifteen minutes the cutter was a dot on the western horizon, headed for Miami.

"Must've had an emergency call, guys. There has to be a mess of problems with the storm," Stan said.

Peter stared after the vanished cutter. "Bloody hell. Damned ship-shape crew, that lot. Her Majesty's lifeboat lads would approve, completely. Right, Catherine?" Stan watched her nod and smile enthusiastically, not forgetting for an instant that she was supposed to be English.

"Peter, Timothy, I need to speak with you," Stan said after everyone finished up the task of getting *Samora* sailing again.

"Right, Skip," the ever-perceptive Peter responded quickly. "Pretty clear that Road Town is out of the question and *Aletheia* needs some port time. So where to?"

"That's right. We'll have to make port in the States. And I have a suggestion. I know I told you that BVI was the end of the line—new crew there and all—but you two have been marvelous. Couldn't ask for better. How about a little shore leave in the cool mountains of Colorado? Get out of this tropical shit for a while. You've both earned it—double time—and things are bound to be a little slow down in the Islands until the storm gets sorted out. A little R&R and then on down to Road Town. How about it?"

"I wouldn't mind that, Captain," Peter nearly shouted as he grabbed his friend. "How about you, Timmy?" Timothy just grinned the widest his facial muscles could manage.

"So that's it, then. Settled. Now, next stop is Galveston. That's in Texas." Stan glanced at Waddy and Kateryna, who were staring blankly at him. Stan's subtle look shook them both into reality.

"Hey, great!" Waddy clapped Peter on the back.

Kateryna embraced shy Timothy. "You're both wonderful."

"So let's start sailing this boat," Stan said after another moment. "Peter, Timothy, come on down below. I'll show you the games we have to play with the Gulf Stream to get around Florida."

17

East Slope of the Uinta Mountains, northern Utah, May 20

The Soil Conservation Service vehicle was unable to travel any farther up the winding road, even in four wheel drive with chains all around. Where the white pickup stopped, a lot of back and fill tracks, now nearly obliterated, could be seen under the freshly fallen snow. They had been left by the county plow when it had turned around the day before. Even with the sun in the latter cusp of Taurus, winter persisted in the mountains ringing the Upper Basin.

"End of the line, Chucky boy," the lead survey man said to his new assistant. He jumped out of the cab, landing in snow nearly up to his knees. "Skis won't work in this slop; have to break out the sixty-inch webs."

Chuck reached into the back of the truck for the heavy, teardrop-shaped wooden snowshoes. "I hate these things. Why can't the Eagle buy us some modern equipment? Sergeant Preston must have used gear like this; it's gonna be like walkin' in wet cement. Why do we have to *do* this, anyway?" Chuck had spent several years in the army before joining the U.S. Soil Conservation Service. He knew better than to ask such questions.

"Not just us, Chuck. Other teams are having to go out in a bunch of places here and in the Central Rockies, down in the San Juans, in the Wasatch, even up in the Wind Rivers. I guess the guys at the Bureau of Reclamation still don't believe the latest SNOTEL data. So we all get to do some more manual rounds."

"I suppose we gotta go into the SNOTEL site, too, don't we? We gotta calibrate the telemetry, huh?"

The team leader grinned. "Save your strength, Chuck. We'll have a long hump up to Lookout Peak after we do the manual course here—got to take a manual up there to confirm the telemetry."

The latest dump of heavy, wet, spring snow made each step up the steep, unplowed road an ordeal. At the end of the road the two men had to climb even more steeply through the forest to the tree-sheltered clearing where the snow course was laid out. Being the junior man—and a trainee—Chuck carried the sections of sample tube, the heavy spring scale, and the several other pieces of gear needed to deal with whatever snow conditions they might encounter. Following in the well-broken snow, the team leader carried the tape measure and the survey log book. It was a standard government operation.

"Son of a bitch. Where're the course markers?" Chuck groused when he struggled to the edge of the nearly level clearing. "Those signs are twelve feet high. How we gonna know where to measure? We're supposed to always measure in the same places."

"Relax, Chuck. The snow's always about uniform here. No drifting. It'll be close enough. The start of the course is about twenty feet in front of that big fir. Here, I'll give you a hand with the sample tube. Guess we'll need all five sections."

The two men screwed the pieces of slotted aluminum tubing together. They wound up with what looked like a vaulter's pole, with graduations marked all along its length.

"Seven stations on this course; each one is a hundred feet. Head for that little clump of aspens. That's about where the end of the course should be."

Chuck shoed toward the aspens but stayed to one side so that he wouldn't be walking right on the course. When the tape ran out, the team leader waved his partner to a point where he felt the line of the course should be. Chuck plunged the tube vertically into the snow, pushing it down through the many and varied, compacted layers. Only the top foot of the fifteen-foot-long tube protruded when he felt the end hit the ground.

When the team leader snowshoed up, Chuck was checking the toothed end of the tube. A few pieces of grass and conifer needles confirmed he'd gotten a complete sample. Some water was running out the end.

"This ain't gonna work," Chuck frowned. "Can't measure this shit in late spring. What's the point measurin' if a bunch'a the sample runs out the end of the tube?"

"Ours is not to reason why, my boy. I'll just make a note about the snow conditions and the unknown quantity of lost water in the sample."

The team leader recorded the distance the tube had extended down into the snow and also the length of the compacted section of snow contained in the tube. Chuck then held the heavy spring scale while the team leader read off the weight of the tube and the sample. He used his little calculator to compute the overall density.

"Point three two, Chuck. Hell of a lot of water."

At the next station the team leader computed 38 percent, followed by one at 29 percent.

"We're gonna be here all day," Chuck groaned. "These readings gotta be within point oh five or we do'em over till they do."

"We'll take some repeat readings is all. It's the water we're losing; depends on how quickly we measure while it's running out the end. I'll just note everything. Not our fault this equipment wasn't designed to measure water."

The two men finished ten samples on the manual snow course and then began the long trudge up the road to the Lookout Peak telemetry site.

"Did you and Alex have to walk up here to calibrate the site last January?" Chuck asked as he struggled under the weight of his heavy backpack.

"Road was plowed then. We just drove all the way up," the team leader grinned.

When they reached the station they could see only the antenna for the radio transmitter protruding from the snow. The antenna was mounted on top of the instrument shed, fifteen feet above the ground, and no sign of the marker posts could be seen. The posts outlined the perimeter of the "snow pillows"—flexible membranes filled with an antifreeze solution and embedded in the ground. The weight of the snow on the pillows was measured by the amount of the fluid pushed out through a tube that ended in a manometer in the shed. The weight was also measured electronically and transmitted to the master station in Ogden.

"Where're we s'posed to measure? The posts are covered. Prob'ly gonna be too deep for the tube. You ever seen this much snow?"

"Not in the twenty-two years I've been with the Service, Chuck. I know about where the pillows are, though. Start right over there, but take it easy. If you puncture one, we're (I'm) dog food."

Chuck plunged the reassembled tube down into the snow. The top disappeared. "So much for the manual measurement. Why don't they make more sections for the tube?"

"Dunno. Maybe 'cause it'll bend too much or something. Well, we gotta dig down to the door so we can read the manometer. We didn't climb clear up here to come up with zip."

"From the height of the antenna left up there, the bottom of the door must be down more than ten feet," Chuck sighed.

"Just part of the job, Chucky boy. I'll spell you on the shovel."

An hour and a half later Chuck was able to pry the door open. In a few seconds he read the level of antifreeze in the glass tube.

"Hell of a lot of work for one little reading. Still amazes me that the signal from this thing goes way up there to bounce off trails of bursting meteorites, and then down to the station at Ogden. I wouldn't trust these gadgets either if I was workin' for the Bureau."

"Come on, Chuck. There's still enough time to check the SNOTEL at Lake Fork Basin. Nice long days now."

When he pushed the door shut Chuck said something the team leader couldn't hear.

Preparing the dam foundation between the two cofferdams, 1960. The diverted river is discharging through the west tunnel. Note the deep keyways for the dam carved into both abutments (*Bureau of Reclamation*).

CONVERGING PATHS

Unnamed tributary to Glen Canyon, 1963 (*Tad Nichols*).

1

Galveston Bay, Monday, May 23

Peter stood in the bow pulpit with a lead line. "Shoaling fast, Skip. Take it slow."

"Chart says fourteen feet at low tide. So does the depth meter." After a voyage of several thousand miles, Stan was not enthused about the prospect of running *Samora* aground twenty yards from the end of the line.

"I've got eleven feet now, Skip," he heard when he edged *Samora* up to the fuel dock in the Galveston Yacht Basin. The big yacht lurched slightly as her keel settled into Texas mud.

"The Eagle has landed," Waddy said.

A lot of years had passed since Stan had brought in a vessel from a foreign port. The old yellow-buoyed quarantine areas, where vessels had to wait for Health Department clearance, were gone; only U.S. Customs and the Immigration and Naturalization Service were involved now.

"Three thirty. Hope the sand crabs make it down before five; otherwise we'll have to just sit here 'til tomorrow morning." With the radio out, he hadn't been able to make an appointment.

"Sand crabs?" Waddy chuckled.

"Government employees. They move sideways or backwards. Never forward."

Stan climbed onto the dock and sat down, leaning against one of the pilings. Twenty minutes later he saw two white shirts coming toward him down the dock. They were followed by another guy with a dog.

"Good afternoon, Captain. Is your entire crew still aboard?"

"Yes, sir. We're all here." A painful experience early in his sailing life had taught Stan the rigid requirement that only the master of a foreign vessel was permitted ashore until the vessel cleared. The old concern was disease; now it was mainly drugs.

"We've sort of been looking for you. Had a call from the Coast Guard a couple of days ago. Said you might stop by. Close shave with Alberto, huh?"

"Yes, sir, your Coast Guard was most helpful. We're en route to the South Pacific, but we need some repairs. The officer aboard the *Valiant* said this was the best place to get the work done."

"May we come aboard, Captain?"

"Of course, gentlemen, please follow me."

This was not according to plan, Stan thought while he escorted the officials into *Samora*'s salon. They were supposed to have anchored off Road Town in the British Virgin Islands, dropped off Peter and Timothy, and been on their way. As British subjects, the crew could have gone ashore and *Samora* would not have had to clear. At Galveston Waddy would run ashore in the dinghy to pick up the boat Malcolm had arranged, with the weapon being transferred offshore, reversing the procedure in the Black Sea. But after the Coast Guard contact they were very likely being watched, if not directly, then at least by one or more of the geostationary satellites, aircraft, balloons, or radars used in the drug war. And Peter and Timothy were still aboard.

"So, the good captain here is springing for a little R&R for you two out in Colorado?" the INS officer asked.

"That's right, sir. Bloody nice chap, all right," Peter answered, with Timothy just smiling and nodding as usual.

"Looks like everything is in order, Captain Thompson," the customs man said before he started dragging the dog up the companionway.

Stan smiled back at the two officers. *The Coast Guard must have given them a good briefing about the boarding in the Florida Strait. Still had to use their own dog, though. Even our own government agencies don't trust each other.*

"We can give you a thirty-day visa; I'm sure that will be sufficient time to arrange your repairs," the INS official said. "Just complete the I-94s and the customs declarations. You will be going on with the vessel, Ms. Follows?"

"That is correct, sir," Kateryna answered with perfect Eastlands inflection.

I'd keep her around, too, the INS officer thought. *Nice work, if you can get it. A slow cruise in this palace to the South Pacific with that beauty. Must be nice.* "You'll be taking on additional crew here, Captain?"

"Yes, we have other crew. Everything's all mixed up, what with the storm and everything, but we'll sort it out." Stan fully appreciated that Customs, Immigration, and the Coast Guard really did give special help to vessels in distress. *Ordinarily, they're all such jerks. Guess I would be too with all the drug trafficking in this area. Thankless job they have.*

"You're all set, Captain Thompson. You can move your vessel across to the boatyard. I'm sure you'll find everything you need there. Good luck and enjoy your stay in the U.S."

Following the long-awaited, long hot showers to purge a month's accumulation of ocean salt, a dinner that had been graciously offered to the foreign visitors by the Galveston Yacht Club, and Peter and Timothy deposited in a cab for Hobby Airport in Houston, Stan was doing his best to prepare for the next step in the odyssey.

For the past month, *Samora* and the security of the sea had served to effectively isolate his mind from the full reality of what they were doing. At sea things were very straightforward: natural laws founded on perfect reason, and the mariners' ancient responses to the laws. Further, there was the isolation, predictability, and peace of mind that came with the laws—what had driven men to the sea for ages. But now he was back—back in the crowded, random, human-dominated world, with its myriad, often irrational rules, and all the dangers that only the fathomless complexities of the human mind could devise. In comparison, dealing with a hurricane at sea was nothing. And instead of being on their anonymous way to California, the weapon transfer accomplished offshore as planned, here they were, like a clutch of flightless ducks, waiting for the inevitable, if entirely unpredictable, human intervention to swoop down on them.

Waddy shared Stan's feelings. "I don't know about the two of you, but I feel like I'm walkin' around with my ass hangin' out," he said humorlessly.

That did it. Stan whirled to face Kateryna. "Look, we have to know more about your acquisition of the weapon. We have to know what we're up against."

"Stanley, I– –"

"We need to know enough so that we have some idea about the time pressure to get that bomb out of the boat. Does every second count, or do we have some time, or a lot of time, or what?" Stan and Waddy shared a long, determined look.

"Both of you, please listen. The weapon was removed on April 22nd—over four weeks ago. We have been contacted by your authorities twice now and there has been no problem."

"That doesn't tell us enough. *So far* we haven't had a problem, but Waddy and I need some facts. Why can't you tell us more?

"I know your authorities use methods similar to our security police to get information from people. If you do not know anything you cannot tell them anything, no matter what they do. I am trained to resist. You are not."

"Do you really believe that?" Stan said incredulously.

"Can you be so naïve, Stanley?"

"Oh, come *on*!" Waddy burst in, almost shouting. "All our butts are on the line here. And how do we know just what *is* in that big tin can?"

"Saul will tell you, soon enough," Kateryna snapped. She stared at each of them for several moments and then concentrated on the waterway. "All right. I will tell you this. As a practical matter, one man, and only one man, is in a position to know the weapon has been removed from the arsenal. I have no way of knowing if or when he will discover its loss; however, if he does discover that it is missing, and if he were to reveal its loss, it would be the end of him, and it would hurt Ukraine very badly. He loves Ukraine as much as I do. There is another thing. As he loves Ukraine, he despises the West—this country in particular. With the disappearance of Sofiia and me, and the missing weapon, I believe he will figure out the general idea of what is going on. He is very competent at such things. He would welcome having one of our nuclear weapons detonated on American soil."

"How is it possible that only one man would know it's gone?" Stan persisted with more disbelief. "Saul didn't believe it either when we talked about it back at Stony Ridge."

"That is what I cannot get into. You must have known there would be a great deal of risk in removing a nuclear weapon from our arsenal. I am trying to tell you that there is, in fact, much *less* risk than you might have expected because of the special circumstances concerning this particular weapon. Now, we have a job to do, gentlemen. May we get on with it?"

2

U.S. Arms Control and Disarmament Agency, May 24

"Eddie, how did this get here?"

"It came in today's courier pouch from Moscow, General," Edward Griggs replied. He always referred to his boss by his former military rank. Edward Griggs respected his boss, Lieutenant General William Grosvenor, more than anyone. He was very pleased to be his chief assistant, implementing the Tactical Arms Reduction Treaty.

Wil Grosvenor did not have to ask whether the envelope had been scanned for physical content and tampering before he opened it. He cut the end off the envelope with a pair of scissors and shook the letter out onto his desk. He held the sheets of paper by just the tips of their corners while he slowly read their contents. Edward Griggs watched his boss's face progressively tighten the further he read. The general reached into a desk drawer, took out a large manila envelope, and slid the letter into it along with the envelope it had been delivered in.

"Eddie, I've got to see the Energy Secretary ASAP. Also, find out when the big guy at the compound is available."

* * *

"You were lucky, Captain Thompson," the yard master told Stan. "The hit you took only got the masthead equipment. The vessel has excellent grounding and circuit isolation systems which protected the really expensive stuff down below. It doesn't look like the sticks or the rigging got fried either; the grounding saved them too. Could have been a lot worse."

"That's great, Mr. Winslow. We really appreciate how soon you got to us." *Of course they got to us soon. Big bucks for this work.*

The yard master knew that a large foreign yacht like *Aletheia* was not operated on a shoestring; accordingly, the forthcoming yard bill for expedited services would be paid without hesitation. The bottomless letter of credit Malcolm arranged had put the officials of Galveston Yacht Services fully at ease. "We were most happy to be of service, Captain Thompson; we fully understand that you are anxious to be on your way into the Pacific. I envy you." Mr. Winslow had also met Kateryna. "It will be a lovely voyage. *Aletheia* is assuredly a very well-found yacht."

"Thank you, Mr. Winslow. Yes, we're way behind schedule, and we'll already have some disappointed charterers in Fiji. Nevertheless, we have to take her out for a shakedown. It's not that I don't have complete faith in your repairs, sir—just good seamanship, that's all. Besides, my owner and the insurance company would expect it."

"Of course. Indeed, you have a great deal of responsibility with this fine vessel. We'll hold her berth until you return; however, I'm certain you will find everything to be in order. May I offer my chief electronics technician to accompany you in case there is any question?"

"No, no, that won't be necessary. I'm sure everything will be perfectly repaired. We can take care of any needed fine-tuning when we come back in. Thanks for the offer, anyway, Mr. Winslow." Stan hoped that his refusal of the routine courtesy would not raise questions. Both men knew that it would be far more efficient for the technician to see for himself the operation of the electronic equipment offshore, away from land interference; but having the man along was impossible, Stan could not explain to the obviously surprised yard master.

"Very well, Captain. We are at your service if you change your mind."

Stan watched the American counterpart of Malta's Mr. Blaquiére walk back across the yard. *I wonder if he's going to give the Customs guy a call . . . No. No, he won't do that. Discretion is as much a part of his business as it is for the yard in Malta—or in Auckland or Cape Town or any of these places for that matter . . . I hope.*

3

Central Intelligence Agency, Langley, Virginia, May 25

"The Director will see you now, sir." General Grosvenor followed Judge Ahmanson's no-nonsense personal secretary into the inner vault of the Director of Central Intelligence. The soundproofed door whispered across the carpet and closed behind him with a quiet click. The office looked like that of any senior federal judge, but larger: an array of law books covered one wall; another wall and the adjacent table were littered with plaques, awards, diplomas, federal service memorabilia, and photographs of the Director with people, most of whom were recognizable at a glance. The other end of the spacious, hardwood-paneled office was furnished like the living room of a comfortable suburban home. Behind the Director's desk, not standard government issue, was a seventh-floor view of an expanse of Virginia countryside, tinted green by the material in the thick window glass that interrupted outside surveillance—and penetration by anything short of a howitzer projectile. But this was not just another judge's office. It was the seat of power of what was now the most powerful intelligence agency in the world. Director Stuart Ahmanson got up from the large circular conference table and extended his hand to him. Secretary of Energy Ronald McAllister waved him over.

"Good to see you, Wil," the Director said. "Have a seat. Doctor McAllister tells me everything's been going well with TART."

"Thank you, sir. Yes, it has been, at least until yesterday." Wil Grosvenor and the Secretary of Energy knew, of course, that the Director did not need anyone from outside the compound to inform him about details of the destruction of a significant part of the world's tactical nuclear weapons. Central Intelligence was virtually independent in its ability to gather its own information on any subject.

"What can you tell us about the author of this letter?"

"Sir, I'm flattered that you would ask, but I'm at a loss. With all the upheaval in the former Soviet military and the disbanding of the KGB, it could be any disgruntled former official. More fundamentally, I'm not convinced that what is set forth in the letter is truthful. A lot of hard-liners would love to create a crisis for President Yarzov."

"We'll get to that later on, Wil; let's concentrate on the ID of the author first. One of the reasons you're so effective in the implementation of TART is your familiarity with the major players in the Soviet nuclear weapons security apparatus. Let me give you a hint. Our linguistics and philology shop feels pretty strongly that it was written by a Ukrainian."

What a patronizing son of a bitch you are. You're an ass-kisser who politicked his way into a federal judgeship and then into directorship of the CIA. And I have to call you "sir." But salute the uniform, not the man. "If your people are quite sure of that, sir, it narrows the field enormously. Whether Russian, Byelorussian, or Ukrainian, he must have been KGB: among such ethnic Ukrainians there are, perhaps, less than a dozen candidates."

"All right, make up a list with a summary of everything you know about the careers, politics, loyalties, enemies, and personal lives of these people. We'll add that to our stuff, then maybe we can figure out who this guy is."

"Judge Ahmanson, have your people completed the analysis of the letter itself and the circumstances of its delivery to the embassy in Moscow?" *That ought to irritate you, you arrogant shit. Now tell me I have no need to know.*

Wil Grosvenor's boss fidgeted in his chair while the Director crafted an appropriate response. "General Grosvenor, our analysis is not yet finished, and so far we have nothing on the courier of the letter. We'll be continuing with that while we work through your list of people. Now, let's talk about the contents of the letter. With all your years keeping track of Soviet nuclear weapons security, do you think that what is set forth here could have happened?"

"If it did, everything depends upon *when* the tactical weapons were secreted. It had to have occurred before there were any big cracks in the KGB hierarchy—before 1989, 1990 at the latest. The persons named in the letter are all known to me; they're in the top echelon of former Soviet ultraconservatives, and given their backgrounds it's possible, if not plausible, that they could have arranged the disappearance of eighty-three tactical weapons. There would certainly be motivation among the hard core to hide the weapons and eliminate any paper trail before the accounting under the treaty began. Of course, to physically remove them and expunge all references, from construction to deployment, would mean the elimination of quite a few people. The KGB has certainly done that in the past with far less motivation, even in the years since the reign of Iron Feliks. Clearly, the coterie would have to be kept tight and highly loyal to each other. The men listed in the letter meet that requirement. What I do find compelling is that the letter sets forth the exact location of the weapons at a reserve materiel depot near Moscow and specifically itemizes each device by model, yield, age, and tactical configuration. Even the permissive action link codes are included. Sir, there's one demolition type on the list that we had no idea the Soviets possessed. They're not covered by TART." General Grosvenor chewed on his lower lip for a moment. "If the Russians are holding back information on whole categories of weapons, that would be the end of the treaty—no question."

"That's right," Secretary McAllister interjected. "How do we know the weapons listed in this letter are the only ones hidden? I mean, this cuts right to the core of the whole TART agreement. We certainly listed all of ours. What a disaster if this information leaked."

"It sure as hell won't leak out of this building. Besides a handful of my best technical people, only the three of us know what's in this letter." The Director got up, lighting his pipe. "We have to move fast on this, gentlemen. I'll go directly to the President as soon as we have our best information. In my opinion, this whole matter is entirely political between the President and President Yarzov. If the President wants to give it to the National Security Advisor or even the whole council, that's his call; I'm certainly not going to risk a leak by going to anyone but the President. Wil's right. If Senator Wheeler found out about this, it would be the end of TART, it would probably be the end of the loans to Russia that we finally got the Europeans to agree to at the Japan meet, and it might even be the end of Yarzov himself and the start of a whole new hard-line regime. Maybe that's what the son of a bitch who drafted this letter has in mind. If this guy's a Ukrainian, maybe his motivation is to hurt Russia. God knows any Ukrainian could feel that way, especially now. The Russians are close to a deal with Ukraine to take over the entire Black Sea Fleet and the port of Sevastopil in exchange for relieving Ukraine's debt and supplying petroleum and nuclear fuel to them. A lot of people in their parliament think it's a complete sellout. You'll take that into consideration when you compile your information, won't you, General?"

"Of course, Judge."

"All right. Have your list to me by six P.M. tomorrow.

* * *

"Wonder why Malcolm picked this place?" Waddy asked. He and Stan watched the bustle of activity among the shrimp trawlers docked along the waterway from Galveston Bay into Clear Lake.

"Do you know who most of those people are, Waddy?"

"Chinese?"

"Vietnamese. Boat people. Remember when they were given sanctuary in the U.S.?"

"Yeah. They were scattered around all over the country, weren't they? I mean, even to places like Iowa and Nevada."

"You talk about culture shock. Practically none of them spoke a word of English, and a typical Asian has a bitch of a time learning English. They had only the clothes on their backs, no money, and except for themselves, no family or even cultural ties in America. Most of these people were fishermen from the Mekong Delta, so they got a break being sent to Houston; then it didn't take long before families were banding together to lease a shrimp trawler. They'd work the boat twenty-four hours a day, seven days a week, finally being able to buy a broken-down boat. Two families would stay aboard, continue to work it like crazy, while the rest, with some new families, would lease another boat, and so on. In about ten years they took over a big chunk of the shrimping fleet here in the Galveston area. Nearly drove the Texans nuts. There was a lot of ethnic backlash, but the Vietnamese held on, with the great majority of Texans finally coming to accept them. Now they're having modern, custom steel trawlers built and their sons and daughters are going to college. Amazing. Just amazing. You sure as hell didn't hear them demanding bilingual education or affirmative action while they struggled to adapt to American culture—and maintaining their ethnic identities in the process. They just worked their butts off; now they're sending gobs of money back to Vietnam to buy the freedom of relatives and friends. Can you imagine what these people would have to say about the crybabies in Berkeley? This is the best of America, Waddy."

Waddy stared at the maze of organized activity. He slowly nodded his head. "Is it because of their ethnicity? Their culture?"

"More fundamental than that, I think. Family. Without strong family support and cooperation, they wouldn't have had a chance. No one would. No matter what the government tries to do, it can't make a family." Stan paused, looking intently at his close friend. "Look at us. We should both be at home, playing with children or grandchildren, instead of doing what we're doing."

Waddy turned away to look down the waterway toward Galveston Bay. He didn't say anything for a few moments. "I still don't understand why Malcolm picked this spot for the shuttle boat."

"They won't recognize or pay the least attention to your ethnicity. Some redneck Texan would be curious—probably think you were stealing the trawler. Even as Americanized as these Vietnamese have become, with a genuine loyalty to the country that took them in, they still have too much fear of authority to be anything but vague in case someone starts asking questions about this boat. Malcolm sure as hell figured this one right. His obsession with things having to do with peoples' cultures really helped here."

"We're going ahead with the transfer tomorrow night?"

"You bet, pal; I don't care how confident Kateryna is. I want to get that damned bomb off the boat and disappear into the backcountry."

"You think the Coast Guard will be watching *Samora*?"

"No way to know. Customs has sure had plenty of time to come down and really take her apart while we've been in the yard. I think we're okay. It's only good seamanship to take her out for a sea trial before heading out on a long voyage."

"What about where I'll be taking the trawler after the transfer?"

"We'll go check that out right now. If Malcolm is true to form, it'll be a nice obscure spot down the Intracoastal Waterway toward Port Arthur. Ready to handle a boat yourself?"

"Why the hell not. Let's do it."

"Okay. We'll drop off the car and pick up the van Malcolm arranged to be left at the storage garage in Houston. Did I give you your set of keys?"

"Yeah, you did. What about the other parts for *Samora*'s water tank?"

"Now, Waddy, is there any doubt that they'll be in the van?"

4

MANOEL ISLAND SHIPYARD, MAY 26

Augúste Blaquiére watched from his office window while a man in a blue tropical suit got out of a taxi and walked into the ship loft. *Ah! Perhaps another productive day.*

"Good morning, Mr. Stiles. We haven't seen you for a while. Did you just arrive from Naples?"

"Good morning to you, Mr. Blaquiére. Yes, I had to take the ferry to Catania, then the hydrofoil over from Sicily. But it was a lovely trip. Expect to have a good season?"

"Oh, indeed, very good. We are the first to see the ups and downs in the economy, and now things are clearly on the way up. These lovely things are so expensive to operate and maintain." The yard master swept his arm toward the rows of gleaming, varnish- and brass-encrusted yachts that filled the huge building. "Many of their owners are very sensitive to fluctuations in the financial markets. I don't know what costs them more, these yachts or their mistresses."

John Stiles, United States Drug Enforcement Administration, could not identify personally with what the natty little man was talking about, but he did have his own interest in the collection of private vessels occupying the Manoel Island Shipyard. Information the yard master had provided to him in the past had been very helpful in intercepting shipments of heroin that originated in Turkey, bound for western Europe or North America. Private yachts were a popular way of moving the merchandise from obscure anchorages on the coast of Turkey to equally inconspicuous landings throughout the Mediterranean.

"Have you seen any interesting activity lately, Mr. Blaquiére?" Agent Stiles asked in the indirect manner the Maltese man was most comfortable with. Directness was only for unsophisticates.

"Yes, I believe so. A large activity. Indeed, a very large, very interesting activity, Mr. Stiles," the yard master replied with his ever-present oily smile.

"Can you attempt to quantify just how large this activity might be?"

"Oh, yes, I would say $20,000."

"I have never heard of such a large activity, Mr. Blaquiére. I have never heard of an activity greater than $10,000."

"I am certain that it was at least $15,000—it could not have been less. Any one of these fine vessels is at least fifty or a hundred times that large." The yard master gazed off at the assembly of treasures of the yachting world.

"Very well, Mr. Blaquiére, I will accept that the activity was as large as you say. Now, can you be more specific?"

"Of course. If you would follow me please?"

"So, what does all this mean?" John Stiles asked while he stared at the collection of line drawings for certain modifications to the ketch *Aletheia.*

"These show that modifications were made to the sole—that is, the flooring—in the salon of the yacht. My craftsmen made the changes. As you can see, the changes make it convenient to remove and replace the flooring."

"What's under the flooring?"

"Among other things, the yacht's fuel and water tankage, Mr. Stiles: two fuel tanks, side by side, near the engine; two large water tanks, fore and aft, under the salon area."

"These drawings of what look like mechanical pieces. What are they?"

"I cannot tell you that. We only fabricated them, and the yacht captain insisted upon installing them without our assistance. They are a most curious collection, are they not?"

"Mr. Blaquiére, given the large activity we are talking about here, I would insist upon your best estimate of the purpose of the mechanical items."

"Clearly, given that *Aletheia* is a wooden sailing vessel, they must be some variety of mounting brackets, perhaps to secure some mechanical equipment. Captain Thompson did say that additional items were to be installed after the yacht arrived in Fiji; perhaps the mechanical bits were for that purpose. But he was most keen that they be fabricated here. We do have the ability to construct anything that a yacht may require, Mr. Stiles," the yard master sniffed with a slight pause. "Now, these curved pieces are most curious. We have had occasion to fabricate oddly-shaped pieces to facilitate the installation of a new type of diesel engine, for example, but such mechanical work was not performed on *Aletheia*. At least not at this yard."

"How big is the water tank under the cabin floor?"

"As I said, there are two. And, Mr. Stiles, as I also said, they are large. Each is about 1,200 liters."

"May I take these drawings?"

"Of course. It is unlikely that we will see *Aletheia* again. Our work here is completed."

"How can you be so sure?"

"When she departed last month she was bound for Fiji by way of the Atlantic."

"How else could the yacht travel to Fiji?"

"Why, by way of the Indian Ocean," the yard master replied with his also ever-present air of smarmy pretension. "Through Suez and the Red Sea, across the Indian Ocean and Indonesia, then into the Pacific, Mr. Stiles. However, as you may know, typhoons can occur in the Indian Ocean at any time of year. Furthermore, there is the matter of a great many pirates inhabiting the Gulf of Aden; and lastly, such a voyage would be nearly entirely to windward."

God, I hate this little slime. But I need him. "When did she sail?"

"I'll check my log. Yes, here it is. She cleared on April 29th. Oh, yes, she went first to Greece for a sea trial, returning on the 27th. She departed again, bound for Gibraltar and Panama, on the 29th."

"Are you sure she only went to Greece? Did you see her clearance papers?"

"No, but I am certain that our customs and immigration officials will have an adequate record, Mr. Stiles."

"Yes, of course, but I'm asking if you saw or heard anything that indicated she went elsewhere than Greece."

"No, not a thing, Mr. Stiles."

"What about her crew?"

"Again, our immigration people will have that information. I know there was a young French couple who crewed with her to Greece. I did not see them when *Aletheia* returned; however, she did take on two British sailing enthusiasts, clearly professional, and a woman as crew here in Malta. She was also British. Very charming."

John Stiles examined the shipyard contract which outlined the yard storage and services for the sailing yacht *Aletheia.* "Do you know any of the individuals involved with this Portuguese corporation, or whatever it is, that owns the boat?"

"No one, Mr. Stiles. All work was arranged and paid through an agent in Naples. I never saw anyone after the delivery crew brought her here last fall from Palma and before Mr. Thompson and his mate arrived in April. You can see from the file who the agent is. That is all I know. All payments were right on schedule, and there was never a question about anything."

"Mr. Blaquiére, are you familiar with yacht travel between here and the Aegean Islands?"

"Yes, of course. I have often sailed to the Aegean. A paradise."

"The . . . let's see . . . the nine days she was gone on the voyage to Greece. Do you know her itinerary?"

"Mr. Stiles. The yacht was preparing to sail approximately halfway around the world. If I were her captain, I would certainly first like to take a little cruise to the Aegean. And it is only good seamanship to be certain that the vessel is ready for a major voyage across two oceans. I am sure that her papers will show where she disembarked the French couple and whatever other port she may have visited. Other than that, who knows exactly what route she followed?"

What an ASSHOLE*!* "She could as easily have gone to Turkey, correct?"

"The Aegean coast of Turkey is equally as beautiful as the Greek Isles. Yes, of course."

"Can you give me a description of her captain and mate, and the crew that left with her on her last departure?" Mr. Blaquiére complied.

"You were particularly observant of the woman, it seems. Why?"

"Oh, Mr. Stiles, really! She . . . you would have had to have seen her. A most charming lady. As you can imagine, I see many beautiful women associated with these yachts and their owners. But this one. Very intriguing. Very unusual. She was British, and well educated, clearly. But I will say this, Mr. Stiles, no English person I have ever seen had her facial features and her eyes. Yes, it was her eyes. In fact, I have only seen people with eyes like hers in one place."

"Where is that?"

"Slavic Eurasian people of Tatar blood, Mr. Stiles. From Crimea."

5

Lena River Basin, Eastern Siberia, May 27

Across a zone girdling the northern polar regions of the earth a war rages. While the theater of war has often changed and moved over the surface of the planet, some form of the continuum of battle has existed since the water seas and the oxygen-dominated atmosphere first formed over three thousand million years ago. The present region of conflict was established following the most recent retreat of the great rivers of ice that have many times advanced over the land masses of North America, Europe, and Asia, and in this most recent history of our earth the war zone has spread over the mid latitudes. Meteorologists refer to the battle line in the zone as the Polar Front, an area of discontinuity between the prevailing winds that circle the earth from west to east, generally above 30 degrees north latitude, and the opposing flows of irregular, easterly winds that lie above 60 degrees north. The tide of battle surges along the Front as the seasons progress: the forces of summer and warmth confining the enemy to its polar redoubt for half the year, while the legions of winter cold intermittently force their way south for the balance of the annual cycle. Cease fires generally prevail at the vernal and autumnal nodes, though not always; and the front line within the battle theater is not of a uniform latitude at any given time, rather it exists as an undulation, with varied and alternating salients to the south and bulges to the north. Most of the sags and bulges are the result of the relative sizes and positions of the land masses and the seas but are more subtly influenced by the topography of the lands and the fluid movement within the seas.

While a war among men may serve to keep the economies and the human populations of the earth in balance, so the war of the atmosphere serves to keep the heat loading of the earth in equilibrium. The individual skirmishes, attacks, and counterattacks are often hostile and destructive, yet the balance and sum of the tide of war is necessary to the well-being of the whole of the planet. The positioning of the earth relative to its sun, its speed of rotation, the mass and chemical compositions of its seas, land, and atmosphere, the present inclination of its axis of revolution, and its internal temperature and density are the dominant reasons for its ability to maintain a steady-state heat loading. Radiant energy from the sun and the earth's internal heat are, presently, in balance with the energy transmitted to space. In recent years a variety of instruments have detected disturbing increases in the normal quantities of carbon dioxide and methane and decreases in the mass and global locations of triatomic oxygen molecules in the upper reaches of the stratosphere; nevertheless, the heat balance of the earth has, so far, remained in steady state. But while the whole is in fragile equilibrium, the heat equation at any given place and moment of time is not.

The vast heat sink of the oceans, their 322 million cubic miles covering over 70 percent of the earth's surface, is responsible for the overall stability and movement of the earth's heat energy; however, these huge, slow-moving legions are not up to controlling the war on a month-to-month, week-to-week basis—to keep the system in short-term steady state. That task is left to the quick strike forces of the atmosphere, whose armies and battle groups must dash here and there to balance the net heat equation. The regular tactic is to direct warm air from the equatorial reaches to travel high in the atmosphere, moving north. Much of this tropical air mass descends in the midlatitude regions, to be swept to the east around the earth by the prevailing Westerlies, while an equal amount of the upwelling volume rises into the polar region where it settles, as cold as Death's breath, its heat absorbed and dissipated in the vast and frozen sunless top of the northern winter world. And the forces of the air must accomplish these battle movements in an incredibly thin layer spread over the planet's surface. Virtually all of the earth's weather is contained in the troposphere which rises only thirteen miles from the surface. With our globe having a diameter of over 8,000 miles, this depth of air is far less, in proportion, than the relative thickness of an eggshell to its mass of yolk and albumen.

This particular year an unusual amount of warm air was swept north by the high sea surface temperatures of the equatorial reaches of the Pacific and Indian Oceans. The phenomenon of the El Niño/Southern Oscillation—the "heartbeat of the earth" as it is called by some peoples of the west coast of South America—greatly increased the northern movement of overheated air, and through the winter the air that settled and froze across the expanse of the arctic zone accumulated hugely as it became more cold and dense. On more than a dozen occasions its dry, frozen bulk massively spilled south, relieving itself through traditional weak points in the circumpolar front line of the war.

This most recent sortie of the current year's battle was marshalled in far eastern Russia's Lena River basin, in the latitudes near the Arctic Circle. The inhabitants of Yakutsk on the Trans-Siberian Railway were still waiting for their overdue spring, but the long winter prevailed. The huge cell of polar air that had lingered over the taiga forest of the Lena River valley began to move, hugging the earth while it built momentum to penetrate the warm defenses to the south. It probed the usual corridors into Eastern Mongolia and over the Gobi Desert, and across the Manchurian Plain, consistently finding the way blocked by the now-dominant forces of midlatitude heat and pressure. In a score of breaks and passes in the chain of mountains it tried to thrust under the warmer air it encountered but failed, its raiding columns quickly diluted and dispersed. Earlier through the winter—a dozen times over the past six months—the north had been successful in thrusting its accumulations of frozen air south to the Yellow Sea, but this last sally was contained until it finally found a weakness in the Front, plunging over the Dzhugdzhur Range and into the Sea of Okhotsk, still held in the jaws of the lingering winter. Soldiers of the eastern army of the Russian Federation assigned to duty stations on Sakhalin Island shivered and stamped their feet as the river of polar air swept over them, toward the expanse of the North Pacific Ocean.

When its broad snout passed over the Kuril Islands to enter the Pacific, the Siberian air mass had intruded well into the enemy stronghold that now dominated the midlatitude reaches. With the traditional summer of the northern hemisphere now closely approaching, the warm moist air from the tropics was constantly reinforcing the midlatitude Westerlies. The southern forces spread into a northerly bulge in the Polar Front and began to climb over colder air still holding forth on the east coast of the Kamchatka Peninsula. At the same time, the surge of Siberian air penetrated a weakness in the southern front line, behind the warm air's incursion to the north, forming an area of low pressure at the point where the fronts collided. The masses of dissimilar air covered an area 900 miles in diameter. They began to move east with the Westerlies, toward the Aleutian Islands.

***

General Nastenko poured the last of the liter of vodka into his glass and tossed the bottle into the wastebasket. He ate the last of the *holubitsi* and *bigos* his aide had brought up from the commissary and got up from his desk, steadying himself with one hand while reaching for the window curtain with the other. The old officer stared out at the array of naval vessels in the sound and hummed the Ukrainian national song, "The Wide Dnieper Roars and Moans."

So now all of the fleet will go to the pig Russians. We will be dependent upon them for our fuel. And we are to give up our nuclear weapons. In return, we will be given oil and gas, even some uranium for our power plants—our sick, ill-designed power plants. Perhaps another Chornobyl one day soon? Even this port, our Sevastopil, will go to the Russians. Well, they will never find the rest of the weapons. They are safely at sea now, on their way to their new hiding place.

The general returned to his desk and unsteadily sat down to stare once again at the Russian intelligence service file, released to him after the Black Sea Fleet arrangement had been reached with the Russians. *So, Katrusia, you are no longer of any concern to them, and I was given the file on your activities in America. How very considerate.* He stared at the photograph of Kateryna and the American physicist, the picture taken in a cafe of some sort. She was grasping the man's arm and laughing, leaning very close as though she were about to kiss him. *So this is what you want, Katrusia? Is this why you betrayed your country? You betrayed me and your country for a Jew? And not just a Jew but a traitor to his country. He sold nuclear secrets to the Israelis. You prefer this vile creature over me?*

He reread the report he had received from the Radiological and Oncological Institute in Kyyiv, where Sofiia had been treated most recently. Academician Butrymenko, an old classmate, had used his resources to try to locate Sofiia. *Many fine oncology centers exist in America, but the report says that Sofiia is most probably at this clinic in the state of Washington, in Seattle. You will certainly visit your Sofiia, won't you, Katrusia? Also, I have the address of the Jew physicist in California. That is enough, Katrusia. I will find you.*

He got up again to take a last look around his office. *Some pig-fucking Russian will soon sit at this desk. It is over here for me—my own country, yet it is over! Very well, when the American scum decide what to do with the little note I sent them and contact the Russians, then by the time my former comrades are interrogated and reveal me, I will be in America. Of course, the Russians will gladly pay to know the whereabouts of the missing weapons, won't they? Oh yes, they will pay. Ukraine will once again have something to bargain with, and I will be paid for my long years of service to the Revolution . . . and you, Katrusia . . . You know I am coming for you, don't you?*

6

Galveston, May 28

"So what's the arrangement, Peter?" Timothy's friend bounded down the companionway and sprawled on the port settee.

"We're to wait here until the new skipper comes up from St. Thomas, then be on our way to Fiji. That trip sounds good to me; this lady is as fine a berth as I've ever had. We can make the delivery and be back in plenty of time for the season down in the islands. "

"Where are Philip, John, and Catherine?"

"Don't know. The yard master said they left the day before yesterday, after *Aletheia*'s sea trial. Her gear is shipshape now, I should think; the log outlines all the repairs that were done and Captain Thompson signed her off as ready to put to sea."

"Look out! Did you hear that?" Timothy looked up at the skylight.

"Yeah, I did." Peter headed for the companionway. "I'll have a look."

He stepped onto the bridge deck, looking aft in the growing darkness. He started to turn and suddenly felt his legs go out from under him while something wrenched his arm behind his back. His chest and the side of his face hit the deck at the same time.

"Don't move, fuck, or you're dead meat!" Peter vaguely heard through the stars and pain. He was aware of a darkly-clothed figure leaping down the companionway, followed by two others, and he thought he saw some large yellow letters on the back of one man's jacket. Through the ringing in his ears he heard shouts and the sound of something heavy falling down below. His other arm was wrenched behind him; by this time Peter was aware of a large, dark-uniformed man crouching over him with a knee pressing heavily into the small of his back while his wrists were manacled. His entire head throbbed. His mouth was filling with blood.

"Okay, fuck, get up and sit there." Sharp pain stabbed though his shoulders and across his chest when he was yanked up by the hand cuffs. "Don't fucking move. Hear me, boy?"

Timothy was pushed up the companionway by the largest human Peter had ever seen, then shoved into the cockpit seat next to him. They stared at the stubby, gray-black barrels of automatic weapons held by four of the men.

"You are both under arrest on suspicion of possession of controlled substances with intent to sell. You have the right to remain silent, and anything you say can and will be used against you in a court of law. You have the right to have an attorney present. If you cannot afford an attorney, one will be appointed by the court to represent you. Do you understand your rights? Fine. Now, what's your business with this boat?"

Peter tried to speak, but the blood running down his throat choked him. He coughed out a mouthful, splattering the shirt and trousers of the officer standing in front of him. The eruption elicited a curse from the splatteree and a chorus of chortles from the rest of the officers.

"Get this guy a towel and button your faces." The man turned to Timothy. "What about you, fella, have anything to say?"

"See here, sir, We are British subjects. We are here legally. We have done nothing. This is some mistake. We demand to speak to a British consular officer."

"All in good time, pal, but right now you're goin' to jail. Where're your passports?"

"I've got 'em, Bobby," another of the officers said as he came up the companionway.

"I say, aren't you required to have some sort of document to search our possessions?" Timothy demanded, now having spoken more than he had for most of the Atlantic voyage.

"Don't need'em, you Limey prick—got'em anyway—your arrest warrants and a warrant to search and seize this vessel."

"Hey, watch it, Bobby," the giant one said.

"Now," Bobby went on, "where're your buddies, Philip, John, and—what is it—Catherine?"

"May I inquire what your affiliation is?" Timothy continued.

"What?" Officer Bobby sputtered.

"We're agents of the United States Drug Enforcement Administration," the giant one cut in. "Those fellows over there are with U.S. Customs. They'll be taking possession of this boat. Now, answer the man's question."

"We have no idea where they are. We just returned from Colorado, and the yard master told us to wait for the delivery captain who is to come here from St. Thomas. We are only crew, engaged to deliver this yacht to Fiji. We have done nothing wrong and I demand that my companion receive immediate medical treatment."

Peter spit out his towel, drooling more blood. "Don't say anything more, Timmy. We're going to sue these cretins for battery, false arrest, and denial of what they call civil rights. I understand their country has some semblance of a functioning judicial system. Our consulate will arrange for a solicitor immediately."

"Look, you smart-mouthed– –"

"Belay that, Bobby," the giant one again interrupted.

"Okay, let's move this gin palace over to the yard so the boys can start takin' her apart."

***

Pacific Ocean, 400 miles south of Acapulco

Thirty hours earlier, the leading edge of the easterly wave crossed over the narrow land barrier between the Caribbean Sea and the Pacific Ocean. Fifteen days previously, the atmospheric disturbance had formed off the west coast of Africa, between Senegal and a cluster of eighteen volcanic islands, long a Portuguese colony and now the Republic of Cape Verde. The wave created an oscillation in the otherwise steadily blowing northeast trade winds. Together with their counterparts in the southern hemisphere, these steady patterns of ocean wind, named for the great sailing ships that were largely responsible for spreading humanity and commerce around the world, are among the most permanent air currents flowing across the surface of the planet. Relentlessly blowing toward the equator as they follow the curve of the earth over the three great oceans, the winds converge in an area known as the Intertropical Convergence Zone.

The ITCZ is a region of unsettled weather: a nearly continuous belt of low pressure girdling the equatorial maritime reaches of the earth. It lies hot and partially clouded in the tropical sun, not stationary but migrating from just below the equator in February to 14° above the earth's midsection in August. The intense heat of the sun in this low tropical region causes the water to evaporate and rise into the atmosphere so rapidly that the temperatures of the ocean and the moisture-laden air are nearly identical. A frequent product of this strong and turbulent mixing of heat and moisture is the formation of numerous thunderstorms, and the localized winds from these savage little squalls are the only breaks in the otherwise stifling heat of the still air.

The wave was centered along a course just a few degrees above the ITCZ when it moved into the Pacific Ocean. It was not truly a wave in the commonly accepted sense: more of a steadily moving trough of low pressure, 70 miles wide in its direction of travel, extending north and south for about 200 miles, and reaching 26,000 feet in altitude. And its leading edge was not a well-defined front like those associated with arctic-origin storms, but rather a gradual change in weather across its direction of travel, with clouds, rain, and convective updrafts occurring behind the passage of the leading-edge region of the wave. Of the scores of such waves, generally separated by about 15° of longitude, which traverse the equatorial reaches of the North Atlantic, Pacific, and Indian Oceans each year, this wave was among the few which interact in a particular way with three other atmospheric conditions they encounter in their travels.

Shortly after it entered the Pacific Ocean a few hundred miles south of Mexico, the wave encountered a region in which a cluster of thunderstorms had developed. At the time the wave intercepted the accumulation of storm cells, it happened that there was a slight bulge northward in the ITCZ, a phenomenon that occurred regularly but at random locations along the belt of the zone. And as had occurred throughout its travel across the Atlantic Ocean and the Caribbean Sea, the wave caused the northeast trade winds to curve more sharply southward ahead of the wave's leading edge.

With the northeast trade winds trending more steeply to the south ahead of the low-pressure core of the wave, concomitantly the southeast trade winds curved toward the north behind the sinusoidally-moving disturbance in the ITCZ bulge. The result was the initiation of a slight vorticity in the low-pressure core of the wave. The angular movement of the mass of air and water vapor was given an additional boost by the Coriolis effect from the earth's own rotation, an effect which increases with distance north or south of the equator. The cluster of thunderstorms was caught up in the air mass as it formed a slow, almost imperceptible counterclockwise gyre, the storm cells beginning to arrange themselves in concentric rings about its center.

Twenty-two thousand three hundred miles above the equatorial eastern Pacific Ocean, the geosynchronous satellite of the National Oceanographic and Atmospheric Administration recorded the barely discernible visual pattern of the joinder of the four atmospheric phenomena that had occurred over the section of ocean south of Mexico. Meteorologists and atmospheric physicists concerned with this particular part of the world identified the event as a tropical disturbance. It showed on their weather maps as a low-pressure area with a single, closed, elliptical isobar. It was 210 miles in its largest diameter.

* * *

"Stanley, it's nearly time for my call to Sofiia. May we stop, please?"

"We're almost there; you can see the lights on the Bay Bridge now. Wasn't she doing just fine when you talked yesterday?"

"I know you are nervous about these telephone calls, but even if your authorities have been told that Sofiia and I have come to America, would they tap into the hospital's telephone line? Don't your laws prohibit such things? For the—I don't know how many times—I have told you that even if the weapon is found to be missing, there is no chance that it would be reported to your authorities. That would have the severest repercussions in Ukraine and for the individual I have told you about."

"What about the guy just comin' over here lookin' for you?" Waddy asked from his perch in the back of the van.

Kateryna's pause told it all. "Yes, that is a possibility. However, he would have very limited resources here and he would not, under any circumstances, contact your authorities. He would work alone. He certainly could not intercept the hospital telephone."

"Okay, but just make it brief. Please."

"Oh, Stanley, Waddy, look!"

They had just passed through the tunnel at Goat Island. From the upper deck of the Bay Bridge the panorama of San Francisco, her downtown, and her waterfront suddenly filled the scene before them: from the Ferry Building on the bay front to the tops of the hills, the city was ablaze with a multi-peaked mountain of lights, reflecting across the bay.

"Why in hell we comin' back this way? What if somebody sees us," Waddy grumped.

"This is the most direct route to Saul's little hideaway up in Marin."

"I still don't like it."

"Hasn't Kateryna convinced you that there's no way anyone over here has a clue about our little cargo?"

"No, she hasn't."

"Saul should have everything else ready. Before we left, he told me it should not take more than a couple of days to install his stuff. Then we'll be on our way back to Arizona to do a little earth moving."

"Oh, Stan," Waddy sighed with a laugh, "I love it when you talk like that. But what if somebody sees you? You're supposed to be dead, remember?"

Kateryna turned fully in her seat. "Stanley, what . . . ?"

"A detail I forgot to mention. Before we went to Malta, Saul and I went out in my sailboat. We'd waited for a good stormy day, then met Malcolm in a speedboat a few miles out past the Golden Gate. We abandoned the boat—made it look like she'd been knocked down. So Saul and I are both presumed dead. No big deal for me, but it's been really hard on Saul. His kids . . ."

"Stanley, I'm sorry if I implied that only I was making a sacrifice here. Poor Saul."

"Well, that was a recognized part of what we've all agonized over in deciding to do this. It's just that theory and practice are different—sort of like why judges don't dine with hangmen."

"Damn, I sure would like to have a couple of things out of my apartment," Stan said, breaking the silence that had settled over them. "Wouldn't dare . . . anyway, by this time it's probably all in storage under order of the probate court. Okay, there's a telephone. Please make it quick."

At half past ten Stan finally found the narrow dirt lane heading up a cedar-forested hillside from an unmarked side road into the seaside community of Bolinas. Several of the art colony's residents made a regular practice of removing the highway sign for the obscure road into their village. They didn't like tourists.

When the van pulled into the illumination of the yard light, Saul came out of the house and ran over to open the door to the barn. He motioned them in. The doors closed behind the van, then a light flicked on.

"Hey, world travelers, welcome to Bolinas, California, also known as BoBoLand." The van's doors flew open, and there was a lot of hugging and four pairs of teary eyes.

"We're starvin', Saul," Waddy said. "What's in your kitchen?"

"I've got a fresh pot of chili and some corn bread. But first, can I see?"

Waddy jumped in the van and unlocked the rear doors. "Not much to see. Just an oil drum."

"Yeah." Saul stared at the light green barrel. He quickly read the cyrillic notations stenciled on the side. "Okay, come on back and see my playpen." Everyone followed him through the door into the rear of the barn. Several fluorescent lights flickered on, revealing a compact, spotless machine shop: Bridgeport milling machine, machinist's lathe, jeweler's lathe, drill press, welding gear, a surface plate, workbenches, stacked tool boxes, and myriad arcane tools and equipment. Two radiation suits hung in the corner.

"You have a glove box." Kateryna walked over to the large steel cube with viewing windows and isolation gloves extending into a sealed container.

"Isn't it a beauty? Couldn't believe it when Malcolm was able to come up with that box—as good as the ones we were using at Pueblo. So, Colonel Kate," he grinned, "are you ready to get to work?"

Waddy: "We've been on the road for two days. Let's eat first."

7

Central Intelligence Agency, May 29

"Thanks for coming over, Dr. McAllister. Have a seat. I want to bring you up to speed on the bomb stash matter. There's no need for General Grosvenor to be in on this. Let him enjoy his holiday weekend."

You two really don't like each other, do you? the Secretary of Energy thought. "Thank you, Judge, I appreciate the courtesy. May I ask who *is* in the loop?"

"I went to the President as soon as I got Grosvenor's list of possible Ukrainian authors of the letter. I can tell you that it happened to be a particularly bad time to meet with him—you know, all the domestic agenda items and the personal mess."

"Yes, I certainly do know. I was at the last Cabinet meeting."

"Well, anyway, he turned it over to Secretary Demoustier for comment."

"State? Shit! His staff, too? It'll go right to the *Times*."

"No, no, just the Secretary. And the President also informed the National Security Advisor.

"That's worse," Ronald McAllister groaned.

"That's as far as it's gone here, but last Thursday the Man talked directly to President Yarzov. I guess the shit really hit the fan over there. The list of names in the letter, it happens, include some of the old guard who've been trying to oust him. Needless to say, he's cooperating with us one hundred percent. Because the storage site at the reserve munitions depot is just outside Moscow, they know we have good eyes on the place. They couldn't move a shoe box out of there without us knowing."

"I guess Boris is happy to have the information."

"Yes and no. Yes because he now has a good reason to eliminate much of his opposition in one whack, and no because he sees the enormous risk of blowing the treaty and the G-7 loans. Apparently, he has arrested the conspirators without explanation. His problem is balancing the outcry over Stalinist tactics in dealing with his opponents versus what could be a worse problem if he explained the reason for the arrests. Anyway, they moved fast. The weapons were there, precisely as described in the letter."

"Damn. I can tell you that clear through the treaty negotiations and its implementation to date, there was no paper or physical trail on them at all. How do we know there aren't others, Judge?"

"We don't, but let me say this. We think President Yarzov is going to make the right move: complete exposure and a grand public trial. He'll be the white hat; all this happened before his time; it's just the sort of thing Russia can't go back to, et cetera, et cetera. We think he'll wait as long as he can, though, just taking the heat from his opponents. When it does come out—and we'll be ready with damage control over here—we think the treaty, the loans, him, and all the rest will be safe. But we've got our own hard-liners over in the Capitol, as you well know. They'll go ballistic when they find out."

"So did they find out anything more from the conspirators?"

"Oh, come on, Ron. Some things haven't changed that much in Russia. Of course. All six of them gave up one of the names on Wil Grosvenor's list: Major General Pavlo Nastenko. The Russians are working up everything in his file, and then some, and will be sending it on to us. We've got a pretty good pile on him too. Real dangerous guy and a rabid Ukrainian nationalist. Sheer ability brought him up in the KGB despite his regular clashes with the Russian hierarchy."

"Was there an admission from the conspirators of more weapons stored elsewhere?"

"No answer on that one. Yarzov waffled and the President didn't press him. Our sense is yes. He's just weighing his options."

"Is that all we have now?"

"No, there's one last item. General Nastenko has disappeared. Not too surprising, given the arrests, but distressing if there are more weapons squirreled away out there."

* * *

Seattle

Pavlo Nastenko looked out the window of the small apartment on the western slope of Queen Anne Hill, overlooking spectacular Puget Sound and the Seattle waterfront. He liked to look out at the water and watch all the activity in a busy port city. But this was so different from Sevastopil. Puget Sound was much larger, it had islands, and beyond the opposite shore was a range of mountains, now just visible after the rains had stopped.

He was pleased with the apartment he had found. He knew that he might have a long wait, so he wanted to be comfortable and close by were all the conveniences he would need. The Ukrainian had been astonished at what he'd seen at the shopping mall.

Ukraine will never catch up to America, the old man thought while he opened the liter bottle of Stolichnaya. As much as he hated America, he had to admire what she had accomplished. He looked at the shiny new telephone on the table by the couch. *At home most citizens wait months, even years, for a telephone. Here I got it the day after I ordered the service. And I was even able to choose from dozens of models in the store at the mall.*

One of these days, perhaps in the next week or two, he would get the telephone call he was waiting for. His old friend at the Oncological Institute in Kyyiv would tell him when Sofiia was going to leave the clinic. Academician Butrymenko had arranged to be notified of her release. After all, Sofiia's physicians in Kyyiv would be entitled to know the status of one of their patients; of course the American clinic was very pleased to keep the Ukrainian official advised. *That is when I will find you, Katrusia.*

He had located Sofiia when he had casually and brazenly walked through the clinic. Pavlo Nastenko was very good at being discreet. Now, with little to do, he regularly watched the front entrance to the clinic—waiting. Perhaps Kateryna would come to visit her daughter—merely a chance; nevertheless, Pavlo Nastenko would be waiting.

* * *

The outer pressure case—twenty inches in diameter by thirty-two inches long and with hemispherical, handle-equipped end covers—rested on the workbench with one of its ends removed. Saul was working on the inner canister, now enclosed in the sealed glove box. The vacuum pump had drawn off the radioactive argon gas into a pressure container, but Saul wanted to monitor the radiation level in the nuclear component canister for a while before he took it out of the box. Even then, he still planned to wear his radiation suit. At Pueblo he'd gotten very handy using a glove box, and he was now twisting off the last of the stainless steel nuts securing the inner canister end cover. He paused a moment after sliding the cover off the studs, then turned the opened end of the brightly machined cylinder toward the window.

"Go on, Saul," Kateryna said over his shoulder, "it's all there."

He focused the high-intensity lamp on the end of the canister and peered in. His first look revealed an entirely alien mechanism; then, as the seconds passed, familiar components began to emerge from the foreign chaos. *Yes, it's a W-45. More sophisticated, though. Highly miniaturized.*

He turned to face her. "Well?" Kateryna asked, smiling. "Is it up to the ones we were taking apart in Pueblo?"

"It's very cleanly done. At least as good as the ones we were taking apart, and the miniaturization is impressive. It looks like I'll easily be able to access the arming and fusing mechanisms. And you're right, it only has a simple, digital permissive action link. I don't suppose you brought along the wiring diagrams, did you?" he grinned.

"You're dreaming, Saul. But between the two of us, we should be able to figure the circuits out."

"I see the capacitor bank and the krytrons. Is that the problematic little piece of equipment?" Saul pointed his socket wrench at a sealed, cold-cathode, ionizing gas switch.

"That's it. Believe me, they are not fixable. There was even much debate about why, exactly, they did not work perfectly all the time. We went to a whole new design."

"What about the PAL combination?"

"Right in my head."

Saul kept staring into the collection of finely machined mechanisms, electronic components, and wiring harnesses surrounding the matrix of high-explosive lenses. The lenses, in turn, surrounded the numerous concentric and precisely machined spheres of tungsten alloy, beryllium, enriched uranium, and plutonium which comprised the weapon's core. Something seemed out of place, though. He couldn't put his finger on it.

Kateryna interrupted his concentration. "Show me what you've put together for the fusing signal."

"They're over on the bench, under the tarp." He walked over and uncovered the collection of equipment.

"How did you get these sonar buoys?"

"Malcolm, again. I was amazed at how much equipment is available through the private arms dealers who supply the Third World. Now, I suppose, the Russians are dealing with those guys too."

"You wanted us to become capitalists, did you not?" Kateryna picked up a sonar buoy. "So tell me, what have you done here?"

"These buoys are perfect. I don't care about return signals and computing direction, distance to target, target ID, and all that. All I need is a coded underwater pulse triggered by a VHF signal. Very simple. I modified the flotation so that they have just slightly positive buoyancy in fresh water, and I changed the power supply. We picked up some multistage lithium-fluoride batteries for these guys as well as for their receiver in the weapon case. Waddy can help us decide exactly where in the reservoir the buoys should be placed as well as these VHF repeaters. They'll relay the detonation signal down to the buoys, which will then send out the sonar signal. The repeaters are needed so that the detonation signal will not have to have line-of-sight to the buoys. It would be impossible to get a single position on the shore that would give a direct line to all the buoys. Of course, you don't need exact line-of-sight with a VHF signal; I just wanted to be certain. The repeaters will have to be placed on prominent points above the reservoir. Waddy's job, along with setting the buoys."

"Have you tested the system, starting with the VHF signal, going through a repeater, to a buoy, then to the fuse circuit?"

"Right. I did it up in Clear Lake, using a sonar recorder to measure the strength of the signal as it would be received by the transducer in the weapon. The system worked perfectly. All I have to do now is install the transducer and the additional power supply in the weapon case to convert the sonar signal to electrical impulse."

"What about the proximity fuse?" Kateryna had not forgotten any detail of their conversation down in Grand Canyon.

"That's not at all as good as I would like it to be. We simply could not acquire a sophisticated mass-volume-density fuse mechanism. I'm going to use two of the units out of the sonar buoys, incorporating the return signal component, but eliminating the target ID feature. They're sort of primitive, and I'm not at all sure my limited testing has proven their sensitivity. They must be able to sense a nonmetallic mass of one hundred pounds or a one-and-a-half cubic foot volume, to detect the approach of a diver or a submersible. These things just were not made to be adjustable. I've done the best I can, but, well, they're crude. All they were designed to do is detect a large ferrous or titanium mass. Because of the uncertainty, I've decided to use two of them, with different modifications to the mass/volume-sensing component and to provide some failure redundancy. The transceivers will be set into the outer pressure case to cover all directions."

Kateryna shook her head. "After thinking about the situation some, it seems to me that there would be little risk of tampering with the device 500 feet under water. I'm not convinced you really need the proximity system. Those sonar units you're using are just—how do you say—too squirrelly."

"Yes, I also thought a lot about that. Not having the proximity fuses would simplify things a great deal. I don't want the canyon wall to detonate the device, and there is the further problem of the sonar signals being a constant drain on the power supply. On the other hand, the weapon is not going to just sit there indefinitely."

"Are you sure a big fish won't trigger it?"

"I'm pretty sure of that. According to my testing it will, indeed, take a cubic-foot-and-a-half or a hundred-pound intrusion to trip the circuit."

"How did you figure out what to do to modify the sensitivity?"

"A lot of research. Again, I was surprised at how much there was in the declassified literature. Kateryna, I told you I'm not an electronics man. I can design and build anything that can be fabricated with a lathe and milling machine. That's my specialty: miniaturization of mechanical components. But electronics, well . . ."

"Nonetheless you're going to keep the proximity fuse system?"

Saul hesitated again. "On balance, I still think it's a necessary precaution."

Kateryna closely examined the rest of the things on the bench. "This is your flotation equipment?"

"Yes. Placement will be very simple. Here, take a look at this." Saul unrolled a detailed plan view of the dam and the canyon.

"How did you get this, Saul?"

"Public document. Just have to know what to ask for."

A pair of highly trained eyes scanned the drawing. "Amazing. This sort of thing would never be available to the public in my country."

"They will be as times change."

She raised her eyebrows. "I'm not going to hold my breath." Kateryna again concentrated on the finely-drawn Bureau of Reclamation document. "So what is your plan?"

"These are the river diversion tunnels. They routed the river around the dam site during construction." Saul pointed out the dashed lines on the drawing, indicating the forty-one-foot-diameter tunnels through both walls of the canyon. "Each one is about 3,000 feet in length. Here, you can see where they're plugged at the point where the spillways now intercept the tunnels. About 1,200 feet of the downstream end of the right tunnel was retained for the outflow of the spillway. The left one's a little longer."

"How are they plugged?"

"At the elbow in each spillway there's a 150-foot section of solid concrete, keyed in fifty-foot sections into the rock. Right here you can see the original inlets to the river diversions on each side of the canyon."

"You plan to place the device at one of the inlets?"

"Exactly. I chose the right inlet because of the condition of the rock in the west abutment. However, there's a problem with using that one. It was the first tunnel closed, so there's a steel gate and then a temporary concrete plug right behind it. They had to do that to dewater the tunnel so that the permanent plug could be constructed. But on the other hand, the gate and the temporary plug were only built to withstand 200 feet of water head. With the pressure from a full reservoir, and after all these years, they are almost certainly collapsed by now—at least partially."

"The right tunnel appears to be about 1,700 feet long, down to the permanent plug," Kateryna said when she looked at the scale on the drawing. "That also puts the inlet about the same distance from the dam face."

"That's right."

"Much of the force of the explosion will have a direct hydraulic connection to the plug in the tunnel, given that the water has at least partially collapsed the small temporary gate and plug." She continued to examine the drawing, slowing shaking her head. "It's too close. Even at 1,700 feet, two kilotons will be too much overpressure on the dam."

"Were in luck," Saul beamed. "The upstream cofferdam is still down there. All the debris from the tunnels, the overburden scraped off the bedrock at the dam site, and rock mucked out of the spillway inlets was used for the river diversion cofferdams. The upstream one was about 500 feet thick at the base and maybe 200 feet high. A perfect blast deflector."

"Are you sure it's still there?"

"Has to be. There was no reason to remove it. When the Bureau closed the tunnels, the reservoir backed up behind the cofferdam until it spilled over the top."

"No sloughing? Settling over the past 30 years?"

"Believe me, it's still there. Look here. I drew this up to show the location of the cofferdam with respect to the diversion tunnels and the dam."

Kateryna concentrated on Saul's drawing. "The right tunnel makes about a 20-degree turn after it enters the rock, Saul."

"Won't matter at all. Have you studied fiber optics theory?"

"No, but I understand the concept: the channeling effect of the shock wave down the tunnel."

"Right. It'll work just like a fiber optics cable. The speed of sound in water is about 1,500 meters per second and through this sandstone it's about 3,500. So the slight bend in the tunnel won't make any difference at all."

"In the time the reservoir has been filled—how long has it been—about thirty years, you said? Won't the tunnel inlet be silted in?"

"No, not after only thirty years. The sediment in the water running into Powell Reservoir precipitates out soon after it enters the slack water, and

Upstream portal of right diversion tunnel, 1958 (*Bureau of Reclamation*).

the closest major river inlet is over fifty miles upstream. Down at the bottom near the dam there is virtually no current. The river outlet works are about 225 feet up the face of the dam and the powerhouse penstock inlets are higher than that, so none of them cause currents on the bottom."

"Do you mean the dam was constructed with no outlet at the bottom? The river outlet works are 225 feet up the dam face?"

"Yes. The designers figured that the accumulating mud would eventually reach the dam, so they didn't want to gum up the outlet works."

"But what if the reservoir had to be drained for some repair purpose?"

"Couldn't do it," Saul shrugged. "Anyway, the detonation will be about 500 feet under water and 1,650 feet from the base of the dam, which is about 300 feet thick at the bottom. I've studied the drilling logs and the geology reports that were done before construction; it's clear that there is plenty of jointing and some shale seams in the right abutment. That's the reason I chose the right side over the left, despite the temporary plug in the right tunnel. Two KT should be enough to severely fracture the rock as well as—I hope—damage the tunnel plug. Even if the plug survives, there should be enough damage to the rock around it to start uncontrolled leakage through the fractures.

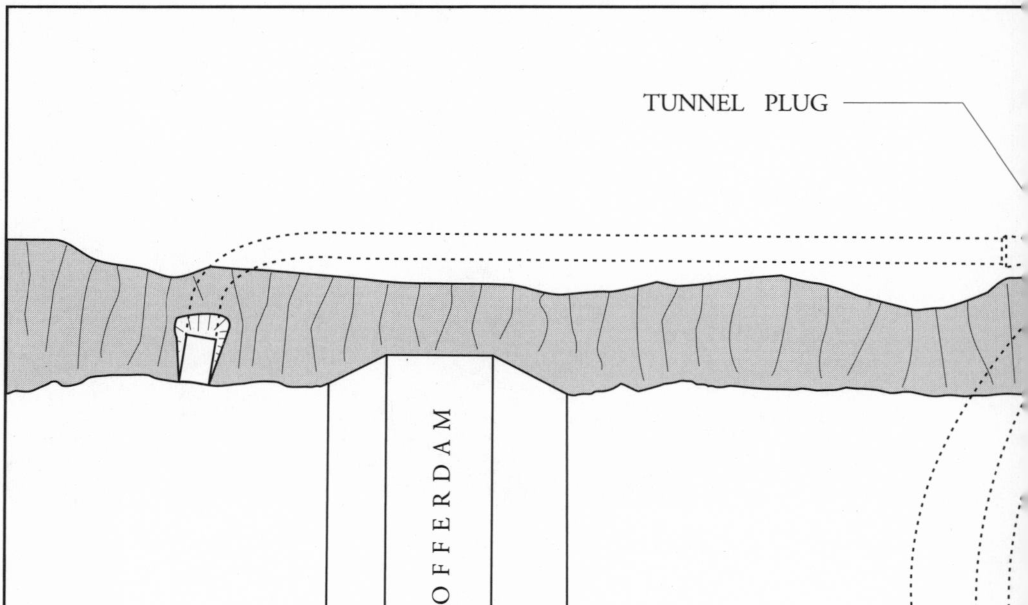
TUNNEL PLUG
COFFERDAM
TUNNEL PLUG

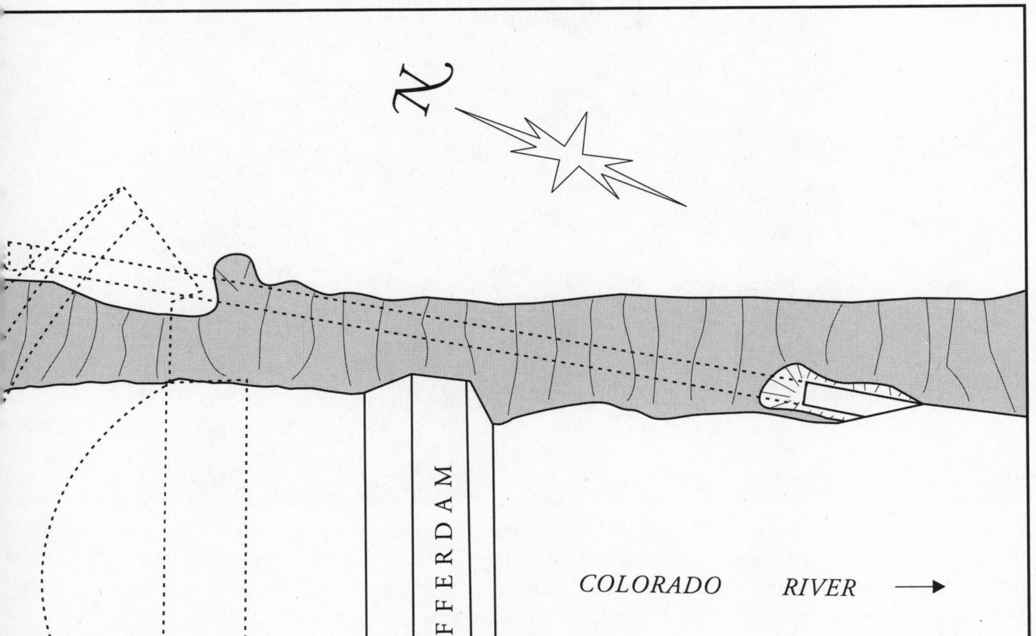
N
COFFERDAM
COLORADO RIVER
0
500
1000
FEET

Dam progress, February 1962. The right tunnel manages the river; the left tunnel portal is thirty feet higher, needed only to accommodate spring runoff. The deep keyways carved into the canyon walls and the inlets for the spillways are clearly shown in this photo. Wahweap Creek aggregate, sorted and piled on the west rim, is constantly replenished while it feeds the nearby concrete batch plant. The "Beehive" on the west rim had to be shaved off to make room for the future visitor center and parking lot (*Bureau of Reclamation, A.E. Turner*).

There will be no way to stop that leakage. The reservoir will drain."

"Are you sure about the joints and seams in the rock? What about faulting?"

"Only vague, conclusory statements were published in the official technical record of design and construction. The specific details were scattered all over so I had to really dig—sorry—to locate them. Back in the early '50s, when the design work was really cranking up, many geologists were very critical of the idea of building such a large dam in the Navajo sandstone. There was a lot of discussion about how poorly cemented the sandstone is, its porosity—even a big debate about the amount of residual stress in the rock as well as the number of joints and seams. I found evidence of only one, apparently inactive, fault across the dam axis. The residual stress, of course, gets greater the nearer the rock is to the wall of the canyon—from the sandstone becoming unloaded by the existence of the eroded canyon. Basically, the rock wants to shear off and collapse into the canyon. Anyway, it was already breaking off in little pieces, so the Bureau had to put in hundreds of rock bolts to hold it. We saw them during our visit."

"So what actual evidence of jointing and seams did you find?"

"A lot in the west abutment. When they got well back into the right wall with the diversion tunnel, a big joint and shear-plane network was encountered. They were committed at that point—couldn't move the dam site, so they just pumped in as much grout as the rock would take."

"How did the engineers know that an adequate grout curtain was established in the abutments?"

"They probably didn't at the time. But no major leaks have developed over the years—just the slow, hydraulic pressure through the sandstone itself and some leakage through cracks that don't flow fast enough to erode the stone. Actually, I guess the engineers figured that since the diversion tunnels would be plugged, the jointing didn't matter. All the details are in the record, scattered through dozens of files. Obviously, the Bureau didn't want to exactly red-flag the situation at the time, what with all the outside geologists trying to make names for themselves. But the best evidence—studies aside—is what happened during the 1983 flood."

"The surging of water and air in the right foundation adit you told me about," Kateryna remembered.

"Correct. It has to be the same jointing, and that proves how extensive it is even though, so far, no big leaks have developed. So the bomb will just help it along, that's all. If we're lucky, we'll fracture the plug too, but that probably won't happen. There's a lot of concrete in there.

"Now, here's how the buoying works. This steel flotation sphere is sized so that the weight of the weapon and the anchor will pull it down. I've calculated the flotation differential so that it will descend at about one and a half feet per second. When the anchor hits the bottom, the sphere's buoyancy will hold up the weapon. The sphere is strong enough to withstand the pressure, and it will float far enough above the weapon to avoid the proximity fuses. You told me the weapon and case weigh exactly 55.6 kilograms; I figured in the extra weight of the new power supply, the proximity fuses, et cetera. Now, to get the rig into position we'll use this inflatable neoprene bladder, sized to hold the lot with positive buoyancy. When it's floated into position, all that needs to be done is to uncoil the anchor rode and the line between the weapon and the sphere, then deflate the bladder. Waddy will handle the placement of the device, as well as the sonar buoys and repeaters. He's confident he can do it all with just a kayak. I've got a nice new one for him."

"What's this?" Kateryna picked up the last item on the bench.

"That's the last piece of stuff to go into the bomb case: the timed arming unit. When Waddy gets to the placement point, he'll enter the code in the PAL which will start this timer. When it runs down, arming will be completed. It's set for six hours; plenty of time to get everything settled into place in the reservoir and everybody out of the area."

"Out of the area? Some doubts, Saul?" She smiled and winked.

"Nobody's perfect. Anyway, once the timer closes the arming circuit, either of the fusing systems will detonate the device."

"What about the detonation signal? Can't it be jammed?"

"Oh, I almost forgot the best part. The transducers in the buoys and in the bomb case have been changed to transmit and receive a whole range of frequencies and signal patterns. They have a large combination of permutations. I don't think the whole array could be interdicted simultaneously, but as a back up, I decided to have land lines to two of the buoys in case the VHF signal is fully jammed."

"I thought you said electronics was not your specialty."

"Right, it's not . . . All I could do was follow a cook book for circuitry that essentially did what I wanted to do."

"Even on that huge reservoir, with airborne detection equipment and enough personnel they will find everything, Saul."

"With the powerful electrical supplies I've installed in the buoys, the sonar signal can run for over sixty miles. That means hundreds of miles of shoreline. An army division couldn't search it all. Waddy will be the one selecting the exact buoy locations; also, he made the decision about which ones are going to have the land lines. No one knows that area like he does."

"Won't your authorities pick up one of the buoys and figure out what your system is, even as complicated as you've made it with the signal frequency and amplitude spectrum?"

"Kateryna, there's no way I could set up a system that can't be compromised. It just gets down to time—the time needed to neutralize the fusing systems versus the amount of time needed to move people away from the dam and down the river corridor. We'll wait a reasonable time for evacuation and then, after a warning, detonate the device before it can be deactivated."

"What about the life of the power supply, Saul? The steady drain from the proximity fuse signals."

"Electronics again. As near as I could figure it, the lithium-ion batteries will be good for a month. We're certainly not going to wait a month to set this thing off."

"I'm surprised Malcolm could not get you a plutonium power cell like we put in the physics package," she said, eyes twinkling.

"Yeah, right. Maybe we could salvage it from one of your space probes that failed during launch."

"How will your authorities know what they are risking when they attempt to disable the weapon?"

"We're going to tell them. I've drafted a letter to the FBI office in Phoenix. Why don't we have some lunch? You can help me fine-tune the letter so we tell them just enough but not too much. Waddy will be leaving this afternoon to get the equipment in place at the reservoir, and I want to get his input on what, if anything, we tell them about buoy placement. I should have the additional stuff into the weapon case and the circuitry changes finished in a couple of days, then the rest of us can head for Arizona."

"Yes, I'd like to go over what you plan to tell your authorities." Kateryna hesitated before she went on. "Saul . . ." she hesitated again. "I'm going up to Seattle this afternoon to see Sofiia– –" Saul started to interrupt. "This is not negotiable. It has been over one month. I cannot wait any longer. You don't need me kibitzing over your shoulder, and there is so little time now. *Try* to understand. And Saul . . . please don't tell Stanley when he gets back from Stony Ridge. Just tell him that I had to get away for a day—to have some space. He will worry, of course, but that is just the way it has to be. I'll be back tomorrow."

***

Office of the United States Attorney, Houston

Jim Peabody glared across his desk at the attorney from the Drug Enforcement Administration. "That's right, Richard, we can't hold her any longer. There's just nothing there."

"But sir," the eager young Harvard Law grad pleaded, "we know a large shipment of heroin arrived in that yacht. We can't just turn it loose."

"*How* do you know? Not the least evidence of drugs was found and no one saw anything loaded aboard or taken off. There is neither testimonial nor physical evidence."

"What about the modified water tank? Why did they cut the big access hole when they were in Malta?"

"Richard, how much do you know about sailing yachts?" From the numerous trophies and photographs in Jim Peabody's office, it was apparent that he knew a great deal about sailing yachts.

"Well, I– –"

"When your people took *Aletheia* apart, all they found was a recently modified water tank with proper baffles installed. Many old yachts did not have properly baffled water tanks. Do you know what baffles are?"

"No, sir."

"A large water tank must have baffles—vertical plates—installed inside to keep the water in a partially full tank from sloshing around. A big slug of water moving across an unbaffled tank can cause quite a force. It can even break the tank loose."

"The drawings from Malta do not show baffles. There is also the size of the access hole," the staff attorney argued.

"Richard, the baffles could have been added later. They're just simple flat plates. All the brackets shown on the drawings and as installed in the tank, while oddly curved, merely hold the baffles in place. The large port in the tank is required to install the new hardware and to enable the tank to be cleaned once the baffles are in place. You have to be able to get at all parts of a water tank."

"Sir, we– –"

"No. That's it. I'm not going before Judge Cisneros again with this dog shit case. It was real thin getting the warrants for the search after the boat was in the yard and to hold the crew based on the profile evidence you had. The credibility of this office is just too important, considering that he hears most of the drug cases in this district. The owner of *Aletheia* has engaged the most aggressive firms in New York and here in Houston; now they've filed a motion for an order to show cause why the vessel should not be released. With the case load in his court, if we push this Cisneros will rip out my asshole and feed it to me. Have you ever appeared before Judge Cisneros, Richard?"

"No, but– –"

"And another thing. One of your agents—what's his name—Ferguson. He got carried away again. Put a leash on that animal. One of these days he's going to screw up a really important case."

"Bobby really *is* a good man, sir. His partner got tortured and killed down in Cali."

"Look, I appreciate that. But if he's carrying too much emotional baggage, he should be reassigned. That English kid got roughed up pretty good, and the guys down in civil claims want to settle with him fast and get him the hell out of here before this whole thing starts making print. I'm going to confess the petitioner's motion, then we're going to release the boat this morning. That'll do us all a favor. I'm sorry, Richard; it just turned out to be a dry hole. After a few more of these you'll start to get a feel for which cases to go to the mat with. This isn't one of them."

8

Naples, June 1

John Stiles was enjoying a long lunch. The assignment in Italy was good duty and after three years he'd gotten fully into the Mediterranean way of life. So had the friend sitting across the table in the waterfront cafe.

"John, you can't take this stuff that seriously—personally, I mean," the CIA station chief said. "You just made a wrong call, that's all."

"I can't let it go, Sammy. There's something there. Something very important. I just know it."

"Okay, I'll do it. I'll send these drawings along to Langley."

"And the file I have on the known movements of the yacht and the descriptions and info on her crew," the DEA agent added.

"Right." Sam Mattingly was primarily interested in calming down his old friend. If sending the information back home for analysis would help, he was more than happy to do it.

"Something important was smuggled, Sammy. Maybe it wasn't drugs, but it had to have been something else. Something big. Those guys went to a lot of trouble using that old yacht to do the job. And there's another thing."

"Yes?" Sam Mattingly said with neutral interest.

"My contact in Valletta has never given me a bad tip. Never."

* * *

Pacific Ocean, 1,200 miles west of Acapulco

The huge cell of rotating tropical air and moisture moved along the path that hundreds of thousands of its sisters and brethren have followed in the era of the current configuration of the land and water masses of the earth: one of the ordained routes that the great cyclonic storms of the tropics have traveled for hundreds of millions of years before man appeared. Mankind has been concerned with tracking their seemingly fickle wanderings for only a few decades, and only since 1966, with the advent of weather reconnaissance satellites, has accurate monitoring been possible. Although he can now gauge and track them, the newcomer is still a long way from predicting just how and when they will form and where they will go in their brief, violent lives. And there is faint hope that he will ever be able to do anything about them other than to try to get out of their way.

Since it had been born four days before, the disturbance in the far region of the eastern equatorial Pacific Ocean had intensified and consolidated. When it first began to form, the nascent storm had faced a capricious, hostile environment, its future by no means certain: it could have languished, disorganized, or it could have been quickly annihilated—ripped apart by the relentless trade winds. Only a tiny fraction of the easterly waves that travel along the ITCZ each year develop into disturbances, then mature storms. So far this season, four of the waves had encountered favorable conditions in the Atlantic and had turned off track to become disturbed areas. Of those, two had developed into tropical depressions; one becoming a tropical storm, then a hurricane.

The youngster in the eastern Pacific also survived. The seedling thunderstorms had coalesced into a symbiotic, revolving mass of warm air and moisture, becoming a tropical depression; then when the winds circulating about its core exceeded thirty-nine mph in tangential velocity, the depression earned the distinction of a name: she was Tropical Storm Carlotta, the third of her kind in the eastern Pacific this season. Carlotta was not at all like the great extratropical cyclones that regularly sweep easterly during the northern winter, one after another across the temperate region of the northern hemisphere. They are born of the clash of cold and dry with warm and moist. Carlotta was a creature solely of the tropics, and the mechanism of her formation, even her function in the grand scheme, was not fully understood. Meteorologists around the world still struggled to find order and predictability in what often appeared to be fathomless chaos in the interaction between the seas and atmosphere of the earth.

The fuel for Carlotta's massive engine, like every variety and bit of energy on or near the earth's surface, from buried coal and oil to warm air and water, began in the sun. The radiant heat beat relentlessly on the equatorial reach of the eastern Pacific Ocean, relentlessly and forcefully enough to continually evaporate the sea's water: a substance which of all the physical elements on the earth required the most heat energy to change its state from a liquid to a vapor. Then as the vapor-saturated air rose from the sea it became slightly cooler, even in the environment of the tropics, condensing the vapor and sending it back to the sea as rain. As it condensed, however, it gave back the latent heat of vaporization the sun originally provided. The massive infusion of heat energy from the re-liquefied water further heated the air, causing faster rising of more saturated air, increasing winds that added to the vorticity of the core of the storm, and lifting ever larger masses of water into the maelstrom.

Like the two tropical storms that had preceded her this early season in the Eastern Pacific, Carlotta had moved nearly west, curving only slightly to the north. But unlike her predecessors, which had formed farther to the south, Carlotta encountered a barrier: an extension of the Pacific High that had slid and elongated unusually far to the south. Atmospheric physicists throughout North America were working to correlate the unusual southern movement of the Pacific High with the massive El Niño/Southern Oscillation event that was currently in progress.

Confronted with the obstacle, Carlotta was unable to slip beneath its southern fringe as her predecessors had done, both going on to whirl harmlessly across the expanse of the Pacific, finally dying above waters too cool to feed them. And Carlotta was now too large to merely collapse and disperse before the barrier. With her way to the west blocked, she began to curve more sharply to the north, her route increasingly encouraged by the Coriolis Effect. While she did so she slowed, nearly stalling, yet her energy machine continued to build over the unusual high-temperature water. The deepening low pressure at her core, now with a well-defined eye, drew the low-level moist air up through the hot convection towers that encircled her eye wall. It rushed and spiraled up the columns at speeds of nearly fifty mph, to be ejected at an altitude of 40,000 feet into the counterclockwise pinwheel of her outflow cloud shield—what is visible in photographs taken from space.

It happened that on this occasion, as it had happened on tens of thousands of occasions over thousands of millennia, the top of the storm was just to the southeast of a tropical branch of the eastwardly-flowing jet stream: the 200-mph freeway of high-altitude air, traveling much higher than its polar branch, was following the eastward bulge of the Pacific High. When the stream rushed past the upper reaches of the storm, it created an anticyclone of the ejected winds, turning them in a clockwise direction. In consequence a hugely decreased pressure in her upper reaches was created. As an increase in air pressure in an internal combustion engine causes a supercharged increase in power, so the pressure decrease in Carlotta's massive engine drew even larger masses of heat up her convection towers from the sea. Her rotational speed increased; as it did so her ring of maximum winds contracted dramatically toward her core and ever larger volumes of moist air were drawn in. She had a total energy content equivalent to a ten-kiloton explosion of dynamite occurring each second: twenty-five times greater than the entire electrical power generation in the whole of the United States. And she was not yet a hurricane.

With her surge of new energy, and aided by the high-altitude winds steering her to the northeast, Carlotta completed a wide, slow recurve that pointed her toward the coast of central Baja California, 1,000 miles away. She began to accelerate.

* * *

Stan had been watching all afternoon. At last he saw the rental car come up the steep hill and into the drive. *Thank God!* He ran down the steps as she leapt from the car. They came together in the middle of the yard.

A long and intense emotional exchange, finally ebbing. "Stanley, I'm sorry; I just had to see Sofiia."

"Damnit, why didn't you tell me you were going up to Seattle? You made Saul and Waddy tell me that bullshit about your just needing to get away for a while, huh? Well, it didn't work. I've been worried sick."

"Stanley, I . . . you never would have understood."

"At least I could have gone with you."

"Please understand, it was much easier—and safer—to travel alone."

"How is Sofiia?"

"Oh, Stanley, she is so much better! She is happy, and the doctors feel that she has a good chance. A *very* good chance. I had a long talk with them . . ."

"What's wrong?"

"Let's go inside." She linked her arm in his and started toward the house. Stan stopped her.

"Wait. I have to tell you something, first. It's Saul. Apparently, there's some problem with the weapon. He's very upset and he won't talk to us about it. He's been keeping to himself, waiting for you to get back."

Saul listened attentively when she told him the good news about Sofiia, but he was politely distracted. "What is it, Saul?"

He frowned at his clasped hands for a few long moments before answering. "That is not a two-kiloton weapon. I sensed something was wrong when I first looked into the case. I cannot measure the quantities of fissile material, or the configuration of the pit and the lenses, but the apparent power of the neutron generator made me question the yield. So I weighed the whole thing. You told me that the gross weight of the two-kiloton weapon is 55.6 kilos. Well, the weight of this device is 62.7. The yield has to be at least fifteen kilotons. Damnit, this was not our arrangement. This changes everything!" He slammed his fist on the table and got up.

"Saul," Stan said after a moment, "I'm sure there's some explanation, perhaps– –"

"Shut up, damnit!" Saul screamed. His friend of thirty-six years had never seen him act this way.

Stan turned to Kateryna. "So what's the deal?"

"You are mistaken, Saul. That device is two kilotons."

"Okay, come out to the shop and I'll show you."

Kateryna looked into the stainless steel canister at the familiar collection of components. She saw that in her absence Saul had completed all the fuse modification work and the additional power supply installation. Everything was beautifully done. She then looked closely at the components that had been created and assembled in Russia. Like Saul, she fully understood that with the modern weapons there was little difference in overall physical configuration between a two-kiloton weapon and one with a twenty-kiloton yield. Besides the fission initiation equipment, there were only small changes in the relative sizes of the fissile materials and the high-explosive lenses, with little visible from the exterior unless the observer happened to be very familiar with the exact design of the particular weapon. Kateryna was very familiar with this device. When she looked closely at the HE lenses and the neutron generator she saw that Saul was correct. Without question, he was correct.

"Well? Do you see what I mean?"

"It's twenty kilotons."

Saul kicked a can of stainless steel mill shavings across the shop, followed by another kick to the wall.

"Okay, folks," Stan said a few moments after Saul perched himself rigidly on his stool, "we're going to go back into the house and talk this through. To start with, Kateryna, you're going to tell us everything about how you acquired the weapon."

She gave him a long, painful look. Then with an intuition independent of any acquired skill, she nodded.

Kateryna did tell them everything, beginning with how she had first learned of the scheme to hide a number of tactical nuclear weapons.

"What happened to the man at Chelyabinsk who told you about the conspiracy?" Saul asked. The shocking revelations had thoroughly quashed his anger.

"He just disappeared, like the others."

"How could you have found out and not been liquidated yourself?"

"Just luck. Misha was never linked to me, and remember, when he told me it was less than a year after Tolik died—only shortly after the conspiracy began. I was still being, well, left alone. That was very apparent. A number of my superiors felt bad about how I had been treated in not being able to go back to Kyyiv until after my husband died."

Kateryna looked over at Stan. He'd been very quiet since she'd told them about her relationship with General Nastenko after her return to Ukraine. "Stanley, I would do anything to save her life. Anything. Any mother would do the same."

Her palliatives afforded Stan only the tiniest measure of relief. "Your knowledge of the existence of these hidden weapons had much to do with your decision to help us, then. You were afraid they would escape into the hands of terrorists," he finally said, not as a question.

She nodded. "I have told Saul—all of you—that the situation in my part of the world is not just a matter of academic interest."

Saul remembered his naïvely academic conversations with Kateryna back in Pueblo and on the river trip. "We should have known there was more to your response than ideological differences. And this information, if discovered by our disarmament people, could destroy the entire treaty arrangement. Set us back years. Even start a whole new cycle of paranoid defense madness in the Congress." Saul paused for a moment. "Were these weapons to be refitted or retired because of the switch problem? Can you tell us about that?"

"Yes. Now that you know about the existence of the conspiracy, the details of how those officers were able to acquire the weapons does not matter. Officially, they were returned to Nizhnyaya Tura for refitting. There was an opportunity, while they were located at the weapons plant, to *lose* them, so to speak. It was still difficult, I am sure, but far easier than trying to spirit away dozens of duty-ready pieces from many scattered locations."

"Kateryna, what else is there?" Stan demanded. "What happened in Seattle?"

Even under her glowing, ocean tan, he could see her face darken. "He is here, in America," she said without emotion.

"Who? Not him! General Nastenko is here? My God!" Stan jumped to his feet.

"Yes. I saw him near the hospital; however, I am sure he did not see me. Stanley, please sit down."

"But there's no security for Sofiia. The fact that you were able to just walk in and talk to her and the doctors makes it pretty clear that the authorities don't know you're here." He sat down. "What if he takes her? That settles it, then; we must make a formal request for her asylum and protection. I'll call Malcolm as soon as he gets back."

"Stanley, the least assertion that a nine-year-old girl needs protection will surely expose all of you. Just *what* would you tell your authorities? As it is, she is doing fine. Just another poor little sick refugee."

"At the least, she must be moved."

"Where? The Alfred Hoskins Center is the very best; she is in the midst of a complicated series of treatments. And there is something else. The clinic administrator told me that the doctors in Kyyiv have asked to be kept informed of Sofiia's progress."

"How could they know she's there? What's going on?"

"They also want to be advised if Sofiia is moved and where she is taken. The academician at the Kyyiv Oncological Institute who made the request is a very close friend of General Nastenko."

"Kateryna! You cannot leave her to the mercy of a KGB killer!" Stan immediately regretted his outburst. Painful silence. He could almost feel the woman sitting across the table saying: *"like me?"*

She continued, more coolly. "He will not harm Sofiia. You do not know this man."

"No, I certainly cannot know him as you do." He immediately regretted that remark more than his last one.

"We will discuss this further only when Malcolm returns," Kateryna said, the coolness now ice. "Saul, why don't we talk about the change in circumstances we now have to deal with?"

He shook his head somberly. "There is nothing to be done."

"We have come so far. There has to be a way to salvage the situation." She was thankful for Waddy's absence. He would only have added fuel to the dry tinder.

Stan desperately wanted to recover from his blunders. "Isn't there some way to decrease the yield?"

They shook their heads in funereal unison. "Stan," Saul answered, his normal patience now fully reverted to type, "these mechanisms are exquisitely balanced, integrated units. At detonation everything occurs in a carefully orchestrated sequence in a matter of nanoseconds. Why in hell do you think it took thousands of people and about twenty billion in today's dollars to figure it out and crudely build the first one? This is a fixed yield device.

Weapons that are designed to be variable yield use a hydrogen isotope, tritium, that is inserted into the pit just prior to the detonation sequence. Yield can be adjusted by changing the amount of tritium. This device does not have that feature. Mission-required reliability and long shelf life precluded the use of that arrangement with these weapons."

"Actually, the yield *can* be reduced," Kateryna allowed, nodding her head. "The urchin redundancy that you compared to a—what did you say—a Model T?"

"Bypass the neutron generator? I thought of that, but the yield would probably be very unpredictable."

"Yes. The limited testing that was done on these devices with the deuterium gun eliminated produced a range of yields with just the urchin and its contained matrix of lithium deuteride. Only slight variances in initial neutron flux resulted in a wide variation in the fusion boost. Yields ranged from three to as high as seven kilotons."

"Can either of you try to explain that to me?" Stan asked. He looked at Kateryna.

"Stanley, an explosive nuclear reaction requires extra neutrons to be inserted into the core prior to the fissile material being crushed to critical mass by imploding high explosives. As Saul said, tritium is the best source of the neutrons, but it has such a short half life that it has to be replaced regularly—impossible for the mission of these demolition munitions. This weapon uses a different scheme. A device called a neutron gun, that injects a burst of deuterium into the core at the precise moment in the detonation sequence, is the primary source of neutrons. There is also a redundant system: an old fashioned assembly of polonium and beryllium in a frangible lattice, statically placed in the core, and with the lattice filled with lithium deuteride, another source of neutrons. The neutron generator is more efficient, but is critically dependent upon a precisely timed insertion. The polonium/beryllium urchin is crude and of low-neutron yield, but it is reliable. Just exactly how many neutrons are there to initiate the reaction, and when they are there, wholly determines what happens. Fast neutron generation time—what may be called a single link in a chain reaction—occurs in ten nanoseconds: ten billionths of a second. The energy release, or yield, of the weapon builds up geometrically, with the very great majority of it occurring during the last few generations. With a 100 kiloton weapon, for example, 99.9 percent of the explosive force is released in the last six of 58 generations, and the whole sequence of generations, or "doublings," occurs in only a little over half a microsecond. With the 100 KT device I mention as an example, a 59th generation, which would nearly double the yield, does not occur because the fissile core is being blown apart to less than criticality in the 58th generation. So what happens in the crucial final stage is wholly dependent upon the efficiency with which the sequence begins."

Saul nodded. "That's one reason why there has been so much testing over the years. The least variance in design or fabrication can have profound consequences."

"And when it comes to fabrication of these mechanisms," Kateryna continued, "far more than mere theory, materials, and sophisticated tools are required. An unbelievable amount of technical skill—artistic skill, really—is required to get the job done. They make a Swiss watch look primitive. We have been very fortunate. A great deal of skill was needed just to make the changes in the fusing that Saul has done."

Stan noticed Saul blush slightly. He smiled at him: "It's clear that all those years rebuilding antique cars have paid off, Saul." He immediately realized that his old friend did not have to be reminded that he would never again see his beloved automobiles. For the third time in less than five minutes, Stan had opened his mouth only to change feet. A withering glance from Kateryna accentuated his regret. Another long moment of painful silence.

Kateryna turned to Saul. "Do you have maps of the configuration of the canyon upstream of the dam? Before it was flooded?"

"Yes, I have the old U.S. Geological Survey's seven-and-a-half-minute topos of the area. Hold on." He returned with a stack of maps and soon found the right quad.

"The canyon walls are very nearly sheer, on both sides, upstream for two miles," Kateryna pointed out. "The floor is also uniform. Of course, the upstream dam face is only gently curved and vertical through most of its height. With such conditions, we should be able to quite accurately calculate shock wave expansion, rebound rates, and energy transmission as a function of progressively distant placement of the weapon upstream from the dam. This is right in my area: detonation physical effects."

Saul stared intently at the contour lines on the old map. "We don't know the exact configuration of the cofferdam you aren't convinced is still down there."

Kateryna ignored the sarcasm. "We will also need to see the cross-sections of the dam and its keying into the sandstone. And we will need the core drilling data you spoke of."

"I've got them." He came back with a pile of drawings and loose-leaf folders.

Kateryna glanced through the compilations of information detailing the hundreds of core samples that had been taken from the canyon rock. "The walls are remarkably homogeneous, despite what you said about the jointing and seams in the west wall. This will make the calculations even easier."

Saul responded with tepid enthusiasm: "Not so. Seams, layers, and fracture planes lace through it, as with any sandstone. Many fractures must exist besides the ones cored or otherwise discovered during construction. I did a statistical probability analysis, given the ones that were discovered. It's in that pile in front of you somewhere. And that rock is certainly not homogeneous. If it was, I probably wouldn't have taken this whole thing on." He was now into full, Saul-mode sarcasm—a common frustration-release modality for a brilliant mind.

Kateryna persisted. "What programs do you have for this little computer?"

"Not so little: a gig, 32 megs of random, and a fast processor." Saul once again left the room and came back with a printout. "I ripped these off from the lab. I needed them when I did the calculations for the device we were *supposed* to get." Saul could not hide his frown.

She briefly perused the list. "Two of these will work fine for what we need to do."

"How could you possibly know?" Now a quiescent spark of interest.

"Oh, we have all of these. Primitive but adequate."

"But how– –"

"We bought them from your software manufacturers . . . and some other persons. It is simply amazing what is offered for sale in this country."

"But some of these are custom designed, even if they are a bit out of date."

"Those are the ones that were acquired on the, uh, secondary market. But that doesn't matter. Come on, Saul, let's get to work. Give me a chance. I'll convince you."

Stan watched in quiet, wholly uninformed silence while the two physicists huddled in front of the PC screen for the better part of the next four hours. They were speaking English, with occasional lapses into Ukrainian, but it might as well have all been an ancient Coptic dialect. Stan had barely managed to survive plane geometry in high school, and he had long ago accepted that his spatial visualization skills peaked with his ability to assemble a sandwich, as Waddy had so cruelly observed. Herculean effort and intense motivation had been required, over many years, for him to become proficient in sailboat navigation. He had no hope of even beginning to understand what Saul and Kateryna were talking about. All he could do to measure progress was to monitor trends of facial expressions and body language, summits of vocal enthusiasm and valleys of silent plodding. He busied himself with supplying food and drink. Abruptly, the intense activity seemed to have concluded.

"Is that sufficient cross-verification for you, Saul?"

"I accept the calculations. It's the physical data in the area of the abutments and the cofferdam situation that are uncertain."

"We're using the same data you used for the close placement."

"Not at the location of the sandstone abutments, I didn't. With the small device, the cofferdam would easily absorb enough of the blast even with the worst assumptions with rebound. And I didn't have to get into the situation with the abutments. Even with more remote placement of the larger device, and assuming the most probable energy transmission to the *assumed* mass of the cofferdam, the concrete can *probably* withstand the higher overpressure. But the patterns of force vectors into the abutments are too uncertain. The confidence factor is unacceptable."

"You had a damage confidence factor of 91 percent with the small device. This one is 79 percent."

"Yes, but there are more assumptions that we cannot as exactly quantify with the detached placement, so the 79 percent is really not that firm. It can't be. Even with the most favorable assumptions about the size and configuration of the cofferdam, the entirety of the concrete dam is now at critical overpressure. We've had to make some pretty thin assumptions about the rebound efficiency off the bottom and sides of the reservoir. And besides the abutments, there is the further uncertainty of the bedrock keying. I was attacking the canyon wall with little collateral effect on the structure. The yield of this weapon is just too much, no matter where we place it. The structure will get too much overpressure."

"It could be as little as three KT."

"Oh, come *on*, Kateryna! We *have* to assume seven. Worst case analyses on everything is mandatory."

"We have done all we can do with the information we have, Saul."

"My point exactly. Besides, we would have to give up the proximity fusing safeguard with the device right next to the canyon wall."

Kateryna plotted the weapon placement point on the old map and then overlaid it with an acetate sheet showing the present reservoir configuration. "So there it is: 9,250 feet from the dam face, immediately adjacent to the right wall. Depth is 490 feet. Water depth at the placement point is projected to be 510 feet on June 5, rising at about point two feet per day."

Maps and nautical charts were back in Stan's sphere of comprehension, so he interrupted. "How is Waddy going to locate the exact placement point in a kayak, right next to a canyon wall on a dark night, nearly two miles from the lights on the dam? We about have a new moon now."

"Shouldn't there be enough residual light above the hills surrounding the reservoir so that he can pick out landmarks?" Kateryna asked. "He could triangulate from these three high points on the other side. Even with only starlight, shouldn't they be visible enough against the sky? He can take bearings with that little hand-held compass we used on *Samora*. What did you call it, Stanley?"

"A hockey puck. I don't know," Stan replied quietly, thinking about the many times he'd groped along a dark and unknown sea coast, uncertain of his position. "Except for Page, maybe the power plant, and whatever there is late at night at the Wahweap Marina, there's no source of background light. It could be raining. And on the other hand, the lights could screw up his night vision."

Kateryna plotted the bearings from the placement point to the three conspicuous sandstone domes the topographic map showed rising above the level of the reservoir. "What is the magnetic variation in the area, Saul?"

"Twelve point nine degrees east."

"Does your hockey puck have any deviation, Stanley?"

"Not in a plastic kayak. But he'll have to drag that big steel sphere well behind him so it doesn't affect the compass."

"I'm sorry it's not stainless," Saul said.

"So. Here are the bearings." Kateryna laid the slip of paper on top of the maps. Everyone stared at the three numbers in silence. Stan went into the kitchen for more coffee. Saul got up and stared out the window at the barn.

"We can't do it. We just can't do it," he finally said in a flat voice. He turned around and faced the others. "There's just too great a risk the whole structure will fail. The flood is unthinkable. That reservoir is nearly full again. It's been snowing steadily in the high country for the past two months and the big runoff is only now starting—a repeat of the situation in 1983 and '84. The goddamn Bureau, once again, has not left enough space in the reservoir, they're so cocksure of their spillway repairs."

"Saul," Stan interjected carefully, "we knew the reservoir would be full or nearly so, we– –"

"I know, I know . . . It would have been nice to delay this whole thing until late winter when the reservoir is at its lowest. I know we can't. I appreciate the time constraints—the situation with Sofiia. And it's just a matter of time before we're discovered." He gave Kateryna a glance. "But the situation now with this weapon. No, this is just too much. We can't. When Malcolm gets back, we'll discuss the whole thing, along with what to do about Sofiia."

Kateryna studied Saul absently, her mind going back over the previous four hours' work. After a long pause, "Saul is correct."

"But your calculations with the new yield," Stan protested. Somehow, probably having much to do with his escort of the weapon across a large piece of the earth's surface, he had lost his inhibition about the project.

"There *is* too much risk. I must agree with Saul."

Helplessly, he looked at each of them in turn. "I guess I can't argue with two physicists. What about Waddy?"

"We will just have to meet him at the rendezvous and explain the situation, that's all," Kateryna said with finality.

Saul looked at her with relief. "Give me a hand closing up the case."

Malcolm listened closely over the telephone, amazingly without interruption, while Kateryna outlined the situation with Sofiia. "Sofiia should stay where she is for the time being. The facilities and staff at Hoskins are not available anywhere else, at least not until I can get a few last things put together out of the country. I'll get some of my guards up there immediately—no one will even notice them. Believe me, Kateryna, even you would approve of these people. They can handle anything."

Kateryna saw that he was correct. That was the end of one issue.

Malcolm even listened patiently while Saul tediously explained why the weapon could not be modified and why a more remote placement in the reservoir was too risky. Saul suffered from the scientist's compulsion to pick all the fly shit out of the pepper. Malcolm finally cut Saul off when he became convinced that it tasted sufficiently like pepper. "As for the bomb, I agree with Saul and Kateryna. This has changed everything. Why don't we go after that friggin' dam plugging up the Hetch Hetchy? Should be able to quiet Waddy down with that alternative. Just blow the shittin' thing to bits. All the water will run down into Don Pedro Reservoir. Plenty of room there since the greedy farmers in the valley keep it sucked dry every year."

"I don't like that idea at all," Stan said angrily in the direction of the speaker phone. "I mean, I like the idea of getting rid of O'Shaughnessy Dam, but there's no way I'm going to have anything to do with setting off a twenty-, or seven-, or three-, or whatever-kiloton atomic bomb in the middle of Yosemite Park, spewing radiation all over the place. Besides, there'll be hundreds of hikers and backpackers in there by now. There're a lot of popular trails in that area, and people will be camped all over the place. Impossible to find them all. No, let's think of something else."

Malcolm: "Why don't we just sit on the whole thing for a while? What's the rush? It's been nearly six weeks since the weapon was removed from Ukraine."

Saul spoke up. "I'm getting real nervous about staying here any longer. That Ukrainian general is over here now and God only knows what he has in mind to do." Kateryna nodded. "Kateryna agrees."

"Well, that's also right," Malcolm said after a beat. "As soon as our authorities do have a clue, it will be the end of our chance to do anything, at least here in the States. I guess I do agree that we're at the shit-or-get-off-the-pot point. I suppose we should just hide the weapon and get the hell on out of here. I'm sure we'll be able to come up with a worthy use for that thing somewhere."

"Aren't we all forgetting the more fundamental reason for taking on this project?" Kateryna asked, this time with Saul bobbing his head in agreement. "This weapon needs to be detonated—the sooner the better—and ideally here in the U.S., where it will have the most, shall I say, *political* effect. Gentlemen, we still have a marvelous opportunity, which may soon be lost, to create worldwide awareness of the dangerous situation with all these weapons. How will we all feel when the inevitable finally happens with another Soviet weapon and we passed up the chance to do something that might have contributed to preventing it?"

"Saul, what about just taking that thing out in the Nevada desert?" Stan suggested. "Maybe somewhere near the current testing range? Touch it off out there. We could even turn it into a big media circus in advance." The room was silent as everyone chewed on Stan's idea and Kateryna's painful observation.

"Stanley," Malcolm said, "risking my whole plan in order to get rid of that dam is one thing, but just to make a political statement? I don't think so. Maybe we should just chuck that thing into the trench offshore and forget it."

"More than a political statement is involved," Kateryna said. "Since General Nastenko is here, he must have moved the rest of the weapons in Ukraine—eighty-one of them, gentlemen. And the reason for our debate right now is that forty of them are twenty-kilotons yield. Detonating the one we have will go a long way toward convincing your authorities that they should find him, before he decides to do something about his hatred for your country."

None of the three old friends had remotely considered that the pilfering of a single, small, atomic bomb from the former Soviet Union could have lead to the present situation.

Malcolm's voice echoed in the room. "Yes . . . you're right, of course. Our little scheme is now out of hand—we have an obligation to do the most effective thing."

"And we'd better get a move on," Kateryna said. "If we're apprehended without the weapon being detonated, our governments will simply handle it all quietly—no dramatic event that could lead to some real disarmament action."

Malcolm: "I agree. You should all clear out of there right now. This Nastenko guy aside, it won't be long before someone finds that stuff we've got spread around the reservoir."

"I don't think we could ever talk Waddy into going back and getting it all," Stan said.

"And I'm worried about his reaction to all this as it is," Saul nodded. Everyone sat in silence, staring at the speaker phone.

"I do know a good place, north of the old Yucca Flat range," Saul finally said. "Don't know what the security situation is there anymore; but for sure there's nobody living in the area and it's already contaminated."

"So we just make another crater out in the Nevada desert and Glen Canyon Dam remains," Stan said bitterly, despite the fact that it was his suggestion. He was thinking about everything he'd been through in the past few weeks.

"Stanley," Malcolm said after a long moment, "I know it's easy for me to say; I wasn't along on that long sailing trip. But you just have to set it aside. We only have what is now. Agonizing over anything else will just make you crazy." Both Saul and Stan understood, after knowing the man for over thirty-five years, that Malcolm never wasted a moment with woulda-coulda-shoulda's. "So, have we got a plan?" the speaker phone asked.

"Yes, let's do it," Saul said. Stan nodded feebly and Kateryna smiled. "Malcolm, we've got agreement. I'll go over to Nevada to scout our way into the old test range. I've been there a lot of times; I have several ideas about how to get in, but it'll take some time. I can meet Stan and Kateryna in Vegas, after their scheduled rendezvous with Waddy Sunday evening. No way to find him until then."

"How do you plan to trigger it now?" Kateryna asked.

"Just a timer, I suppose. I've got a couple since at one point I was still thinking about a timed detonation." Saul thought a moment. "But the way I've got things wired, I'll have to do that *after* the permissive action circuit is closed—that means after we place the weapon. Can't have you driving that bomb from here with the PAL closed."

"How do you say?—'you have got that right,'" Kateryna smiled.

"Okay, I'll stand by," Malcolm said. "When you tell me everything's set, I'll take care of the media contact. What should I say—that's it's booby-trapped and set to go off nearly immediately?"

"That'll work," Saul said. "As soon as the Energy people find out, they won't let anyone get within fifty miles, anyway. Okay, let's do it. We can meet at the Hilton in Vegas Sunday night. Will eleven o'clock give you enough time?"

Stan nodded. "Yeah, should be. Shall I unload all the rest of the crap—all the flotation stuff—from the van?"

"Oh, hell, leave it in there. Good way to get rid of it—and the van."

9

West Wing of the White House, Thursday noon, June 2

The President's chief of staff stepped into the anteroom. "Is everyone here? Good. Come in, gentlemen."

Wil Grosvenor tried not to gawk, but he couldn't help it. In his military career, and then during his tenure as director of the Arms Control and Disarmament Agency, he had been in on many high-level meetings with puffed-up politicians and glittering with brass. But this was the Oval Office, and he was one of a party of six seating themselves on the rose and ivory damask sofas near the fireplace. The President, dressed casually in a polo shirt and slacks, was pouring himself a cup of coffee from a silver service next to a bronze bust of Abraham Lincoln.

"Coffee, anyone? Help yourselves." The President sat down in one of the gold silk armchairs facing the group. "Okay, Judge Ahmanson, tell us where we are now."

Stuart Ahmanson really did not want to be here. This meeting with the President had all the indicators of being one in which he would be put on the spot with inquiries about specific intelligence matters. His deputy director of intelligence, a career officer with the agency, would be far better prepared to answer the President's questions. The Director couldn't gain a thing at this meeting—only possibly lose political points. He cleared his throat and began in his sonorous, controlled voice. "Mr. President, since you last spoke to President Yarzov we've had more developments. Prior to the disappearance of the last known conspirator, this General Nastenko, we have been advised that one of his senior staff also vanished: Lieutenant Colonel Kateryna Romanivna Kovalevska. Incidentally, I am in direct communication with my counterpart in the Russian Federation Foreign Intelligence Service, so we are getting fresh information. Everything that is verifiable has been spot on. It's clear that President Yarzov was sincere in his promise of full cooperation."

"If he wants his seven billion dollars, I guess he *would* cooperate," the President said dryly.

"Yes, sir. It seems that the relationship between the general and his aide was complicated. They were intimately involved." Two pairs of legs uncrossed and recrossed, followed by some shifting of bodies on the couches.

"Okay, he took his girlfriend with him," the President snapped. "Get to the point, Stuart."

"Sir, the evidence is compelling that this Colonel Kovalevska has arranged the smuggling of a fully operational tactical nuclear weapon into this country. We believe it arrived at Galveston on May 23."

The President stared intently at the CIA Director for several long moments. "*How* compelling is the evidence, Stuart?"

"Very, Mr. President."

Another long pause. "Okay, give me the details."

"Colonel Kovalevska has a gravely ill daughter, her only child, suffering from radiation poisoning from the Chornobyl incident. The colonel's husband, a physician, died treating the victims of the disaster, and the daughter, Sofiia Anatolovna, is now at an oncology clinic in Seattle. With the treatment she was receiving in Kyyiv, it was apparent that she would not survive. I'll tell you what—the little girl's mother is gutsy. She visited her daughter yesterday morning. Even talked to the staff. We didn't find out that the child was at the clinic until last night. Just missed the woman. Anyway, there's the colonel's motive.

"She was a group leader on one of the TART teams last winter, and she disappeared for about a week under very suspicious circumstances. Moscow tells us she was able to elude the three very capable agents who were assigned to watch her team. The matter of her intimacy with General Nastenko is next. Moscow does not believe it was innocent. They believe she used him to gain access to other caches of secreted weapons that the conspirators claimed were in Ukraine. The storage locations in Symferopil and Odessa have been investigated, and indeed, a single marine container has recently been removed from each location. Mr. President, this woman is a former KGB officer with a specialty in nuclear demolition—at least we deduced that from the information the Russians provided. Her dossier was a little vague about the details of her assignments. Finally, she has a doctorate in plasma physics from the Physics/Technological Institute. Those were the principal reasons she was on one of the TART teams. She really knows her business. Next, her counterpart at the teardowns at Pueblo was Dr. Saul Kalinik, from Livermore. His doctorate is in high-energy physics, from Cal Tech. So, that was her opportunity. Now, as to her means– –"

"Wasn't he the one involved with the Israeli agent we caught two years ago?"

"That's correct, sir," the Director nodded.

"Mr. President, if I might," Secretary McAllister interrupted. "Dr. Kalinik was not prosecuted; all charges were dropped. He was innocent. I personally selected him to head the Pueblo team."

"You mean, don't you Dr. McAllister, that there was not sufficient evidence to prosecute him—to convict him beyond a reasonable doubt?" the CIA Director said acidly. "That's a far cry from innocent. Hell of a poor choice to hold a highly sensitive TART assignment."

What a backstabing son of a bitch you are. No wonder Wil hates your guts. "Mr. Ahmanson, your own office and State agreed that his background, plus the fact that he was ethnic Ukrainian, made him an excellent choice." Ronald McAllister looked to the Secretary of State for confirmation while he finished his retort. He didn't get it. *You're both going to leave me twisting in the wind on this one, aren't you?*

"All right! Stow it, you two," the President growled impatiently. "Go on, Stuart."

"Right. Yes, sir. It seems that Saul Kalinik has also disappeared. He supposedly drowned sailing a small boat outside the Golden Gate. His close friend and sailing companion, Stanley Bellamy, a professor at the San Francisco College of Law, was also allegedly lost. Now, here is another bit of compelling information that goes to the perpetrators' means. A DEA agent assigned to Naples passed on some information to our chief of station in Italy. There was a set of drawings for some work done on a large sailing yacht at a yard in Malta, and the agent specifically asked that we look at certain mechanical parts that were fabricated. Together with other factors, he felt that the parts were meant to accommodate the storage of a large, heavy container. He was right. We ran them through a modeling program, and the best fit indicates that the parts, assembled in the yacht's water tank, could have been used to restrain a cylinder-shaped object. It happens that the object size conforms exactly to the configuration of a Soviet 200-liter fuel drum. All of the Moscow weapons were in 200-liter drums."

"Where is the yacht?" the President asked.

The Director hesitated a moment before continuing. He was now confronted with having to tell the President something he particularly did not want to hear. Above all other considerations, indeed the most fundamental, albeit never mentioned, mandate of his agency, was to never—*ever*—tell the President of the United States something he did not want to hear, when that something involved a particular presidential idiosyncrasy or political hot button. The policy had produced the failure to anticipate the disintegration of the Soviet Union and the Iran-Contra affair, among many other presidential administration embarrassments. "Mr. President, on May 23 the yacht *Aletheia* arrived at Galveston, ostensibly for electronic repairs. Work was done at Galveston Yacht Services to enable her to continue her declared voyage to the South Pacific. She had been boarded and inspected by the Coast Guard in the Florida Strait. Then she was inspected again by customs, and DEA conducted a complete teardown. She– –"

"*Where* is the yacht *now*, Stuart?"

"Uh, sir, she has put to sea. She's through the Canal and into international waters, bound for the Marquesas and Fiji. Probably approaching the Galapagos at the moment."

More leg crossing activity and shifting on the silk couches. Deadly silence. The President concentrated on Ronald Reagan's Kentucky oak and walnut flooring, visible around the edge of the huge oval rug.

"Judge Ahmanson, are you telling me that yacht was just turned loose, given the information we had?"

"Sir, the DEA was looking for drugs. They took her apart. Nothing was found. The U.S. Attorney in Houston decided that there was no cause to hold her."

"You just told me it was a DEA agent who turned up the evidence that the yacht could be carrying a nuclear weapon. Did the U.S. Attorney know that?"

"Uh, no, sir, he did not." Another deadly silence. This time the President got up and walked over to the glass-paneled door that opened onto the colonnade. He stared out at the perfectly manicured garden.

"Why, Judge Ahmanson?" he asked icily as he rocked back and forth on his toes and heels. More than anything else the President hated to hear about interagency ball-dropping and, worst of all, the often intentional disconnects among the branches of his administration.

"The DEA didn't pass on Agent Stiles's information to Justice or our office, sir. So the U.S. Attorney was only looking at the drug situation. We only took our look after Agent Stiles gave his file to the station chief in Naples."

"Okay, that's the last straw." The President wheeled around. "We're going to transfer that DEA outfit into the Bureau." He turned to his chief of staff. "Start the ball rolling, Arnold. Set up a meeting with the Attorney General. This time we're going to do it. We now have a nuclear bomb loose in this country because, once again, one hand didn't know what the other was doing. I'm *sick* of this turf-protection crap! This is all supposed to be one frigging government, isn't it? We are *going* to coordinate all these scattered fiefdoms!" Wil Grosvenor noticed a flicker of a smile pass across the face of the FBI Director.

The President returned to his seat, focusing again on the rigid Stuart Ahmanson. "So Stuart, your people were denied the opportunity to verify what the computer told them about this mechanism in the bilges of the yacht, right?"

"Yes, sir."

"All right, what about the people aboard the yacht? Tell me about the people."

"Agent Stiles's information contained detailed descriptions of the persons aboard the yacht when it cleared Malta. The same people were aboard when it arrived in Galveston. The captain, carrying a Canadian passport identifying him as Philip Thompson, matches the identification of Stanley Bellamy in his State Department file—he supposedly drowned along with Saul Kalinik. A woman, holding a British passport, who reportedly came aboard in Malta, matches the photographs we have of Colonel Kovalevska. There were two young Englishmen, crewmen, who we have verified with British intelligence, but they do not appear to be part of the conspiracy. Then there was a fifth person, a man, also carrying a Canadian passport—John Barrows. His true identity is unknown at present. Both the Canadian passports and the woman's were fraudulent. And another important piece of information was in the DEA agent's report, Mr. President. Prior to its departure for the Atlantic, the yacht made a voyage to the Aegean Sea. With that information, we verified that she called at the Island of Limnos in the northern Aegean."

"Do you have a chart of the area with you?"

"Yes, sir. Here is Limnos, just west of the entrance to the Dardanelles."

"Not very far into the Black Sea, is it?" the President mused.

"In there and back to the Aegean, four days at the most. Another thing, Mr. President; crew that were aboard the yacht when it departed Malta were left at Limnos. Just Bellamy and the unknown man would have remained to sail the boat."

"After the yacht left Malta, was there time to make the whole trip to the area of Crimea and return to Malta?"

"Yes, sir. Easily. That brings us to the final point. Moscow has told us that within that period of time, Colonel Kovalevska ordered an army unit to deliver a drum of diesel fuel to the commercial dock at Sevastopil."

"The drum of fuel was taken from a marine container in the reserve depot at Symferopil, correct?"

"Yes, sir." Another long pause.

"Stuart, after the DEA inspected the yacht at Galveston, could you verify the fingerprints of the Ukrainian officer and the two men with Canadian passports? Most importantly, why couldn't you ID the unknown man through his fingerprints?"

"The DEA did not lift fingerprints, Mr. President."

The President cupped his forehead in the palms of his hands, his elbows on his knees. In the silence that followed, Wil Grosvenor glanced at the FBI Director. He was the only one in the room who was completely at ease, again with a wisp of a smile on his face.

"The unknown man's identity might very well tell us what in hell is going on!" the President barked. More silence when he got up and walked into his adjacent study. He returned, puffing on a cigar.

"Any doubt in anybody's mind?" The President turned to each of the people in the Oval Office, ending with Roger Chedworth. "Okay, Roger, looks like you pick up the ball from here."

"Yes, Mr. President," the FBI Director answered. "Stuart and I have already coordinated. We've run as much background on the California men as we have, and we've cross-referenced them. First of all, the principals graduated together from the University of California at Berkeley. Since– –"

"Berkeley. That explains it," the President interrupted with more than a touch of sarcasm. "Sorry. Go on."

"Kalinik and Bellamy have been very tight with Malcolm Renslaer since they all graduated from Berkeley in '62." Another pregnant silence gripped the room. With the exception of Wil Grosvenor, every man present was aware that Malcolm Renslaer had managed, through myriad devices, to contribute more than $3 million to the President's campaign, dispensing his largess fluently wherever it would do the most good. "And, sir, Mr. Renslaer, it seems, has also disappeared."

"You're not suggesting are you, Roger, that Malcolm Renslaer is involved with these people?" The President immediately thought about the investigations several House and Senate committees would gleefully start when the whole thing finally surfaced. "Disappeared? How in hell does a man like Malcolm Renslaer just disappear? He's so screwed into the woodwork out there in California, if he left he'd take half the state with him."

"Apparently, Mr. President, he has done just that," Director Chedworth answered. "From the information we have so far, it's clear he's been planning to leave for the past three years. He must have had a hundred accountants and lawyers scattered around the world involved in dispersing and moving his assets offshore. He's left a big chunk of the California and New York financial communities holding bags with big ragged holes in the bottoms. I've got a team tracing his assets, but we've seen enough to figure out that everything is kept on the move faster, so far, than we can follow it. The whole pile seems to be rolling constantly from corporation to limited partnership to holding company, in and out of jurisdictions all over the world. We're going to need a lot of help from Treasury and the SEC. So far as we can tell right now, Malcolm Renslaer does not now own a single piece of real or personal property in the United States. His business empire still appears to be functioning normally, it's just that he no longer owns it, or so it seems. And, sir, we suspect that Renslaer owns the yacht *Aletheia*. On paper, she's owned by a Portuguese holding company, but like everything else, the trail from that outfit leads to an endless string of entities, also scattered around the world."

"Do you have enough to arrest him?" the President asked tentatively. He thought again about the investigations that would erupt.

"At this point, I don't think so, sir; and besides, we have no idea where he is." The FBI Director paused. "As soon as Malcolm Renslaer is arrested, the whole thing could be public."

The President frowned. "How much of a head start do these other four people have, Roger?" he asked with resigned composure.

"Sometime around May 26, Bellamy, the Ukrainian, and the unknown third person left Galveston. We know the bomb was not on the yacht on May 28 when the DEA seized the vessel. We also know the yacht was taken out into the Gulf, supposedly for a sea trial. The weapon could have been removed to another vessel."

"Is there any evidence it was taken to the Panama Canal?"

"We just don't know at this point. She'd been completely taken apart by DEA before she left; of course, the weapon could have been put back aboard out at sea. Sir . . . uh, I should add . . . there was another reason the U.S. Attorney in Houston released the yacht." Another uncomfortable pause. "The DEA agents got a little too aggressive with one of the two English fellows who were innocent hired crew. I guess he saw it as a way to avoid a lot of bad PR, and his civil claims people quietly paid $50,000 to settle. Letting the yacht go also got rid of the Brits." Everyone was aware of the veins and tendons bulging around the President's polo shirt collar. He turned to his chief of staff.

"Arnold, when that DEA outfit is reorganized into the Bureau—and I say *when*, not if—I want that man Stiles promoted. *Promoted*, do you hear? He's the only one in that whole sorry outfit who didn't have his head wedged clear up his ass. He had the instinct and guts to push his good information outside of channels while his bosses were rotating on their thumbs, protecting their turf. No wonder the goddamned Colombians are winning the war."

During the President's outburst, Wil Grosvenor noticed a slight increase in the tiny smile on the FBI Director's face.

"Okay, Roger, go on, please." The President got up again, walked across the room, and stared out the reinforced windows at the South Lawn. The day after taking office he had ordered the removal of the stand of trees that had long blocked the beautiful view down to the Jefferson Memorial.

"The three men: Bellamy, Kalinik, and Renslaer, have a number of commonalities. But there is a dominant one—one that has persisted since they met at the university. They are environmentalists, sir. They've all been active in numerous environmental and conservation organizations in the Bay Area and elsewhere. In recent years, Renslaer, as you know, has become increasingly outspoken about various environmental concerns, backing it up with donations all over the world. Mr. President, everyone involved who we've identified is very highly educated, extremely intelligent, and aggressively motivated when it comes to environmental matters. Even the Ukrainian had something in her file about complaining about radiation contamination somewhere. But there is one thing, sir, that I think we can take some comfort in. Excluding the Ukrainian, these are not the kind of people who will detonate a nuclear weapon in an urban area, and targeting the Panama Canal does not seem to fit into an environmentalist's agenda. We have no evidence at this point that the weapon is even intended for the U.S. With Renslaer moving out of the country, he could have something else in mind . . . Perhaps Japan."

The President was well aware of the trade restriction strings Malcolm Renslaer had tried to attach to his campaign donations and all the rest of the increasingly effective, anti-Japan pressure that a great deal of money spread around in Washington could effect. The Director was right. It wasn't at all clear that the bomb was intended for the United States. "What type of weapon is it? What did the Russians tell you, Stuart?"

"Sir, we don't know the configuration of the weapon. Moscow tells us that missile warheads and atomic demolition munitions, both land-use and naval varieties, were in the Odessa and Symferopil caches. They claim there is no way to know what configuration it was. The weapon could have been taken at random from either lot."

"You don't really believe, Stuart, that this Ukrainian woman—a former KGB officer and a nuclear physicist—would just select a weapon at random, do you?" the President asked, not turning around.

"We just don't know. We need more information on their intent."

"What's the yield of the weapon?"

"Uh, we're not certain about that either. Could be either two kilotons or twenty."

"Is that what the Russians told you?" The President headed back to his chair in front of the fireplace.

"Yes, sir. Only two-KT weapons were supposed to be stored at

Symferopil, according to five of the conspirators; however, the sixth one insisted that the weapons at Odessa had been switched with the ones in the Crimea when they were secreted in 1989. The weapons intended for Odessa were all twenty kilotons."

"This is just great, Stuart. Two kilotons is one thing, but twenty is quite another. Just what we need, another Hiroshima." *Even Malcolm Renslaer wouldn't do that. Would he? On the fiftieth anniversary? Jesus.* "Is there *any* evidence the weapon was put back aboard the yacht after the DEA inspection? That the port call at Galveston was just a ploy to put us off the scent?"

"No, sir." The FBI and CIA directors shook their heads in unison. Director Ahmanson: "The electronic repairs were legitimate. They'd been hit by lightning in the Atlantic."

The Japanese would change their constitution and rearm immediately. We'd be at war with them again. Renslaer would love it. "I'm not convinced that this doesn't have something to do with Japan. Let's board that yacht again to have another look. And keep the lawyers out of it. I don't give a damn about legal jurisdiction and all that crap—just finding that bomb, okay?" The President thought for a moment. "No point, right now, in saying anything to the Japanese."

"No, sir," the Secretary of State said. "And that could also make it public. Their leaks are getting as bad as ours."

"Even if it's not on board that yacht, I want you all to stay on top of the Japan scenario. Renslaer has plenty of ships and aircraft to move that thing anywhere he wants. Understood? All right, let's move on. Roger, is there any hard information on the identity of the fourth man?"

"As we speak, Mr. President," the FBI Director answered, "we're investigating our best lead. The three known men were members of a lunch club—the Cactus Club. It's in Berkeley."

"Ah, yes, the Cactus Club." The President beamed. "I know it. Renslaer took me there for lunch during the campaign. Amazing collection of people: very conservative and very liberal at the same time. I don't know what it is. Everybody is so absurdly honest or something. It's kind of frightening, actually. Good move, Roger; that may be the key to finding these guys. Do we have a good physical description on the fourth man? I can tell you there's quite a spectrum of humanity at that Cactus Club."

"Sir, the description we have is confusing. Obviously, the Maltese who gave Agent Stiles the description was not familiar with the ethnicity of this Mr. Barrows. He could be Hispanic, a West Indian– –"

"What about an American Indian?" the President suggested. "Seems to me there were a couple of them at the club. The damned place looked like the UN."

"Yes, sir, certainly. An American Indian. This afternoon we have a team from the San Francisco field office going there to interview members.

Other squads are going out to Livermore, to the law school, and to the Mayacamas offices, but that Cactus Club is our best shot at present to get information on possible bombing targets—and we will certainly find out who this Mr. Barrows is if he has anything at all to do with the club. Like you said, we know things are discussed pretty openly there."

"They sure ripped me up with a lot of questions I'd never heard anywhere else during the campaign." The President frowned. "Hold on a while, Roger." He chewed on his Havana. "There are quite a few influential and very nosey people in that club. When you get through there today, and everywhere else your people are going, the leak pressure around here will jump to a couple hundred psi." He turned to the JCS Chairman. "General Westfeldt, how long would it take to find that yacht and board her?"

"Since she cleared the Canal only yesterday, locating her will be easy. Southern Command has a couple of sea stallions. We could be aboard the yacht this afternoon, sir."

"Roger, if all your agents sniffing around out in the Bay Area today force a leak, and if we don't know where that bomb is, we'll have instant bedlam. I think there's a good chance that bomb is headed for Japan. If it is aboard the yacht, no one else need know this thing ever happened."

"Sir, if I may. If Renslaer is taking the weapon to Japan, why didn't he send the yacht across the Indian Ocean? It's only half as far going that way."

"You didn't serve in 'Nam, did you? Do you have any idea how much pirate activity there is in southeast Asia? And it's about as bad down through the Red Sea. Besides, that yacht would get the crap pounded out of her going to windward clear across the Indian Ocean. No, Renslaer is a very cautious man. He'd take the safer route." The President stared at the floor for a few moments. "Yeah, hold your troops out there in the Bay Area until tomorrow, Roger. We can afford one day . . . And another thing. Those two Brits had to have heard something. I mean, the Ukrainian would handle it, but that other, Bellamy fellow can't be a pro—he might have let something slip, something that might help us locate them or ID the last man. Yeah, when you take a look at that yacht, have your intel people talk to those two sailors, General Westfeldt. Maybe that $50,000 will help . . . *Damn* those DEA thugs . . ." The President turned to his energy secretary. "Okay. Dr. McAllister, have you got NEST up to speed?"

"Yes, sir. The regular unit at Nellis Air Force Base is awaiting deployment orders, and we've alerted the entire 800-member standby team."

"Mr. President," Director Ahmanson interrupted, "Moscow tells us that all the weapons were in shielded drums, so it is likely that the missing one is still being transported in it. A nuclear energy search team would have to be very close to have any chance of detection."

"Sir," the Energy Secretary replied, "the Director may not be familiar with the current level of sophistication of our radiation detection equipment.

The current situation is precisely what NEST was set up for."

"That's right, it certainly is," the President said abruptly, with a glance at Stuart Ahmanson. *Agency rivalry is going to destroy this government.* "If it's not aboard the yacht, we'll put NEST to work on every piece of Renslaer's equipment we can find."

The President turned to the seventh person in the room, his national security advisor. "Emil, I think we have to go to the Council with this. What do you think?"

"Mr. President, the key people are already in the loop. I think we should keep it tight until we have a likely target. This is not a military matter."

"It will be when we find that bomb," the President said peremptorily. "If it *is* here, I'm going to use the army to evacuate the area. The whole thing is going to be organized before I go to whichever governor is involved—no national guard or state police or whatever. We have to be able to move fast and be fully coordinated before our media friends create their nightmare. Any hint of a leak so far?"

"Sir," Ronald McAllister said cautiously, "after we alerted NEST, we got a call from Peter Argyle at the *Post*. I think he bought our training exercise explanation, but you know Mr. Argyle."

"Yeah. When it does finally leak, we have to be ready. I'll have to let the Press Secretary in on this." A uniform exhalation came from the other six men in the Oval Office.

"I know, gentlemen, I know. But you all realize, of course, that when this gets out it won't be just the media. The boys and girls down at the end of the Mall will launch into orbit, the European leaders will be demanding information about the possibility of nukes loose in their part of the world, and there could be an instant free-for-all in Russia. Yarzov has his hands full as it is. Of course, we'll have millions of panicked citizens, and local authorities will not be able to cope. There will be rumors, fueled by the media, that these things are scattered all over the countryside, that it's all part of a giant plot by the Russians. Use your imaginations to take it from there, gentlemen. We have simply got to have everything spun into shape to answer all the questions when it does get out. General Westfeldt, get the military cranked up for instant deployment. Anything else, people? Good. And Roger, if we strike out down there in the Pacific I want an immediate report on your investigation at the Cactus Club tomorrow. I want you to be in touch with your field people personally."

10

Hoover Office Building, June 3

"What in hell? Closed?"

On the other end of the connection, Special Agent in Charge Thomas J. O'Flannery could not believe he was speaking to the Director in person. "Yes, Mr. Director. The Berkeley Health Department closed the club this morning. Something to do this time with inadequate toilet paper capacity in the john and a scoop being left in the ice machine."

"What do you mean, *this* time?"

"It seems that it's a regular occurrence, sir: health code violation, fire code, architectural code—something. Anyway, there was no one at the club when our team arrived. Not even the cook who lives upstairs."

"Have you got a warrant?"

"No good, sir. All the federal judges were gone by three, when we got back over to the city. Wasn't even a magistrate around."

The Director gripped the telephone until his knuckles were white. *Country club, frigging judges. A hundred thirty-four G's of taxpayers' money a year, and they're gone at three in the afternoon.*

"Sir, we did locate Judge Pollack at his home in Millbrae. We can go down there to get a warrant. He'll be upset, our going to his home—you know, his being the chief judge, but perhaps– –"

"Kick it in, Mr. O'Flannery."

"Sir?"

"I said kick the damned door in and toss the place. Take anything with a name, address, or telephone number on it. *Find* the people belonging to any name, address, or telephone number. You know who we're looking for."

***

Gulf of Alaska

The *Batavian Princess* rose and fell rhythmically as her bows plunged into the gray-green twenty-foot seas. She was Swedish built, Greek billionaire owned, and Liberian registered; she carried a Taiwanese crew of nine, commanded by four Dutch officers, and was under contract to another billionaire, a Texan, to transport several million board-feet of unprocessed old-growth spruce logs and a load of chips from Alaska's Tongass National Forest to Yokohama. Her flag of "convenience" enabled her owner to avoid unnecessary inquiries about her maintenance and the health and safety of her crew, who had never heard of a government agency known as OSHA, and who never under any circumstances said a word, to anyone, about her operation. The Greek and the Texan had never met or even spoken to each other, both heavily insulated by reams of paper; and in the event of some dispute, incident, or tragedy, in accordance with their charter party the business aspects of the matter would be quietly resolved by a tightly knit group of maritime law solicitors in London.

"Looks like we're through the warm front," the first officer said, squinting up at the wall of cumulonimbus ten miles ahead of the ship. The steadily increasing rain and the lowering and thickening stratus clouds they had experienced for the past two days abruptly ended. The barometer quit falling, but the humidity was 100 percent with surface fog fleeing ahead of the now-fitful southeast wind, strangely warm at their latitude of 53° North.

The radar return showed a dense mass of heavier air directly ahead. The second officer switched the display to a larger scale. "She's a hell of a big one for this late in the season," he said, watching the sporadic flickers of lightning between the base of the cloud bar and the sea. "Looks like a nasty squall line across the cold front. Better send the men forward to check the chains and tie downs."

Despite the heavy seas the ship was making a steady eighteen knots and the distance to the wall of heavy cloud, iron black at its base and rising to over 40,000 feet at its billowed white anvil summit, was crossed in less than 30 minutes. The erratic southeast breeze abruptly changed to a surging forty-to-fifty-knot blast on the starboard bow of the ship, the northwest wind shoving mountains of spume-capped water before it. The fog was instantly gone, replaced by sheeting rain and a thirty-degree plunge in temperature. Waves of hail swept over the piles of thousand-year-old former trees, the deluge accompanied by cannonades of thunder and latices of lightning tines. Forty-seven hundred tons of Swedish steel and ancient spruce rolled, shuddered, and groaned, the deck cargos straining against their heavy chains as the steep plow blade of tropospheric tantrum swept across the North Pacific, in close pursuit of the warm front sprinting ahead.

In less than forty minutes it was over, and the ship churned steadily toward the Japanese archipelago, 4,100 statute miles to the southwest. The sky was bright and sunny with scattered puffs of cumulus clouds; the barometer had leveled out at 1,015 millibars; the temperature was 60 degrees.

"Passed right through the center of the low," the first officer said as he walked out onto the bridge wing to get a good view of the mountains of eight-to-ten-foot-diameter spruce cadavers lashed to the deck of his vessel.

The crew of agile Taiwanese were scurrying among the piles, checking the tie downs. Upon their arrival in Japan, the huge logs would be carefully examined, the inspectors searching for particularly fine-grained specimens whose perimeter flesh would be fashioned into sound boards for expensive pianos destined for return to the United States, the initial value of the spruce components having been increased several thousand percent. But most of the Engelmann trunks would be put in storage in the backwaters of several coves on the northern island of Hokkaido, where the icy brine would preserve the wood indefinitely. The Japanese fully appreciated the enormous value the ancient, fine-grained timber would have in the not-too-distant future, when no more of the giant trees stood alive on the earth. The ship's hold was also full of trees that had gone down to the sea in chips, and the remainder of the deck cargo would be disassembled into millions of throwaway chopsticks: the Japanese counterpart to the American Styrofoam cup.

The first officer had had about enough of heavy weather on this trip. After clearing Yokohama, they'd deadhead to Rangoon for a load of teak; then it was across the Indian Ocean, around the Cape of Good Hope, and home to the little farm outside of Groningen, his plump and pretty wife, and their three butter-blond children. "Better send along the met data to NOAA," he said. "Looks like the Canadians and Yanks are going to take another hit. Damndest weather this year I've ever seen."

* * *

The seas were confused, with large colliding waves. Overhead, patches of blue sky appeared in the high clouds; a slight, erratic breeze moved the 96° damp air. Nine miles away in all directions around this particular spot in the eastern Pacific Ocean, 700 miles west of Cabo San Lucas, the weather conditions were very different. To the northeast the nine miles, the skies darkened, turning a strange purplish-green color. The sea itself assumed the same hue, and where the sea stopped and the air began was difficult to distinguish. The ocean waves were monstrous: more than sixty feet from trough to spume-capped crest. Over a distance of less than a quarter mile, the light, intermittent winds were replaced by a rain- and foam-saturated blast from the east-northeast, surging between 130 and 160 miles per hour, driving before it the rain that returned to the sea at a rate of ten inches per hour. Hurricane Carlotta was now a mature tropical terror. The whales, dolphins, and fishes of the pelagic sea had fled before her approach, creating a marine desert in her wake. At this moment she was the most powerfully concentrated natural force on the surface of the earth.

In its ten-day cycle, examining the entire surface of the world's oceans below 66° North latitude, Topex/Poseidon had spotted Carlotta several days before, as well as the extratropical cyclone 5,000 miles to the northwest that was moving east-northeasterly toward the Gulf of Alaska. The satellite's precision altimeters located the growing equatorial storm by sensing the slight increase in the surface elevation of the sea in the center of the revolving mass of water vapor and air. At first the water was only a few centimeters higher, on average, than that of the surrounding sea, but on this overhead pass, on this day, the bulge was nearly four feet closer to the satellite than the encircling plane. To the precision altimeters, the pimple on the vast ocean 830 miles below might as well have been Mount Everest.

Meteorologists at the National Center for Atmospheric Research in Boulder, Colorado, would quickly use the altimeter data to calculate that the atmospheric pressure above the bulge had fallen from 1,013 to 875 millibars, making Carlotta the most powerful eastern Pacific hurricane recorded in the twenty-eight years since accurate monitoring of tropical storms had been possible. She was almost a category 5: the most severe. But the meteorologists and atmospheric physicists had no means to compare the monster they were observing with other tropical storms that had formed in this area of the Pacific Ocean over the past two hundred million years.

The same scientists and their companions in oceanography were also observing the greatly elevated sea surface temperatures extending now to the latitude of Ensenada. Boundless energy was available to sustain and strengthen Carlotta all the way to her projected landfall on the coast of Baja California.

11

Kanab, Utah, Sunday, June 5

Stan and Kateryna had been waiting in the True Grit Saloon and Cafe for over an hour, sitting at the front table so they could watch the van through the greasy, fly-shit-specked window. The hard looks they'd received from the group of locals strung along the bar had relaxed as most of the cowboys refocused their attention on the grainy TV, their long-neck bottles of beer, and, principally, the tight Levis and halter top worn by the bartender. A few of them divided their attention between the activity at the bar and the tall foreign-looking woman sitting at the front table. From the rear of the room the sporadic click of balls on the pool table mixed with the moaning of a country-western singer on the juke box, competing with the TV sports announcer and the Budweiser ads. A pall of cigarette smoke drifted through the room, mingling its stale aroma with the fragrance of rancid deep-fryer grease coming from the direction of the kitchen. Stan and Kateryna had had a long drive through the backcountry of southern Utah and were famished when they arrived in Kanab. They'd completely lost their appetites while waiting for Waddy.

Unable to occupy themselves with food, they'd ordered beers in an attempt to blend in, but the accumulation of spilled ketchup, dried beer goo, and sundry other organic matter on the table top had made even the consumption of the beer a challenge. Stan spent much of the wait discreetly watching a group of three cowboys clustered near them at the end of the bar. One of the three was constantly playing with a small knife—one of those razor-sharp skinning knives Stan had seen advertised in the hunting and couch-macho magazines that were always in his dentist's waiting room. In the hour he and Kateryna had been waiting, the bartender had set up six rounds for the team at the end of the bar. The daylight was just gone and the neon beer signs had been turned on when Waddy came through the door.

No one seemed to know or even recognize him. The bartender gave him an indifferent glance when she looked up from the sink she'd been leaning over, washing beer glasses; but all of the men at the bar turned their gazes from the pink, bouncing halter top toward Waddy. Unlike the casual but undisguised curiosity the ranch men had displayed toward the two tourists who had invaded their bar, Waddy might as well have been a Palestinian walking into a temple in Jerusalem.

"Hi guys," he said as he sat down. He scanned the row of deadly stares along the bar. "Have a nice trip?"

Kateryna's discomfort with the place Waddy had chosen to meet took another downward plunge, matching the chill settling over the barroom. "Waddy, let's go somewhere else," she whispered.

"Piss on these cowboy assholes," he answered, in a tone calculated to be almost perceptible along the bar. "I'm not goin' anywhere."

She forced herself to focus on what she had to say. "Waddy, there has been a development we need to talk about . . . ." She outlined, quickly and succinctly, the situation with the weapon; the decision they had reached.

Throughout the explanation, Waddy sat rigidly, not interrupting. When it was over, he looked intently at each of his friends. He understood the decision was irrevocable.

For months now, his mind had been filled with the prospect of releasing the great canyon and the river of his people. Nothing—*nothing*—was more important to him. He had helped bring the needed weapon across an ocean, clear back to California, all the while with his expectations rising. He had spent the past three days getting the sonar buoys in place in the reservoir and the repeater transmitters set on two nearly inaccessible sandstone spires. Travel was not easy in the canyon country. Everything had been moved in the kayak or overland on his back, and all at night. He had bites from one snake and two scorpions as a result of crawling around in the darkness, with all three venomous wounds still very painful. Even the loss of sensation in his leg and nausea from the snake bite persisted. Now everything was canceled. The big dam and the reservoir would remain. His dream was lost.

"Well, what the goddamn fuckin' shit!" Waddy screamed as he bolted from his chair. The click of pool balls stopped, along with all conversation at the bar. Only the whining, phony-Southern-accented voice from the jukebox speaker and the excited babble of the TV sports announcer remained.

In an instant the three men at the end of bar were standing over the table. "'S'cuse me folks. Is this here dirty little Navajo nigger givin' you trouble?" the one with the knife drawled.

What happened next was entirely predictable. Waddy spun around to deliver what was intended to be a bone-shattering punch to the face of the redneck, fat-bellied *pahana* who was calling him a nigger. Worse than that, he'd been called a *Navajo* nigger. But as he turned, his snake-bitten foot betrayed him. He stumbled. The other two cowboys grabbed him and pinned him against the bar. The one with the knife stood in front of him.

"Hey, Ben," came a shout from the other end of the room, "send that little war whoop back to the reservation."

"Yeah'n explain he shouldn't come back," came another voice.

Kateryna started to get up but then stopped, easing back into her chair. She looked quickly around the long, narrow room. At the same moment, the man standing in front of Waddy—Ben, apparently—drove his fist into Waddy's stomach, to an instant roar from throughout the bar. Waddy sagged in front of him, still pinioned by Ben's companions. The man wound up and hit him again.

"Why don't you go back to the reservation, Navajo nigger, an' get back to sparkin' them sheep? Prob'ly got a few good stump-broke ones." Louder yells and hoots from the crowd when Ben ripped open Waddy's shirt.

"Well look at that. Look at them nipples. Black, jus' like a nigger. An' not a hair, jus' like a goddamn snake. Yup, a Navajo nigger snake. Tell ya what," Ben shouted, pumped up by the crowd and ten bottles of Bud, "how 'bout a couple'a tattoos? These here Injuns, jus' like them other niggers in Africa, like to decorate their bodies. How 'bout a couple'a 'Ns'—for Navajo nigger—carved right over them ugly black nipples?" More shouts of encouragement.

"Do it, Ben! Do it! Carve that dirty little fucker!"

Stan started to get up, but Kateryna grabbed his arm. She was a hair trigger of anticipation—not fear—not uncertainty—but something explosive. In that instant Stan realized he did not know the woman. She was not watching the action at the end of the bar but was looking at the others in the room, her eyes darting from person to person. She had her hand in the little waist belt bag she always carried.

Stan looked back to the end of the bar in time to see Ben cut a four-inch-long slice deep into the upper right side of Waddy's chest. For an instant there was no blood. Then a dark, veinous stream began to spread fluently down his body.

In the next moment, too much happened for Stan's mind to register. The end of the bar was a blur of bodies and flailing arms. One of the men holding Waddy started to slide to the floor, clutching his neck; the one on the other side appeared stunned, eyes staring and unseeing. Ben was doubled over with both hands to his groin. As he hit the floor, an arc of puke fountained from his mouth. In another instant, Waddy was astride him with the skinning knife in one hand, reaching toward Ben's vomit-spewing mouth with the other. Blood, barf, and Budweiser splattered everywhere.

Kateryna was out of her chair. The 54-year-old lawyer willed his body to follow the 38-year-old former KGB, but Stan seemed to be caught in slow motion, his eyes and mind trying to focus on the mêlée on the floor.

"I'm Hopi, you cocksucker!" he heard; then he saw Waddy's knife hand rip through Ben's mouth, accompanied by a drawn-out, gurgling scream. Waddy's left hand drew back, flinging a bloody object across the room.

What had been a peripheral view now came into full focus. He saw three men lunge toward the mess on the floor—the man in front pulling a short-barreled revolver from his jacket pocket. In the same drawn-out moment, Stan saw Kateryna blend into the group of three. His initial propulsion out of his chair had been the assault on Waddy; but now seeing Kateryna surrounded by the strangers, he instantly forgot that he'd left his Irish will to brawl on a bloody field at Da Nang.

Her right hand was a gloved fist. Protruding from both the top and the bottom were what looked like knife blades, about four inches long. A chorus of thuds, groans, and screams erupted from the group Kateryna intercepted. The one with the revolver sank to the floor clutching his arm, the weapon gone from his hand; another went down in a perfect imitation of Ben's groin-clasping collapse to the floor. The third man turned and started a limping run toward the back of the room. Everyone else in the bar was frozen in his chair or atop his stool. The cutesy bartender was rigid, her mouth gaping in a silent scream. Nothing remained to attack after the few moments it took for Stan to react.

"Go! Go! Go!" he heard as Kateryna yanked his arm. Waddy was at the door, waving them on. They were suddenly in the dark parking lot, surrounded by four-wheel-drive pickups and stock trailers.

"Help me with this!" Stan yelled. A carved log bench was soon wedged between the door and a porch pillar.

While Stan started to concentrate on the location of their van, he heard hissing air. Waddy and Kateryna were running among the trucks, jabbing their knives into sidewalls. He got the van started, then Kateryna was knocking on the passenger side window. He reached over to pull up the lock.

She fell in as he spun the van in the dirt lot. The van struggled to follow Waddy's rapidly accelerating truck down the highway.

"Lights out," he heard from the passenger seat. He clicked the switch, decelerated involuntarily in the sudden blackness, recovered some vision, then jammed down his right foot to catch up with the lightless, camouflaged truck speeding ahead in the dark. In snatches of light from street lamps he had glimpses of Kateryna removing the glove from her hand. Attached to the palm was a vicious double-ended dagger, stiletto thin and double edged. Glove and sleeve were spattered with blood.

In a few minutes they were off the highway on a gravel road. Now in full darkness, away from the town, Stan saw the truck had dim lights, like World War II blackout lights, meagerly lighting the road. They raced along in the dark.

"Waddy cut out that guy's tongue," he said.

"Yes."

His mind kept repeating, over and over: *'ur'ee 'ih'uhl 'avaho 'igger.'*

Stan followed the truck through the back streets of St. George, ending the long, wild ride. They had trailed Waddy on a circuitous route, first south into the Kaibab Mountain Indian Reservation, then west through the red rock, sage, and juniper hills and canyons of southern Utah ranch country. The truck finally stopped across the street from an all-night pharmacy and grocery store. Waddy limped back to the van.

"Go in and get some stuff to patch me up. If a cut-up Indian walked into that Mormon joint, the police would be here in about a minute. And get some food. I haven't eaten in two days. We gotta keep movin' fast to get that bomb over to Nevada. Shit's gonna go down hard any time now."

Kateryna and Stan leaped from the van and ran across the street. She headed for the pharmacy in the back while he roamed the isles of the market section, tossing quick food into the shopping cart. In five minutes they met at the checkout counter.

"Stanley!" Kateryna was grasping his arm and looking out the window of the market. The van was gone.

* * *

SAN FRANCISCO, LATE SUNDAY AFTERNOON

Special Agent in Charge Thomas J. O'Flannery was under more heat than he'd known since he'd joined the FBI after law school. Like a lot of other agents, he'd turned to the FBI when he'd been unable to pass the California bar exam. He didn't want to be a lawyer anyway. Lawyers were the assholes who spent their lives trying to figure out ways to get the guilty criminals off.

Whores. Not for Tom O'Flannery. He liked being a cop. A very special kind of cop. He had the full weight and authority of the United States government behind him, and he got to wear a suit—like a real gentleman.

Why in God's name is the Director himself checking on the details of finding some members of a weird lunch club over in Berkeley? And any evidence we get from the kick-in won't be usable.

The SAC now had some information. His agents had spread out all over the Bay Area to track down every member they could find from the list they'd taken from the chef's room at the club. On this lovely June weekend the agents had found only a few of the members who had not scattered to weekend hideaways, but they'd finally identified the unknown subject. There was no doubt the unsub was a Wadsworth Temeseh. The physical description they had matched the person who occasionally lunched with Renslaer, Kalinik, and Bellamy at the club.

A Hopi Indian. What in hell is a Hopi Indian doing there? Like a lot of Bureau men, Tom O'Flannery was burdened with uncompromising preconceptions about many things, most having to do with rigid definitions of legal and not-legal; of "right" and "wrong." As field offices went, his San Francisco outpost was about as liberal as Bureau traditions and the current curriculum at Quantico permitted—decidedly more so than the Mormon Mafia that populated the L.A.F.O. down the coast. But Tom O'Flannery still had a difficult time imagining a Hopi Indian being anywhere other than on the reservation, where he belonged.

And Special Agent in Charge O'Flannery had more information. As soon as they had the name, it was run through the National Crime Information Center. Bingo! It seemed that their suspect had recently been involved in a little altercation in Grand Canyon: a felony assault warrant for Temeseh had been issued by the Coconino County Superior Court. The NCIC report also showed that he'd had some criminal activity in Colorado, with his defense successfully engineered by Stanley Bellamy. But the fact of acquittal didn't matter to the police agency that had submitted the report to the national center, and it certainly didn't matter to Special Agent in Charge Thomas J. O'Flannery. If the police—any police—had charged him, he was guilty. It didn't matter that some smart lawyer had managed to fool a jury.

Tom O'Flannery placed his call to the Hoover Office Building. He'd waited until he had something worthwhile to report, was decidedly nervous about bypassing the chain of command, and was positively amazed that he was calling the Director personally. He was fully astonished when the call on the secure line zipped right through and he was hearing the distinctive voice of Roger Chedworth.

"What have you got, Tom?"

Shit, now it's "Tom." "Good afternoon, sir." Tom O'Flannery checked his watch. *Three hours ahead.* "I mean, good evening, sir."

"Yeah, right. Well? What?"

"The last man is a Wadsworth Temeseh. He's Hopi Indian; lives most of the year on the reservation and works seasonally for the Canyon Park Company. He comes to the Bay Area to peddle Indian trinkets."

"Good work. Anything on where they are?"

"Negative, sir, but NCIC turned up a recent felony warrant for Temeseh. The report says he assaulted some teenage boys—local kids, from Menlo Park—without provocation, injuring one of them severely. It must have been bad, sir. All three of them have lawyers and they're suing the Canyon Park Company and the Park Service—even a guy who owns some mules down there. It was last February 18—in Grand Canyon."

"Grand Canyon? What happened?"

"Sir, I've just got the summary. Apparently, he beat the crap out of a seventeen-year-old boy and both his friends. It occurred on a trail that runs down into the canyon from somewhere on the south side of the park. Unprovoked assault. That's all that's here."

"Were any of the other people we're looking for involved?"

"The report does say there were three possible witnesses: a woman and two men. No names or descriptions."

"Anything else?"

"Sir, there is one other thing. Minor detail, perhaps."

Nothing is minor here, you twit.

"We contacted the Park Service. Four days before the assault, Temeseh had taken a party on a river rafting trip, on the Colorado River . . ."

Something was vaguely starting to come together in the FBI Director's gut. It had begun when he first heard the reference to the Grand Canyon. It coalesced further when Agent O'Flannery mentioned the river.

". . . some place called Lee's . . . Lee's Ferry is where they started. I looked it up. It's right below a big dam out there. Glen Canyon Dam."

Sweet Mother of Christ! It's Glen Canyon Dam!

Agent O'Flannery heard what sounded like a soft groan over the telephone. "Sir . . . ?"

"Tom, stay in your office. I'll be back with you shortly."

* * *

Waddy stopped the van on the dark highway running east from Page toward the Navajo Generating Station. *No time to diddle with lock pickin'.* The three-foot-long bolt cutters bit through the padlock hasp, and Waddy was soon driving down the road below the huge smokestacks of the deserted Navajo- and Hopi-Indians', Black-Mesa-coal-fired power plant. The road ended at the uncompleted Antelope Creek Marina, a few miles upstream from the dam. The Navajo Nation had planned to build its own marina on the reservation side of Powell Reservoir, but work had been stopped.

Son of a bitch the water's high. He stopped the van on the slope of the intended boat-launch ramp. *It's come up two feet since I left here.*

He retrieved his kayak from behind the pile of boulders where he'd hidden it. Back at the van he soon had the top half of the lead-lined barrel removed, but was having no luck pawing around in the dark looking for the come-along they used to lift the cylinder out of the barrel. *Don't dare use a light.* He couldn't find it; then he remembered. *Oh shit!* He could picture it lying on the shelf in the barn at Bolinas. *Now what? No way I can lift this fucker out by myself—not sliced up like this. Might drop it.* He tried to think, but the pain was making him dizzy. Blood oozed from beneath the wadded-up tee shirt he'd tied to his chest with a leg from his trousers. *Slow down. Go through everything in the van.* His search didn't take long because there was little in the van except his pack, some tools, the green drum, and the pile of flotation gear. *The float line. I can make a tackle rig out of the float line and then tie it back together.* He cut four short lengths from Saul's pre-measured line, intended to connect the bomb canister with the flotation sphere, then assembled a rope-sheaved block and tackle using the rest of the float line. With the tackle tied to the hook in the roof of the van and the other end on the bomb case handle, Waddy walked the barrel to the back door of the van and slid it over the bumper. The bottom of the barrel fell off. It was all he could do to hang on while he eased the canister to the ground with the improvised 4:1 tackle. A warm stream erupted from beneath the blood-soaked tee shirt. He concentrated on not paying attention to the blood or the throbbing, stinging pain.

He started to disassemble his tackle but had trouble with the knots that had pulled tight, compounded by difficulty in reaching over his head. The fingers in his right hand weren't working right. *Be forever undoin' these knots. Never tie'em all back together. Might be too short, anyway. Saul said the steel float has to be kept away from the bomb. The proximity fuses.* He crawled back into the van and dug through his backpack. *My climbin' rope. Should'a thought of that first. Not thinkin' right.* He stared for several moments at the trusty nylon rope that had managed to extricate him from a number of difficult situations. *Fuck it; have to use it. Four years old. Time to retire it anyway. How long? Should have measured the float line before I cut it up. Well, doesn't matter how far the sphere is above the bomb. Just can't be too close.* Waddy cut a long length from his climbing rope.

Out came the spherical steel float, the anchor, and the neoprene bladder. Waddy started to pump up the bladder with the foot pump he used to inflate the river rafts. *Spillways are runnin' big. Dumb shits miscalculated again.* He'd come across Glen Canyon Bridge, rather than the Navajo Bridge, to scout for any sign of unusual security. When he crossed, he'd seen the plumes of water erupting from the river outlet works' hollow jet valves and from the portals of both spillways. Lots of hard hats had been scurrying about on the top of the dam.

Looks like the beavers are busy with all that water. Well, that means the river's clear. No way anyone's down the canyon with all that water. Park Service's closed it by now. Everybody'll prob'ly be run off Mead, too. Waddy stopped pumping for a moment, thinking about the nuclear bomb at his feet detonating right behind Glen Canyon Dam. *TWENTY kilotons—not just two!* His smile broadened when he thought of the dam, the power plant, and the bridge vaporizing in a white-hot explosion. He imagined the 600-foot-high wall of water, blown backward by the shock wave, hesitating for a moment before realizing it was free, then exploding down the canyon. He thought of the rocks and falls in Hance, Crystal, and Lava rapids—how they would be scattered before the greatest rush of water the canyon had ever known. *No way Buck and the mules are still down at Phantom. No, everyone's been run out of there, too.* Then the gigantic surge would hit Mead Reservoir, forcing a cascade over Hoover Dam. He laughed out loud when he thought of the wall of water bearing down on Laughlin. He pumped harder.

As the bag swelled, he went over what had to be done, concentrating on Saul's instructions about how to set everything up. He had to think slowly and carefully because of the thought-interfering pain in his chest and arm—the pain from the venom in his foot was nearly masked. When the bladder was firm, he attached Saul's pre-measured line between the anchor and the bottom handle of the canister, his length of climbing rope was tied between the upper handle and the flotation sphere, then he knotted the neoprene bladder to the top of the sphere. *Saul said this sphere is sized to float the bomb, but not the anchor. And this bladder is supposed to float the whole works when I paddle out there. Hope he was right.* He tied everything into a bundle.

The pain from the knife wound sapped his strength. *Why'd you pick that place, dumbshit. Should'a known there'd be dung-stompers. Puttin' the fat-cat ranchers' range maggots out to destroy the public land. I hate 'em all.*

He was nearly ready. *Gonna be a bitch gettin' into this wet suit. Gotta have it in case I fall outta the boat.* Waddy had particular difficulty getting the top pulled on over the bulge of the sticky tee shirt. He dragged everything down to the water's edge, again becoming aware of the snake bite; the pain in his chest and down his right arm made the work excruciating. He had to get everything floating before he got into the kayak—he would have no leverage at all once he was in the little boat. After ten minutes of effort and endless curses in two languages, with the assembled cargo finally free of the shore, Waddy scrambled into the kayak and started to drag his load into deep water.

He was in the arm of the reservoir between the reservation side and Antelope Island. The usually narrow passage was now wide with the reservoir above its maximum "conservation pool" elevation. While he paddled, he went over Saul's instructions.

"When you're in position, lower the anchor first. Make sure the line uncoils properly. Then punch in the PAL code. Read back the code to me." Waddy recited the arming lock combination in his mind. *"Correct. From the moment the combination is put in, the proximity and sonar fuse circuits will be accessed in six hours. In case that thing screws up, we have six hours to get you off the lake and all of us out of there. That's not going to happen, though. Now, lower the bomb case and the flotation sphere. Okay, the anchor, the bomb canister, and the flotation sphere are hanging down, and the arming circuit in the bomb is on a six-hour countdown. Everything is being held up by the bladder. Check to be sure the kayak is not hung up on anything. Then open the valve on the bladder. Make sure nothing is attached or the kayak'll go down with the lot. You clear on everything?"*

Waddy and the trailing equipage were soon two barely-discernible forms on the dark surface of the channel between the shore and the island. With his black boat and wet suit, and with all the gear painted black, he was quickly lost on the reservoir's expanse. Only the rhythmic motion of his paddle might reveal him.

The kayak and its baggage moved easily across the dark, quiet water. As he came out from behind the south end of the island, Waddy scanned the reservoir in the direction of the Wahweap Marina, two miles up the west side. He saw no activity around the resort or on the pontoon docks. *Bound to be some tourists out screwin' on a houseboat. Maybe they've all been run out with the reservoir in flood. Good, not a runnin' light anywhere. No night fishermen. Just a barkin' dog over there somewhere. Car drivin' along the road from the bridge. Damn, sound travels on this water.*

In fifteen minutes he was in the middle of the reservoir, between the sandstone walls. He turned toward the string of lights across the top of the dam, now just above the surface of the water, then soon passed the cable and buoys strung across the reservoir that marked the boat exclusion zone above the spillway inlets. The lights from the dam, the bridge, and those marking the power cable towers on the west canyon rim cast reflections on the water. Even a few of the windows in the visitor center offices were lighted. *Beavers are workin' late.* Across the dam, near the east elevator where the employees went down into the structure, he could see hard hats moving around in the overhead lights.

Each stroke with the paddle sent a ripping pain from his neck, to his groin, and down his right arm. From the elbow down, it was nearly numb. He could feel blood pooling in the folds of his wet suit.

While he paddled across the smooth water Waddy was thinking about a great many things. He thought of his people and the ancestors of his people who for millennia had known intimately the great river canyon submerged beneath him. He thought of the land around him and what only a few generations of *pahanas* had done to it. Without the bar fight back in Kanab he would have gone along with the others—reluctantly, but he would have gone

Antelope Island at its to-date smallest on June 18, 1983 (*Bureau of Reclamation*).

along. They were a team, after all, and the team had decided what to do. But now things were different.

They're all the same. That guy just said what most of them want to say. How many of my people—all Indian people—have you pahana *fuckers raped, maimed, enslaved, and murdered? You multiply like rabbits in your cities, and you destroy my country so you can continue to multiply. We're being exterminated. Huddled together on a few mesas. Okay, it's payback time.* Waddy was paddling mechanically, in a trance, numbed by the searing pain in his body and the hotter burning of his thoughts.

Got to stay out here in the middle, away from those spillway inlets. Hate bein' out here, though. Too easy to spot me. But I can't get close to the walls. He shuddered when he thought of being drawn into one of the notches in the canyon walls, leading to the spillway gates. *With this load'a crap, I wouldn't have a chance. Get sucked in like a bug.*

He paddled closer to the dam and then reverse-paddled when the bladder and its suspended load drifted past. Stopping the momentum of the assembled equipment was difficult. His right arm was now entirely numb. Each rotation of his wrist as he twisted the paddle sent stabs of pain from where the numbness ended, across his chest, then down to his waist.

He stopped in the water, verifying that he was motionless by watching two lights lined up on the shore. He carefully studied the top of the dam and the parking lots on either side, trying to determine how far out onto the water the illumination extended. *They're blinded by the lights. Can't see out here.* He struggled to get his cargo moving again. *Got to get closer. Don't want one cubic yard of that fucker to survive. Twenty kilotons! About what was dropped on the poor bastards at Hiroshima and Nagasaki. Now we'll see how you* pahanas *like it.* He kept paddling closer to the dam. This time he turned the kayak and paddled in the other direction to stop the load. Once again he watched the rim of the dam and the access roads running out to it. *No one's seen me. Right here. This is perfect. Plenty of room for the proximity fuses. I'm sorry, ancient rock. You have to go, along with the* pahana *monstrosity. It will soon be over. Your torment will soon be over, and the river will be free. The river of my people will be free!*

Waddy concentrated. *Anchor first.* He cut the ties holding the bundle together, and then cut the anchor line tie and slowly payed the line out. *DON'T tip the boat over.* The weight now suspended from his hands caused intense pain in his chest, but soon the anchor was hanging free beneath the bomb case. He was dizzy from the pain as he started to cut the canister tie, to let it sink below the sphere. *Oh shit, the arming lock! Stop and THINK, asshole!* He forced himself to wait a few moments to settle down. *I'd never've been able to haul this sucker and the anchor back up. Okay. Now the combination.* He concentrated on the list of numbers and weird Russian letters, struggling to remember them correctly through the stinging throb in his chest; then, slowly and deliberately, he punched the list into the waterproof keyboard. A little light in the panel winked twice. *It's supposed to blink THREE times! Oh, SHIT!* Waddy's heart was pounding; all consciousness of his several pains vanished. *What did Saul say? It's not limited try. I can do it again.* Once more he made himself think of the numbers and letters, but now his certainty was gone. Again he punched in the nine integers and letters, ending with the particularly strange one that looked like two Ks, back to back. Three red blinks immediately greeted him. Waddy sagged in his seat. A minute passed while he murmured some things known only to the people of his Snake Clan.

Okay, the fucker'll be armed in six hours. Now, pahana *establishment, we'll just lower your very own little petard.* He cut the tie to the bomb case, watching it disappear beneath the black water as he eased it down on the climbing rope. *What was that!* He thought he'd felt something on the rope. *Too late now.* Next, he cut the tie to the sphere and watched as it too sank into the void. Only the flotation bladder remained. He untied the tow rope, checked to be certain he wasn't snagged on anything, and then unscrewed the valve. The air rushing out seemed explosively loud beneath the sides of the canyon. His mind flashed back to the bar parking lot.

Waddy anxiously watched the men on the top of the dam while the air rushed out of the neoprene bag. Still deflating and half full, it sank under the surface with a final hiss, bubbles continuing to come to the surface around the kayak for another minute. He was now alone in the quiet dark. He turned his little boat and paddled back toward the Antelope Creek Marina. Rain started splattering the surface of the water.

On the crest of the dam, a lot of men were moving about in noisy confusion, their voices raised above the roar below them. Randy MacConnell zipped up his parka when the rain started to fall. He looked away from the eruptions down the canyon and glanced back over the surface of the reservoir, its surface now stippled with heavy drops of rain. Something on the water caught his eye—right where the lights from the dam faded into the veil. He squinted into the rain-streaked darkness, shading his eyes from the quartz flood lamps. He could see a rhythmic, oscillating motion on the reservoir surface. *Son of a bitch. Some jerk is out there in a boat. Looks like a little canoe or something. Dipshit's inside the exclusion area.* In a few more seconds, the apparition was lost beyond the illuminated curtain. Randy MacConnell shrugged and walked back toward the elevator. He had far more important things to worry about than some tourist out on the reservoir.

One minute, fifty seconds after the dam superintendent's attention had first been drawn to the reservoir, a mushroom anchor thudded into the scoured out bottom of what had once been the channel of the Colorado River, 720 feet behind the dam and 662 feet beneath its rain-sprinkled surface. Seventy-one feet above the anchor, the bomb canister hung in ink-blank, 45°F stillness, suspended by a length of kernmantle climbing rope, itself attached to the flotation sphere. The deflated bladder drifted alongside.

Saul had sized the sphere so that the weight of the water it displaced was slightly less than the combined weight of the anchor, the canister, the deflated bladder, all connections, and less the buoyancy of the weapon case. But the anchor and the objects connected above it had descended toward the bottom at six feet per second—four times faster than Saul had intended due to the unanticipated weight of the larger weapon. When the anchor abruptly stopped in the layer of silt, the rest of the equipment tried, for a long moment, to continue the descent, but with the weight of the anchor now relieved, the flotation sphere asserted its new dominance in buoyancy, decelerating quickly and immediately beginning to obey the command to rise to the surface. The result of this sudden reversal of motion and change of momentum was a sharp pull on the length of climbing rope connecting the sphere to the bomb canister, still obeying its own command to continue downward, albeit relieved somewhat by the buoyancy of the weapon's two sealed containers.

Approximately mid way along its length, the five-year-old synthetic rope was partially severed—cut by a fractured piece of 1.7-billion-year-old naturally metamorphosed Vishnu shist in the Pipe Creek Canyon wall. Each of the constituent elements in the rope's braided kernmantle core had been cut more than three-quarters through; therefore, the sudden force of the sphere trying to return to the surface caused the remaining, intact strands to stretch and part further. When equilibrium was reached, the rope was being continually tensioned by a 241-pound pull of the opposing forces of gravity and water pressure. Adding to the rope's burden was the circumstance that it did not happen to be what mountain climbers call a "dry" rope—protected by a Teflon-based coating. Its non-water-repellent filaments would, over time under water, lose approximately 30% of their dry strength.

Between the anchor and the sphere, the Kharzov-series atomic demolition munition hung motionless. Inside its outer pressure case, a digital timer precisely ticked through the remaining 21,185 seconds of its programmed 21,600-second countdown, at the conclusion of which it would do three things: activate a pair of independent, proximity fuse mechanisms, each of which was wired directly to the detonation circuit within the nuclear package; turn on the similarly-wired sonar fusing system; and open the last link in the arming circuit. The fuses would then wait for an instruction from the void.

***

Malcolm sank into his chair when he heard what Stan was telling him over the telephone.

"My God, Stanley, he'll set that thing right behind the dam! Some local cut him with a knife? . . . Yes, that had to have been it . . . Yes, I agree, I'm sure you and Kateryna could have brought him around . . . I know, it wasn't me getting carved up by some cowboy cretin. Okay, this forces everything. Sofiia's getting moved today. I'll have a plane down to Vegas to pick you up this morning after Saul drives up there to get you. Kateryna's right; don't use Waddy's truck . . . Yeah, we gotta tell the feds. Give them everything. And Stanley, ask Kateryna if she's ready to move to the Seychelles Islands . . . Yes, I do like Africa."

12

Seattle, Monday morning, June 6

Pavlo Nastenko looked out at the pleasant scene from his snug little apartment high on the west slope of Queen Anne Hill. The rain had stopped earlier in the morning and the sun was breaking through the cloud cover. Like flowers in a spring meadow, sailboats had sprung up on the water, scattered in the reaches of bright blue among the forested islands in the sound.

"Such a pretty place," the old man said out loud. "I could be content here."

Earlier that morning he had watched Sofiia being wheeled out of the hospital and into a van. A group of orderlies, doctors, and nurses had accompanied her. To Pavlo Nastenko the highly trained security personnel in the group might as well have been in uniform.

He watched a cluster of sailboats coming together for the start of a race. *It is just as well. Prevents me from doing something foolish. My mission is the defense of Ukraine and the acquisition of funds necessary to live and to carry out my work. Foolish to draw attention to myself here—to jeopardize everything. Besides, they have interrogated Captain Khalavchenko by now, so they know I was looking for Kateryna. They will now look here. Foolishness, driven by senseless revenge.* Pavlo Nastenko smiled when he realized that his thoughts were mirrored in the old Slavic saying: "pride and stupidity arrive on the same tide." *Let her go. She has also suffered at the hands of the Russians. She only did what she was trained to do . . . And we trained her so very well.*

* * *

"Get a tag on this call *now,*" Tom O'Flannery ordered above his hand cupped over the telephone. The automatic recorder captured everything the intense voice at the other end of the line was saying: ". . . you'll find a package in the mailbox on the Turk Street side of the federal building. It has everything you'll need." The caller hung up.

Tom O'Flannery now fully understood why the Director was handling this personally and why the San Francisco field office had not been told anything.

"Okay, everybody out," he curtly told the agents assembled in his office. "We'll do the case summaries later." They filed back out into the bullpen (not *called* a bullpen in deference to the sexual orientation of a few of the agents—a "steer/heifer pen" had been suggested in an anonymous fax they'd received from the L.A.F.O.). When the room was cleared he picked up the secure line to Washington. No anxiety this time.

"We started things rolling Sunday night when you called, Tom. We were pretty sure that was the target. Now, when you get the package, have a plane standing by in case some of it can't be faxed—I mean things like photos. We have to have originals of photos."

I KNOW that, Tom O'Flannery thought as he hung up the telephone. *I've had a lot more years in the field than you have.*

Roger Chedworth hung up the telephone and turned to the man standing by his office window. "You mean we had to just let her go?" The FBI Director could not believe it.

"That's right," the head of the criminal division at Main Justice told him. "About a half dozen of New York's finest, with their local counsel *pro hac vice* sponsors in tow, convinced a federal judge in Seattle that we couldn't hold the little girl. They had three oncologists, a neurologist, and two shrinks testifying. Like in a custody battle, it just got down to what was in the best interest of the child."

"But we're talking about the worst kind of felonies here," Roger Chedworth protested. "About our only chance of catching that woman is through contact with her daughter."

"The child is not a perpetrator. Doesn't matter what her mother or someone else did; can't use her as a lure. She's gone, sir. Left on a private international flight this afternoon, right after the hearing."

* * *

Santa Rosalillita, Baja California Norte

When the outer bar of the storm reached the Baja peninsula, 200 miles to the southwest Carlotta's eye entered Sebastián Vizcaíno Bay. The pods of California gray whales that congregated to breed in the warm, shallow waters of the bay were long gone, traveling north to the Bering Sea. The hurricane was moving faster now, its forward motion twenty-five mph as it continued its course to the northeast. In less than seven hours the storm's eye wall slammed ashore, wholly inundating the little fishing village and trapping its inhabitants who had had no warning from their government of the severity of the approaching cordonazo. The people were well aware of the terror that could come from the sea—the "Lash of Saint Francis" that visited only rarely and then almost always during the time of the saint's feast in October—but they had nowhere to go to avoid the monstrous surge of water or the several tornados that were spawned in the hurricane's path. Few of the inhabitants of the little community survived.

Carlotta was now a category 5 storm. The winds in her eye wall were 175 mph over a one-minute mean, gusting to 210. She had compacted as she intensified, her spiral rain bands drawn inward toward her inner wall as the energy exchange intensified; but she still spread over a diameter of nearly 400 miles, with her leading edge now extending to the Sonora/Arizona border. In four more hours, Carlotta crossed over the narrow peninsula and entered the upper end of the Sea of Cortés where the water in the shallow desert-surrounded gulf was thirteen degrees above the 76° temperature needed to sustain the hurricane's heat engine.

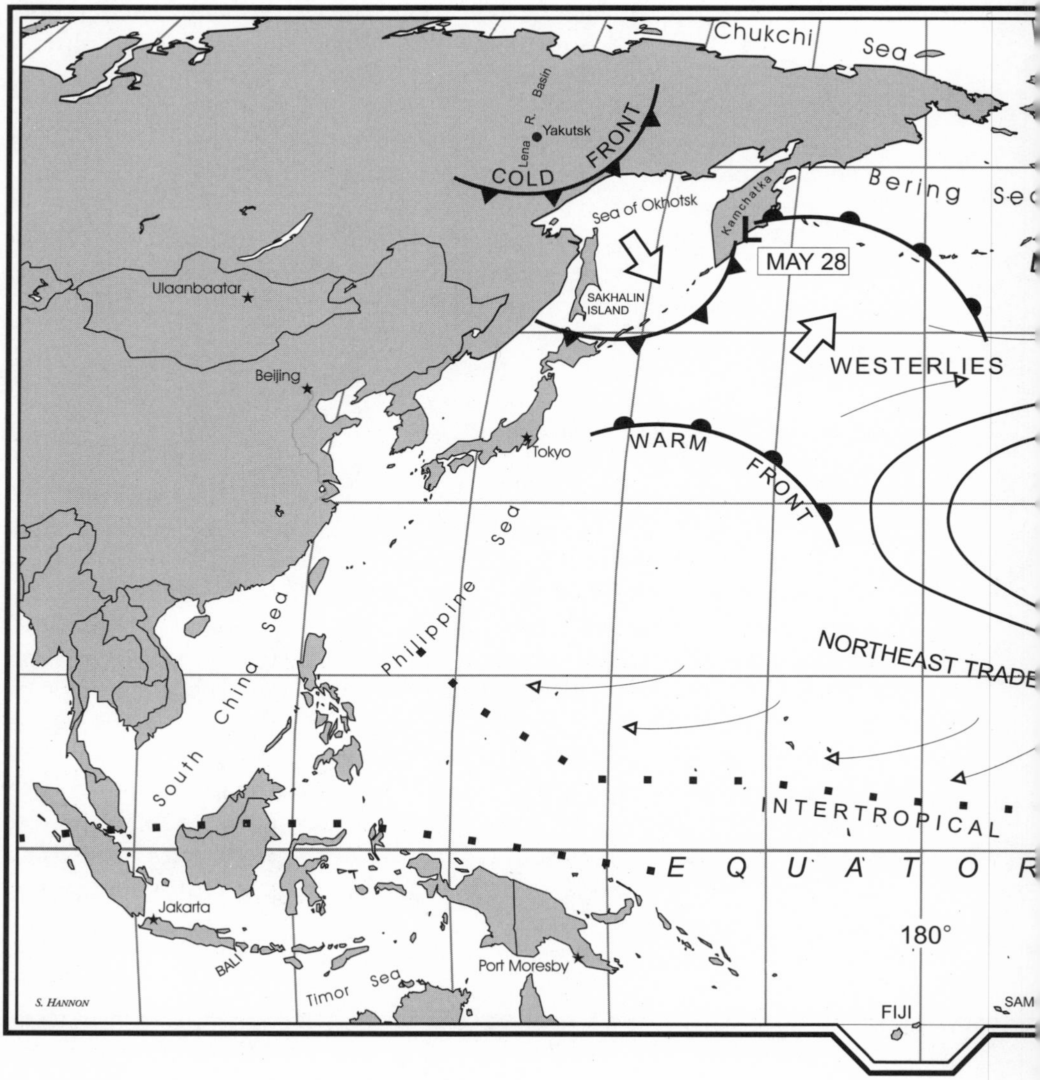

Chukchi
Sea
Lena R. Basin
Yakutsk
COLD FRONT
Bering Sea
Sea of Okhotsk
Kamchatka
L
MAY 28
SAKHALIN ISLAND
Ulaanbaatar
Beijing
WESTERLIES
WARM FRONT
Tokyo
South China Sea
Philippine Sea
NORTHEAST TRADE
INTERTROPICAL
EQUATOR
Jakarta
BALI
Timor Sea
Port Moresby
180°
FIJI
SAM
S. HANNON

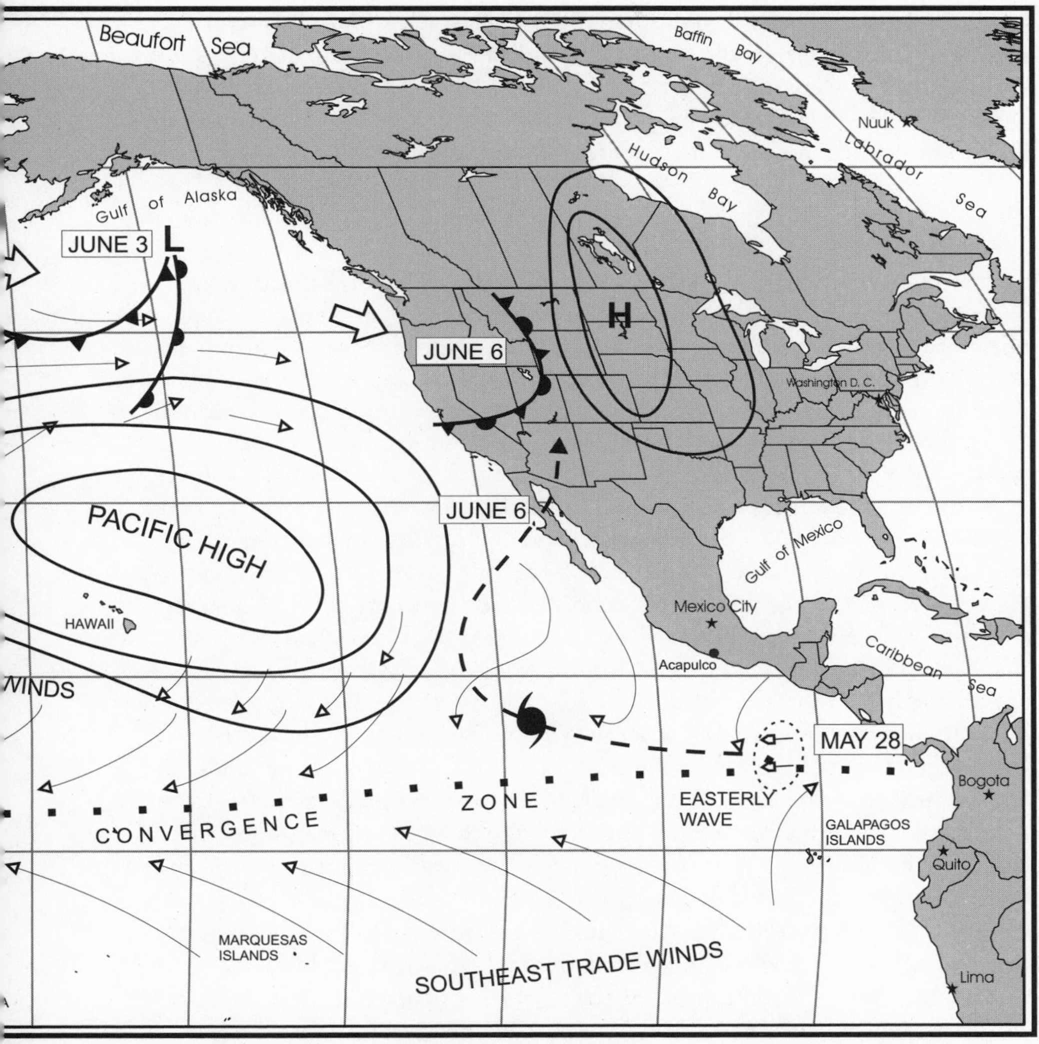
Beaufort Sea
Baffin Bay
Nuuk
Labrador Sea
Hudson Bay
Gulf of Alaska
JUNE 3
L
H
JUNE 6
Washington D. C.
JUNE 6
PACIFIC HIGH
Gulf of Mexico
HAWAII
Mexico City
Acapulco
Caribbean Sea
WINDS
MAY 28
Bogota
ZONE
EASTERLY WAVE
CONVERGENCE
GALAPAGOS ISLANDS
Quito
MARQUESAS ISLANDS
SOUTHEAST TRADE WINDS
Lima

Carlotta absorbed more billions of BTUs and more hundreds of thousands of acre feet while she moved across her last source of energy and moisture. The giant storm's cyclonic motion imperceptibly started to decelerate when her core left the sea for the final time, but with her enormous store of energy she would maintain her atmospheric rotation far into the interior of the desert land mass. Torrential rain began to fall in Organ Pipe National Monument on the Arizona side of the border; immediately, severe storm warnings were sent throughout southern Arizona, the Imperial Valley, and, belatedly, Baja California Norte and Sonora. Un-leveed areas around Yuma flooded. By noon, rain was falling heavily in Phoenix.

* * *

The northern Pacific storm had consolidated when it swept over the coast range and the Cascades, much of it squeezing through the wide break in both mountain chains that is the valley of the Columbia River. Its fronts had combined; the mass of cold air had caught up with the warm air to create what meteorologists call an occluded front—the remaining cell of warm air being forced upwards, over the following cell of atmosphere that had originated in the frozen tundra of arctic Siberia. Little of the storm's remaining moisture was shed as it raced over the Columbia Plateau and the Snake River Plain, then headed toward the Rockies and the expanse of American heartland beyond. But for the first time since its formation off the east coast of Kamchatka, the storm met a serious obstacle. A huge ridge of high pressure, which in a normal year would have extended from the Great Plains west across the Great Basin and would have shunted the storm well into Canada as it approached the coast of North America, had stopped east of the Rockies. With its forward progress blocked, the mass of saturated air slowed its race, consolidated, then began to settle southward: into a large basin ringed by the San Juan Mountains, the central Rockies, and the Wind River range to the east; by the Wyoming, the Uinta, and the Wasatch Mountains and plateaus to the west. In less than twenty four hours the eastward progress of the storm halted, its central core of occluded low pressure remaining stationary at an elevation of 18,000 feet where the ambient pressure was 500 millibars—half the pressure at sea level. The bulk of trapped saturated air began to settle earthward, chilled by the combined cell of cold air beneath it. In its descent it cooled enough to condense—to fall as a steady, heavy rain over nearly all of the 108,000 square miles of the Upper Basin of the Colorado River.

13

The White House, Tuesday, June 7

The five men jumped to their feet when the President and his chief of staff walked into the Roosevelt Conference Room in the West Wing, just across the hall from the Oval Office.

"Arnold," the President motioned to his chief of staff, "we need the map of the Colorado River Basin. Seats, gentlemen. Okay, George."

Commissioner of Reclamation George Ricketson stepped up to the large map of the southwestern United States. The whole Colorado River Basin was outlined in red. The Basin covered the eastern half of Utah, nearly all of Arizona, the southwest corner of Wyoming, western Colorado, a piece of western New Mexico, and a little bit of southern California and Nevada. The reservoirs stood out in blue; below Hoover Dam was a crosshatched area in red extending down the lower Colorado River, clear to the Gulf of California. The several water diversion canals and pipelines were also shown. The map dramatically underscored political reality as well as physical detail: although California occupied only a tiny fraction of the Colorado River Basin, it received the greatest share of the river's water.

"Point out Glen Canyon Dam for us," the President said as he sat down. Like most of the powerful politicians in Washington who had clawed their way into long-term seats of power, he was an Easterner. Excluding California with its huge block of voters, to the President the West was a largely unknown part of the country: a land of anonymous square-bordered states that produced few electoral votes; lots of cattle, timber, and particularly-rabid environmentalists; and incessant carping about water and public land use. And it took too long to fly over the huge area to get to California. The President rarely even looked down at the dreary expanses of monotonous brown drifting by 35,000 feet under the wings of Air Force One.

The Commissioner's pointer landed about midway along the Utah/Arizona border. A long jagged piece of blue extended to the northeast, well into Utah. "This is Lake Powell, above the dam, which extends about 185 miles upstream to here."

"How much water is in that thing?" the President asked, standing up and squinting closely at the map.

"It's full now, sir, so it contains twenty-seven million acre feet."

"Tell me in English, George."

"An acre foot would almost cover the area of a football field, minus the end zones, with one foot of water. It's 43,560 cubic feet."

"So there's twenty-seven *million times* that much?" The President scowled and sat down. "Where would the flood extend?"

"Mr. President, the red crosshatched area down the lower Colorado would be the inundation zone in the event of a catastrophic failure of Glen Canyon Dam." The map showed an area alternately widening and narrowing as it extended down the river, finally spreading out in a large area near Yuma and extending to the Gulf of California.

"That's all desert, isn't it?" the President asked. To most Easterners, everything west of the 100th meridian—about mid-Nebraska—was desert. If the land was not profusely lush and green like the Maryland countryside, it was desert. With his exposure to the western United States largely limited to what he could view from 35,000 feet, everything had always appeared to be an endless, uniformly drab expanse of wasteland.

"Yes, sir, most of it is. But there is population along much of the course of the river, mainly concentrated in several resort areas. Here's Laughlin, Lake Havasu City, the Parker Strip, Yuma, and there are Mexican villages down in this area."

"Oh, that's great. We're going to flood the Mexicans. Have to tell 'em, I guess. George, how many people? How many people are there along the river now?"

"Sir, I don't know, I– –"

"Those are your dams and reservoirs, Mr. Ricketson—perched above all those people. You have to have *some* idea."

The Commissioner of Reclamation, being both a supervisory engineer and a long-tenured bureaucrat, was used to having a cadre of assistants around him at any meeting. Scores of people in his bureau and in the rest of the Department of Interior could answer the President's question in an instant. "Mr. President, I can find out with a call to– –"

"Commissioner Ricketson . . . all of you . . . listen. Right at this moment, we have very strong reasons to believe that a twenty-kiloton nuclear bomb is sitting right behind that big dam out there. So far, outside of the people in this room, no more than a dozen people in this government know about the situation—at least the whole situation. Until our planning on how to deal with this thing is in place, and until we have everything ready to move, we have *got* to keep a lid on this. We'd have wholesale panic in the communities along the river, the media would work everybody into a frenzy, including my loyal opposition down the street, and the madman with his finger on the trigger might freak out, too. Mr. Chedworth, how much time do we have?"

The FBI Director squirmed in his seat slightly in response to having to answer a very specific question. "Not much—about four days." The

Reclamation Commissioner could not stifle a little groan.

"Okay, thank you. Now give me some details, Roger. You can sit down, George."

"It appears that the conspiracy broke up right about the time the bomb was placed. We believe that occurred Sunday night. Yesterday the San Francisco office was contacted by one of the conspirators, Saul Kalinik, who advised us that although they had decided to abort the plan, one of the group, this Wadsworth Temeseh, probably set the device by himself, he– –"

"Roger, hold on. Didn't your people gate crash the Cactus Club last Friday to identify this—what's his name—the last of the conspirators?"

"Uh, yes, sir. Well, it happened that the club was closed. We lost a lot of time by not being able to interview club members then. Practically all of them would have been there on a Friday, but we had to track them down individually over the weekend until we found one who identified the last conspirator." The Director had no difficulty resisting his impulse to say that they should have gone to the club on Thursday, as originally planned, when most of the members would also have been present—rather than waste precious time chasing a boat across the Pacific.

"Closed? On a Friday? It's a lunch club. Friday's the best day to go to a place like that."

"Yes, sir, the Berkeley Health Department closed it. Happens pretty regularly. If we'd gotten to those club members right away on Friday (Thursday) we'd have surely ID'd Temeseh immediately. The woman we finally located on Sunday—the one who named him—goes to the club nearly every day (probably Thursdays). We'd have then had the NCIC info on Temeseh, and we'd have identified the target, Mr. President. Enough time to get people out to the dam."

"Why in God's name does the City of Berkeley give them such a hard time?"

"It's not just the city, sir; it seems the whole university establishment is offended by the club. They don't like what's discussed there."

The President exploded. "Well, *I* know what's discussed there. What the hell! Berkeley! I've had enough of those arrogant bastards. This time their attitude may well result in a lot of dead citizens. Okay, Ron," the President turned to his energy secretary, "at your earliest opportunity (Ronald McAllister knew that meant within one hour after he got back to his office), give me a rundown on the current funding for the radiation laboratory on the Berkeley campus—not Livermore. Make that *all* federal funding that finds its way into Berkeley. Maybe it's time those portside assholes got their Washington teat dried up. I'm sure the people in Sacramento will love to pick up the tab. Okay, go on, Roger." The President glanced around the familiar room, still decorated to celebrate T.R.: his 1906 Nobel Peace Prize displayed along with pictures of his beloved horses and scenes from the old west. The

President knew his reaction was relatively mild, compared to what the first Roosevelt president would have done.

The FBI Director struggled painfully to swallow the smile his face was still trying to make. "Right. Yesterday our Phoenix office got a call– –"

"Excuse me, Roger. General Westfeldt, didn't your intelligence people talk to those British sailors aboard the yacht—to find out if they had any clue about the real identity of the last man?"

"They wouldn't talk to us, sir. We had a couple of our best people give it a try, but they knew we had no jurisdiction to be boarding the yacht. Then when we tore their boat apart again, without being able to tell them what we were looking for, well . . . they were uncooperative, to say the least."

"Yeah . . . Can't really blame them." More unkind thoughts about his drug enforcement administration. "Okay. Sorry, Roger, go on."

"We got a telephone call from someone who claimed the bomb was set behind the dam. We assume it came from the man we'd just ID'd—Wadsworth Temeseh. Very little detail was given."

"What did he say?"

"Sir, do you mean exactly what did the caller say?"

"Yes, Mr. Chedworth, yes."

The FBI Director clicked on his laptop. The reclamation chief glanced over. He really wished he had a laptop. His key staff—and his ten-year-old grandson—were fully at ease with the information-crammed machines, but the old engineer had been unable to bring himself to learn.

"The recording of the perpetrator's voice says, quote: *There is a twenty-kiloton atomic bomb set in the reservoir behind Glen Canyon Dam. You* pahana [sic] *motherfuckers have exactly five days to clear the people away from the river before I touch it off. Try to diddle with the bomb and it detonates immediately.*"

"What's a *pahana*?"

"It's the Hopi word for a white person, sir. Not a derogatory term. Well, sort of—depends on how they say it. Just their word for, well, *us*."

"When's the deadline, exactly?"

"The call came in at 1630, so that means the same time this coming Saturday, mountain standard time. Arizona doesn't use daylight savings."

Commissioner Ricketson raised his hand. "Sir, I believe the Navajo reservation—it borders Lake Powell—*is* on daylight time." The President scowled. "But, then again, sir, the Hopis are *not* on daylight savings, even though they're surrounded by the Navajo Reservation. You see, the Hopis don't much care for the Navajos . . . so . . . how do we know which time he means, his being Hopi and all, I– –"

"Oh, *Jesus*, Mr. Ricketson!" The President glowered at his commissioner of reclamation. *God, what if I had to deal with him every day? The old fart probably counts the toilet tissues he uses.* "Let's just assume the earliest time, okay? Now, Roger, what do we know about this Indian crazy?"

"Quite a bit now, actually, but I can give you a quick summary of his current state of mind by something that happened Sunday. We just picked it up from NCIC." The Director again referred to his computer. "On Sunday, Temeseh, the woman, and Bellamy met in a restaurant in Kanab, Utah." He pointed to the map. "Here's Kanab, right here, about sixty miles northwest of the dam. According to more than a dozen witness reports, all customers and employees in the restaurant, Temeseh attacked three men with a knife. It was totally unprovoked, without warning, and very vicious. One man was severely injured. Temeseh cut out his tongue."

The Energy Secretary and the President's chief of staff groaned in disgust. The old engineer, the Joint Chiefs Chairman, the BATF chief, and the President just stared impassively at Roger Chedworth.

"Nice fellow," the President said.

"There's more. In the same incident, and also unprovoked, the woman waded into another group of innocent bystanders in the restaurant and sliced up two of them with her own knife. We know, of course, that the woman is a lieutenant colonel in the Ukrainian state security and she's ex-KGB. Even though she's a scientist, she went through the whole KGB training program at the Manger—something to do with her principal assignment that the Russians glossed over in their report."

"She would have had a great deal of close combat and special weapons training—probably assassin training, too," General Westfeldt added. "The only way you can handle people like that is to kill them."

"Okay, we certainly know what we're dealing with. Have you worked up the stuff the other conspirators delivered to you, Roger?"

"It arrived by courier last night. Our people, together with some from Energy, have worked on it nonstop. No individual on the analysis team knows the context, only individual bits and pieces."

"All it takes is one of those people to go to the papers."

"It won't happen, sir—at least not my people."

"Not mine either, Mr. President," the Energy Secretary said. The BATF and Reclamation chiefs joined the unanimous shaking of heads.

"So. Punch line, Roger. Is it legitimate?"

"Yes, sir. We believe it is. The detailed photographs in the package conform exactly to the information we got from the Russians. The fusing of the device has been modified to be activated by either a sonar signal or proximity volume or mass—that is, if anything approaches the device it detonates. Kalinik provided detailed specs on everything, including the sonar transmitters. They're merely modified navy units. We're working on a way to intercept or mask the sonar signal or to disable the units themselves."

"Dr. Saul Kalinik," the President snarled. "Should have prosecuted his ass back when that thing with the Israeli went down. Where there's smoke, there's fire. Okay, the sonars. They're in the lake? How many?"

"Yes. Six of them."

"Have they been located yet?"

"Sir, we can't be out in that lake fishing around. That would freak the guy for sure."

"Use our overhead spooks. They can't all be looking for Russians anymore. Might give the National Reconnaissance Office something to do to justify their nice new buildings," the President said caustically. He was still smarting from the media heat he'd taken over the CIA's latest secret undisclosed-dollar-amount boondoggle.

"Right, Mr. President, NRO's using what they have, but it seems we're limited to one of the old KH-11s that's tasked over a relatively low priority area east of the Urals. Its backside pass takes it over the dam area. But, we have a problem. The one in place lost its infrared downlink a couple of years ago. It's the storm out there, sir. We can't see through the heavy cloud cover without the infrared."

"Well, how soon can we get a look? What's the weather prediction?"

Roger Chedworth twisted in his chair again. "Uh, little problem there too."

The President glared at the floor, and the Director twisted a little more. "Sir, the biggest combined storm system on record is coming together over a big part of the southwest. NRO's best estimate is that we probably won't get a peek for seventy-two hours. And, Mr. President, about using the spook– –"

"Oh, no! Not this time. The fucking ACLU can go piss up a rope. This is *not* domestic surveillance. This is foreign terrorism that happens to be taking place here. We are *going* to use that satellite. I don't give a damn about building a case to prosecute those guys . . .We'll handle it another way, when the time comes . . . Okay. Are we ready to go on the ground?"

"Yes, sir," the BATF chief answered. "We have a team at Page, Arizona, and we're covertly dispersed around the reservoir for several miles upstream from the dam. The army's deployed Delta teams."

General Westfeldt nodded. "Six assault squads in Blackhawks are standing by at the staging area at the Page airport. We can drop people into any part of the country surrounding the reservoir."

The President turned back to his BATF chief. "After that mess your people created down in Texas, Billy, here's your chance. See if you can keep the testosterone level under control this time. Put one of your nastiest bulls in charge of those young studs—that ought to sort things out."

The tiny smile crept back onto Roger Chedworth's face, but this time the President caught it. "You, too, Mr. Chedworth. Your Hostage Rescue Team thugs with their tanks did a fine job when they took over down there—managed to kill about eighty men, women, and children, didn't they? And your sniper heroes also handed this administration that debacle up in Idaho."

The nascent smirk left the Director's face without effort.

The President fired up a Havana. "Damn, I wish we could straighten things out with Fidel. Gettin' real hard to find these guys. Don't suppose the Russians would be any help now. Okay. We're not going to rely on the cavalry saving the day. I hope you can, gentlemen, but we are not going to depend upon it. General Westfeldt, how soon can you start evacuation?"

The Chairman went over to the map and used the pointer. "Mr. President, we started deployment to these posts and bases in southern California and Arizona just after you spoke to me yesterday morning. We'll have sufficient people on the ground by tomorrow morning, all along the area. So far it's being handled and explained as a fast deployment exercise. I just need the word and we can move into the area along the river in a matter of hours . . . Sir, I'll have to coordinate with the local authorities. Have the governors been notified?"

"Not yet. Too soon for all those questions. But I'll tell you this—the state and local authorities are going to stay completely out of it. This is a federal matter and I want a tight chain of command. If we got the national guards, county sheriffs, state police, highway patrols, and municipal police involved, it would just be a giant cluster fuck. We do not have three months to coordinate this thing. All we need to do is move people out of that cross-hatched area. Looks like Yuma will be the biggest problem, but we'll have the most time for that job. Be nice to know how many people are down there." The President scowled in the direction of his reclamation commissioner for a long moment. "George, what will be the flood transit times to the key points, the major communities along the river?"

Commissioner Ricketson swallowed hard. His flood section people out in Denver could tell him immediately. "Sir, I can find out– –"

"Jesus, Mr. Ricketson, what in hell did you think we were going to be doing here this morning? Damnit, you're an engineer—been with the Bureau nearly forty years. Give us your best estimate. General Westfeldt needs that information."

"Sir," the general interrupted, "I can wait a few hours. It's most important that I have accurate information. It's not a problem." Ending a career in the armed forces with four stars required far more than being a good soldier; General Westfeldt just wore a uniform instead of a business suit. He now had the Commissioner of Reclamation securely in his corner.

"And, sir," the general continued, to further deflect the issue, "I would be more comfortable if I knew exactly what your communication with the governors involves."

"All right, you'll be on the line when I place the calls. The whole point here is that the operation has to be set up and under way before the crap hits the media fan."

"Concerning the media, sir, I see a big problem. Part of the army's mission will be to secure a perimeter around the dam, away from any influence from the blast or fallout. Of course, Page will have to be evacuated as well as the people at the Navajo Generating Station and the marina at Wahweap." He pointed out the places on the map. "Sir, we can live with all the media hype and interference along the river, assuming we have things well along when they show up, but we simply cannot have news helicopters fluttering around the dam."

"General Westfeldt, I'm going to declare martial law for the area along the river corridor and within a sufficient perimeter around ground zero. We cannot risk spooking that Hopi madman."

"We'll have to be crystal clear on the news exclusion," his chief of staff spoke up.

"This is war, people—just like the situation down in Waco turned out to be." The President glanced at the BATF chief. "The media were kept out and they went along—bitched and moaned, but they went along. In an area under martial law, the military shoots first. Correct, General Westfeldt?"

The general nodded.

"So if some newsie wants to be a hero looking for a Pulitzer or a fast track to an anchor chair, he gets blown out of the sky. Understood?"

Commissioner Ricketson raised his hand again. "Sir, excuse me . . ."

"Yes, George."

"We have a situation at the dam that may be very fortuitous. We're having to spill, since there's an unusually high runoff, so– –"

"Yes, we've all seen the news, George," the President snapped, puffing impatiently on his cigar. "Kept that reservoir too full again, like you did in—how long has it been? Ten years ago?"

"Uh, yes, sir. But what I wanted to say is, when this occurred back in 1983 we had some damage in the spillways– –"

"That's right," the President said with some enthusiasm. He had a glimmer of what the Reclamation chief was getting at.

"Well, sir, the damage was repaired, but it seems to me that we could claim that there was again some problem with the spillways, there was going to be an unusually high runoff, and, so, prudence demands that we evacuate. Just as a precaution. That way there need be no mention of the bomb."

"That'll work," Roger Chedworth nodded.

Everyone's previous assessment of the stolid old engineer ratchetted up several notches.

"But it wouldn't explain why we need such a tight exclusion fifty miles from the dam and why we have to evacuate Page and the Navajo power plant," General Westfeldt said quietly.

"We'll work that out, General. George is on to something here."

"And if I could add something else, sir, we could say that there is the matter of a possible overtopping of Hoover Dam."

"I almost forgot about that, George. Let's go back to the dam explosion situation. Does the flood map we've got here include the consequential failure of Hoover Dam?"

"Sir, we've looked at that in the past—what would happen to Hoover if there were a catastrophic failure at Glen Canyon. We don't think there'd be a problem."

"What do you mean *think*, George? And tell me what you *think* WOULD happen."

The Commissioner was very sorry he hadn't shut up while he was ahead. "Sir, Hoover Dam was massively overbuilt back in the '30s. It's not just an arch dam, it's a gravity dam as well. We've concluded that there would be up to a 150-foot overtopping, and the peak flood would occur over two days. Of course, the power plant would be totally destroyed, but there is little risk that the toe of the dam would be undercut enough that the dam would tilt. The canyon walls are not sandstone, but a very dense volcanic substance. Sir, the analysis is very complex. I would have to– –"

"Okay, George, we'll accept your answer as: 'No, the flood projection does not include the water behind Hoover Dam.' How much water is in there right now?"

"About twenty-four million acre feet. It will likely fill from the anticipated runoff this season."

"Why in God's name don't you people keep more flood storage space in those giant reservoirs?" The President had no way of knowing that an adequate answer to his question would require a careful understanding of political wrangling that had started over twenty years prior to the authorization of Hoover Dam in 1928, that had lasted until Glen Canyon Dam was authorized in 1956, and to a milder extent, that had continued until the present time. Even if he were inclined to learn, the Eastern politician-president would never fully understand the details of Western water politics and the powerful agribusiness and electricity industry forces that fueled the politics. Commissioner Ricketson probably knew as much as any man still alive about that particular political morass.

"We did have the authorized amount of flood space reserved, but snow runoff and rain in the basin between Hoover and Glen Canyon have taken much of it. Sir, the matter of allocation of storage in Lake Mead is, well, it's very complex, and . . . Do we have to get into all that now?"

"George, let me just verify one thing. It is correct that the Bureau of Reclamation has no duty to maintain *any* flood capacity in Lake Powell?"

"That is what the congressional authorization for the dam and reservoir specified, yes, sir."

"So if the water is available, the Bureau must fill it?"

"Yes, sir. If the reservoir is full or nearly so, we manage winter releases to accommodate the spring runoff."

"And your people did a fine job this year, right? Like they did in 1983."

"Mr. President, the heavy, late spring snowpack, combined with these two very unusual storms, has created an anomalous situation, and– –"

"Anomalous. Is that the word you would use to explain to the people downstream that their homes are going to be washed away, George? But you don't have to talk to the American people, do you? Is that the appropriate word *I* should use when I have to go on the tube to try to explain why this has happened twice now in a little over ten years?"

"Mr. President– –"

"Okay, George, that's enough. You're right. We don't need to discuss the piss-poor planning for those reservoirs. But I want that whole question on next year's legislative agenda." The President turned to his chief of staff. "Arnold, take care of that, will you?" The Eastern president had no way of knowing the full extent of the array of political power that would be brought to bear by the municipal, electrical power, agriculture, and livestock industry lobbies. Even with a powerful ally in the insurance industry, the President had exactly zero chance of changing the manner in which the big Colorado Basin reservoirs were managed—any more than he could change the way in which the insurance companies and the AMA ran the country's health care system.

"Roger, what about disabling the fusing signals?"

"We've located one of the radio signal repeaters Kalinik reported to us and we should have the other one shortly. However, that's not the end of it because the Indian can still send a signal directly to one or more of the buoys. If he's close enough he doesn't even have to have direct line of sight. Additionally, there are the land lines. The material from Kalinik says there are land lines to two of the buoys as a backup."

"Okay, but what's the plan to disable the sonar system? I understand you can't just go out there and start picking up his buoys, but what *can* you do?"

"We will electronically override or mask the signals. Once that's done, we'll remove the buoys. But the way Kalinik set up the signal frequencies and patterns, and with the overkill power they have, so far our people say they can't nullify or mask the signals—not for sure, anyway. Frankly, if we hadn't had the detailed data from Kalinik, we'd have a real hard time even figuring out what's going on."

"I'm sure the judge will take that into consideration when he sentences the guy," the President said icily. "Let's move on. Roger, any hope of negotiating with the Indian?"

"Mr. President, we have no idea where he is, other than he has to be somewhere around the lower third of the reservoir."

"Well, if he contacts you, what do you have in mind for negotiation?"

"From the little we got from Kalinik's conversation with the San

Francisco office, and what we know about this person, there'll be no negotiation. This guy is not a terrorist in the classic sense. That is, he's not threatening something or doing something to accomplish some other agenda. He just wants the dam gone . . . Period."

Several long moments of silence followed. The President puffed on the stub of his cigar. "Get your people moving, General Westfeldt. We'll call the governors right now."

The telephone rang. The Chief of Staff picked it up and then handed the phone to Roger Chedworth.

A smile spread over the FBI Director's face. "Mr. President—gentlemen—Saul Kalinik just walked into the San Francisco office."

14

Glen Canyon Dam, June 8

The dam superintendent slammed down the telephone and stomped out of his office in the Carl Hayden Visitor Center. "Helen, no more calls from news people. I've got my hands full here and I don't need any more of their silly questions. Just refer them to the official release from Salt Lake." He got into his heavy rain pants and jacket. "I'm going down below for a while."

Randy MacConnell stared at the surface of the reservoir disappearing into the shroud of rain pelting its surface, now less than five feet from the crest of his dam. After the snow runoff had begun, followed by the Upper Basin storm surge, the spillways had been in operation for twelve days. The tunnel overflows were being opened more and more as the inflow to Powell Reservoir climbed steeply.

"Spillways are working fine, Randy," his O&M chief said. The men were standing on the crest of the dam near the right abutment, below the visitor center. Far beneath them, the canyon was filled with spray and the churning white water being ejected through the river outlet works and the spillway exits from the walls of the canyon. "Good sweeps on both sides." He peered through the sluicing rain with his binoculars.

"Yeah, but the vibration has gotten worse—seems stronger than it was in '83, and this rain sure has gotten worse. Never seen anything like it."

"Bound to be some vibration with all that water, Randy. We're at 60,000 on each side. The ROW's at seventeen."

"Damn, I hate this business of trying to outguess the runoff each year when the reservoir happens to be up. Inevitable we'd get caught again. Damnit,

I wish Salt Lake would listen to me." Randy MacConnell loved the big dam he was responsible for. He'd been assigned to Glen Canyon for eighteen years. He knew every inch of the giant mass of concrete and equipment: every tunnel, gallery, adit, walkway, and room; every piece of plumbing, machinery, and electrical equipment.

"What's the latest on the weather, Johnny?" The dam superintendent had been so busy and was so upset with the unremitting calls from media people that he hadn't even turned on his television for the past three days.

"It looks like the front that's been moving across the Upper Basin has stalled over the western slope of the Rockies, so there's gonna be a whole lot more rain on top of all that snowpack. We've been getting the fringe of it here for the past three days. The report also said it's going to get hot, all over the basin, when the storm clears out; and the sudden increase in rain here is from another system coming up from the south. A big hurricane came ashore down in Baja, so we're starting to get the rainout. I just picked up the latest projection from Salt Lake—calls for a surge in inflow, and they won't know where it'll peak until these two storm systems crap out or move out of the basin."

"No choice but to bump up the spillways again," the superintendent nodded. "The reservoir's come up a foot and a half in the last twenty-four hours."

"Salt Lake says we're to run 'em both up to seventy-five kay."

"Yeah, that should do it."

* * *

Carlotta was no longer an identifiable cyclone when she moved over the Sonoran Desert into central Arizona on the morning of June 8. Although her core's rotation had finally stopped, the huge mass of water and heat energy continued to move upslope toward the mountains rimming the Phoenix basin to the northeast. No longer being fed and rejuvenated by warm ocean water, the mass of moisture slowly released its burden in the endless meteorological cycle of ocean to cloud to rain to river to ocean.

Recurving tropical cyclones entering the desert southwest were by no means unknown phenomena. Long before the first white settlers came to the region around the confluence of the Salt, Verde, and Gila Rivers, the Hohokam Indians had known and respected the huge storms that occasionally came across the desert from the great ocean. The natives learned to recognize the unmistakable signs in the approaching clouds and fled to high ground as the torrential rains swept over their valley and occasionally even over the mountains that rimmed it. The current inhabitants of Phoenix, with their relatively brief occupation of the valley, were nearly unconscious of the storm threat from the southwest; yet in recent times three major tropical storms had

Left spillway test, June 24, 1980, the day after the reservoir filled for the first time. The short test revealed no hint of the latent problem with the spillways which would arise three years later (*Bureau of Reclamation, Vern Jetley*).

penetrated into Arizona. In 1951, 1970, and 1982, the rainout from tropical cyclones deluged the deserts of Sonora and southern Arizona. In the 1970 dispersal of Hurricane Norma, rainfall of nearly six inches occurred over the Mogollon Rim above Phoenix. It had even extended into western New Mexico.

When Carlotta passed over Arizona in a four-hundred-mile-wide swath, she continued to move northeast over Phoenix and up to the Mogollon Rim, the arc of mountains separating the Verde and Salt River watersheds from that of the Little Colorado. Flood control and water supply reservoirs in the Phoenix-side headwater basins quickly captured much of the rainfall, but the city and practically all of the cotton fields in the lower valley were inundated by the water spilling from the structures and falling heavily from the passing storm.

Water from the Verde and Salt Rivers poured, in turn, into the Gila, already running in flood; and with the other rivers' additions it carried 125,000 cfs when the it joined the Colorado River at Yuma. The levees around the old city contained the flow despite the heavy rain that had been falling for the past two days: they could withstand a flood of 145,000 cfs before the water invaded the city. Beyond Yuma the water diverted into the Mexicans' Alamo Canal or found its way around their Morelos Dam to proceed across the Colorado River Delta to return to the sea; but before the flood surge reached the Mexican diversion structure, the water badly eroded the old earthen plug and levee that had been constructed after the 1905 flood into the Imperial Valley. The Colorado River maintained its channel to the Gulf of California, even though the levee that kept it from turning to the west and down into the below-sea-level sink of the Imperial Valley was badly damaged.

In her dying drive from the Gulf, Carlotta had lost nearly a quarter of her moisture and energy, much of it sheared off by the 6,000-foot heights of the Mogollon Rim. The remaining storm was drawn north by the existence of a large low-pressure region stalled over the Upper Basin. Inexorably, Carlotta's mass of heat and moisture was pulled toward the low pressure area in the skies like a huge bowl of soup spilling upwards; then, in the hours following the storm's surge over the Mogollon Rim, another chunk of its moisture rained out in the desert basin of the Little Colorado. All of the uncounted, normally dry washes, from the Continental Divide in New Mexico, through the Painted Desert, and across the Navajo and Hopi reservations, gathered the rain, joined, and finally converged in the Little Colorado Gorge, which twisted down into the lower end of Marble Canyon. For three days the Little Colorado ran over the travertine springs of the Hopi Sipapuni at a peak rate of 170,000 cfs, with all the aggregated 1.5 million acre feet flowing down the Grand Canyon and into Mead Reservoir, adding to the accumulated spring runoff from the 59,000-square-mile basin between Glen Canyon Dam and Hoover Dam. The Lower Basin reservoir was rapidly using up its five million acre feet of flood capacity.

The bulk of Carlotta, now drained of less than 40 percent of her moisture, moved over the Hopi's and the Navajo's Black Mesa, past the low divide separating the Little Colorado from the San Juan River. The 400-mile-wide, tropical-origin storm and its millions of acre feet of suspended moisture surged into the lower expanse of a closed basin to join the dying remainder of another storm that had begun in the arctic, half the world away to the west. Nearly every drop remaining in the combined system would wring out in the 108,000-square-mile, already saturated, snowpack-rimmed basin upstream of Glen Canyon Dam.

15

GLEN CANYON DAM, JUNE 9

The continual vibration from the massive surges of water through the canyon walls was shaking the entire 9.25-million-ton dam. The spillways were more than half full, but unlike the situation in 1983, nothing could be done to curb the flows through the ravaged tunnels. With the reservoir elevation at 3,713 feet, if the gates were closed the flashboards would be overtopped by five feet, tearing them off. The flow in each bore was now 105,000 cfs, over three times the peak rates they had carried in 1983, and with the river outlet works contributing another 17,000, the total discharge down the Colorado was 227,000 cfs. Seventy-six miles down the river, at the foot of Marble Canyon, the flow jumped to over 345,000 with the addition of the remainder of the runoff draining from the basin of the Little Colorado. The most wild-eyed river rat would not even think of getting into a raft to give the Colorado a try.

No water flowed through the Glen Canyon power plant. Even with two of the eight units down for repair, the discharge through the six remaining fifteen-foot-diameter penstocks would have contributed another 24,000 cfs to relieving the rising reservoir. At 11:00 that morning, Randy MacConnell had gotten a terse call from the Upper Basin headquarters directing him to shut down the power plant. Furthermore, after the penstocks were closed, he was to evacuate all personnel from the dam except the few needed to operate the spillway gates. Salt Lake had told the superintendent that with the unexpected inflows from the snowmelt and the combined storms, now forecast to rain out entirely in the Upper Basin, it was likely that the dam would be overtopped; of course, the power plant would suffer massive damage and the penstocks exiting the base of the dam would likely be breached. The latter event would mean that the high-pressure water would discharge from the broken ends of the powerhouse flumes until the reservoir dropped 245 feet to their intake level on the upstream dam face. It had taken several hours to lower all eight, fourteen-by-twenty-two-foot, 213,000-pound, fixed-wheel gates over the inlets on the reservoir face of the dam. With the job completed, the superintendent, his O&M chief, and four other men were the only people left.

There's something else going on, Randy MacConnell thought. *Something else besides safeguarding the structure and my people.* The whole town,

Wahweap Marina, and even the Navajo Generating Station, six miles from the reservoir, were being evacuated while the military swarmed over the whole area to secure a huge perimeter around the dam. Randy MacConnell wasn't buying the earthquake and landslide threat story—that if a catastrophic failure of the dam occurred, there was a possibility of substantial seismic activity when the trillions of tons of water were suddenly released. *There has to be something else.* He'd seen six C-130s land at Page and unload Blackhawk assault helicopters.

We'll get through this. He stared down into the canyon below his dam, watching the 120-mph jets hitting the flip buckets at more than 3,000 tons per second; the resulting plumes, like snow-white rooster tails, arced halfway to the rim. He squinted into the cloud of mist filling the canyon. He thought he could see bits of debris in the jets. *The aeration slots must have failed! What's happening to the spillways?* For several days he'd been hearing the rumbling sounds from deep in the walls of the canyon that he'd heard in 1983 when the spillways were seriously damaged; now, even clear up on the west rim, he could feel the vibration. He was worried. Very worried. In 1983 the Bureau had known the tunnels would be kept far below their capacities and the flows would fall off quickly. Not so this time. Even before the dam overtopped, the tunnel design capacities would be exceeded; then with only a modest overtopping they would be completely filled.

God help the tunnels if they run full. Randy MacConnell knew enough about tunnel flow hydraulics that he didn't want to even think about the tunnels trying to run full—under pressure. And there was something else he was thinking about: the evidence of faulting in the right abutment—the one he was standing over—which had showed up in the surges in the lower foundation adit during the 1983 episode. *What about the increased drainage the E&R people shrugged off?* But the dam supervisor would have been even more worried if he knew and fully understood all the details of what had occurred during the construction of the diversion tunnels.

Beginning in 1957, sixteen months of blasting through the ancient rock with tons of high explosives had been needed to excavate the tunnels. In many places the vibration and shock waves from the explosions had fractured or opened up shear planes, joints, and seams that ran through the stone—discontinuities formed during the several million years that the Jurassic Period, cemented sand dunes of the Navajo sandstone had been slowly uplifted along with the rest of the Colorado Plateau. Where the joints and cracks had been encountered, most extensively in the right abutment, they were pumped full of concrete grout in accord with standard engineering practice at the time. The engineers were satisfied, particularly so since the problematic sections of tunnel were to be plugged. However, many other cracks existed which were not detected and grouted.

During the 1983 incident, when water and air had surged through the drain holes in the abutment adit above the right spillway, the vibration from the cavitation had managed to extend and further open a number of the seams and fissures in the sandstone. Although the problem drain holes into the adit had been sealed with grout, the network of cracks remained, extending over the area between the spillway tunnel and the adit—clear back to the plug in the diversion tunnel. A number of the cracks also connected to the drain holes in the concrete lining of the right tunnel, and the small flows through each of them added another 225 gallons per minute to the existing hydrostatic pressure flow through the porous rock. Because the cracks were so small, the flow of water through them was slow: the leaks remained at their steady state, 225 gpm.

Yet another potential problem lay adjacent to the diversion tunnel plugs. With the state of the art in placing concrete that existed in the late 1950s, fully lining a tunnel through rock had been difficult. Forms were placed around the inside of the tunnel, then concrete was pumped into the void between the forms and the sandstone wall of the rough bore. The problem lay in filling the small space at the very crest of the tunnel, between the tops of the forms and the rock ceiling. Many small voids remained, where grout did not completely fill in the spaces. These voids added to the latticework of natural, construction-explosion-formed, and cavitation-vibration-formed cracks in the sandstone above and around the tunnel plugs.

The steady vibration and shock waves from the erosion in the right tunnel had been occurring for eleven days. The cracks in the sandstone and the voids in the concrete above the plug were now interconnected for the whole length of the tunnel barrier, with one branch of the network situated just behind the point where the cavitation erosion of the spillway tunnel was occurring. The speed of the leaking water was ten feet per second, enough to start a slight erosion of the crack when it was suddenly connected to the bore of the spillway as the cavitation and mechanical cratering ripped away the concrete lining. A labyrinthine conduit now existed between the water at the bottom of the reservoir and the right spillway. The crack around the tunnel plug was 150 feet long and not very large—less than one-quarter of an inch at its widest point—but behind the crack was the full pressure at the bottom of the reservoir: 240 pounds per square inch. For over thirty years the Navajo sandstone abutments had dutifully withstood the pressure, allowing only a gradual infiltration through their porous structure and paper-thin fractures, never before experiencing a stream of water racing through their cemented sands. Now, concentrating its energy at the narrowest constrictions in the tiny channel, the water gradually accelerated from ten to 220 feet per second—150 mph—cutting like a liquid laser through the aeolian rock. The leak was insignificant: entirely undetectable when it joined the huge flow in the right spillway.

At nearly the same time, water began flowing through another segment of the network of cracks and fissures into two of the drain holes in the right abutment adit. The flow through the drains was so powerful that it soon began to cut a crater in the bare sandstone ceiling of the tunnel, seven feet above the holes. After impinging its jet on the ceiling, the water ran down the gutter in the floor and into the gallery in the bottom of the dam, in the process running across sensors placed there to measure drainage. The sensors were electronically connected to computers in the Instrumentation Section at the Bureau's headquarters in Denver.

"Randy, you've got a problem in the bottom right adit. Send someone down there to take a look. The flows have really shot up—may be a couple hundred gpm. Call us right back."

I knew it, Randy MacConnell thought. He'd gotten used to the steady vibration, numbed by all his other concerns, but now the shaking seemed much stronger. *Got to be a shitload of cavitation down there . . . and it's going to get a lot worse.*

Twenty minutes later the maintenance technician stepped off the elevator at the top of the dam. "Big leak, Randy. I couldn't get clear back there, but there's flow like it was a fire hose. Water's running three inches deep across the whole floor of the adit."

"Thanks, Sam. Could you tell if it was coming from the floor drain holes?"

"Definitely."

Randy MacConnell had not gotten a good night's sleep for nearly a week. The inflow to the reservoir was currently about 600,000 cfs: only an estimate because a great deal of un-gauged water was coming down the myriad streams along the now-190-mile length of Powell Reservoir. The surcharged, 193,000-acre surface was also receiving heavy rainfall.

All the major reservoirs upstream were full and spilling: Flaming Gorge on the Green; Blue Mesa, Crystal and Morrow Point on the Gunnison; Navajo on the San Juan; McPhee on the Dolores; Granby at the headwaters of the Colorado; Green Mountain and Dillon on the Blue River. The latest gauge reading above Green River, Utah, by itself showed a flow of 185,000 cfs. The reservoir inflow was clearly going to continue to increase, so Randy MacConnell had been told to bump the flows to 125,000 in each spillway. Even with that, a net capture of over 300,000 cubic feet would occur each second. The reservoir elevation now stood at 3,713 feet: two feet below the crest of the dam and six feet below the tops of the parapet walls.

16

Laughlin, Nevada, 0700, June 10

The manager of the Golden Dream Hotel and Casino, along with all of the guests and employees in the fourteen-story building, was being herded into the street toward a long line of busses, some green, some dark blue, parked in front of the nine mid-rise hotels strung along Casino Drive, Laughlin's single main street. Hundreds of young men and women in military fatigues, all armed, surrounded the evacuees. The rain had just stopped. Everything glistened in the bright morning sunlight.

"All right, if you've got a vehicle, get in it and drive where you are directed. Move along quickly, please. If you haven't got a vehicle, get in a bus. This area is now under military control. Keep moving, please. Laughlin is being evacuated."

The manager had learned earlier in the morning that there was no point in trying to ask questions. A young Ranger lieutenant with no neck and a shaved head had told him, politely but summarily, that he was to awaken all his guests and staff and advise them of the evacuation. At 4:30 A.M. he'd been given two hours to get the building organized, and for the past two and a half hours he'd heard a steady barrage of complaints, yelling, cursing, crying, whining, promises of lawsuits, and threats of bodily injury. All he knew for certain was that the entire populations of Laughlin and Bullhead City across the river were being moved up their respective hills, out of the bottom of the river valley.

The public information officer for the 3rd Brigade had his tent set up in the command post area. Outside, a collection of seventy-five television and newspaper reporters waited impatiently. The big studio tractor-trailer rigs were arriving regularly, parking in the media area and setting up their satellite dishes.

Before he had to go out to face the horde of reporters, Major Armando J. Armijo sat down to arrange his thoughts and decide what he would say to the people. He had to be sure he had the parameters straight on how far he could go in answering their questions. That was easy, really; Major Armijo did not know very much. He knew only the particulars of how the evacuation below Hoover Dam was being accomplished and that it had to be completed by 1600 hours. General Hardwicke would go on television in the evening to further explain things to the public.

"Good morning, ladies and gentlemen, I will assume that you've all read through the public information release you've been provided. If you have any additional questions, I will be glad to answer them according to the information I currently have." Major Armijo knew that a few of the little black apertures pointed at him were sending his picture all over the world.

During the next thirty minutes he patiently re-answered all the questions that had already been carefully, fully, and clearly answered in the press release. But the written press release did not play well on television. This was, after all, show business, so the media needed a star. Right now he was all they had.

"Yes, that's right," Major Armijo answered for the third time, "we're just requiring people to move out of the flood plain. At this point on the river it's less than a quarter mile up the hill . . . Yes, everyone is free to go. They just cannot go back into the restricted area . . . Yes, ma'am, just like the police authority during the earthquake in L.A. and the riot the year before, and then during the fires and then the floods and mud slides . . . No, ma'am, I'm not advised that the river-boat-shaped casino will float . . . Yes, similar action is being taken all along the course of the river . . . Yes, it's a very large operation to evacuate Yuma . . . I can't tell you, sir, if all the money has been taken out of the casinos . . . I'm not advised about salvage rights . . . including the money, ma'am; probably have to wait until the debris is in international waters . . . Most certainly, ma'am, we're cooperating fully with the Mexican government." And so it went until a reporter from Flagstaff got his turn.

"What's going on up in Page, Major? Every road into the dam area is closed to traffic going in and all aircraft are being kept out. We haven't had any flood coverage up there for over a week."

"Sir, there's another command in charge of that operation, so I'm not able to answer your question in detail. I can only say that precautions are being taken in the remote event—I mean the *very* remote event—that the dam should fail. In that situation, we have been advised that there would then be some risk of seismic or landslide activity in areas immediately adjacent to the canyon. Page and the Navajo Generating Station are in the risk zone, so they're being evacuated as a precaution."

"Why is it necessary to exclude aircraft?"

"The military evacuation requires complete control of the situation. We cannot risk interference with necessary military use of the airspace."

"Major, there are reports that both the FBI and the Bureau of Alcohol, Tobacco and Firearms are up at the dam area. What would those agencies have to do with earthquakes and landslides?"

"Ladies and gentlemen, I have no information on that subject. I'm sure that it's just a rumor. Now, if you would please excuse me . . . ."

* * *

Waddy hurried along the ridge toward Kane Point, above a little side canyon that would eventually wind down to the north side of the reservoir. The side canyon was similar to hundreds of other little gorges that found their way down to what had once been Glen Canyon of the Colorado River.

He would make much better time if he could trot along the sandy bottom of the narrow, twisting canyon rather than have to weave his way in and out among the crevices, potholes, and precipices on its rim. He looked down into the deep, normally dry cleft in the sandstone. The water was running nearly halfway up the sides. He knew that if he slipped on the slick sandstone and fell in, he would be reduced to a mass of hamburger by the time he was spit out at the reservoir. He was headed for a point overlooking Padre Bay where he would have a good line of sight to one of the repeater antennas and also directly to two of the sonar buoys, one of which had a land line to shore. His deadline was four-thirty, Mountain Daylight Time, tomorrow afternoon. He intended to keep it. Payback time.

* * *

Paul Heartwood finished the last of his lunch while he sat outside on the deck of the Mesa Laboratory building. The modernistic structure, designed by the renowned architect I. M. Pei, blended perfectly into the Flatirons foothills that overlooked the city of Boulder. A large number of the young men and women attending the University of Colorado were there because of the Flatirons. Some of the best rock climbing in the country was found in the hills above the campus.

"Nice view of the People's Republic of Boulder today, Dr. Heartwood." Willie Jefferson Davis was also enjoying the warm Colorado sun.

"Boulder's not that bad. Ever been to Berkeley?"

"No, I haven't. Hey, that's right. You're a Cal grad, aren't you?"

"Boulder just doesn't have anywhere near Berkeley's whine coefficient." Professor Heartwood turned his gaze past the university town below them, out to the Great Plains horizon. It was as flat as the sea meeting the sky. Forty miles away on the horizon to the southeast, and partially obscured by the curvature of the earth, the atmospheric physicist could just make out a slender tower and what looked like a large white building standing alone on the prairie. "Well, they did it. Built that big new airport right in the middle of the worst tornado area in the whole Front Range."

"Sir, Colorado doesn't get really horrific tornadoes like in the Plains states or the Midwest. Besides, the new Doppler radars should give adequate warnings of wind shears and micro bursts."

"So you think it's as safe out there as Stapleton Airport is."

"Uh . . . no, sir."

"You finished, Willie? Let's go back and see what we've got."

Paul Heartwood finally had the revised projections for the Upper Basin of the Colorado. Most of his staff had struggled for the past nine days to modify the Upper Basin precipitation model to include Hurricane Carlotta, a task he'd ordered when he first saw the projections of the big storm's interaction with the southern extension of the Pacific High and the record high sea surface temperatures extending up to southern California. The base model was not designed to include such a deep penetration of tropical cyclone activity into the southern intermountain region. The model anticipated tropical storm penetration into the Sonoran Desert and beyond—ample historical evidence documented such events—but to have the bulk of the storm mass extend into the Upper Basin and to have an obliging 500-millibar low waiting there to help draw it in—that was unanticipated. Recognized as possible, but unanticipated. The maximum flood study done by Appleton-Thompson Engineers for the Bureau of Reclamation had envisioned such an event, but it had been considered too remote a possibility to be worthy of any attention in the Upper Basin model.

"What we have here is a classic example of the results of human arrogance."

"What do you mean, Dr. Heartwood?"

"Arrogance, Willie. Plain old, common, everyday arrogance. What is this big model based on? Theory? Sure. Good theory? Sure, again. But most importantly, it's based on demonstrable experience. And look at the experience we have to demonstrate: in the Upper Colorado River Basin, at best, no more than a hundred years of records, with the early records often suspect. We talk about 100-year and 500-year floods. Engineers design and build water impoundment and diversion structures based on what they know and can reasonably expect. That's the key word. *Reasonable.* Of course, engineers by their very nature are reasonable people. We scientists, however, we're not supposed to be bound by the pedestrian realities of design and construction limitations and cost-benefit analyses. We're supposed to be free to really examine what's going on in the world. Well, we failed here, Willie. We failed big time. We failed because, deep down, we suffer from the same shortcomings as the pragmatic, plodding engineers. This isn't science fiction; it's supposed to be real. And being real, we fall back on real numbers—real numbers we can count and massage and analyze, just like the engineers. A hundred years, Willie. How long has it been raining in the Upper Basin of the Colorado River?"

"Nearly two weeks now. Steady."

"No, how long in history?"

"Who knows? Probably hundreds of millions of years before the Grand Canyon started to form five million years ago."

"Exactly. We have not the faintest damn idea what the meteorological history of that region of the earth is other than vague estimates of overall climate changes over tens of thousands of years. We have no idea whatsoever about short-term events in that basin. And so, like the engineers we have been taught to disdain, we fall back on *known* data when we simply cannot handle the great unknown."

"But the program model uses lots of paleo data, much of it based on tree-ring studies. That goes back a couple thousand years. Statistically, that makes a good sample."

"For overall trends, even annual summaries, yes. But no dendrochronologist can tell you about specific storms or rainfall events, only that certain years were either wetter or dryer than normal, whatever normal is. That's all they can in-*fir*."

Willie Davis grimaced.

"Look at this data," his boss smiled. "What's going on right now, this morning as we talk, is a bigger precipitation event than I thought should even be anticipated in the program. Remember last November when I mentioned the A-TE study the Bureau commissioned? What they called the 'upper limit design rainstorm'? Well, here it is, Willie, and I was too arrogant to even stick it into the program. Even so, we still cannot say where this occurrence lines up in the whole scheme of possible events. This thing provides some evidence that the Grand Canyon was not worn away one grain of sand at a time but largely was created in thousands of events like we are seeing today: catastrophism, not solely uniformitarianism."

"Dr. Heartwood, it's nearly noon. Don't we have to get our summary ready for the director?"

"You're right. Sorry about getting carried away on primordial ramblings. But you do see what I mean by arrogance, don't you?"

"Yes, sir. I certainly do."

"Let's go look at the final numbers."

They watched the printout of the isohyetal rainfall contour map for the Upper Basin. Next came the computer's numerical projections from all the rainfall gauging records and the modified meteorological model of the interaction of the two storms overlain on the existing snowpack.

"Hard to believe, isn't it, Dr. Heartwood?"

Over the next seven days, 9.3 million acre feet of water was going to land or melt in 94,000 already-saturated square miles in the Upper Basin of the Colorado River. The law of gravity would assure that all the water would head toward a relatively tiny arch of concrete in the lower end of Glen Canyon.

17

GLEN CANYON DAM, JUNE 11

Randy MacConnell picked up the telephone and heard his boss's voice up in Salt Lake. "Randy, open all the spillway gates fully and evacuate the structure."

"Doug, is there any way I can find out what in hell is really going on? I've got the military, the ATF, the FBI, and God knows who else running around all over the place. I can't just walk away from here. The reservoir is about up to the parapets. With the current inflows, we're going to overtop soon."

"That's the point. The structure has to be evacuated until the water recedes."

"But there's no danger in my office in the visitor center. It's ninety-five feet above the dam crest."

"Look, Randy, these are orders from Washington. Just do it and get out. Now!"

"Wide open."

"Randy, with the head we have now, tunnel capacities will be exceeded."

"Got to do it, Johnny."

At each spillway, two 326,000-pound radial gates slowly winched to the tops of their arcs. When they shuddered to a stop the reservoir surface was still standing above their lower edges, but as the gates rose the flows under them increased explosively. The water surged through two forty-by-forty-seven-foot openings into each spillway mouth, pouring into both yawning maws at nearly 200,000 cfs, more than 60,000 cfs above the design flow rate. There was no more effect from the air slots because there was no air. The tunnels were now pressure conduits. The rumbling and vibration in the abutments and throughout the dam increased sharply.

"Johnny, we're outta here."

* * *

Waddy checked his watch. *Just past four.* The heavy rain provided good cover for his final climb to the top of a rock dome rising above the reservoir, but the slightest misstep on the slick sandstone would send him sliding over the edge to plunge 150 feet to the water. Even if he survived the fall, there was no place to crawl out. He stopped and glanced over the edge: the canyon walls below him rimmed the reservoir like a giant bathtub, only rarely interrupted by a section of steep, boulder-strewn shoreline. *Be trapped like a rat in a rain barrel.* Waddy had to stop often while he scrambled over the polished rock. Although his body had managed to metabolize the snake and insect venom, it still struggled with the oozing wound in his chest.

He sat down on the dome, just below the top so that he would not be silhouetted: legs crossed beneath him, facing the east, hands folded in his lap, back ramrod straight. For nearly thirty minutes he sat motionless in the pelting rain, his lips moving in silent recitation of ancient prayers known only to his Snake Clan and to the Motswimi, the Hopi warrior society.

He got up and walked over to where he'd left his backpack under a ledge of rock. He hadn't needed to look at his watch to know that 4:30 had arrived. He opened the top flap, unfolded the plastic trash-bag liners, and took out one of the two identical VHF radio transmitters.

The dome of rock he was standing on was twenty-five miles up the winding reservoir on the north side: less than twenty miles from the dam by a crow flight. One of his repeater antennas was located down the reservoir on a pylon of sandstone on the other side, about four miles away. Although he couldn't see the spire through the rain, he knew he had a direct line of sight, just as he had to two of the sonar buoys below him in Padre Bay. The powerful sonar transmitters in the buoys were capable of sending a signal readable up to sixty miles away by the sensitive receiver in the bomb case—more than sufficient at this location.

Padre Bay, Waddy thought with disgust. *What'd they call it? Crossing of the Fathers? Been used by my people for 2,000 years before a couple'a wanderin'* pahanas *finally stumbled on it.* Beneath this part of the reservoir the Franciscan explorers, Silvestre Vélez de Escalante and Francisco Atanasio Domínguez, had found a way across the canyon on the return leg of their failed 1776 expedition to the missions of California. Waddy thought of the centuries of suffering his people had endured at the hands of the Spaniards and then the Mexicans and, always, in the name of their church. *Arrogant,* pahana *religions. How many have died because of them?*

The time had arrived. Waddy's heart was pumping fast while he dialed in the frequency. He lay down on the rock, looking away from the direction of the reservoir, and pressed the transmit key. Seconds passed. Nothing happened. He squeezed again, this time holding the key down for several seconds. Nothing. He sat up, checked the frequency, then pressed the battery button: the little red light came on. He reset the transmitter for frequencies on either side of the one he was supposed to use and tried again. Still nothing happened.

He went back to his rucksack for the second transmitter, readied it, and resumed his prone position, his pulse racing again when he squeezed the key. Once more the gigantic explosion did not happen. He went through the same exercise with the second radio as he had with the first. Still nothing. Then he tried keying both transmitters at once, with no result. The driving rain was not the problem. Both transmitters were marine instruments.

Waddy went back to the little ledge of rock and sat down. In his entire life he'd never felt such despair; then for the first time in more years than he could remember he began to cry. He sat on the high sandstone promontory for nearly half an hour, unconscious of the driving rain, his thoughts focused only on the biggest disappointment his life had yet presented him with. At length he got up; he began putting on his backpack for the long, dangerous, now-uninspired trek back to . . . to what? *For* what?

Wait! He spun around. He looked down at the reservoir.

"The *water*!"

Over a week had passed since he'd finished setting the sonar buoys and repeater antennas. In that time the reservoir had risen. He didn't know how far it had come up, but it had to be over ten feet. He'd set the buoys just out from the shore, anchored in places where the reservoir banks were only slightly sloped. He had to be certain they couldn't move around—to maintain line of sight to the repeaters.

The anchor lines are too short! Saul had weighted the buoys so that they would have nearly neutral buoyancy. The old storage batteries he'd brought in strapped to his kayak were heavy enough to hold the buoys down while the reservoir rose above them. *The antennas are under water—too far under water.*

"All *right*!" Waddy shouted out loud again. *Take me a few hours to get around to the land line. It's okay. Just a short stay of execution, that's all.*

* * *

Hoover Office Building, 8:30 p.m.

"What's going on?" the Director asked over the telephone.

"Don't know, sir," the supervisory special agent said. "He's two hours past his deadline, even figured on daylight time. Could be a lot of things. The rain. Our security . . ."

"Evacuation done there at Page?"

"Yes, sir. Everyone's gone except us troops. Hell of an operation to get all those people out of here. Didn't know the army could organize things so quickly."

"The President's bugging me. Let me know immediately if anything happens."

10:30 P.M.

Roger Chedworth snatched the telephone from its cradle midway through the first ring. The next thing he heard was laughter.

"We've got it, sir," came the choking voice over the telephone. "The buoys are *under water*. The dumb shit must have anchored them too short. The reservoir's come up twelve feet since he set them."

"Now's your chance! Get teams out to those buoys with the land lines." Saul had told the FBI everything he knew about where the buoys were to be placed and which ones were to have the land lines. He and Waddy had spent a long time scanning the topo maps of the reservoir area, selecting general locations, but it had been left up to Waddy to pick the actual points.

"We're on it as we speak, sir. Our guys and ATF special response teams are heading up the reservoir now."

"Still raining out there?"

"A deluge, sir. We could sure use that satellite info. We don't know exactly where to look, and the rain cuts visibility to nearly zip."

With just a snatch of clear weather during a pass, the KH-11 could find the buoys, even through twelve feet of water. The Director thought of the NRO reconnaissance satellites and the agency's land-based equipment directed at Soviet hardware in orbit; then his thoughts were followed spontaneously by a memory of how the agency's covert photographic capabilities had been inadvertently revealed. On one of the early shuttle flights, NASA reported that several of the heat shield ceramic tiles had detached during launch and that there was concern about reentry. How did NASA know about missing six-inch-square tiles? a bright reporter had asked. The astronauts could not see the area of the shuttle where the tiles were said to be missing. The simple report about the missing tiles had been picked up immediately, then transmitted to the old gray men in the building at No. 2 Dzerzhinsky Square in Moscow. More than a few shivers had rippled through the Soviet intelligence community.

"You have *got* to get to the land-lined buoys before he does," the Director commanded unnecessarily.

"We've got every boat available out on the lake, sir, and even in this ratty weather the army has six Blackhawks in the air. We'll get him."

***

Waddy was making slow progress. It had taken him five hours to coon his way around the edge of Padre Bay, partly because of his uncooperative arm, but mainly because he'd forgotten about a long side canyon, full of water. Now, in the dark, he had to move largely by feel on the slick rock, and he dared not use his flashlight. The incredibly bright searchlights from a helicopter swept over him just moments after he'd ducked behind a rock.

Even in this rain they'd see a flashlight in a second. Prob'ly got infrared. Fuckers are out in force now. Prob'ly figured out what the little problem is. Out on the lake lookin' for those buoys. Knew I shouldn't've given them a specific deadline. Should've just blown the sucker after waitin' a couple'a days.

Waddy heard the unmistakable, throaty roar of one of the big inboard-engined launches the Bureau used. *It's slowin' down right out there on the bay somewhere. 'Bout a quarter mile to go now.*

"Can't see squat, sir," the ATF agent said as he examined the foggy-green image of the shoreline revealed by his Noctron scope. The big inboard launch slowed and settled into her wake.

"Infrared isn't finding him," another man said. "Must not be in this end of the bay—or maybe it's the rain."

The agent in charge examined his map. He disregarded five of the locations the FBI had marked, concentrating instead on one of the two buoys with a trigger line that was supposed to be in this corner of Padre Bay. *How in hell am I going to find a piece of wire when I can't see twenty yards through this crap?* "There's supposed to be one right over in that corner." The AIC checked their location with the GPS receiver. He had the military model, so he knew where they were within thirty feet, not the 300 feet the civilian versions were restricted to. The problem was that he didn't know precisely where he was going. "Okay, course 335, and take it slow. It's gonna shoal up fast. You got the army on the horn, Ralph?"

"Yes, sir," the radioman said. "One's heading over this way right now."

The eerie, throbbing sound of the helicopter could soon be heard over the rumble of the inboard and the rain spattering the water and the deck of the launch. The AIC didn't hear the familiar *whop, whop, whop* of the Hueys he remembered from the rice paddies in 'Nam, just a growing, undulating whine coming from somewhere in the dark behind them. "Get the light over there," he said, pointing toward a spot on the shore.

The quartz halogen spotlight came on, glaring back at the men in the boat, reflecting off the heavy rain and immediately destroying everyone's night vision. Simultaneously, the command to turn on the light had not registered with the agent concentrating on his view through the Noctron. His screamed curse pierced the din of rain, approaching helicopter, and idling Cadillac engine.

"Shit! Okay, move in. To hell with the rocks. That land line's got to be somewhere right over there."

The boat advanced more quickly toward the shore. A ragged jumble of boulders became visible in the harsh light, even through the curtain of rain. The man in the bow cried out: "There he is! I see him!"

A dark figure moved quickly down through the boulders toward the water's edge. "He's getting closer!" The AIC shuddered, thinking of what would happen when the dam exploded. *The water will drop hundreds of feet. We'll be swept away as it goes down.*

Through the rain-streaked light he could see intermittent flashes of movement among the boulders, steadily progressing—getting closer to the water. "Take him out!" Six automatic weapons sent a spray of rounds into the jumble of sandstone blocks.

"Oh, shit!" The darting figure was now only about thirty yards from the water's edge. *All he has to do is get to the end of that signal cable.* The Blackhawk was suddenly overhead, its powerful downwash cutting off the rain, replacing it with a vertical blast of air. The shore of the bay, now fifty yards away, was awash in brilliant light, the rain becoming millions of dangling, shining threads in the blue-white illumination.

"He's almost there!" two of the agents cried out in unison. At the same instant, the big Sikorsky fired three rockets. A moment later they exploded among the boulders in a ball of bright orange. The sound of the detonations engulfed the motor launch in another moment.

The AIC saw something move between two large rocks right at the shoreline. "There he goes again!" Overhead, four more rockets launched in quick succession. The beach again erupted in a huge splash of orange. The Blackhawk advanced rapidly toward the edge of the bay, then flared and hovered out from steep shore, its rotor tips only a few feet from the sandstone wall. A half-dozen men dropped down cables, swam ashore, then spread out among the piles of blocks at the base of the cliff.

Long seconds—a minute—passed. The squad leader came on the radio. "We got him. Not quite dead. Get that launch in here to pick him up."

Two of the Delta Force men heaved Waddy over the gunwale, dumping him headfirst at the AIC's feet. "Easy, we're gonna need that shithead." The rest of the rapid-assault team were already being hoisted back into the Blackhawk.

"Good work, guys, see you back in Page. Ralph, tell the other boats they can relax."

RIVER

Entrance to Cathedral Canyon from Klondike Bar Trail, 1963. The reservoir was just beginning to fill (*Tad Nichols*).

Cathedral Canyon entrance, with some of Powell Reservoir, 1970 (*Tad Nichols*).

Cathedral Canyon, 1960 (*Tad Nichols*).

1

Glen Canyon Dam, June 14

The water inched over the top of the four-foot-high parapet wall, ran down the other side, and spread across the dam crest roadway. It leaked through the cracks between the sliding glass doors to the elevator towers, then flowed across the floors of the lobbies to the stairwells descending into the dam. It seeped through the doors to the elevators to run down their 503-foot-deep shafts.

The reservoir elevation was 3,719 feet. With the huge radial gates fully opened, water surged under their lower edges and plunged down the steep slopes of the tunnels, filling them entirely, but it was not enough to curb the rise of the reservoir. Inflow through the gauged rivers in the Upper Basin was now over 750,000 cfs: the average flow rate of the Mississippi. Rain continued to fall, collecting in myriad side canyons that carried their contributions into the low point of eastern Utah's canyon and slickrock country. Besides the falling torrent from Hurricane Carlotta and the stalled midlatitude front, the massive load of snow ringing the 108,000-square mile basin was relieving itself into the hundreds of streams that found their way to the Colorado River.

Each spillway now carried overflow at nearly 200,000 cfs. When they had filled, the character of their flows changed entirely, abruptly transforming from an already-turbulent jet surging and boiling from the outlets because of the eroded linings, to a coughing, explosive flow—like water being dumped from a jug. Without an atmospheric connection, the pressure increased enormously, far exceeding the loading the tunnels were designed to withstand. The average speed of the water dropped as it stalled and then surged again in its effort to find the portals, but the scores of millions of pounds flowing through each bore, under wildly fluctuating high pressure, were too much for the remaining concrete linings to resist: rapid destruction replaced the earlier cavitation and mechanical cratering. Down the lengths of both spillways the concrete peeled and ripped away from the rock it was installed to protect. Overpressure surges entered the hundreds of drain holes drilled into the sandstone, further increasing the loading on the now-exposed porous rock. The relentless shaking was transmitted directly to the structure wedged between the ancient walls of cemented sands that defined Glen Canyon.

The dam was not a solid, continuous piece of concrete. It had been built as a double row of stacked blocks: twenty-six stacks forming the arch of the dam. Each stack was divided into lifts, seven and one-half feet high: long lifts at the 330-foot-thick base of the dam and short ones in the thin upper part of the structure, with the concrete in each lift having been allowed to harden before the next higher lift was poured on top of it. The resulting stacks of blocks, piled up in the twenty-six double rows, were not keyed together or connected with reinforcing bars; rather, all the irregular cubes of concrete were designed to be held together by their own weight and the force of the water pressing against the outer curve of the assembled dam—like a Roman arch doorway lying prone. When the stacks were completed, they were full of seams and cracks between the individual pieces. All the voids had been filled with grout pumped through a labyrinth of piping throughout the dam, and watertight expansion joints were also placed at intervals in the structure. In its finished form, the 9.25 million tons of dam was, in a sense, a solid mass of concrete. Actually, it was a pile of blocks with cemented seams.

The dam had been designed to withstand seismic and water pressure loads greater than any predictable earthquake or flood of water could produce. Everything the engineers did was based upon predictions that were, in turn, based upon probabilities. What was the probability of an earthquake of a

Under construction, 1960. The penstocks are seen protruding in the downstream row of lifts, with the pillars to hold them being erected between the dam and the power house. The river outlet works' plumbing is in the top of the picture (*Bureau of Reclamation*).

certain magnitude? What would be the probable stresses on the dam? What were the probable inflows to the reservoir? What was the probability of the dam overtopping? What was the probability that the spillway tunnels would ever run full? How large did they have to be so that the probability they would have to carry excess flow would be low enough? What was "low enough?"

Within the dam, plumb bobs descended in vertical wells through the height of the structure. The slightest tipping of the dam would be revealed by the movement of the bobs at the ends of their several-hundred-foot-long, steel-wire lines. Trilateral laser sights pinpointed precise targets to monitor the least movement of the face of the dam—accurate enough even to sense the concrete's expansion from the sun's heat. Uplift and deformation pressure gauges at the base and the abutments, and strain gauges embedded across the interfaces between the concrete and the sandstone, also monitored the forces bearing on the structure. All the devices measured movement to within hundredths of an inch.

The shocks from the cataclysmic forces in the spillways were, indeed, stressing the dam. The grouting between the blocks and lifts cracked in random places, but the huge chunks of concrete did not move out of position. The technicians at the instrumentation section in Denver, closely watching their computer printouts, saw no movement other than the continual vibration. The engineers who had designed the great dam had built in factors of safety far above the probable loadings and stresses they had foreseen. However, the technicians did see another, very bothersome, set of numbers on their computer screens and printouts: leakage in the lower right-hand side of the dam, with the sensors now showing a flow of ten cfs—over 4,500 gallons per minute. The flow into the lowest gallery and out through the dam had surged shortly after the seismic readings shot up—when the spillway gates had been opened fully.

But the Bureau's staff in Denver had no way to measure or even to know about another escape from their reservoir, presently taking the shortcut around the right-hand river diversion tunnel plug to enter the spillway. Although the high-pressure hemorrhage around the plug ran at 175 cfs, the flow was wholly swallowed in the 200,000-cfs torrent exploding down the spillway from the surface of the reservoir.

The water moved slowly around the partially-collapsed temporary gate and concrete bung at the inlet to the diversion tunnel, then proceeded even more slowly down the forty-one-foot-diameter length of the tunnel before it entered the crack network around the permanent plug. The now-well-defined conduit through the faults and gaps in the rock and concrete was at the lowest point in the reservoir. Under the pressure at that depth the water moved at more than 250 feet per second through the aperture, soon joined in its transit by particles eroding from the surfaces of the crack, the combination creating a sandblast jet, rapidly cutting a hole through the Navajo sandstone in a fast-frame version of the process that had created the myriad slot canyons throughout Glen Canyon. As the hole enlarged, the flow increased, but not at the same rate as the expanding diameter of the hole. When the diameter doubled, the flow had gone up fourfold. By the time the width of the hole increased three times, the volume racing through it each second had gone up nine times. The process continued at a steady rate.

Meanwhile, the dominant flow through the spillways was still struggling to force its way to freedom. In both tunnels it finally found some relief.

In order to repair the damage in 1983, it had been necessary to bore seventeen-foot-diameter access adits through the canyon walls from the transformer deck of the power plant, intercepting the spillways just downstream from their elbows. The engineers had decided that method was the most efficient way to get all the necessary repair equipment and materials into the eroded tunnels.

Cutting the adits had been difficult and expensive, so when the job was completed the engineers decided to retain the tunnels rather than fill them with concrete. Engineers hate to throw anything away. One day they might have to get equipment and materials into them again; furthermore, the

Left spillway construction adit, September 6, 1983. Access to the right spillway was similar (*Bureau of Reclamation, Tom Fridmann*).

retained adits provided easy access for inspection. Accordingly, they were only partially plugged at the spillway ends, with watertight steel man-doors located above the level of the designed maximum flow. The engineers did not foresee any problems.

However, with the tunnels running full under violently surging pressure, the river was about to create a problem. In its desperate search for escape, the plunging water found a particularly weak place in each of the tunnel walls: the man-doors, together with the concrete plugs that held them, blew out like ruptured diaphragms, permitting the water to rush toward additional exits. From the left spillway it jetted out of the canyon wall above the four hollow jet valves from the river outlet works, which were dutifully sending their streams down the river. The angle of the new, unintended, river outlet works, however, was such that its jet was directed nearly straight across the power plant tailrace, where it impinged at the base of the opposite canyon wall.

The situation with the right spillway was a little different. When they

Right spillway repair tunnel portal and transformers, June 21, 1984 (*Bureau of Reclamation*).

visited the dam, Saul had pointed out to Kateryna that the construction adit into the west wall had been cut into the rock right at the end of the transformer deck, where twelve 345,000-volt transformers were lined up across the front of the powerhouse. The transformers' function was to boost the power plant's output voltage before it was sent up the cables to the switching station on the west rim. When the small plug of concrete at the end of the construction tunnel broke out, the seventeen-foot-diameter jet of one-hundred-mph water was lined up nearly perfectly with the row of transformers. All but the last three of the ninety-ton electrical units were sequentially blasted off the front of the power plant building like bowling pins.

On the crest of the dam, the level of the 193 miles of surcharged reservoir, which extended back up Glen Canyon, Narrow Canyon, and into the lower reaches of Cataract Canyon, had risen above the 3,719-foot elevation of the top of the upstream parapet and quickly filled the area between the safety walls. With the spillway tunnels full, the rising water had nowhere to go but down the steeply sloping front face of the dam. At first, as it inched over the precipice, the water sheeted thinly down the 75° ramp, barely wetting its surface. Soon it would flow more vigorously.

Thirty-six hours before, a surge in flow had come down all the tributaries and the main stem of the Colorado, caused by the combined effect of the rainout from Carlotta, the moisture remaining in the stalled midlatitude front, and the snow, now melting with a vengeance in the warm rain. The saturated earth could absorb and retain no more. Every drop that fell or melted became runoff. All the great rivers of the basin—the Green, the Yampa, the White, the Colorado, the Gunnison, the Dolores, and the San Juan—were running at flows never before recorded or even predicted. But in the five million years that rivers had been flowing through this present configuration of the land mass of southwestern North America, many such flows had come down the river now named the Colorado.

Nine hundred thousand cubic feet were augmenting Powell Reservoir each second, meaning that the present and steadily increasing influx would add over 600,000 acre feet to the artificial impoundment over the next twenty-four hours. With only a short time lag, the inflow affected the flow over the dam: because water is incompressible, the water coming in soon forced the level of the whole reservoir to rise. At the dam, the water was creeping up at three inches per hour, and very soon the rate of rise would accelerate. In less than twenty-four hours Powell Reservoir would be spilling eight feet deep over the parapets. The Bureau's engineers estimated that in two days the overflow would top out at least thirty feet above Glen Canyon Dam's 1,560-foot-long crest.

* * *

The steadily increasing river from Glen Canyon had been taking about twenty-three hours to reach Mead Reservoir and then Hoover Dam. Between the two big dams, the 56,000-square-mile basin had also received a lot of rainfall from each of the storms before they combined. The principal flood control structure for the Colorado River had nearly used up its five million acre feet of flood storage capacity. The outflow through Hoover's spillways, power plant, and outlet works had been held to the crucial 40,000-cfs level as long as possible, but it had slowly been increased to the current 80,000—already causing heavy flooding nearly to Yuma. With their reservoir nearly full, the managers at Mead Reservoir would very soon be powerless to contain the more than 400,000 cfs presently moving around, and over, Glen Canyon Dam. But that was just the beginning. The Bureau was about to upgrade its forecast to predict that in another thirty-six hours the flood would crest at 1,400,000 cfs.

"My God! It's a good thing the army moved in when they did to evacuate all those people," the Hoover Dam superintendent said as he watched the giant plume of water filling the bottom of Black Canyon below his dam. "It's gonna be the end of every community along the river. How'd they know to move so fast? How'd they get the authorization? Sure as hell isn't in the Bureau's SOP."

"If we'd gone through normal channels with this unexpected storm flood, there's no way the local authorities could have handled it," came the reply from the other man standing on the crest of the beautiful art deco structure. "Whole lot of people would have died. Just would have refused to believe the kind of water that's going to go down there. Total chaos."

"That's for sure," the superintendent said. "Those people—the authorities, too—they treat this river like it was a goddamned lake. Authorize building right to the very edge of the 20,000-cfs river."

"Practically no one down there remembers the regular peaking flows we had to release before Glen Canyon was built. Except for the few weeks in 1983, all they've known is a nice, steady 20,000 cfs. And since 1983, well, shit. The construction along the river has mushroomed. Look at Laughlin. A gamblers' Disneyland right on the river."

"It's all gonna go. The whole jackass, Coney Island, neon tourist-trap operation. Every last crap table, roulette wheel, and slot machine—right down the river. Havasu City and the Parker Strip too."

"You bet."

As bad as the two old Bureau men really did feel about the great loss of property that was occurring down the river and the absolute devastation that would take place in the next week while the flood moved clear to the Gulf, they also had a very strong "I told you so" feeling. The dam they were standing on had been here only sixty years. The river's canyon, five million.

2

Flagstaff, Arizona, 9:00 a.m., June 15

Randy MacConnell could not believe what the people in Salt Lake were telling him: inflows exceeding 1,300,000, perhaps as high as 1,400,000. Although the storms had about rained out, it would still be at least thirty hours before the flood crested. After that, the hydrograph would slowly diminish over about ten days, then gradually rise to a lesser crest and fall again after the snowmelt peaked. Already overtopping the dam by nearly twelve feet, the anticipated reservoir elevation of thirty-one feet over the parapets was still to come. Randy MacConnell tried to imagine what the toe of his dam and the power plant would look like after the river got through with them. He had a pretty good idea.

The good news was that despite the intense seismic waves from the overpressure flows in the spillways and the water crashing into the penstock well at its toe, the dam had moved only very slightly, about two-tenths of an inch—so far. It was standing up to the (assumed) worst that Mother Nature could throw at it. But no one could see what was going on within the dam since the television circuits had been lost the evening before. The water overtopping the crest had finally broken through the glass doors in the elevator towers and flooded the galleries within the dam, taking out the television circuitry and all the monitors within the structure. Before the gallery flow data were lost, the leak in the lower right abutment was something in excess of 1,000 cfs—only an estimate because the sensor scale had been exceeded. Obviously, the engineers concluded, a serious connection existed between the right spillway and the dam, probably through the lower foundation adit.

"Excuse me, sir," a crisp army major said as he stuck his head around the door. "You've been cleared to go on up to the dam for a look-see."

Randy MacConnell was in his car, heading toward highway 89 in less than a minute.

The ground beneath his feet shook violently enough that he had to keep his feet spread apart to remain standing. From his vantage on the east rim, Randy MacConnell had an unobstructed view of the wall of water falling from the dam's crest, clear green at first, then turning into a sheet of white as it disappeared into the abyss. Although the base of the dam had fully

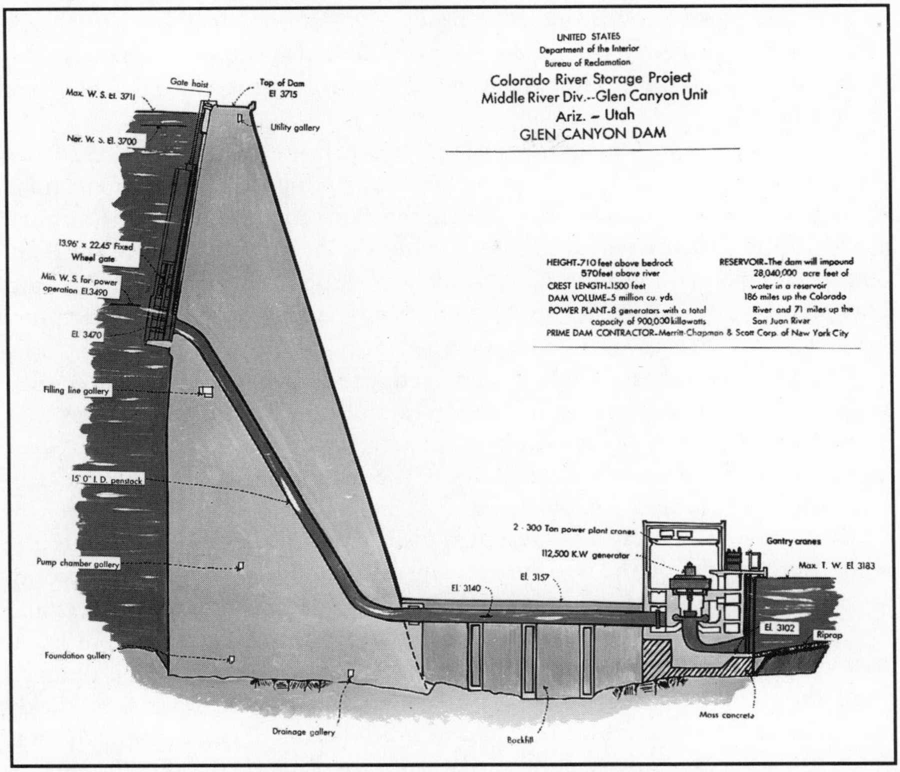

A Bureau of Reclamation sketch, 1961. The generator output was later upgraded to 1,350,000 kilowatts.

disappeared in the churning cauldron of white water and mist, through intermittent breaks in the veil he thought he saw a jet of water emerging straight out of the west wall, near the transformer deck. Then for the first time he noticed the transmission cables hanging slack from the towers on the west rim.

"Son of a bitch, the transformers are gone!" Then he caught a distinct glimpse of the jet of water emerging from the west wall, a moment later its east wall companion. "Oh, my God, the construction adits!"

The man standing on the rim of the canyon could not see it through the giant cloud of mist that rose nearly to his feet, but at the toe of his dam, between the base of the dam itself and the powerhouse structure, the cascade from the crest nearly 700 feet above was wreaking monumental havoc on his power plant.

As the dam was keyed into the bedrock of the river channel, the powerhouse structure rested upon a massive block of concrete that was also set into the Navajo sandstone. The heavy foundation was needed to absorb and transmit to the riverbed the force of 32,000 cfs (1,000 tons per second) plunging through the penstocks and being suddenly turned into the wheels of the turbines.

In its normal operation, water drawn from the reservoir, 320 feet from its bottom and 230 feet below the nominal high-water line, descended through the eight penstocks embedded in the dam's concrete to emerge through the fifteen-foot-diameter conduits just above the downstream base of the dam. The penstocks then crossed a 150-foot gap, supported on concrete pillars, between the two structures to enter the concrete mass of the powerhouse foundation. When the dam and power plant had been completed, the void around and under the flumes had been filled with sandstone rubble and topped with a layer of topsoil that soon sported a carefully mowed growth of bluegrass, about one and one-half football fields in area.

When the water first inched over the parapets and slid down the dam face, the first thing it encountered was the football field, not in need of irrigation thanks to Carlotta's recent transit. Now, at 610,000 cubic feet per second, it was hitting the bottom at a rate of 38,000,000 pounds per second, at a velocity of 130 miles per hour. Though the bedrock of sandstone could absorb this kinetic energy, the man-made structures in the area were in no wise designed to stand up to it. As the steadily increasing volume plunged from the dam crest, the first few million tons of Powell Reservoir quickly scooped out the layer of bluegrass and topsoil, then all of the backfill, and was soon attacking the concrete pillars that supported the penstocks. The rubble fill was scoured cleanly when the flow was forced to change its direction through nearly 160° as it hit the bottom and then deflected up and over the powerhouse. Shortly, the concrete pillars were knocked out and the unsupported lengths of penstock were ripped and twisted out of both the dam and the base of the powerhouse to be launched in graceful, cartwheeling arcs down the canyon, like giant pieces of broken macaroni.

Although the dominant force vector was vertical, aimed at the sandstone bedrock, the unintended plunge pool and flip bucket at the base of the dam, not streamlined and shallow like the ones at the outlets of the spillways, directed a portion of the flow squarely at the back of the powerhouse. The steel-fabricated stories of the superstructure were blown off the concrete base like the houses of the two brothers of Practical Pig were lost to the Big Bad Wolf.

Eight General Electric generators were lined up within the powerhouse across nearly the full width of the canyon, their 155,000-horsepower water turbines embedded well down into the concrete foundation beneath them where the penstocks had ended their descent. Under normal operating conditions, the water, having transferred its energy to the turbines, exited through deeper sections of the foundation and out through draft tubes into the bottom of the tailrace pool where it swirled about before heading on down the river. Two stories above the concrete-embedded turbines, the 168,000-kilowatt generators, attached by shaft to the turbines, protruded up into the powerhouse above the giant slab of foundation concrete. Each of the eight generator units weighed 1,550,000 pounds, with the assemblage of rotating parts in each weighing in at 740,000 pounds. Despite its great mass, when the core of a generator, attached to a turbine two floors beneath it, was rotating at its design speed of 150 rpm, it was an amazingly delicate machine turning upon perfectly leveled, plumbed, and lubricated guide and thrust bearings. In its designed operating condition, each turbine rotated under a carefully balanced loading of the water force offset by an opposite torque from the electrical resistance of the power grid it was connected to. But for nine of the generators there was no counterbalancing electrical resistance. The transformers and their connections to the switching yard on the west rim were gone.

With the penstock gates closed, as directed by the Region headquarters, water now entered the turbines by the more direct, airborne route; and with no electrical resistance counter-torque, the nine turbines and the generators shaft-connected to them spun out of control, accelerating rapidly above their intended 150 rpm. As their angular speeds increased, the generators and their more slowly rotating, power-grid-connected three companions, also received the full blast of the waterfall, now unimpeded by the vanished superstructure of the powerhouse. Thrust, rotational, and bending forces overcame the turbine and generator shafts and bearings, and as close whirling tolerances of metal-to-metal clearances were lost, each of the three-quarter-million-pound rotating masses succumbed. Their banshee screams of scoring and ripping steel pierced the cannonade of cascading water. The torrent that had only days before been alpine snow, tropical moisture, and a saturated Siberian air mass, then began to disassemble the complex assemblies of stator windings and the lamination bundles in the generators' rotors.

The destruction at the base of the dam had not been instantaneous but had occurred in logical sequence as each component shattered, ripped, or exploded and was swept away before the river's relentless and increasing attack. By the time the assault from the parapets had reached 600,000 cfs, all that remained of the powerhouse and its contents were the mangled stumps of the generators and some twisted and broken sections of the I-columns and concrete pillars that had supported the powerhouse. What was left of the transformers outside on the transformer deck had been sheared off cleanly.

Randy MacConnell accurately imagined most of what was happening at the base of his dam, and like Wadsworth Temeseh less than two days before, he experienced a sense of defeat and despair such as he had never known. The very focus of his life and career was being wrenched apart in the canyon below him by forces beyond the control of any human effort. He did not even notice that the rain had stopped. Bright shafts of sunlight invaded the canyon and refracted through the billions of droplets drifting on upwelling eddies to create numerous full-spectrum rainbows. Nearly any person alive—not a veteran employee of the Bureau of Reclamation—would have found the sight beautiful: beautiful in the display of Nature's water and sunlight; and, for many persons, beautiful in both the physical and the political consequences of Her wrath. As the many people like Randy MacConnell loved the grand dam, there were also many who hated it and the dead politicians and greed merchants who had demanded that it be built.

Laying blame on the Bureau of Reclamation for the existence of Glen Canyon Dam is easy, but such blame is nearly entirely misplaced. The great political and financial forces of water, electric power, livestock ranching, and corporate agribusiness had put the dam in the canyon, not the collection of dedicated, hardworking engineers and technicians who carried out the best work they could when the final order had been given. And once the dam was a reality, it had also been very easy to place blame squarely on the Bureau when the giant malfunctioned, as it had done in 1983 and as it was doing on this day. Randy MacConnell, though not a part of the team that had designed and built the massive dam and its power station, had been very much a part of the cross fire of forces that dictated their operation—and that kept the reservoir too full.

The politically powerful farmers of the Imperial/Coachella, and the Salt/Verde/Gila River Valleys, who had paid not a cent for the construction of the dam, yet who reaped enormous profit from the water and electrical power it delivered, were the core reason for its destruction. Their lobbyists and political power brokers donated, pleaded, and coerced to keep the reservoir as full as possible as a hedge against times of drought. The ag barons' water-selling, municipal counterparts in the Los Angeles Basin, in San Diego, and in Phoenix did the same, operating from differently-funded financial and political bases. The electric power brokers and their electricity-devouring public utility clients also screamed long and loud not to "waste" lucrative power head in the reservoir. To be sure, the federal government reaped the initial reward from the great cash register dam, but it was fundamental American capitalism that guaranteed that each middleman down to—but not including—the final consumer got his markup and profit.

Commencing shortly after Powell Reservoir began to fill in 1963, a water recreation industry had begun to assemble around and become dependent upon the reservoir. To maximize the profit-making size and minimize the unsightly bathtub ring, the lake-top entrepreneurs also wanted the reservoir kept as full as possible. How many times had Randy MacConnell had to endure the protests from the marina operators and the calls from their lawyers and political dogs of war when the reservoir level had fluctuated? Every time the level rose or fell, the marina concessionaire had to move its corporate pontoon docks and the attached collections of yachts and houseboats. When the water fell, there was the inevitable odor that accompanied the dead, slimy ring of bleached rock along 1,900 miles of shoreline. Inevitably, well-lubricated tourists, driving speedboats flat-out across the reservoir, would hit unmarked domes of rock that were almost awash. More screams of protest and the also-inevitable lawsuits.

Both private and commercial river rafters complained loudly about fluctuating flows from the power plant, but, again, it was not the Bureau's fault. The Western Area Power Administration, which decreed the outflows through the power plant, was responsible for the daily rise and fall of the river level—fluctuations that swamped favorite camping spots or left the rafters' heavily-laden boats high and dry on beaches along 225 miles of river from Lee's Ferry to the slack water of Mead Reservoir.

Now environmentalists, conservationists, and collections of scientists of every stripe and discipline—even the U.S. Park Service, part of the Bureau's own Department of the Interior—also demanded that outflows below Glen Canyon Dam be kept to a steady 20,000 cfs, or reasonably close thereto. The "environment" along the river below the dam, an environment that did not exist in its present form before the dam had been built, was now threatened by daily-fluctuating flows. But water fluctuated wildly as it entered the reservoir during the course of a year, so how could Randy MacConnell and the staff in Salt Lake manage the reservoir properly if they could not, to some extent, balance outflows with inflows? And the rafters'/environmentalists'/scientists'/ Park Service's cry for a steady flow down the river would also be fiercely contested by the electrical power industry because the big hydro plant had the unique ability to meet a sudden spike in electrical demand by a corresponding spike in the flows through the dam's penstocks. It didn't have to wait for coal to burn, to heat water, to make high-pressure steam, and finally to maintain turbine speed against increased electrical load. The Western Area Power Administration insisted upon taking full advantage of the convenient attribute of hydroelectric power generation to supply the instantaneous demand for electricity—and to set the much higher rates it charged to meet the peaking power demand.

On top of everything else, if the reservoir was full or nearly so, each year Randy MacConnell's bosses at the Upper Basin headquarters in Salt Lake City had to play the delicate game of juggling releases with anticipated spring runoff—trying to keep the reservoir as full as possible and all the while trying to keep the several competing interests happy. The inevitable result was what he was seeing below him in the canyon, albeit a lot worse than even the most timid hand-wringer in the Bureau had predicted. The dedicated veteran of the U.S. Bureau of Reclamation now staring into the bottom of Glen Canyon wanted to both cry and scream out loud. He kicked a chunk of sandstone over the edge and watched it disappear into the boiling cloud. But despite what he felt about the scene he was witnessing, his thoughts shifted to the greater tragedy occurring down the river.

What if the army hadn't cleared out all those people below Lake Mojave? How did they know? Randy MacConnell also thought about the beautiful old structure far down the river at Black Canyon gorge. Hoover Dam, along with the then-recently-constructed dam suffering before his eyes, had been the inspiration for him to become a civil engineer. While he was very concerned about his own dam—the remaining structure itself—he knew that Hoover would survive even if severely overtopped. The massive block of concrete, nearly as thick at the bottom as it was high, was wedged between dense, granitelike walls of andesite breccia. It would lose its power plant as Glen Canyon Dam had lost its own, but Hoover Dam would survive.

Below Hoover was an entirely different story. The sixty-seven-mile-long thread of Mojave Reservoir ended at Davis Dam, an earth-fill structure just above Laughlin and Bullhead City. Randy MacConnell knew the impending flood would easily take out the three and a half million cubic yards of fill, releasing an additional 1.8 million acre feet into the river, with the disaster repeated at Parker Dam, a concrete arch that impounded Lake Havasu. Billions of dollars in property damage would be inflicted, but there was little excuse for loss of human life if the riverside residents did what they were told.

3

Mayacamas Island, Republic of Seychelles, June 16

"They got Waddy," Malcolm announced as he hung up the telephone. "Day before yesterday, while he was trying to get to one of the land lines. He's injured badly. In a hospital in Phoenix."

"Stanley!" Kateryna called out to the patio. "Waddy has been captured. He's in hospital!"

Stan stepped into the shade of the big open-air living room. "When? How badly is he hurt?"

Malcolm eased himself into his oversized chaise. "Day before yesterday. It was at night on the north shore of the reservoir, at Padre Bay. Dunno how bad he is. No details available from my people in Phoenix."

"I guess Saul must have told them how to find him." Stan sighed. He stared out at the brilliant blue ocean.

Kateryna repeated Stan's unfocused view out through another of the open archways. "I knew from the last time we talked to him, after Malcolm picked us up at Las Vegas, that Saul was going to turn himself in." Stan and Malcolm looked at her in surprise. "I just didn't believe him when he said he wanted to stay in California for a couple of days, to ship one of his cars or something, before coming out here." A breeze blew through the room and rustled the leaves of the palms and the brilliant bougainvilleas ringing the patio. "I just knew, that's all. I should have confronted him. He had no right to keep it to himself. Now Waddy has been badly hurt."

"Hey, enough of that. It wasn't your fault." Stan got up and joined her on the window seat. They all stared out across the gardens that spread down the hillside to the sea.

"I feel so helpless!" Kateryna said, getting up and then promptly dropping into a chair next to Malcolm.

"I know," he said. "But there's nothing we can do. My people in Phoenix are arranging the best lawyers."

Stan tried to break the somber mood. "Perhaps Mother Nature will take over where we failed."

"Yeah. Must be a hell of a flood back there," Malcolm said. "Listen! Here comes the chopper from Victoria." He lurched out of his big lounge chair and headed for the patio.

Kateryna was ahead of Stan, trotting down the crushed coral path as the Sikorsky settled onto the pad. They saw Sofiia jump down the lowered stairs, clutching her backpack.

"Mama! Stanley! Uncle Malcolm!" the little girl cried as she ran across the painted concrete toward her mother, her sun-bleached pony tail bouncing and swinging.

Stan watched Kateryna sweep the little girl into her arms. *God, she looks so much better now*. Malcolm puffed down the path and wrapped his huge arms around them both. "I'll bet you're ready for a ride on your new pony, aren't you?" Malcolm clearly enjoyed his newly acquired avuncular duties.

"Oh, yes! Oh, yes! Mama, can I wear my new boots?" Sofiia bubbled while she towed her mother up the path.

"All right, we'll both go upstairs to change. Coming, Stanley? Malcolm? It was your idea."

"Sure, I need to go down and take a look at the plantation anyway. Meet you at the stables in twenty."

"Stan and I have to run over to Nairobi tomorrow; want to come along?" Malcolm asked when they finished their supper on the lantern-lit patio. Being only a few degrees south of the equator, the spectacular Seychelles Islands sunset had vanished in a matter of minutes.

"No, I don't think so. Sofiia and I have a lot to talk about; and there is so much to do to get this place organized."

"I know there's still a lot to do. I've had it all under construction for nearly two years. Took me six months just to cut the deal for the island. Remember when I couldn't meet you for the river trip? That was the week the closing was scheduled. I'd already poured a ton into this place before I even had a deed; so, in place of the long-term lease, they finally agreed to let me buy it. That big hospital over in Victoria was also part of the arrangement—one of the things it took to convince them to sell this island, and, well, to sort of look the other way on a few details."

"The hospital is wonderful, Malcolm," Kateryna said, watching Sofiia play hopscotch on the patio with the plantation foreman's daughter. "It has helped the island people so much . . . Sofiia too."

Malcolm smiled contentedly.

"It's all still such a shock," she said. "I had no idea you were really so . . . so serious about all this. I mean, you've moved your whole—how do you say—your whole *thing* here."

"A lot of it is here, but I'm still plenty diversified." He stared out at the sea, his happy demeanor slowly dissolving. "Are you about ready to *really* get back to work? It's about time we started getting into the other projects I have planned."

"Malcolm," Stan said, glancing over at Kateryna, "we really need to take it easy for a while. Just give us a little more time, okay?" He turned back to the view of the Indian Ocean. "Where's *Samora*?"

"She's just past the Marquesas. Had a bit of a delay in the Galapagos when the feds took another look in her bilges. Ha! Probably thought that bomb was going to Japan . . . Not a bad idea, actually. Hey, I'm just *kidding*. She'll won't be to Fiji for another two and a half weeks. I'm sure the skipper will want a little stopover in Tahiti or Bora Bora."

"Will you bring her here?" Kateryna asked.

"Wait a while! How about you two going out there? Bring *Samora* through Indonesia and across the Indian Ocean. You could take a nice long rest stop in Bali."

Stan and Kateryna looked at each other with big smiles and nodded.

* * *

All personnel in the fifty-nine-year-old Hoover Dam and its power plant had been evacuated. On both the Nevada and the Arizona sides, huge throngs watched in fascination as the water slid past the protruding tops of the penstock towers and poured over the crest of the dam, the 1,244-foot-wide Niagara disappearing into the cloud of spray filling the bottom of Black Canyon. The nearly completed, $123 million ($32 million cost estimate) Bureau-of-Reclamation-designed visitor center and garage, carved into the dense andesite at the Nevada abutment, absorbed the widening fringe of the cascade plunging over the dam. The imported-from-Italy, bronze-tinted windows imploded and water filled the structure embedded in the canyon wall, including the elevator shaft down to the power deck. By the time the elevator-water conduit was able to deliver its full stream at the bottom of the shaft, there was little of the power plant awaiting demolition.

Overhead, several media helicopters jockeyed for position—to avoid each other and the power cables strung across the chasm—while they awaited their turns for a pass close to the rim of the waterfall. They had been prohibited from flying below the crest of the dam, but two or three had come close when the nearly frantic, story-crazed reporters aboard exhorted their pilots to risk their licenses and both their lives. For the pilot, it was $125 per hour no matter where he flew. For the bouncing, babbling, twenty-four-year-old beside him, it was a potential launch into the big time. No more sleeping with people you didn't want to sleep with.

In studios in Los Angeles and New York, equally frantic television production supervisors agonized over the possibility of missing some uncovered disaster. They might not catch something really awful and the competing stations or networks would scoop them. Nielsen ratings, promotions, the new Mercedes, the rarefied air of ego center stage on the evening news: all were at stake. Armani-clad old men in mansions in Bel Air and Greenwich intently watched multiple channels simultaneously for evidence that their teams were missing something big. A lift of the telephone would end a career. Adrenaline pumped through the veins of every news peddler, great and small. *This* was a *story*! But if they had known about the story suspended seventy-one feet above the bottom of the reservoir behind Glen Canyon Dam, there would have been near-fatal, super-orgasmic hysteria.

* * *

Following the initial then gradually increasing releases from Hoover Dam, the large but relatively slow-moving flood had inundated but not terminally damaged many structures in the communities down the river. The Bureau of Reclamation managers had done their best to control the discharge from Mead Reservoir to avoid a sudden surge in flow that would increase the water's velocity; however, as the bulk of the flood began to descend, the Bureau was obliged to follow its prime mandate: protection of the Hoover Dam structure. The spillways had to be fully opened. The Bureau men did it as gradually as they dared, knowing what was coming down the canyon above them, but the outflow from Hoover was soon running at 400,000 cfs, almost immediately followed by the very rapidly expanding flood overtopping Glen Canyon Dam and ravishing its spillways. With only one of the big reservoirs deployed to control the river, the Bureau's options had been severely limited.

The Colorado River was now in uncontrolled flood, exceeding anything known or suspected by the modern inhabitants of the river valley.

The members of the several Indian tribes along the river had quietly left several days before the residents of Laughlin, Bullhead City, Needles, Lake Havasu City, the Parker Strip, and the several other streamside developments had been forced from their homes and businesses—in some cases kicking and screaming and in others crying, arguing, and promising legal action. For those who managed to avoid the military and remain, their survivors would later sue the federal government for wrongful death.

The gradually increasing flood down Boulder Canyon had been kept within the Davis Dam spillways, well below their 214,000-cfs capacity. But the ensuing 400,000-cfs, full-bore afflux from Hoover's spillways quickly overtopped the dam; then it wasn't long before the zoned earth-fill structure began to cave in beneath the relentless water when its volume climbed to over a million cfs in less than twenty-four hours. The 1.8 million acre feet behind Davis Dam also joined the march to the sea.

Two miles below Davis Dam, Laughlin, Nevada, lay basking—glittering—in the hot June desert sun. Except for an occasional dog trotting down the litter-strewn streets, the town was deserted, eerily silent in the still, 110-degree air. Before the vanguard of the giant flood arrived, the Colorado River had risen steadily, engulfing the foundations and street floors of the row of casino/hotels built along the west bank of the river. So confident and unconscious were the owners of the buildings that they had built docks out into the expected-constant-level water, fronted and overlooked by their casinos, restaurants, bars, and patios. The speedboats, outboards, and pontoon craft heretofore moored at the docks were now floating above the patios and crashing through the ground floor windows.

The 400,000-cfs flood, followed by the million-cfs monster on its heels and augmented by the contents of Mojave Reservoir, arrived in Laughlin over a single day, followed in another day by the gradual crest of the full 1,400,000 cfs effort by the river. The entire town was engulfed. The huge twelve-story, steamboat-shaped casino gradually lifted off its foundation, as a slow-motion surfer would do near the sloping crest of a wave, but the steamboat's one-hundred-foot-diameter side-wheels did it no good. When the River Queen finally tried to become the boat that it resembled, the neon-pink, yellow, red, and white hotel and casino failed on its maiden voyage—disassembled into its hundreds of thousands of component parts. The tall black smokestacks with their ornately flared yellow tops were tossed and rolled before the flood, following the three-story-high sign in the parking lot with its flashing electronic display advertising Double Slam 777 and prime rib and lobster dinners for $5.95—ripped from its steel pedestal and flung against the side of the next building in the row along the riverfront.

Contributed by each of the nine high-rise casinos strung along the bottom of the river valley, roulette wheels and crap, blackjack, and poker tables bounced along on the crest of the flood, side by side with every variety of bedroom, dining room, lobby, and office furniture, liberated boats, and palm trees. Unseen beneath the surface, the heavy slot machines, dominated by the huge "Quartermania" devices with their four-foot-long handles, were rolled along the bottom of the river, being converted into eighteen- to thirty-inch-diameter balls of stainless steel, chrome, and plastic; little rows of cherry clusters, oranges, and sevens; and coins—lots of coins. The casino owners had plenty of time to evacuate the people, as it turned out, but the United States Army had refused to allow them to reenter the town to unload their tons of coins. For years after the flood, but then only following tedious courtroom debates in the three involved states over salvage rights in the thread of a navigable river, with the squabbling reminiscent of that for the treasure of the *Nuestra Señora de Atocha*, a local cottage industry would blossom, fueled by the search for the little bonanzas hidden in the river's sands.

The parade of slot-machine balls was joined in the mass being propelled down the river bed by hundreds of thousands of poker chips, $-signs in every conceivable shape and size, Keno chairs, and crushed and balled-up municipal trash cans, formerly unique in their Laughlin-pink livery. The forty-by-one-hundred-foot Keno boards and heavy oak and marble cocktail bars were driven into the bottom of the channel, crushed under the concrete fragments of multilevel parking garages and chunks of the Davis Dam power plant, automobiles, trucks, construction derricks, bulldozers, cement trucks, dumpsters, and RVs whose owners had left them in Laughlin for weekend retreats. The *Little Queen* river cruise boat was found far downriver two weeks later, upside down in an alfalfa field half a mile from the channel. In its later life, the little paddle-wheeler would serve as a horse loafing shed on the Chemehuevi Indian Reservation where the river had placed it, Ark-like.

Just downstream from the demolished riverboat, the city's four-story-high steel cowboy in his jeans, checked shirt, and cowboy hat waved his arm from the roof of another casino. When last seen the cowboy had been driven hat first through the windows of the grand ballroom on the third floor of the Golden Dream Hotel and Casino. The Golden Dream disintegrated minutes after the cowboy entered the ballroom.

During the ensuing day, while the river rose and then gradually fell from its 1,400,000-cfs peak, its work at Laughlin, Nevada, would be completed. Weeks hence, with the vanished flood replaced by the Bureau's 20,000-cfs artificial river, all that would remain to suggest that a cluster of high-rise hotels and casinos had once proudly stood on the bank of the languid stream would be sand-blown patches of asphalt parking lots; expanses of concrete slabs, still partially painted green to look like grass; and the stubs of building foundations. An occasional raccoon would wander up from the riverbank, dimly remembering the goodies he used to find in the dark places around the dumpsters.

On the Arizona side, Bullhead City also disappeared. The original village had been constructed in 1945 to house the builders of Davis Dam, needed to regulate the river for delivery of Mexico's 1.5 million acre feet of treaty water. Below the "old" town, the newer Bullhead City, necessary for Laughlin's thousands of casino employees, had been constructed in an area defined by the inside of a large loop in the river, bulging to the west. The subdivisions of Riviera, Holiday Shores, and Riverbend consisted almost exclusively of thousands of mobile homes and double-wides. Assisted and encouraged by the army, the casino workers and their families watched from the safety of the eastern bluff of the river (conspicuous evidence of previous high-water lines) as the river-level municipality vanished. After the flood, not a trace of the densely packed, mobile home communities, or even the stump of a tree, remained in this almost-oxbow course of the Colorado River. Below Bullhead City, the miles-long strip of tourist businesses extending to, and intruding somewhat into, the Fort Mojave Indian Reservation, was also peeled off the earth like paint before a window scraper.

The Mojave Indians—they and their predecessors having occupied the area for several thousand years and with a good oral history to tap into—had permitted little construction in their river bottom, restricting development to a segment of the commercial strip along highway 95 that ran through the reservation from Bullhead City south to Needles, California. Resort entrepreneurs in Laughlin, Las Vegas, and Palm Springs had been driven nearly crazy seeing the Laughlin-proximate, eminently-developable land occupied almost exclusively by livestock, alfalfa, and field crops. When the flood receded, the Mojaves would be left with a deep new layer of very rich topsoil, albeit interlarded with a sundry collection of Laughlin memorabilia and the shards and shreds of Riviera/Riverbend/Holiday Shores. Additionally, the Mojaves would have no need to plead with insurance agents or government employees doling out reluctantly released insurance funds or the taxpayer-subsidized, low-interest, disaster-area loans.

Needles was next. Fortunately, the old part of the town was partially spared by two circumstances. Through the Indian reservation the river valley expanded to a width of three miles, permitting the flood to spread and slow; and most of the old town had been built on the bluff overlooking the river. Everything below the high bank, including the new luxury homes, condos, and marinas built along the edge of the river, disappeared in the debris-laden brown flow. Below Needles, the Havasu National Wildlife Refuge on the Arizona side also got a new layer of soils and nutrients, though it also got much of the newer Needles town and the more buoyant Laughlin detritus.

The river had one more canyon to transit before it entered the series of broad bottomlands extending to the Sea of Cortés. Just above the gorge at the head of the canyon, dominated by the ragged spires of the Needle Mountains, the torrent encountered the four spans crossing the channel at Topock, Arizona. The Atchison, Topeka and Santa Fe Railroad bridge was neatly lifted off its pillars and sent crashing against the new Interstate 40 highway span—no match for the massive steel truss designed to carry triple-headed steam locomotives. The tangled assembly of heavy spans then sadly eliminated the old Route 66 bridge in a quick swipe. The last and newest arch over the channel, also supporting a gas pipeline like the one the old highway bridge had carried in later life, also disappeared in an instant. The army had seen to it that the high-pressure gas lines from Texas had been turned off, ignoring the screams of protests and the usual, California-style threats and dashes to courthouses by L.A. Basin utility company attorneys. Martial law, by order of the commander in chief, took precedence over whatever the lawyers could convince one of their black-robed brethren to do.

The flood concentrated when it entered the last canyon on the Colorado River's long migration from the high alpine valleys of the Wind River Range. Instead of descending through a seventy-five-mile-long series of gorges and valleys, created long ago by the river, the flood encountered another reservoir which began shortly after the steep and rocky Mojave Canyon was entered: "Lake" Havasu, backed up forty-five miles behind Parker Dam. The flood plunged through the narrow gorge of the canyon, spreading out and inundating occasional broad expanses of the Havasu National Wildlife Refuge and the Chemehuevi Indian Reservation, where the hapless *Little Queen* was shunted off in an eddy to its final rest. The last 22 percent of the remaining, most reluctantly sinkable, components of Laughlin were also deposited here.

Lake Havasu City, incorporated in 1978, was capable of accommodating over 80,000 people. Thankfully, on the very hot June Wednesday when the army had moved in to clear the flood zone, the population had been only about 28,000. The hordes of young people who flocked to the reservoir and to the Parker Strip below the dam on the weekend were largely gone—back to Los Angeles and Phoenix. Since the army commanders were anticipating a catastrophic failure of Glen Canyon Dam and the possible failure of Hoover Dam in consequence, the people were moved much farther up the slope than the actual flood now demanded. It had indeed been fortunate that the flood had not occurred in January, when Lake Havasu City and the scores of campgrounds farther down the reservoir would have been bursting with the tens of thousands of northern snowbirds who flocked to the area each winter. But as it was, the army still had its hands full forcing the reluctant residents out of harm's way. Practically all of the people remaining in June lived in Lake Havasu City year-round. Many were burdened by physical disabilities, and most had vowed, after a lifetime of moving, never to move again. Nearly all of the residents had come to the area since Glen Canyon Dam had been built, so, of course, they had not the least idea that there was such a thing as a flooding Colorado River. They lived on the shore of a constant-elevation lake—it did not even look like a river—and the municipal, state, and federal authorities who knew better, or should have known better, had said nothing.

The lowered crest of the flood across the three-mile-wide lake should have saved Lake Havasu City. Unfortunately, the core of the city had largely been built upon what had been a ridge thrusting into Mojave Canyon and the land to the immediate east. In 1943 the Army had built an R&R camp above the recently formed reservoir, complete with a 6,000-foot runway across the top of Pittsburgh Point. When Robert McCulloch, Sr. first saw the area and envisioned his new resort, the ridge—then a peninsula into the lake—was soon transformed into an island, with a bridge. Naturally, the city was designed to grow up around its gemstone attraction.

The flood was forced to concentrate again. No way remained to spread out, so the water had to spread back up and go around—and over—all of the island and much of the city-choked shore to the east. As it swept through the narrow channel between the island and the "mainland," the flood disassembled the lovely old bridge. Its ten-thousand-odd granite blocks were rolled down into the bottom of Mojave Canyon, where they would forever lie, their square-hewn shapes scattered upon the irregular shapes of nature. London Bridge had fallen down, a victim of a flood the Thames could never have managed; but—at last—the wags in the London pubs would be silenced.

When the flood concentrated in the again-narrow reservoir below Lake Havasu City, little commercial damage was accomplished until it arrived at Parker Dam. The dam had been built specifically to create a sump from which the already-huge L.A. metropolis and the planned-to-be-huge Phoenix metropolis could suck their millions of acre feet of water. After the flood passed by, destroying the suck pumps and the impounding structure for the suck pond, it became clear that many swimming pools, fountains, golf courses, and lawns would go hungry in L.A., Phoenix, and Tucson. A lot of cotton plants would also die on thousands of acres broiling in the 115° inferno around Phoenix.

Parker Dam was built in a narrow, steep part of the canyon—a perfect place to build a dam cheaply; however, the deep canyon further concentrated the river's flow. The spillways were overwhelmed in an instant when the water exploded over the old concrete structure, built along with Hoover Dam in the mid-1930s. While the river proceeded inexorably in its quest for the Gulf, the arch dam, its footings reaching 235 feet to bedrock through the Colorado riverbed, resisted for most of the day but ultimately succumbed, adding Lake Havasu's 650,000-acre-foot contribution to the river's effort. What would be left of Lake Havasu City would look down on a broad river, and the stripped, bridgeless island would once more be just a muddy ridge on the slope of Mojave Canyon.

Past the dying Parker Dam, the flood scoured out the densely packed corridor along the series of narrow gorges and valleys between Parker Dam and the Colorado River Indian Reservation. The Parker Strip had partially overcome the army's efforts to remove its stubborn residents and the not-to-be-told-anything teenagers who had remained beyond the weekend. The river took just over 300 lives as it rushed through what had been the Parker Strip, with many of the victims' bodies disappearing permanently. The next town, on the east bank of the river, Parker, Arizona, survived because it was an old community, built high on the bluff over the river channel. Below Parker and the reservation, the river valley spread to a broad area of croplands, undeveloped wetlands, and wildlife refuges, with occasional accumulations of Bureau of Reclamation plumbing and enclaves of riverside RV communities. The army had not reached them all, had not evacuated a few who had elected to remain in the 115° June temperatures and whose bodies also disappeared with the river.

Even though the flood was spreading out as it approached Yuma, it still had enough head to wreak havoc at Imperial Dam, a few miles above the old city. The long low dam, the sediment-settling ponds, and the head gates for the All American Canal were breached, flooded, or swept away. Seventeen thousand cubic feet per second filled the canal to brimming and headed for the bountiful lands of the Imperial Valley, sixty canal-miles away to the west, but the great bulk of the flow proceeded past this route to the Imperial Valley and continued toward Yuma. The water that had so recently passed high overhead in the swirling vortex of Hurricane Carlotta was on its way back to its place of origin. Most of the water, however, would not make it that far.

***

Isolated from the chaos, deep in the still water behind Glen Canyon Dam, the stainless steel canister drifted back and forth almost imperceptibly in the tiny currents that curled to the bottom of the reservoir from the flow across its surface. Silently, the sonar transceivers sent periodic signals into the surrounding water in search of a threat. Ninety-three feet above the canister, the steel sphere relentlessly pulled on the climbing rope that kept the canister from plunging to the bottom—an event that all the proximity fuse transceivers would perceive to be a threat as soon as the reservoir bottom came within their zones of tolerance. The injured length of rope continued to do its work, although as the hours and days passed, filaments of kernmantle in its partially severed core failed, thereby minutely increasing the load on the remaining filaments. All the while, the surrounding chilled water kept at its work of altering the rope's chemical composition—and its tensile strength.

***

The flood officially crested 32.6 feet above the top of the dam: a bit higher than the Bureau had initially predicted because the inflows had risen to

1,485,000 cfs. With approximately 400,000 cfs forcing its way through the ravaged spillway tunnels, the remaining 33,900 tons per second accelerated down the steep face of the dam, achieving a terminal velocity of 137 mph at the bottom. With the power plant superstructure and machinery swept cleanly off their foundation, the flood went to work on the mass of concrete that formed the foundation. Under the relentless load of water, transferring a portion of its kinetic energy directly to the upstream face of the huge block, the forces holding concrete to Navajo sandstone were finally overcome by the river. The foundation first slipped a fraction, then a larger fraction, and then broke out of its pad notched into the riverbed stone. It moved enough to permit the water to begin shooting freely over the block rather than against it. Equilibrium was reached when the massive footing had been tilted and displaced about forty feet. It would never again support a 1.35-gigawatt hydroelectric power plant.

Things were also not going well in the spillways. Whereas the power plant penstocks had been designed to run perfectly full with an even, streamlined flow directed at the blades of the water turbines, the spillways, not in the least designed to operate as pressure conduits, were suffering grievously. With the increased head of water, the flows were forced even more violently down into the deeply eroded tunnels and continually surged under the relentless overpressures. The situation in the tunnels was at its worst at the elbows below the plunge from the inlets. Here the erosion, which had started as cavitation damage, was the most severe—a greatly aggravated version of what had occurred in 1983. The millions of tons of falling water had long since worn through the three-foot concrete linings and had attacked the much softer sandstone. The dense concrete of the 150-foot-long tunnel plugs was encountered, so the water began to cut the more friable natural material from around the plugs. Sections of the plugs broke off as they were released from their imprisoning rock and, with their sandstone companions, were ejected like missiles from the tunnel portals.

In the right tunnel, the high-pressure water at the bottom of the reservoir was also helping with the effort to dislodge the remaining ninety-foot-long section of sandstone-encased plug. The small flow that had begun with a jet tracing through a labyrinth of cracks in the rock had now enlarged to a six-foot-diameter, twisting, high-speed, sand-and-water-filled pipe around the concrete. The army of the river was seeking to consolidate its forces at the obstruction in the hole through its sandstone wall. The river wanted to flow at its accustomed level, where it had run for several million years before the bothersome obstacle had intruded a mere thirty-odd years before.

4

Las Vegas, June 18

Lisa Montgomery couldn't sit still. When something was bothering her, when something was just not *right*, when she wanted to be out digging up information, she could not stay at her cramped little desk in the congested news room. But Lisa knew that if she were ever to rise above the level of general assignment reporter, she would have to learn to sit at a desk and write news copy, draft special events coverage proposals, and in general do all the other paper-shuffling crap necessary to pay her dues and be a proper reporter. With her Gidget-like bubbly smile reinforcing a pert brunette face and saucy personality, Lisa knew very well that she had a good television "presence." And she also knew that she was a lot brighter than any other reporter she had ever met. When the opportunity came along, she was convinced that she'd have a good shot at sitting in one of those chairs on the set in the studio—probably just a special-interest slot on the noon news, but Lisa was determined that her career wouldn't stop there.

Nonetheless, she was not entirely enthusiastic about a career that would keep her locked up in the studio, on a rigid schedule, spitting out other reporters' stories. There was a big price to be paid for the glamour, prestige, and salary that went along with a center-stage news chair, and in many respects she was happy being out in the field investigating and covering her own stories. Nearly all the other reporters were content to sit around waiting to be assigned. Not Lisa. When she wasn't on an assignment she was out on her own, digging up the information needed for whatever special coverage she had convinced, or would convince, the news room editor that it was in the station's interest to develop.

Lisa had been with KNOB for three years, only her second job since college. Although she hated Las Vegas, it was a logical step in her reporting career so she was probably stuck at the station for at least three or four more years. Then maybe Phoenix and eventually, with luck, a big West Coast station. In the interim, Lisa intended to concentrate her efforts on a specialty she'd developed. A national-interest specialty was a good way to open a door into a major station.

Shortly after she'd gone to work for KNOB, Congress had enacted legislation ending the nuclear weapons testing moratorium. The legions of lobbyists for the high-priced contractors in the nuclear weapons business had finally convinced enough congresspersons that it was necessary to "keep current" in the endless pursuit of ever more sophisticated weapons of mass destruction. Lisa had gotten one of the first assignments when the story broke about the Department of Energy's intent to resume a regular program of exploding giant bombs under the desert less than 100 miles northwest of Las Vegas; unfortunately, the program had slowed, almost stopped. She was back to reporting the celebrity entanglements and peccadilloes, mob-related murders, and all the usual crash-and-burn stuff that made up the bulk of local news in cities like Las Vegas. Her carefully planned specialty was disappearing.

To try to get out of the rut, Lisa was struggling with a proposal for a special interest item about the city's latest scheme to steal water rights from northern Nevada's ranchers. Every municipal and agricultural planner in southern Nevada now realized that their state had not gotten its proper share of the water stored behind Glen Canyon and Hoover Dams. But the compact could not be changed: Arizona and California would never agree to give up a drop. It was all very complicated and Lisa struggled with her writing—the writing stuff she had always hated, really learning to hate it during her first year in the business at the little station in Flagstaff. At this moment the assignment editor was leaning over her shoulder, reading her latest effort as he scrolled it down the screen.

"Lisa, this is crap. After the first two paragraphs it just turns to mush. I have a pretty good idea where you want to go with the story but I still can't understand it. No way any of our viewers will. Tighten it up. We have to make a scheduling decision this morning—in about half an hour, in fact. Why'd you leave this to the last minute?"

I know it's crap. Lisa also read through her mess as her anxious, sweaty boss wheezed his breath past her cheek toward the PC screen. The normally-pestilential odor, overlain with the residue from the Greek specialty he'd had for lunch, was more than whelming. Lisa willed her gag reflex not to reflex.

When he left, she electronically cut, pasted, and rewrote. *God, this is tedious.* Lisa forced herself to concentrate on the details of water diversions, the city's condemnation powers, and the point of view of the ranchers, but her mind was far away on something she sensed was much more important. Fifteen minutes later, her boss was back.

"Quasi-crap this time, but we gotta go with it. What in hell's the matter with you? This is even worse than usual. Hope you've got a good date tonight," he muttered before he scurried back to his office. Lisa did have a date that evening: a Saturday night date with the new sports guy just up from Albuquerque, and her boss was certainly right about her needing a good date. She sighed, realizing she was not sure she could concentrate even on that.

Damn, I'd like to get out of here today. Anybody could learn to write readable copy, she thought, but it took talent—unteachable talent—to dig out both the background and the core story information: to just talk to people and get them to tell her what she wanted to know. Lisa particularly liked to probe deeply into a brand-new political/environmental brouhaha. The resurrected nuclear testing program had brought the environmental community into full battle formation, and Lisa's job—she had been very successful at it—was to juxtapose the people/environment concerns about the testing with the strategic/political viewpoints of the decision makers in faraway Washington. Although Lisa had a difficult time with scientific things, she had quickly proven to be such a good investigator that the news room editor allowed her to continue to cover the testing story. Over the past year, she had learned much of what was knowable about the plans to resume tests out in the desert, and, most importantly, she had become acquainted with many of the military and Department of Energy people involved in the new program. She'd gotten access to the test site and been all over Nellis Air Force Base—she'd even talked her editor into letting her take a couple of trips to Washington. Lisa seldom had trouble locating and meeting key people and getting interviews. She had learned early on that although she often couldn't grasp the mechanical fine points of what was going on, the men she wanted to talk to were nearly always willing to bend over backward to help her understand. Besides being a very bright and determined young woman, Lisa had long ago discovered that men had a hard time saying no to her.

What made it increasingly difficult for Lisa to concentrate on her work in the past couple of weeks was that she suspected the Energy Department was up to something besides the nuclear tests. Even during the slowdown, the program had been following a regular routine for months, with the same Energy people involved who had always been very cooperative with her; but she'd seen a whole team of new people arrive and now she hadn't even been able to get in to the Department's compound at Nellis to talk to them. Lisa had long cultivated her latent instinct that questioned coincidences, now the coincidence that attracted her attention was that the new activity had begun when the flood story had begun to break: more particularly, the activity at Nellis had begun the same day the army began to move everyone away from Glen Canyon Dam.

As a junior reporter, Lisa had been denied the chance to cover the flood, a story reserved for the old, connected reporters—until the media focus shifted to the temporary Bureau office in Flagstaff. Because she knew her way around the town, she had gotten to tag along a couple of times with the senior reporters who had set up camp near the military's public-information office in the northern Arizona city. It had been on the first trip to Flagstaff that she noticed something that really aggravated her dormant discomfort.

She and one of the senior reporters had been out at the military staging area at Pulliam Airport. All civilian air traffic was excluded; the military had taken over everything, but despite all the confusing comings and goings, Lisa quickly noticed a particular airplane that she had seen before at

Nellis. In her investigation of the preparations for the new tests, Lisa had learned that the unmarked transport belonged to the Nuclear Energy Search Team. She had never been able to learn anything specific about NEST or its duties, knowing only that it was a highly clandestine agency within the Department of Energy and that it often worked closely with federal security and law enforcement agencies: CIA, FBI, and BATF.

On the next trip to Flagstaff, Lisa saw something else that further tickled her antennae. She'd been one of the reporters assigned to stand around down in Waco to monitor the Branch Davidian siege by the Bureau of Alcohol, Tobacco and Firearms. Naturally, she had gotten to know several of the BATF agents. She saw two of them in Flagstaff, and—what really got her attention—one of them had been talking to a man she was pretty sure was a NEST member. Lisa had said nothing to the other reporters, then she'd been unable to go along on any more trips to Flagstaff. It was driving her crazy, her assigned work was going to hell as a consequence, nevertheless she was nervous about trying to get too nosey with the new people out at Nellis.

Lisa decided what she had to do. One of the top Energy guys in the testing program loved to go to Las Vegas to play golf, hit the casinos, see some shows—and go out with her. She had to wait until he was at his office on Monday to call him.

5

YUMA, JUNE 19

The army set up its command post and staging area at the Marine Corps Air Station on Yuma Mesa at the southeast corner of the city. The site was selected for the relocation of the city's residents because it was 213 feet above sea level, safely above the expected crest of the flood, and because the Southern Pacific Railroad's main line from Los Angeles went right around the northeast corner of the city on the crest of the mesa and passed just to the north of the air station, with a convenient government spur branching into the station. By utilizing another railroad spur circling the northwest sector of the city on the crest of Yuma Levee, the army would have a direct means to evacuate the thousands of people living below the levee. Accordingly, the army commandeered every piece of available motive and rolling stock and herded the residents aboard trains for transport to the high ground. The evacuation was orderly, the more so when the area commander was notified that the big dams up the river were not immediately at risk. C5s carrying the supplies needed to set up a giant tent city at the air station were able to land easily because the military base had one of the longest runways in the world, an alternate landing site for the space shuttles.

At this most populated point on the river, the army managed to organize the move of the 40,000 people in the flood plain in the northwest sector of the city and adjoining Yuma County in less than a week. Had it been January, nearly 125,000 people would have been in and around the area. Only the portion of the city lying in the Yuma Valley east of the historic Old Town and under the Yuma Levee would be flooded as the main body of water found its way along the general course of its ancient bed.

The Colorado River delta covers an area of about 4,700 square miles. Over the course of the creation of the delta, as the sands and sediments eroded from the Colorado River's basin, the channel of the river intermittently swung like a pendulum from its fixed point near Yuma. The arc of the pendulum swing was from a southerly course into the Gulf of California to a westerly route that curved to the north and down into the Salton Sink. The topographic divide separating a southerly flow from a westerly one was on a southwest line between Yuma and a small mountain named Cerro Prieto, about twenty-five miles southeast of Mexicali. So long as the river stayed to the south of the gradually sloped divide in its broad delta, the water would flow to the sea, but during the many periods in the geologic past when the river had elected to wander to the west, its entire flow, generally about fifteen million acre feet in a year, would descend into the Salton Sink. Uncounted times in the past the entire Sink had filled to the level of the sea, almost and perhaps actually connecting with the Gulf at the head of tide water near the base of Cerro Prieto.

The Colorado River in its delta has always been a shallow, meandering stream, wandering about on the top of its giant mound of sand, forever seeking the easiest path to a lower level and never developing a regular channel to contain its periodic flood flows. Overflows from the floods would spread out across the vegetation-choked delta, causing the river to rapidly drop its load of sediment and continue the process of building the delta. And after each flood, the river would choose a slightly different course over the broad sand cone, endlessly selecting overflow channels in myriad directions.

The river's pendulum swing to the west in 1905 was triggered by the works of man, not a vagary of Nature. Immediately thereafter, the Ockerson Levee was constructed along the west side of the river around and below Yuma to contain another attempt at a westward course, while on the opposite bank the Yuma Levee encircled the northwest sector of the city which lay in the historic flood plain. That the levees were effective was periodically demonstrated by their containing the uncontrolled floods: even the record 1916 flow of 250,000 cfs at Yuma had been kept in check and the regular surges between the levees flushed the accumulating sediment and vegetation out of the channel. Then when Hoover Dam was completed in 1935, the threat of flood on the Colorado was nearly eliminated, with flows thereafter kept at or below 30,000 cfs. Only a rare torrent down the Gila River, such as the 1916 event or the one that occurred during the winter of 1992, challenged the levees. Such a Gila flood would be short-lived, unlike the long-duration snowmelts that had historically come from above the site of Hoover Dam. The filling of Powell Reservoir over a period of seventeen years also helped control the river at Yuma, where its volume was kept to 15,000 cfs or less—the event of 1983 being the only exception. Accordingly, for the past sixty years, no regular, scouring floods had occurred to keep the channel between the levees clear. The river had steadily deposited silt and sediment into its course around the city, with the channel becoming further choked with heavy accumulations of vegetation.

The 1,000,000-cfs flood began at Yuma early on the morning of June 19, soon inundating the expanse of farmlands in the Gila Valley at the confluence of the Gila and the Colorado Rivers below Yuma Mesa. When it encountered the obstruction of the mesa, the traveling lake turned westward toward its historic channel—what is present-day Old Yuma. The original city had been built on the southern bank of the river near the promontories of rock between which the river flowed: Indian Hill on the California side and Prison Hill on the Arizona side also marked the site of the historic Yuma Crossing, regularly used since prehistoric times as a fording point. The flood leaped into the old city after passing the promontories and removing the Southern Pacific and highway bridges in the process. The remainder of the water, not taking the shortcut across the city and continually overtopping the flanking levees, proceeded down the overwhelmed channel toward Mexico's Morelos Dam.

The last impoundment structure on the Colorado River extended nearly across the channel between the two levees, with a small bypass around its east side. Below their dam the Mexicans used the original Alamo Canal, which still followed the course of the ancient Alamo River, and which, in normal years, diverted the last drops of water in the river for consumption in the Mexicali Valley, the so-named southern reach of the Salton Sink south of the border. Since the Mexicans nearly always diverted the entire remaining flow of the Colorado River into their canal, they had failed to maintain or even be concerned about the twenty lift gates through the dam that would be needed to bypass large flows to the Gulf. The lift gates had been damaged during the 1992 flood down the Gila, and when Hurricane Carlotta passed over southern Arizona the floods that had not been contained in the Gila at the Corps of Engineers' Painted Rock Dam had caught Mexico's Ministry of Agriculture and Hydraulic Resources unprepared. Since the water was unable to escape around the end of the dam quickly enough, its passage complicated by the accumulated sand and growth in the river bed and the additional mountain of channel vegetation the 1992 flood had collected in its travels down the Gila—plus the pile the current inundation shoved before it—and further because it was only able to pass through the three gates that were operable, the water backed up behind the dam, overtopping it to pour into the Alamo Canal and over both levees into Mexico and Arizona.

Just upstream from Morelos Dam on the outside of the curve, where the leveed river made its sharp turn from its western heading around Old Yuma to proceed southerly toward the Gulf, was the location of the original headgate into the old Alamo Canal: Rockwood Landing, constructed at the turn of the century by the original Imperial Valley developers. As flooding rivers always do on the outside banks of turns in their channels, the Colorado started to erode the levee where the Rockwood Landing headgate had been plugged, the crush of water boring like a team of giant moles through the soft sands. Long before the peak flood hit the area the next day, the river was flowing vigorously west through the old diversion point. Neither the Mexicans nor the Imperial Irrigation District was able to stop the flow into the rapidly expanding canal née the Alamo River née the ancient and sometime Colorado River.

Beyond the Ockerson Levee, the second line of defense against a westward flow of the river was a network of leveed irrigation canals crisscrossing the Mexicali Valley. But the flood, now directed into the ancient river channel and continually carving deeper and deeper through the sands that had once existed as rock in the Colorado River Plateau, would not be deflected by the man-made obstructions. When the growing volume tried to make its turn from a westerly heading to its currently-normal route to the south and the Gulf, more and more swept into the expanding breach in the levee. The pendulum had swung again.

Down the course of the Alamo River the water proceeded at a gradient of two feet per mile, like the historic gentle flows in Glen Canyon. As it overwhelmed wholly unprepared Mexicali and its companion across the border, Calexico, the flood turned north to begin a steeper descent toward the Salton Sea. The water was now exactly at sea level. With its new slope of seven feet per mile, it proceeded at a rate much like its travels below Lee's Ferry where the river starts into the rapids of Marble Canyon.

In this area of the Salton Sink, the New River—consistently the most polluted stream in the United States—also flowed north, carrying pesticide- and fertilizer-laced drain water and hideously poisoned sewage from the many factories and maquiladoras that American companies had set up in Mexicali to take advantage of Mexico's cheap labor and lax environmental laws. The New River channel had never been restored since it was gouged out during the 1905 event: it had provided a convenient conduit to transmit the witches' brew of agricultural and industrial exports to the Salton Sea. At first the flood remained within the New River channel, carved fifty feet deep and six or eight times as wide in 1905; however, with the peak surge the channel was quickly overwhelmed, permitting the flood to spread out, occupy, and further contaminate many of the drain-water channels heading north to the pool in the bottom of the Salton Sink.

At the end of the last leg of its long journey, the runoff from the headwaters of the Colorado River spread onto the still, hot surface of the Salton Sea, 226 feet below the level of the Pacific Ocean. After the first flood flows entered, it was not long before the waters topped the dikes that had been constructed to hold back the inland sea from the valuable lands at its southern shore. The stolen properties reverted in a rush to their rightful place on the floor of the Sea. When the peak of the 1.4-million-cfs flood arrived at Yuma over the next day, the great majority of it would turn into the Imperial Valley. Once again the Salton Sea was trying to join with the Pacific Ocean's Sea of Cortés, 110 miles to the south.

6

Las Vegas, June 25

"Your call couldn't have come at a better time," Ralph Canterbury gushed as he beamed across the table at Lisa. "How'd you *know* I'd be coming out for a little temporary duty at Nellis? I mean, this is just *fantastic* that we can spend some time together." Ralph was sixty years old and highly placed in the Energy Department—his latest and last berth at the government trough after a career jockeying for ever more elevated positions in various bureaucratic offices through six administrations in Washington. He and his wife of thirty-two years were woven into the social fabric of Silver Spring, Maryland, and after his imminent retirement, with a big payoff for taking an "early out," he was primed for a nice job with one of the energy contractors with which his department was doing a lot of business. But tonight, after the lovely dinner they had just ordered at the Las Vegas Grand Hotel and after the Barry Manilow show—at about quarter past twelve, if things went according to schedule—he'd be slipping off Lisa's tiny black lace panties, ending the day that had started with a good round of golf and doing what had come to be the most important and constantly anticipated thing in Ralph Canterbury's life.

Lisa was not pleased with the prospect of an evening with Barry Manilow. Her idea of a good time was a late disco party in the company of a young male hardbody. Last Saturday with the new guy on the sports staff had been fun, and Lisa was looking forward to a repeat of what had turned out to be a very long, very satisfying evening. But tonight, for business, she had to join the geezer brigade. She knew she'd be the only woman in the theater under fifty-five. Ralph was a great fan of the still-popular crooner, who only rarely did a dinner show, so Lisa knew Ralph would want to sit as close to the stage as he could. She'd been embarrassed when she called her good friend at the Las Vegas Chamber office who could always get her whatever show tickets she needed: "Oh, God, Lisa, Barry Manilow? And you want a front table? This *has* to be business."

Lisa knew she only had the time during dinner to make her move. Ralph would drink a lot during the show, and it would be impossible to get any serious talking done at a theater front table. After the show, Ralph would have only one thing on his mind; he'd last about a minute, then be asleep in another one. Early Sunday morning he'd be on the golf course again; he always worked on office stuff late Sunday afternoon and evening, talked to his wife, and went to bed early after an exhausting weekend. Ralph had learned a long time ago that the secret to getting a lot of nice TDY was to travel out on a weekend, get his playing in, then get back as early as possible Monday before being seriously missed. Important meetings in Washington were almost never held first thing, Monday mornings. The last thing you wanted to do was to be off on a party trip midweek, and *never* on a Friday.

"So, tell me what your creative little mind has been investigating since I last saw you," Ralph said, unable to keep from glancing at Lisa's small, very firm, unsupported breasts poking against her satin chemise.

"Well, you guys haven't got much new going on out in the desert, so I've been spending some time down at Flagstaff covering the flood. Sure would like to get a peek at what all that water is doing to a couple billion dollars' worth of government property wedged into Glen Canyon."

"I can tell you this much, Lisa: a friend of mine over at Interior tells me that repair costs are going to be in the billion-dollar range. And—this is a new thing—the Reclamation people think there's a chance the whole reservoir could drain before it's all over. Seems there may be a leak through one of the old river diversion tunnels around the dam."

"So all that stuff about earthquakes and landslides is legitimate—what they've been telling us might happen if the dam failed, releasing the water?"

"Uh, yeah, I guess that's right." Ralph twisted in his chair a little bit.

"Must also be why they've had to evacuate everyone from around the canyon—even Page and the Navajo Generating Station." Lisa had not missed Ralph's squirm. She watched him carefully. She'd gotten pretty good at detecting if he was holding something back.

"Well, yeah, that's right." Ralph twisted a little more.

There IS something else. HAS to be.

Ralph had answered her as he always did when she started to intrude on sensitive information. He knew full well that there was a definite price to be paid for the wonderful times he got to spend with the delightful little Lisa, and short of an outright breach of security he'd tell her anything that could not be traced directly to him. It was always worth the slight risk. Lisa never revealed her sources.

She leaned forward. "Can you tell me anything else?" Ralph was unable to not stare at what he'd get a really close look at later.

"Lisa, I just don't know. Not really." He hesitated again. *What the hell. This is public—sort of.* "Remember Dr. Kalinik? Saul Kalinik? From Livermore? You met him two years ago out at the test site."

"Yeah. He gave us a briefing. He was involved in actual weapon development wasn't he?"

"That's right. But he hasn't been doing weapons R&D the past couple of years. He's been with the NOVA laser program ever since he was accused of giving information to that Israeli."

"But he was cleared of that, wasn't he? Everything was quiet after the first bunch of stuff surfaced."

"Yes, officially, yet he was still reassigned to NOVA. Most recently, he was detailed to one of the TART teams—the one at Pueblo—and now he's been *arrested*," Ralph said conspiratorially, taking advantage of an excuse to lean even closer. "He's in a maximum security jail out near San Francisco."

"What for?"

"Lisa, I don't know. I really don't. It was an FBI arrest. I know Saul pretty well, so I tried to find out what was going on. Almost immediately, I got a call from a guy at Main Justice telling me to butt out. The same day my boss said he'd been called by the Secretary with the same suggestion."

"Was Dr. Kalinik at Pueblo when he was arrested?" Lisa was beginning to think the evening would be worth having to endure Barry Manilow and whatever she'd have to do later.

"I don't know, but here's the strange part—I mean even more strange than his arrest. A couple of months ago, the end of March sometime, Saul was reported missing and presumed drowned while sailing with a friend off the coast near San Francisco. The next thing we know, he's arrested by the FBI."

"What about the sailing friend? Is he missing?

"Stan Bellamy was a law professor in San Francisco. I met him once when I was out at Livermore, when Saul took me to some lunch club up in Berkeley. Boy, I'll never forget that day. Anyway, when I heard about Saul back in May, I found out the lawyer guy was drowned too."

"Ralph, tell me something . . . Honestly." Lisa reached across the table and took hold of both of his hands. "Why did you bring up Saul Kalinik when I was asking you about the situation at Glen Canyon Dam?"

"Lisa, I don't *know* anything. It was just a coincidence that came to mind when you mentioned the dam."

"What coincidence?" Lisa squeezed Ralph's hands more tightly.

"Remember Dr. Bonn? Jonas Bonn? He was the fellow who gave one of the first briefings out at Nellis."

"Yeah, he was explaining a whole bunch of stuff about the new testing. You know that technical crap gets past me pretty quickly. So what about him?"

"He supposedly came out to Nellis two weeks ago. You know I'm right at the center of what's going on with the new tests, and I'm pretty familiar with Jonas's work . . . There was absolutely no reason for him to come out here. The whole test works has been on hold for a couple of months, so I got sort of curious about why he made the trip. He's not like me; he hates Vegas."

And I'm sure he doesn't have a nice tight young squeeze out here, either.

"Well, I checked with a friend down in personnel who cuts the travel papers. You know I'm familiar with the details of that pretty well, as much TDY as I get. Anyway, I found out he didn't go to Nellis at all. He went to Page. He went on a government plane right to Page."

"What does Dr. Bonn do?"

"Lisa, that's getting into some touchy stuff. You know I can't– –"

"Just his job description, Ralph . . . Not what he actually *does*."

". . . Okay . . . Nuclear weapon triggering."

Ralph's answer jolted her. Then, immediately, the many loose ends that had been bugging her for the past few weeks started to weave. "Nothing else?"

"That's all, Lisa. That's absolutely all. Now here's the coincidence. His oldest friend and closest associate at Energy is Saul Kalinik. They worked closely at Livermore right up until Saul was reassigned. And finally . . ." Ralph paused again. His mind flashed to the king-sized bed in his room at the Hilton. *Oh, what the hell.* "Jonas has traveled to San Francisco twice in the past two weeks. Believe me, he has no business at all right now out at Livermore or the Berkeley lab."

"Ralph, are you suggesting . . . could it be . . . there's a nuclear weapon at the dam? Is that what you think? How long have you known about this?"

"Lisa, like I said, I don't *know* anything. This is all way over my head. If this got back to me, I'm dead meat. Maybe *actual* dead meat. Besides, it's just speculation. There could be a perfectly good explanation for Jonas to have gone to Page."

"What? To go fishing during the flood? To do Anasazi research? Come *on*, Ralph." Lisa then did something she never did: she decided to tell Ralph about the information she had. Good (successful) reporters never share anything. "Ralph, I've seen a new bunch of Energy guys at Nellis, even though nothing's going on out there with the tests. The NEST plane was at *Flagstaff*—

that was also about two weeks ago—and I also saw some ATF guys I met down in Waco. What in hell do *they* have to do with a flood, or even an earthquake?"

"Oh shit, Lisa." Ralph was starting to wish he'd stayed home.

"When was Kalinik arrested?"

"It was the same weekend the army moved in to evacuate the people and when the security went up around the dam area. Near as I know, they were virtually coincident."

"But not a coincidence." She did not ask a question. "Everything started happening at the same time."

"What are you going to do with this?" Ralph was now convinced that he should have stayed home.

"Nothing until I can get some hard evidence." Lisa knew exactly what she had to do to get it.

* * *

Randy MacConnell looked down into the lake at the toe of the dam. Water jetting from the spillway construction adits and from portals in the face of the dam kept the lake full while it tried to leak out around the dislodged power plant foundation. He stared in resigned fascination at where his smoothly running power plant had been. About three-quarters of a billion dollars in structure and equipment had vanished.

Even before the water had stopped spilling violently over the crest of the dam, the engineers at the Bureau headquarters in Denver concluded that they had a serious problem with the right spillway. The surface of the reservoir was dropping much faster than the overtopping and the calculated inflows to the spillways should have produced. Furthermore, the outflow from the right portal was much higher than that of its companion across the canyon. Clearly, a big leak had developed around the diversion tunnel plug. Inspectors also observed that the entire lining of the right tunnel was gone at the exit, its portal diameter appearing to have been enlarged to nearly sixty feet. Both tunnel exits continually spewed out amber-colored water and chunks of sandstone, but pieces of concrete and rebar were now only seen in the turbulent boil emerging from the right wall. Quietly and grimly, after carefully reviewing all the evidence available, the lead engineers in the concrete dam division concluded that Powell Reservoir was going to drain.

As soon as the cataract over the parapets began to subside, the engineers were also shocked to see that water was gushing from every portal in the face of the dam. The hallway from the bottom of the visitor elevator had exited the dam face to a walkway spanning the gap to the powerhouse. The eight-by-nine-foot exit, now an isolated rectangular aperture about 150 feet above the scoured-out toe of the dam, was discharging water in near duplication of the streams coming from the spillway repair adits. Companion streams were also erupting, less vigorously, from the other elevator hallway exit across the dam and from the several dam face portals next to the canyon walls. Obviously, the engineers decided, a massive connection existed between the right spillway tunnel and the galleries within the dam. In addition to their conclusion that the reservoir was going to drain through the conduit around the tunnel plug, they were very concerned that the extensive leak from the spillway into the galleries could compromise the dam abutment, causing a catastrophic failure of the structure before the reservoir drained. In any event, the engineers and their counterparts in the U.S. Army Corps of Engineers were convinced that most of the water impounded behind Glen Canyon Dam was destined to occupy a large part of the Salton Sink.

The media frenzy over the continuing flood had decreased as the river flow had subsided from its nearly million-and-a-half-cfs peak. Little additional damage was possible along the river, excepting the slow inundation of the Imperial Valley, where a cadre of reporters dutifully chronicled the creeping spread of the ancient sea and the valuable land it slowly swallowed. Tens of thousands of acres of alfalfa were slowly being transformed into duck food, meaning the price of Big Macs and Whoppers would probably have to go up about a nickel. But the dramatic flood story was over. Investigative reporters had dredged up every available foot of film on the 1905 flood and were having great fun juxtaposing the current situation with the historical occurrence. The central theme of the ongoing coverage was that the river was now reclaiming the fertile lands it had created and man was helpless in his efforts to stop it, no matter the hopeful schemes of the engineers or the arm-chair recriminations of the politicians, lawyers, and talk-show hosts.

7

Page Airport, July 4

A little tap on a sliding glass pane had given her access to the deserted steel building and Lisa was now reasonably comfortable in her perch by an overhead window in the U.S. Park Service's hangar next to the passenger terminal. But she was very tired, a lot more dirty than she had grown accustomed to being during the past few years, and more than a little nervous. With the highway across Hoover Dam closed, she'd had a very long trip across the southern Utah and northern Arizona canyon country by way of St. George, Zion National Park, Bryce Canyon National Park, Escalante, Capitol Reef

National Park, Hanksville, Hite Crossing, Mexican Hat, Kayenta, Tuba City, and finally an obscure jeep track across the Navajo Reservation commencing near Cow Springs, Arizona. From the point where she'd left her car, the last eighteen miles had been covered on her mountain bike. The sandstone slickrock country around Powell Reservoir was very familiar to Lisa. Growing up in Flagstaff, she had spent much of her pre-employment youth exploring the vast and rugged country on both sides of Powell Reservoir and Grand Canyon: from the forested plateaus of the Kaibab on the north to the arid reservation lands of the Navajos on the south. Long before she had been attracted to the intoxicating world of the news media, Lisa had come to be comfortable getting along by herself in the Arizona and Utah outback.

The gaps in the army's perimeter were large where Lisa had entered, but she decided not to push her luck by driving any farther. The army had spread itself very thin in its attempt to secure the hundreds of square miles of arroyo-latticed slickrock, sage- and juniper-covered backcountry within the fifty-mile security radius from the dam. Most of the soldiers, many of them reservists on rotating duty, knew little about the desert, had not a clue about the network of labyrinthine canyons with their Indian trails and jeep roads surrounding Glen Canyon, and at night were very concerned about snakes and scorpions. The soldiers did not patrol much after dark. Lisa had little difficulty slipping through the cordon; then with the Navajo Generating Station evacuated, she'd had an easy approach to the Page airport.

Lisa had made a calculated decision in making her move on the Fourth of July weekend. Although she had scheduled time off, more importantly she figured that she'd have a better than average chance of spotting the traffic she was looking for during a time when government employees were never expected to work. Maybe, just maybe, Energy Department and military hotshots would use the cover of the holiday to move about. She had enough trail food to last until the day after the holiday weekend. The well-equipped government airplane hangar had even offered up a rest room and a coffee machine.

She twisted the 600mm lens onto the old Nikon F2. Her faithful cameraman had loaned her the necessary equipment and had patiently explained the fundamentals of 35mm photography when she'd announced that she wanted to spend her holiday weekend photographing landscapes in the Kaibab. Shutter speeds, F stops and ISO numbers had never been vital to Lisa's life—that's what cameramen were for. But now she had a real need to know. Her cameraman had been particularly concerned about his beloved old 600mm lens, eventually relenting when Lisa assured him that his equipment would be safe. He always had a hard time saying no to her.

She already had some nice wide-angle shots of the equipment sitting on the airport tarmac, including a dramatic frame of the NEST airplane huddled next to the fleet of Blackhawks; now the long lens gave Lisa an intimate view of the rockets nestled inside their launching tubes on the assault helicopters, even some clear shots of the sundry numbers stenciled on the aircraft and their armaments. With the telephoto she also got some good full-frame close-ups of several of the people coming and going from the NEST plane, as well as a number of the men in camouflage fatigues visiting the helicopters. From her experience at Nellis, Lisa knew that the men in fatigues were not regular army troops. Several times the army had deployed Special Forces at Nellis, and these guys looked like the same people. She got an added bonus when one of the BATF men she'd seen at Waco came outside for a smoke. *Nice profile, just like a police mug shot. Okay, all I need now are some real people from Energy. Some recognizable faces.*

Lisa had been cramped on her perch by the hangar loft window for most of the day when some unusual activity jolted her out of her drowsiness. A Page Fire Department pumper unit drove out and parked next to the runway, an activity Lisa had seen occur at Nellis whenever a general officer arrived at or departed from the air base. *Got to be somebody heavy coming in.* A few minutes later, an unmarked Lear touched down on the runway. When the plane pulled up in front of the passenger terminal, she got nice close-ups of everyone who got off. Lisa didn't need a program to identify Roger Chedworth, Director of the FBI, and exiting just behind him was Dr. Jonas Bonn, followed by the Director of the Bureau of Alcohol, Tobacco and Firearms. She quickly changed lenses to get a picture of the whole entourage against the backdrop of the government perk jet, the Blackhawk helicopters, and the NEST plane. *That ices it. I'm outta here.* Lisa faced a punishing bike trip in the dark and a repeat of the long, circuitous drive back to Las Vegas, but she had one more stop to make in the morning.

8

Flagstaff, July 5

"Sir, I spoke with you a couple of weeks ago, after the evacuation began. I'll bet you're pretty tired of answering all our dumb questions about the dam, huh?"

"Yes, I remember you, Ms. Montgomery. What can I do for you?" Randy MacConnell was relieved that it was just a reporter this time and not a television camera shoved into his face.

I'll use the shock/confrontation routine here. "Sir, I'll get right to the point. What can you tell me about the Special Forces and ATF activity up at the dam?"

"Uh . . . how do you know about that?" Randy MacConnell had reported what he'd seen only to his boss in Salt Lake.

"Mr. MacConnell, I'm not permitted to reveal my sources. Just like the public will not know that I learned anything from you. Why would elite military and civilian people be setting up camp? There's no one there now except the government, right?"

"Ma'am, I don't know."

"When did you first see them? What have they been doing?"

Randy MacConnell realized the reporter had solid information. If he lied, she might find out and report it. Far more importantly, however, the very devout member of the community of Saints had always had a hard time trying to tell a lie—in fact, he had never yet in his life managed to do it. "The C130s with the Blackhawks arrived the weekend of the evacuation. Up until my people and I had to get out, I saw the military setting up at the Wahweap Marina, and there were some unidentified civilians spending a lot of time on the rims above the dam. I know they weren't Bureau people. Even when I was permitted to go up there during the height of the flood, the people I saw didn't seem to be interested in the flood itself. They had some kind of equipment. Looked like they were trying to measure something in the water behind the dam."

"You weren't introduced to anyone?"

"No, ma'am."

"Could they have been trying to measure the seismic threat to the dam abutments?"

"That wasn't any kind of seismic equipment I've ever seen, Ms. Montgomery."

"Anything else?"

"Well, the ATF people appropriated our inboard launches. They went out on the lake a couple of times—not for long, though. Seemed to be searching for something. We were ordered out just after all that started. That's pretty much all I can tell you. Did you find out about this from our Salt Lake City office?"

"Like I said, I cannot reveal my sources. Thanks for your help, Mr. MacConnell."

* * *

This time Lisa did not have to write up a tedious special coverage proposal for submission to the senior news staff. She laid out what she had at a closed-door meeting with the newsroom editor, held fifteen minutes after she'd gotten her film developed. The editor had then quickly assembled his senior staff and called the station manager.

"Do we confront Washington? Give them one chance to admit or deny?"

"If we do, they might just admit it, and we lose our exclusive. Seems to me they wouldn't dare deny it. This is bound to come out; then how would the Administration look? Its current approval rating on the candidness scale is about at whale-shit level as it is."

"Whatever the terrorist weapon is in that reservoir, they may be gambling that they can quietly remove it and the story just goes away."

"The flood has stabilized, and people are starting to move back down to the river. The military can't patrol the whole length of it. If the public isn't warned of the real threat up there and the dam gets destroyed, a lot of people are going to get caught."

"Gentlemen, we still don't have any hard evidence."

"Jonas Bonn and that NEST outfit aren't on vacation down there."

"The ATF and what can only be Delta Force assault teams in Blackhawk gunships don't have anything to do with earthquakes or evacuating civilians."

"Saul Kalinik had his hands on tactical nukes right up until he was arrested—after he supposedly drowned."

"Lisa's photos put everybody right there at Page. She confirmed with the dam supervisor. Hell, even the FBI director and the ATF chief were there—on the Fourth of July, no less."

"Okay, people," the general manager spoke up, "we're going with this. Preempt the network news. No ads. I know that violates our contracts and the network agreement, but it'll give us our best exposure. Dealing with the advertisers, the network, and the station owner is my problem. We only have one crack at this. Let's do it by just laying out the evidence. Continual graphics overlay—something like, 'Is there a nuclear bomb at Glen Canyon Dam?' Excellent job, Lisa. You'll have the number two chair at 5:30. Ready for it?"

9

The White House, July 6

Twenty-five minutes after an obscure television station in Nevada broadcast its story about Glen Canyon Dam, the President was in his office with his chief of staff, his press secretary, the Energy Secretary, the

Commissioner of Reclamation, and General Westfeldt.

"Okay, Edgar, where are we now?"

Edgar Peoples, the White House spokesman, had a ready opinion, as usual. "No way to contain it, sir. The networks and everybody else have just dropped everything to go on this thing. Just a matter of time before someone pays for a big leak."

"How much time do you think?"

"You should have a press conference right away in the morning."

"No effort at genie containment in the Nixonian style, Edgar?"

"Definitely not, sir."

"Dr. McAllister, how close are your people to disabling that thing?"

"Mr. President, with the flood we've had a problem– –"

"Dr. McAllister, how soon?"

"Uh, no estimate, Mr. President."

"What's the problem?"

"It's the proximity fuses, sir. With what we know now, we can't risk getting near the device."

"Best solution—from what you know right now?"

"We may have to wait for the reservoir to drain. At least that way we don't risk a catastrophic flood."

"I'd say it's been pretty catastrophic so far, Ron."

"Sir, we'd be talking about twenty-seven million acre feet all at once. That could cause the failure of Hoover Dam, which is also full, adding about another twenty-seven million. Yuma would get wiped off the map, and we'd have an even bigger problem with the Mexicans than we have already."

"Yeah . . . the Mexicans." Once again, the President's East Coast perspective did not permit him any knowledge, much less understanding, of the country's neighbor to the south. It was just a source of unremitting illegal immigration problems that were seriously undermining his voter base in California.

The Reclamation chief was shaking his head. "Sir, we don't think there will be a problem with Hoover."

"We've been through that, George. How long for the reservoir to drain?"

"Mr. President, the flows have not yet stabilized—neither outflow through the tunnel breach nor the snowmelt and storm inflows, and– –"

"How long, George? How long!"

"Sir . . . uh . . . probably four weeks. I– –"

"How probably, George?"

"Ahhh . . . five weeks, for certain."

"Jesus, we have to sit here with that damn thing boiling away on the front burner for another month? I might as well just move into the press room." The President turned back to his energy secretary. "Ron, if I manage to live through the next month, then what? What will be the situation with that bomb when the damned lake finally drains into Mexico or wherever it's going?"

"Two possibilities, sir . . ."

"Oh, Jesus!" The President got up from his desk and turned around to view the result of Frederick Law Olmsted's marvelous design of the South Lawn environment. He loved the inspiring vista, extending past the Ellipse and the Washington Monument to the Tidal Basin and the Jefferson Memorial. It always managed to calm him down. He was standing in the shoes of Washington, Jefferson, and Lincoln. He could handle whatever the tedious, physics Ph.D. and the equally pedantic engineer could confront him with. "Okay, Ron, go on." He resignedly took his seat.

"The proximity fuse sonars are a constant drain on the batteries. We're not sure when they will be drawn down. That's the first possibility: that by the time the reservoir drains, the proximity fuses will be depowered. Secondly, the bomb could settle to the bottom and detonate if the batteries still have power . . . At least there wouldn't be a flood."

"Sir, if I might . . ." George Ricketson interrupted, hand raised. "There is a variation on the second possibility the Secretary mentioned."

The President stared sullenly at his reclamation commissioner.

"Sir, it's the cofferdam. When Glen Canyon Dam was built, an earthen cofferdam was constructed across the canyon above the construction site to keep the river out of the area. The river was diverted through the canyon wall tunnels above the cofferdam. Well, it's still down there. So when the reservoir drains, there will be a pool remaining between the dam and the cofferdam. The bomb could remain suspended in that pool. We don't know – –"

"Okay, George, that's enough." The President looked closely at Secretary McAllister, now fidgeting in his chair. It was apparent that the Energy staff had not considered the cofferdam situation. "Ron, you and your people are going to spend as much time as is necessary with George and *his* people to find out *everything* you need to know about that dam. Okay?"

"Yes, sir."

"Suppose that bomb does wind up just hanging there in that pool in the bottom. How long until you can safely get in to take it out?"

"Mr. President, we just don't know about the power supply Kalinik installed. I can't answer you exactly."

"I wonder if Yarzov would let me borrow a couple of his best KGB people—whatever he calls them now. I'm sure we'd know all we need to know from that traitor in about five minutes."

"Sir, Dr. Kalinik *has* told us everything. We've been over and over what he did. The problem is, the oddball way he wired the two proximity fuse circuits, we just don't know what the power drain is and we don't know about residual fuse sensitivity as the power supply diminishes. It will just get down to a statistical guess."

"General Westfeldt, any problem maintaining tight control along the river corridor and around the dam?" *God, I wish I had more like him around this place.*

"Just manpower, Mr. President."

"Yes, I understand. All right, gentlemen, that's it. It seems we have to keep all the balls in the air for at least a month and perhaps for some indefinite time after that. Edgar's right. We'd for sure have a leak, probably worse than the one out of that reservoir. But on the other hand, there'll be relentless pressure on us to disable that thing once the story is out—admitted, that is. Well, we'll have to handle that. Edgar, Arnold, set up the press conference for eight o'clock in the morning. Get the speech people over here immediately."

10

Flagstaff, July 10

With the bomb revelation, no one other than a lot of Bureau people was paying the least attention to the fact that the flow from the bottom of the dam was still increasing. The left tunnel was carrying an estimated 130,000 cfs from the still-full reservoir, but the discharge from the right tunnel was 270,000 and rising steadily.

The junior reporters consigned to the sweltering tedium of reporting the slow inundation of the Imperial Valley clamored and begged to be reassigned to the new, potentially spectacular, career-enhancing disaster. The creation of an expanded, inland sea in southern California was forgotten while television, radio, newspaper, magazine, and tabloid reporters concentrated on the colossal story centered at Glen Canyon Dam. Accordingly, Randy MacConnell was very glad to have the military perimeter around the dam where he could escape from his temporary office in Flagstaff. The lovely northern Arizona resort town had become media central, and to the now very tired dam supervisor, the continual questions and demands for information were like being nibbled to death by a flock of ducks.

Three newspapers and a television network had filed suit to gain access to the dam area. A federal judge in Phoenix had granted a temporary restraining order allowing them limited access, but the Ninth Circuit Court of Appeals in San Francisco, overcoming its normal judicial routine that advanced at glacial speed, immediately ordered the TRO dissolved, saying that, on balance, public safety concerns outweighed First Amendment right-to-know concerns. A battery of New York lawyers was prosecuting an appeal to the Supreme Court, demanding a forthwith hearing due to the exigent circumstances.

Of course, speculation was rampant. Talk shows across the country switched from the usual fare of the latest sexual indiscretions and/or mayhem and murders of and by prominent people to dark discourses about every conceivable type of bomb conspiracy, from the lowliest terrorists to the highest levels of government, domestic and foreign. Beyond the conspiracy theories, a regular theme was the irony of the speedy evacuation initiated by the then-secret bomb threat. If there had been no bomb, it was generally concluded, thousands of people would have died in the unexpected and sudden flood. The local authorities, even the states, would have been helpless. Some even suggested that the bomb conspirators should not be charged with any crime: they were, in fact, unwitting heroes. The involved federal and state prosecutors were not moved by the argument, however. Among the more bizarre fringe stories, one newspaper even suggested that the bomb had been placed in a scheme by California to get back its water, stolen by Arizona.

The font of news was limitless once the President held his second press conference to inform the citizens that the bomb was, indeed, a weapon from the former Soviet Union. Of course, the U.S. nuclear stockpile was fully secure. And yes, this incident epitomized the crucial need to get on with the matter of complete nuclear disarmament. Immediately following the President's revelation, unnamed sources revealed the details of the weapon's size (still uncertain), placement, and fusing arrangements. Leaks from the involved government agencies—the FBI, the Department of Energy, and the ATF Bureau—had become a hemorrhage. The President was furious, but there was little he could do given the highly heated state of public concern: he dared not fire a single person in his administration. The media, the President's enemy politicians, and a growing segment of the populace made continual and unanimous demands to know what the government was doing. What was being done to defuse the device; and if there was a detonation, what would be the result? All attempts to keep the domestic agenda on track had been derailed.

Following the revelation of the right tunnel leak and the conclusion that the whole reservoir would drain, a few old Bureau men began to see a small silver lining in the great storm cloud. At least now the structure would be fully dewatered so that repairs could be made. As designed, and under normal circumstances, Powell Reservoir could not be fully drained. Once the reservoir fell below the level of the river outlet works, located on the upstream dam face 225 feet above the original river bottom, a two-million-acre-foot dead pool would remain in the narrow inner canyon: a thin thread of reservoir reaching over 100 miles up the canyon, with the river continuing to flow in faster than the Bureau could ever hope to pump it out of the deep hole. The uncertainties involved with managing water standing that high behind the dam and leaking through the porous sandstone would have presented incalculable problems for the engineers as well as hugely increased construction costs.

Moreover, before they could even start the task of reconstructing the power plant from the foundation up, the enormous block of concrete from the old foundation would first have to be removed. The engineers, together with the big construction contractors who were already lining up for the very lucrative and pork-barrel-filled windfall project, would also face the job of re-plugging the right diversion tunnel and relining both spillways. By the time the reservoir finally drained, the damage to the right tunnel would be massive—almost unimaginable—but the biggest concern was with the dam itself. The structure had moved less than two inches, but even the relatively tiny displacement meant that a wholly different and unknown loading pattern was pressing onto the sandstone abutments. A great deal of core testing and study would have to be done before the repairs could even be assessed, much less engineered and started.

11

Glen Canyon Dam, July 20

When the level of the reservoir had fallen below the intakes to the spillways the previous week, the flow in the right tunnel was measured at 390,000 cfs using an improvised river gauge at Lee's Ferry. Now, five weeks after water first inched over the crest of the dam, the right tunnel outflow seemed to have stabilized at 425,000 cfs—an equilibrium having been achieved between the increasing erosion of the tunnel and the decreasing pressure from the falling height of the reservoir. At the stabilized flow down through Grand Canyon, the spillways and the still-surviving outlet works at Hoover were now just barely able to keep the river from pouring over their own dam. It didn't matter much, anyway; the power plant at Hoover looked much like the one at Glen Canyon. On down the river, the steady 425,000 cfs kept the river channel for its own exclusive use.

Amazingly, the loss of the two huge hydroelectric plants at Glen Canyon and Hoover Dams had little impact on the delivery of electricity anywhere in the western United States—unless and until the unseasonably cool weather in the L.A. Basin got back to normal. Even the shutdown of the Navajo Generating Station, with more output than the two big hydro plants combined, had little effect on the whole system: the three generating plants amounted to only about 6 percent of the output of the interconnected power grid in western North America. As the summer wore on, however, the Western Area Power Administration would be forced to impose rolling blackouts in the high-consumption areas of Phoenix and the L.A. Basin. Many residents of Phoenix would learn, finally, that they indeed lived in a broiling inferno from which they could not locally escape.

***

The resurrected course of the Colorado River into Mexico and back into the United States was carrying the entirety of the Powell Reservoir escapee. With the deep, right-turn trench the flood had scoured in the vicinity of the old Rockwood Landing, not a drop was able to proceed to the Gulf. The gap in the sand levee above Morelos Dam was now nearly a quarter mile wide, and following the first quick buildup and then the great peaking surge from the storms in the Upper Basin, the river had settled down to transporting between reservoirs all of the millions of acre feet remaining behind Glen Canyon Dam, as well as the quantity still melting in the mountains ringing the Upper Basin.

The accumulated water had spread the banks of the Salton Sea twenty miles farther south, swallowing the city of Brawley, the commercial hub of the billion-dollar, valley agriculture industry. The Corps of Engineers calculated that by the time the last water drained from behind Glen Canyon Dam and melted from the high mountain tundra, Brawley would be under twelve feet of water, the surface area of the valley's sea would double, and its shoreline would reach south to the town of Imperial. Nearly one-half of the Imperial Valley would be reclaimed by the river. On the brighter side, the EPA would soon note that the Salton Sea's level of pollution was substantially reduced.

The powerful valley landowners, with their lobbyists, politicians, bankers, and lawyers in tow, made continuing demands that the Bureau of Reclamation and the U.S. Army Corps of Engineers "*do* something." But until the flow under Glen Canyon Dam finally abated, nothing could be done to redirect the river to the south. The valley farmers even suggested that Morelos Dam should be blown up to relieve the obstruction blocking the flow of water to the Gulf. The fact that the dam happened to belong to Mexico gave the farmers little pause in their proffered partial solution. With nothing to be done to fix the problem, all energy was spent in planning litigation and bemoaning the dollar losses. Great teams of lawyers searched for any person, governmental agency, insurance company, or other entity which had money and could be the target of a lawsuit. Somewhere in the process it had been forgotten, or never even understood, that the flood was merely a natural part of the ages-old processes that had created the fertile lands—and the very rich farmers—in the first place.

12

Department of Energy, July 26

Secretary of Energy Ronald McAllister and Commissioner of Reclamation George Ricketson faced the packed conference room. The President had detailed to them the task of keeping the public informed about the status of the situation at Glen Canyon Dam. Although creative news people and their paid experts could dream up issues in near-endless variety, they all, essentially, got down to two questions: (1) When is the bomb going to hit the bottom of the reservoir? (2) Will it retain sufficient power to set off a proximity fuse? Since the honest answer to both of the questions was "we aren't sure," the press conferences were quickly reduced to uncounted questions about why the government did not know. But today, the officials had a bit more information.

"Commissioner Ricketson, tell us why you don't know how deep a pool will remain between the cofferdam and the base of the concrete dam."

George Ricketson stepped over to the chart stand with his pointer. Unlike his lonely, sweaty meetings with the President, this time he had all the assistants and visual aids necessary to keep an engineer happy. "Miz Roberts," he said to the woman from the Miami Inquirer, "as shown here, the crest of the cofferdam is estimated to be about 140 feet above the level of the original riverbed. Since the reservoir started to fill thirty years ago, we believe there has been some settling and sloughing of material. As also shown here, the bottom of the reservoir in front of the cofferdam—between it and dam itself—is lower than the original river bottom. A lot of material was taken out so that the dam could be built on bedrock, and that material was used to build both cofferdams. Now, when the right diversion tunnel was closed, the reservoir started to back up behind the upper cofferdam. About a month after the left tunnel was closed, the rising lake reached the top of the earthen dam, and when the water broke through it cut a trench down through the dam. We don't know just how deep a trench was cut, so therefore we don't know what the present vertical distance is from the lowest point in that trench down to the bottom of the reservoir—that's the elevation at which the water will stand between the dam and the cofferdam when the reservoir finally drains. The problem is complicated by the fact that the material eroded out of the cofferdam somewhat filled in the area between the two dams. Our best estimate is that when the reservoir drains, we will be left with a pool about ninety feet deep." The room erupted in a chorus of unintelligible, shouted questions. The Commissioner's pointer aimed at a reporter belonging to one of the 175 raised hands silenced the room.

"Can't you use depth-measuring equipment? Wouldn't it tell you exactly what the bottom contour is?"

Secretary McAllister stood up. "Let me answer that, George. Of course we could. But any such equipment relies upon some kind of an electronic signal, usually sonar. The sonar fuses in the bomb are still active, so it's just too risky. I can tell you that we have had some military volunteers out on the reservoir using mechanical plumbing equipment to map the bottom, but we have a large area to cover; and furthermore, we have no clear information about even the general area where the device was set. Every time those men send down the plumb line they run the risk of passing it by the bomb. If I might add, we also cannot use electronic equipment to pinpoint the position of the bomb float so that we will know exactly when the surface will fall to the level of the float."

"You've been unable to get that information from Wadsworth Temeseh?"

"This isn't the former Soviet Union, sir. So far, he has refused to say anything." The Energy Secretary was not known for his diplomacy, and he had almost had quite enough of press conferences. He selected another hand thrust up from the crowd.

"What about all those reconnaissance satellites the CIA has? Surely they have the capability to see into that reservoir."

"I am not able to respond to that. But I will tell you that the mission of the CIA does not include domestic surveillance. In fact, that activity is specifically prohibited by law. Certainly you should be aware of that. I can say that all permissible equipment is involved in our investigation, and we do have some information in that regard. I cannot say anything more on that subject." The military services, the Defense Intelligence Agency, and the CIA had argued forcefully against exposing the country's capabilities (or lack thereof) in the matter of seeing into the waters of the world.

"Dr. McAllister, I understand that you cannot use electronic means to locate the bomb, but what is your current information on how high above the bottom the float is located? That's as important as knowing the depth of the reservoir, if I understand the situation correctly."

"Yes, how far the float is above the device will determine when the bomb will begin to settle toward the bottom. We know the line from the anchor to the bomb canister is seventy-one feet, but that doesn't matter. It's the distance between the canister and the float that's critical. As soon as the reservoir level drops to the position of the float, the bomb will start to fall at the same rate as the surface of the reservoir. We have found out from Saul Kalinik, when he reviewed the inventory of the material found in the van, that his intended float line was not used.

"Now, this next chart . . ." The Secretary nodded and one of his assistants leaped into action. ". . . shows that Kalinik's intended line to connect the float to the bomb was sixty feet long. So, if Kalinik's line had been used—when the reservoir level drops to and then remains at the ninety-foot depth at the bottom of the notch through the cofferdam—there would be no problem. The bomb would remain suspended about thirty feet above the bottom. We would simply wait until we were certain that the batteries had completely run down and then just go in and remove the device. But that's not the situation we're dealing with. After reviewing the contents of the van, Kalinik concluded that Temeseh had forgotten the winching device needed to remove the bomb from its can and had used pieces of Kalinik's float-to-bomb line to jury-rig a winch. Then, since he'd cut the line into a number of pieces, he must have used a portion of a climbing rope he had in the van to use as the float-to-bomb connection. The problem is that we do not know how long the rope originally was—all we have is what remains. As you might expect, climbing ropes of this kind come in a number of standard lengths, 50 meters and 60 meters being the most common, and we don't know if it may have been shortened at some time. So, therefore, if you've followed me this far, you can see that if the actual length of rope he used was much longer than sixty feet, the bomb will settle close to the bottom as the lake level drops to the ninety-foot level. Specifically, if the line he used is eighty-three feet or longer, the bomb will descend to within the sensitivity range of the proximity fuses when the lake drops to the ninety-foot level." The room erupted into another chorus of questions.

"Mr. Secretary, have you been able to make any estimate about the length of the rope he used?"

"Based upon Kalinik's recollection of the climbing rope that belonged to Temeseh—assuming it was the same one Kalinik saw—as well as some other factors, we believe that the line length is, indeed, about 80 feet—right at the borderline of the critical distance between the float and the bomb canister. And Mr. Delaney," the Secretary turned to a previous questioner, "same answer why we have not gotten that information from Wadsworth Temeseh."

"So what you're saying is that there is a good chance the device may actually come within the proximity fuse sensitivity range when the reservoir bottoms out."

"Yes."

"Do you have any estimate as to when that may occur?"

"I'll ask Commissioner Ricketson to answer that."

"As we speak, we still have about six million acre feet in the reservoir, and the depth behind the dam is 340 feet." Another of the Commissioner's assistants sprang forward to change charts. "As you can see from these cross-sections of the reservoir, the canyon narrows considerably throughout most of its length: that's why it's still 340 feet deep, even though we only have six million acre feet; but the rate of fall of the surface will accelerate now that the level is approaching the inner, narrow part of the canyon. Present outflow through the diversion tunnel is 360,000 cfs; inflow is 40,000. So, based upon everything we know about the rate of fall of the reservoir and the length of line from the device to the float, the critical time period will be between noon, July 31, and midnight, August l." The room exploded again. Several reporters ran for the telephones in the lobby; most thumbed the keys on their cellular units.

"And that, of course, brings us back again to question number two, doesn't it?" the Secretary said to a wave of laughter in the hall. "Nothing more to tell you, really. Saul Kalinik is cooperating fully, but we just have too many uncertainties about the remaining state of the power supply in the weapon. We know that the sonar transmitters for the proximity fuses are still sending out signals; however, I can report to you that the signal strength has weakened somewhat. But if sufficient signal strength continues until the critical time—five days from now—we have no reason to believe the device will not detonate. And that's *if* the line Temeseh used is long enough and *if* we're correct about the ninety-foot-deep residual pool. We have carefully reviewed all of the information from the defendant and from the Russian authorities, and we believe that we do indeed have a fully operational nuclear device out there, ladies and gentlemen." Several more reporters hurried from the room. "I know you are getting a great deal of opinion from various experts in the private sector, but I can tell you that you are receiving the best information right here. I hope you will all do the responsible thing and urge your readers and viewers to make no attempt to penetrate the exclusion area. No one would think, I hope, of walking out in the middle of our nuclear test area in Nevada. The same situation should apply at Glen Canyon. Thank you very much. We will call another conference if anything further develops."

* * *

Lisa clicked off the television at her desk. In the great surge of media coverage of the dramatic situation at Glen Canyon Dam, station KNOB—and Lisa Montgomery—had been quickly forgotten. The networks and the big independents had fully taken over, overwhelming Lisa and her studio by the sheer weight of money, geographical coverage, and power: transmission wattage and the other kind. She had uncovered the biggest story she'd ever heard about in her whole life, and here she sat at her little desk in a studio with a market listing of over 100. The heavy hitters at the big-city studios with their single-digit market listings had had their war correspondent and other high-visibility assignments to move them up. Others had managed, with great persistence and luck, to get into the right beds on enough occasions. Now

Lisa was watching her chance of a lifetime being gobbled up by the big guys. This was *her* story. Well, Lisa decided, she wasn't through. She still had an advantage not possessed by the network darlings. Because it was such a big story, only the elite of the elite got to cover it. The big-deal television personalities living in and around New York and Atlanta and being paid millions every year were not the sort to attempt another penetration of the now-tightened military perimeter around the dam.

The military had been embarrassed by Lisa's close-up photos of the doings at the Page airport. Prosecution had been threatened; but so far the studio's lawyers had held off the Justice Department. Feeling that it had been duped, the public was in no mood to see the dupe-exposer prosecuted, a situation the President had quickly seen, followed by his immediate command to bring the government's three-piece warriors to heel.

An exclusive on a big story required taking a big chance. Furthermore, the story demanded proper television coverage, which meant her cameraman would have to go along. He had questioned the sanity of her decision to travel to the vicinity of ground zero of an imminent nuclear detonation, but Lisa had pointed out that the location she had in mind on the west rim would be nearly three miles from the base of the dam if the thing went off; and where they would be hidden, they would have adequate protection from the radiation flash and the blast shock wave. They would be in position to get footage of the immediate aftereffects of the explosion, and then, with two coups to her credit, the brilliant young reporter would rocket to stardom. Of course, her cameraman would go with her.

The cameraman had also questioned Lisa's plan to try to breach the army perimeter in nearly the same location she had used before. Lisa reasoned that it would be the last place they would think would be tried again. Besides, it would remain virtually impossible to close off the vast network of interconnected canyons and trails in the reservation area southeast of the dam, no matter the army's half-vast effort to do so.

13

Powell Reservoir, July 30

Lisa, like Waddy, knew about the uncompleted marina at the foot of Antelope Canyon. Once they had gotten through the army's somewhat tightened perimeter, struggling with backpacks and saddlebag-burdened mountain bikes, the route she knew through the reservation and power plant property down to the marina remained wide open. With a nuclear detonation threatened, very few people remained within the perimeter. Under Lisa's direction, her photographer had been able to remove one of the skiffs left at the marina, drag it down to the edge of what remained of the reservoir, and then row them around Antelope Island and over to the west shore, below the site of the Wahweap Marina. Antelope Island was actually a large flat butte sticking up in the middle of the lower canyon, and it had very nearly reverted to its former status by the time Lisa and her cameraman slipped through the narrow, deeply recessed patch of water separating the butte from the Navajo Reservation. When the reservoir finally drained, the Navajo Nation would reclaim the former island as part of its lands to the south of the river.

The climb up the slope of the canyon on the other side of the rapidly dwindling reservoir, in the dark with their equipment and camping supplies, had been a nightmare. Thirty years' accumulation of underwater slime on the sandstone made the already difficult ascent nearly impossible. Lisa's photographer had fallen numerous times in the several trips needed for him to transport their heaviest gear, but Lisa had diligently urged him on from her perch on the rim. And as the critical day and hour arrived, they were ensconced near the top of the west canyon wall with a clear view three miles down to the vertical face of the back of Glen Canyon Dam, rising above the top of the cofferdam where the surface of the reservoir was just starting to fall into the notch in its earthen rubble.

Once in position, early on the morning of July 31, they dared not take even a little peek over the rim of the gully where they had set their camp. They spent the time under the cover of their sand-colored tent, immune from detection from any reconnaissance excepting the possibility of exposure from a satellite- or aircraft-carried infrared camera. They sweltered in the still, midsummer heat, waiting for what could happen at any moment in the next thirty-eight hours. A few seconds after the explosion they would peer over the edge and start the camera to record what every other news person could only dream about. Lisa's cameraman had already recorded scenes of the newly exposed canyon that had not been viewed in thirty years: what the canyon below the reservoir looked like and what the reservoir had done to it. They already had a hell of a story. But it was not enough for Lisa. She demanded—she had to have—the *big* story.

***

Ninety-three feet below the surface, in the pool between the dam and the eroded crest of the now-exposed cofferdam, the Kharzov-series atomic demolition munition imperceptibly sank through the dimly lit water toward the mud. Thirty-seven hours before, the level of the reservoir had dropped to 166 feet, exposing the flotation sphere. Now as the surface continued to fall, the sphere fell with it, along with its suspended canister. The nylon climbing rope had faithfully performed its intended duty: preventing objects from falling with disastrous consequences, but it was near the end of its rope. The water-weakened filaments were failing at an accelerating rate while the survivors were subjected to an ever-increasing loading.

Within the bomb's pressure case, three lithium-ion batteries, wired together in parallel, continued to provide a voltage differential and a tiny surge of amperage, as required, to two sonar fuse mechanisms also securely affixed to the battery-case mounting brackets. The sonars' several highly sensitive little noses protruded slightly through the skin of the pressure case.

For fifty-seven days, five hours, and thirty-one minutes, fed by the required voltage and current flow from the batteries, each of the sonars had sent a periodic signal, in the form of a sequence of pulses of varying duration and amplitude, into the surrounding liquid medium. Also contained in each of the two sonars' electronic mechanisms was a sensor that was intended to react when it detected a certain type and quality of pressure wave returning, in a precisely ordered time interval, from its outward-bound journey into the liquid. The little sonar transceivers in the fuse noses were very simple, by current computer-chip-driven design standards, but they were rigidly uncompromising with respect to the subtle pressure waves they would respond to. They could not interpret or "think" about the return signals they received. They could only react to a very specific one, with a specific duration and amplitude, and one at a very specific time delay—and they could only react Yes or No. Unlike the ability of a fifteen-year-old male human to react in the rear seat of his car to a Maybe signal sent by a fifteen-year-old female human, the sonar receivers only had their black/white reaction choices—no shades of gray.

Over the past fifty-seven days, five hours, and thirty-one minutes, none of the sonar transceivers had detected a return pulse that permitted anything other than a "No" response. Hundreds of thousands of No's had been registered when the transmitted pulses had not been returned within the required parameters.

Yes. The canister was exactly seven feet, three inches above the soft layer of sand, silt, and mud at the bottom of the pool.

Upon completion of the Yes reaction the little electronic brain of the successful sonar unit immediately caused an electrical pulse to be sent through a shielded coaxial cable extending through the wall of the inner case and into a piece of equipment in the physics package known as an event counter, an electronic device that was perhaps the most highly sophisticated—and had been the most carefully guarded—element among all the components in the nuclear weapon. The event counter then began a series of events which would end the counter's electronic life precisely 11.202800127 seconds later. The counter's function with respect to the weapon was much like that of a conductor with respect to his orchestra.

Within the inner case was a separate plutonium-cell power supply, fully charged, unused, and ready to work. The event counter activated a switch connecting the power output to a transformer—unique to the Soviet weapon—which changed the plutonium cell's output from 32 volts and a large current flow to 4000 volts and a small current flow. Over the next 11.2 seconds, the released electrical energy flooded into a bank of capacitors where it was stored at the high voltage for a later event. The event counter was poised to initiate its second instruction. From this point forward, it would carry out its functions in a manner which fully justified its highly guarded status.

While the intervals of time that were about to occur may be described and mathematically defined, and equipment constructed to react in accordance with the necessary time intervals, the human mind cannot comprehend—*really* comprehend—the time lapses. At ski racing events, winning times are often determined by hundredths of seconds. Scoreboards record such times, but no truly rational person can claim to sense the difference between 98.00 seconds and 98.01 seconds. We are comfortable, nonetheless, with the distinction. If the one-hundredth second is then divided by ten, a millisecond results: entirely beyond comprehension. In the world of nuclear physics, however, relevant time intervals are measured in one-millionths of that one-thousandth of a second: a nanosecond. Wholesale nonsense in human terms, but the mechanism within the Kharzov-series ADM suspended in the water behind Glen Canyon Dam was set to commence a delicate sequence of events that if they were to proceed as intended had to be choreographed in terms of those millionth-thousandth seconds.

The event counter instructed a switch to open, to release the energy stored in the capacitors to a junction where the electrons would be divided into thirty-two equal-length cables containing an equal number of devices known as krytron switches. The krytrons, employing a radioactive inert gas, had the ability to close and open their circuits in a period of two nanoseconds, with all of the thirty-two switch openings occurring within another two nanoseconds of each other—a remarkable achievement of the event counter as well as of the switches themselves. Once through the krytrons, the electrical pulses were destined to travel down their cables to a cluster of three gold-filament detonators embedded into each of the twenty hexagonally-shaped and twelve pentagonally-shaped high explosive lenses surrounding the fissile core of the weapon.

But the one-in-12.5 chance that the central switch would not open occurred, halting the genius-designed sequence of events. Hang fire. The surge of 4,000-volt-driven electrons never made it to the krytrons and thence to the detonators. The sonar fuses—both of them now—continually sent their little "Yes" commands to the event counter, but it was unable to do anything effective with the instructions. The counter had recognized the interruption in the program and had immediately (0.000000004 seconds later) shut down the sequence. At the same time, it instructed another switch across the still-charged capacitor bank to open, to drain off the charge of stored electrons. Then it turned itself off. It could no longer hear the insistent little signals coming from the sonar transceivers.

The Kharzov-series atomic demolition munition continued its slow descent toward the mud, 720 horizontal feet from the base of Glen Canyon Dam.

14

The White House, August 2

Three press conferences had been held while the critical day at Glen Canyon approached, with world attention riveted on the slow countdown. As the day arrived and the hours moved by, the President—privately—did not much give a damn anymore if a block of concrete in some obscure piece of a wholly uninhabited canyon in the even more broadly obscure, few-votes-producing southwestern desert was blown into oblivion. The big threat—the threat to thousands of lives from the flood—was over. This whole thing was now seriously interfering with his desperately needed domestic work.

"Okay, where are we now, Dr. McAllister?"

"Mr. President, the oblique camera views from the satellite show that the device had to have hit the bottom yesterday morning. We then verified it actually was on the bottom when the flotation sphere started to drift around. The pool level dropped a little bit more and stopped at eighty-six feet. The Indian's flotation line was a little over ninety feet long, a bit longer than we'd figured."

"So that's it, then. Great. We don't have to sit around for another month wondering when the batteries will run down. When are you going to move that thing out of there so this country can get back to more important disasters?"

"Sir," the Secretary said, pausing uncomfortably, his face presenting a premonitory cringe. "Sir, it seems that there is one last problem." He swallowed hard.

"Oh, that's fine, Ronald. Tell me about another problem with that goddamned bomb," the President said in a rising but remarkably calm voice.

"Even with the device sitting on the bottom, the sonar fuses are still transmitting."

"Okay, Kalinik's mickey-mouse fusing system didn't work. Get that damned thing out of there."

"Sir, since the device came within the sensitivity range, yet failed to detonate, it was evident that something else—another problem—existed. We have consulted at great length with Dr. Kalinik as well as the Russians. Sir, we believe we have a significant problem."

"*Consulted* with Dr. Kalinik? We should draw and quarter that traitor." The President stared at his energy secretary, who was now starting to perspire below his hairline and on his upper lip. "Okay, what's the *significant* problem?"

"Mr. President, it's the detonation system. The high-voltage electrical impulse to the detonators around the HE matrix comes from a capacitor bank, through a central switch, then krytron switches, and into the leads to the detonators. We believe that– –"

"Jesus, Ronald, just tell me what the problem is. I don't want the goddamned details!" In the last month, the President had learned far more about the intricate workings of the inside of a nuclear bomb than he had ever wanted to know.

"I'm sorry, sir, but it's important that you know exactly what the situation is. We . . . You . . . will have a very difficult decision, I'm afraid."

"Okay, Dr. McAllister, go on." The President sighed heavily and lit one of his Havanas. The Energy Secretary hated cigars. *Maybe this will help cut this short.*

"I'll try to be concise, Mr. President."

"That would be a breath of fresh air."

"Sir, we believe that the detonation sequence in the weapon actually started but then stopped due to the failure of a component in the system."

"Is that thing going to go off or not, Dr. McAllister?" A long pause. "Well?"

"The short answer is, we don't know."

"Oh, *bat SHIT!* How many of you eggheads have we got over there in that department of yours?" The President watched the perspiration run down from the vicinity of the Secretary's nostrils to the upper edge of his lip, where it remained, constrained by surface tension. "All right, Dr. McAllister . . . explain it. Slowly and carefully, so I can understand."

"Mr. President, the Soviets had a problem with a component in the detonation circuit in a number of their tactical weapons. It is a high-speed switch, used in the portion of the system active after the detonation sequence begins, that discharges a burst of electricity into the detonator leads. Well, they recognized the problem and recalled the weapons using the defective switch, but the weapon involved here retains one of those switches. They have a low percentage failure rate, but we feel, upon all the evidence, that the one in our weapon malfunctioned."

"Okay, it failed. Get that bomb out of there."

"Sir . . . please . . . the situation is more complicated. Part of the Soviet fail-safe system in weapons of this type is to provide for a drain of the electrical charge in the capacitor bank—what sets off the detonators—in the event that the sequence to detonation does not finalize. Well, we've just found out, in our last talks with Saul Kalinik, that he may have inadvertently interrupted the circuit that allows the capacitors to discharge—that is, to drain off—outside of the detonator circuit. Sir, without the drain pathway open, those capacitors will just sit there fully charged. Now, here is the specific problem . . ." From the expression on the President's face, Ronald McAllister knew he had only a little more time to finish his explanation. "The suspended charge in the capacitors is delivered to the detonator leads through what is, essentially, a krytron switch. Well, it's not exactly a krytron . . . it's a . . . well, it's a very sophisticated switch that operates in less than a 'shake' . . . uh, just a few nanoseconds, that is, just a tiny fraction of a microsecond." *Oh, shit, hurry up.* "The Soviet switch, as it turns out, is very sensitive in addition to being occasionally prone to activation failure. Sir, the weapon is set to discharge in the event that switch decides to activate. We believe that just a small physical disturbance could activate it." *Made it.*

"You mean we still have a bomb with a hair trigger out there."

"Yes. Yes, that's it exactly." Ronald McAllister did not have, nor would he ever have, the President's ability to concentrate information and thoughts—one of the many reasons why the tall, gruff man sitting across the old carved-oak desk was President of the United States.

"And now we have to send our NEST people down there to defuse that thing. What are the chances that disturbing the bomb case will set it off, Ronald? Somebody's got to move that thing out of the water."

"A very big chance, sir. We think more than even money—perhaps a 70 percent probability. And, sir, the Reclamation people tell us not to hold our breaths waiting for the water to seep through the cofferdam to expose the bomb on the bottom, to make it easier to work on. That could take a year, in all probability."

Probabilities, the President thought. His entire function got down to the sifting of probabilities, starting each morning with his briefing from the CIA lady who came to his office to tell him about the subtle changes in the state of the world that had occurred over the night and what the *probabilities* were of such-and-such occurring. *I'd like to be the Pope. He knows there is a God, nothing else matters, and that is that.* "Why not suspend charges around it and blow it up? We've certainly managed to blow up a few of those things in Air Force crashes without creating a nuclear detonation."

"Sir, we've taken a long look at that. Unlike the accidental explosions you described, none of the usual nuclear system safety links are in place here. A demolition charge pressure wave will travel more slowly through the pressure case and then the inner case than will the reaction of the charged circuit to send the impulses to the HE detonators around the fissile core. The central switch will release a 4000-volt charge that will reach the detonators in a matter of a few milli-microseconds. It would then be a race between the demolition charge shock wave trying to blow the pit apart and the implosion wave trying to create critical mass in the pit. We think the implosion wave would win the race, Mr. President."

The President stood and turned to look out the window at his favorite view down the South Lawn. Ronald McAllister waited quietly while the President remained in his position for nearly a minute, slowly rocking back and forth on his toes and heels. He abruptly turned around.

"Ronald, why don't we offer Kalinik the job? He's been in that little cell out in California long enough now to have thought a great deal about spending the rest of his life with no sunlight. I may have misjudged the man—the way he turned himself in right after that Indian put the bomb in the lake. Well, he's obviously a caring individual. Maybe he'll just see it as his duty. Better him than some poor slob from NEST."

Ronald McAllister, Ph.D., now saw yet another reason why the man was President.

* * *

"Good morning, Andrew," the President said to the Secret Service man sitting in the anteroom just outside the Oval Office. Even though it was 3:45 in the morning, a Secret Service agent was on duty. The office of the most powerful man on earth was always guarded.

"Good morning, Mr. President." The young agent wasn't at all surprised to see his early morning visitor.

The President had to have these quiet times to do his thinking. The short naps he caught in the late morning and again after dinner enabled him to conserve his energy. His senior staff was in a near-constant state of panic knowing the Man, more often than not, had a few hours' head start on them each morning. God help them if they were not at least as well informed as he was when they gave him his 9:40 A.M. briefings.

In the quiet of his famous office, its thirty-six-by-thirty-foot dimensions surprisingly small in relation to its significance in the world, the President could sift and condense and analyze his thoughts. He could do that better than any other man in the chaos and noise of a campaign meeting or speech or in a staff conference, but he could do it with startling efficiency while sitting in his chair alone in the dark behind his desk. Although he had a more comfortable study, including a softer chair and a larger, more modern desk immediately available in the next room, the President preferred to do his most important thinking in the place that had witnessed so many difficult decisions since its construction during William Howard Taft's administration. The President smiled when he recalled the historically rumored Washington joke at the time of its construction that the room had been designed to conform to President Taft's rotund form. In its current, post-1934 incarnation, the office occupied the southeast corner of the West Wing, positioned to permit the President's favorite views of the lovely Rose Garden as well as the expanse of the South Lawn and beyond. The old oak desk, carved from the timbers of *H.M.S. Resolute* and a gift from Queen Victoria during President Hayes's tenure, was too small, inefficient, and uncomfortable. Nevertheless, and far more important to this president, it truly reeked of the American history he loved. The whole environment of the executive sanctum helped immeasurably in his struggle to do the best job he was capable of.

And the President knew exactly what his job was. While his cabinet members, his military commanders, and the legions of staff in his administration could analyze mountains of information, conclude issues, and make recommendations in their individual areas of responsibility, it was up to him to bring it all together: to resolve and make compromises among conflicting forces and interests. Sitting at the very apex of the federal midden, only he had the responsibility to keep the entirety of the big picture in crystal focus, despite the pretenders to that distinction who occupied a number of the 535 seats in the big building at the end of the Mall.

This early morning the President thought about the risk to the individuals who would be required to try to defuse the nuclear weapon resting in the mud under eighty-six feet of water at Glen Canyon Dam. It was a hell of a thing to ask even Saul Kalinik to bargain for his freedom with a 65/35 risk of losing his life: the refined odds the dweebs over at the Department of Energy had come up with. *But it's got to be Kalinik. He'll do it,* the President concluded after several minutes thinking about all the things he had come to know about Saul Levi Kalinik, Ph.D.

The President thought about the dam. Right or wrong, good or bad, whether or not it ever should have been built in the first place, millions of people in one way or another had come to depend upon it—to use its water and electrical power and the big reservoir behind it. Over the past couple of weeks the Bureau had gotten a reasonably good handle on what the repair costs would be, even without being able to send hundreds of specialists out there to crawl over every inch of the dam, the remains of the power plant, and the spillway tunnels. They had to guess, nonetheless the Bureau people were pretty confident about their guesses. The whole thing, fully back up to speed: about $1.7 billion—and for a certainty, much more if the slight shift of the dam had caused unexpected loading of the sandstone abutments. Of course, the President had little doubt that the entire project would be constantly over budget and delayed—and with the inevitable new problems surfacing as work progressed. *We'll have to let the bids cost-plus. A dream come true for the contractors. They'll milk that job for years.*

Repair of the dam would become an enormous political issue. Things had been bogged down for weeks as it was, and the environmental community would surely launch a campaign unlike any yet seen in the country. The question of whether the dam should even *be* repaired would drag on for years, with the repair costs, of course, going up in the interim. Lawsuits. Endless lawsuits. Environmental impact statements. Experts in disciplines that no one had even heard of before would argue endlessly. Everything the President was trying to do would be infected by the old West-versus-East divisions in Congress: the conservative Western livestock, water, and electrical-power combine versus the Eastern, environment-voting, liberal wing. And the outcome was anything but certain. The President could not look far enough down that particular road to see who would prevail. But whoever won in the end, the protracted battle would be enormously divisive, and it was uncertain how it all would finally play out politically. He also thought about the election he had to face in a little over two years. *This thing will just drag me down.*

He thought about the nation's need for the reservoir. Its water and power production capacity. The recreational use. *A lot less land to irrigate now, down in the Imperial Valley.* Of course, the lobbying had already started. There was not only growing pressure to quickly repair the dam and power plant, but, incredibly, to spend some ghastly sum to drain the Salton Sea back down to its old level. *The Mexicans are already so pissed off about the gringo flood they'll refuse all cooperation with any scheme to pump water out of that hole and across their property. Can't really blame them, I guess.* The President was just now starting to really appreciate what his predecessors must have gone through back when the Imperial Valley farmers and electrical power brokers were pressing for new dams on the Colorado River. The California and Arizona governors and a solid block of Senate and House members from the Southwest, joining forces across party lines, were standing ready to throw their considerable weight around in the Capitol. The great political wrangling would reach into all corners of the government. *No, that all must be avoided.*

The President got up from his desk to leave his office. He wanted to go out through the Rose Garden door to walk back in the warm night air along the colonnade, but he exited the Oval Office the way he had entered. To do otherwise would create some anxiety among his Secret Service staff, who were duty-bound to know the exact whereabouts of "Boomer" at all times. They were always standing closely by, except when he was upstairs in the mansion's family quarters. His ever-present military aide, who carried the "football," would also be frantic.

Retracing his normal route, he went upstairs and into his wife's study, where he searched the shelves of the bookcases until he found what he was looking for. It was a slim, oversized book: a coffee-table book. The President returned to his office and set the volume under the little pool of light from his desk lamp. The book was not new; its dust jacket was chipped and yellowed. He looked carefully at the color picture on the front: a view of the fluted and rose-black walls of a narrow, serpentine canyon of stone. Below the photograph, he read the title:

THE PLACE NO ONE KNEW
Glen Canyon on the Colorado
by Eliot Porter

The President opened the book, pausing at the copyright page. It had been printed by the Sierra Club in 1963. On the opposite page, he read the first three sentences in the foreword, written by David Brower, who at the time had been the club's executive director:

> "Glen Canyon died in 1963 and I was partly responsible for its needless death. So were you. Neither you nor I, nor anyone else, knew it well enough to insist that at all costs it should endure."

He turned the pages of the volume slowly, examining the beautiful photographs of scenes in the great canyon, occasionally stopping to read the quotations from the best of the environmental writers.

After forty-five minutes the President closed the book, turned off the desk lamp, and got up to look out at the first hint of light in the Rose Garden. He was thinking about where Glen Canyon Dam was located, remembering in detail the map of the Colorado River Basin he had examined so many times in the past few weeks. Excluding a few wide places in the road and the city of Page, now evacuated, the nearest town was over fifty miles away in a direct line. Other than Kanab to the west, there was only the tiny hamlet of Escalante and some place called Henrieville—maybe it was Hanksville—even farther away to the north, near Bryce Canyon Park. Eighty-or-more miles to the southwest was the expanse of Grand Canyon. The rest of the surrounding area was either BLM land or Indian reservation, largely deserted. *That place is almost as isolated as Yucca Flat—less than a hundred miles from Las Vegas—where we blew up how many atomic bombs in the atmosphere?*

The President struggled with his Eastern perspective of the United States. It wasn't that he was prejudiced against the far Western states, California excluded; it was just that they meant little to him. He had always felt like a foreign visitor when he campaigned out there, no matter the warm smiles and apparently sincere welcomes he had received.

His mind then shifted gears, directing his thoughts to the role of the United States in the world at large. Besides his domestic programs, his abiding concern was nuclear disarmament. The President firmly believed that the United States was letting a never-again opportunity slip through its fingers while the situation in the former Soviet Union rapidly deteriorated. Mere economic pressure had not been enough to do it—had not convinced the Russians that the big bombs were no longer needed. The President believed that in order to convince the Russians the American people had to be convinced first. And the American people were forgetting about the nuclear threat. The fact that an atomic weapon had been smuggled into the country had certainly reawakened the people to some extent; unfortunately, it was not enough. They would simply expect the bomb to be deactivated. Somehow it would be deactivated, the media coverage would end, and the incident would quickly fade from the public's memory.

The President sat in his chair, staring at the awakening morning in total concentration for another ten minutes. He decided what had to be done and went back upstairs to bed. Four hours later, when Washington was awake and functioning, the President called the FBI Director and told him to arrange for Saul Kalinik to be brought immediately to Washington. He also wanted what's-his-name—the Indian—brought along. He should be recovered enough by now.

* * *

The basement below the President's and his senior staff's offices was largely used for service facilities—kitchen and dining rooms, barber shop, and so on. One of the most coveted perks of White House service was the mess privilege: to be able to use one of the three West Wing dining rooms, decorated with a nautical flavor by the boat-loving Franklin Roosevelt and still operated by the navy. Only persons sufficiently advanced in the White House food chain and who were particularly in the President's favor were accorded the honor. The basement also housed the Situation Room, in place since John Kennedy's failed effort in 1961 to oust Fidel Castro, and since Kennedy's time, every president had been linked to the Situation Room through the equipment carried by his military aide. It was to a small room adjacent to the White House nerve center that Waddy and Saul were being led.

Waddy's stomach growled as they were hurried along, passing the dining rooms. He had not eaten for nearly a day. The delicious smells were excruciating. *Sautéed pork loin with plum/fig coulis. Lavender rice. Cumin vinaigrette veggies. Apricot cobbler*. Adding to his discomfort were the short leg chains connected to more chain around his waist and then to the cuffs that secured his hands. While he shuffled along he was closely accompanied by a United States marshall who stood about a foot above him. Saul also had an escort. Very quickly he and Saul were pushed into the small, lead-shielded conference chamber adjacent to the Situation Room that was the most secure area of the White House. It was wholly isolated from any possible surveillance.

They had been sitting in the little room for half an hour when the

President walked in and closed the door. To Waddy he looked just like he did on television except a lot older. Waddy started to stand, only to be yanked back into his chair by the giant federal policeman—the activity instantly reminding him of several of the barely healed tears and holes in his body.

"Take it easy with him, mister!" the President barked. "Now, both of you, remove their restraints and leave the room."

"But, sir . . ."

"Do it."

Saul and Waddy were permitted to stand while the two officers removed their chains and shackles. With reluctant glances at the President, the marshalls left the room.

"Sit."

They sat rigidly-still in their chairs, alone with the President of the United States while he slowly scrutinized them across the polished walnut conference table.

"I'm going to give you two one brief chance to avoid spending the rest of your lives in prison. This is between just the three of us. We'll soon find out what kind of men you are." The President let that sink in for a few moments.

"Dr. Kalinik, you and Mr. Temeseh are going to go out to Glen Canyon. When you get there, you are going to do whatever needs to be done to detonate that nuclear bomb." The President had the benefit of psychological profiles of the two men sitting across from him, prepared as soon as they'd been identified. He was almost certain he knew how they would react.

The impact of what had just been said by the President of the United States took a moment to register in Saul's head. "Can you tell us why you want such a thing done, Mr. President?"

"We're not here to talk about that. We're here to give you a chance to not spend the rest of your lives in the maximum security prison at Marion."

Waddy: "We'd get immunity from prosecution?" These were the first words he'd spoken since his capture nearly two months before. He'd even refused to talk to Malcolm's lawyers.

"Well, you *can* talk. Sure do appreciate all the help you gave us." The President glowered at the muscular young man sitting across the conference table. Waddy stared back, unblinking.

"Can't do that," the President answered curtly, breaking their mutual stare down. "Let me make it very clear what's happening here. Only the three of us will know about this. That is, the three of us and your friends out in the Seychelles, if you survive. You two are to go out to the dam—full public exposure—to disable the bomb. Dr. Kalinik knows about the little problem that's recently come up with the detonation system, and he knows what the risk is, probably better than all those nerds in the Energy Department. While you are doing the job—being heroes trying to win back your freedom—there will be a terrible accident. What I am saying is, if you pull it off, it won't be an accident."

"There's still a big risk that there *will* be an accident, sir." Saul turned to look at Waddy. "There's better than an even chance the device will detonate if it's disturbed. It's a problem with the switch Kateryna told us about, compounded by a mistake I made when I wired in the fuses."

Without hesitation, "I'll take those odds. Beats the hell out of rotting in some *pahana* prison."

"Understand, there won't be changes of identity, relocation, and the rest of that crap, either," the President added abruptly. "You two will be on your own. But if you succeed, you'll be free—dead and gone so far as the rest of the world is concerned. And I'm sure your friend Malcolm Renslaer will help you out. I can't do anything except give you this opportunity." Saul and Waddy continued to stare across the table at the very large and very calm man. The President lit a cigar, taking his time. "Can you do it, Dr. Kalinik? Can you do it with just the tools you'll be provided to defuse the weapon?"

The large, dominant man sitting across the table, puffing on a slug-green Havana, asking him to do something he did not want to do, momentarily sent Saul back to the director's office at Lawrence Livermore and what had started this madness. This time he *could* say no. "Sir, I don't know. The failure occurred within the detonation sequence. I don't know with this Soviet weapon if I can just back it all up and start over to give the switch another try." *God . . . electronics.* "With the detonation sequence started, the event counter probably cycled through the quick sequence, including the firing of the neutron gun, I– –" An upraised hand across the table ended Saul's intended long recitation.

"Are you willing to make the effort?" The President could not listen to another physicist picking through the details of exactly how a nuclear weapon came to life.

"Willingness is not the issue, Mr. President. I'm not sure if anything I could try would work, especially since I'm not going to have any of my own equipment."

"Well, it seems to me that it would be quite reasonable, given that you are going to be more than seriously risking your lives, that you should have your own tools. We'll send somebody out there to get them. Just don't ask for particular equipment that could not have anything to do with defusing the thing."

"Of course not, sir." *What can I get away with asking for? Shit, why am I even CONSIDERING this insanity?* "Sir, what if it doesn't work? I rig it to go off and it doesn't work? They'll be back when we don't check in."

"They'll hunt you down and kill you both . . . on my specific instruction." The President let that register for a few moments.

Waddy looked at the President, then back at Saul. *They'll never find me in that country—not alive, anyway.* "Saul, let's just do it. I have faith in you. Nothin' like a little pressure to make somethin' work."

"I like your attitude, young man," the President said between puffs. "I could use some people like you around here." He meant what he said.

"Well then, get rid of some of those gutless *pahanas* and pick out a few people who really *care* about this land and not just their wallets and stayin' in office. I could give you a nice list." Once again the Southwestern desert Hopi and the Eastern establishment president, as dissimilar as it was possible for two American citizens to be, stared at each other, unblinking. The President now knew more about Wadsworth Temeseh than all the government shrinks had been able to deduce.

"And sir," Waddy finally said, "no TV bullshit. If we're supposed to just hide out after we do this, I don't want my face on the evenin' news. Those old Colorado mug shot pictures in the papers—well, they don't really look like me, especially with this short hair. Do you see what I mean?"

"Done," the President said as he stood up. "While the Energy people are collecting your tools and equipment and whatever, we'll keep you isolated out at Andrews." He turned before opening the door. "Now remember . . . if you're successful, it's imperative that you completely disappear. Let your friend Renslaer take care of that."

The following morning, at what he sincerely hoped would be his last press conference on the subject of the frigging dam out in the desert, the President announced that the two Glen Canyon suspects in custody had volunteered to attempt to defuse the bomb. ". . . and despite their terrible criminal acts, I'm proud of their coming forward to attempt to atone for their conduct . . . In the final analysis, true American character has shone through . . . if more criminals accepted responsibility for their conduct there would be less need for building more and more prisons . . . These are very brave men . . . in the finest American tradition . . . The NEST team members and their families will be spared the terrible risk that the defusing work entails . . . We're very sorry, but the defendants will not be available for interview . . . very high security risk . . . ."

The networks now had the makings for the greatest true-life drama ever to be made into a prime-time miniseries. To their great frustration, however, the studio front men were firmly and summarily denied access to the principal characters who would be offered millions for the necessary details of their stories—and the television writers *had* to have those many details to make the lucrative drama real. Manufacturers of hair colorings, corn chips, toilet bowl cleaners, and throwaway baby diapers would pay a ton to sponsor the program.

15

Flagstaff, August 6

Lisa hadn't been able to take any more days in the stifling tent without a bath, some real food, and a beer. For three days she'd dreamed about nice cold bottles of beer. When it became clear that the bomb wasn't going to go off, she and her cameraman had gone home. They had some good shots of the canyon anyway, and Lisa was carefully deciding how, when, and where would be the most advantageous time to release them.

Then with the news from the President's press conference, she decided they had to go back. They just *had* to go back. This was going to be even better. The two crazies were actually going to try to defuse the bomb so there was no question that Lisa had to have action footage. Her cameraman refused to go back, particularly when he realized that they'd (he'd) again have to haul the boat and their equipment, probably through deep mud, all the way from the Antelope Creek Marina to the river, again flowing at Nature's intended elevation. Eventually, Lisa had found a way to change his mind. She could always make men do what she wanted them to do.

Then Lisa decided at the last minute that they'd go in from the north side. They didn't have time to go clear around, and with the reservoir completely gone it could be impossible to drag their gear across all that mud and up the cliff to their campsite. They could avoid going down into the canyon altogether—no more climbing down and then up through the slimy glop—however, they wouldn't have the perfect cover of the myriad canyons on the reservation side. Though faster and easier, the north-side approach would be much riskier.

It turned out that the army's security perimeter was particularly thin through the isolated Paria Canyon Wilderness route Lisa selected for their approach to Glen Canyon's west rim. And given the very high chance of a nuclear detonation, the army had only a few well-dug-in soldiers inside the perimeter. In the words of General Westfeldt: "Actually who cares? People who sneak in there now probably won't have the opportunity to pass on their felony-stupid genes. Good candidates for the Charles Darwin Award."

Once they'd penetrated the perimeter, using a logging road that had been long-abandoned after the 800-year-old ponderosa yellowbellies had been mined from the Kaibab, they'd had a relatively easy bike ride, even with their heavy packs, back to their spot on the west canyon rim overlooking the dam.

Bureau of Reclamation geologists at the mouth of Wahweap Creek, next to the base of Sentinel Rock, 1956. The creek's alluvium, only a few miles from the dam site, yielded ideal aggregate for concrete (*Bureau of Reclamation, Fred Finch*).

This time Lisa decided they weren't going to sit in their tent roasting. That wasn't necessary, at least until the men started working on the bomb.

Late the next afternoon the FBI jet landed at Page, 125 miles from Flagstaff and the mobs of reporters—and the studio people, still desperate for fodder for their screen writers. A few of the media employees stood around at the perimeter check point on highway 89, but the rest preferred to stay in Flagstaff, where hotels, restaurants, bars, and air conditioning were close by.

The helicopter settled in the mud next to the river, about five miles up from the dam. From the west, a little stream flowed past a giant sandstone monolith and into the river: Wahweap Creek was again joining its resuscitated parent, as it had done for millions of years.

With their tools, an inflatable, and camping gear, Saul and Waddy were suddenly alone in the bottom of the canyon, listening to the fading sound of the helicopter, now vanished over the rim. It was going to be back to get them in two days—unless events made its return unnecessary.

They stood still, surrounded by the furnace-hot silence, now amplified after the clattering ride from Page. Even the brown river sliding by a few feet away was strangely mute. They stared at the scene around them: everything encased in a uniform, gray-brown layer of dried or drying goo, extending from below the bathtub ring high on the canyon wall to the river bottom. Excepting the large pond trapped behind the cofferdam, the river had only just completed its task of draining the reservoir to the floor of the narrow inner gorge. The river-level goo was beginning to dry and curl into flakes in the 115° heat.

"What a stench!" Saul said disgustedly, looking around at the many evaporating pools dotting the canyon floor. Saul was not given over to hyperbole, and all but the most olfactorily challenged would have agreed with his assessment. Several ravens, two golden eagles, and a turkey vulture were pulling at the rotting flesh of a few of the hundreds of fish floating in the hot and shallow, fetid ponds or lying in the muck- and slime-covered sand. A couple of scrawny coyotes and a raccoon had also found their way into the canyon to join the feast. Saul looked at the turkey vulture and smiled. *Maybe it IS Cactus Ed; he always said he'd come back as a turkey vulture. Yeah, he'd be the first one down here.*

Saul pointed downstream. "Waddy, look at that," he laughed. They walked down along the river to investigate. At the base of the slimy, steep slope of the west canyon wall, a huge heap rested in the mud: hundreds of crushed and shattered floating docks, houseboats, speedboats, skiffs, rowboats, a few sailboats, and several jet skis. High above, the broken ends of the marina mooring cables dangled over the rim.

"Look at all this crap," Waddy said, surveying the refuse surrounding the boat and pontoon pile: rusted outboard engines; broken propellers; houseboat toilets, bathtubs, shower stalls, and kitchen sinks; countless beer cans; broken or lost pieces of every variety of marine and personal equipment—even a few unwanted automobiles that had made their final, driverless, late-night trip down the boat ramp—littered the canyon floor. Hundreds of plastic bags still containing garbage and human waste tossed into the reservoir over the past twenty-five years lay among the lost and discarded equipment. The marina operator, enjoying a government-sanctioned monopoly in the Glen Canyon National Recreation Area, had used its money-making reservoir as a convenient trash dump. Everybody knew Lake Powell could never be drained.

They walked back up the river, pumped up the raft, and loaded in their gear. Floating around the corner, past the field of boats and trash, they soon saw the gray wall far down the canyon, rising above the intervening slope of the cofferdam. Watching the huge plug of concrete growing in size ahead of them, Saul and Waddy both experienced the same strange feeling. The river still carried nearly 15,000 cfs. Their sense, independent of their minds' knowledge, was that it should have been forming a lake at the end of the giant cul-de-sac. But it just disappeared.

The raft passed a narrow side canyon on the left, separating the east wall from the butte that had been Antelope Island. In its descent through its reborn channel, Antelope Creek had already cut a course through the mud to the river. Waddy thought back to the night he had paddled around the island, nearly 600 feet above where they now floated.

"How long do you think it'll take Nature to start repairing this place?" Saul was looking at the leached sandstone surfaces and the endless expanse of the gummy coating. The anonymous filth even sheathed the trunks of huge cottonwood trees, still rooted in the mud where they'd stopped growing thirty-one years before. Their bare gray branches, like suppliant claws, reached mutely for help.

"Already startin', up near the top. Most of this layer of shit'll get blown, flaked, and washed off in a few years. Underneath, where the color's been leached out of the rock, that'll take longer. But you know, the discolored layer is very thin and partially disintegrated. It'll start to spall and flake off pretty quickly too, revealin' the native rock underneath. Up in the bathtub ring, you can already see where the sandstone is showin' through in a lot of places where it's been out of the water for a few years."

"What about the desert varnish and the runoff streaking? The tapestry?"

"Don't hold your breath there, Saul. The patina of the desert varnish—the oxides of iron and manganese—that won't recover for a lot of human lifetimes. Look at how the clan stories of my people are still visible around the canyon country, etched into the varnish a thousand years ago and more. The tapestry? Long time for that too, but not as long as with the varnish. But take heart. Within fifty years, seventy-five at best, there'll be mostly lovely orange walls risin' up out of this canyon. Mother Earth will repaint her varnish and her tapestries in her own patient time, and of course all the vegetation will be back. It'll come back in a hurry, actually, 'cause all this nice fertile, moist soil won't sit here alone for long. And another thing. With all the water that reservoir forced into the sandstone, I think seeps all over the canyon will run for a long time. Look, you can see lots of places on the walls where the water is runnin' out. Tapestry will form pretty fast below those seeps, like it did in the canyon walls below the dam abutments—you know, where it was bein' forced through the sandstone by the impounded water. Won't be long before all the little side canyons will be burstin' with maidenhair ferns and flowerin' plants of all kinds. Cottonwoods'll breed like Navajos, and maybe, just maybe, we'll be rid of all that damn tamarisk the *pahanas* brought in."

High on the west rim, the cameraman had his telephoto lens focused sharply on the object drifting toward the end of the box canyon. "This is perfect, Lisa. We're going to have some good stuff, but it'll be dark soon. I wish we had one of those surveillance gizmos so we could hear what they're saying."

Lisa wasn't paying attention. She was concentrating on what her next job would be. San Francisco. Maybe even New York.

Waddy pulled the raft ashore, where the river ponded briefly behind the cofferdam before it sluiced into the black hole in the west wall. The mire and mud pile rose steeply above them, between the river and the big dam, now nearly obscured. They unloaded their gear from the raft.

"Well, what's easier?" Saul asked. "Hump the boat up right here or carry it over to the notch?"

"I say we go up and over from here. Hard to walk along the slope in this glop." Forty-five minutes later, and after another trip down to the river to get the gear they'd need, they were organized on the edge of the cofferdam pond. They stared up at the slime-draped immensity, at the much-reduced Lake Powell it presided over, and the black sphere floating nearly midway across the lake.

"You sure put that bomb right where it would do the most good." Saul almost gagged at the odor, now at its nasally offensive zenith in the vicinity of the rapidly warming pool, with its steadily increasing litter of expired fish.

"Saul, I . . . I've never had the chance to apologize to you, and all. I mean, I just freaked after that shit happened up in Kanab."

Saul had a flash of memory of his earliest childhood and what he had been told of his parents' fate: a man and woman, holding hands, herded with hundreds of others to the edge of a bulldozed pit . . . Men in gray uniforms. A machine gun . . . "Forget it, Waddy. I understand completely."

Saul pushed the boat into the water and started to load their equipment. "Frankly, I don't think that switch is all that sensitive. I mean, we don't want to drop the thing, but I think it'll be okay. Ready to go get it?" Saul didn't know if he believed what he just said or not. It really didn't matter. If they tried to run, they'd be tracked down and shot like rabid dogs. No due process next time. A president's credibility was directly at stake.

They rowed out to the sphere. Waddy reached down and carefully pulled up a length of the slack flotation line.

"Well, there's your climbing rope," Saul laughed. "Do you realize how much anxiety you caused by using that rope?"

"Little details." Waddy joined Saul's laughter. "You never can know how little details can change things. If I hadn't forgotten that damned comealong and just used your flotation line, as planned—well, shit, that bomb would be just hangin' there, they wouldn't'a known about the switch, and we wouldn't'a got our chance. With more waitin', who knows what the President would'a decided." Waddy's smile faded. He stared across the pond and up the hundreds of feet of slime-covered concrete. "Saul, what I really think is . . . what happened is what was *intended* to happen, even that shit up in Kanab."

He followed Waddy's gaze at the Bureau of Reclamation's soulless treasure. "It's not just you Hopis who believe in fate." Waddy nodded, smiled. They listened to the silence around them on the vile, stinking lake.

"Come on, it's going to get dark soon. Time to try this nifty little winch my former employers gave us." Saul lashed the cable drum to an oarlock. "We can just crank it up by taking a few wraps of the rope around the drum. You tail the rope like you were using a sailboat winch."

"Guess we both better sit on the other side to balance the weight of the canister and the anchor," Waddy said.

Saul reached across the raft and started to crank the winch handle. "We'll soon know—actually we won't have enough time to know—if that little piece of equipment down there objects to being moved."

The climbing rope was suddenly under tension again, starting to lift the canister. In the minutes immediately preceding the canister's settling into the mud the rope had nearly parted; now the remaining kernmantle filaments were strained almost to their limit. The buoyancy of the water negated much of the canister's 62.7 kilogram weight, but it was not enough. One after one the remaining strands failed.

Waddy was spelling Saul on the winch. "Still no increased load. Not liftin' the anchor yet." Then he saw it. "Oh, fuck!"

"What?"

"Ease over to this side of the boat. Easy, but do it fast."

Saul slid across the thwart tube. The boat almost capsized from their combined weight and the strain on the winch. "Oh, my god!"

"Reach down and grab the line," Waddy said, unconsciously whispering. *How'd that happen?* He thought back over the last times he had used the rope. He remembered the summer before when his climbing partner had taken a long fall. *Should have retired it after that. But I know I checked it for cuts . . . the climb down to the mule . . . didn't check it . . . the night climbs to set the VHF repeaters. Could have busted any time . . .*

"I got it." Saul had hold of the rope below the break, but he was not supporting its full load. A moment later the rope broke and Saul started to go over the side, still clutching the slick nylon, now slowly sliding through his grip. Waddy lunged for the rope and the raft started to capsize, spilling both of them into the water. They thrashed to grab something—anything—with their free hands. Waddy's found the bow line as the boat completed its turn. Saul immediately followed the example. Once again time was standing still for Waddy. His mind tried to go back to that day at Hance Rapid.

"Saul! Can you hang on by yourself for a little bit? I gotta try to get up on the boat."

"I think so." Saul struggled to stay afloat, his left hand death-gripping the bow line. He twisted his wrist to wrap the taut climbing rope around it, then the load on his now-stinging right arm increased with a shock when Waddy released the rope.

"Glad we don't have that anchor, too. We'd be completely fucked."

"Can you get up on the boat?" Saul gasped, between frantic, leg-scissoring moves.

"Nothin' to grab. We're gonna have to swim this thing to shore."

"It must be over two hundred yards."

"You got a better idea? And before your arm gives out we gotta get that rope tied around your waist." With one hand each, they managed to pull up the canister and get a loop tied around Saul. "Now we gotta get rid of that anchor. We'll never be able to lift that sucker. How much rope you think we pulled in?" They both looked at the tangle still attached to the winch and tried to remember the cranking.

"I think about fifty feet. So the canister's about forty feet down."

"Me, too. Saul, just hang on to the bow line. I gotta go down and cut the anchor free."

"Forty feet! You'll never make it."

"We got no choice. I'll pull myself down the rope as fast as I can." Waddy checked his belt knife, gulped down several deep breaths, and started hand over hand down the rope.

Saul felt the tension on the rope slacken in jerks. Seconds passed. Ten seconds. Steady tension returned. *He must be going around the canister . . . don't . . . bump it.* A few more seconds. Then the tension on the rope shot up, jerking the bight around his waist. *He's pulling himself back up the rope. Can barely hang on.* Interminable time. Waddy burst out of the water.

"My ears! Fuck!" He hung on the bow line for a couple of minutes, gasping and coughing. "It is about 40 feet down. Okay, let's go."

"Waddy, wait a minute. When we get close, the canister will hit the slope of the dam."

"If we stay out here it's gonna hit the bottom a lot harder." With the boat-end of the bow line in his teeth, in perfect swashbuckler tradition, and with Saul clutching his belt, Waddy started for the cofferdam.

"Son of a bitch," the cameraman muttered.

"What? Lemme see." Lisa snatched the Betacam. "Wha . . . why are they in the water."

"Their boat turned over. They're going to *drop* that thing. Lisa get *down*!" He ran for a boulder, away from the rim of the canyon. There was a limit to his loyalty.

In an instant, Lisa followed her cameraman. The full realization of what was happening finally penetrated.

"Hang on Saul. Just a little farther."

"My back's about busted." Saul's attention was not fully focused on the agony in his back. *What's the slope of that dam? Probably 45 degrees, like the other side.* He tried to estimate the remaining distance to the shore. *About sixty feet away. Forty-five degree triangle.* "Waddy, we're getting close. Slow down." They both started dog paddling, barely inching toward the muddy slope.

"Waddy! I think I felt it hit. Stop! Thank God this dam is mostly mud and not rocks."

"Well, if that didn't set the sucker off, guess nothin' will. Saul, we gotta pull it up and then set it down farther up the slope. You gotta stay out here while I get the boat ashore and turned over." Once again the weapon canister was nudged by the soft goo. Saul treaded water while Waddy got the boat upright and returned. "Okay, gimme the line and climb in. Just vault over the tube. I'll counterbalance." They soon had the black stainless steel canister pulled up to the side of the perimeter tube. Saul eased the raft close to the shore and then slipped down into chest-deep water. Waddy found himself in water nearly up to his chin.

"Easy, easy," Saul said.

"What the hell, it's touched the bottom twice now. That switch must be okay."

Saul didn't know what to say. "Why push our luck?" After much careful struggling, the canister was soon resting on the slope of the cofferdam. The dam's coating of curled, drying sediment flakes were rapidly becoming proper mud again. It was starting to rain.

"Need any help takin' the end off?"

Saul behaved as if he hadn't heard. He was focusing on the wet steel cylinder resting at his feet.

"Well?"

"I don't dare work on that circuitry in this rain."

"We can rig the tarp. I'll go get it."

"It's more than that, Waddy. It's the yield . . . We've got to take it through the tunnel—to the dam abutment."

Waddy stared at him. "Up in Kanab, they told me you were afraid to set this thing two miles away. And now you don't think it'll do the job right here?"

"There's a very good chance, even if it detonates, that the yield won't be anywhere near twenty kilotons. Before I ask you to help move it, I think you should know just what the problem is."

Waddy was already running through his mind what would be involved in carrying out Saul's bomb move. "Okay, tell me."

"This weapon uses a device called a neutron gun to initiate the fission reaction at detonation. I'm not at all convinced that the gun will fire this time because a piece of equipment in there called an event counter—a sort of timer—could have cycled through the whole firing sequence, setting off the neutron generator. The generator on this Soviet device can only fire once. And without the neutron injection there is only a primitive system in the core to deliver enough neutrons to get the process going, but not enough for full yield. The yield could be as high as seven kilotons, but it could also be as low as three. We're nearly a thousand feet from the dam face here, not a whole lot closer than where I intended to set a weapon of two kilotons that wouldn't have ruptured the dam. And even without the cofferdam as a barrier, now we've got an air connection instead of a water connection to transmit the shock wave." Saul paused again. "Waddy, we're seriously risking our lives to blow that thing up. Even without moving the device, there'll be a significant gamble when I start messing around in there and get into the rewiring. I'd just as soon take a little more risk and get it inside the dam abutment, where it'll for sure do the job. Even with only three kilotons, that dam would not be reparable. At least the whole right side would get blown out."

"What are *all* the possible results with this thing, Saul?" Waddy sat down in the mud and grinned up at his friend.

"A whole range of things *could* happen. To start with, no matter what I'm able to do in there, the detonation sequence may not be repeatable. Next, even if the event counter can be re-initiated, the capacitor discharge switch could fail to activate again. Third, we could have a detonation, but with only a yield of between three and seven kilotons. Finally, the device could function clear up to the design level if the neutron gun fires."

"Without burying me in a pile of physics, tell me what you think will happen."

Saul smiled. "Well, we're back to where we started, aren't we? I don't think we'll have the use of the neutron gun, so we're somewhere in the range of three to seven kilotons—at least that's what Kateryna said the testing of these devices taught them. Well, I really doubt what she said, based on the testing of some of our first generation weapons. I think there's a strong possibility of the yield being even lower."

"How much lower?"

"Probably less than one."

"What will one kiloton do—right here?"

"Not nearly enough." Saul smiled again, this time starting to laugh. "But, my friend, this hotshot physicist you're talking to is just not that certain about anything with this damned weapon."

"Let's move it, Saul."

Saul looked at his watch. "It'll be dark soon. The NRO boys sitting back there in their nice new building will get a peek at us, real time, in a little while. That old KH-11 is due over in a few minutes."

"But with their infrared supersnoop stuff they can watch us at night too."

"We have a little break there. During all the sessions out in that jail, while I was helping the Energy guys try to figure out how to undo our little project, I found out that they have a dysfunctional bird up there. It lost its infrared downlink. And a comment one of the guys made about its mission over the Urals clued me to the orbit schedule. Despite how much you may love the area, Waddy, this part of the world has not been of pressing concern to the National Reconnaissance Office. I guess they were simply unable, or unwilling, given the amount of nitrogen tetroxide and monomethyl hydrazine they would expend in the thrust rockets, to move a fully equipped bird over this area."

"No moon tonight, Saul. Be black as a well down here."

"Great. We'll sit here, looking busy, and wait until it gets dark . . . well, almost dark. We should wait until we have barely enough light to see without having to use a light. There's always the chance they have an aircraft up there looking at us, but I doubt it—not with the possibility of a twenty-kiloton detonation." Saul hesitated. "They could have a drone, but we'd hear it—I think." He looked at the muddy slope. "It's going to be touch and go carrying this thing through this crap."

"Aren't you gonna make the changes here?"

"Nope. Gotta do it where we finally place the bomb. When I'm through, that detonator circuit *will* be sensitive. Relax, it's not going to be a problem. We've just demonstrated that, right? Just have to make it over this mud pile and float it into the tunnel."

"What're they doing?" Lisa demanded as her cameraman decided to take a quick look over the edge of the rim. He knew that if the weapon went off he wouldn't have time to duck. His head would be fried before he could duck. He wished they were a lot farther away, but they were already near the place where the canyon turned, blocking the view down to the dam.

"It . . . it looks like they're moving it. Pretty dark down there now."

"Here, gimme that." Lisa peered through the telephoto lens. "They *are* moving it. Looks like they're heading over toward the river. The raft looks like it's down by the river too. Shit, what's going on? Here." She handed the Betacam back to the cameraman. "Get some of that."

The cameraman knew that Lisa had not the foggiest notion of the greatly reduced light-gathering ability of a telephoto lens in dim light. A videotape is nowhere near as sensitive as the human eye. He ran the Betacam anyway.

Lisa stared down into the darkening canyon bottom. What the men were doing just didn't make sense. The news reports from the Energy Department had made it very clear that any movement of the bomb could cause it to detonate. "They must be taking it over to the raft. That means they're . . . they're going to go into the tunnel!"

"Maybe they're going to float it downriver—so if it does go off, the dam won't be destroyed."

"Yeah. Yeah, that must be it," Lisa said, not fully convinced. "We gotta go down there and see what's going on. C'mon, let's go back and get one of those rowboats we saw in the pile. It's only three or four miles to where we can find a way down." The cameraman grumbled but started to pack up their gear. He knew that Lisa Montgomery was a very determined woman.

"Leave all the stuff here," Lisa commanded. "We don't have time, and I don't want (you) to carry all this crap down a cliff in the dark."

Saul and Waddy had a lot of trouble carrying the bomb case through the slime, up and over the cofferdam. Now they didn't have the water's buoyancy to help. Hump fifty feet through the slippery goo and set it down—carefully. Hump another fifty feet and set it down again—carefully. Up the slope of the cofferdam; at least a half-dozen stops and as many near-disaster slips; finally to the top. Even harder carrying it down the other side. Nearly an hour passed before the bomb case was resting on the floor of the raft.

"Waddy, I don't know," Saul said when he tried to see into the tunnel. In the almost-night, the black, rushing water disappeared into the blacker void in the base of the canyon wall. Saul was predisposed to claustrophobia in addition to the acrophobia he'd been reminded of on the mule ride. He was now having a lot of trouble with his bright idea. "You know, it'll probably work right here. Thinking about it some more, the yield is probably– –"

"Oh no, you don't. We're takin' that sucker in there. We've moved it a bunch already and nothin's happened. Relax, we've got a light."

Saul pointed the light into the gaping hole, shielding the lens from any overhead view. The beam was swallowed abruptly by the blackness, the swiftly flowing water seeming to just disappear into a bottomless nothing. Seeing where they had to go made it even worse.

"Let's do it, Saul. There's no problem."

Easy for you to say. I've not spent most of my life skunking around alone in the desert backcountry. Saul shivered and climbed into the raft.

The little raft was quickly caught in the current and swept into the tunnel, the air instantly becoming cooler as they entered the underground river. Waddy was on the oars with Saul perched behind him, shining the light down the void. Saul imagined he was falling into a deep, dark sewer beneath the streets of New York.

"Shit, this is weird," Waddy said in the darkness ahead. They floated along on the river, invisible beneath them. Saul was thinking about the tunnel growing smaller in diameter until the water would fill it completely. Intellectually, he knew that was impossible, considering the flows it had carried, but his mind made him think it anyway. His shivering grew worse.

The tunnel made a slight turn to the left. Desperately trying to control his fear, Saul made himself remember the drawings of the right diversion tunnel. *Yes, I know where we are.* He glanced back, now unable to see the faint gray spot of the tunnel entrance. *Like Jonah sailing to Tarshish. Swallowed alive.*

The tunnel took a jog around a huge mass of concrete, visible as a glistening bulk of gray in the cone of light. *The remains of the plug.* While they passed the broken concrete, the lantern beam revealed extensive erosion of the sandstone. Caverns a hundred feet deep disappeared back into the walls and overhead in the tunnel ceiling.

"Mother Earth taking back her canyon, Saul."

Saul thought of the violent, explosive flows the tunnel had carried. A chunk of rock from high overhead crashed into the river in the ink blackness behind them. "Sounds like she's still taking it back." He imagined the whole crown of the ragged ceiling crashing down.

The water driven deep into the sandstone from the many years of hydrostatic pressure was weeping out of the rock everywhere, running in rivulets down the seams and indentations in the walls and sprinkling into the river from overhead.

"This should be about it, Waddy. Let's pull over. Got to be sure not to go too far. We'd never get back against this current."

Waddy pulled to the left side and found an eddy pool where the wall of the tunnel had been deeply carved. "Hand me the light." He played the beam over the oozing sandstone.

"Saul, look up there."

A hundred feet above them a small tunnel opening emerged, barely visible in the flashlight's feeble shaft through the delicate rain. When Waddy moved the light across the cavern's ceiling, another hole appeared.

In his mind's eye, Saul leafed though the many diagrams of the dam he'd examined for so many days. "That must be one of the abutment adits from the dam. Yeah, it's the lowest adit. It went back about 400 feet in the rock. It went right over the spillway, and now it's been exposed. The adit connects to the network of galleries in the dam."

"We gotta get the bomb up there."

"It must be nearly a hundred feet, Waddy. It's not necessary. Even with only one kiloton, that's enough to do a fine job right here. That adit up there proves we're right at the abutment."

"We've come this far. Why don't we just take a little look around? Maybe we can find an easy way up into that tunnel. C'mon. It's worth a try."

Saul realized that no matter what he said, he would be unable to adequately communicate to Waddy the extent of the explosive force involved in what he casually described as *only* one kiloton—two million pounds of TNT. Concentrating on what the detonation would do, Saul was temporarily oblivious to his fear and the sounds of the dark river flowing through its tunnel.

"Come *on*, Saul. Just a little snoopin' around."

The voice echoing in the tunnel shook Saul back to reality. He remembered being told by the Energy people that the spillway repair adits had blown out during the flood. "Okay, I think we have one chance. It should be down just a couple hundred feet."

Waddy grabbed the two pieces of his climbing rope and they started down the sloping side of the tunnel. The river had massively hogged out a ragged junction as it split its flow between the two routes of escape; soon they were scrambling up the sloping bore of a side tunnel. They could feel warm air rushing down from above. It had to be leading out. Saul had never felt such elation.

Dim starlight greeted them when they climbed out of the earth. They could see the spectral outline of the crest of the dam and the canyon walls far above. Saul remembered the day back in February when he and Stan and Kateryna had stood at about this spot: on the transformer deck, below the multistoried superstructure of the generator building. In the near blackness he realized that the power plant building was gone. Everything was just gone. The penumbra of the lantern beam revealed what looked like a huge, grotesquely tilted block of concrete between the base of the dam and the river channel.

"Saul, look! Back there!"

Waddy was pointing the light at the face of the dam. The Bureau people had erected a scaffold and ladder up to the exit of the visitor tunnel, where only a small rectangular aperture in the face of the dam remained. The

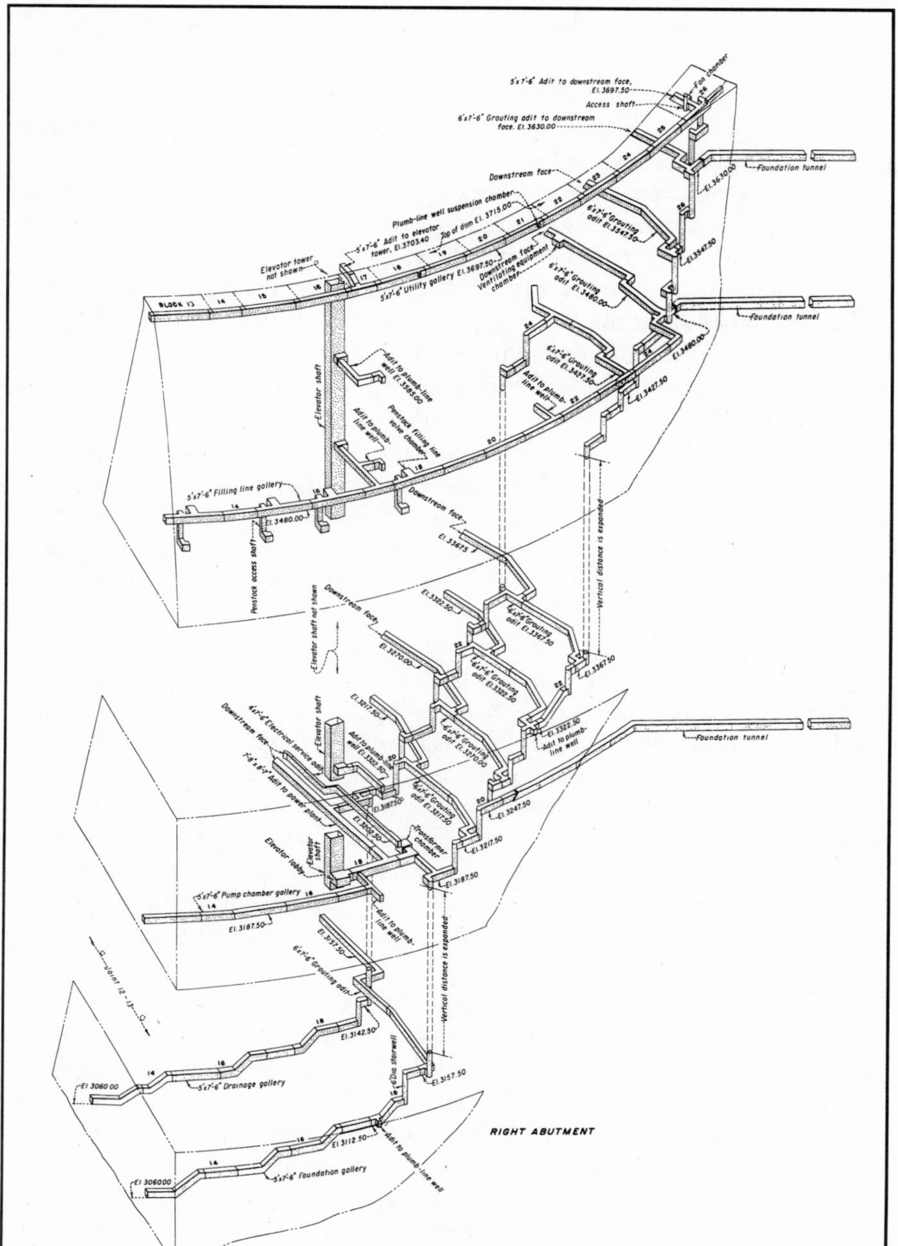

Dam galleries, right abutment.

bridge was gone, along with the powerhouse it had led to. Waddy played the light along the base of the dam. They could see the black, gaping holes of the eight penstocks—sheared off where they exited the wall of concrete.

They picked their way along the steep sandstone slope back to the dam and climbed the makeshift ladder. From the portal they walked down the long hallway into the dam, then stopped about 200 feet in, where the passageway turned to the right and lead to the little lobby at the base of the visitor elevator. At the turn, an intersecting hallway disappeared back toward the dam abutment. From their tour on St. Valentine's Day, Saul remembered there had been a steel mesh gate here. The gate and its frame were gone, wrenched out of the concrete walls by the water exploding through the galleries from the exposed river diversion tunnel. Waddy turned around and pointed the flashlight down to the elevator lobby. The gate was crumpled against the dead end of the lobby where the rush of water had deposited it.

The gate still had the dam gallery tourist display bolted to it. Waddy examined the diagram. "Look there, Saul. There it is—the foundation adit. It shows to be up just a little higher than we are here." Waddy studied the diagram carefully. "C'mon. Let's go back there."

Saul followed Waddy and the flashlight beam through the ink blackness of the gallery passageway, much narrower than the tiled visitor hall they had just left. He was getting claustrophobic again. The tunnel turned and then turned again at an intersection. Waddy stopped to make a scuff in the thin layer of wet sand on the floor.

"Better mark where we're goin' so's we don't get lost in here."

Saul shivered and followed Waddy up a spiral staircase. They went farther along a level hallway and up another spiral of stairs in a narrow cylinder through the concrete. Saul had completely lost his sense of direction. At each intersection, Waddy made a mark in the sediment glistening on the wet floor.

Saul was now conscious of a faint draft blowing from behind them. They were walking down a long reach of tunnel. He noticed that they were no longer surrounded by smooth planes of concrete but by rough surfaces of oozing and dripping sandstone. Waddy suddenly stopped, and Saul could no longer see the walls of the tunnel ahead of them. He crept up beside Waddy and then jumped back. The beam of light was shining down into the river flowing in the darkness nearly a hundred feet below them.

"There's the raft, Saul. This is it."

"I saw it," he said from his position now several feet behind. Saul was once again reminded of his fear of heights, now compounded by the strangling claustrophobia and the wet darkness. The mule ride out of the Grand Canyon had been a severe test, but at least it had been in the daylight and out in the open. He sat down on the floor of the adit, his back pressed against the cold, wet sandstone, his arms wrapped tightly around his knees.

"Hold the light." Waddy tied the rope together with a double fisherman's knot and tossed it over the edge. He took the light from Saul. "Shit. Too short." He stared down at the tiny rubber dinghy. "Here, take the end, I gotta go back down there."

"I can't get too close to the edge, Waddy. I just can't!"

"Just move over a couple more feet. I gotta be able to reach the end of the rope down there."

Saul inched closer to the precipice and took the end of the rope. Waddy and the dancing beam of the flashlight disappeared back toward the dam, leaving him alone in total darkness. He put his hand before his face, an inch away, but could see nothing. He could hear the river rushing past, far below the drop off just two slippery feet to his left. He sat motionless in the enveloping black, his back forced against the rock as tightly as the friction between the bottoms of his shoes and the wet floor would permit. His seat and his back were soaking wet. *Get back fast, Waddy. I can't take much more of this.*

An eternity passed until Saul saw the reflections of the light shining on the ragged ceiling of the tunnel. He was unable to look over the edge.

"Saul, I can't reach it."

Oh, God!

"You gotta get it lower," echoed from far below. "Just reach over the edge. That should be enough." Saul inched closer and stretched his arm as far as he could reach. There was nothing to grab with his free hand. Everything was smooth and slick.

"Not enough. Lean over the edge."

"I can't!"

"Yes, you can. Just get on your stomach and reach over the edge. That should be enough."

Saul laid flat, wetting his front side to match his back. He reached forward and skidded himself toward the edge until he could just see over. The flashlight beam gave glimpses of the black river and the huge ragged cavern sloping down—and under him.

"Little farther. I gotta be able to tie on the dinghy bow line."

Saul wriggled forward. The edge of the tunnel floor pressed into his chest. He could feel tugs on the end of the rope. "Shit, don't pull me over the edge!"

"Okay, haul it up," he heard after an eternity—the most recent eternity.

"What, the bomb case? Are you crazy?"

"No, the winch. I got the end of the winch cable tied to the bomb case."

"I have no leverage up here. I might drop it."

"Okay, hang on. I'm comin' back up."

Another aeon passed until Saul saw flashes of the light down the adit and heard Waddy's footsteps.

"Here, give me the rope and hold the light." Waddy stood on the lip of the precipice and hauled up the rope. "Now, give me a boost. And try to hold the light up there."

"Waddy, I might slip. I can't. What are you doing?" Saul's knees were shaking uncontrollably when he tried to stand up. He made it to his knees.

"You gotta get closer, Saul. Just press tightly against the wall and give me a step. I think I can reach it if I can step on your knee." Saul squirmed a half step closer to the edge and willed himself into a crouch. Waddy stepped up on his thigh and tugged on several of the many rock bolts protruding from the dripping sandstone overhead. The dam builders had even been concerned about the stability of the rock in the inspection tunnel. He finally selected one, out over the edge of the void. "That's a tight one. Should hold." He stepped down.

"Just a little closer, Saul. I gotta use both hands to tie the winch on. Hang on to my belt. Point the light farther out."

"I only have two hands." Saul really wanted to have one of his hands on the floor for reassurance. The ice cold knot in his gut demanded it.

"Well, use 'em. Grab my belt." Saul complied as Waddy reached out over the edge. If his weight pushed Saul along the slick floor, Waddy would plunge to the river. A Saul-eternity passed. "There . . . Got it." Waddy reached back for one of the other bolts and swung back into the adit. The winch hung from a piece of the bow line. "Well, let's crank it up."

Saul made himself think. "Shouldn't one of us go down there to keep it from swinging? The canister could hit the wall if it swings." Saul thought to himself about the unknown Soviet krytron-like switch and the reservoir of 4000-volt energy poised just above it, waiting to rush through the open krytrons to the detonators. *Maybe there won't be enough current without the krytrons cycling. Probably will be, though.* For the first time since they'd been volunteered down into the canyon, Saul fully appreciated—made himself appreciate—the risk they were taking. His mind focused on the delicate piece of electronic equipment nestled in the inner canister, next to the cable bundle leading to the detonators. The gas-filled switch, though understood exactly by Saul in general function and structure, was wholly unknown in its foreign details. Only the vagaries of a small piece of electronic hardware separated them from oblivion. In just a fraction of a microsecond, they would be reduced to subatomic particles, instantly comingled with companion fractured nuclei from the surrounding rock and concrete. What had been flesh and what had been stone would be identical in the multimillion-degree proximity of the fission energy release.

"Yeah, you're right. I'll go down and tie the rope onto the bottom handle to hold it steady while you crank it up."

"It's going to be a lot harder to lift, not being in the water. I won't be able to do it alone."

"Look, just get it started, runnin' straight up with no swingin'. I'll come on back to help you." Once again, Saul was alone in the dark.

"Isn't this great, Saul? Usin' the government's own equipment to make sure this little puppy gets to do its best job."

"Easy! Don't bump it!" Saul shouted when the bomb case appeared at the lip of the tunnel. They swung the steel cylinder over the edge and backed off the winch, easing the steel case to the floor.

"Okay, just a little more humpin'," Waddy said, catching his breath. "Gonna be a bitch gettin' this mother down those spiral stairs. 'Least it's all downhill."

In forty-five minutes, they were back in the visitor tunnel. "Hey, you brought up my tool boxes."

"One of us has to keep a level head," Waddy chirped.

"Well, you better hope mine's level when I go to work on this thing," Saul answered, watching Waddy's smile fade.

Saul examined the tourist diagram. "Okay, that looks like the spot. Doesn't show completely here, but I remember that right at this level the pump chamber gallery goes clear across the dam to the other elevator. If we go halfway, we'll be right in the transverse center of the dam: 100 feet from the reservoir face, 200 from the front, and about 150 feet above bedrock. Couldn't have designed a more ideal place to put this little piece of equipment."

Like most of the gates in the dam galleries, the one leading to the pump chamber gallery was gone, ripped from the walls and carried away by the violent rush of water. In their final haul of the bomb down the long corridor, Saul and Waddy were unconcerned with the several rest stops they had to make. They were nearly to their final destination: the end of a trip that, at least for Waddy, had started over a third of the way around the world.

"Okay, I'll pace it to the other elevator lobby—to be sure we're right in the middle."

"Waddy, it's not *necessary*."

"Humor me."

He was back in a few minutes. "Well, we're a little too close to the east side."

"Damnit, I'm not moving this thing another inch. Now, why don't you go get the tools while I try to get my head working right."

"Hold the light on the end." Saul used a ratchet wrench to twist the nuts off one end of the cylinder. Waddy, if not Saul, had nearly forgotten about the sensitive detonator circuit in their struggles to move the bomb case through the dam tunnels, stairwells, and galleries. Saul's hands were sweating when he removed the last nut and carefully jiggled the hemispherical cover off the studs at the end of the pressure case. He then went to work on the inner canister, now empty of its protective, and deadly, radioactive argon gas.

"Okay, hold the light real steady while I go over these drawings." Saul carefully examined his own sketches and the prints he'd received from the FBI. The latter were covered with notations in cyrillic. Saul read them easily, admiring their intricately and beautifully drawn schematics.

While Saul worked, regularly studying the drawings and the exquisitely organized maze occupying the inner case, Waddy stared at the flat-black-painted cylinder resting on the floor of the gallery. He thought back over how far they had come: Malta, the Black Sea, the Atlantic, back to California. Now it was time. *The river of my people will be free!*

"Bingo!" Saul's voice echoed down the narrow corridor. "The event counter has a reset circuit. Supposed to be a quarter-turn screw on the side." He bent down to look. "Yeah, there it is." He looked up at Waddy. "Ready? This is the moment of truth, my friend." Saul took several deep breaths, exhaling them slowly. *Electronics!*

While Waddy pointed the flashlight beam into the open end, Saul worked on the hundreds of millions of rubles' worth of precision equipment and materials inside the steel case. He labored very, very slowly. Deliberately. All fear was soon gone. He was back in his shop, working on one of his beloved cars.

"An alarm clock?" Waddy couldn't believe it. They only did that in movies.

"What'd you expect? Was I supposed to ask the Energy guys for a digital timer? We're supposed to be *de*fusing. No one would question us having a windup alarm clock since we're supposed to be on a time schedule. This little clock will complete the circuit just fine." Saul went back to work inside the nuclear components case, pausing occasionally to stop, think, and stare at the drawings.

"Boy, it's real hard to see in here. Point the light to the left."

"Saul, take a break for a minute."

"Yeah. I need a breather." He stood up to relieve his knotted back.

"Tell me, as simply as you can, what you're tryin' to do."

"It *is* simple. I'm just putting in a circuit to start the whole detonation sequence over, with the clock used to close the circuit. Trouble is, I have to be sure I'm in the right wire. I've told everyone all along that I'm not an electronics whiz."

Saul's last comment had not put Waddy at ease, and twenty long minutes passed with Saul in trancelike concentration on his work and Waddy finally in an equally detached reverie involving his land, his people, and his river.

"There, that's it. I got it. Hand me the voltmeter again. Yep, that should do it. Still a full charge across the capacitors. What time've you got?"

"Nine forty-five, nearly."

"Me too." Saul stood up, much relieved—physically *and* emotionally. "Okay, let's go. We've got exactly five hours."

"Aren't you gonna put the covers back on? And what about your tools?"

"Waddy, I don't plan to work on any more bombs, and that device just doesn't care if it has an end cover. C'mon."

Waddy didn't move. He stared rigidly at the cold, deadly weapon at his feet, its black form inert in the lantern beam now beginning to yellow from its continual use. "Saul, hold it a minute. While we're still here, standing right over this thing—here inside this big dam—tell me . . . just tell me . . . what's this thing gonna do? I mean, describe the effect when it goes off . . . We won't get to see it."

Saul smiled at his friend. He also appreciated the intense moment they were sharing, the near culmination of a long-held dream. He studied Waddy's face in the dim light, seeing a close friend but also realizing that their deepest thoughts and driving forces were so very different.

"Again, everything depends upon the yield—and if that switch works. Let's think positively. With a full, twenty-kiloton detonation, the fireball will be about 500 feet in diameter, I think. I don't really know, for sure, given the incredible mass of all this concrete, but the fireball will certainly extend outside of the dam. Everything—*everything*—within the plasma ball will disappear. Just beyond the fireball, the surrounding stone and remaining concrete will be melted. But it will be blown away by the overpressure wave, traveling at several thousand meters per second. It will nearly pulverize everything in the canyon—down into the bedrock and maybe back into the canyon walls. Contained as it is, the shock wave will be amplified. Small fragments of concrete and sandstone will be blown up and down the canyon and far into the sky. Just a crater, well down into the riverbed, will remain. You can scale down what I just described for a smaller yield. At the very least there will be nothing left of the whole middle section of this dam."

"A new Lake Powell," Waddy said. "Maybe nice rapids goin' in and out. Actually, it might be kind'a nice if some of this fucker remains—to remind people what was here."

"Time to go, Waddy. We need to get the hell down the river, and we may have to stop at the end of the tunnel and haul the raft down if there's anything left of the flip bucket."

Thirty minutes later, the little raft floated out the end of the ravaged tunnel, now completely free of any remnant of the kinetic energy dispersal ramp that had once graced its portal. By 2:45 in the morning, Saul and Waddy would be well up the Paria River from its junction with the Colorado at Lee's Ferry. The Paria led up into very remote country to the north.

* * *

The aluminum skiff floated down the dark tunnel through the west wall of Glen Canyon. A flashlight beam played off the glistening rock.

"Did you get all that going in?" Lisa called back to her cameraman. "The networks will kill to get their hands on this footage."

The cameraman was struggling to juggle the Betacam, the oars, and the wrenching claustrophobia in his gut. With its single light, the camera would pick up little other than reflections off the wet sandstone and the flowing water they were riding on.

Lisa called out suddenly from her perch in the front of the boat. "Hey! Hold it! Stop this thing. Pull over to the left." The Sony nearly went over the side as the cameraman struggled to pull the boat into an eddy pool.

Lisa was shining her flashlight up at the ceiling. "Look at that hole up there! And what's that thing hanging down from the ceiling?"

The cameraman looked up through the lens, twisting the magnification ring. "Hold your light steady, Lisa, the camera light isn't enough." The now unshielded lens was spattered with water from the gentle rainstorm in the tunnel. "It looks like a winch. Yeah, it's a winch."

"What's that?" Lisa was twenty-six years old and a public relations major. Except for some pieces of camping gear and her bicycle, her knowledge of things mechanical ended with her blow dryer.

"It's used to lift things."

"C'mon. They must have gone up there. We gotta find how they did it."

Lisa and the cameraman groped their way down the river tunnel, found the construction adit, then made their way out to the canyon. The brilliant canopy of stars that had invaded the evening through intermittent rain clouds was gone now, obscured by a solid cover that had moved over Manson Mesa and the canyon slicing through it. The dim sky abruptly ended at the outline of the crest of the dam and the canyon rims.

She played the flashlight beam over the shattered remains of the powerhouse, her mind holding only one thought. "Damnit, damnit! If only we had more light to show this. Except for maybe some government people, no one's seen what's happened. Can't you get *anything*?" she implored. "Maybe with the flashlight and the camera light we'll get it. Try." Lisa had been to the dam many times. She knew that what she was seeing was very, *very* newsworthy.

While Lisa pointed her light around the base of the dam, the cameraman noticed the only human exit from the place they were standing, other than the way they'd arrived. They were soon climbing up the ladder and into the hole in the dam face. Finding the gateless corridor at the turn in the visitor tunnel, Lisa started roaming around in the galleries and up a spiral stairway that she thought led to where they'd seen the winch. The cameraman finally convinced her to go back before they got hopelessly lost. It took them over half a cameraman-desperate hour to find the visitor hallway again. Lisa found another passage and then led the way down a long gallery that seemed to go across the width of the dam. After a few hundred feet, she called out.

"Look! Up ahead, on the floor!" They were soon looking down at a black cylinder lying on the wet concrete. Next to the cylinder were two large plastic tool boxes, a half globe of black-painted steel, a round stainless steel plate, and a collection of hex nuts and lock washers. Lisa peered into the cylinder with her light.

In a few moments, things began to register in the perceptive young woman's mind. "Look at that! A clock! Do you know what this means?" Lisa's patient porter was thinking only about their being in a tiny wet corridor in the abyssal center of a massive block of concrete—and standing right next to a hair-triggered nuclear bomb.

"Think about it. Those two didn't do this alone—I mean, without the government knowing. They must have half a dozen of those surveillance thingies up there watching. My God! Do you realize what's going on? Here, get a shot inside this thing. There's enough light with all that shiny metal and stuff."

The cameraman shivered and then got down on his hands and knees and ran about ten seconds of tape.

"We've got it *now*!" Lisa bubbled. "Let's get that tape back to the studio."

The cameraman was about to ask her how she planned to get back when Lisa crouched down beside him and again peered into the bomb case, pointing the flashlight closely at the face of the clock. She looked up at the cameraman, all excitement in her face gone, replaced with horror.

"What *TIME* is it!" she screamed.

The cameraman stuck his wrist under the flashlight beam. "I've got quarter to three."

* * *

"You think anybody will find the raft and the other stuff?" Saul asked while they picked their way up the twisting bed of the Paria River. During the past thirty minutes a steady rain had started to fall, quickly swelling the little stream's meager flow.

"Maybe an archaeologist in about a thousand years. Don't worry, I know how to hide shit where it won't be found."

"*We* should find a place to hide pretty soon. It's almost time."

"Saul, we're twenty miles away. Maybe about eight in a direct line."

"I don't think you understand. Come on. Under that overhang."

"What time you got, Saul?"

"Two forty-five, nearly. How about you?"

"Yeah."

"There won't be any danger from the radiation burst down here, but there will be some ground shock and the narrow canyons could concentrate things. For sure, some rock will be shaken loose from the walls in this canyon. We have to assume the worst case with that weapon."

"You mean the *best* case, don't you?" Waddy grinned as he followed Saul under the sandstone ledge.

At twenty-one seconds past 2:46 A.M., Mountain Standard Time, a thirty-two-volt-driven electrical current jumped across a metal-to-metal connection in a mechanical clock. Five years previously, the little alarm clock had been assembled by a twelve-year-old Indonesian girl in a sweatshop factory in Taipei. Past the clock connection, the current entered another piece of hardware, about fifteen years old, this one assembled in a sterile environment by a robotic machine operated by a highly skilled technician at a Most Secret, heavily guarded facility in Krazniarsk, Russia.

Once inside the second piece of equipment, the electrical pulse was acted upon by a remarkably sophisticated—for its age—and fail-safe redundant collection of electronic chips and circuits. As it had done eleven days previously, the event counter instructed a plutonium power cell to deliver a load of wattage through a step-up transformer to a bank of capacitors. But this event was unnecessary since the capacitors were fully charged. Eleven and two-tenths seconds elapsed—the capacitor charging time—before the counter sent a signal to a cold-cathode, ionizing gas-filled switch and junction where the 4,000-volt discharge pulse from the capacitors was to be divided into thirty-two branches. This time the pulse leapt across the radon-gas switch, with a rise and fall time of less than four nanoseconds (0.000000004 sec.), and split into the thirty-two branches, each controlled by a similar, but normally-open, krypton-gas-filled switch. Responding to instructions from the event counter, each of the krytrons cycled on-and-off several times in a period of less than seventeen nanoseconds to effectively compress the high-voltage current to a higher amperage: to provide more current for the electricity's intended task. Down the thirty-two, twenty-five-centimeter lengths of cable the divided and compressed surges of electricity went, the first krytron-switched pulses reaching the end of the line in two nanoseconds and each of the cables delivering its load of electrons at least as "simultaneously." The destinations were ninety-six detonators: three per lens of plastic-bonded high explosive. At least one of the detonators on each of the lenses had to activate—to flash from massive overloading by the compressed current. But seven of the hair-thin gold wires were already broken, victims of the many moves and rough handling the ADM had been subjected to over its lifetime, and two of the failed bridgewires were on pentagon number four, leaving only one to perform its crucial task. It was enough: the weapon designers' double redundancy was vindicated. Something slightly less than six nanoseconds later, each of the twenty hexagon-shaped and twelve pentagon-shaped blocks of high explosive, arranged in a perfect Buckminster Fuller sphere—like a soccer ball—were starting to explode. The explosion outward was irrelevant. It was the explosion inward—the implosion toward the materials spherically contained within the lenses—that was the HE's mission.

The finely-machined and precisely-fitted lenses were composed of a highly refined form of a commonly used military ordnance explosive (the Soviet equivalent of Octol), and they were sculpted from layers of slightly differently-composed materials that had progressively faster detonation speeds as the shock fronts moved radially inward. The incrementally advancing detonation speeds and carefully programmed spaces within the explosive materials served to direct the bulk of the thirty-two shock waves toward the center of the spherical collection of fissionable materials and their fission enhancers.

Ahead of the shock wave, the innermost surface of the high explosive material pressed against a thin layer of metal, dominantly composed of tungsten and placed there by the designers of the device because of its high rigidity and thermal properties and to protect the layer of the softer and operationally crucial metal just beneath it. The half-inch-thick beryllium "reflector" was a window to gamma and X-rays, but it provided a closed door to the flood of neutrons that would soon try to escape from the sphere. Next, the shock front would encounter a shell of uranium 238: the "tamper." While it was not a fissile material—its atoms could not split under a bombardment of neutrons as could its slightly lighter but natively much rarer relative, uranium 235—at the very end of the upcoming fission reaction, the heavier isotope would serve to contain the reaction for a few nanoseconds to permit the final, yield-doubling generation of fissions to occur.

Precisely concentrically levitated by a layer of polyurethane foam within the outer shells of tungsten, beryllium, and uranium 238, was the last assembly of materials that were the principal targets of the chemical explosive shock waves now progressing inward: six pounds of plutonium 239 and fourteen pounds of highly enriched uranium (92% uranium 235) were formed into two pairs of nesting shells, with a 1.85-inch void in the center. Had this been the most fission-efficient creation of the Soviet designers, a considerably smaller mass of these painstakingly manufactured and separated materials would have been used to produce the same yield. The two materials were at the center of the device because they were the only elements known to have the properties of being both fissionable by low-energy neutrons and stable at room temperature.

One and a half microseconds (1,500 nanoseconds, an eternity to the event counter) after it detected the successful detonation of all thirty-two high explosive lenses, and another microsecond before the outwardly-expanding gasses from the detonating explosive ended its life, the event counter performed its final act. It instructed a companion piece of equipment, the neutron generator, which was also located just out of the reach of the 21,000-feet-per-second rush of dissociating high explosive, to inject a load of deuterium through a still-intact conduit into the weapon's pit. The stream of "heavy hydrogen," each atom containing a valent-genderless neutron in its core besides the native, positively-charged proton, was targeted at the void in the innermost shell of plutonium. Although the HE implosion had already started, with its shock waves also traveling inward at 21,000 feet per second, the deuterium, traveling at a significant fraction of the speed of light, easily arrived in the pit first. Within the void was a lattice of polonium and beryllium—to provide an additional source of the operationally-crucial neutrons—with the interstices of the lattice filled with a compound whose molecules consisted of a radioactive isotope of the very light metal, lithium, and a hydroxide of deuterium.

By the time the chemical explosives had completed their work, the shock waves they had generated were traveling toward the center of the collection of spherical shells at nearly 28,000 feet per second and the assembly had been compressed to one third its original volume. While solid to human touch in their native states, all of the metals in the sphere were in fact nearly entirely composed of nothing, their constituent atoms separated by vast distances in relation to their sizes. Now under the effect of the chemical explosives, with the void volumes in the metals reduced by two-thirds, the pressure was over a million times the pressure of the earth's atmosphere at sea level, with the concomitant temperature many millions of degrees Centigrade.

So far, everything that had transpired had been mechanical, electrical, or chemical. But now the stage was set for the occurrence of a series of phenomena that are not entirely understood, despite the claims of most of the current generation of physicists and mathematicians who concern themselves with the fundamental nature of matter and energy. The stelar inferno in the core now contained a supply of "low" energy neutrons from the injected deuterium and the crushing of the polonium-beryllium urchin with its matrix of lithium 6 deuteride. Immediately adjacent to the neutrons was the surface of the innermost shell of compressed plutonium.

Among the stable chemical elements, plutonium 239, created from uranium 238, and its companion uranium 235, possess the unique property of being relatively weakly held together. If a sufficiently large collection of the atoms of either element are contained in a sufficiently-small space ("critical mass"), unattached excited neutrons in the vicinity may intercept the atoms. A penetrating neutron will then cause the plutonium or uranium atom to fragment into smaller elements, liberating either two or three unattached neutrons—and a quantity of energy that had theretofore been bound up in the uranium or plutonium atom's constituents. It is the exact *source* of that energy that is the subject of continuing debate among physicists. All that is known to an absolute certainty is that the net mass of the atom's fragments is less after the release of the energy—energy that had been bound up in the parent Uranium 235 and 238 since the elements were formed in billions-of-years and billions-of-light-years time- and distance-away supernovas.

The two or three freed neutrons—statistically more than slightly doubling the number of neutrons that existed before the fission—were now able to intercept other nearby fissionable atoms. In the initial low-energy-neutron-induced fission process—called a "generation" or a "doubling"—billions of atoms were involved. But the generations were not precisely predictable since either two or three neutrons were released each time and not all of them found fissionable targets in that generation. Additionally, the fission fragments (over 300 have been identified so far) started getting in the way. But, statistically certainly, the process proceeded at the rate of two exponential: 2–4–8–16–32–64–128–256–512–1,024–2,048–4,096–8,192–16,384–32,768–65,536–131,072–262,144–524,288–1,048,576, representing twenty generations: less than half the total number that were programmed to occur in the entire fission reaction currently underway.

With all the generations occurring within the same confined space, and with the geometrically progressing, massive amount of energy that was being released also remaining in the same space—about seven percent escaping in the form of gamma and x-ray electromagnetic radiation—the pressure and temperature also increased geometrically. "Slow" neutrons became "fast" neutrons, further increasing the number of atoms that were targeted in each generation. Temperature and pressure now exceeded that in the center of the sun.

Accordingly, within the tiny core of the Kharzov-series atomic demolition munition in the process of detonating, the temperature and pressure were high enough for two additional atomic events to occur among the elements strategically located in the munition's pit. One of the elements, the astoundingly versatile, lightest metal that has been long used pharmacologically because of its ability to provide relief to the sufferings of schizophrenics, had also been discovered by the Berkeley lab's nuclear schizophrenics to be of service to the mutually antagonistic and contradictory (physically schizoid) events needed in the core of a second generation atomic weapon. The lithium deuteride fissioned to helium, deuterium, and the triatomic isotope of hydrogen—tritium—releasing more energy:

$$3Li^6 1D^2 + n \rightarrow 2He^4 + 1D^2 + 1T^3 + 4.6 \text{ Mev}$$

and then in momentary imitation of the steady-state processes that have taken place in suns throughout the universe for the past 15 billion or so years, the deuterium and tritium came together to form more helium, liberating from atomic bondage about four times the energy that materialized in the fission reaction—thermonuclear fusion:

$$1D^2 + 1T^3 \rightarrow 2He^4 + n + 17.6 \text{ Mev}$$

The two core reactions did not produce more neutrons to join the mêlée in the fissioning plutonium and uranium, but along with the marginal neutron contribution of the polonium and beryllium urchin in the pit they created a sharp burst of energy to speed up the existing, critically important, initial neutron flux—the "boost." And it could have been a great deal larger if tritium had been injected into the core ahead of the stream of deuterium from the neutron gun. But not with this device. The mission of this atomic demolition munition demanded a shelf life and a predictable yield that the short-lived tritium would not permit.

The doublings continued at a fantastically accelerating rate, with the outer beryllium reflector keeping the legions of neutrons within the core where they would do the most good. But even the most sophisticated fission weapons, developed and tested over decades, cannot use all of their available plutonium and/or uranium. At some point the enormous amount of energy contained in the mass of fissioning material can no longer be contained. The explosion point begins to occur between the 53rd and 58th generations, depending upon the particular design of the device, its size, the means used to initiate the fission, the configuration of the fissile components, tamper, reflector, and many other factors. With the particular weapon located in the bowels of Glen Canyon Dam, number 55 was the last doubling. The reaction reached steady state as even the uncountable number of neutrons then available could not find enough targets to cause doubling number 56, which would have increased the yield of the weapon from approximately twenty kilotons to nearly forty. And even the last full doubling was permitted only by the presence of the inertial mass of the uranium 238 tamper that kept the core together for the ultimate yield of the weapon to increase from ten kilotons to twenty. Both a highly precise design and human and robotic fabrication perfection had been required to produce the predictable yield.

What had started out as a release of energy from a chemical reaction in the high explosive lenses—a violent enough implosion to crush a six-inch sphere of lead-dense material into the shape of a slightly oversized baseball—was about to reverse direction and proceed outwardly with an explosive force well over two million times greater than the initial event. Such is the difference between the forces chemically linking molecules and those contained within the atomic constituents of the molecules.

Besides the initial flash of very high frequency, short wave length electromagnetic radiation—the photons of gamma- and x-rays—that raced out of the device at a good fraction of the speed of light as the fission reaction rose to its peak, the vast bulk of the atom-released energy consisted of thermal radiation and the kinetic energy contained in the expanding shock wave. The medium of the shock wave—for a distance of three and one half feet—was air. Then the kinetic and thermal energy encountered a much more dense medium comprised of a chemically bonded assembly of sand, variously-sized gravel aggregate, pozzolan, cement, and dissociated water.

Over a period of more than two years, approximately 200,000 tons of the pozzolan had been hauled, truckload by truckload, 110 miles from a pumice deposit north of Flagstaff. Very nearly three million barrels of portland cement had been trucked 188 miles from the Phoenix Portland Cement Co. plant at Clarkdale, Arizona, fifty miles southwest of Flagstaff, where it had been manufactured from locally-available deposits of Redwall and Lakebed limestone, clay, and gypsum. The balance of the concrete constituents used in constructing the 9.25-million-ton dam and the adjacent power plant foundation had been assembled from water, and sand and gravel, transported from deposits located in the ages-old channel of Wahweap Creek, a small south-flowing tributary of the Colorado River about five miles upstream of the dam site. The concrete had been mixed and slumped into the dam's forms at an average rate of 335 cubic yards per hour over the two years, with production proceeding 24 hours per day, five to six days per week. The result of the effort by hundreds of workers and extensive assemblies of massive equipment was about to be disassembled in a much shorter time.

The overpressure/fireball front was traveling at 35,000 feet per second when it encountered the concrete wall of the pump chamber gallery at a location just a bit east of the midpoint of the gallery's traverse of the 300-foot-thick base of the dam. A small sliver of the radially-expanding, multi-million-degree wave proceeded westbound in the transverse tunnel and quickly overtook two 98.6°F assemblies, largely composed of carbon, hydrogen, and oxygen, which were traveling at about fifteen feet per second down the tunnel. Back at the air/concrete interface, the overpressure wave had paused not a measurable period of time when it entered the denser medium. The many chemical constituents of the concrete were immolated to incandescence in the thermal front as it continued to expand up, down, and sideways.

In the downward direction, the expansion of the fireball halted at a distance of 250 feet: 150 feet through concrete and the remaining distance into Navajo sandstone. Everything within that distance was converted from stable mass to several-million-degree-hot molecules and ionized atoms—and into nutrinos, hadrons, quarks, gluons, and numerous other defined and undefined subatomic constituents of matter that have been the object of close scrutiny by the Lawrence Berkeley Laboratory cyclotron physicists for nearly half a century. At the outer edge of the incinerated crater the sandstone was converted to glass, but the shock wave continued into the stone, pulverizing another 100 feet as its front proceeded in the direction of the center of the earth. It crumbled and then merely cracked the next 300 feet before it dissipated with only elastic deformation of the rock in the planet's huge, energy absorption sink.

Upward, the fireball consumed another 250 feet of concrete before the shock wave detached from the decelerated white-hot sphere and began its mechanical pulverization work on the remaining 350 feet of structure overhead. But this time the overpressure wave did not confront the ultimately unyielding mass of the earth. Rising skyward, it encountered less and less of the concrete as the dam cross section thinned. The wave progressively broke free into the air on either face of the dam, with the shock front only slightly affected by the gravity-induced force of the remaining mass of concrete. Fragments of the shattered man-made stone, from fine dust to Volkswagon-sized chunks, were propelled high above the rims of the canyon, the heavier ejecta soon falling back into the canyon/crater but the finer particles being carried high into the atmosphere by the surge of air that rushed in to fill the low-pressure void behind the column of debris and heated air. But because of the heavy rain now falling on this part of the Colorado Plateau, all of the debris cloud, much of it radioactive from the contained fission fragments of the weapon's core and other portions irradiated by the surge of high energy particles when the atom-fracturing process had reached its peak, was also carried back to the earth in the near vicinity of the dam. The rain and the river would soon carry all but the larger pieces of non-soluble material down the canyon to settle into the mud in the upper reach of Mead Reservoir. The soluble radionuclides: strontium, cesium, and iodine, dominantly, would be diluted beyond detection in the millions of acre feet of water standing behind Hoover Dam.

The sideways effects of the shock wave were much the same as those proceeding vertically. On the upstream side, the blast had merely 100 feet of concrete to disassemble, most of it consumed in the fireball and the rest carried away by the breakaway shock front, to be propelled over—but largely through—the cofferdam and then several thousand feet up the canyon. On the way by, the front vaporized the remainder of Powell Reservoir, which joined the rest of the material heading up the canyon. On the downstream face, the fireball barely broke through, but debris was fired well down the river canyon, ricocheting off the sides of the 600-foot-deep gorge. And before heading down the last fifteen miles of Glen Canyon, just a couple of hundred feet south of what had been the dam face, the shock wave encountered a large, tilted block of concrete that had only recently supported a 1.35 gigawatt hydroelectric power plant. Nearly all of the block joined that portion of the dam that was heading downriver. And lastly, on its way down the canyon, some of the air-transmitted shock wave slapped the canyon walls, contributing another layer of pressure on top of the now complicated series of waves expanding outward from ground zero through the Navajo sandstone.

With the escape of the fireball from the mass of the dam, the nuclear detonation displayed the normal air burst signature of a double flash of light. When the fireball cooled to 300,000°C and its rate of expansion was the speed of sound in air, the detaching shock wave heated the surrounding air to incandescence: the first flash. The hot air then absorbed visible radiation and the fireball could not be seen until the gasses cooled enough to permit visible light to escape: the "breakaway" point of the second flash.

On this early morning in an isolated and now deserted area of the Colorado Plateau, two pulses of orange-blue light lit up the western rim of the canyon high above the Paria River. Besides the distinct, momentary glow on the rock, the rain-saturated air in the canyon brightened over a period of several seconds, the pulses of light being refracted and scattered through billions of water droplets.

"The fireball broke out!" Saul yelled. "The gun fired! The ground shocks will hit next!"

Saul had not quite gotten the words out when the P wave arrived. Traveling steadily at an average speed of two and one-quarter miles per second through the nearly homogeneous sandstone, but reflected and refracted by faulting, seams, joints, shear planes, and density changes in the rock, the compression and dilation wave passed under the bed of the Paria River Canyon, followed shortly by the undulant S wave. The bed of the river canyon seemed to roll. It kept rolling, slowing, finally stopping after the surface-traveling Rayleigh and Love waves raced by. Time seemed to stand still. A few rocks that had broken loose from high on the rim thudded into the stream bed.

The expanding energy sphere had initially broken out of the debris at Mach 21, to head up and down the river gorge and over its rims, its thermal and mechanical work at the dam completed. Shortly after the passage of the overpressure front, air rushed in to fill the vacuum occupying its wake, in the process creating a reversed blast-like effect that carried hundreds of tons of debris up into the cloud rising in the rain above Glen Canyon. Meanwhile, the overpressure at the face of the shock wave rapidly lessened with the front's spherical expansion; but since it had gotten a very much faster start, it remained ahead of the sinusoidally-moving sound wave, traveling steadily outward at a mere 1,000 feet per second. Since the explosion had occurred in the bottom of a deep canyon, the sound wave disturbance would fade from perception by the normal human ear at a surface distance of approximately 50 miles. On this early rainy morning, none of the reporters who normally kept a vigil at the roadblock on highway 89 remained to hear the faint rumble from the north. A few people, still awake in Flagstaff, Kanab, and scattered places throughout the red rock country, did notice an odd double flash that lit up the cloudy night, followed by a slight tremble in the earth.

Eight and one-half miles from ground zero, both the shock front and the sound wave remained distinct. The first to arrive at the floor of the Paria

River Canyon, four miles up from its junction with the Colorado River at Lee's Ferry, was a jolt of wind, tapering quickly to a breeze that continued until the sound arrived: an intense roar, lasting several seconds before fading to a throaty rumble. For perhaps twenty seconds more, the dying breeze continued up the canyon and plunged from its rim, swirling the rain now falling as a fine mist. The air was again deathly still. A few more rocks bounded down the canyon slopes and plopped into the stream.

Waddy stuck his head out from under the ledge. "Son of a bitch! How big you think it was?"

"Had to have been the full twenty kilotons. At much less, I don't think the fireball would have broken through the dam." Saul followed Waddy out.

"I sure would like to see what it looks like up there," Waddy said when they headed up the canyon. They had to wade the calf-deep water that filled the bottom of the gorge.

"We'll find a newspaper when we get up out of here. There'll be plenty of pictures in the papers. And by the way, how do you like being dead?"

Waddy smiled at his friend between glances upward to watch for rocks. "You know I'm gonna come right back here after the heat's off."

"I know."

"The President must be pretty confident none of us will ever say anything."

"He knows we won't."

"Pretty smart *pahana*."

"Yeah, Waddy, a pretty smart *pahana*."

Fifteen river miles northeast of Lee's Ferry, up the twisting gorge of Glen Canyon, the Colorado River abandoned its temporary passage through the canyon's western wall, the route now blocked, and began to descend a cataract of warm, freshly fractured stone to a depression in its ancient bed. A small lake soon formed, the water heated several degrees as it patiently removed a transient source of energy from the stone. Then the river spilled down another ragged fall to continue its passage from the alpine mountains of its birth—to continue its long and winding, its fierce and gentle, its ageless and relentless, journey to the sea.

GENTLE CANYON

1

Colorado River, April 19

The journalist and his assistant got out of the raft and helped the boatman drag it up the long, broad beach on the inside of the turn in the river. Up the beach and running down the length of the amber-colored reach of fine, soft sand, a thicket of willows and chokecherry bushes grew profusely. Behind them, stands of hackberry, box elder, and cottonwood trees stood in clusters along the base of the high orange cliff. Across the river, a huge sandstone monolith dominated the canyon's opposing wall. *This is the place,* the journalist smiled to himself. It looked exactly like the view he'd seen in the simulator back at the studio. He could have run the whole river in the simulator, but for his story he wanted to actually experience the canyon as it had been before the dam was built.

High overhead a raven soared, its tail and wing feathers spread in the thermal rising from the depths of the canyon, already hot on the brilliant early spring day. Near the river's edge in the reed-choked water, he saw what looked like a large humpbacked fish wriggle out of the shallows and disappear into the red-brown current. Then the journalist's attention was again drawn upward in search of a high-pitched call he heard—not the deep croak of the raven but a sort of *kaaak-kaaak-kaaak* sound, shrill and quavering as it echoed in the deep canyon. It seemed to come from somewhere on the pinnacle centered on the outside cliff.

"Boy, look at that old raft." The boatman walked over to the scarred and scraped hypalon inflatable resting on the sand. Patches overlaid patches around the navy gray perimeter tubes, nearly hiding the distinctive yellow stripe that girdled them. "What an antique. And look at them wooden oars. No way you'd get permission to cut pieces of lumber like that now."

"He's here!" the journalist said excitedly. "That's got to be his boat." He had worked for nearly a year to arrange this meeting, but the man he wanted to talk to had refused to even discuss doing the interview in the simulator.

"What a delightful place this is," he thought out loud. He stared across the river at the sandstone wall rising above the opposite bank, trying to find the source of the intermittent but persistent calls he heard from high on the cliff. Broad, vertical streaks were faintly visible on the bright orange surface of the rock. The journalist's contemplation was interrupted by his assistant nudging his arm.

Three people walked down the beach toward them. A woman, about sixty years old, strode briskly ahead of two younger men. She was slim and moved gracefully—like a dancer, the journalist thought. Her thick straw-blond hair contrasted sharply with her tanned olive-toned complexion. One of the men was about ten years younger than the woman and very tall, with deep auburn hair and dark, faintly Asian almond-shaped eyes, while the other man appeared to be in his late thirties, shorter, thickset and broad shouldered. His heavy thatch of hair, more blond than his closely trimmed beard, complemented a ruddy, freckled face, grooved with deep smile lines. While the group walked toward them, the journalist's attention was fixed on both the woman's and the younger man's faces. They each had the most startling bright blue eyes he had ever seen.

"Hello, we've been looking for you," the woman said. "I'm Sofiia Wallach . . . my son, Anatoliy, and this is Richard—Richard Bellamy," the woman nodded to the younger and then the older man, respectively, while they all exchanged hand shakes. "Have you enjoyed your trip through the canyon?"

"It's been lovely," the journalist said, uncomfortable under the woman's steady gaze. "You must be . . . are you Kateryna Bellamy's daughter?" Sofiia's smile widened, she nodded. "And you must be Kateryna's son," the journalist said, turning to the older man.

"Yes, Stanley Bellamy was my father."

"Will you join us in our camp? We're back in there," Sofiia said, gesturing toward a cluster of trees above the dense thicket of bushes lining the beach at the foot of the canyon wall. After they started up through the soft, amber-brown sand, the journalist thought he heard music coming from the direction of the cliff.

They pushed their way through the thick tangle of willows and chokecherry bushes, the latter already blossoming with promise of the masses of bitter, pungent berries they would host early in the fall; then headed toward a big grove of cottonwoods, box elders, and hackberry trees standing near the cliff. The journalist noticed a pair of squirrels leaping from branch to branch in the hackberries, chasing each other through the trees that were their favorite source of food.

The visitors followed the others into a high, narrow slot in the canyon wall. Upon entering, the air suddenly cooled; the music grew louder, the sharp notes echoing from somewhere down the stone corridor. *It sounds like a quartet of flutes.*

They stopped at another stand of trees: smaller than the ones in the big grove at the entrance but displaying the most brilliant iridescent red blossoms the journalist had ever seen. A puff of breeze soughed through the delicate branches, waving their heart-shaped leaves. *Those must be Judas trees.*

The simulator sure didn't do them justice. And look at all the little blossoming hedgehog cactuses.

Following the others, turning to the right, the journalist found himself in a huge amphitheater, half bathed in sunlight. He stopped abruptly, startled by what he saw. The simulator had failed again. It hadn't even come close to capturing what he was seeing. From high above in the vaulted ceiling, a thin stream fell into a pool under the overhang of the great cavern. Along seeps in the back of the grotto and out into the sunlight, the walls were covered with a profusion of glistening mounds of moss, delicate ferns, and a riot of flowers—mostly bright yellow mimulus. The notes of the flute were now loud and sparkling, their echoing effect resonant, seeming to come from all directions. The aeolian voices suddenly stopped, but a few moments passed before the chamber was silent.

Near the center of the cavern a large boulder rested in the sand. The journalist saw an old man sitting down, leaning against the boulder. A small boy was playing at his feet. The old man struggled to get up when the group entered the amphitheater, and as he did so the journalist saw that he was Native American, about five-seven: he wore only a sort of loincloth, made of rough cotton, and a finely woven headband—light blue, tan, and black in color. His hair was snow white, in bangs beneath the headband, falling nearly to his shoulders on the sides. In the back it seemed to be tied up in some way. The only other clothing the man wore were a pair of sandals that appeared to be made of course, twilled plant leaf. About his neck a simple lignite medallion was suspended from a choker of stones and beads which contrasted sharply with the deep reddish nut-brown color of his skin. The journalist noticed many long-healed scars. A particularly large one extended across the right side of his chest.

"Good afternoon. I'm Waddy. Have a seat." The journalist shook the old man's hand. It was thin, the grip weak. "This is my grandson, Tuvi." The little boy smiled shyly and stared unblinking at the journalist. A duplicate of the old man's headband was the little boy's only clothing.

"Mr. Temeseh, please continue to play, I– –"

"Waddy. Just Waddy."

"Very well, Waddy. I . . . We didn't mean to interrupt your playing."

"That's it for today. Hard to do anymore with the teeth I have left." Waddy laid the flute on top of the boulder, then resumed his seat in the sand. The journalist thought the flute looked very old.

Everyone sat down in the warm sand between the boulder and the shaded pool. A calliope hummingbird darted through the cavern, pausing before the monkey flowers along the sunlit seeps. The thrum of the bird's wings blended softly with the delicate patter of the water falling into the pool.

"Did you see the peregrines up there? Outside—up above the river?" Waddy asked the journalist.

"The what?"

"Peregrines. Peregrine falcons. They've got their aerie on a ledge up on that pinnacle across the river. The falcon always makes a racket when a raven or an eagle flies by or when someone's out on the sandbar. Her tiercel's usually out grabbin' cliff swallows. I like to watch'im catch those cliff swallows—hell of a show."

"Yes, I did hear something, but I didn't see anything but a raven."

"Hard to spot 'em on the cliff if you don't know where to look." Waddy concentrated again on the stream falling from the roof of the cavern. "Had a good rain couple'a days ago. Still some runoff from the upper canyon." He gestured toward a notch in the rock, high in the ceiling of the grotto. "I'd like to go on up the steps out there to take a look, but . . . guess I can't do that anymore. You fellas ought'a try it, though."

"You mean the Anasazi steps?"

"Hisatsinom. They were Hisatsinom."

"Mr. Temeseh . . . Waddy, as I told you, our com net is doing a story on the destruction of the old Glen Canyon Dam. It's a matter of continuing public interest, especially now with the fiftieth anniversary this coming August. I won't bother you with rehashing what has been well documented. Just a few questions."

"Okay, I said I'd do it. But I don't wanna talk all afternoon. I'm kind'a tired."

"Sir," Sofiia interrupted, "please don't be too long with your questions. Waddy's had a long day." From the look on the woman's face, the journalist realized she'd cut him off summarily at any time.

"Go ahead, my friend," Waddy smiled. "Nice place to talk. Very appropriate. Have at it."

The journalist gathered his thoughts. He stared up at the sculpted sandstone towering overhead. As in most places throughout Glen Canyon, the bright orange rock had the beginnings of dark streaks running in parallel columns down its face. Below the overhead notch, on either side of the thin stream of water, the rock was a glistening indigo, brightening to cobalt and then to white on its dried edges. Whiffs of musty dampness drifted out of the shade into the harsh dryness of the sunlight.

"It's been over forty years since you were last interviewed, hasn't it?"

Waddy also took his time responding. He examined the back of his hand, then slowly nodded his head. "Yeah, I guess that's about right."

"You have said—in your initial interview and the later one—that Dr. Kalinik insisted that you go on down the river to safety while he worked alone to defuse the bomb. It detonated while he was working on it. Some years later, the government announced that you and the others would not be prosecuted for anything having to do with placing the bomb in the lake and all the rest. Well, what I want to ask about . . . if I could, that is—you know, our viewers' interest in anything having to do with this canyon is insatiable." *Shit, how do I get into this without offending him?*

"Go on, spit it out."

"Well, it's been so long and . . . and you're– –"

"I'm gettin' real old, and when I die there'll be no one left. Right?"

"Uh, I don't mean to . . . well, yes, sir." *Damnit!*

"And you want to know if I have anything to add?"

"Yes. Yes, that's it—some more details, particularly about Dr. Kalinik and what he was doing. In your interviews you said that he had to work on the bomb out of the direct sunshine because the electronic components were very sensitive to heat, making the work even more dangerous. So, he had to work in the boat, in the only available shade right next to the dam. Also, you wouldn't have to take the risk of moving the bomb onto the cofferdam."

"Yeah, that's about what I said."

"Well, can you tell me anything more? Perhaps some more detail to flesh out those last minutes with Dr. Kalinik, your conversation with him . . . It must have been very intense. Some personal things, perhaps, that our viewers might like to hear about—things to include in our narrative when we visit his memorial at the dam site." The journalist's assistant was busy with his surroundcam, capturing the entire scene and the conversation.

Waddy leaned back against the boulder, his fingers laced behind his head. For nearly a minute he stared up at the finely sculpted patterns of cross-bedded sandstone, studying the relentless, patient efforts of Mother Earth to reclaim her canyon. "Yeah, we blew the fucker up."

"I'm sorry . . . you *what*?"

"I said, we blew it up."

"You . . . you *purposely* set off the bomb?"

"Yeah, we hauled it into the dam, Saul set a clock in the detonator circuit, and we got the hell out. Went off while we were walkin' up the Paria."

"You took the bomb into the dam? How could you? I mean, weren't the detonator circuits very sensitive? In everything that was reported, there was no question about that right from the beginning."

"Yeah, it was pretty hairy—'least I thought so at first. But ol' Saul, he didn't think there was gonna be a problem, so we just did it."

"How did you manage such a thing?" The journalist and his assistant stared at the old man, along with Sofiia, Richard, Anatoliy, and the boatman.

"Floated down through the river tunnel, then winched the bomb up into another tunnel that went back into the dam. Set it right in the very heart of the sucker—right down near the bottom. Perfect spot."

The journalist thought for a moment. "Yes, early on there was discussion about how . . . well, how completely the dam was destroyed. But right from the beginning, experts assumed that he had to work out of the sun right next to the dam, which you later confirmed. Also, the consensus was that the device must have been of a larger yield than had been supposed. But I don't recall that there was ever any suggestion that it had been moved from behind the dam."

"Well, we did a good job, didn't we?" Waddy smiled. "I mean, ain't hardly shit left, is there?"

This is absolutely amazing. "You said Dr. Kalinik used a clock?"

"Yeah. Just a plain old-fashioned windup clock. Feddies didn't think to question Saul havin' an alarm clock in his personal gear. Pretty smart man, ol' Saul. What you *pahanas* call American ingenuity, right?"

"Then you escaped down the river?"

"Floated right on out the tunnel and down to the Paria. Buried the raft and the rest of the crap near Lee's Ferry—above Lonely Dell. No one's found it yet," Waddy chuckled. "*Pahana* anthropologists . . . Anyway, we were climbin' up Paria Canyon when the sucker went off." The journalist was about to ask what happened next—where they went—when Waddy continued. "Tell ya' what. I'll just tell ya' where we hid the raft. You fellas go on down there and take a good look at the stuff we left—lot of it is Saul's—that'll prove he was with me. We just had too much shit to haul clear on up the Paria. I'll draw a little map for ya', later on."

"That would be wonderful, Mr. Te . . . Waddy." *This is going to be outstanding!* "So, how did you . . . Where did you go?"

"Snuck into Escalante. Got ahold of Malcolm, and he arranged for us to be picked up. Went to his place in the Indian Ocean. Real nice spot."

"Then where did Saul Kalinik go? . . . All these years . . . he's been remembered for having taken a huge risk—risking his life to save the dam, but losing." The journalist had recovered enough to begin to see the humor in it all. "That big monument the Park Service erected . . ."

"Yeah, told Saul about that. He got a big kick out it. Now, with your story, the environmental groups'll prob'ly wanna put up a bigger one. Anyway, Saul moved to Ukraine, where he lived out his life. In Lviv. That's in the foothills of the Carpathian Mountains. Beautiful country, Ukraine . . . Malcolm set up everything. Sofiia's mother, Stanley, Malcolm—we all went to visit there a lot of times. Saul married again and had another family." The journalist and his assistant were stunned. So were all of Kateryna's progeny sitting around the circle. The boatman was getting bored.

"When did he die?"

"Let's see," Waddy hesitated, distractedly concentrating on a little crevice in the jumble of rocks in the back of the cavern where he knew one of the canyon's unique rose-colored rattlesnakes liked to coil up and doze during the day. "It's been nine years. Yeah, Saul died nine years ago. He was ninety-five. Malcolm, Stanley, Kateryna, and I—we all saw him together—the last time, about, oh, eighteen years ago—just before Malcolm died."

"But . . . but Saul Kalinik had a family—I mean, his first two children.

They lived in Israel, as I recall. Didn't he ever contact them?"

"Sure. Saul went to Israel a lot. And they went up to Ukraine."

"But, how could this have been kept . . . well, not revealed all this time?" Sofiia, Anatoliy, and Richard were looking intently at each other, shaking their heads.

"He pretty much kept his mouth shut. That's one of the reasons I always liked ol' Saul. Same with his family. So now I suppose you want to know why I'm telling you this?"

"Well . . ."

"The last time I saw him—when we all visited there—we talked about tellin' the story. Saul just said that after he died he'd leave it up to me. His family, Malcolm, Stanley, Kateryna—they all agreed."

"So why *are* you telling us? After all this time."

"Don't know, really. Guess it's 'cause my time's so short now, an' . . . I guess it's time, considerin' how well-loved this canyon is, that people know that it'd still be flooded 'cept for what Saul—and someone else—did on *purpose*. The world should know that just *one* time—*once*—one of those damn bombs got *intentionally* put to a *good* purpose."

"This . . . this is all quite a revelation, Mr. Temeseh."

"Waddy."

"Right. Waddy." The seasoned journalist didn't know what to ask next.

"Your next question is, 'did we act alone, Saul and I?' The answer is no, we did not. Well, we physically acted alone, but the inspiration—let's say the motivation—came from somewhere else."

"Who?" the journalist asked cautiously.

"The President."

"The President of the United States?" *My god!* The journalist tried to remember who had been president in 1994. He was drawing a blank, but he remembered a detail. "He was the first one who . . . it was his reelection inaugural. Just a ten-minute ceremony in the Oval Office instead of the scores of millions they spent back then celebrating reelections—you know, the parades and parties and all the crap. I remember the story now. At the end of it there wasn't even a speech. He just said, 'Now, let's get back to work.' There were highway signs and whatnot all over the place after that—with his picture and the comment from the end of the swearing in . . . Uh huh, he was a smart one, all right."

Waddy thought back to that day a half a century ago in the basement of the White House. *Yeah, a REAL smart* pahana. "He gave us the choice of sittin' in jail all our lives or takin' the risk of tryin' to touch off the bomb. Easy choice—for me, anyway." More stunned silence. Sofiia, Anatoliy, and Richard had never heard a word about anything Waddy was saying.

Shit, what a story! "But how could he have made such an arrangement?

How could such an explosive thing be kept secret?"

"Because it was just the three of us—me, Saul, and the President. He came up with the idea and we did it."

"But . . . this is incredible! Why would he sanction—ask you to do such a thing?"

"Never told us. He must have had his reasons, just like we had ours. I'd say his reasons are pretty clear now."

"You mean the disarmament?"

"Yep. That and the love affair you *pahanas* been havin' with this canyon over the last fifty years."

The journalist remembered more. "Right after the dam was destroyed, he *did* launch his campaign in the U.S., in the old United Nations, over in Russia," he thought out loud. "I guess the early successes got him reelected." The journalist stretched his memory to recall all that he'd read about the big disarmament push that had begun back in the mid '90s. Every nuclear weapon in the world had been gone by 2015. Laws had been passed throughout the world making it a capital crime to even possess fissionable material.

"How soon did you come back here after the detonation?" He had to make the best of a few more questions. The old man was getting tired, and he could see that Sofiia was getting antsy.

"Helped out with Malcolm's projects for a while. Had a couple of my own . . ." Waddy stared up at the vaulted ceiling again. "I came back here for a visit the third year after it blew up. In those early years, the Park Service ran everybody outta the canyon. Too dangerous, they said, 'cus'a the rock slides and all the quicksand. Worked out fine for me, though. Nobody was down here in those days. Spent most of every year down here 'til they finally found me—spotted one of my garden terraces. By that time I guess a lot of people sort of thought we were heroes, Saul and I. You know the rest."

"Where did you live? I mean, you've said you came back here; but, I mean, have you been here all along?"

"Oh, after I went over to Malcolm's place, I moved to Ethiopia for a while—it's close by, just over in Africa, and Malcolm liked to go over there occasionally. Real nice country, Ethiopia . . ." Waddy smiled and went back to studying the fluted and sculpted surfaces of orange rock soaring above the cavern.

"Why Ethiopia?"

"Just a real pretty place, that's all. Real pretty, in more ways than one. Sofiia, can we have some lunch, I'm starvin'."

"I think that's enough for now," Sofiia said to the journalist. "Waddy will want to take a nap after lunch."

"After I snooze a little bit, I'll draw your map and then let you in on some details about what Malcolm and the rest of us were up to. You might find it interesting. But first, I gotta have somethin' to eat." Waddy retrieved the flute and settled back down against the rock, one ankle resting on the other knee.

***

Waddy watched the boatman organize his raft. The canyon floor was moist and cool, contrasting sharply with the yellow-hot splash of sun, high on the pinnacle across the river. The falcon was upset again. "You folks gonna head on down right away?"

"Yes," the journalist answered, shaking Waddy's hand. "We want to get some shots of the restored ruins, and tomorrow we're looking forward to seeing the detonation site. What do they call it now? Lake Powell?"

"Yeah, that's what most call it. Not on the official maps, though," Waddy smiled. "And I hope you enjoy the best rapids on the river—the one goin' into the lake and below the old power plant site: the Carl T. Hayden Memorial Falls and Floyd's Run."

"The simulator did show big rapids going in and out of the crater. Didn't see any evidence of the dam, though. Even the power plant foundation is nearly gone; just some rubble in the falls below the pool."

"Yeah, twenty kilotons," Waddy mumbled.

"What did you say?"

"Nothin', just talkin' to myself is all. Old men do that a lot."

"What you told us last night. Whew! The rest of those Soviet nuclear weapons. None of the things you described has ever been made public."

"Yeah," Waddy said, staring down the river, remembering. "Be sure to watch for the eagle aerie at the dam site. It's on the lip of the tunnel up on the right wall—one of the old inspection adits in that little piece of concrete that got rammed back in the wall up there. Guess the Park Service's gonna knock it down, though; too much of a hazard, they say, but the historians are goin' bonkers about destroyin' historic sites . . . Perfect spot for the birds too. But they'll just build another nest in the rest of the tunnel that goes back into the sandstone."

"Waddy, there's one other thing I almost forgot. Back at the time, a TV reporter and her assistant disappeared. Their camp was found on the west rim, a couple of miles up from the dam site. Did you see them?"

"Before we moved the bomb out from behind the dam, while we were waitin' for it to get dark, we did see somethin'. A couple'a flashes from up on the rim. Must'a been off a camera lens. We figured it couldn't be government people, bein' so obvious, so we just went ahead after it got too dark for anybody to see what we were doin'. Had'ta been just somebody snoopin'. Guess they must'a been peekin' over the rim when the bomb went off. Big mistake."

"But no trace of them was found up there."

"Maybe they followed us down to the dam. That was a real big mistake. See what your *pahana* ambition and greed does to people?" With the information the journalist had gotten in the past day, he knew exactly what the old man was talking about. Waddy looked at him steadily, then gave him a big grin and a wink.

"Have fun, you fellas," he said as the boatman pushed their raft into the warm, milky-brown river current. "There ain't gonna be any more interviews," he shouted after the retreating boat. "You got an exclusive. And don't forget to dig up the dinghy and stuff."

Waddy went back into Music Temple. He was alone when he walked around the pool and back to the very farthest recess in the cavern. Sofiia, Richard, and Anatoliy had taken the boat across the river to show Tuvi Hidden Passage. After lifting out a few slabs of sandstone, he reached down and removed the lid from an old kiva jar. Inside, he placed the little bone flute and another prayer stick to lie next to a delicate and very old, feather *paho.* He sprinkled the collection with some white corn meal. *Twenty seasons I spent snoopin' around in here before I found this. One of the old people really didn't want it found.* Waddy sat in the sand for a few minutes, quietly said some words, then sealed the lid with a mixture of piñon pitch and cotton wadding. He carefully replaced all the slabs and rocks. *Nobody'll find it now—'cept maybe an archaeologist in about a thousand years.*

"Waddy, *please* come back with us to Stony Ridge," Sofiia pleaded. "Mother would so much like to see you, and . . . there may not be another chance."

"You have to see what we've done with the vineyards. The latest *meritage* is outstanding," Richard said. "Tolya and I are very proud of what we've done. So is mother."

"And so is *my* mother," Anatoliy said, giving Sofiia a little squeeze.

"All the children would love to go riding with you," she said.

The old man hesitated. "Don't have a passport. They wouldn't let me in. It's been years since I was out there." He had a feeling this would probably be his last spring in the canyon. The remaining time in this most special place was very precious to him.

"I'm sure we can arrange something. Right, Richard?" Sofiia said in a convinced way.

Her half brother nodded. "Sure. We're pretty well connected in our country. Won't be a problem."

Waddy thought of California—so many thoughts over so many years. "Glad your flag is accurate again. Took a long time."

"Yes, the grizzlies are well established now in the Sierra and up in the northern forests. Hasn't been a problem since we got the last of the ranchers off the public lands. Just the other day there was a report of several bears feeding on a whale carcass on the Humboldt coast."

"That little red star on the flag is appropriate, too," he winked at Richard.

Richard laughed. "We're not that bad, Waddy—except maybe Berkeley, of course."

He looks just like Stanley when he smiles. He thought again about Kateryna; about Stony Ridge, rides with the children, the redwood grove. "You're right, the time *is* almost gone. I'll go back with you. I need to visit with Malcolm and Stan too." He thought of the quiet meadow near the lodge, where the two old friends rested in the shadow of the great trees.

"We can go for lunch at the Cactus Club," Richard suggested.

"Damn, is that place still there? I thought the university would have condemned it by now. Almost had it surrounded the last time I was out there. Those people still givin' the club a hard time?"

"Nothing's changed," Richard said, "and the government did try to condemn the property, saying it was needed for the university. Father's idea a long time ago put a stop to that, though."

"What? What did Stanley do?" Waddy grinned, very interested.

"I don't know how long ago it was. Had to have been back before you even met him. He advised the club that it should convey away the property to all the members, all their immediate and distant family, and even a whole bunch of other people. Everybody was deeded a couple of square feet—thousands of conveyances. Well, by the time the California Republic tried to condemn the property about forty years later, the deeded properties had passed into the hands of heirs and been further conveyed or given away, with the owners scattered all over the world—hundreds of them untraceable. The government even tried a quiet title action, but the legal costs were getting astronomical and auditors questioned the propriety of the whole thing. So they finally had to give up. Right now, the club is an enclave wholly within the campus; and what's really great, the university has to keep a road through the campus for access—what the lawyers call a 'way of necessity.' It goes right to that great big parking lot. The club still keeps lines painted on old-style asphalt—like there were still automobiles driving in to park. It's just great. They hate us more than ever."

"Good old Stanley. Always knew he was a smart *pahana.*"

"I've got another idea," Richard said excitedly. "We'll take *Samora* out. The weather has been lovely, and mother said just the other day that she'd like to do that. She and father spent so much time aboard her."

Richard had inherited his father's love for the old Renslaer yacht as well as his love of sailing. *Samora* was tenderly cared for, with a ready contingent of talented crew always available to sail the grand old lady. Her amber varnish and polished brass gleamed, her teak decks were stoned to a smooth milky gray, and her topsides glistened a glossy black, perfectly complementing her suit of tanbark sails. She was the undisputed queen of the bay.

"No spinnaker, though," Waddy laughingly chided. "Too much wind on the bay. Scares the shit outta me."

"Okay, no spinnaker," Richard smiled, shaking his head. "But that's what all those young gorillas down in Sausalito look forward to. We're training for the Tahiti race this year."

"You takin' that antique across the Pacific? She's older'n I am."

"She's fine, Waddy. Perfect, actually. Want to come along?"

"Pass, thanks."

"Waddy, I have another suggestion," Tolya said. "Why don't we all go up to Hetch Hetchy for a few days? Grandmother said she'd like to do that too. The California Conservation Corps has done a terrific a job restoring the valley since the dam was removed."

Government never would have taken this one apart. Even took those San Franciscans forty years debatin' whether the world could use a copy of Yosemite Valley.

"Maybe we'll see one of the bears."

"Yeah. Yeah, I'd like that," Waddy said. He remembered another old man who had long ago fought for his own river canyon. They both had finally triumphed.

AFTERWORD

The Hisatsinom (Kayenta Anasazi) and their predecessors occupied or frequented the Canyon and its environs for hundreds of years before the end of the thirteenth century, as evidenced by the archaeological work done by the University of Utah and the Museum of Northern Arizona in the years preceding the flooding of the Canyon in 1963. While the characters in the opening segment of the first chapter are fictional, the available history of the Hopi people and the findings of the Canyon investigators confirm the factual details presented. The reasons for the late thirteenth century abandonments remain the subject of ongoing debate.

The chronology and the descriptions and personal interactions of the members of Major John Wesley Powell's 1869 expedition are factual, subject to the usual disagreements common to an accounting of any historical event.

The chronology and the physical descriptions of events that took place at Glen Canyon Dam in the late spring and early summer of 1983 are accurate, based upon the official record of the U. S. Bureau of Reclamation, including the "Final Construction Report on Repair, Spillway Tunnels, Glen Canyon Dam, Colorado River Storage Project, Page, Arizona," December 1984.

Descriptions of Colorado River history and politics, including the 1905 flood, and of the construction and operation of the dam and other impoundments in the river basin are accurate, although arguably—if only occasionally—embellished in some respects by the author's viewpoint.

The storm interactions described in the story are based upon two Bureau of Reclamation studies entitled: "Determination of an Upper Limit Design Rainstorm for the Colorado River Basin Above Hoover Dam," September 1990; and "Colorado River Basin Probable Maximum Floods, Hoover and Glen Canyon Dams," September 1990.

Descriptions of nuclear weapons and their functioning and effects are generally accurate but have been intentionally altered in some particulars.

Book Ordering Information

If you cannot find this book in your local retail outlets, BookMasters' order fulfillment department will mail it to you directly.

Price, Tax, and Shipping

Price	$28.95
Domestic shipping, per book	3.00

Colorado Residents add 3% state sales tax plus any applicable local taxes, on book price only

Books are shipped UPS ground within 48 hours. Faster service is available for an additional fee. Call the 800 number for details.

Ordering

MAIL your check or money order to:

BookMasters, Inc.
P. O. Box 388
Ashland, OH 44805

Include your name, mailing address, daytime telephone number, the book title, and number of copies ordered.

CALL 1-800-247-6553, 24 hours, every day.

Mastercard, Visa, American Express, or Discover cards are accepted.

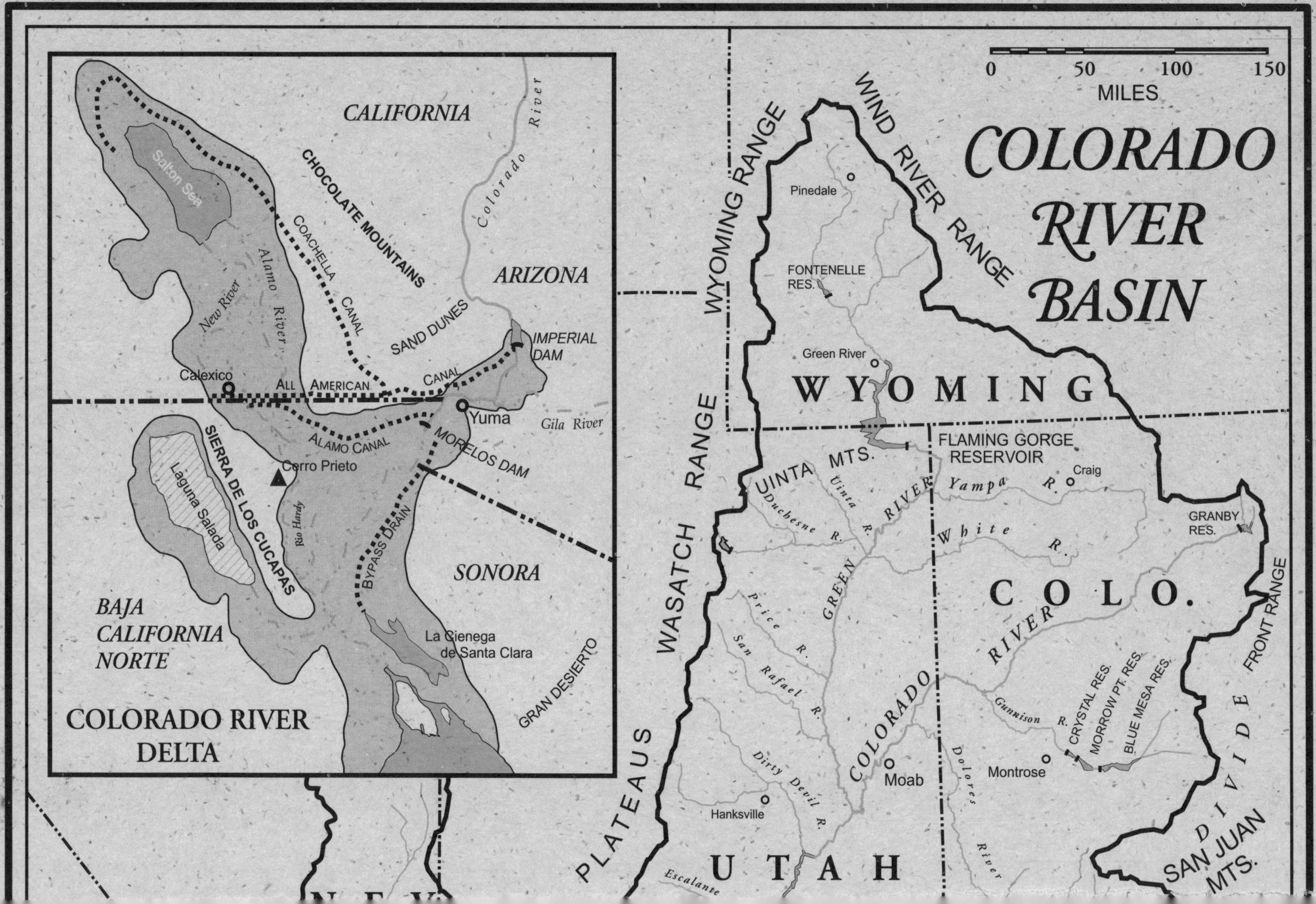
COLORADO RIVER BASIN
0 50 100 150
MILES
WIND RIVER RANGE
WYOMING RANGE
Pinedale
FONTENELLE RES.
Green River
WYOMING
FLAMING GORGE RESERVOIR
UINTA MTS.
Craig
Yampa R.
White R.
GRANBY RES.
FRONT RANGE
COLO.
RIVER
Duchesne R.
Uinta R.
GREEN RIVER
WASATCH RANGE
Price R.
San Rafael R.
COLORADO
Moab
Gunnison R.
CRYSTAL RES.
MORROW PT. RES.
BLUE MESA RES.
Montrose
Dolores River
DIVIDE
SAN JUAN MTS.
Dirty Devil R.
Hanksville
PLATEAUS
Escalante
UTAH
CALIFORNIA
ARIZONA
Colorado River
CHOCOLATE MOUNTAINS
COACHELLA CANAL
Salton Sea
New River
Alamo River
SAND DUNES
IMPERIAL DAM
Calexico
ALL AMERICAN CANAL
Yuma
Gila River
ALAMO CANAL
MORELOS DAM
SIERRA DE LOS CUCAPAS
Cerro Prieto
Laguna Salada
Rio Hardy
BYPASS DRAIN
SONORA
BAJA CALIFORNIA NORTE
La Cienega de Santa Clara
GRAN DESIERTO
COLORADO RIVER DELTA